# The Punishment She Deserves

# ALSO BY ELIZABETH GEORGE

*A Great Deliverance*
*Payment in Blood*
*Well-Schooled in Murder*
*A Suitable Vengeance*
*For the Sake of Elena*
*Missing Joseph*
*Playing for the Ashes*
*In the Presence of the Enemy*
*Deception on His Mind*
*In Pursuit of the Proper Sinner*
*A Traitor to Memory*
*I, Richard*
*A Place of Hiding*
*With No One as Witness*
*What Came Before He Shot Her*
*Careless in Red*
*This Body of Death*
*Believing the Lie*
*Just One Evil Act*
*A Banquet of Consequences*

YOUNG ADULT

*The Edge of Nowhere*
*The Edge of the Water*
*The Edge of the Shadows*
*The Edge of the Light*

NONFICTION

*Write Away:*
*One Novelist's Approach to Fiction and the Writing Life*

ANTHOLOGY

*A Moment on the Edge: 100 Years of Crime Stories by Women*
*Two of the Deadliest: New Tales of Lust, Greed, and*
*Murder from Outstanding Women of Mystery*

ELIZABETH GEORGE

# The Punishment She Deserves

A LYNLEY NOVEL

VIKING

VIKING
An imprint of Penguin Random House LLC
375 Hudson Street
New York, New York 10014
penguin.com



p. xi: Excerpts from "That Lives in Us," by Rumi, and "The Moment's Depth," by Rabia are from *Love Poems From God: Twelve Sacred Voices From the East and West*, translated by Daniel Ladinsky. (New York: Penguin Compass, 2002.)

ISBN 9780525954347 (hardcover)
ISBN 9780698411654 (ebook)

Printed in the United States of America
1 3 5 7 9 10 8 6 4 2

Set in Bembo Std
Designed by Amy Hill

*FOR TOM, IRA, and FRANK*

*With thanks and love.*

*Somehow, I got lucky.*

Why lay yourself on the torturer's rack
of the past and future?
The mind that tries to shape tomorrow beyond
its capacities will find no rest.

—Rumi

The moment's depth is greater than that of the future.
And from the fields of the past,
what can you harvest again?

—Rabia of Basra

# PART I

# 15 DECEMBER

BAKER CLOSE
LUDLOW
SHROPSHIRE

The snow began falling on Ludlow town in the evening, while most people were doing their post-dinner washing-up as a prelude to settling down in front of the television. If the truth be told, there wasn't much else to do in the town after dark beyond tuning in to one programme or another or heading out to a pub. And since Ludlow had, over the years, become more and more the choice of pensioners seeking tranquility and early bedtimes amidst the mediaeval buildings and cobbled byways, very few complaints concerning the dearth of evening entertainment ever occurred.

Like so many others in Ludlow, Gaz Ruddock, too, was doing the washing-up when he first noticed the snow. He stood at a sink whose window looked out at the darkness. Mostly, he could see his reflection and the reflection of the old man who wielded the tea towel next to him. But a light in the narrow back garden illuminated the flakes as they began to come down. Within minutes what had seemed to be only a gentle dusting altered to a real curtain of the stuff, waving in a developing breeze that made it look for a moment like lace window coverings.

"Don't like that, do I? I keep saying. Fat lot of good it's doing me, though."

Gaz glanced over at his companion of the tea towel. He didn't think the old bloke was talking about the snow, and he saw that he was correct since Robert Simmons wasn't looking at the window but rather at the washing-up wand that Gaz was using on one of their plates.

"In't sanitary, that," old Rob said. "I keep saying and you don't change over like I want."

Gaz smiled, not at old Rob—he always thought of his housemate with that adjective preceding his name as if there were also a young Rob in the house with them—but rather at his own reflection. He and window Gaz were sharing a knowing look. Rob nightly complained about the wand, and Gaz nightly reminded him that it was far more sanitary than filling a basin with soapy water in order to swirl glasses, crockery, cutlery, pots, and pans round it as if the water miraculously redeemed itself after every dunk of something into it.

"Only thing better than this," Gaz would say, with a shake of the washing-up wand, "is a dishwasher. You say the word and I'll fetch us one, Rob. Easy as anything. I'll even install it."

"Bah," Rob would reply. "Got along till eighty-six years and counting without such a thing and I expect I can make it to the grave without one just as well. Mod cons, bah!"

"You've a microwave, mind," Gaz would point out.

"Different, that is," was the curt reply.

If Gaz asked why possession of a microwave was different from the purchase of a dishwasher, Rob's answer was always the same: a huff, a shrug, and a "Just is, is all," and the discussion was finished.

It mattered little to Gaz. He wasn't much of a cook so there was never very much to wash. Tonight the meal had been jacket potatoes stuffed with chilli con carne from a tin, with a sweet corn and lettuce salad on the side. Half of the meal had been prepared via microwave and the tin hadn't even required an opener, possessing a pull ring instead. So all there was to wash was two plates, one wooden spoon, some cutlery, and two mugs from which they'd drunk their tea.

Gaz could have done the washing-up and the drying on his own, but old Rob liked to help. The old gent knew that his only child, Abigail, phoned Gaz once a week for a report as to her dad's well-being, and Rob intended Gaz to declare that his charge was just as full of piss and vinegar as on the day he'd moved in. Even if Abigail's phone call hadn't been a regular feature of their life together, Gaz suspected old Rob would still have insisted on doing his part, though. It was the only way he'd agreed to admit someone into his house in the first place.

Once his wife had died, he'd gone on living on his own for six years, but his daughter thought he was becoming too forgetful. There was his medication that wanted taking twice each day. There was also the concern that if he fell, there'd be no one in the house to find him. Abigail needed someone to be in charge of her dad, she had declared, and faced with the choice of sharing his home with a carefully selected stranger or leaving Ludlow for a life with Abigail, her four children, and a husband whom her dad had disliked from the day he appeared on the doorstep to take his only daughter clubbing in Shrewsbury, Rob had pounced on the idea of a housemate like the lifebelt it was.

Gaz Ruddock—given name Gary—was that housemate. He had another job as Ludlow's PCSO, but that was mostly during the day and since he generally walked or bicycled his beat like a 1920s bobby, he could stop in and check on the old gent daytimes when necessary. It worked a perfect trick for him anyway: his wages as the police community support officer were meagre, and acting as Rob's live-in companion gave him not only free accommodation but a small salary as well.

His mobile rang as Gaz was wiping down the draining board and Rob was neatly folding the tea towel onto the rack above the cooker, where it would dry. Gaz shot the mobile a glance to see who was phoning. He gave thought to ignoring the call as old Rob gave him the eye. They'd lived together long enough for Rob to know what would happen next. A phone call in the evening usually meant a disruption to their plans.

"Near time for *Strictly Dancing,*" Rob reminded him, naming the programme he favoured above all others. "An' Sky has a Clint Eastwood film as well. The one with that barmy woman."

"Aren't they all barmy?" Gaz decided to let the mobile go to message. He needed to get Rob settled with the telly and the remote.

"Not like this one," the old man said. "This's the gel who wants that radio song played for her. You know. Then she 'cides that Clint Eastwood must be her man—maybe they do the job on each other or somethin' but I don't recall 'cept men are that foolish when it comes to women, eh?—and she commences to break into his house and chop up his belongings."

"*Play Misty for Me*," Gaz said.

"You recollect it, then?"

"Oh, that I do. It put me off women altogether, that film."

Old Rob laughed, which segued into a cough that didn't sound all that good to Gaz. Rob had been a smoker till he was seventy-four, when a quadruple bypass had finally convinced him to give up the weed. But that didn't mean that the sixty years of smoking preceding the bypass hadn't done enough damage to fell him with cancer or emphysema.

Gaz said to him, "You all right there, Rob?"

"'*Course* I am. Why wouldn't I be?" Rob gifted him with a glare.

"No reason, 'f course," Gaz told him. "Let's get you settled with the telly, then. Need the loo first?"

"What're you on about? I know when I have to piss, boy."

"Not suggesting you don't."

"Well, when I need someone to shake off my—"

"Point taken." Gaz followed the old gent to the sitting room at the front of the house. He didn't much like the tilt to Rob's gait or the hand he put on the wall to steady himself. He needed to use a walking stick, he did, but the bloke was a stubborn bastard. If he didn't want a walking stick, he was going to be Gibraltar when it came to anyone's recommendation that he use one.

Once in the sitting room, old Rob lowered himself into his armchair. Gaz lit the electric fire and closed the window curtains. He excavated for the telly remote, and he found the right channel for *Strictly Come Dancing*. Five minutes before the programme would begin, he saw, enough time for him to make the Ovaltine.

He found Rob's nighttime mug in its place in the cupboard, decorated with a transfer picture of his grandkids gathered round Father Christmas. This had faded with subsequent washings, and the ivy-and-holly wreath that formed the handle of the mug was chipped. But Rob wouldn't hear of having his Ovaltine from anything other than this particular mug. He made a big thing out of muttering complaints about the grandkids, but Gaz had learned soon enough that old Rob properly adored them.

Ovaltine in hand, Gaz returned to the sitting room. His mobile began to ring again. Again he ignored it in favour of getting old Rob settled. *Strictly Come Dancing* had just begun, and its opening moments were the special ones.

Rob loved to gaze upon the ladies, those who were contestants and those who were the professional dancers meant to teach the bloke contestants the cha-cha, the fox-trot, the Vienna thingy, and whatever else. Old Rob ate up the costumes with a spoon because they were fashioned to display a good mile and a half of cleavage and the sight of those ladies shaking their tits was a blessed reminder that, at eighty-six and counting, Robert Simmons was still alive.

"Lookit them, will you, lad?" Old Rob sighed. He held his Ovaltine up in a salute to the television screen. "You ever seen milkers 's pretty as those? 'F I was even ten years younger, I'd show those ladies how milkers like that are meant to be used and wouldn't I just?"

Gaz chuckled, but it was in spite of himself, as where he came from women were worshipped, up on the pedestal and all of that. They were sexual, sure. But they were sexual because of God's plan for them, and that plan didn't include making themselves available to men for purposes of displaying their "milkers," especially on telly. But there was no changing old Rob, who was a randy bloke, and *Strictly Come Dancing* was the highlight of his week.

Gaz fetched a blanket from the back of the sofa. He tucked it round Rob's sapling legs. He checked the *Radio Times* to make sure *Play Misty for Me* was actually showing later on in the evening, and when he saw it was, he left his companion chortling at the inane conversation going on between the presenter and the judges on the dancing programme.

He'd left his mobile in the kitchen, and he took it to the table, where he flopped into a chair. He had an uneasy feeling about the call. It was end of autumn term at West Mercia College. With exams finished and students readying themselves for the Christmas holiday, loud parties and binge drinking were probably going to be on the night's agenda.

He tapped on the mobile to return the call. Clo answered at once and said to him, "We've snow here, Gaz. What about you?"

Gaz knew that she wasn't interested in a report on the topic of the weather, but it was a way to begin a conversation that, he also knew, was going to progress towards a request that Clo knew she probably shouldn't give voice to. He wasn't going to make it easy for her. He said, "Here, too. It'll make a dog's dinner of the roads, to be sure, but at least it'll keep everyone inside."

"End of term, Gaz. Kids won't be inside. They don't care about snow, sleet, rain, or whatever when it comes to the end of term."

"They're not delivering the post," he pointed out.

"What?"

"Snow, sleet, rain. Postmen?"

"Believe me, they may as well be postmen. The weather isn't going to stop them."

He waited, then, for what was coming. It took her only a moment.

"Would you check on him, Gaz? You can make it part of a regular round. You'll be doing a round anyway, won't you? Considering the weather, I expect you're not the only PCSO being asked to go out tonight to check on young people in the pubs."

Gaz rather doubted that. West Mercia was the only college in all of Shropshire, and it was hardly credible that the rest of the PCSOs in the other communities were going walkabout in the snow with no reason for doing so. But he didn't argue the point. He cared for Clo. He cared for her family. Although he knew she was playing on those feelings, he could easily go along with her request.

Still, he said, "Trev's not going to like it if I do this. I expect you know that, eh?"

"Trev's not going to learn about it because you're not going to tell him. And I'm certainly not going to."

"It's not me you should be worrying about when it comes to grassing, though, is it."

There was a pause as she took this in. He could visualise her. If she was still working for some reason, she'd be sitting at a desk, which would be perfectly neat and orderly in the way she was neat and orderly. If she was at home, she'd be in the bedroom, kitted out in something that she deemed wife-appropriate, and this would be for her husband's benefit. She'd told him more than once in joking that Trev liked her soft, sweet, and compliant, all characteristics that weren't exactly natural to her.

She said, "As I said, end of term, streets getting icy, kids engaged in post-exam booze-ups . . . No one is going to question why you're out and about, making sure everyone's safe, Finnegan included."

That wasn't unreasonable. Besides, being out and about did have benefits beyond mere exposure to bracing air. He said, "All right. Will do. But it only makes sense if I'm out there later on. Just now? No one's going to be up to anything."

"Understood," she said. "Thank you, Gaz. You'll let me know what he's up to?"

"'Course," he told her.

ST. JULIAN'S WELL
LUDLOW
SHROPSHIRE

Missa Lomax gazed upon the clothing that her friend Dena—commonly called Ding—had laid out on the bed. Three skirts, one cashmere pullover, two silk blouses, a pullover top hung with silver dangly bits akin to icicles. She'd removed all this from a capacious rucksack, saying, "The black one's the best, Missa. It's real stretchy."

Stretchy was necessary. The clothing all belonged to Ding, and she and Missa did not share a similar physique. Where Ding was petite and curvy, possessing a woman's full body but not much height, Missa was pear-shaped, given to hips if she wasn't careful about her weight, and she stood six inches taller than her friend. But she had brought nothing with her to Ludlow that would serve as a festive outfit for a night out. She'd not even considered nights out when she'd joined the college because she'd not come to Ludlow to party but rather to study biology, chemistry, maths, and French prior to attending university.

She said, "These'll all be too short for me, Ding," and gestured to the skirts.

"Short is the style and what difference does it make?"

It made plenty of difference to Missa, but all she said was, "I won't be able to ride my bike."

"*No* one's riding a bike in this weather." This was said by Rabiah Lomax, who came through the door to Missa's bedroom, a purple tracksuit hanging on her lithe frame and nothing at all on her feet save polish on her toenails, appropriately red and green for the season with the big toe additionally decorated with a golden tree-ornament painted upon it. She went on to say, "You'll be taking a taxi. I'm paying both ways."

"But Ding's come here on her bike, Gran," Missa pointed out. "She won't be able to—"

"Completely foolhardy, Dena Donaldson," Missa's grandmother countered. "You can take the taxi and fetch your bike at another time, can't you?"

Ding looked relieved. She said, "Thanks, Mrs. Lomax. We'll pay you back."

"Don't be ridiculous," Rabiah said. "'Paying me back' will be your going out and having a good time." To Missa she went on with, "Enough of studying for at least one evening. Life's about more than schoolbooks and keeping your parents happy." At that, Missa glanced at Rabiah but said nothing. Her grandmother continued briskly. "Now. What have we here?" She walked over to the bed. She took in the clothing with a single glance and chose the black skirt. Ding, Missa saw, beamed with pleasure.

"Put this on," Rabiah ordered. "Let's see how it fits. I'd lend you something of mine, but as I've reduced my wardrobe mostly to my dancing kit and my running kit, I've nothing suitable. Except, perhaps, for shoes. You're going to need shoes." She fluttered her fingers and went off in the direction of her bedroom as Missa stepped out of her trainers and her blue jeans and Ding rustled round in the chest of drawers for, she said, "a pair of tights that don't look like something from Oxfam."

Missa eased herself into Ding's skirt. The fact that it stretched made it wearable, although it still bit into her stomach like a ligature. She said, "Ooof, I don't know, Ding."

Ding turned from the chest of drawers, having scored a pair of black tights. "Fabbo!" she cried. "It's just the thing. Lads'll melt when they see you in that."

"I don't especially want lads melting."

"Yes you do. It doesn't mean you have to *do* anything with them. Here, take these. I've got something special to show you." She handed over the tights and went for her rucksack, from which she brought forth a lacy bra.

Missa said, "There's no way that'll fit me."

"It's not mine," Ding told her. "It's an early Christmas gift from me to you. Here. Take it. It's not going to bite."

Missa never wore lacy bits of anything. But clearly Ding wasn't having it as far as refusals went.

"Now that thing's gorgeous," was Rabiah's comment when she saw what was dangling from Ding's fingers. "Where did it come from?"

"My gift to Missa," Ding told her. "She's going to graduate from vests."

"I *don't* wear vests," Missa said. "I just don't like . . . Lace is itchy."

Rabiah said, "Small price to pay for . . . Dena Donaldson, is that a push-up bra?"

Ding giggled. Missa felt her face going hot. But she took the bra, turned her back modestly, and tried it on. She looked in the mirror and what she saw of the mounds of her breasts made her face hotter.

"Here, here, here!" Ding scooped up the icicle pullover, whose neckline showed off the products of the push-up bra to best advantage when Missa cooperatively donned it. "Fabbo-licious," she declared. "Check it out. And, oh Mrs. Lomax! Gorgeous! Are those for Missa as well?"

She was referring, Missa saw, to the shoes. She gave them a look herself and wondered when her grandmother had last worn them. The

Rabiah she knew generally wore running shoes or cross-trainers when she wasn't barefoot or dressed for square dancing. She'd given up anything remotely fashionable when she'd retired from her teaching job at the comprehensive. But this pair of shoes looked older than any that would have come from the days of Rabiah's teaching career. These had to have come from her earlier dancing life.

"I don't know," Missa said doubtfully.

"Horse manure," was Rabiah's reply. "You can walk in these as easy as anything. Put them on. Let's check the fit."

They fit, just. Rabiah declared that Missa would wear them and "no nonsense about it. It's not as if you're hiking all over town in this weather anyway. Now, Dena Donaldson, I suspect you've brought makeup in that rucksack of yours, so see to Missa's beautification while I ring for a taxi."

"Should I tweeze her eyebrows as well?" Ding enquired.

"We're requiring everything," Rabiah told her.

QUALITY SQUARE
LUDLOW
SHROPSHIRE

It wasn't a taxi, as things turned out, but rather a minicab. Missa's gran made an extremely big deal out of paying for it all in advance—going into the town centre *and* coming back—so, as she put it, everyone would be absolutely clear on what was owed at the end of the evening: nothing.

"I hope you see that, my man," Rabiah said pointedly to the minicab driver.

The man barely spoke English, which didn't give Ding much faith that he'd get them to Quality Square in the first place, let alone back to St. Julian's Well. But he nodded at Rabiah, and he created a supremely serious show of seeing that both Ding and Missa were belted into the backseat of his Audi.

An Audi, Ding reckoned, suggested that business wasn't half bad. On the other hand, the fact that it slid around the corner on the icy road suggested that it needed better tyres. Still, she settled back, gave a squeeze to Missa's hand, and said, "We're going to have a wicked good time. We both totally deserve it."

Of course, the truth was that it was Missa who totally deserved it since Ding made certain she herself had a good time as often as possible. But things were rather different for Missa.

It had long been Ding's habit to Google every person with whom she thought she might want to strike up a friendship, and just three lectures into their mutual maths course, she'd decided that the attractive mixed-race girl with the perfect skin and the charming little gap between her front teeth might be someone she'd want to know. So she'd checked her out via the Internet, she'd followed a link or two, and that was how she'd discovered that Melissa Lomax was one of three daughters and that the middle daughter had passed away ten months previously. She also knew where Missa was from: Ironbridge. Her dad was a pharmacist, her mum was a paediatrician, and her gran Rabiah was a former Rockette, a retired teacher, and a current champion London Marathon runner in her age group.

Ding liked to know things about people. She assumed everyone else was the same way. It was always a surprise to her when she learned that others didn't gumshoe round the Internet upon considering someone girlfriend or boyfriend material. To Ding, doing the gumshoe bit saved a lot of time. It was always good to know if someone had previously displayed a tendency towards psychopathy.

The ride from St. Julian's Well to Quality Square wasn't a long one, although the falling snow made it longer than usual. Because of the weather, virtually no one was out and about—which was unusual at the end of term—but Corve Street and then the Bull Ring were brightly lit, and the seasonal fairy lights outlining shop windows created a cheerful atmosphere in which one half expected to see Dickensian carolers on every street corner.

Ding wasn't looking forward to Christmas. She hadn't looked forward to any holiday in years. But she was willing to put on a face of merriment if she had to, so she said enthusiastically, "Gorgeosity in the *extreme*. It's like being in a fairyland, isn't it."

Missa gazed out of the window, and Ding could see on her face the doubts she had: not about the beauty of the scene through which they were driving but rather about the partying that Ding intended them to experience. "D'you think anyone else's even going out tonight?" she asked.

"End of term? Exams all finished? There'll be plenty of people, especially where we're going."

Ding had a good idea of the best spot since she lived not particularly far from any of the faculties of West Mercia College, and she'd spent a significant number of evenings having a booze-up with her other mates at the same pub: the Hart and Hind in Quality Square.

The minicab was taking them as close to this spot as it could reasonably get. They were in the oldest part of Ludlow, working their way past mediaeval buildings and through narrowing streets towards Castle Square, where the twelfth-century castle ruins looked out upon a lengthy rectangle of cobbles and gravel. Here open-air stalls had, for hundreds of years, offered everything from pork pies to porringers at daily markets. Here also was a tangle of lanes overhung with shambling buildings that represented shops, accommodation, cafés, and restaurants.

By using King Street, the minicab was able to deposit them at the only access to Quality Square. This was a short and narrow passage through which braver drivers could pilot their cars should they wish to do so. However, once they were inside the square, there was no exit other than through the passage again, so the only souls who took on the challenge of getting inside the place by vehicle were the residents who lived above the shops, boutiques, and galleries that formed three of the quadrangle's sides.

A cobbled lane formed the fourth side. It led to a large terrace, and it was towards this that Ding intended to lead Missa once the minicab driver handed over his mobile number, which they were to ring when it came time to fetch them. Ding said, "Come *on*, girl," as Missa took the card with a grateful smile and tucked it into her shoulder bag. "We have some serious partying to do."

They ducked into the passage and took care with the cobbles since walking in this area in anything but flat-soled shoes was to risk turning an ankle. Beyond lay the square, where the snow made the stones slippery and the pavements difficult to negotiate. They manoeuvred between two residents' cars and passed a gallery outside of which a lacy-dressed metal sculpture of a woman wore a mantle of snow. The branches of the evergreen shrubbery surrounding it were beginning to droop with white weight.

They weren't alone in their choice of destination, as Ding had reckoned they wouldn't be. When they turned into the lane that formed the square's fourth side, they saw on the terrace ahead of them that despite the snow, a large group of smokers were balancing their drinks on the window ledges of a pub, while others sat on blankets at tables above which outdoor heaters were warding off the chill.

This, Ding informed her friend, was the Hart and Hind, a sixteenth-century coaching inn and the favourite gathering spot for boozers attending West Mercia College. While there were, she admitted, plenty of other pubs in the town, this one had long been everyone's pub of choice not only because one could stop there directly one's lecture or tutorial ended so as to become pissed in a pinch, but also because the proprietor was willing to turn a blind eye to the occasional exchange of money changing hands for "mind-altering substances of the illegal kind."

Missa said, "Ding, I'm not taking any drugs."

"'*Course* you're not," Ding agreed. "Not when you've never even had a drink." She went on to confide, "There's some bedrooms upstairs 's well. Course, there would be as it's an old inn. But he doesn't let them out."

"Who?"

"Jack. Bloke who owns the place. There's two of them—bedrooms, I mean—and if you've got the cash, you c'n use them for a bit if you want to."

Missa frowned. "But if he doesn't let the rooms out . . . ? What're they for?"

Ding nearly said, "*You* know, for God's sake," but the truth was that Missa wouldn't understand unless you spelled it out for her.

Ding had learned early on that Missa made a Very Big Deal about her virginity. She was like someone from another century, saving herself so that when her prince came along, bearing a ruby slipper and looking for a virgin, she'd be the only one within one thousand miles and two continents.

Ding herself had lost her virginity when she was thirteen. She'd tried for it earlier, but no one was interested till she got decent breasts. When it happened, the act was a meganormous relief: just to get the deflowering of herself over and done with in order to have one less thing to worry about. She didn't know what Missa was saving it for anyway. Her memory of the Big Moment began with her horrified albeit drunken "You're going to put *that* in me?," continued with the uncomfortable positioning of her body on the seat of a wooden pew near the back of St. James Church not far from Much Wenlock, and ended with her suitor thrusting nine times and grunting with completion on the tenth.

The pub door opened as they approached it through the crowd. A blast of music assaulted them. Bee Gees, Ding thought. Good Lord. ABBA wouldn't be far behind. She grabbed Missa's hand and pulled her inside, where a long corridor panelled in ancient black oak was packed with bare shoulders, bare legs, spangles, sequins, glitter, tight trousers, and the heave-ho of dancers taking advantage of "Stayin' Alive."

The corridor opened into the public bar. Music was shaking the floorboards. This was meant to promote dancing, which was meant to promote thirst, which was meant to promote the purchase of lager, ale, cider, cocktails, and the like. Ding had to struggle to get through the great glomerations of kids who were gyrating to the music, texting, or taking selfies and the equally great glomerations of kids who were crowding the bar where the publican and his nephew were doing their best to keep up with orders.

Ding could pick up only snippets of shouted conversations:

"He didn't *ever.*"

"He bloody well did!"

". . . *and* he missed the loo by a mile. Blokes are *so* . . ."

". . . over hols and I'll let you know if . . ."

". . . bloody coast of *France* for New Year's and don't ask me why . . ."

". . . actually thinks if I fuck him, he can . . ."

Ding almost lost hold of Missa's hand in the middle of the crowd, but she managed to hang on to it long enough to see one of her two male housemates sitting at a table beneath a slew of old pictures of Ludlow in Bygone Days. This was Bruce Castle, Ding's frequent bedmate. Eternally called Brutus in humorous contradiction to his diminutive size, he was, she saw, swilling cider. If the two empty pint glasses in front of him were anything to go by, she knew what he was up to: he wanted to become drunk enough to have an excuse if some girl tried to slap him into next week for sticking one of his hands up her skirt.

Brutus was dressed to the nines, as usual, and when Ding and Missa joined him at the table, the first thing the boy said was "*Very* hot," to Missa, in obvious reference to her figure-hugging clothing. "Sit here so I can feel the flesh."

Ding sat down next to him and pulled Missa onto one of the other chairs. She said to Brutus, "Shut your gob. D'you think women actually *like* to be talked to that way?"

Brutus wasn't embarrassed. He merely went on with, "I dunno where to grab her first: arse or tit," which earned him a punch on the arm, delivered accurately, where it would hurt. It prompted a "Jesus, Ding! What's crawled up *your* arse?"

Ding said, "Go get us a drink."

Missa said, "Oh, I don't—"

Ding waved her off. "It's not a drink like in a *drink*. It's just cider. You'll like it." She gave Brutus a look. He heaved himself upwards and lurched through the crowd to the bar. She watched him, frowning. She didn't like it when he got drunk. Tipsy was fine. High was okay. But Brutus was never the real Brutus when he was drunk, and she couldn't understand why he'd got himself soused so soon into the evening, as that had not been part of the plan at all.

Missa, she saw, was gazing round the pub, taking everything in: the jostling, laughing mass of scantily dressed females and the boys standing as close as they could, trying to chat them up. She wondered if her friend was catching the action near the bar. There, the publican Jack Korhonen was tossing a room key to a boy who had his arm round a somewhat staggering girl in a sequined tube of a dress. The boy caught the key in one hand. He turned the girl towards the stairs.

Brutus returned. He had three pints. When he set one down in front of Missa, Ding watched carefully as her friend took a sip. She waited to see if Missa would note the alcoholic nature of the drink. She did not. It was carbonated and very tasty, a pleasant way to get happy that didn't take long.

Brutus scooted his chair closer to Ding. He said into her ear, "You smell like a goddess tonight." He slid his hand onto her thigh. It began to travel upwards. She caught his fingers and sharply bent them backwards. He cried, "Hey! What the hell is *wrong* with you tonight?"

Ding didn't have to answer because they were joined just then by the third member of their little household, who said, "Fuck, Brutus. Try romance next time."

Brutus said, "But that's what I want. Someone to fuck Brutus."

"I'm howling at that one, lad." Finn Freeman yanked a chair away from a nearby table, ignoring a girl who cried, "Hey! We're *using* that."

He plopped onto it, grabbed Brutus's cider, and took an excessively large swig. He grimaced, saying, "Fuck's sake. How c'n you *stand* that shit?"

Missa, Ding saw, had lowered her gaze in reaction to Finn's coarse language. That was another thing about Missa that Ding found endearing. She didn't ever swear, and she made no effort to hide her embarrassment when someone swore in her presence.

Ding knew that Finn meant nothing by it. He was generally all right for someone who'd shaved one half of his head in order to tattoo his skull. This wasn't a particularly appealing look, but the way Ding saw things, it was a case of what*ever.*

"Who wants to buy me a Guinness?" Finn asked the table at large.

"Speaking of shit," Ding commented airily.

Brutus cooperated, though. If he hadn't done so, Ding knew that—no matter how he had evaluated the cider—Finn would down Brutus's and move along to Ding's or Missa's. He had a bit of a problem with the drink, but as Ding had learned in the past few months, it was only one of his problems.

The biggest one was his mum. He called her the Hovercraft for her propensity towards monitoring his life, like someone working for GCHQ. It was because of her that Finn had come up with a plan to avoid the Christmas hols at home and instead take off for Spain to spend the time with his grandparents. Trouble was, he didn't have the necessary money to get there, and when he'd phoned his gran to ask for the funds, he'd ended up speaking with his granddad instead. Unbeknownst to Finn, once Granddad had agreed to the dual request of an invitation to Christmas in Spain along with a ticket to get there, he'd then rung Finn's mum to make certain it was fine for her only child to skip Christmas in the bosom of his parents.

That had put an end to that. He'd managed to get his mum to agree to two extra days in Ludlow by lying to her about a children's holiday programme he was meant to attend, one put on by a local church. Only God knew why Finn's mum had gone for that story, but she had done. Two days of post-exam freedom, however, were all that Finn was going to be allowed. He wasn't happy about that.

"So," he was saying to Missa, "how the hell did Ding get *you* to come out? You always got your head in a book, far as I ever saw."

"She's a *serious* student," Ding informed him.

"Unlike you," was Finn's reply. "I never seen you studying *any*thing."

Brutus returned with Finn's Guinness. He said, "You owe me."

"As usual." Finn saluted them with the drink. He said, "Seasonal bah humbugs," and poured a quarter of it down his throat. "Let's get serious, you lot," was his next remark. "Our mission: complete obliteration."

Ding had to smile. Finn didn't know it, but they were actually on the very same page.

QUALITY SQUARE
LUDLOW
SHROPSHIRE

The troubles with binge drinking had always been manifold. They were represented by girls sicking up in gutters, boys having a piss wherever and whenever the fancy took them, rubbish being scattered all over the pavements, broken bottles lying in the streets, property being damaged in the form of trampled gardens and overturned rubbish bins. Shrill arguments, cat fights replete with hair pulling and eye gouging, fist fights, stolen handbags, snatched smartphones . . . The list of what accompanied binge drinking went on and on, although it was worse in the big city centres where late-night clubs allowed young people to drink themselves into folly till dawn.

In a town like Ludlow there were only pubs, but Gaz Ruddock had discovered that the lack of late-night clubs made no difference when it came to bingeing, though. In his first week as Ludlow's PCSO he'd come to learn that, faced with a population swollen more and more each year by pensioners, the pub owners had learned to attract and accommodate the kind of crowd who regularly kept far later hours.

It was after midnight when Gaz finally reached Castle Square. He'd worked his way from pubs on the outskirts of Ludlow because he reckoned that if Finnegan Freeman wanted to engage in a truly proper booze-up, he wouldn't be so stupid as to do his drinking in the pub nearest West Mercia College, where he was a student. But Gaz was proved wrong, as things turned out.

He parked the panda car in front of Harp Lane Deli, which as usual had entered the town's seasonal window-dressing competition. It had taken first prize during Halloween, and from the look of things, it was going to take first prize again if a half-size Father Christmas with a line of similarly sized children waiting to climb upon his lap was any indication. At one of his shoulders stood a perky-faced elf with a pile of gifts in his arms.

Gaz shoved open the car's door and swung himself out. Snow had begun to heap onto windowsills, and it formed a pristine carpet down the length of the market square. In the distance the lights that shone on the castle walls made the scene look like an enormous snow globe. It was quite beautiful and Gaz would have admired it had he not been bloody cold and equally anxious to have his search for Finnegan Freeman over and done with.

Gaz strode into the passage that led from the marketplace to Quality Square. Once through, he could hear the noise. Music, loud conversation, and laughter reverberated in the square as if the pub stood within an echo chamber. He wasn't surprised to find five understandably angry residents gathered outside their homes in parkas and hats and scarves and boots. Two of them approached him as he walked into the first pool of light from a streetlamp. It was, he learned from them, "about bloody time that *someone* had arrived to do *something* about this." *This* didn't need clarification.

He advised them to go indoors and told them to leave the situation to him. Considering the noise, there were going to be a good number of drinkers both inside and outside the pub, so moving them along would take some time.

He rounded the corner. Striding towards the open terrace, he encountered some two dozen drunken young people hanging about beneath outdoor heaters. They were swilling down drinks of every kind; they were leaning against the pub walls; they were having a snog in the multitude of shadows. The acrid odour of marijuana grew stronger as he approached the pub door.

He blew his police whistle shrilly, but it was practically impossible for it to be heard over "Waterloo," which was blasting through the open door of the pub. He would have to deal with the music first, so he went inside. There, in the entrance corridor, the drunken condition of two young ladies was allowing five well-dressed boys to grope them while betting each other—in language that Gaz wouldn't have repeated even to old Rob—just how far along the road they were going to get before the girls understood what was happening.

Gaz's face pinched up. He bloody hated this sort of thing. He forced his way into the group and broke up the action. One of the boys swirled round on him, ready to give him a taste of something he had no appetite for, but when he saw Gaz's uniform, he dropped his fist.

"That's right," was Gaz's remark. "Clear out of here and take your mates with you."

He kept a firm grip on each of the girls as he forced his way through the crowd and into the public bar. He caught the stench of someone's vomit nearby, and he dropped the girls into chairs at the table from which the stench appeared to be coming. That would sober them up or prompt them to be sick. Either was fine with him.

The publican Jack Korhonen was chatting up a girl at the bar. She looked to be in the vicinity of fifteen years old. He didn't see Gaz till

Gaz had his hand on the back of the girl's neck and was barking "Underage" into her face.

"I'm eighteen years old!" was her slurred defence.

"You're eighteen like I'm seventy-two. Be on your way before I haul you home."

"You can't—"

"Can do, have done, will do again. You can tiptoe inside Mum and Dad's house with none the wiser or have me banging on the door to hand you over to them personally. What'll it be?"

She graced him with a nasty look, but she also took herself off. He watched till she disappeared into the corridor that would take her outside, and he was satisfied to see three girls of similar age and appearance follow in her wake. He turned to Jack, who held up his hands in a don't-blame-me gesture. He said to him over the noise, "Turn it off. Time to shut things down."

"Not closing time yet," Jack protested.

"Make it last orders, Jack. And who's upstairs in the rooms?"

"What rooms're you speaking of?"

"Right. What rooms, eh? Tell whatsisname over there"—with a nod at Jack's nephew—"to knock them up and let them know the fun is finished. Seems that'd be better than myself breaking in on whatever's happening. Are you going to turn off the music or am I?"

Jack sneered, but Gaz knew it was merely for effect. He did as he was told. Shouts of protest rose at the cessation of ABBA, but into it Jack called, "Last orders. Sorry."

More protest followed. Gaz ignored it and began to move among the tables. He still had to have a look for Finnegan Freeman, and he found him at a far table against the wall. At the moment, his head was in his arms, which were themselves crossed on the tabletop. Next to him was a nattily clad boy holding a smartphone while a mixed-race girl leaned into him and together they laughed at something they were watching on the smartphone's screen.

Gaz strode over to the group, but stumbled when he got to them. He glanced down to see what was on the floor, and there he found another girl relaxing sleepily against the wall. He recognised her:

Dena Donaldson, Ding to her friends. To Gaz she was someone developing a very serious problem with the drink.

He bent and, his hands in her armpits, jolted Dena to her feet. When she saw exactly who was gripping her, the sight appeared to be enough to sober her up. She said, "I'm okay, I'm okay, I'm perfect."

"Are you now?" Gaz enquired. "Happens things don't look that way. Happens this could well be the time I cart you straight home so Mummy and Dad can have a proper look at—"

"No." Her face hardened.

"No, is it? So you're thinking Mummy and Dad—"

"He's *not* my dad."

"Well, love, he is whoever the hell he is and he might be interested in seeing how little Dena spends her evenings. Don't you agree? Or not? And *if* not—"

"I can't leave Missa. I promised her gran I'd stay with her. Come *on,*" and she struggled to get away from the grip in which he held her. She called out, "Missa, let's go. You got that bloke's card for the minicab, right?"

Missa looked up from whatever she was viewing. So did the boy. Both of them clocked the PCSO. The boy said to Gaz, "Hey. She's not hurting you. Let her go. Pick on someone—"

"Fuck it, Gaz." This came from Finnegan. He'd raised his head and, of course, he understood in two seconds what Gaz was doing in the pub.

"Get up now, Finn," Gaz told the boy. "Got to get you home and tucked up in bed."

Finnegan came straight up at that. He reared back against the wall. "No bloody way!"

The rest of them looked confused by the exchange as well they would, since it would have been out of character for Finn to tell them that he had more than a passing acquaintance with the town's PCSO. Gaz said, "I don't mean Worcester, do I. I mean home here, tucked up in your bed here, and whatever else you require *here.* Hot cocoa if you want it. Bournvita. Ovaltine. What you will."

"You *know* this filth, Finn?"

The other boy had said it, and Gaz's blood bubbled, quick as could be. He hated kids who dripped privilege, and he turned towards him.

Dena said, "Brutus," in a tone that apparently told the boy to back off. He shrugged, went back to his smartphone, and continued watching whatever was on it.

Gaz snatched it out of his hand. He had it into his pocket before Brutus—and what sort of name was *that* for a kid who looked to be the size of a scrum half rather than a second row?—knew where it had gone. He said to him and to the rest, "You lot are going home as is everyone else in this place." He shouted, "Last orders, like you heard. And I'm giving everyone five minutes to down them." He was gratified to see some of the kids already leaving. He was equally gratified to see four kids coming down the back stairs in the wake of the younger of the barmen. They looked disheveled and in need of a talking to, but Gaz had enough on his hands with the four in front of him.

To Dena he said, "You best think about your choice, missy."

To Finn he said, "I'm taking you home."

To the others he said, "And you two scarper before I think of something else to do with you."

Dena said, "Fine. I'm choosing. You can take us all," and before Gaz could inform her that he wasn't running a bus service for the likes of this group, she announced, "We live together, as if you didn't know. I'm quite happy for the ride, and my guess is everyone else is as well. You lot coming?" she asked her friends airily as she reached for her coat and scouted round the floor till she came up with some kind of ancient evening bag. "We can carry on our partying at home, which is what, I believe, this officer is suggesting. Isn't that *right*, constable?" she asked him.

Gaz heard the harmony that accompanied the melody of her final question. It spoke of triumph at having bested him. Yes. Well. They would see about that.

# 4 MAY

SOHO
LONDON

First had come the requisite clothing, and her choice was simplicity itself. She already had dozens of slogan-bearing T-shirts she could wear—only some of them being truly objectionable—so the single purchase she made was two pairs of leggings, black in colour since black was supposed to be slimming and God knew she wanted to look slimmer than she actually was. Next, naturally, had come the footwear, with an astonishing array of choices she had absolutely *not* known could exist online or anywhere else. Black, of course, there was lots of black, but there was also the choice of beige, pink, red, silver, and white. One could have glitter as well. One could choose from soles of leather, resin, rubber, or a synthetic material of unnamed and, one hoped, eco-friendly origin. Then came the ribbons or the laces. Or the ankle straps with buckles. And finally presented were the taps themselves. Toe, toe and heel, none at all . . . although why one would purchase tap shoes without taps didn't make much sense to her. She ended up choosing red—it was, after all, her signature colour when it came to footwear—and she went with straps and buckles as she could not see herself being responsible for keeping either laces or ribbons tied for the length of time that they would need to be tied: ninety minutes each lesson.

The last thing Barbara Havers had ever expected when she'd agreed to tap-dancing lessons in the company of Dorothea Harriman, the department secretary of her division in the Metropolitan Police, was that she would actually enjoy the activity. She'd gone along with the plan merely because she was worn down after listening to relentlessly given arguments on the subject of the benefits of tap dancing as exercise. Although most forms of exercise that didn't involve pushing a shopping trolley up and down the aisles of the nearest Tesco had long been anathema to Barbara, she'd fairly quickly run out of excuses on the subject of being too busy.

At least she'd managed to remove Dorothea's hands from her love life or, more specifically, from her lack thereof. To do this, she'd invoked the name of an Italian policeman—Salvatore Lo Bianco—with whom she'd become acquainted during the previous year. That had stirred Dorothea's interest, which was further stirred when Barbara informed her that she was expecting a visit from Inspector Lo Bianco and his two children round Christmastime. Alas and alack, that hadn't happened, a sudden appendectomy performed on twelve-year-old Marco having prevented this. But wisely, Barbara hadn't shared her disappointment with Dorothea. As far as the departmental secretary knew, the visit had occurred and bliss of some acceptable sort was just round the corner.

Dorothea was not to be so moved regarding the tap-dancing lessons, however. Thus, for the last seven months, Barbara had found herself once each week in a dance studio in Southall, where she and Dorothea learned that a shuffle was a brush followed by a spark, a slap was a flap without the weight transfer, and a Maxie Ford involved four different movements that the faint at heart and clumsy of foot were never going to master. Nor were those individuals who did not practise daily between lessons.

At first Barbara had simply refused to practise. As a detective sergeant at New Scotland Yard, she did not have a plethora of open hours in which she could shuffle off to Buffalo or, frankly, to anywhere else. And while the instructor had been good enough to start his neophyte tappers gently and with mounds of encouragement, he wasn't entirely pleased with Barbara's progress, and after the tenth lesson he let her know it.

"One must work at this," he told her as she and Dorothea were restoring their tap shoes to the cloth bags in which they were religiously carried every week to Southall. "If you consider the progress that the other ladies have made and with far more impediments . . ."

Well, yes. Of course. Righto and all that. Barbara knew he was speaking of the group of young Muslim women who were part of the class in which she and Dorothea had enrolled. They were learning to tap while still maintaining their modest garb, and the fact that more than half of them were actually able to execute a Cincinnati while Barbara could still only manage a simple slap was due to the fact that they did what they were told to do, which was practise, practise, practise.

"I'll bring her up to speed," Dorothea promised their instructor. He was called Kazatimiru—"You are, of course, to call me Kaz"—and for a recent Belarusian immigrant, he spoke astonishingly good English, with only a slight Slavic accent. "You're not to give up on her," Dorothea informed him.

Kaz, Barbara knew, was smitten with Dorothea. Men generally fell for her many charms. So when Dorothea prayed, charmingly, that his patience would hold, Kaz was warm putty in her manicured hands. Barbara reckoned she was completely off the hook at that. She could show up, mess about on the tap floor, pretend she knew what she was doing as long as she made appropriate noise with her shoes, and all would be forgiven. But she hadn't taken Dorothea into account.

They were going to hold post-work practice sessions, Dorothea informed her in very short order. No messing about with excuses, Detective Sergeant. There was a list of women eager to enroll in Kaz's class, and if Barbara Havers did not soon cut the metaphorical mustard with her tap shoes, she was as good as sacked.

It was only by swearing on the life of her mother that Barbara was able to convince Dorothea to relent. The secretary's plan had been to hold their practice sessions in the stairwell at work, close to the vending machines where there was room enough to shim sham, scuffle, riffle, and riff. That, Barbara had decided, was *all* she needed to complete the picture of who she was in the eyes of her colleagues. She promised she would practise nightly, and she did so. For at least a month.

She improved enough to earn Kaz's nod and Dorothea's dimpled smile. All the time she kept her dancing a secret from everyone else who touched upon her life.

She'd lost an entire stone, she found, quite effortlessly. She had to move to a smaller skirt size and the bows she tied on her drawstring trousers were getting larger by the week. Soon she would have to move to a smaller size there as well. Perhaps eventually she'd also become the picture of lithesome beauty, she decided. Stranger things had happened.

On the other hand, that lost stone *was* the open door to tucking into curry two nights a week. Plus, it allowed for absolute piles of naan. Not the plain sort, mind you, but naan dripping with garlic butter, naan with butter and spices and honey and almonds, naan any way that she could find it.

She'd been on her way to a massive weight regain when Kaz brought up the Tap Jam. This was seven months into her lessons, and she was thinking about dahl heaped upon naan alongside a lovely plate of salmon tagliatelle (she was not averse to mixing ethnicities when it came to dinner) when Dorothea said to her, "We must go, Detective Sergeant Havers. You're free on Thursday night, aren't you?"

Barbara was roused from her vision of carbohydrates gone wild. Thursday night? Free? Could there ever be a different adjective applied to *any* night in her life? Dumbly, she nodded. When Dorothea cried, "Excellent!" and called out to Kaz, "You can count on us!" she should have known something was up. It was only after the lesson as they were walking to the Tube that she discovered what it was she'd committed herself to.

"It will be such fun!" Dorothea exclaimed. "And Kaz is going to be there. He'll stay with us on the renegade stage."

*Stage* was what informed Barbara that come Thursday night, she would have to invent a sudden debilitating illness directly related to her feet. She had, apparently, just committed herself to some kind of tap-dancing extravaganza, which was among the very last things she wanted to give a place on her bucket list.

So she made a decent attempt at excuses, touching upon fallen arches and bunions gone quite mad. Dorothea's response was a pretty, "Don't even attempt to get out of this, Detective Sergeant Havers," and to make things worse, she let Barbara know that she was to bring her tap shoes to work on the day in question, and if she did not, Dorothea was utterly certain that Detective Sergeant Winston Nkata would be *pleased* to fetch Barbara home to get them. Or Detective Inspector Lynley. He loved going out and about in his fancy car, didn't he? A drive up to Chalk Farm would be the very thing.

"All right, all right," had been Barbara's surrender. "But if you even *think* I'm planning to dance, you're dead wrong on a dish."

Thus she found herself in Soho on a Thursday night.

The streets were packed, not only because tourist season had officially begun, but also because the weather was pleasant and because Soho had long attracted clubbers, theatre-goers, diners, gawkers, dancers, and drinkers. So it was a case of muscling through the hordes to get to Old Compton Street. There, a club called Ella D's was situated.

On an upper floor of the nightclub, twice each month, a Tap Jam occurred. This, Barbara quickly discovered, comprised a Jam Mash, a Renegade Jam, and a Solo Tap, all of which she vowed to eschew the moment she learned what each one demanded.

The Jam Mash was already in progress when they arrived. They waited outside for a quarter hour to see if Kaz was going to show up and introduce them to the promised delights of Ella D's. After that, however, Dorothea announced impatiently that "he's had his chance," and she led the way into the club where, from above their heads, they could hear music coming, along with what sounded like a herd of newly shoed ponies on the run.

The noise intensified as they climbed. Along with the sound of "Big Bad Voodoo Daddy," they could hear a woman shouting over a microphone: "Scuffle, scuffle! Now try a flap! Good! Now watch this."

They hadn't, after all, been abandoned by Kaz. They discovered this as they entered a large room with a raised platform at one end, some two dozen chairs pushed to the walls, and a smaller crowd than Barbara would have hoped. It was clear she wasn't going to be able to escape notice if she mingled among them.

Kaz was on the platform with a stout-looking woman in swirly 1950s gear. No high heels, naturally, but gleaming tap shoes that she was employing to serious effect. She was calling out the steps and doing them with Kaz. Before the platform three lines of tappers were attempting to duplicate the movements.

"Oh, isn't this brilliant!" Dorothea exclaimed.

For reasons obscure, she had costumed herself for this event. Whereas she had so far always gone to their lessons garbed in a leotard and tights—the leotard covered over by trousers till she reached the dance floor—tonight she'd decided on a period kit. It featured a poodle skirt, a blouse tied up beneath her breasts, and a perky ribbon round her head à la Betty Boop. Barbara had decided it was an effort at incognito, and she wished she'd thought along those lines herself.

Dorothea wasn't, however, incognito to Kaz. He clocked them within about thirty seconds, and he leapt off the platform and Cincinnatied in their direction. With the sixth sense of a seasoned dancer, he spun round just as he reached their immediate vicinity. Another two steps and he would have knocked both of them to the floor.

"What a vision!" he exclaimed. He was, of course, speaking of Dorothea. Barbara had gone for simplicity: trainers, leggings, and a T-shirt printed with I'M NOT LAUGHING AT YOU. I JUST FORGOT TO TAKE MY MEDS.

Dorothea dimpled and brought forth a quick curtsy. She said, "You looked *brilliant*!" in clear reference to his dancing. "Who's she?" she asked.

"*That,*" he said with some pride, "is KJ Fowler, the number one tapper in the UK."

KJ Fowler was still calling out the steps. When the music ended, another piece began. "Johnny Got a Boom Boom," came over the speakers. Kaz said to them, "Put your shoes on, ladies. It's time to buck."

He bucked his way back to the platform, where KJ Fowler was executing a series of steps that made the efforts of those attempting to follow her look like the Underground in rush hour. Dorothea's eyes were alight. "Shoes," she told Barbara.

At the side of the room, they put on their tap shoes. While Barbara desperately sought a believable reason for sudden paralysis, Dorothea pulled her onto the floor. A cramp roll was being executed on stage by KJ Fowler, and Kaz followed this—upon her instruction—with a dizzying combination of steps that only a fool would have attempted to emulate. Nonetheless there were takers, Dorothea among them. Barbara stepped to one side to observe. She had to admit it: Dorothea was good. She was, in fact, on her way to a solo. And with Barbara and the Muslim women as her main competitors, she was going to be there before she knew it.

They managed close to twenty minutes in the Jam Mash. Barbara was dripping sweat and thinking about the possibility of making an escape without Dorothea noticing when the music stopped—for which she fervently thanked God—and KJ Fowler informed them that time was up. At first Barbara thought this meant a blessed escape. But then KJ announced a real treat for them all. It seemed that Tap Jazz Fury were paying a visit to Ella D's.

Shouts and applause greeted this news as a small jazz band appeared out of nowhere. The assembled crowd got to it when the band did its stuff. Some of the dancers, Barbara had to admit, were so fleet of foot that she gave half a thought to continuing with tap, just to see if she could become one tenth as skilled.

It was, however, only half a thought, and it was interrupted by a vibration emanating from the area of her waistband. There she'd tucked her mobile phone, for although she'd committed to this Thursday evening extravaganza of tap dancing, she was still on rota. A vibrating phone meant only one thing. The job was ringing her.

She excavated for the phone and glanced at it. Detective Chief Superintendent Isabelle Ardery. She generally rang Barbara only when Barbara had committed some malefaction or another, so before answering, Barbara did a quick look-see at her conscience. It seemed clear.

Considering the level of noise, she knew she'd have to take the call elsewhere, so she tapped Dorothea on the shoulder, held up the mobile, and mouthed *Ardery*. Dorothea wailed, "Oh no," but of course she knew there was nothing for it. Barbara had to answer.

Still, she wasn't able to get to it before the call went to message. She shouldered her way out of the room and made for the ladies', down the corridor. Once inside, she listened, and the DCS's message was brief. "You're being called off rota, ring me at once, and why the devil aren't you answering in the first place, Sergeant?"

Barbara returned the call, and before Ardery could cook up an accusation about why she hadn't answered, Barbara said, "Sorry, guv. Noisy where I am. Couldn't get to you fast enough. What's up?"

"You're going up to West Mercia Headquarters," Ardery told her without preamble.

"I'm . . . But what've I *done*? I've not once been out of order since—"

"Ratchet down the paranoia," Ardery cut in. "I said you're *going*, not being reassigned. Bring a packed bag tomorrow and get to work early."

WANDSWORTH
LONDON

Isabelle Ardery had quickly concluded that the investigation she'd been told to conduct was going to be awkward. An enquiry by the police *into* the police was always touchy. An investigation by one police body into another owing to a death of a suspect in custody was much worse. Worst of all, however, was the intrusion of anyone from the government into the mechanics of a police enquiry. Yet within minutes of reaching the office of Assistant Commissioner Sir David Hillier, Isabelle understood she'd be dealing with all of this.

Behind her secretarial desk, Judi-with-an-i MacIntosh gave a modest indication of what was afoot, telling Isabelle to go in directly as Sir David was awaiting her arrival, with a member of Parliament. "No one I've heard of," she admitted, which told Isabelle that the MP in question was an obscure back-bencher.

"Do you know the name?" she asked Judi before she turned the knob on the door.

"Quentin Walker," the secretary replied. She added, "Not the least idea why he's here, but they've been talking for sixty-five minutes."

Quentin Walker turned out to be an MP representing Birmingham. As Isabelle opened the door, he and Hillier rose from chairs drawn round a small conference table on which a carafe of coffee stood, two cups of which were already in use. A third awaited. Once introductions had been made, Hillier indicated that she was to help herself, and she did so.

The AC made short work of telling her that on the twenty-fifth of March in the jurisdiction of the West Mercia police, someone had died while in police custody. The incident had been investigated by the Independent Police Complaints Commission as per usual, and although the IPCC had concluded that things had gone badly amiss, the investigators had also concluded that there was no reason to pass their report along to the Crown Prosecution Service, as there was no criminal charge that could be laid at anyone's feet. It was a straightforward suicide.

Isabelle glanced at Quentin Walker. There seemed to be no reason for him to be there unless this death took place while someone was in custody in Birmingham, the MP's bailiwick. But the location of the death—in the jurisdiction of the West Mercia police force—indicated that this could not be the case.

She said, "Who was the victim?"

"Bloke called Ian Druitt."

"And where was he in custody?"

"Ludlow."

Curious. Ludlow was not even near Birmingham. Isabelle glanced at Quentin Walker another time.

The MP's face was impassive, but she took in that he was a nice-looking man with a head of well-groomed chestnut hair and hands that appeared as if he'd never ventured anywhere in the vicinity of manual labour. He also had extraordinarily gorgeous skin. Isabelle wondered if someone appeared in his parliamentary office daily to shave him and administer the hot towels afterwards.

"Why was Druitt in custody? Do we know?" Isabelle asked.

Again, Hillier was the one to answer. "Child molestation." His voice was dry.

"Ah." Isabelle set her coffee cup on its saucer. "What's the brief, exactly?" She was still waiting to hear from Quentin Walker. He can't have come to the Met on a social call. He was also at least a decade younger than Hillier, so that eliminated the old school tie.

"Hanged himself while waiting to be fetched from Ludlow to the

Shrewsbury custody suite," Hillier told her. "He'd been taken to the Ludlow station pending the arrival of patrol officers." He lifted his shoulders, but his look was regretful. "It was quite a cock-up."

"But why was he taken to the Ludlow nick in the first place? Why not directly to Shrewsbury?"

"Someone seems to have felt that the allegations called for immediate action. As there's a police station in Ludlow—"

"Was no one watching him?"

"The station's unmanned."

Isabelle looked from Hillier to the MP and back to Hillier. A suicide in an unmanned police station wasn't a cock-up. It was a disaster that heralded a serious lawsuit.

It was very odd, then, that the complaints commission had taken a decision not to hand their report over to the Crown Prosecutors. The affair was irregular and Isabelle had a feeling that the answer Hillier gave to her next question was going to make it more irregular still.

"Who made the arrest?"

"Ludlow's PCSO. He did exactly what he was told to do: pick the bloke up, take him into the Ludlow station, and wait for patrol officers to come from Shrewsbury to fetch him."

"I know I don't need to mention how strange this is, sir. Ludlow's community support officer making the arrest? The newspapers must have had a field day with that once this bloke . . . what was his name again . . . Druitt, was it? Once he killed himself. Why on earth didn't the complaints commission kick this along to the Crown Prosecutors?"

"As I've said, they investigated—the IPCC—but there was simply nothing to prosecute. It was a disciplinary matter, not a criminal act. Still, the fact that Druitt had been taken to wait at an unmanned station, the fact that a police community support officer had made the arrest, the fact that the suicide was about to be questioned on the topic of child molestation . . . You see the problem."

Isabelle did. Cops hated paedophiles. That did not bode well if a paedophile died in custody. But for there to be anything additional required—once the IPCC had concluded its investigation with the decision of no criminality—indicated that something more was going on.

She said to the MP, "I don't understand why you're here, Mr. Walker. Are you somehow involved?"

"The death appears suspicious." Quentin Walker took a white handkerchief from the breast pocket of his jacket and pressed it delicately to his lips.

Isabelle said, "But it obviously wasn't suspicious to the IPCC if they concluded suicide. It's unfortunate. It sounds like dereliction of duty on the part of the PCSO. But why is it suspicious?"

Walker told her that Ian Druitt had established an after-school club for boys and girls, associated with the parish church of St. Laurence in Ludlow. It was a successful organisation and much admired. Not the slightest breath of scandal had ever touched it, and none of the children involved with the club had ever come forward with a single concern about Druitt. These facts alone had raised questions in certain quarters. Those quarters had turned to their member of Parliament in order to produce some answers.

"But Ludlow isn't part of the area you represent," Isabelle said. "Which seems to suggest that the 'certain quarters' you refer to have a personal connection to you or to the dead man. Is that right?"

Walker glanced at Hillier. The look suggested to Isabelle that her questions had somehow reassured the man. She prickled at this outward sign of the doubts he apparently had about her. It was infuriating that women were still considered so bloody secondary in the world, even here.

"*Is* there a personal connection, Mr. Walker?"

"One of my constituents is Clive Druitt," he told her. "Are you familiar with the name?"

It sounded only vaguely familiar. She couldn't place it, so she shook her head.

"Druitt Craft Breweries," the MP said. "Combination brewery and gastropub. He started his first one in Birmingham. Now there are eight."

Which meant he probably had money, Isabelle thought. Which meant he had the MP's attention when he wanted it. She said, "His relationship to the dead man?"

"Ian Druitt was his son. Understandably Clive doesn't believe his son might have been a paedophile. Nor does he believe he was a suicide."

What parent ever wanted to believe his child was engaged in criminal behavior? Isabelle thought. But surely a thorough investigation into the suicide in custody had told the dead man's father that, as regrettable and terrible as it was, Ian Druitt had died at his own hand. The MP must have explained this to Mr. Druitt. As far as Isabelle could see, there was no reason to involve the Met.

She said, with a glance at Hillier, "I still don't quite see—"

Hillier cut in, "There've been enormous cutbacks in the force up there. Mr. Walker is asking us to make certain those cutbacks have no bearing on anything related to this suicide." He'd emphasised one word: *certain*. It would be her job to assign someone to smooth the waters of Mr. Druitt's concern in order to avoid a lawsuit. This didn't please her, but she knew better than to argue with the assistant commissioner.

She said, "I can spare Philip Hale, sir. He's just finished—"

"I'd like you to handle this personally, Isabelle. It's going to require quite a delicate hand."

She kept her expression steady. This was an assignment for a detective inspector at most. Even if that were not the case, the last thing she needed at the moment was to be asked to travel up to Shropshire. She said, "If we're speaking of delicate hands, this sounds like something more suited to DI Lynley, then."

"Perhaps. But I'd like you to take it on. With Detective Sergeant Havers, by the way. I daresay she'll be an excellent second. As she acquitted herself so well in Dorset, doubtless she'll do the same in Shropshire."

Isabelle did not miss the implicit message here. Having received it, she finally recognised the matter in hand. She said, "Ah. Yes. I hadn't thought of the sergeant. I do agree, sir."

Hillier twitched a smile in her direction and said, "I did think you would." He then turned to the MP and went on. "I'll be frank, Mr. Walker. We're stretched thin everywhere and that's owing to decisions that have been taken by the government. We can give you five days only. After that, DCS Ardery and DS Havers must return to London."

Walker seemed wise enough not to argue the point. He said, "Thank you, Commissioner. Understood. Let me be frank as well. I was opposed to what's been done to reduce the police force nationally. You have a friend in me. You'll have more of a friend when this is completed."

He took his leave soon after that. Hillier had already gestured Isabelle to remain where she was. When the door had closed upon the member of Parliament, Hillier returned to his seat. He examined Isabelle, and his look was speculative.

"I trust," he said, "that this adventure in Shropshire will suffice to meet our ends at long last?"

Isabelle fully understood the AC's plan. "That would be my intention," she told him.

WANDSWORTH
LONDON

At home later, Isabelle turned her attention to packing for her trip to the Midlands. First, however, she sought the vodka. She'd already had one martini, but she told herself that she was owed another as the day had been long and the developments had been unexpected.

As she sorted out underwear, trousers, jerseys, and nightclothes for the Midlands jaunt, she enjoyed the cocktail. She'd taken to stirring instead of shaking the vodka and the ice, which provided the drink with so much more power to alter the way she looked at life. And she needed to start seeing life differently now, thanks to her shit former husband and his Necessary Career Step, Isabelle. You might consider coming out at holidays, he'd told her with unctuous pleasantry. We'll have a big enough house, and if that doesn't appeal, no doubt there'll be suitable hotels nearby. Or B & B's? That wouldn't be bad, would it? And, no, before you ask. The boys may *not* come to spend holidays with you. It's out of the question.

Isabelle would not give her former husband the pleasure of hearing her upset. Were she even to say, *Please, Bob,* she knew where that would take them: into the realm of You Know Why This Is Necessary. That would lead them directly into their shared history, yet another pointless discussion that would deteriorate quickly into accusations and denials. There was no point.

She finished her martini before she finished her packing. There was little enough left to do, so she knew she couldn't bugger anything up at this point. She was quite pleased with her level of sobriety, so she topped up her martini and then slipped the bottle of vodka carefully into her suitcase. She'd not been sleeping well lately, and she'd sleep worse in a bed that was not her own. The vodka would act as a soporific. No harm in that.

Having completed her preparations for the trip and having also placed her suitcase by the door, she finally went to the phone. She knew both of his numbers by heart, and she punched in one of them, ringing his home and not his mobile. If he wasn't there, she'd leave a message. She didn't want to disturb him if he was spending the night elsewhere.

Lynley recognised her voice, as he would do. He sounded surprised and, so completely like him, rather suspicious. After, "Guv. Hullo," he went on with, "Everything all right?" far too casually.

She schooled herself. Proper diction and cool assurance were called for. She said, "Quite fine, Tommy. Am I interrupting something?" which was a veiled way of saying, "Is Daidre with you?" and "Are you and she in the midst of what lovers are often in the midst of after ten o'clock at night?"

"You're interrupting something, but it can wait," Lynley said pleasantly. "Charlie has persuaded me to go over his lines with him. Have I mentioned that he's captured quite a good role in a Mamet play? Admittedly, it's not the West End. It's not actually in London at all. But apparently as long as it's somewhere in the Home Counties, one is meant to be impressed."

A voice spoke in the background. Isabelle recognised it as belonging to Charlie Denton. Denton had long kept lodgings in Thomas Lynley's Belgravia townhouse. In exchange for room and board, he acted as manservant, valet, cook, housekeeper, and general dogsbody, with the understanding that he would require time off to audition for anything of a thespian nature that came along. So far he'd managed a few small roles here and there, but mostly there.

"Yes, of course, you're absolutely right," Lynley was answering Charlie. "It's Mamet that counts." And then to Isabelle, "He's also waiting for a callback from the BBC."

"*Is* he?"

"His experience here in Eaton Terrace has given him—what do they call it?—serious street cred when it comes to roles in costume dramas. If his luck holds, he's to be an irascible footman in a twelve-part series taking place in the 1890s. He's asking one and all to keep fingers crossed."

"Tell him mine are."

"He'll be delighted."

"D'you have a few moments?"

"Of course. We're finished up here. Or at least I am. Charlie could go on till dawn. Has something come up?"

Isabelle gave him an abbreviated version: suicide, the West Mercia police, the IPCC, a member of Parliament, and his wealthy constituent. At the conclusion, Lynley said what was logical: "If the IPCC have indicated that there's no further case to pursue, what does Walker expect someone to find?"

"It's all pro forma, a pouring of oil on the water with the Met doing the pouring for an MP who'll doubtless be called upon later to repay the favour."

"That sounds like Hillier."

"Doesn't it just."

"When would you like me to leave? I've a jaunt down to Cornwall I intended to make, but that could easily be put off."

"I do need you to put it off, Tommy, but not in order to head to the Midlands."

"Ah. Then who . . . ?"

"Hillier's asked me to take this on."

Lynley's silence greeted this. He, too, knew how irregular it was that she would be doing a job that generally would have been taken up by a member of their department whom she outranked. Additionally, there was the not small matter of who was going to replace her while she was gone.

In answer to this, she said, "I'm leaving you in my place. This Midlands situation isn't going to require a great deal of time, so you won't have to put off Cornwall for long. I do hope all's well, by the way."

She was speaking of his family, living in Cornwall on what was purported to be a walloping great estate somewhere near the coast, which they'd so far managed to hold together without having had to wave the white flag and hand the heap over to the National Trust or English Heritage. He reassured her. This was merely something of an annual trip, he told her, made slightly complicated this season by his sister and her adolescent daughter having sold up in Yorkshire to join his mother and brother in Cornwall. "But, as I said, the trip's easily put off," he finished.

"That's helpful, Tommy. I know you're owed the time, by the way."

They had now reached the more delicate part of the conversation. Thomas Lynley was many things—urbane, educated, blue-blooded, and in possession of a dusty old title that he probably used to book tables more easily at London's most renowned restaurants—but the one thing he wasn't was a fool. He'd know something was up and he'd work it out soon enough. Still, since she was leaving him in charge, she had to tell him, so she said, "I'll be taking Sergeant Havers with me. She's reporting to work with her rucksack packed, in case you arrive after she and I have left and you begin wondering where she's got herself off to."

This, too, was met by silence. Isabelle could picture the wheels spinning in Lynley's brain. He arrived quickly at, "Isabelle, wouldn't it be wiser—"

"Guv," she corrected him.

"Guv," he agreed. "Sorry. As to having Barbara accompany you . . . Wouldn't DS Nkata be the better choice? Considering what's happened, isn't this going to require . . . well, a softer touch?"

Of course Nkata would be the better choice. Winston Nkata was a man who knew an order when he heard one, a skilled detective who had so far managed without a hint of difficulty to work in concert with the entire cast of detectives under her command. DS Nkata was the better choice for virtually anything. But he did not suit her larger purpose, and Lynley was certain to winkle that out.

"I'd like to witness Barbara back in form," she told him. "She's had some success since that Italian business and this is—at least for me—her final hurdle."

"Are you saying that if Barbara manages to carry off this enquiry without"—Lynley seemed to search for a term, choosing—"without colouring outside the lines, you'll tear up the transfer paperwork?"

"Destroying her girlish dreams of a future in Berwick-upon-Tweed? I shall put the paperwork through the shredder," she assured him.

While he seemed satisfied, she knew he would harbour enough suspicions about her intentions towards Barbara Havers that the first thing he'd do upon ringing off would be to contact the detective sergeant and give her a talking to that he hoped would get through to the exasperating woman. She could almost hear it: "Barbara," in that smooth voice of his, a mixture of Eton and received pronunciation, "this is an opportunity to determine your future. May I encourage you to see it that way?"

"I'm on board," Havers would tell him. "On it, over it, under it, and whatever you want. I'll even do without fags on the drive up there. That should impress, eh?"

"What will impress," he would counter, "is the offering of ideas instead of arguments, a dress sense that speaks of professionalism, and an adherence to procedure at all times. Are we clear?"

"As water in the Caribbean," she would say breezily. "Trust me, Inspector, I won't cock things up."

"See that you don't," would be his final remark. He would then ring off, but he would have his doubts. No one knew Barbara Havers better than her longtime partner. Cocking things up was her stock-in-trade.

Isabelle had very little doubt that she was providing Barbara Havers with sufficient rope. She herself merely had to stand back from the gallows in order to have a better view as the body plunged through the trapdoor.

# 5 MAY

HINDLIP
HEREFORDSHIRE

The first thing Barbara Havers clocked when they were finally admitted onto the vast grounds of West Mercia Police Headquarters was the isolation of the place. They'd had to stop at a lone reception building first, both to show their police identification and to inform the officer behind the counter that they were expected by the chief constable, who should have made arrangements for them to be allowed in at once. This hadn't turned out to be the case, so Barbara reckoned that the higher-ups at West Mercia Headquarters weren't exactly going to be strewing rose petals to herald their arrival.

When they finally received permission to proceed, they climbed back into their car and passed through several gates as they coursed along a drive from which not a single building could be seen. What *was* in sight were CCTV cameras. They were everywhere. But the only things they seemed to be documenting were the acres of lawns across which no terrorist—domestic or otherwise—in his right mind would have attempted to cross. For there wasn't a single tree behind which to hide. Nor was there a bush. Nor was there even a convenient sheep. Nor was there anything until they finally reached the car park.

The administrative offices were in a former great house that was sumptuously draped with Virginia creeper. The path to this imposing structure was softened by the presence of shrubbery, and in a few neatly kept flower beds roses were beginning to bloom. In addition to the great house, institutional purpose-built structures served as the rest of the headquarters, and from somewhere on the vast grounds around them, the sound of barking suggested police dogs were also trained in this place. Some kind of police cadet activity was ongoing, Barbara saw as they drew closer to the main entrance. An arrow-shaped sign reading JUNIOR CADETS THIS WAY indicated the route to a building whose shape hinted at its being a chapel that had once served the occupants of the great house.

It had taken them four and a half hours to make the drive up from London. There was no simple route. One had to choose among various motorways and primary roads with—if one was lucky—the occasional dual carriageway not afflicted by roadworks. By the time they finally reached Hindlip, the only thought in Barbara's mind was how she was going to manage a fag and where she was going to find a very large steak and kidney pie. For although Ardery had stopped for petrol along the way, she was otherwise not one for taking breaks unless the loo beckoned with considerable urgency. And even then it was a matter of in, out, and on their way. Barbara had thought it wise not to suggest an interlude somewhere that might involve lunch.

"This is an opportunity you may not have again," DI Lynley had told her privately before she'd set off with Ardery. "I hope you make the most of it."

"I plan to do some *serious* forelock pulling," Barbara had assured him. "I'll probably be bald by the time we return."

"Don't take this lightly, Barbara," he'd said. "Unlike me, the superintendent has a much lower tolerance for creative initiative. You're going to need to play by every rule. If you can't, there'll be heavy consequences."

She'd felt impatient with him. "Yes, yes, and all right. I'm not a *complete* fool, sir."

Their colloquy had been interrupted by Dorothea Harriman. The departmental secretary had obviously been put into the picture either by Lynley or by Ardery because she gestured to Barbara's small wheeled suitcase, and she said, "I hope you've got your tap shoes in there, Detective Sergeant. You know how easy is it to fall behind. And why on earth didn't you tell me last night what was going on?

I'd've asked Kaz to make a music tape for you. You can always practise in your hotel room, and now you'll have to do it without accompaniment. How many lessons will you miss? With the recital in July—"

"Recital?" This came from Lynley, who looked far too interested in the conversation for Barbara's liking.

Dorothea informed him that "there's to be a dance recital July sixth and the beginner's class is to take part in it."

"A dance recital?" He raised an aristocratic eyebrow. Barbara knew at once that their little chat with Dorothea had to be cut off.

She said hastily, "Right. Well. Yes. Whatever. Now, as to Shropshire, sir," in the hope that this would derail any other conversation.

No such luck, of course. Dorothea Harriman was the European champion of not being derailed. She said to Lynley, "*You* remember, Detective Inspector Lynley. I did tell you the detective sergeant and I were going to see about tap dancing."

"And you have, have you? *And* you've mastered it enough to be part of a dance recital? Impressive indeed." Lynley nodded at Barbara and said, "Sergeant, you're full of surprises. Where in July is the recital so that I might—"

"No need to tell him." Barbara shot a warning look at Dorothea. "He's not going to be invited." And then meaningfully to Lynley, "No one I know is going to be invited, sir, so don't take it personally. If all goes well in the Midlands, I'll break a leg and not be able to do it at all."

"Pshaw!" Dorothea said. "Detective Inspector Lynley, *I* shall invite you."

Lynley's response was a mild, "Dorothea, did you actually just say *pshaw*?"

To which Barbara said, "She's full of surprises herself, Inspector."

Now, though, there was no surprise in the fact that once she and Isabelle Ardery entered the great house and identified themselves at the huge round reception counter in the rotunda of the place, they discovered they were meant to wait. The chief constable was at present in a meeting. He would get to them when he could.

HINDLIP
HEREFORDSHIRE

Isabelle hadn't expected to be welcomed warmly by the West Mercia police. Her presence was a signal to them that someone believed they'd stepped afoul of proper procedure, and that same someone wasn't happy.

Generally, this unhappiness took the form of solicitors participating in what could be a very costly lawsuit or it took the form of unrelenting phone calls from tawdry tabloids and respected newspapers still in possession of funds for the sort of investigative journalism that most people—not to mention most organisations—preferred to avoid. But neither of those possibilities had occurred. There were no solicitors involved, no legal case threatened, and the papers that had covered the death in custody and the subsequent investigation had ultimately moved on to something else. So for there to be *another* investigation and for this current investigation to be instigated by the careful manoeuvrings of a member of Parliament . . . It was no wonder to Isabelle that she and Sergeant Havers were left cooling their heels for a full twenty-five minutes.

After the first five, Havers had politely requested permission to step outside the building for a fag. Isabelle gave idle thought to ordering her to remain where she was, but she had to admit that on the drive north, during which she had deliberately not paused for anything save petrol and then the use of a lavatory at one of the service areas, Havers had been a model of cooperation. She had even dressed with care, although where on earth she'd found the hideous cardigan she was wearing—grey decidedly did not become her nor did the pills that dotted the garment like an outbreak of smallpox—would remain a mystery. So to the query about a single cigarette, Isabelle nodded. She told the sergeant to be quick about it, and so the sergeant was.

A uniformed female officer came to fetch them at long last. They went up a grand staircase and through great double doors at one side of a large landing. Behind these doors was what had probably once been the drawing room of the former great house. A large room with spectacular windows, it retained its ceiling of impressive plasterwork, the original chandelier still hung from a medallion ornamented with a plethora of plaster fruit, and an enormous marble fireplace still possessed its huge caryatid-supported mantel on which two wedding photographs and a plaque of some sort were displayed.

Once told that the chief constable had only stepped out of the office for a moment and would be with them presently, Isabelle crossed her arms and stifled what she felt like saying, which was along the lines of "He's already *made* his point." Instead, she forced herself to consider the room and its past as a drawing room. The furniture made it difficult to imagine groups of period pieces arranged artfully for coffee, tea, and polite postprandial conversation. The chief constable's desk took up a vast amount of space, and an institutional bookshelf behind it offered a score of unattractive three-ring notebooks with covers of plastic or of canvas. These were held in place by stacks of manila folders in various degrees of disintegration. On top of the folders sat a collection of dust-covered wrought-iron toys and three cricket balls held in a basket. To one side of the room a coffee table stood between two heavily curtained windows. Five chairs surrounded this, and a glass jug of water along with five glasses suggested that this was where they were going to have their meeting with the chief constable.

Sergeant Havers had gone to one of the windows. Doubtless she was wishing she were outside where she could suck down another fag. Doubtless also, she was hungry. Isabelle herself was famished, but food was going to have to wait.

Both of the office's doors opened simultaneously, as if two unseen footmen were without on the landing and doing the honours. A uniformed man looking vaguely like the Duke of Windsor ten years into his marriage to Wallis strode inside. He didn't extend a welcome. Instead, he said, "Superintendent Ardery," and gave Havers a glance that plainly indicated that an introduction to her was not going to be required.

He didn't give his name, but Isabelle didn't allow her hackles to rise at this, nor at his mistake about her rank. She already knew his name anyway: Chief Constable Patrick Wyatt. She would correct him about her rank in due time.

He also didn't invite them to sit. Instead he said, "I'm not happy you're here," and he appeared to be waiting for her response.

She cooperated. "And I'm not happy to be here. Neither is Detective Sergeant Havers. Our intention is to be as brief as possible in order to craft a report for our superiors and then to be gone."

This appeared to thaw the chief constable slightly. He gestured to the coffee table with its five chairs and he said, "Coffee?" to which Isabelle demurred. She shot a look at Havers, who did likewise. Isabelle said that the water currently on the table was fine, thank you very much indeed. She didn't wait for the chief constable to pour. She took a seat and did the honours all round. Havers also sat. She sipped. Her expression said she was expecting hemlock, but as this was the only liquid available she would at least die slaked.

Wyatt finally joined them, and Isabelle went at their situation directly. "Sergeant Havers and I have been put in a difficult position. It's not our intention to blacken anyone's reputation up here."

"I'm glad to hear that." Wyatt took up his water, gulped it all down, and poured himself another glassful. Havers, Isabelle noticed, looked relieved that he hadn't keeled over after downing the first.

"Cutbacks are making a hash of things everywhere," Isabelle said. "I know you've taken an enormous hit—"

"Our 'hit' is that we're down to eighteen hundred officers policing Herefordshire, Shropshire, and Worcestershire. We've not a single bona fide constable walking a beat any longer, and entire towns are now in the hands of police volunteers and the Neighbourhood Watch. At this point, it takes—minimally—twenty minutes for one of our officers to arrive at a crime scene. And that's only if the poor sod isn't already dealing with something somewhere else."

"It's not that much different in London," Isabelle said.

Wyatt harrumphed and shot a look at Havers as if she were the embodiment of what cutbacks in policing had reduced the world to. Havers met his look but said nothing. She didn't appear cowed.

"I want to make a few things clear," Wyatt said. "On the night of the incident, an ambulance was dispatched at once when the first call came through. When it was clear to the paramedics that the man could not be revived, the call centre was informed and the duty detective inspector was sent in. *Not* a patrol officer first, mind you—had there even been one available, which there was not—and not a duty inspector. The force incident manager sent a detective and that officer went to Ludlow straightaway. She initiated an investigation at once, and in due course she phoned the complaints commission."

"In due course?"

"Within three hours. This followed her inspection of the scene and her interview with the paramedics and the officer present at the station, as well as the arrival of the Home Office pathologist. Everything was done by the book."

"I appreciate that information," Isabelle told him. The West Mercia police had adhered to an understandably foreshortened version of standard procedure. Receiving the news from the paramedics, they had cut to the chase instead of sending a patrol officer followed by a duty inspector followed by a detective. A death in custody was going to require special handling, and the officer on duty at the control centre, having taken note of the contents of the 999 call, would have known this at once.

She said, "Was a parallel investigation going on, then, while the IPCC was investigating?"

"An investigation into how the cock-up occurred in the first place? Yes, there was," Wyatt told her. "Both investigations were thorough. Both reports were shared with the victim's family, and the IPCC's report was made available to the public and the press. To be frank, why the Metropolitan Police have decided to intrude at this point is beyond my ken."

"We're here as reassurance for a member of Parliament. He's taking considerable pressure from the dead man's father."

"Bloody politics." The phone on Wyatt's desk rang, and he stood to answer it. He said only, "Speak," and then listened to the reply. "Send her up at once," was his next statement.

He went to the bookshelves behind his naval destroyer of a desk, gathered a stack of manila folders, and returned with them to his chair, where he placed them on the coffee table.

Isabelle glanced at them but did not take them up for a look. There would be plenty of time for that later. For now, she wanted to be put into the picture from the CC's point of view. She said, "We know the death occurred at the Ludlow station. We know the place was unmanned on the night of the death. But what's the actual situation there?"

"We've had to close down stations in all three counties," Wyatt told them. He gestured to a large map on the wall between the two windows of the room. It hung just above where they were sitting, and Isabelle recognised it as comprising Herefordshire, Shropshire, and Worcestershire. "In Ludlow's case, the station's unmanned, but it's not unused. Officers stop in when they're out on patrol, in need of computers, or establishing an incident room."

"Is there a custody suite?"

He shook his head. There was no place in the building for suspects in a crime to be held under lock and key. Nor were there interview rooms, although it wouldn't be entirely irregular for someone to be taken there to be questioned if a patrol officer felt it necessary.

"We've been told that a patrol officer didn't make the arrest, that a PCSO did the job."

Patrick Wyatt confirmed this. The individual who'd died inside the Ludlow police station had been taken there by a police community support officer. He'd been informed by his guv that the regular patrol officers would be driving down later from Shrewsbury when they finished dealing with a string of burglaries. Eight homes were involved along with five businesses in two different towns, and the Shrewsbury patrol officers had been assisting the very few detectives that could be mustered to attend the scenes of the crimes. They'd reckoned four hours before they could get to Ludlow.

"Why the rush to bring him in?"

The CC didn't know, since the order to bring in the alleged paedophile would have come from the PCSO's own superior, who'd be in charge of all the support officers in the area. What he *could* tell them was that a phone call had been made accusing Ian Druitt of child molestation. It had been made anonymously. It had come into 999 and not 101, and it had been made from the external emergency intercom at the Ludlow police station.

"External intercom?" came from Havers. Isabelle saw that the sergeant had produced a fresh-looking notebook from her shoulder bag along with a mechanical pencil.

At all closed or unmanned police stations, Wyatt informed her, external intercoms now allowed members of the community to be put in touch with the control room that handled emergencies as well as major crimes.

"So because of that call, someone was dispatched at once?" Isabelle asked. "Surely it was something that could have waited a few hours, even a day, for a patrol officer to be free."

Wyatt didn't disagree. He said that he reckoned this unfortunate circumstance had been the result of a confluence of two issues: the extent to which the regular patrol officers were involved in the burglary situation and the fact that the call involved paedophilia, which was an accusation that the police had learned over time to take very seriously.

A knock sounded on the chief constable's office door, and he strode to admit a woman with a dress sense not dissimilar to Barbara Havers's. Wyatt introduced her: Detective Inspector Pajer. She looked frazzled. While her smooth black hair was cut in an attractive style that cradled her oval face and fell to her jaw, beneath her eyes there were unappealing bags, which were darkly fleshed. Her lips were so chapped that they looked painful. Her hands were reddish, as if from rough work. Had she not been carrying a briefcase, Isabelle might have assumed she'd come to clean the office.

DI Pajer said, "It's Bernadette," to Isabelle as she crossed the room, offered her hand first to Isabelle and then to Havers. She took one of the vacant seats. She poured herself a glass of water without being bidden. Then she opened her briefcase, brought forth a stack of labelled filing folders, and waited as the chief constable joined them.

Pajer folded her hands on what she'd brought with her and said, "Before we go into anything, I'd like to be told the brief."

"Your work isn't being questioned, Bernadette," Wyatt explained.

"Due respect, sir? If I'm asked to headquarters in order to speak to officers from the Met, I suggest that's not the case," Pajer replied.

Thus Isabelle understood that Pajer was the detective inspector who'd been on duty the night of Ian Druitt's death. It was her investigation—along with the IPCC's—that she and Havers had come to look into. Much as she'd done for Wyatt, Isabelle explained the politics of the situation to Pajer, ending with her intention to be on the road back to London as soon as possible.

Pajer listened, nodded, and placed her filing folders on the coffee table near to those Wyatt had already put there. She began to share her information.

Present when she arrived at the Ludlow station, she said, were the paramedics who'd worked on Ian Druitt and the PCSO who'd arrested him: one Gary Ruddock. The body had been moved, and the ligature Druitt used had been taken from his neck.

"What was the ligature?" Isabelle asked.

Here Pajer took from a file the photographs taken of the scene. Among them was one of a long band of scarlet material perhaps four inches wide. This, she told them, was a stole. It was part of the vestments worn by clergymen when doing a service.

"Was the dead man a clergyman?" Isabelle asked.

"He was. You've not been told?"

Isabelle glanced at Havers, whose lips had formed an O. She, like Isabelle herself, had to be wondering why this was a detail they hadn't been given in London. She said, "I see. Please go on."

According to the arresting PCSO, Druitt had just completed evensong when Ruddock arrived to fetch him to the station, and he was in the vestry of St. Laurence Church in the midst of removing his vestments. Evidently, he put the stole into a pocket of his anorak.

"Could Ruddock have pinched it?" Havers asked. "When he fetched the deacon, I mean."

DI Pajer had considered the possibility, she told them. But she thought it very unlikely. For pinching the stole suggested some kind of plan, and it was a matter of pure chance that the PCSO had been the one charged with hauling in Druitt. And of course, he would know—as they all did—that a death while in custody was going to trigger not one but two investigations.

It seemed that Pajer had done everything as it was meant to be done. She'd rung for a Home Office pathologist; she'd removed the paramedics and Ruddock from the scene; she'd taken their statements separately; she'd phoned for the scenes of crime officers as a precaution and when they'd arrived, they'd taken clothing, fingerprints, and everything else necessary should it be decided that a crime had been committed rather than a suicide having occurred. She had not made that determination. She'd merely done what she was supposed to do, given the circumstances she found herself in. It was all, she said, in the material she'd brought with her. Each interview she'd conducted: from the operator at the call centre who'd taken the PCSO's panicked call to the paramedics who'd used the paddles to try to shock Druitt's heart back to beating.

"And the IPCC?" Isabelle enquired.

Pajer confirmed that she'd rung for a complaints commission investigator directly upon the Home Office pathologist's formal look at the body. The IPCC had sent someone the next day. She was the first person who was interviewed, after which the investigator went on from there.

It was clear to Isabelle that this was the conclusion of Pajer's remarks. The DI replaced the photos into their folder and centred it along with other files on the table. She also gave Wyatt a look asking if that would be all, since she was—as they all were—increasingly overburdened.

Wyatt said to Isabelle, "If you've no further questions . . . ," and DI Pajer started to rise.

Isabelle said, "I'm wondering if anyone made certain that this PCSO—Ruddock—was truly the only available choice to arrest Ian Druitt."

Wyatt said sharply, "'This PCSO' has been a good officer, and he's taken what's happened damn hard. Not only because someone died on his watch but also because he knows what that means for the rest of his career. His brief was to take the man to the station and to wait for the patrol officers who would remove him to Shrewsbury. And that's exactly what he did."

"Why didn't he just take him directly to Shrewsbury himself?" This from Havers again, pencil poised for the CC's reply.

"Ruddock did what he was told to do by his superior," Wyatt told them. "That would be the local sergeant in charge of all the West Mercia PCSOs. I assume DI Pajer has also interviewed this individual," with a look at Pajer.

She said, "The problem—you'll read it in the report, of course—was that Ruddock also had to deal with an incident of binge drinking in the town."

"Do you mean he left the police station once he fetched Druitt?" Again, from Havers.

"Of course he didn't leave the station!" Wyatt declared.

"But then how—"

At this, the chief constable stood, in the act of examining his watch. He said, "We've given you all the time we have. Everything you need to know is in the files, and I assume you're meant to read them. Would that be correct?"

Of course it would, Isabelle thought. But she said nothing as, obviously, the chief constable knew the answer already.

LUDLOW
SHROPSHIRE

Ding had spent the afternoon just outside Much Wenlock, watching her mum play tour guide to the few paying visitors who actually wanted to have a look at the Donaldsons' mausoleum of a house. Ding hated this. It wasn't so much that she had to put up with strangers breathing on the family silver—especially as there *was* no family silver—but rather it was that she had to put up with her mother's desperation to please. This showed itself in the ridiculous stories she concocted about what she'd decided to refer to as the King James Room, the Queen Elizabeth Chamber, and the Roundheads Hall. Ding gritted her teeth practically down to her gums each time she heard her mother say, in artificial pear-shaped tones, "Now it was here in 1663 . . . ," because this signalled the launching of the Capture of Cardew Hall and God only knew what else because Ding tried not to hear anything more of it. Most of the time she succeeded since her job was to remain in the entry hall in order to sell tickets to tourists and to take money for her mother's homemade chutneys and jams. At least the chutneys and jams were the real thing, although Ding wouldn't have put it past her mother—in a bad year for fruit—to purchase a few cases of Sainsbury's strawberry jam and just repurpose it as her own.

The fact that their home was called Cardew Hall was the only part of the tour that was true. The place had always been Cardew Hall, although Ding's mum knew nothing of a single ancestor who might have lived in it, having herself inherited the virtual pile of rubble from a childless great-uncle and also having made the completely mad decision *not* to unload it at once onto an entrepreneur eager to turn it into a Relais & Châteaux hotel.

So because of all this and, more, because of the family's desperate need for funds to repair the plumbing, restring the electrical wiring, modernise the kitchen and the bathrooms, and rid the entire rubbish tip of mold, mildew, and more pests than one could begin to enumerate, Ding was forced to show up two afternoons each week during summer term and every single afternoon during summer hols, and do her daughterly duty by keeping her post at the front door. While she despised every moment that she had to do this, it was the deal she'd made with her mother: Ding could enjoy the freedom of living-in accommodation in Ludlow provided that she returned on the afternoons when Cardew Hall was open to view. But the entire experience always put her on edge.

She was looking for some kind of respite when she got back to Ludlow, but when she reached the house in Temeside, she knew it was going to be difficult if not impossible to achieve that inside the place. For she recognised the Volvo parked mostly on the pavement in front of the house, and she realised that Finn Freeman's mum had decided to drop by. Knowing that a visit from her would result in a row—because it always did whenever Finn spoke to his mum—Ding decided to seek a few minutes of peace by the river. She knew just the place: up along the way at Horseshoe Weir. There, from the pavement above, she'd be able to look down on the pool. As waterfowl had taken up residence with spring's arrival, she might manage a glimpse of ducklings. Ducklings *always* improved her spirits.

That was how she ended up catching sight of Brutus and Allison Franklin, lip-locked on the River Teme with their kayaks lashed together to make the lip-locking easier. Her afternoon had been the camel. Seeing Brutus and Allison was the straw.

She felt something fracture within her. Brutus was *supposed* to be the one person in her life whom she could rely on now that Missa was gone from Ludlow. Yes, yes, even to believe that was completely ridiculous since he'd told her from the first that they would only be friends with privileges. But when she'd agreed to that plan, she'd also assumed that he wouldn't be seeking "privileges" with anyone else, let alone doing so less than two hundred yards from the home he lived in. The home he lived in with *her*, with Ding.

She was staring at the two of them—Brutus and the loathsome Allison—when a car's alarm began blaring just nearby. This caused several of the mallards to squawk and take flight. In the river, Brutus and Allison parted and, as luck would have it, Brutus caught sight of Ding. She spun round to leave, only to hear his friendly call of, "Hey! Dingster! How did it go this time?"

She spun back to the sight of him and to the sight of Allison looking so smug that Ding wanted to launch herself into the river, walk across the water like an enraged cartoon character, and rip off the other girl's face. But instead all she did was shriek, "You . . . you!" on a rising note that sounded like a cat whose tail is caught in a slammed door. This was more humiliating than seeing Brutus and Allison in the first place—not to mention being seen *by* Brutus and Allison—so she whipped back round, stepped off the pavement, and was nearly hit by a city bus. That shot adrenaline through her and shook enough sense into her that she was able to get home without being the victim of a roadway incident.

Inside the house, she could hear Finn and his mum going at it. The situation, she reckoned, had to be serious because they generally went at it over the phone, not in person. Indeed, she'd only actually seen Mrs. Freeman once before now, along with Finn's dad when they'd delivered a bookcase and a chest of drawers for Finn's bedroom back in the autumn. And that had been a very brief visit. Finn couldn't have hustled them out of the house any faster had the building been on fire.

Now in the sitting room Finn's mum was in the midst of saying, "If I hate anything—which I do not—what I hate is how that man pulled the wool over your eyes."

"He didn't. He was a decent bloke. He was my friend as well. And you bloody hate it when I have friends. Just fucking admit it, Mum."

There was a moment of silence. Ding could hear an intake of breath, probably an attempt to get calm. She knew she should have taken this moment to announce her presence, but she didn't do it. She remained where she was and she listened. At least it took her mind off Brutus and off Cardew Hall.

Finally, Finn's mum said, "Do you actually think . . . ?" And after another pause, "Are you trying to protect Ian Druitt? Is that what this is?"

"Fat lot I can do to protect him since he's dead," Finn replied.

"Listen to me, Finnegan. I've been told there's a new investigation being launched with officers from Scotland Yard. They very well might want to speak with you."

"Why?"

"Because they're here to conduct an investigation *into* the investigation that was done following Ian Druitt's suicide."

"No *way* did Ian—"

"All right. Whatever you wish to call it. But they're investigating and chances are they're going to come across your name. If that happens and if you deny something you know to be true—"

"I don't know *anything* to be true," he broke in. "Except Ian was my mate and I know my mates. No way am I denying that. D'you think I wouldn't have *known* it if he was messing round with little kids? He was a good bloke and good blokes don't ever—"

"Oh for God's sake! D'you actually think child molesters hang round the local infants' school drooling, with their cocks hanging out of their trousers? Just because you think you know someone doesn't mean you have the slightest clue who they really are. I want you to promise me that you'll stay clear of anything having to do with the wretched man's death."

"You just told me some Scotland Yard people're going to want to talk to me. Am I s'posed to leave town?"

"I said they *might* want to talk to you. I said if they do, you're to tell them the truth."

"Oh, I know a few truths they'd be chuffed to hear."

"*What* is that supposed to mean? Finnegan, do I need to make clear how little more it will take before I pull the plug on this entire college experience you claim to be having?"

Ding thought this might be the moment to intrude, so she opened and closed the front door again—this time employing a slam—and she passed by, then executed a backtrack to put herself in the doorway to the sitting room. She saw that Finn was deliberately slouching on the sofa, a posture that was guaranteed to drive his mother straight round the bend. For her part, Mrs. Freemen was standing practically on top of him. She turned at the sound of Ding's saying, "Oh. Hullo," to which Finn responded with, "Don't come in 'less you want her to sort you as well."

"Dena." Mrs. Freeman wore an expression that told Ding she was meant to move along, up the stairs and out of earshot.

Had Ding not already had her day driven into the ground first by Cardew Hall and second by Brutus, she would have sauntered into the sitting room and plopped onto one of the huge beanbags, just to irritate the woman. But since her day had already gone from bad to worse, she wanted just to be alone. Besides, she had an essay to write, so she gave a desultory wave to Finn, and she went for the stairs.

"Let's get back to it," was the last she heard, spoken by Finn's mum.

"Oh right. Let's *do* that," was Finn's sarcastic reply.

Since her bedroom was at the back of the house, Ding heard nothing more. She closed her door to make sure that remained the case.

She had an electric kettle in her room for early morning tea, and she switched this on.

She was just settling down to do some work, cup of tea on the desk next to her notebook, when her bedroom door opened. She swung round, and when she saw it was Brutus she wanted to spit fire at him.

"Leave me alone," she said. "I've had a rotten day."

"No one showed up?"

How infuriating it was that he was speaking about her afternoon at Cardew Hall when he bloody well knew he'd made a ruin of what could have been their decent evening because of his antics on the river. She said, "That's not what I'm talking about, *Bruce*."

He ignored the *Bruce* and said, "Had a good number of visitors then?" and damn him if he didn't close the door behind him and *snick* the lock, as if he thought he'd be getting some.

"If you must know, three Germans and one American lady with a notebook and a tape recorder. Now if you don't mind . . ." She swung back to her desk.

Brutus came to her. He played the masseur with her shoulders and her neck. He knew she liked that. He'd used it as a prelude to sex often enough. Was he *actually* thinking she'd be doing it with him not a half hour after she'd seen him sticking his tongue down Allison Franklin's throat?

She shook him off. "Go away." Then, "Leave me *alone*," when he kept up the massage action.

He dropped his hands. But he didn't leave. Instead he said, "So you saw me with Allison. The whole deal, right?"

"*What* whole deal? Did you actually go further than tasting her tonsils? What was 'the whole deal,' then? Sticking your fingers up her pussy?"

He was silent. She was forced to turn on her chair and look at him. His thick blond hair was tousled, suggesting Allison's having had her way with it, and one of his shirtsleeves was rucked enough that Ding could picture Allison's nasty little hand snaking up it to feel the muscles she'd find there. And he *did* have muscles, did Brutus. He'd been a weightlifting fiend from the time he'd concluded that five foot four was going to do it as far as his height was concerned.

"So?" she said. "Are you going to answer?"

"I thought we agreed. It doesn't mean shit."

"Which *part* of it doesn't mean shit? The you and me part of it? The you and Allison part of it? Or the you and the everyone with a vagina part of it?"

"We aren't exclusive, Ding, you and me. I was upfront from the first. I *told* you how I needed it to be. It's how I'm made. It's how most blokes are made. They act faithful because if they don't, they won't get any. So what you should feel is—"

"*Don't* you tell me what I should feel!"

"—grateful that at least you *know* where we stand. I always told the truth about that."

"Oh. Pardon me for not being grateful. I see I should have *applauded* your openness. I should congratulate you for feeling free to get into some other girl's knickers one hundred yards from our front door and in bloody plain sight!" She hated herself for shrieking the last four words.

He said, "If you knew that you couldn't be what me and you are, then you should've told me upfront. But you didn't tell me. Why? 'Cause what you thought is that the way I am—the way I *told* you I am—wouldn't apply in your case."

"I never!"

"So why the freak-out? You always like it well enough. You don't fight me off, even when you know I've already been with—"

She shoved him away from her. "Get out!" she shouted. "Get bloody out of here because if you don't I'll start screaming. *Then* I'll tell everyone that you . . . I'll tell . . . I swear . . ." She threw a textbook at him.

He dodged the book, but it was perhaps her words that kept him inside her room. "Tell everyone?" His tone was deadly serious of a sudden. "Tell everyone what, Ding?"

"I woke up," she said. "All right? I bloody woke up, and you weren't here."

LUDLOW
SHROPSHIRE

They found their hotel in the mediaeval part of town, just across from the great ruins of Ludlow Castle. This sat splendidly upon a promontory high above the River Teme, which curved round the castle on the west and south, a peaceful tributary overhung with willows and beeches. That, along with the River Corve to the north, acted as good as a moat.

Griffith Hall had apparently lived many lives from its time as a residence for the Griffith family, retainers to successive Earls of March. It had endured a lengthy period as an exclusive school for young boys and wartime use as a recuperation site for the wounded. It had served as a town museum and from that it had become what it was today: a dispirited hotel in need of a deep infusion of cash. Even the peonies and hydrangeas, which massed brightly along a stone wall separating the car park from an expanse of lawn, could not do much to change the air of better times gone by that hung over it.

Isabelle's digs were high in the building and accessed by so many staircases, fire doors, and corridors that she reckoned she would require a trail of breadcrumbs to find her way down to breakfast in the morning. But they also had the virtue of being two spacious rooms and a bathroom, although their windows looked out upon rooftops from one, a corner of the castle from another, and from a third—heavily curtained—the building next door. When she opened those last curtains to let in more light, she was greeted by the sight of an elderly gentleman wearing what appeared to be a onesie. This was unbuttoned, displaying his concave chest through whose grey hairs he was meditatively running his fingers. He saw Isabelle and waved gamely. She jerked the curtains closed and vowed not to open them again.

She unpacked quickly. She'd rung down to reception for ice and lemon, and while she was laying out her toiletries on the white wicker cart that served as the bathroom vanity, the ice and lemon arrived. Room service was the same person who'd checked them into the place and carried their bags to their rooms: a boy in the vicinity of twenty who favoured false eyelashes and black liner and whose ear gauges had created holes through which a golf ball could have been hit. She saw that he'd brought her a single drinking glass with two pieces of ice in it and one slice of lemon lying perkily at the top. She'd assumed requesting ice meant a bucketful—small though that bucket might have been—and that lemon would mean a plate of slices, but that obviously was not going to be the case. She stopped herself from complaining so early in the game—for all she knew, the poor boy would serve the dinner as well, and she didn't fancy him spitting into her food—and she thanked him as graciously as she could. Then she went to the bedside table where she'd stowed her vodka and tonic. Considering this was going to be her only drinking opportunity while in her room just now, she went for strength. A quarter cup of tonic accompanied vodka that topped up the glass. She drank deeply. She was owed in more ways than one.

It was clear that Thomas Lynley had managed a few words with Sergeant Havers before their jaunt to Shropshire. The woman had been cooperation personified from first to last, no matter the tests that Isabelle devised for her. On their one brief stop for petrol and their second to use the ladies', the sergeant hadn't flickered an eyelash at Isabelle's "Buy yourself a bag of crisps or something as we won't be stopping again." Rather, she had returned from her trip to the ladies' with two virtuous apples, one of which she handed over to Isabelle.

She'd maintained this persona all the way through their interview with the chief constable. If she minded not being introduced to the man—something Isabelle was certain the supremely well-bred DI Lynley would never have failed to see to—she gave no indication of that. She'd merely taken notes, asked a question here and there, and waited for further instruction.

The sergeant had also made no comment when shown her accommodation in Griffith Hall, which Isabelle had made certain in advance would be suitable only for a novice in a cloistered convent. She *had* relented about the bathroom—shower, loo, and sink, but that must be the absolute limit, do you understand?—and the bed needed to be a single, she'd instructed the hotel. If it was more like a camp-bed than something suitable for a hotel, all the better. Isabelle had long since discovered where Barbara Havers lived, in something of a hut that looked as if it had earlier served as a garden shed, so if the sergeant had thought to utter a word of complaint, Isabelle was ready with a reply. But she did not complain. She merely entered, slung her bag on the bed, and asked if the telly worked. Apparently she'd been watching *EastEnders* from her mother's womb.

"You'll have little enough time for television," Isabelle had informed her before heading off to her own room. She'd handed over the pile of folders that DI Pajer and the CC of the West Mercia police had given to them. "Have a look through these."

Havers had blinked. But she gave no hint that dividing up the folders might expedite the process.

Before dinner, she met Havers in the bar, as arranged. Someone—no doubt Lynley—had put the sergeant into the picture of changing for dinner, but she'd misinterpreted the idea of changing, reckoning it meant just altering one's outfit. All she'd come up with was beige trousers, brown brogues, and a blue blouse that was only travelling towards threadbare instead of having already arrived at that destination. Isabelle's vodka and tonic had mellowed her, though. She didn't mention the sergeant's attire. Instead, she sat upon one of the leather sofas and gestured for Havers to take the other.

The sergeant looked confused. Then she cast a glance in the direction of the dining room. She went for apologetic as she said, "Sorry to bring this up, but . . . I mean, as we didn't have lunch . . . ?"

It was clear she'd never been to a hotel, fine or otherwise. A B & B probably, a pub with rooms maybe, but a full-service hotel with a bar and restaurant in addition to a breakfast room . . . ? Not at all. The poor woman didn't know what to do with herself.

"This is how we begin, Sergeant," Isabelle told her. "Do sit. They'll bring us menus. I'm ordering a drink. Have one yourself. It's after hours, and we're officially off duty."

Havers hesitated. She'd brought several of the investigation's filing folders with her, and she clutched them defensively to her chest.

Isabelle said, "Surely Inspector Lynley hasn't *always* forced you to have your meals in . . . I don't know . . . Little Chefs? I can't think that would quite be his cup of tea. *Do* sit down. Someone will be along. Hotels have a sixth sense about these things."

Havers relented, but she perched on the edge of the sofa. She kept the filing folders hugging her body, clearly expecting this to be a working dinner, and she managed to look as if Isabelle would leap to her feet at any second and announce that the joke was on her.

Within moments, Isabelle's promised someone arrived, menus in hand. As she'd suspected, it was Mr. Eyelashes Et Cetera. She asked him his name.

"Peace," he said.

"I beg your pardon? Your name is Peace?"

"Peace on Earth," he told her. "Mum liked to make statements."

"Did she indeed? Have you siblings, Peace on Earth?"

"End of Hunger," he told her. "After that, she couldn't get pregnant again. Just as well, you ask me." He handed them the menus, saying, "Drinks?" as he did so.

Isabelle was more than ready for her second of the evening. She said, "Vodka martini, straight up, with olives. Stirred, not shaken, if you will. Sergeant, what will you have to drink?"

Havers, she saw, was studying what appeared to be the fancy cocktail list. Her brow was furrowed, and her lips were moving as she read the names and their accompanying descriptions. She finally said airily, "I think I'll have the same. The vodka thing."

"You're certain?" Isabelle doubted Havers had ever even had a martini.

"Certain as there's snow in the Alps."

Isabelle nodded at Peace on Earth. "Two vodka martinis, then."

He said, "Will do," and took himself off to the bar to do the mixing there.

Isabelle wondered if he was also the chef. So far there appeared to be no one else working in the place.

"Wonder if he's got his mum's skeleton kitted out in the attic," Havers murmured, glancing round the lounge in which they sat. They were its only occupants.

Isabelle frowned. "His mum?"

"You know. Beware of the portrait with moving eyeballs and taking a shower if there's a curtain and not a glass door? Anthony Perkins? Janet Leigh? The Bates Motel?" When Isabelle made no reply, Havers went on. "Good God, guv, have you never seen *Psycho*?" She made stabbing motions along with a *wee, wee, wee* sound. "All that blood swirling down the drain?"

"I seem to have missed it."

Havers looked astonished. "Missed it?" Her expression suggested that she wanted to ask if Isabelle had been in a coma for several decades.

"Yes. Missed it, Sergeant. Is it required viewing for anyone considering a holiday and looking for accommodation?"

"No, but . . . well, some things are cultural touchstones. Aren't they?"

"I wouldn't disagree, although I'm not sure violent death through shower curtain is one of them."

Peace on Earth brought them a bowl of mixed nuts and another of cheese straws. Havers looked at them longingly, but she didn't help herself. Isabelle reached for a cheese straw and offered the bowl to her. The sergeant took one and held it, cigarlike, between two fingers, as if waiting permission to put her teeth upon it. When Isabelle crunched down upon hers, Havers did the same. Her unnerving accuracy in duplicating Isabelle's movements made the DCS wonder whether she'd been practising the art of mirroring in her spare time.

"What have you gathered so far?" Isabelle asked her, with a gesture at the files they'd been given.

Havers referenced the anonymous call that had come into the 999 control centre. It had been a man's voice, no name given, and as all calls were, it had been recorded. The IPCC files had contained a transcript of the call, and it was the transcript that had caught the sergeant's attention. After making the claim of child molestation against Ian Druitt, the voice had said, "I can't abide the hypocrisy. That sod goes after children—boys *and* girls. He has done for years, and *no one* wants to see it. It's like the goddamn Catholic Church."

Havers said, "First I wondered why anyone took the call seriously, guv. It was like an anonymous letter when you think about it. Someone decides to cause this bloke Druitt aggro, so he rings 999 and makes a claim about him. He doesn't offer proof, but the coppers rush out and make an arrest."

"Paedophilia being something the police are going to take on board at once, Sergeant . . . ," Isabelle pointed out, leaving the rest hanging there because Havers would know it. The phone call was not unlike someone anonymously ringing the coppers to indicate a neighbour had been seen shoving a body under the patio. Wheels were going to be set in motion.

"Oh, I understand that. But it was the last part. The Catholic Church bit."

Isabelle had taken another cheese straw, but she held it midway to her mouth. "The Catholic Church bit?"

"Child abuse and the Catholic Church. Doesn't that suggest anything to you?"

"Should it? I mean aside from the fact that it's come out that Catholic priests were diddling children, and their superiors knew it and did nothing about it."

"Exactly, guv. This bloke Ian Druitt? Turns out he was a *deacon*, not a full-on priest. So he had a superior right here in Ludlow, a superior who could have known all along what he was up to but did nothing to stop him."

"You're suggesting that that's the reason behind the anonymous phone call: that the Anglican Church did exactly as the Catholic Church has done. Well and good, but where does that take us?"

"To the fact that an Anglican deacon offed himself in the Ludlow police station without ever being told why he was there. Because 'cording to the IPCC report, the PCSO brought him in but said nothing to the bloke because *he* didn't even know why he'd been told to fetch him. And then the bloke offed himself? That doesn't make sense."

"It makes sense if you consider that, being a deacon of the church, Ian Druitt could have read the handwriting on the wall the moment the PCSO showed up to collect him. What was his name again?"

Havers consulted her paperwork. Peace on Earth came to their table with their martinis. She said, "Gary Ruddock. And what I'm saying—"

"Thank you, Peace. May I call you Peace, by the way?" Isabelle said all of this with meaning. Her discussion with Havers wasn't one that she wanted anyone—let alone a hotel factotum—to overhear.

"Fine by me," Peace on Earth said as he placed the drinks in front of them.

Hastily, then, Havers closed the file. She took up her martini and before Isabelle could mention that it was something she might want to savour, she swigged a mouthful as if it were mineral water. Thankfully, the top of her head did not burst into flames, although her comment, "Strong," barely made it from between her lips afterwards.

Peace had, in the meantime, transformed himself into their waiter. He produced a pad and pen and asked them about their menu choices. Isabelle went for the soup followed by the lamb medium rare, and Havers, who hadn't looked at the menu and possibly hadn't even seen the menu, said in something of a post-vodka murmur that she'd have the same, although her expression suggested that she didn't know lamb could be cooked in any way other than to a crisp.

When the young man had taken himself off—possibly to do the cooking as well—Isabelle pointed out to Havers that the fact that Ian Druitt was an Anglican deacon explained two elements of the case. The first was why the phone call to 999 had been made anonymously. "Most fathers wouldn't want their sons or daughters to be questioned by the police about molestation. They'd want it even less if the molester was a deacon as it would easily come down to the child's word against a churchman's." The second was that the deacon had been collected sooner rather than later after the phone call. "The MP who came to see Hillier—Quentin Walker—told me that Druitt had a boys' and girls' club here in town. If that's the case, he was in a position of such trust that he needed to be stopped at once if he was messing about with any children in that club."

Havers didn't look convinced, though. Instead she looked thoughtful before she said, "Or there's always this, guv: Someone was trying to get Druitt stitched up for something he didn't do."

LUDLOW
SHROPSHIRE

It was half past eleven, but Barbara knew she had to get out of the hotel and into the air. She also knew that she'd buggered things. The predinner martini had been followed by two bottles of red wine. One cup of coffee—black, strong, and sugarless—had done nothing to slap her into sobriety. If the drinking had been designed by Ardery to see what she would do when offered it, Barbara reckoned she'd failed the test.

As for the DCS, she'd not shown the least sign of being even tipsy. Instead of coffee, she'd also had two port wines after dinner. Her capacity for drink was astonishing. The only indication she'd given that the drinks were getting to her was when she'd taken a phone call during their dinner. She'd given it a glance and then said to Barbara, "I must take this," and rose to leave the dining room. She headed for the doorway, and she'd veered off course a bit. But even that could have been due merely to a ruck in the carpet.

Barbara had heard her say, "But I've hired you to *deal* with this, haven't I," before the DCS went out of earshot. Upon her return, Ardery had looked stony in the face, but whatever the phone call had been about, she'd left the matter wherever she'd rung off on the caller. She seemed expert at compartmentalising things.

After the meal as they climbed the stairs, Isabelle laid out their plans for the following day, which would begin at half past seven when they met for breakfast. The day would include speaking to the PCSO who'd been in charge of carting Ian Druitt to the Ludlow station. It would also include a drive to pay a call on the dead man's father, and a conversation with the vicar of St. Laurence Church, which, according to their paperwork, turned out to be where Ian Druitt had his position as deacon.

"Goodnight to you, Sergeant," were Ardery's final words, along with, "I hope you sleep well."

Barbara surveyed her room on unsteady legs and knew how unlikely was the probability that she would sleep at all. First of all, the room swam round her in such a way that she thought she might not make it across the carpet to the bed. Second, the bed was so narrow and looked so uncomfortable that even if she managed to fall upon it, she reckoned she'd spend the night feeling like a prisoner stretched out on the rack.

Not born anywhere *near* yesterday, Barbara had understood what Ardery was up to on the journey to Herefordshire and then to Shropshire. As soon as the DCS had announced there would be no stopping for lunch, she'd reckoned that Ardery was going to use this excursion as an opportunity to push her not only to the edge but over it. Ardery's dislike of her had been established early into her tenure at New Scotland Yard, and while Barbara had done nothing to garner anything *other* than dislike from the DCS, she'd managed to stay clear of absolute malfeasance until she'd taken herself off to Italy in defiance of Ardery's orders. Providing information to a reporter working for the nation's worst tabloid hadn't helped matters. Doing it more than once had done the job to seal her fate. So now in Ludlow, Barbara found herself quite adept at reading the tea leaves. DI Lynley might have seen this as an opportunity for redemption, but Barbara knew what it actually was: a design to sink her permanently and to guarantee her transfer to Berwick-upon-Tweed.

This room in the hotel was part of it. She didn't need to see Ardery's own digs to know that they wouldn't resemble this, which had to be the quarters of a former scullery maid shared, undoubtedly, with a laundress and the dairy maid had Griffith Hall had a dairy in its glory years. But Isabelle Ardery was *not* going to hear a complaint from DS Havers. So if Barbara had to sleep on the floor to achieve any comfort at all, she would do so.

The drinking, though, had blotted her copybook after an entire day of keeping it pristine. She was pissed all the way to the stars, and this did *not* bode well for the morrow. She needed to sober up. She also needed a fag. The hotel was a nonsmoking establishment—wasn't *everything* these days, she asked herself bitterly—so she decided that a walk in the night air might suffice to meet those two needs. After splashing water on her face in a bathroom the size of a church confessional, she grabbed up her shoulder bag, made sure she had her fags, and staggered down to reception.

No one was there, but she found a neat pile of tourist maps on the counter, along with postcards of the castle and dozens of brochures for various "Days Out" in Shropshire. She took up one of the tourist maps and unfolded it. Her vision was doing the polka, but she could still see that the map was heavily given to advertisements for shops, cafés, restaurants, and galleries. In the middle of all this was a fairly usable plan of the mediaeval centre of the town. The presence of the castle made it simple for her to see where she was in Ludlow—across the street from it—and despite the swirling sensation in her head, she was able to plot out a route that would take her through the narrow streets and ultimately deposit her in front of the police station, from which she could then find her way back.

Town plan in one hand and fags in the other, she went outside to find that it had rained while she and Ardery had been at dinner. The cool night air promised sobriety. On it hung the sweet, sharp smell of woodsmoke from a fire nearby, something utterly foreign to London, where wood fires were no longer permitted. People cheated on the law and burned them anyway, but it was rare enough that the scent of them in Ludlow was like being thrust back in time.

The buildings had the same effect on her. Griffith Hall was part of a line of dwellings that lay claim to the passage of centuries. A plaque on one of the houses indicated that a mediaeval range of buildings here had been transformed into a Regency terrace by means of altering what faced onto the street, while at the corner where the lane opened onto Castle Square, a twentieth-century café shared a plot of land with a half-timbered Tudor town mansion.

Barbara felt like a traveller caught between several time periods, although the sounds of nearby music and happy conversation fixed her in the present. She recognised the chatter of drinkers whose habit with fags did not allow them to do both—drink and smoke simultaneously—inside a pub that was not in view. She reckoned the drinkers and smokers were mostly students, for across the square she could see a wrought-iron archway that spanned two buildings and made an entrance that was identified by glittering stainless steel letters that indicated the route to West Mercia College.

The last thing Barbara wanted to do was seek out a pub. So she lit her first fag and continued on her way. Her head was muzzy. A weekly pint of ale or lager was her usual limit, and she cursed herself for feeling she needed to acquiesce when offered another kind of drink. As for downing a sodding martini? She had to ask herself where congenial cooperation ended and utter mindlessness began.

On the High Street, she encountered only one individual: a man carrying a sleeping bag under his arm and a carrier bag in his fingers. He wore a rucksack and was accompanied by an Alsatian. He looked to be getting ready to doss in the doorway of a distinguished stone building identified on her town plan as the Buttercross. He was opposite the pavement on which she was walking, so she couldn't get a clear look at him, but she made note of the idea of someone sleeping rough in Ludlow. It seemed unusual.

There was no traffic in town just then. Ludlow's nightlife appeared to be restricted to a few pubs, and its restaurants seemed to cater to those who ate early and retired to bed soon afterwards.

Following her designated route, Barbara found herself ultimately in a pedestrian passage where the now-gated Renaissance Flea Market promised her a variety of goods that she had no use for. This passage was dimly lit, and she paced along it quickly to emerge onto a curve that her map defined as the point where Upper Galdeford Street met Lower Galdeford Street.

Here everything was much different, for emerging from the vicinity of the flea market she found that she'd left the mediaeval precinct entirely. The roadway was wider, indicating its purpose as a route bypassing the old part of the town. Along it, a terrace of houses stood, faced either in dismal grey stucco or in brick with single steps to serve as their porches. The breeze was brisker here, and brisker still when she reached her destination.

The town's police station had its position at the corner of Lower Galdeford Street and Townsend Close, not far from Weeping Cross Lane, which, according to her map, dropped down to the River Teme. It seemed to Barbara that it was from the river that the breeze took some of its chill.

She was surprised by the size of the station. A two-storey structure faced with red brick, it was larger than she thought it would be, its traditional blue and white-lettered police light extending from the southeast corner of the building. Wide stone steps led to a substantial oak door hung with a simple overdoor that was less decoration than shelter from the rain.

Barbara climbed the steps. She was sober enough to note that the police station—despite its present disuse—was hung with a CCTV camera that was pointed upon the steps she'd just climbed as well as upon the pavement and at least part of the street. She also saw what hung to the left of the front door, which was a phone receiver above which potential callers were informed that lifting the receiver would connect them to the operations and communications centre, where what would be asked was: the location of the station at which they were standing, their name, their contact number, and their address. "Any communications about the 2003 Sexual Offences Act need to be made at one of the following stations," the message concluded. Barbara read those stations and saw from the list that not one of them was Ludlow.

This gave her pause. The allegations against Ian Druitt fitted into the 2003 act. She wondered if the person making the report to the operations centre had been informed of that. Indeed, she wondered again as before why the operations centre had moved on an anonymous message at all, considering that the basic requirements of identity, phone number, and address had evidently not even been met. However, if the location of the intercom had been identified by the previous investigation, it stood to reason that the digital recording from the CCTV camera pointed at the steps could have shown the person who had used the intercom, once the time of the phone call and the time from the CCTV camera were noted. But all of this went no distance at all to explain why the police station's external phone had been used in the first place when surely a call box somewhere in town could have served the same purpose.

Barbara left the front door, went down the steps, and had a longer look at the station. Several windows on the upper floor were cracked open, which confirmed what CC Wyatt had told them: patrol officers whose beat included Ludlow still used the station when they were out and about. The place was dark now, save for lights on the ground floor that appeared to illuminate the former reception area.

In the back of the building, there was a car park designated for official use. Here, she saw, a single police car sat in deep shadow, parked at some distance from the building. It stood in a corner with its front end pointing forward into the car park as if a quick response from someone might be necessary. She was about to turn away from this and continue on her route when she saw that the vehicle was not unoccupied. Movement from within on the driver's side caught her attention, and from where she stood she managed a glimpse of what looked like a man who'd adjusted his seat so that he could lean far back. Considering the hour, the place, and the situation in Shropshire vis-à-vis policing, she reckoned she was looking at one of the patrol officers assigned to police a large area that included Ludlow. He was having a kip while, no doubt, a fellow patrol officer kept up appearances by cruising through some of the other towns. When naptime was finished, the other officer would rouse this one by radio. An exchange would be made, another kip enjoyed, after which their policing would resume. It wasn't unheard of despite its being unprofessional. But Barbara concluded that the more cutbacks fell upon the shoulders of the local rozzers, the more those cops would cease caring about doing the job as well as it should have been done.

QUALITY SQUARE
LUDLOW
SHROPSHIRE

"The nephew, is it?" Francie Adamucci asked Chelsea Lloyd. She did one of her signature moves, the one with her hair: casually flipping it off her right shoulder while allowing the rest of it to drape sexily over the left side of her face. "Really? The *nephew*? He's seriously too young."

"Which means you fancy th'other, I expect?" Chelsea gestured sloppily with her lager—it was at least her fourth, but who was counting?—aiming vaguely at Jack Korhonen. He was waiting for the foam to allow more Guinness into a pint for a bloke who looked about one hundred and eighty-three years old. "I hear he's married, Fran."

"I hear that doesn't make a difference."

Ding listened to her two mates having yet another typical Francie-Chelsea conversation. No matter where a discussion between them began, if they were drinking it always came down to who fancied which male in the immediate vicinity. In this case, there were only three in their line of sight: the old gent eagerly grabbing up his Guinness, the middle-aged owner of the Hart and Hind, and his twenty-something nephew, whose name Ding could never remember. There were others here and there in the pub although the pickings were virtually nonexistent. Ding reckoned Jack Korhonen won Francie's interest by default.

She'd come out with her friends because she couldn't stand to remain in Temeside. Finn had been forced out to dinner with his mum, after which he'd come home in a mood so foul Ding had not wanted to be anywhere near him. As for Brutus . . . She'd decided to take his interpretation of friends with privileges straight to heart, which was why she'd joined Fran and Chelsea.

"You did *not*! You never!" This came from Chelsea, who spoke behind her hand like a fifteen-year-old, all astonishment or what*ever.*

"Of course I did," Francie told her. "God, Chels, what's the point of fancying someone if you don't make a move?"

"But he's . . . God, Francie, he's, like, I don't know . . . *forty* or something?"

"It was just a bonk," Francie said indifferently. "It's not like I'm planning to marry the bloke."

"But what if his *wife*—"

"Separate lives." Francie mentioned this in a dismissive tone that indicated the wife was a rather boring issue for her. "They own the pub together and they live together, different bedrooms in the same house. She goes her way and he goes his."

"How do you know?"

"He told me."

Chelsea's enormous blue eyes grew, if possible, more enormous. "Are you thick or something? That's what married blokes *always* say when they want it!" Her expression grew shrewd as she considered what Francie had been telling them. "I don't believe you. Where exactly was this heavenly bonk with Jack Korhonen s'posed to have happened?"

"Don't be such a dim bulb. It happened where bonks *always* happen in this place. Everyone knows 'bout the rooms above." And to Ding, "Ding knows, don't you, Ding?"

Ding didn't need to reply since living proof was just coming down the stairs behind the bar in the persons of two suspiciously bright-eyed individuals: a curvy girl in a leotard and her male companion, from whose fingers dangled a room key with a fob the size of a shoe. He handed this over to the Korhonen nephew along with what appeared to be two twenty-pound notes. The nephew nodded, gave the couple a grin, and placed the money not in the till but rather in what looked like a miniature coal scuttle behind it. Quickly enough another couple took the room key in hand and climbed the stairs.

"OMG," was Chelsea's reaction. "Don't they even change the *sheets*?"

"They were clean enough when *we* used them," Francie told her.

"Clean enough isn't clean at *all*. You could get some gross disease!" When Francie shrugged—a girl who didn't have time to consider diseases—Chelsea shook her head. "I do *not* believe you. I mean, what d'you want with an old man, Fran?"

"Like I said. I fancied him. Still do, in fact. *And* I wanted a bit of a laugh. It's only sex, Chels. If I didn't have to swot for an exam tomorrow, I'd have a go with him tonight as well."

Having said this, she downed the rest of her lager. Ever her cohort, Chelsea did the same, as Francie asked Ding if she was ready to leave. But Ding wasn't ready, so she said she'd stay and she'd see the other two girls in the morning.

This was agreed to and the girls went on their way, leaving Ding at the bar asking for another lager from the nephew while also eyeing the pub owner and wondering why Francie Adamucci—who, let's face it, could have any bloke she winked at—would allow Jack Korhonen to poke her.

He wasn't bad looking, Ding had to admit. While he had salt-and-pepper hair, he had plenty of it and it curled appealingly. If his beard was also greying, it was neatly trimmed and attractive on him. He wore trendy specs whose round frames gave him an elfin appearance. *But* he used braces instead of a belt. These were seasonal or holiday-oriented or political, and Ding had always thought—when she thought about Jack Korhonen at all, which was hardly ever—that wearing braces made the bloke seem ancient. *Definitely* too ancient to want to bonk. Unless, of course, he was a wizard in bed.

Ding considered Jack, and her consideration led inexorably to Brutus. Was *he* a wizard in bed? No. At eighteen years old, what boy could *possibly* be, even someone like Brutus, who was going at sex like someone thinking women were about to disappear from the earth? But Jack Korhonen . . . a man whose age had given him decades of experience . . . His sexual expertise had to be either what Francie had been told or what she'd learned firsthand from experience. Else she'd be taking note of the nephew—did any of them actually know his name? Ding asked herself—which she hadn't done, not even when Chelsea had said she fancied the boy. All of this amounted to evidence, Ding decided. If Francie Adamucci fancied Jack Korhonen, there was going to be a very good reason.

She saw that he was glancing in her direction. He would do, naturally, as not only was she a paying customer, but she was also the only female alone at the bar. She cocked her head and met his gaze with hers. She lifted her lager to her lips and drank. When she put the pint back onto the bar, she ran her tongue over her upper lip to remove the nonexistent foam.

The nephew moved from the bar to several of the tables that had been abandoned by other college students who, like Francie, had exams or papers that wanted writing or early lectures or tutorials. He set about gathering glasses and wiping moisture rings from tabletops, and in doing so he didn't see that another couple had descended the stairs.

Jack Korhonen dealt with them: key returned, money handed over, money deposited, and off they went into the night. He turned from that coal scuttle depository and came to the bar to gather the glasses left by Francie and Chelsea. He said to Ding, "Friends abandoned you, eh?" and while she could have allowed that to be the conversation starter about Francie and Chelsea, she opted instead for, "I didn't think you were the one who handled the rooms."

He said as he doused the glasses in whatever substance cleaned them beneath the bar, "Which rooms?"

"*You* know."

"Fact is, I don't. What about the rooms?"

"Oh really, Jack." She surprised herself when she used his Christian name, knowing that it signalled something but at the same time still not entirely sure that she wanted to signal anything just yet. "That bloke just gave you back the key. With money as well."

"What bloke?" he asked. "What key? Are you hallucinating? Or is it fantasising?"

Then he gave her what she could only call the Look. It consisted of a very slight upturn of his lips, an even slighter flare of his nostrils, and a dropping of his eyes to her chest and a subsequent raising of his eyes to her face.

She understood that he was testing. She leaned over the bar to shoot him some additional cleavage. She ran her index finger round the rim of her pint. She said, "You're having me on, aren't you? Francie tells me you use those rooms yourself."

"Does Francie indeed?" He was drying the glasses. His nephew brought a plastic tub of more glasses to the bar. Jack didn't acknowledge him with so much as a glance. He said, "Francie's been naughty, then. I thought she'd keep our little secret."

"And I wager you have lots of little secrets." Ding ran her finger round the rim of her glass another time. She lifted that finger to her lips and slowly sucked it into her mouth.

Jack eyed her. "Girl, you best be careful with that. Blokes'll get the wrong idea if you keep it up."

"What makes you think it would be the wrong idea?" Ding asked him.

He was silent for a moment before he said, "If you've got yourself into that frame of mind, it's not a problem to accommodate you." It took only three seconds for him to slide onto the bar the room key he'd just been given by the latest couple to have used one of the two rooms upstairs. "Or," he said, "are you just a tease? You have the look of a tease. Come down to it, I wager off you'd scarper."

"I've never been a tease," she said.

"Your words, not mine," was his reply. He moved off and took up the tub of glasses. As he did so, the nephew rejoined them. He eyed the room key, then he eyed Ding, then he eyed his uncle. He left the key where it lay.

Ding took two deep draughts of her lager. She was pleasantly lit up and she asked herself what was the harm, really. It's what everyone did. And in her particular case it was a statement that needed making.

She'd thought that she and Brutus had actually had something. She'd thought that when he'd told her that they would only be friends with privileges, it would be easy enough to alter the relationship into something more. But now she knew that was nowhere near to being likely. So she closed her hand over the key.

She saw that its fob said it fitted room 2. All she would need to do was to climb the stairs and find the door. She also saw that Jack Korhonen was watching her, his expression a dare: Was she a tease or was she the real thing, like Francie Adamucci?

She took up her lager and made for the stairs. She shot him a look. There was no doubt in her mind what he would do.

Two ceiling fixtures in the upstairs corridor shed dim light to direct the way to the pub's two bedrooms. Between them an open door displayed what would be a shared bathroom for anyone stopping overnight, but she reckoned sharing that bathroom during overnight stays was a rare occurrence since the pub owner would be making far more money from letting the rooms out on an hourly basis to anyone wishing to have a bonk.

Behind the door that bore the number 1, she could hear both grunting and moaning along with the rhythmic mating call of mattress springs. As she passed, a girl's voice cried, "Yes, oh my God!" and the mating call intensified, turning her cries into short, pleased shrieks.

Ding paced past, gulping more of her lager. It was her intention to down the rest of it. For once she was feeling absolutely free.

She paused in the loo. Wisdom suggested that she use it. As she did so, she heard the grunting from room 1 more clearly. She wondered how long it would take him to finish and at what point sheer exhaustion might bring on an unsatisfactory conclusion for him. For the girl, it seemed the encounter had been a smashing success. She was no longer shrieking but had grown silent as her partner labored on.

To flush or not? Ding asked herself. She thought not. She didn't wish to embarrass the couple in room 1—although something about the entire room-for-hire situation at the pub suggested they weren't the type to be embarrassed—and she also didn't want to distract the boy from what was seeming to be his extended efforts. So she tiptoed out from the bathroom and made her way to room 2, where she let herself in as quietly as she could.

The scent assailed her, coming at her like a hostess overeager to welcome her company's arrival. It was a blend of unwashed female, undeodorized male, sex, unlaundered sheets, and a heavy application of room spray that failed to cover the other odours. No one had thought to open a window, and Ding went to do so. It was, she discovered, painted shut and with panes so filthy that she could barely distinguish what it overlooked, which was the cobbled way of Church Street, its streetlamps shedding cones of light on two art galleries and a cheese shop.

She turned from the window to look at the room. She hadn't switched on the lights, so she saw in the semi-darkness that the furniture had been kept to a minimum: a chest of drawers, a seat-sagging armchair, a full-size bed, one bedside table with lamp. Above the bed some sort of print hung, but she couldn't tell what it was. She *could* tell by the precision of its hanging that it probably had been nailed in place. There were no other decorations, and the bed itself was mattress only, as someone had rid it of its ill-smelling sheets, which now were balled up in a corner.

On the top of the chest of drawers stood a large basket filled with potpourri, which she discovered smelled mostly of dust, and next to this was the air scent bottle, which she took up and sprayed till there was none left. Then she downed the rest of her lager. Then she sat in the armchair and waited.

He was there more quickly than she expected, not ten minutes after she'd climbed the stairs. He didn't knock but merely came into the room. He coughed at the smell, saying, "Jesus Christ! D'you have a thing for lavender?"

He made no mention of the room's overall condition. He merely shut the door and, like her, did nothing to illuminate the space.

Instead, he slid the braces from his shoulders, pulled his shirt from his trousers, and crossed the room to her. He said, "Not a tease, eh? Am I meant to take that for the truth?"

"You can take it any way you want. You didn't drag me up here, 's I recall."

He chuckled. "You're a bit of a thing, aren't you? College girl or something else?"

"What do you think?"

"Don't think a thing other than not wanting to get myself stitched up for having a fifteen-year-old to bed. How old're you then?"

"Eighteen. What about you?"

"I like you," he said.

"That's not what I wanted to know."

"Oh, I expect it isn't. But that's all I'm saying. C'mere then," and he drew her to her feet and was kissing her before she was prepared for him to do so. He certainly knew how to kiss, she discovered. He kissed in a way that made her want him to go on kissing her into next week. As he did so, he took her hands and put them under his shirt and put his own on her hips to pull her closer and then on her waist and then up and up till he had her bra unhooked and was squeezing her nipples just to the edge of pain and then releasing them the very moment before she cried out as if he knew and he certainly knew and it was pure pleasure shooting down her body just where he wanted that pleasure to go.

He released her. He nodded as if she'd somehow proved something he'd been wanting to know. He moved to the bed and there he pulled his shirt over his head in that way she'd seen men do on the telly when unbuttoning the shirt was just too much trouble for the hurry they were in. He tossed it onto the bed, and then he kicked off his shoes and lowered his trousers and she saw he wore nothing else beneath them.

She knew she was meant to be doing something: either helping him out of his clothing or removing hers. But she was arrested by the sight of his muscled back, his buttocks with deep creases defining the muscles there as well, his legs and his arms and as he turned back to her—

Which was when she saw the mat of hair on his chest how the grey mixed with the dark and how it narrowed at his waist till it spread thickly like a nest for his erect penis and how it climbed to just below his neck where the rope, the rope, or was it a tie or was it the belt of a dressing gown—

"Like what you see, eh? Most girls do."

—and she hadn't known what to do or what it meant so she'd not said a word how could she say a single word about the rope the tie the dressing gown's belt—

"What're you about, then? Get your kit off, girl. I'm not intending to stand here forever." And his hand closed over his penis to give it a boost because she wasn't doing what she was supposed to be doing, which was undressing and crossing to him and straddling him and rubbing herself up and down him so that he could feel how excited she was by the sight and the feel of him only she wasn't not now not ever not like this.

She headed for the door, but she had to pass him and he grabbed her, saying, "Hey! What's this, then? Not what you thought? Not hearts and flowers and music and some bloke kissing your neck or whatever instead of this?" He clutched her crotch, saying as he pulled her against him, "Believe me, girl, you'll like it rough. Why d'you think they keep coming back, those mates of yours, those college girls?" He turned her to the bed. He lifted her skirt. His hands were on the waistband of her tights. She started to scream.

"What the . . . What're you *on* about? Shut the fuck . . . Jesus!" He released her.

She went for the door, thinking he might try to stop her, but he didn't, of course, because he wasn't a rapist, he was a bloke who had women every which way he wanted them whenever he wanted them and if it wasn't going to be her—which it clearly wasn't—he wasn't about to force it to be her.

She was down the stairs in a flash. In another flash she was stumbling across the old pub's floor and pushing out into the night.

# 6 MAY

LUDLOW
SHROPSHIRE

Barbara rang DI Lynley in the morning. Despite her walkabout on the previous night, she was so hung over that she found that she was actually still pissed. She had barely slept. The reason for this was not only the room heaving to and fro like a ferry on a very bad crossing to France, but also that, upon returning from her walk, she'd roused Peace on Earth from wherever he'd taken himself off to and she'd asked him to brew for her an entire pot of coffee. Her room being far too small to do any real work in, she'd occupied a table in the residents' lounge where she'd had her first—and it would be her last—martini earlier in the evening. During this time of swilling down coffee, she went through every one of the filing folders of information they'd been given. She also made notes dealing with her evening's stroll.

She waited till quarter past six to ring Lynley from her room. She decided the castle, which she could see from her window, was as good an excuse as any. It was early yet, but he was an early riser.

A woman answered his mobile, however. She said, "Barbara, hullo. We're at a critical moment. He's not quite available," so Barbara knew she hadn't misdialled. She understood she was speaking to Daidre Trahair, whose employment at London Zoo resulted in hours as early as the inspector's.

Barbara searched for words. She knew the inspector was involved with the zoo's large animal vet, but he played his cards very close when it came to his love life post the terrible death of his wife, and he'd never directly told her that some of his nights were spent with

Daidre Trahair. She said, "Not sure I want to know what the critical moment is. Can you have him ring me when it's passed?" and realised as the remark left her lips that she might have been wiser to head in a direction different to double entendre.

But Daidre laughed. "He's scrambling eggs. I'm spellbound by his method. I've never seen them scrambled quite this way."

"Word of warning," Barbara told her. "I wouldn't eat 'em. Far as I know, he can't even make toast."

"That's very good to know. Your phone call is a brilliant excuse, then. I'll hand you over to him and finish the eggs myself."

In a moment, Lynley's voice said, "Barbara. Has something gone wrong?"

She replied with, "I passed every test until dinner, and believe me, sir, she was tossing them in front of me like hay for the horses right from the start."

"Tell me," Lynley said.

She gave him the *A* to *Z* of it: from the journey to Ludlow with its one stop for petrol and one for the loo to the shared drinks and dinner. She didn't spare herself. What she needed from him was a way to proceed at this point, as she would see the DCS in some thirty minutes. Her insides were telling her that confessing her sins to Lynley might prevent her from committing more of them.

"A martini *and* wine?" Lynley said at the conclusion of her confession. "That's rather heavy going for you, Barbara. Did you not think—"

"That's just it. I didn't think. She said we could have something since we were off duty and there was this bloke standing there—his name is Peace on Earth if you can credit that—and so we could have . . . whatever. There was this drinks menu with all sorts of names—what the bloody hell is a Sunset in New Mexico anyway?—and I reckoned . . . I don't know what I reckoned, so I said I'd have what she was having. Some kind of vodka in a glass the size of my mum's Easter bonnet. Then wine. I had coffee after, but the damage was done and she knew I was pissed. I mean, how could she *not* know? I'm lucky I didn't throw up on the stairs. Meantime, she's not even the tiniest . . . I mean, she stumbled a bit when she was leaving the room to take a phone call but that was it. She wasn't even slurring her words."

Lynley took this on board for a moment before saying, "I shouldn't worry."

"But do I say sorry? Do I tell her I generally only have ale or lager and one at that and mostly once a week anyway?"

"Don't do that." Lynley's answer was swift. He went on to say, "Aside from testing you—and you *had* to be expecting that, Barbara—how is she otherwise?"

"Herself. The Queen Bee, the legend, the goddess, whatever. Only, like I said, she had a phone call last night from someone. She took it but all I heard was that she was employing someone to handle something and she didn't sound chuffed about the call."

He was silent a moment. She wondered if he was asking himself whether he should hand over some information to her. She wished he would. It might serve to make her time with Ardery easier. But she decided not to put him in the position of having to make a choice. He was first and foremost a gent. If Ardery had confided in him, he wasn't going to break that confidence for love, money, or loyalty to Barbara Havers.

He said, "If you think the drinking last night was a test—"

"*If*?" she said.

"—just be warier. No need to accept when something's offered. A polite refusal is all that's necessary. How are you feeling this morning?"

"I don't have a word for it."

"Ah. Do your best not to let her know how badly it's sitting with you, and I expect you'll be fine."

"I just . . ." Barbara saw how badly she wanted to blurt out the real reason for her call: She wished he were there in Ludlow, either acting the part of Isabelle Ardery's second or acting the part of her—Barbara's—guv. She understood quickly enough that the latter was the case. So it was best not to conclude the sentence.

"You just . . . ?" he prompted her.

"I just hope I can swallow some breakfast."

"Yes. Well. We've all been there at least once, Sergeant. Soldier on."

He rang off then. Barbara wasn't sure she felt any better than she'd felt before making the call. There was no help for it, however: she had to go down to breakfast.

She found the DCS just ending a call on her mobile. Peace on Earth was arriving at the table with a coffee press. Ardery asked him to do the honours and added, "We're going to need more than one, I dare say," after a glance at Barbara.

That alone put Barbara into the position of having to say something, so she chose a hearty "I'll be drinking tap water from now on. I might go out on a limb and add one piece of ice and a slice of lime, though."

Ardery's lips moved in a smile so faint it could have been a tic. She said, "You might get two pieces of ice, I've found. Have some coffee." She reached for her own and had it black. There was a tremor in her hand.

Barbara said, "I went walkabout last night."

"That's admirable." *Considering your condition* was something that Ardery didn't add. "How did you find fair Ludlow?"

"Not as well lit as it might've been. A few back lanes waiting for the next mugging to happen. But I located the police station, which's what I set out to see."

"And?"

Peace on Earth showed up with the second coffee press and his waiter's pad. Ardery went—astoundingly—for the full English breakfast. Barbara chose porridge, reckoning she might be able to gag that down. Peace looked as if he expected more of her. Certainly one couldn't cope with the day ahead without piling on the grub. She said, "That's it, then," and refrained from mentioning that her usual fare was a Pop-Tart or two and a cup of tea.

When he'd taken himself off to see to the meal, Barbara told Ardery what she'd discovered at the unmanned police station. She included the information about the CCTV camera, the location of the intercom phone, the notice informing users what to do in the event their report concerned sexual offenders, the open window at the police station indicating its occasional use just as the chief constable had explained it, and finally the panda car in the car park with the police officer lounging within it.

"I had a think about that," she said to Ardery. "The bloke inside the car last night? I figured him for one of the area's patrol officers having a kip while the other does part of the nighttime drive about in the district. He gives this bloke an hour—p'rhaps two—and then they switch it up and its naptime all over again, this time for the other patrol officer."

"How does that relate to the matter in hand?" Ardery spoke over the top of her cup. She'd downed her first coffee and had gone for a second.

"Could be the PCSO was snoozing that night when Druitt died, this Gary Ruddock bloke. Could be he was outside in a car—"

"But why would he do that? There was no one in the building aside from himself and Ian Druitt, was there?"

"—*or* he was having a kip in one of the offices inside the station. Point is that it's the kip part that got me thinking. It doesn't make sense that Druitt was able to off himself while the PSCO was in the building *and* fully functioning on duty and all that. Something had to be different about that night. I'm just suggesting that the PCSO asleep might be it."

Ardery nodded. "That would certainly put him into it, wouldn't it? All right, then. Have at the PCSO this morning. See what you can get beyond what we already have. Compare what he says to you with what he said to DI Pajer and the IPCC. He'll be in the picture about our being here, though, so there's no point to thinking there might be a surprise involved when you turn up. Also, have him show you where the suicide occurred."

"Right. Can do. But I'm also thinking we ought to—"

"Yes?" Ardery sounded interested, but her eyes narrowed in that way she had.

"The PCSO," Barbara said quickly, changing course. "Can do, will do."

Ardery gave that tic of a smile. "Very good. Meantime, I've been in touch with Clive Druitt. One of his breweries is just in Kidderminster. I'll be meeting up with him there and smoothing the way *opposite* the direction of a lawsuit. Evidently, he wishes to give me an earful on why the boy—as he calls him—would never have hanged himself since 'suicide is an abomination before God,' as he put it. We shall see about all that, I dare say."

LUDLOW
SHROPSHIRE

When she made a phone call to PCSO Gary Ruddock to arrange an interview, Barbara discovered that his availability was dependent upon someone called old Rob, who turned out to be an elderly pensioner in whose home Ruddock had a room. He needed to see his doctor this morning, did old Rob, and as this visit to his doctor had to do with the old bloke's bladder, his prostate, and his worsening incontinence, it wasn't something that could wait. But Ruddock would meet DS Havers at the police station after the appointment. Round half past eleven?

He sounded a nice enough bloke. Having an elderly parent herself, Barbara was sympathetic to his situation, although she did not live with her mum and hadn't done in quite some time. But seeing to old Rob's needs appeared to be part of Gary Ruddock's remit as his living companion, so she agreed to the plan.

This left her at loose ends. She wondered if she should ring DCS Ardery and ask what the other officer would have her do while Ardery herself was attempting to make nice with Ian Druitt's dad. But she dismissed this plan as completely lacking in initiative. Lynley wouldn't have expected it of her.

She had the time to walk over to St. Laurence Church—if she could find it in the rat's nest of Ludlow's ancient lanes—and nearby would probably be the vicarage. Questioning the vicar about his deacon, along the lines of what did he know and when did he know it, seemed a viable alternative to lounging round the hotel waiting for Gary Ruddock to be free.

Outside, she found that the morning was due to unfold into a glorious day. Across the street, the lawns in front of the castle glittered with the previous night's rain, and in the flower beds spiky blue flowers mixed with cheerful white and yellow blooms.

Her plan of the town told her that a route diagonally through Castle Square would put her roughly in the vicinity of St. Laurence Church, buried amidst mediaeval buildings that had sprung up round it through the centuries. The square itself was peopled by merchants who were setting up for the day's open-air market, one that was going to feature mostly foodstuffs heavily given to baked goods if the aromas were anything to go by.

At the north end of the square, Barbara found Church Street, one of two exceedingly narrow lanes that led east, along which a variety of tiny shops offered everything from cheese to chess sets. St. Laurence was tucked just beyond this area, with its west side facing a horseshoe of curiously high-end-looking almshouses. There were two entrances to the building: on the south and the west, with the southern entrance seeming the main one. Since the church itself suggested someone's presence within it and since someone's presence suggested information as to the location of the vicarage, Barbara decided she would have a look round.

The church was certainly unexpected, not only in location—hidden away as it was save for its crenellated central tower—but also in its size. The place was huge, which suggested the wealth of the town in the distant past from the wool trade, as was usually the case. It was constructed of sandstone, ruddy in colour, with distinguished buttresses, Perpendicular windows, and spires surmounting each corner of its tower. At its north end, a small churchyard took shade from ancient yews, and above, jackdaws wheeled noisily in an azure sky.

The place was open. Barbara ducked inside, where she found herself not in contemplative silence as she thought she might be, but rather in the position of eavesdropper upon an argument between an older and a younger woman about how many floral displays were going "to be *truly* necessary, Vanessa," to decorate the place for an upcoming wedding. "We're not exactly paupers, Mum," Vanessa was petulantly pointing out. "And I don't intend to become one," Mum said. "You've two sisters and they're going to want weddings as well." They drifted towards the end of the chancel, where a Perpendicular window dazzled with ancient glass that had somehow escaped Thomas Cromwell's notice.

Barbara left them to it because she'd seen a man heading in the direction of a chapel that featured yet another enormous window—again stained glass—and a small altar beneath this. The man wore garments suggesting priesthood, so she decided to give him a try. She fished for her identification, said, "'Scuse me," and approached him.

He swung round. He looked to be in his late sixties, with an impressive mound of iron-grey hair that swept back from his forehead and was sculpted to his head. His face was unlined, but his eyebrows were thick and heavy, and his ears on their way to enlargement. He cocked his head, saying nothing, although he did cast an anxious look in the direction from which the voices of Vanessa and her mother were emanating. Probably worried that he'd be asked to intervene in the flower dispute, Barbara reckoned.

She introduced herself and explained why she was there, taking time with how it had all come about and ending with a request to have a few words with the vicar about Ian Druitt, if he *was* the vicar. Indeed, he was. His name was Christopher Spencer, and he was only too happy to accommodate her. He seemed happier still to get out of the church, since the argument over wedding flowers was becoming ever more intense. Vanessa sounded like a girl who knew that raising the volume always led to getting her way.

The vicarage was just nearby, the Reverend Spencer told her, across from the churchyard. If she didn't mind having a chat there instead of here . . . ? It was just that he had his wife's to-do list to see to, and he'd been derailed by a meeting with "the ladies," as he put it, inclining his head in the direction of mother and daughter. Barbara told him she didn't mind at all.

At the vicarage, Barbara was offered coffee, to which she demurred. She was offered tea, which she also turned down. Spencer said if she positively wouldn't mind their having a chat while he was seeing to the birds' cage, he would be ever so grateful, as cleaning it had topped the to-do list, his wife being too terrified of budgerigars to see to it herself, God bless her.

Barbara told him she had no problem at all with birds and cage cleaning, as long as she didn't have to participate. He looked startled at the very thought that he would append such a requirement to their conversation, saying, "Good gracious, no! Please do follow me."

He led her through the kitchen to what had been the larder of the old house. There on one of the marble shelves, a very large cage was occupied by two colourful budgerigars. They eyed the approach of the vicar with some interest.

"We don't *keep* them in here," the vicar told Barbara. "Too little stimulation for them. They're usually in the sitting room near to the window, save on cage-cleaning mornings."

"Got it," Barbara said.

"They're called Ferdinand and Miranda," he went on. "This rough magic and all of that."

"Ah." Barbara wasn't sure what to make of his remark. She reckoned, however, that Lynley would have been all over it like flies on cut fruit.

"They came to us named," he said. "Not the best choices, 'f you ask me, but at least it wasn't Romeo and Juliet. I must confess that I don't actually know which of them is which, though. I've never seen them get up to any business, which would otherwise be helpful. As it is, they don't appear to know their names anyway. Would you like a chair? I can bring one from the kitchen. Or a stool. Would you prefer a stool?"

Barbara said that standing would be fine as it gave her a better view of the birdcage cleaning for future reference in the very unlikely event that she might want a bird of her own. He set to, then, beginning with opening up the cage, sticking his hand inside like a blade, allowing both the birds to perch upon in. He withdrew it, and they cooperatively hopped onto the top of the cage. There, one of them said, "Coffee ready?" and the other replied, "Milk and sugar?"

The vicar explained that those were the only phrases the birds had ever managed to learn, and no one had taught them. They had merely picked them up, as birds would do. As if in reaction to this, both of the budgerigars squawked and took flight. Barbara ducked as they went straight for her and then beyond her into the kitchen.

"Never mind them," Spencer said casually as he removed the

bottom of the cage by sliding it out. It was, Barbara saw, a depository for an astounding amount of budgerigar guano. "They'll come back eventually when they're hungry." He bundled up the newspaper lining the tray that served as the cage's bottom. He removed the dirtied paper and reached for several new sheets from a neat pile inside a basket that sat on the floor. He said, "How can I help you? What would you like to know about Ian?"

"Whatever you can tell me," Barbara said.

He seemed to consider what he wished to say as he folded the sheets of paper to fit the bottom of the cage. He removed all of the perches for cleaning, and he began to speak.

Barbara learned that Druitt had studied to be an Anglican priest after having graduated university with a second-class degree in sociology. It was after attaining this degree that the young man had decided upon the church as the best way to put his studies to work. Although he'd completed all the necessary coursework that would have led him to the priesthood, he'd not made it all the way. The vicar explained that, unfortunately, Druitt had been unable to pass the required exam that would have led to a ministry of his own.

"Took it several times." Spencer gave this information with a regretful shake of his head. "Poor man. Nerves. He simply could not do it, so he settled for deaconry. He did an excellent job there, by the way." Here Spencer paused to rustle round a plastic bucket in the corner of the room. He brought out a wire brush and applied it to the first of the wooden perches, dislodging more of the birds' droppings onto another sheet of newsprint. Barbara took note of the fact that there was certainly nothing wrong with the creatures' bowels . . . if birds actually *had* bowels. She knew nothing about bird anatomy beyond wings and beaks. Spencer went on to say, "It turned out a blessing for us that he never made it to full priesthood. He was here in Ludlow from the first. Of course . . . ," Spencer hesitated, a perch in one hand and the wire brush in the other. From the kitchen one of the birds spoke of coffee again. The other did not reply. "Actually, to be honest, I must say he was a bit of an overachiever in the blessing department."

"How so?"

Spencer went on with the brushing. He did it with vigour, placing each perch to one side as he finished with it. "He ran his life by the Beatitudes," Spencer said. "I think it's fair to say he was governed by doing good works, but sometimes this took him to extremes. He started our after-school children's club years ago, he did meals for the housebound and the elderly, he was a crime victim volunteer—a good use of his sociology degree there, I dare say—he recorded books for the blind, he helped out occasionally in the primary schools, he took part in maintaining public footpaths. He was just establishing a street pastors programme as well, which we need rather badly in town because of the drinking that goes on amongst our young people."

"How did he collect the children for his club?" Barbara asked once the vicar had completed the list of Ian Druitt's admirable efforts on behalf of the community.

"Gracious." Spencer seemed to be considering the question and wondering why he didn't know the answer. He rustled round the bucket again and brought forth a spray bottle that he began to use liberally on the wire bars of the cage's sides. "You know, it's been part of the town so long that I'm not sure how to answer that, Sergeant. I believe the club came about through the town council as well as the schools. As a request. The children came via both those sources, I think. As I said, I'm not sure. I can tell you, though, that as these things do, the club started slowly as something to occupy children after school, and it gained members over time. Enough so that Ian generally had a college student come in as a helper each year."

"A college student." Barbara underlined this in her notebook. "Can you give me any names?"

"Unfortunately, no." He wiped down the wires of the cage with a rag. He said, "However, I can tell you that Ian kept records, so there'll be a list somewhere. I expect you'll find something amongst his things."

"My guv's gone to meet with his dad. Could be he's got some clobber to hand over. Is anything of his left here, though? I'd like to check through it if you have something."

Spencer looked surprised. He set his rag to one side. "Oh, he didn't live here at the vicarage, Sergeant. I offered. My wife and I rattle round this place and have bedrooms aplenty. But he preferred the privacy of his own establishment. Let me find the address for you, shall I?"

Without waiting for her reply, the vicar left her. Barbara found her fingertips tingling at the information he had just shared. Why would Druitt need his own private place when here in the vicarage he could easily have lived close to the church for very little rent or for none at all? While that suggested a desire for privacy, it also suggested a desire—or a need—for secrecy.

Spencer returned, in his hand an envelope upon which he'd scrawled Ian Druitt's home address. She read it—it meant less than nothing since she didn't know the area—but the fact of it led to her next and, she reckoned, most reasonable question.

"Can I assume you knew why Mr. Druitt was arrested, Vicar?

Spencer nodded, although his cheeks flared an unnatural colour. He seemed to wish to hide his embarrassment because he quickly left her to fetch a large box of birdseed. He filled a container that hung from the side of the cage. He said, "I don't believe he was a paedophile, Sergeant. He's been part of this parish for more than fifteen years, and there's never been even a whisper of any kind of impropriety."

Barbara let the words hang there. It was something she'd long ago learned from DI Lynley: Sometimes silence is better than a question. She watched the vicar fasten the feeder to the cage and bustle out of the room for water. Outside, a very loud motor started quite close by. Someone, she thought, was seeing to the lawn in the churchyard.

Spencer returned, water in hand. "Of course," he admitted as he fastened the container to the cage, "who could have possibly guessed the extent of the paedophilia that existed in the Roman Catholic Church? *And* in our Anglican Church, as it turns out. There it all was, hidden for generations by bishops and archbishops . . . disgraceful and unforgivable." He looked up then and his expression spoke of a concern that he, too, had failed in moments when he'd been most needed. He said, "I must assure you . . ." He gave a small shake of his head as if it were a feeling and not a thought that he was dismissing.

"What?" she said.

"That had I known anything, had I had an inkling, had I even *suspected* Ian of that, I would have done something at once."

Barbara nodded, but one thing was certain. Christopher Spencer's final declaration was very easy to make, after the fact.

BEWDLEY
WORCESTERSHIRE

Isabelle parked across the street from the Druitt's brewery, which turned out to be not in Kidderminster as previously indicated but rather on the Kidderminster Road, just west of the smaller town of Bewdley. It had been easy enough to find, an establishment that was positioned quite within walking distance of the River Severn as well as close by the Severn Valley Railway. From both the river and the rail tracks the brewery could be seen. Occupying a large, historic, and picturesque river warehouse, it was just the place for people to make a stop if they were travelling to or from Ludlow and Birmingham or points beyond.

Isabelle took a moment before making her way to her meeting inside the building. She was earlier than she thought she'd be, and a coffee she'd stopped for along the way had given her something of a thirst. Without a bottle of water with her—a foolish omission she wouldn't make from now on, she assured herself—she rustled in her bag and found one of her airline bottles. She generally drank the same vodka, but on the occasion of supplying herself with mini bottles suitable for her shoulder bag for this jaunt to Shropshire, she'd opted for variety in addition to the larger bottle of her regular that she had in her hotel room. This particular vodka was Ukrainian in origin, she saw from its label. It contained two gulps, no more, but she decided it would do to quench her thirst for now.

Her breakfast phone call had been from her London solicitor, ringing another time in what Isabelle knew straightaway was going to be one of those calls in which he was asking himself mentally if he could possibly "get this woman to see reason." She could tell this from Sherlock (his parents had truly been mad, she thought) Wainwright's voice, not to mention the placating tone he was beginning to develop with her. He claimed he was trying to guide her away from a costly legal battle that she was certain to lose, but she was beginning to think he was really trying to maintain his professional track record. She'd hired him in the first place because of that track record. However, with each argument they had, her conclusion that he only took on dead certs was getting firmer.

"May we turn once again to the terms of your divorce?" he'd asked her. "Essentially, you see, the difficulty we're encountering arises from your agreeing to the custody arrangements in the first place. Because Robert Ardery has full custody and because you made no effort to fight him on this during the initial proceedings, when the boys were young enough that making an argument regarding their need for Mummy—"

She'd gritted her teeth at the term and considered herself virtuous for saying nothing.

"—it becomes especially difficult to make that argument now the boys are older. His side will declare that they've had a mummy all along in the person of Robert's wife, Sandra, and in all this time the situation has worked quite well. You've had your visits—"

"Supervised," she said. "Supervised by *them*, by the way. To use your term, 'in all this time,' I've had the boys to myself exactly once, and that was when Bob and Sandra had a dinner to go to in London so they brought the boys to me for an overnight while they had some sort of romantic interlude in a hotel. *One* overnight, which started at five o'clock in the afternoon and ended at ten o'clock the next morning. Let me ask you, Mr. Wainwright, how would you feel in my situation?"

"I'd feel as you do: frustrated and passionate about trying to change the course of events as they are being laid out."

"The course of events, as you call it, involves New Zealand." She could hear the ice in her tone. "Auckland. New Zealand. Moving house. Leaving England."

"I understand completely. But we have a legal document that says nothing at all about the boys' residence and in which country it must be. I remain mystified as to why the solicitor you engaged for your divorce didn't prevent you from accepting some of the terms of it, especially those referencing the boys' country of abode."

Because I had to accept all of Bob's terms, Isabelle thought but did not say. Because had I not, he would have opened my life to the scrutiny of my superiors. Because if *that* occurred, I was done for and he knew it. Because I drink. But I am *not* a drunk. Bob bloody well knows that, but he was willing to use anything to keep the boys with him and—a mere four months after our divorce, thank you—with his sodding Sandra.

She said, "I didn't understand the terms at the time," although this was, of course, a lie. What she hadn't understood was that Bob might receive an offer that allowed him to leap up the ladder of success. Despite this ladder's being planted in Auckland, there was part of her that couldn't blame him for climbing it. Both of them were professionally ambitious.

But that was *not* the point. The point was New Zealand and how often she could realistically travel there to see her sons.

"I'm not sure what will be made of that if we insist upon a proceeding," Wainwright said.

"I want him stopped," was her reply. "I want access to my children. I don't care what it costs. I'll find the money to pay you."

It was then that she'd caught sight of Barbara Havers—green about the gills but upright—heading in her direction, so she'd ended the call. Her hands were shaking with rage and with the aftermath of her vodkas, wine, and port, and she realised she should have had a few mouthfuls of the hair of the dog before meeting the detective sergeant, but that couldn't be helped. She got through most of a disgusting full English breakfast for show, she and Havers had parted, and she'd had an inch of her stowed-away supply of vodka before leaving the hotel with extra bottles of the drink in her bag.

Now, she tossed the empty one into the glove box. Four strong mints took care of any problem she might have had with her breath, and once she'd finished touching up her lipstick, she checked for traffic and crossed the road to the brewery.

It wasn't open hours yet, but a late model Mercedes sitting in front of the establishment suggested that Clive Druitt was somewhere within.

He seemed to have been watching for her—she hoped he hadn't seen her down the vodka and a glance across the street at the position of her car said this was unlikely—because he or someone she assumed was Mr. Druitt opened the frosted, translucent front door. On this *Druitt* was decoratively etched in lettering that matched the neon sign hanging high on the warehouse that announced DRUITT CRAFT BREWERY and below it in roman type FINE LAGERS, ALES, AND CIDERS.

"Detective Chief Superintendent?" His words sounded stiff, as if the man were trying not to judge her in advance before he understood her intentions and heard her thoughts on the matter of his son's death. When she nodded, he said, "Clive Druitt. Thank you for coming."

"No thanks necessary. I appreciate your meeting me here rather than Birmingham."

"There were things to see to," he said. "Come in. We're mostly alone. Kitchen staff don't start arriving till half past ten."

He closed and locked the door behind her and gestured her to follow him across a reclaimed wooden floor that was fashionably distressed. It was dark with age as was most of the interior of the old warehouse, which offered a long and scarred bar as well as tables with chairs of various periods and styles. Contrasting with this, five enormous stainless steel tanks glittered behind a pristine glass wall in a room behind the bar. Pumps, tubes, and pipes sprouted from them, and the scent of yeast and hops and roasting grains rendered the air a veritable advertisement for the product being made.

Druitt led her to one of the tables, this one long and in a refectory style. It had benches instead of chairs and upon it were lined a row of cardboard boxes, some of them sealed and some of them gaping open. He said, "My boy didn't kill himself," and as if he had definitive proof of this, he reached into one of the boxes and he pulled out a largish family photograph in a frame. He handed it over.

It depicted what Isabelle assumed was the entire Druitt clan: mum, dad, adult children, their spouses, numerous grandkids, and a perfectly groomed springer spaniel. They'd been arranged artistically by a professional photographer, who'd wisely told them to wear similar clothing. Their choice had been blue jeans and white dress shirts, although two of the men and one of the women—it had to be said—would have done better to have selected something more suitable to hiding what could only charitably be called their muscles and curves.

She could easily tell which of the family members was the son Ian. He stood in the middle of the adult children, and he was the only person not wearing jeans and a white shirt. Instead, he wore clerical garb. She assumed the photo memorialised his ordination, or whatever it was that officially proclaimed someone a deacon.

Aside from DI Pajer's photos of his body, this was Isabelle's first look at Ian Druitt. Like his siblings, his parents, and several of the grandkids, he was ginger-haired. He was also bespectacled and pudgy, with a rounding of the shoulders that suggested a wish to hide his height or, what was more likely, to make himself into someone who might go unnoticed. For those three characteristics—the ginger hair, the specs, and the pudginess—had long served as a mating call to bullies. She wondered if he'd suffered at the hands of more aggressive children when he was young. She also wondered how that might have affected him.

"He would *not* self-harm," Clive Druitt said as if he'd read her thoughts.

Isabelle glanced at the man. She could see what grief had done to Druitt since his son's death. The weight he'd lost made his face look drawn and creased, and while he was already slender in the photograph of his family, now he had an emaciated look. Cheekbones had become predominant as had the crevasses beneath them. His eyes were sunken and his wrists were bony. His hair had faded. From ginger, it was heading towards the colour of straw.

She hadn't been sent to Shropshire to prove or disprove anything about the dead man, but she didn't tell his father as much. She was there to look into the conduct of the two investigations that had occurred, which was an entirely different matter having to do with how the police had behaved and not how Ian Druitt's life may have led up to his suicide. Done properly and with any putative irregularities duly accounted for, her investigation's results would be identical to those that had already been reached.

Still, she needed to be careful here, since the fact that there had not also been an investigation by the Crown Prosecutors did indicate there might be cause for concern on Mr. Druitt's part. So she said, "I met your MP—Mr. Walker—in London, along with the assistant commissioner of the Met. Mr. Walker's expressed your concerns as well as his own, Mr. Druitt. I'm fully on board." This was something of a lie, but she was here to reassure the man that his disquiet was being taken seriously. "My sergeant and I will be looking at the previous investigations that resulted in the verdict of suicide at the coroner's inquest."

Druitt was no one's fool. He quickly surmised that her presence did not constitute a reopening of the case. He said, "Ian had no *cause*. You ask anyone and they'll tell you as much." He moved to one of the sealed boxes and opened it. He riffled through its contents—Isabelle could see it was mostly clothing—and when he didn't find what he was seeking, he opened another. This time, he found what he wanted after removing a stack of neatly folded woolen sweaters. He handed over to her a wooden plaque and he instructed her to "give it a look."

She saw it was fashioned of fine cherry and it had a large engraved brass plate fixed upon it. Across this were the words *Ludlow Man of the Year* and beneath them *Ian Druitt* followed by the date, which was in early March. Above this was etched Ludlow Castle on its hill with a flag waving above its central tower. The award, Isabelle thought, was quite nice, not just a second-rate nod of obligatory gratitude from the town.

"They gave him this," Druitt said. "The mayor and the town council. Had a ceremony in the council chamber: speeches, refreshments, musicians from the college. I'm telling you, he had *no* reason to kill himself. He had friends. He had people who loved him. He had everything he could have wanted."

He also, Isabelle thought, had an allegation of paedophilia hanging over him. She didn't say this, however. She knew that a plaque actually meant nothing in the greater scheme of things; while lovely, it was only a gesture. Additionally, in the case of Ian Druitt, a plaque and a ceremony and a band and all the trimmings could have served as a means of pushing someone already angry into anonymously setting the ball in motion.

Clive Druitt went on. "Our Ian? Never depressed a day in his life. Never one to be sad, to be looking for more than what he had. Does that sound like a suicide to you?"

At this, she wondered if Druitt even knew about the allegation of paedophilia. She assumed that he must. How could he not? He wouldn't want to face that, though. No father would want to hear that about his son.

"And this," he said. "You look at this." Now he'd removed from the same box a folder newspaper. She saw it was local: the *Ludlow Echo.* It carried a front-page story about the ceremony at which Ian Druitt had been named the town's Man of the Year. It listed his activities in Ludlow as well as his accomplishments past, present, and coming in the future. They were, admittedly, very impressive. But none of them went any distance to proving he wasn't a suicide. And if he wasn't a suicide, then someone murdered him or he'd died accidentally. The first was improbable considering where he'd been when he died, and the second was impossible for the same reason.

She said, "Mr. Druitt, I assure you my colleague and I intend to look into every aspect of what happened that night at Ludlow police station. We'll examine the reports that were written about it and we'll look at the procedures that the responding officer and the IPCC followed. If there's something untoward in what was reported, we *will* find it."

He turned to face her and she could see him trying to read exactly what was meant in her words. A few moments passed in which she saw that they weren't alone as she'd previously thought because a young woman wearing a boiler suit was dealing with the tanks beyond the glass wall and making notes on a clipboard she was holding.

Druitt finally said shrewdly, "This isn't to be reopened, is it? You've come to sweep things beneath the carpet. You listen to me, Detective Chief Superintendent Whatever Your Name Is. I'm not having that. I want this whole matter reopened, and that's what Walker assured me was going to happen once he talked to the Met."

"This is how it begins." Isabelle aimed for reasonable in her voice. "Once my colleague and I conduct our investigation into the enquiries that went on in Ludlow, we fashion a report for our superiors. A recommendation is made based on our report. But we don't have the power to make that recommendation ourselves. That's done by our higher-ups." A borderline lie, but it was close enough to the truth to serve. They could investigate as much as they wanted to investigate, fine-tooth combing their way by speaking to every person who had already been spoken to. But as far as Isabelle could see at the moment, that would be a largely unnecessary expenditure of their time and the Met's resources.

Druitt said, "I want *everyone* talked to, and I mean everyone who knew my boy. I particularly want someone to grill that police whatever-he-was who left Ian alone for however long he left him alone *and* for whatever reason. If I don't get that, you're going to hear from my solicitors. All of them."

Well, this wasn't going quite as planned, Isabelle thought. Another call to his MP was doubtless going to be his next move if he didn't like how things were arranged. Before they reached that pass with each other, she needed to placate him. Hillier would not be pleased to hear from either the man's solicitors or his MP. Nor, she expected, would Chief Constable Wyatt or anyone else be pleased. She ran her hand over the most recently opened box. She said, "Completely understood, Mr. Druitt. May I take these with me, please?"

"These belongings of Ian's? What do you want with them? I expect you mean to toss them, don't you?"

"Absolutely not! There could be, amongst your son's belongings, something to aid us."

"I'll get them back, won't I?"

"Of course you will. And you'll have a receipt for them."

"I ask because I don't trust you lot, not when you say Ian did himself in. Men of God don't do themselves in. And Ian was a man of God."

LUDLOW
SHROPSHIRE

In daylight the L-shaped police station wasn't much different from what it had been at night, although now there were no lights on inside, no windows open, and no panda cars in the car park. Indeed, there were no cars at all, which told Barbara that the community support officer had not yet arrived. This gave her a chance for a daylight recce of the place, which she started to make at once.

The building was fronted by a slope where trimmed shrubs edged the top of a lawn. Barbara discovered that one could, without trouble, walk behind these shrubs and along the side of the station. This she herself did, in order to reach the car park behind it. There she saw a CCTV camera hanging above the door that led from the car park into the back of the building. Other than the additional camera above the front door, though, there didn't appear to be any more visual security.

Returning to the front, she looked up at the CCTV camera, which she'd noted on the previous night appeared to be directed towards the street, taking in at least part of it, the concrete steps that climbed up from the pavement, and the pavement itself. She wondered how wide the lens on it was. In addition to documenting whoever came up the stairs and walked towards the station, was the lens wide enough to allow the camera to take in the door and the intercom hanging to one side of it? Was the camera's position fixed or did it swivel if a different angle was wanted?

She was pondering this when a patrol car drove by. She returned to the car park, where a young man was just climbing out of the car. He called out, "Sergeant Havers, is it? Sorry for the wait. Old Rob took his time about settling when I got him home," all of which announced him as the PCSO.

Gary Ruddock was, she saw, a good-size bloke. He stood just over six feet tall, and although there was a roundness to his physique, this suggested muscle rather than fat. His dark hair was cut short, but not in the fashion of a football hooligan. His face was oval. He was squeaky-clean looking and perfectly shaved.

His handshake was firm. "Gary Ruddock," he said. "Gaz, actually. Have you been here long?"

"It's Barbara," she replied. "Just a few minutes. Is Rob your granddad?"

"My landlord, more or less. He won't go into a home. He's too feisty by half for that. *And* he won't live with his daughter. That's Abby. So I'm the compromise. I see to him nights and mornings, and there's a neighbour who looks in on him when I'm at work. Let's go inside."

"Does that swivel?" she asked him.

He turned from the door into which he'd inserted a key. He followed the direction of her gaze. "The camera?" he asked. "I haven't a clue. I don't even know if it's still functioning now the station's not manned. We can try to swivel it later, though. There's going to be a broom somewhere inside."

He led the way into the station, saying, "Coffee? Water? Tea? It's filtered. The water, I mean. What I mean is there's a Brita jug in the fridge."

She said water would be good and he told her he would have a coffee, if she didn't mind. He took her to what had probably been a lunchroom for the officers in the days when the station was being fully used. Now it was part storeroom, and there were cardboard boxes with various dates upon them, which were stacked in one corner of the room along with paper for printers and boxes of ink cartridges for the same.

She said, "What a shame."

He looked over his shoulder and clocked her looking about. He said, "Cutbacks've gone deep. It's one of the reasons I couldn't ever get onto the regular force. And now, 'course . . . after what happened . . . I'm lucky to have a job at all. 'Course, I reckon that was rather the case from the first as I'm not much for reading."

"Reading?" Barbara wasn't at all sure where he was heading with this.

He went on with his coffee making, pulling some Nescafé and an electric kettle from a cupboard along with a large mug celebrating the work of the RSPCA. "I turn words and letters round," he told her. "For a long time I thought it had to do with how I was schooled. But when I ran off to Belfast and tried special classes, it was just the same."

He let the water run in the sink and kindly washed out a glass for her. He handed it over then, let her pour for herself from the Brita jug.

"What d'you mean: 'ran off'?" she asked him.

He filled the kettle and set it to boil. "Oh. Sorry. I lived in a cult till I was fifteen. Donegal this was."

"That's quite something."

"Oh aye, it was. They were very big into increasing and multiplying, but not equally big on educating the kids. I reckoned at the time

I might be able to catch up on my schooling once I got away from them, but like I said, it was no go. Something's wrong with the way I see words. I'm crap at spelling as well. That's why PCSO was the best I could manage, as there's not a lot of forms wanting to be filled out like if one's a regular. But I expect you know all that."

Barbara waited while he made his coffee once the kettle clicked off. He nodded at the long table beneath the room's only window, where two plastic chairs were tucked. They sat, and when Ruddock circled his hands round his RSPCA mug, Barbara saw he bore a tattoo across the top of his left wrist. It was very thick, very dark, and all uppercase: CAT. She nodded at it, saying, "You're an animal person, eh?"

He gave a laugh. "Cat's my mum. We all had 'em. All the kids. To identify the mums."

"You all had tattoos?" Barbara said and when he nodded, "Bit odd, that. Usually it's the dads needing identifying."

"That wouldn't've ever been possible without DNA tests being done. It was all part of spreading the seeds. The cult was big on increasing and multiplying, like I said, but small on who did the increasing and multiplying when and with who."

"But you'd know who your mum was, wouldn't you?"

"Only 'cause of the tattoos is how we'd know. We never lived with our mums once we were off the breast. We got taken to a sort of nursery, and after that, our mums didn't see us much because of . . . well the increasing and multiplying thing, which was sort of their job, if you see. So the tattoos made sure a lad didn't seed his own mum or his sister when he got old enough for sex."

Barbara took this in for a moment before saying, "Sorry, but that sounds . . . can I say . . . over the top?"

"Oh, massively," he agreed, unoffended. "You can prob'ly work out why I left soon as I could. Once I ran off, I never went back." He took a sip of his coffee. He wasn't a slurper. Lynley, Barbara thought, would have approved. Where Lynley came from, learning never to slurp was a skill mastered at one's nanny's knee and doubtless from the silver christening cup. Ruddock put his mug back on the table and said, "How did the Met get involved in all this?"

"Weren't you told?"

He shook his head. "I only talked to the IPCC and to the detective who first came round. That's it."

"The House of Commons has taken an interest. Sorry about it, but we have to start from the beginning." She took out her notebook and mechanical pencil. She saw Ruddock blow out a breath. She said, "Sorry."

He said, "It's only like this'll never end. I know you're doing your job, but still . . ."

*Job* was where she began, with the enquiry about how he'd managed to keep his after a potential suspect in an alleged crime had killed himself while at the Ludlow police station waiting for transport to Shrewsbury.

"It came from West Mercia Headquarters," he said frankly. "What I got told by my guv is someone over there argued to keep me on, someone ranking."

Barbara made note of that. It seemed odd that a higher-ranking officer would take this sort of stand, considering the commotion that Ian Druitt's suicide had caused. Better to shuffle the offending community service officer under the carpet or, more likely, out of the door altogether. She said, "Any idea why?"

"Arguing to keep me on?" he clarified, and when she nodded, "Some of 'em did training sessions when I was in Hindlip, and I got to know three or four of 'em. Just to talk to, if you see what I mean. I reckoned that was a good idea, in case I ever was able to have an interview for something more than PCSO." He shrugged but looked mildly embarrassed. "It was . . . well . . . I guess you'd call it a political thing."

"A clever thing as well," she replied. Ruddock may have had trouble with his letters and such, but he was no dummy if he'd thought of that one. "So that's where the training school is? At police headquarters?"

"Yeah. So it's easy enough for officers there to give some courses now and then." He took another sip of his coffee and with his thumb traced the letter *R*. "Truth, though? After what happened, I reckoned I'd be sacked straightaway. I'm that grateful I wasn't."

Barbara said nothing. At the training school for PCSOs, she thought, he must have learned to be quite a wily political animal.

He went on. "I was so bloody *stupid.* When I fetched him, he was taking off his kit after a service. I waited for him to finish it all up but I didn't think to watch his every move. Why would I? He was just some bloke taking off his kit. When he was ready, he grabbed up his anorak from a hook on the door and off we went."

"Did he ask what he was being questioned about?"

"Over and over. But I hadn't the first clue. I only knew what I was supposed to do, and I didn't think about asking my sergeant why I was meant to do it. And then, about an hour after I got him here, a binge drinking situation developed that I was meant to handle."

"By leaving the station?"

"Oh no. Not ever," he said. "I couldn't do that because of Mr. Druitt being here. But I had to make phone calls to all the pubs. Christ. I wish they'd stop serving kids when they're pissed, but it's all about money in the till, so they just keep on."

His mind had been on other things, then, Barbara reckoned. Thus far, from her nighttime reading of the reports she'd been given, his story was the same as it had been all along. She was impressed that Ruddock didn't try to sugarcoat things. She said, "Would you show me where it happened?"

He'd obviously known this would be part of their talk because he rose without hesitation, left his coffee on the table, and said, "It's this way."

They headed deeper into the building. The walls—institutional yellow, and Barbara wondered if there was an unwritten law that corridors in government buildings had to be painted this unappealing cross between mustard and algae—still had bulletin boards hanging upon them with posters and notices now curling at the edges, and within several of the rooms that they passed, a few computers indicated that the building was still in use by patrol officers when they were in the immediate area. All of this caused her to understand why an officer wanting to have a bit of a kip at night would do so in the car park and not inside the station.

She said, "How many officers actually use this place?"

He was opening a door. It had an empty nameplate on the front of it, the sort that generally was used to identify the office of one of the station's bigwigs. "Aside from the patrol officers assigned to this area?" He took a pause as if trying to visualise who else might need to use the building for something related to policing. "Detectives, I reckon, needing to log on to the system. Major crime team members for the same reason. Vice officers. Officers who patrol the district, like I said. Myself, as being assigned to Ludlow."

She followed him into the room where Ian Druitt had killed himself. According to both DI Pajer's report and the report made by the IPCC, he'd managed the act using his stole and a doorknob on the coat cupboard, but there was a detail in the DI's report that Barbara had underlined, and she brought it up now. She considered it a singular irregularity.

When a suspect was arrested or brought into a station for questioning not of his own volition, handcuffs were used. And that had been the case here, since the postmortem report had noted that the handcuffs—these were the plastic variety that were ratcheted round the suspect's wrists—had produced abrasions on Ian Druitt's. This suggested that the plasticuffs had been put on Druitt too tightly in the beginning or that he had struggled when he had them on. Or both, she reckoned, since he would have wanted to get out of them if they were too tight.

She said, "DI Pajer's report says you took the plasticuffs off Mr. Druitt because he'd complained about his hands getting numb. Was he fighting the cuffs? Attempting to get out of them? And why plasticuffs and not ordinary handcuffs?"

"They were what I had on me," Ruddock told her. "And they weren't too tight. I never do tight. Just secure is all."

"But you still cut them off him?"

Ruddock rubbed his forehead. "He kept going *on* about 'em. Complaining how they were hurting his hands, how he couldn't feel his fingers. He was insistent. He got louder 'n' louder. So I went back to the room and cut 'em off."

"Why didn't you stay with him?"

"No one ever said I was *supposed* to stay with him. Like I said, I didn't know the first thing about why he was even there. All I ever got told was pick this bloke up and keep him at the station till the patrol officers fetched him to Shrewsbury. I wish to God they'd told me why I was bringing him in, but all I knew was that he was wanted for questioning. Full stop. And I'm not meaning to excuse myself when I say that. I'm the one caused this whole mess."

"What were you doing, then? While he was alone."

This had been in DI Pajer's report, but Barbara wanted to hear it from him directly. "Like I said, I got phoned about this situation going on in the centre of town with kids and their drinking. There wasn't anything I could do about it from here except to ring the pub in question—it's called the Hart and Hind—and tell them to stop serving young people. Then I had to ring the rest of the pubs round about, so if the kids moved on, they wouldn't get served anywhere else."

"Where were you, then, making these calls?"

"Just in one of the other offices. While I was doing that is when it happened. I didn't leave the building. I wouldn't've done that. I just wasn't in the same room as him. If someone had *told* me he was a risk, I wouldn't ever have left him on his own. But no one did. So what I thought was that it would be okay to ring the pubs."

That he'd left Druitt alone was a phenomenal blunder. But it wasn't the only blunder that had occurred.

Suicides had happened before in custody. Suspects being held for questioning had been known to use restraint belts to hang themselves, to bash their heads into walls in the hope of achieving a deadly haematoma, to slash their wrists on a small piece of protruding metal previously not noted on the bottom of a toilet or basin. Where there was a will, there was generally going to be a way, including a man who'd once used his socks as a garrotte. It was impossible to take into account every permutation of self-harm. The police did their best but on occasion they were outsmarted.

What gave Barbara pause, though, was how convenient this particular place was for a suicide to occur. Druitt could have been murdered by Ruddock or by any officer who showed up and for whom Ruddock was now covering. Since the case in hand was about paedophilia, Druitt was going to be loathed on general principles. The only stumbling block in this line of thought, though, was Gary Ruddock's contention that he had not known why he was meant to fetch Druitt, aside from the man's being needed for questioning. Unless, of course, he'd been given the word and was now lying about it.

She said, "I've seen the transcript of the 999 call that prompted Druitt's arrest."

He looked wary, as if he were about to be blamed for a phone call on top of Ian Druitt's death. He said, "Yeah?"

"One of the things the caller said was that he couldn't abide the hypocrisy of it. My guv thinks that refers to the paedophilia and Druitt's being a churchman. What do you think?"

He considered this. Barbara nodded that she was ready to leave the room. She'd seen nothing that might have given any kind of mute testimony regarding the death that had occurred. There were only the usual signs of wear and tear that an office shows once someone moves from it: smudges on the window, scuff marks on the lino, picture hooks where certificates once had hung, slut's wool in the corners.

Back in the corridor, Ruddock said, "Only thing I can think of was this honour he'd been given. Even old Rob saw it in the paper, and p'rhaps the caller saw it as well and his ire got lit by it."

"What honour?" Her paperwork hadn't mentioned any honours.

"Ludlow Man of the Year. Rob always reads the local paper and he's fond of talking it over at dinner. There was a story."

"About Ian Druitt as Man of the Year? When was this?"

He looked thoughtful. "I'm not sure. P'rhaps four or five months ago? He was receiving something from the town council. There was a picture of the mayor and him, Druitt. So . . . Man of the Year and paedophilia? That'd be hypocrisy, wouldn't it?"

It would, Barbara thought. But the first question was whether it was enough to prompt Ian Druitt to kill himself when the word got out about an investigation into his behaviour. And the second question was whether being named Man of the Year was enough to prompt someone to kill him before an investigation into his behaviour could take place.

LUDLOW
SHROPSHIRE

"So he's a nice enough bloke," Sergeant Havers said to Isabelle in conclusion. "And dead grateful still to be in uniform. He knows he's at fault for leaving Druitt on his own, but he also says he hadn't the first clue why he was fetching the bloke to the station."

"Anything he said that wasn't in Pajer's report or the IPCC's?"

"He didn't go into his own background with them, so that's new information, for what it's worth."

They were standing outside the Charlton Arms, at the far end of the Ludford Bridge. It was an attractive inn across the river from Ludlow, bordering on the ancient hamlet for which the bridge was named. The building was shaded by leafy beech trees from which birds were raising a ruckus of song when they weren't rocketing into the sky, and Isabelle had directed the detective sergeant to it when Havers had rung on her mobile announcing that she'd finished her interview with PCSO Ruddock. She'd described him as a "bit of a slow learner, seems like. But that appears to relate to reading and spelling."

"Why in God's name is he still employed? Have we any idea?"

"He says he was told an officer at headquarters took his part, someone who gave courses at the training centre when he was there."

"He must have been one hell of an impressive student, then," Isabelle said. "Which doesn't *quite* square with the reading and spelling bit, does it."

"He says he sucked up to the officers. Reckoned it might help him advance."

"Well that's been scuppered," Isabelle noted.

Havers nodded. She was dragging in on a cigarette, obviously taking the opportunity to toke up on the nicotine before Isabelle gave her another assignment. But Isabelle didn't wish to assign her to anything at the moment. What she wished was to enter the Charlton Arms, to sit at one of the tables overlooking the river, and to do something to still the tingling that was going on in her nerve endings. But it was hardly an hour at which a drink would be excusable in any eyes but her own, so she said, "Our suicide's dad wants another full investigation, with bells, whistles, and dancing girls."

Havers blew out a lungful of smoke and tossed the dog-end of her cigarette into the river. Isabelle gave her a what-the-hell look after watching the dog-end hit the water. Havers said, "Sorry. Wasn't thinking."

"Let's hope a swan doesn't take it for a nibble."

"Right. Won't do it again. What did you tell him?"

"Mr. Druitt? I've brought back nine boxes of our Ian's belongings and I've told the dad we'll be digging through them. Sifting for evidence. Looking for clues. Tossing out red herrings. Reading the entrails of slaughtered oxen. God knows what else. The point is to keep him away from the phone because he assured me that his next move is to ring his solicitors. In the plural. We need to forestall him."

"That's next then? The boxes?"

"God no. What else do you have?"

"The vicar, I suppose."

Isabelle cast another glance at her. She turned away from the sight of the Charlton Arms because its presence was proving more of a temptation than she could abide. She said, "What about the vicar?" And when Havers looked tentative, Isabelle said impatiently, "Let's have it, Sergeant."

Havers explained that when Gary Ruddock hadn't been immediately available to see her, she'd decided to speak with the vicar of St. Laurence Church. She hoped that was all right, guv.

Isabelle said, "For God's sake, Sergeant. It was on the list. Why wouldn't it be all right? Get on with it."

Havers did so. She'd taken notes of their conversation—just as she'd done for her colloquy with Ruddock—and she flipped to that part of her notebook. She listed for Isabelle what turned out to be all the various reasons that Ian Druitt had probably been named Man of the Year. There was no particular change from what Isabelle had read in the newspaper that Clive Druitt had shown her. The deacon had put a thumb into every pie of social responsibility that existed in Ludlow. Havers concluded by referencing the after-school children's club that

Druitt had established, saying, "There's some college boy who assisted with this. I'm thinking we should speak with him."

"Why?"

"Seems that if this whole bit of Druitt being a paedophile *is* true, we need to—"

"Sergeant, we aren't here about the truth or falsity of the paedophile bit. That's not our brief. I expect you know that. In case you don't, I'll remind you that we're here to see if DI Pajer and the IPCC did what they were supposed to do. We're here to follow *their* reports to make certain they didn't miss something connected to the suicide. If we talk to anyone else at this point, it's going to be the forensic pathologist."

Havers didn't reply to this. Isabelle could see that she was gnawing at something mentally, though.

"So far is there anything that Bernadette Pajer or the IPCC missed?" Isabelle demanded. "If there is, I want to know it."

"It doesn't seem like it," Havers admitted. "But—"

"There is no but. Either there's something or there isn't, Sergeant."

"Well, if the vicar and this bloke's dad both say—"

"What they say has nothing to do with what actually *happened*. When someone kills himself without there being an obvious, outward reason, people want to think it wasn't a suicide. That's human nature. Overdose of pills? Accident. Gunshot? Murder. Self-immolation? Either one."

"But you don't *accidentally* kill yourself in a police station, guv," Havers protested. "Which makes it—"

"Suicide. Because have you any idea how difficult it is for someone to fake suicide by hanging? And in this case, according to what you've told me, suicide by hanging from a *doorknob*? Besides that, the point of our presence *isn't* about trying to discover if the man had a reason to kill himself. For all we know, he's Rebecca de Winter and he just had a diagnosis of cancer."

"Except . . ." Havers hesitated.

"What?"

"Well, it's only that she was murdered, guv."

"Who?"

"Rebecca de Winter. Max killed her, remember? The cancer thing was how he got off. See, she really wanted him to kill her since she knew she was going to die anyway, and if he did the job for her *and* got caught, she'd be ruining his life, which is what she'd wanted all along."

"Oh for God's sake," Isabelle said. "We're not living in a 1940s melodrama, Sergeant."

"Right. 'Course. But there's this as well: Druitt didn't live with the vicar and his wife though they had plenty of room. He wanted his own place, the vicar said. He said it was because of privacy. What I'm wondering is what he wanted that privacy for. Because if someone knew why he needed privacy, that same person—"

"Enough." Isabelle threw up her hands. "We're going to talk to the forensic pathologist. I can see only that is going to convince you that the first two investigations were sound."

THE LONG MYND
SHROPSHIRE

Instead of at the hospital where the postmortem examination of Ian Druitt had been performed, Dr. Nancy Scannell informed them that they would have to meet instead in an area of Shropshire called the Long Mynd where, it turned out, the doctor was a member of a consortium of pilots who had pooled their money to purchase a glider. The Long Mynd was the location of the West Midlands Gliding Club, and it was here that Dr. Scannell was duty-bound to assist a member of the group in launching the consortium's glider that afternoon.

Reaching the Long Mynd involved a drive of some miles to the north of Ludlow. It was an area of vast hilltop moors of grass, accessed by coursing along roads and lanes that became progressively steeper and narrower, until barely a single vehicle could be accommodated. Here male and female pheasants darted in and out of the hedgerows, and sheep lay about the roadway as if in ownership of the asphalt. The fact that cars didn't travel this route often was indicated when a flock of mallards—males, females, and ducklings—plopped down from a slope directly in the path of the DCS's car, either oblivious to its presence or overly sanguine about their safety. Ardery swore and hit the brakes. Barbara was relieved that she didn't flatten the lot of them.

The DCS was on edge. Barbara had seen that during their conversation on the Ludford Bridge and now she saw it more in Ardery's driving. She'd thought about offering to take the wheel when they reached a weathered directional sign at a barely inhabited hamlet called Plowden. It indicated the route to the West Midlands Gliding Club, and she got a glimpse of the lane, which looked more like a cart track climbing upward at an alarming angle. She shot a glance at the DCS. Ardery was white-knuckling the steering wheel.

They made the turn and climbed to a hamlet that proclaimed itself as Asterton, which looked less like a hamlet and more like someone's farm. There, yet another indicator demanded that they squeeze by a BT call box and engage in a steeper climb on the roughest lane yet. Finally, they arrived at what appeared to be the gliding club, or so a very large sign indicated, printed complete with photos of smiling pilots and passengers who grinned and appeared to be attempting to look at ease while soaring, motorless, in the blue.

The place was accessed through a gate that gaped open despite being hung with a sign reading KEEP CLOSED AT ALL TIMES. It was a collection of corrugated metal wartime huts sitting on a vast acreage nearly bare of all vegetation save grass upon which a good number of plump sheep grazed. Various other buildings constructed of various other materials partnered the huts, and in front of these a line of gliders waited for someone's use while others were in the process of being removed from the low-slung trailers in which they were stored. Behind the gliders, cars were parked, and behind the cars a more formal-looking building announced itself as the clubhouse, which contained a reception area, offices, meeting rooms, and the cafeteria. It was in the cafeteria that they were set to meet Dr. Scannell.

They were late. A wrong turn had taken them a number of miles off course, delivering them into one of the multitudinous hamlets that dotted this section of Shropshire. So while they found Dr. Scannell waiting for them, they did not find her in good humour. Barbara's conclusion was that the forensic pathologist and Isabelle Ardery were well matched at this point.

"I've ten minutes left," Dr. Scannell told them. She'd risen from her place at a long table in the club's cafeteria when they'd come into the room. She was casually dressed in blue jeans and a flannel shirt. Piles of her salt-and-pepper hair sprang from beneath a baseball cap. "I'm due on the runway," she went on. "Sorry, but it can't be helped."

There were other pilots who were having meals in the cafeteria, a loud group of them talking and guffawing about "Number One's bollocks of a briefing this morning" at a window that served as one entire wall and overlooked a sweeping countryside. Dr. Scannell wanted their conversation to be a private one, apparently, as she led them to another room. This had the looks of a briefing room since it was hung with charts and it possessed a whiteboard. Scannell didn't stop there, however. Instead, she went on to a final room, which turned out to be the gliding club's bar, and no one was in it at the moment.

Barbara glanced uneasily at Ardery. Ardery's gaze was fixed steadily forward, placed upon a table at the far side of the room. As if reading her gaze, Dr. Scannell took them there.

She looked at her watch—it was very official, Barbara thought, with lots of dials and gizmos to give her endless bits of information—and said, "Nine minutes. What do you want to know?"

Barbara had Scannell's report. Ardery took it from her, slid it to the pathologist, and said, "My sergeant has some concerns about your conclusion of suicide."

"Has she indeed?" Scannell gave Barbara an indifferent look. She removed her baseball cap. Her hair bounced out like a litter of puppies being freed from a pen.

"It's only because of the doorknob bit," Barbara said, and the pathologist's fierce expression made her rather more tentative than she'd thought she would be. "Plus this bloke doesn't seem the suicide type from what I've come up with about him."

"Disabuse yourself of that notion." Scannell brought forth a pair of half-moon spectacles that she dug out of the breast pocket of her shirt and perched on her nose. "There is no type. There is only whether the death was suicide, accident, or murder, and in this case it was suicide."

She opened the folder and set out its contents, which consisted of postmortem photographs, a transcript of what she'd recited into the recorder documenting the examination of the body as she'd conducted it, the report she'd compiled when her examination had been completed, and the toxicology information that had been supplied. She referred to her report and to the photographs. These latter she set out for Barbara to look at. Because of the paucity of time they had, she spoke quickly, without a pause, to ask if there was anything unclear in what she had to say.

Venous congestion was where she began. It, combined with asphyxia, was the cause of death. The venous congestion had been effected through use of a priestly garment as ligature, a stole, which was not dissimilar to a rather narrow scarf. The stole was broader than the normal sort of ligature that suicides used, and it was soft, so it was unable to sink into the tissue of the neck at any depth. Did the sergeant know what this meant? No wait for an answer. It meant that instead of cerebral anaemia caused by pressure on the arteries, what they had was jugular veins being blocked through compression. This resulted in loss of cerebral circulation—"blood flowing into, out of, and around the brain in layman's terms," the doctor said—which caused venous pressure in the head to rise. Death would have come in three to five minutes, since only two kilos of pressure on the jugular veins were needed to close them.

She began to indicate each of the photographs as she went, taking a second to give her wristwatch another look. The body, if the sergeant would care to look at the photos of it in situ, bore all the signs of suicide as well. Note the distortions of the face. Examine the degree to which the eyes have become prominent. Observe the minor bleeding sites—"These are called petechiae"—that one can see on the inside of the lips. But most important, note the bruising on the neck.

Barbara said, "I see all that. Only . . . what I *don't* see is how using a doorknob can possibly work if someone wants to hang himself."

"It has everything to do with intention," Dr. Scannell said. "The individual leans forward and allows his body weight to do the work:

to render him unconscious quickly. This causes the venous congestion I spoke of, which triggers the loss of cerebral circulation. While accidents are known to occur this way—autoeroticism is a good example—to murder someone like this . . . ? The ligature would show it."

It all had to do with the neck and the marks that the ligature left on the neck. These marks had to match with any number of points of interest: the weight of the body suspended and the degree of suspension, whether the ligature was wrapped round the neck once or twice, the type of knot used, the length of time the body was suspended from the door knob, a single versus a double impression of the ligature, whether there was an impression of the ligature at all.

"There was nothing to indicate that this incident was anything other than suicide," Scannell concluded.

"Even his wrists?"

"What about his wrists?" She looked at the photos and compared them to her notes. "You mean the abrasions? Consistent with what the arresting officer reported. The handcuffs—these were of the plastic variety—were put on too tight, according to what the victim said to the officer. He was, naturally, foolish to remove them—"

"But what if he didn't?" Barbara cut in. "He could've staged the suicide then, couldn't he? Or someone else could've come into the station, done the job on this bloke Druitt, and then the PCSO found him, panicked, and tried to make it look like a suicide. Couldn't that be what happened?"

Dr. Scannell's expression indicated she was considering or at least *had* considered this premise at some point. She said, "It *could* have happened in one of those two ways," and when Barbara was about to give Ardery a pointed look, the pathologist continued, "And the angel Gabriel could have put in an appearance and done the job as well, but I rather doubt it. Now—" and here she stood—"I'm wanted on the launching field. Have you seen a glider being winch launched? No? Come along, then. You might want to watch."

Barbara wasn't the least bit interested in watching a glider get itself launched. But if it gave her another few minutes to question Dr. Scannell, she was going to take them. So before the DCS could demur,

Barbara jumped to her feet and indicated that she was wild about winches. She was gratified when Ardery didn't follow her, remaining instead in the bar where they'd been sitting.

Outside, the wind was gusting more fiercely than when they'd arrived. Smoke from a fire at a caravan park to one side of the gliding club made the air acrid, and additional odours mingled with the smoke: chemicals, petrol, and a vague scent of manure.

Nancy Scannell strode in the direction of a distant grassy moor, and Barbara scurried to keep up with her. Across from the building from which they'd emerged, she saw that someone was driving a tractor round what appeared to be the single runway of the airfield. This activity served to move the grazing sheep out of the way, and it seemed to be the case that the launch of the glider waiting at the end of the runway had to occur fairly quickly once the sheep scattered since, given enough time, they would merely place themselves in the line of fire once again.

Two four-wheeled vehicular contraptions stood at either end of the runway, which looked to be at least a mile long. They each accommodated a driver and contained an enormous spool at the front. Barbara assumed that these were the winches. Between them ran a thick steel cord, and from this another steel cord extended perpendicular to it, presumably waiting for a glider to be attached.

Dr. Scannell didn't appear to be inclined for more conversation, but Barbara decided that couldn't matter because there was something more she wanted to know. So she said rather breathlessly, "What about strangulation?"

The pathologist was cramming her wildly blowing hair beneath her baseball cap, and she said, "What *about* strangulation?" as she waved at the pilot who stood next to the open cockpit of the glider, studying some distant clouds for whatever they were apt to tell her. "Coming!" Nancy Scannell yelled. "Woohoo! Coming!"

The pilot turned; another woman. Barbara wondered if the whole group who owned the glider consisted of women as well.

"Why couldn't someone have strangled him?" she asked. "Why not strangle him with that priest thing he was wearing and then string him up to the doorknob to make it look like suicide?"

"Because the marks on the neck would be different." Scannell made no effort to hide her impatience. Barbara couldn't blame her, really. They were, after all, questioning her competence.

"How?" Barbara asked her.

"Turn around, then." The pathologist dug a handkerchief out of her jeans.

"Why?"

"Just *do* it. You have a question. Here's the answer."

When Barbara turned obediently, the pathologist slipped the handkerchief—folded into a very short ligature—round her neck. She tightened it slightly, saying, "If I strangle you, Sergeant, the mark of the ligature is straight round your neck. I could hang you then, of course, but the primary mark straight round your neck would be there for everyone to see. If you hang yourself, the ligature mark is at an angle, like this." She demonstrated. "That's the short and sweet of it. Now if you'll excuse me . . ."

That said, she walked off, balling the handkerchief into her pocket again. Barbara watched while she joined the other pilot at the glider. They engaged in what appeared to be an inspection of the craft, and they were joined by a man who walked from the winch to look over the wings and several thingummies here and there. When he was finished, the glider was hooked onto the perpendicular steel cord extended from the cord that ran between the two winches. The man walked back to his winch, and as Dr. Scannell steadied the wing of the glider and held it parallel to the ground, the pilot climbed into the cockpit and sealed herself inside.

It was all a matter of less than a minute: Dr. Scannell thumbs-upped the winch man. The winch man flashed his lights at whoever was at the other winch one mile away. All systems were go, the steel cord began to be drawn from the closer to the farther winch, the glider was pulled, and in what seemed like less than fifty yards, it was in the air. It soared to about eight hundred feet, where the secondary steel cord that had held it to the moving line was released. The rest was gliding.

Pretty bloody incredible, Barbara thought as she watched the glider soar in silence into the air. What sort of fool would even try it?

THE LONG MYND
SHROPSHIRE

Left alone in the bar, Isabelle told herself she would not. Still, across the semilit room, the line of bottles glittered on the two shelves that held them, suggesting to her that, really, it would be a matter of two minutes at most to duck behind the shoplike Formica counter serving as the bar itself and there merely peruse for curiosity's sake the various brands and types of spirits the glider pilots went for when they were finished with their soaring for the day. Presumably, they kept an eye on each other so that no one imbibed *before* said soaring.

Isabelle assured herself that she had an academic interest in what the glider club's bar served its members: Did the club go for price over quality? What about quantity over quality? Were their vodkas flavoured? Were their gins infused? Was that the Macallan she spied and, if so, how old was it? Merely an interest, a casual curiosity, a momentary desire to breathe in the scent once the bottle was opened and to let that scent do what scents could, which was to prompt memories to flood the mind in place of what was in the mind *now.* Only what was in the mind now was, as she knew, identical to what had been in the mind then. Just one, just one and that would be all because no one would know and the twins were, thank God, down for a nap after a morning an entire morning and then this segueing into an afternoon of first one then the other refusing to *settle* becoming the full manifestation of fuss until—

Isabelle stood. She grabbed her bag and got out of the bar. She strode through the meeting room and into the cafeteria, where the previously guffawing pilots had been sitting at the huge picture window. There were only two of them left now, and they were huddled together in earnest discussion over something of consequence to them, if their hushed voices were anything to go by. They took no notice of her, which was just as well considering the state of her screaming nerve endings.

For a moment, she tried to distract herself with the view of the Welsh Marches which, she could absolutely understand, anyone would find astounding as the panorama went on for miles and miles. In the distance she could see the cumulus clouds and spiralling up beneath them a glider and then another and was it soundless up there or did one hear the wind?

She felt her fingernails digging into her palms, and she wondered at what point during her mental maundering her fingers had tightened to the extent that she knew she'd see four deep crescents in each hand if she looked down to examine her own flesh which she didn't want to do at the moment because of what it would tell her about herself so now this very instant she needed and indeed wanted to get out of this place as quickly as possible because she did recognise that the edge was just there in front of her and it would take little enough for her to step over because it would indeed be similar to soaring like those distant gliders wouldn't it?

"Guv?"

Isabelle swung from the window to see Barbara Havers. She had no idea how long the DS had been in the cafeteria. She told herself that Havers didn't sound concerned, that she merely was letting Isabelle know she'd returned from wherever she'd gone with the forensic pathologist. "Have you seen what you need to see?" Isabelle asked her. "Heard what you need to hear?"

Havers nodded, although her words, "More or less, I s'pose," weren't exactly reassuring.

Isabelle said to her, "Then let's be off," and she directed the sergeant back the way she'd come, which took both of them past the toilets. A stop there prior to their journey was reasonable, so Isabelle told Havers that she would meet her at the car and indicated with her thumb that a visit to the necessary was next on her agenda. As she'd reckoned, the sergeant said she'd use the time to have a fag if the guv didn't mind and at that point the guv didn't mind at all.

The airline bottle wasn't nearly enough but it was something, and Isabelle hastily downed it when she'd locked the door behind her. Then she buried the empty deep within the rubbish and examined herself in the mirror. She used her lipstick. She also put two spots of it on her cheekbones and blended the circles of colour into her skin. That done, she popped a breath mint into her mouth, left the building, and went to rejoin Havers, who was doing her usual sucking down of nicotine as quickly as possible as she studied the airfield and gnawed unattractively on her lower lip.

There was an attitude about her that could have been interpreted in several different ways. It also could have been ignored, which Isabelle was inclined to do. But as a cop who was supposed to be at least moderately competent, she knew that it had to be mentioned. So she said, "Something's on your mind, Sergeant."

Havers turned from her perusal of the airfield. She said with a shrug and a half smile, "Everything looks dotted and crossed from where I'm standing." She tossed the dog-end of her cigarette onto the hard-packed ground and made sure it was dead. "Ready when you are," she said and then added, "Want me to drive, guv? You've been doing the honours so far and—"

"No." Isabelle spoke more sharply than she intended because there was something in the offer that she didn't like. Hearing herself, however, she added with a smile that she hoped looked genuine, "I promise not to endanger the mallards along the way. Come along."

Havers used the drive back to Ludlow to bury herself in the filing folders she'd brought. Studiously she compared the information in them to whatever she'd written in her notebook. The degree to which she concentrated on this activity seemed unnatural to Isabelle. Like her earlier scrutiny of the airfield, it suggested more than one thing, so after a quarter hour of a silence that became—at least to Isabelle—more and more tense, she said to the sergeant, "You're unconvinced. What point do you wish to argue, Sergeant?"

Havers looked up then. A deer-in-the-headlights expression was on her face, and she attempted to alter it quickly. She said, "It's just . . . Have you noticed how convenient it all is, guv? There's a string of burglaries happening round Shrewsbury, so the Ludlow PCSO is the one gets told to bring in the deacon. Then a situation of binge drinking starts up in town and he's meant to deal with that so the deacon has to remain at the Ludlow station. Burglaries, an arrest, binge drinking, suicide. All on one night?"

Isabelle took care with the lane. Two sheep had taken up residence in the middle of it. She blasted the horn at them. They glanced in her direction indifferently. "Oh damn and blast," Isabelle said. She shoved her car door open, leaned out, and shouted, "Off with you! Go on! Get off!" They took their time about lumbering to their feet. She pulled her door closed with a slam and said to Havers, "Are you suggesting that all of this was orchestrated? A string of burglaries, an arrest, a bout of binge drinking that had to be dealt with? D'you have any idea the size of the collusion that would have had to occur?"

"I'm on board with that. But all of the coincidences . . . They tell me this whole thing *should've* been handed over to the CPS. And since it wasn't . . . I mean, don't you think . . ."

Her hesitation was maddening this time. Isabelle said, "Spit it out, Barbara."

"It's just that . . . There's a difference between massive collusions and massive cover-ups. And looking for one sometimes gets in the way of seeing the other."

They'd reached the call box where a left turn would take them down the rest of the hill and put them on the route back to Ludlow. Isabelle jammed on the brakes more heavily than she'd intended. She said, "Meaning what?" and she didn't hide the exasperation in her voice.

"Nothing really. But if we're dotting and crossing things . . ."

"As I've said before, we're *not* here to make this into a murder enquiry. We're here to look at two investigations into a suicide. We can't keep going back and forth on this point as it's going to mire us in minutiae and we can't afford that as Hillier hasn't given us the time."

"Got it," Havers said. "Like before. But since we have a little time—just now, I mean—I've got the deacon's address 'cause the vicar handed it over. And it's strange, don't you think, that he didn't want to live with the vicar and his wife?"

"No, I do not think it's strange. And you've already made this point. So let me ask you this: Would you want to live with the vicar and his wife?"

"Me? 'Course not. But if I was a deacon at the church and I needed a room and they had one on offer and the church was, like, twenty yards away . . . ? Why not take it? If nothing else, it'd be a real money saver. But he didn't want to live with them. Could be there's a reason. And in the two investigations, guv? There's not a single word about where the bloke lived."

Isabelle sighed. Really, Havers was a most exasperating woman. "All right," she said to the sergeant. "I see where this is heading. Your feeling is that we must search out this address and scrutinise the property for . . . what? A skeleton in the basement? A skull in the barbecue? Never mind. Don't answer. Just give me the bloody address."

BURWAY
SHROPSHIRE

Ian Druitt had lived outside of Ludlow on a small housing estate comprising two cul-de-sacs and an unnamed lane. The houses were semi-detached, each with a garage on the side. At Ian Druitt's house, a yellow van stood in the driveway with its side panel open. Upon the panel was painted a skillful depiction of high-end ceramic pots and urns, burgeoning with greenery and flowers. Along with this were the words Bevans' Beauties, a phone number, a website, and an email address. A woman in camouflage dungarees and a short-sleeved T-shirt was loading enormous bags of potting soil into the vehicle. Around her neck a kerchief was tied, and on her head sat a hat with a brim looking large enough to shade her and several passersby.

"This was the address?" Isabelle said to Havers, who checked her notes a second time. When Havers nodded, the conclusion was before them. Ian Druitt had not lived alone. Then the woman turned from the van, and Isabelle saw she was of Druitt's age. Somehow this seemed surprising.

By the current standards in which people of sixty-five were called middle-aged as if they were going to live to be one hundred thirty years old, this woman was a veritable youth somewhere in the vicinity of forty. She was wearing sunglasses of John Lennon vintage and style, and she pushed these up her nose and ceased her work as Isabelle and DS Havers approached her. Isabelle could see that she'd already stuffed the van with the sort of pots featured on its exterior, as well as dozens of summer plants of various types.

Isabelle introduced herself and Havers. Both of them showed the woman their police identification. She looked unsurprisingly confused by this intrusion of New Scotland Yard into her life. But she said in a perfectly friendly fashion that she was Flora Bevans and added, "I know. It's a joke. Flora. It's like my parents already knew."

Isabelle told her that the vicar of St. Laurence Church had given this address as Ian Druitt's, and they quickly learned from Flora Bevans that Ian Druitt had been her lodger. It turned out that she was a member of St. Laurence's church choir, and from one of the elderly members—"You know how women can be with matchmaking?"—she'd discovered that while Ian Druitt was living at the vicarage with Mr. Spencer and his wife, he'd not liked to disturb them with his music and so he was seeking another place to live.

"I had an extra room and I can always use the cash, can't we all," she said frankly. "I reckoned that if his music got too loud for me, I could just remove my hearing aids. So I mentioned it to him, he came over and had a look, and there you have it. There was nothing between us," she added pointedly. "Chemistry and all that? It wasn't there. But he was a lovely bloke. *And* he kept the bathroom like a picture from a magazine, which, you ask me, is a hell of a lot to expect of a man. There's only one. Bathroom, I mean. We shared it and we shared the kitchen and aside from learning not to slam the bloody door when he got in late, we were fine from the start."

"'Got in late'?" Isabelle asked it at the same moment as did Sergeant Havers.

Flora Bevans said, "That man was plugged into every possible organisation that came along. Twenty-four hours were never enough for Ian."

"We've been told he received an award for that," Havers noted.

"Oh yes. And *quite* proud of that plaque, he was. I'd show it to you, but his family came for all his belongings once the dust settled on how he died. Poor bloke." She removed the kerchief from round her neck and used it to blot her face, although it wasn't a particularly warm day and she was not perspiring. She went on to say, "One feels somehow responsible. Suicide. I wouldn't've expected it. He was a man of God, and men of God are supposed to have . . . what would one call it? . . . more spiritual resources, I suppose. It was a shock. He didn't come home that night, as far as I could tell, but I'd no idea he'd been taken off to the gaol. And then word got out about *why* he'd been taken to gaol, and that was all rather dreadful. I don't mean just for me, having possibly had a paedophile under my roof. I mean his family as well. I felt terrible for his family. *Distraught* doesn't describe how they were when they came to collect his things. And who could be surprised by that? One hates to learn something dreadful about a family member at the best of times. But to learn a family member—a clergyman, mind you—has been messing children about . . . That would be absolutely crushing."

"Did you believe he was actually doing that?" Havers asked.

"Oh, what do I know?" Flora said. "When you consider the wives who haven't a clue that their husbands are Peter Sutcliffes cruising the streets with blood-dripping hammers in the boot of the car or whatever he had, what's a landlady actually supposed to know about her lodger? It's not as if the man did anything here in the house, God forbid. But I *must* say that if Ian *was* doing whatever he was suspected of doing, I don't have the least idea where he found the time. Come to think . . ." She knotted her eyebrows.

"Yes?" Isabelle said.

"I've still got his diary. I'd forgotten all about that. I should have handed it over to someone—the man had appointments every hour of the day—but it never crossed my mind till now. You probably want it, don't you? Or perhaps I should send it along to his dad? He kept it in the kitchen and when I packed up his belongings, it slipped my mind that the diary was still where he kept it under the phone."

The diary would open the door to more than Isabelle particularly wanted to get into. But Havers responded before she herself could say anything, and of course the maddening woman said that the diary would be just the ticket thank you very much.

"Come along then." Flora Bevans headed to the front door and ushered them inside.

They found themselves in a small, square entry hung with photographs of what Isabelle assumed were Flora Bevans' planted urns. The woman was quite an artist if the pictures were anything to go by. Isabelle's idea of a planted urn was ivy and the hope that it didn't die should she forget to water it for a few weeks.

Flora took them to a nicely appointed and neatly kept kitchen, where she opened a drawer and brought out the diary, which she handed over. It was standard enough: days of the week and hours of the day, with an inspirational quotation at the top of each page. Havers began to flip through it. From where she was standing, Isabelle saw that it was packed with appointments, as Flora had suggested. While Havers studied these, Isabelle became aware of raucous noise that was coming from the back of the house. It was the unmistakable sound of children playing: shouting, thumping, laughter, and the occasional adult voice raised to get someone's attention.

"School's just beyond the garden," Flora told her. "It's a little chaotic three times a day but it's heaven on the weekends and during holidays. The most peaceful neighbourhood in town, you ask me. I think Ian found it so, as well."

Havers raised her head from the diary. "You can't hear them from the front of the house," she noted.

"Hmm, no. That's correct," Flora said. "My bedroom's above the street so I don't hear them. Ian had the back bedroom, so he got the brunt of the noise if he was here when the children were in the schoolyard."

"Can we have a look?" Havers asked. She added, "That okay, guv?"

Isabelle nodded. Flora took them up the stairs. There she said they could have a look round—not that there was a lot to see—but she herself had to get on with her work, if they didn't mind. No need to lock up when they left, she told them, as she never locked her doors because there was absolutely nothing worth stealing.

Inside the dead man's bedroom, they made two discoveries. The first was that the schoolyard noise would have been quite an assault if one wished for peace and quiet during the day. The second was that the bedroom window afforded a complete view of the schoolyard where, on the tarmac, a hundred or so boys and girls were at play in the springtime sunshine. The children looked roughly the age of third-formers and like most children that age, they were very efficient at raising hell as they jumped rope, dodged balls, threw markers for hopscotch, and engaged in a quite rough activity that looked like a rugby scrum but turned out to be a group of boys attempting to stamp on a helium balloon. All of this was watched over by a scowling woman, arms crossed, who was wearing a police whistle round her neck.

"Wonder if this's what made him go for the room here." Next to Isabelle, Barbara Havers murmured the observation upon joining her at the window. She went on with, "Nice view if you want to daydream what you could do to one of 'em if only you could get yourself and your mitts over the wall without being seen, eh?"

The children in the schoolyard, Isabelle saw, seemed close to the age of her own sons. They played just as determinedly as did the twins, and with just as much abandon. She'd known from the first that twin boys would be an enormous challenge for a mother like her. But she had never once thought or intended or wished to lose them. But *What you're doing to them when you're like this* hadn't been enough to stop her. That was the worst of her sins. God knew there were others.

". . . could get his jollies just standing here as well, I expect," Havers was saying meditatively. "There's that to be thought of. And no one would be any the wiser."

Isabelle roused herself. "What?"

"You know. Jerkin' the gherkin, guv."

"I beg your pardon?"

Havers was hasty with, "I meant . . . sort of . . . having one off the wrist . . . ?"

Isabelle took this in. "Ah. Masturbation as he watched the children?"

"Well, yeah. It's a good spot for it with the school just behind the house like it is. And who would know, right? Flora's out and about with her pots and plants, he's got the place to himself, he hears the kids, and there you have it: Willy wants a handshake."

"Sergeant Havers, are you generally this colourful with DI Lynley?"

The sergeant grimaced. "Sorry," she said.

"Because," Isabelle continued, "I can't honestly imagine DI Lynley being equally colourful with you."

"Oh, dead right, ma'am. He wouldn't. Silver spoon and all that. He'd have his tongue cut out first. Only it wouldn't even occur to him anyway. I mean, to be colourful. It'd more or less get in the way of his upbringing, if you know what I mean. That is, well, everyone knows he's a born gent so no one likes to . . . you know . . . see what he'll make of the . . . I s'pose you'd call it the seamier side of . . . whatever."

"I see." Isabelle knew Lynley fairly well. They'd been lovers for a time and, while it was true that he was the personification of gentlemanly discretion, there were certain aspects of a man's upbringing that went by the wayside if a woman was determined enough. And as Isabelle had been determined enough with Thomas Lynley, she'd heard more from him than, she expected, Barbara Havers was ever likely to do, albeit nothing remotely like the sergeant's own comments. She turned back to the window and said to Havers, "I don't disagree. About the possibility of Ian Druitt's sighting of the children. We both know by now that anything's possible when it comes to humanity."

There was nothing in the room save the furniture: a bed, a chest of drawers, and a narrow desk with a single central drawer, a chair. The drawers in the chest held nothing, the same applied to the desk's single drawer, and on the walls nothing hung. A small hole in the wall above the bed suggested something had been placed there at one time, and considering the monastic nature of the room, Isabelle could picture a crucifix.

There was nothing more to take note of as far as Isabelle could see. The diary seemed to prove the point that had been made about Ian Druitt by more than one person: he was an inveterate volunteer. This was more exhausting than was it suspicious, Isabelle thought. They were, as a result, finished here in Shropshire.

Of course, this was not how Sergeant Havers saw matters, since she said as they descended the stairs, "I expect we ought to go through all that lumber the dad gave to you. It might match up to what he's got set up in his diary, eh? 'Specially if there's information like files and such. I mean, this would be just for consistency. Just to make certain we've touched on everything." And she added as if with the expectation that Isabelle would protest, "I expect the dad'll be looking for that. Don't you think?"

No, Isabelle thought. She *didn't* think. But Havers did have a point regarding Clive Druitt. *And* there was now the matter of that bloody diary. She sighed and said, "And what do you recommend as the best way to do the matching up, Sergeant?"

"Those boxes from his dad? We might find something there that got overlooked." When Isabelle didn't reply at once, the sergeant added, "I c'n look through it all on my own, if you've something else on, of course."

What Isabelle had on was vodka and tonic, very light on the tonic. But she could hardly order Havers to go through the boxes of Druitt's clobber alone while she removed herself to another location. So she agreed that the boxes asked to be gone through, and now that they had the miserable man's diary that was something additional they had to consider, since it constituted an object related to the dead man that the previous investigations had apparently overlooked.

So she said, "Let's get on with it then. We can do everything at the hotel and perhaps Peace can manage a sandwich for us."

As things developed, Ian Druitt's belongings were mostly nonstarters. They carried the boxes of his things into the hotel, lined them up on the floor in the residents' lounge, and began to unpack them while Peace on Earth cooperatively supplied them with marginally edible ham and boiled egg sandwiches. Isabelle ordered the vodka and tonic she desired and instructed Havers to indulge herself if she wished. The sergeant, however, appeared determined to remain abstemious, venturing as far as fizzy water and no further. She was, however, willing to indulge in a packet of crisps to accompany her sandwich.

They made their search through the boxes a division of labour. Isabelle began with one that contained a portable CD player and an eclectic collection of music, from classical to American country. There was also an iPod as well as a stand from which it, too, could provide tunes for the deacon.

Next to her, Havers was unpacking a box that appeared to contain Druitt's nonreligious clothing. As fitting for one devoted to the religious life, he hadn't appeared to own a great deal, and unsurprisingly everything was neatly folded, of muted colours, and generally undistinguished. Tucked among them and perhaps to protect it, Havers found a wooden cross, plain with no corpus upon it. Its wood was fine and polished, however, and on the back of it was a small plaque indicating it was "To Ian with love from Mum and Dad" and a date, presumably the day he became a deacon of the church. At the bottom of this box, a filing folder held a list of male and female names, addresses, and phone numbers presumably representing the membership of the after-school children's club as the given identities of men and women in parentheses after each name suggested the parents of children in the club. And beneath the filing folder a newspaper lay along with a stack of what appeared to be advertisements of appearances for some kind of band called Hangdog Hillbillies. Each of these bore a different venue, a different date, and a different picture of the band. Ian Druitt, it turned out, was a member and the pictures depicted him playing the washtub bass. Other members appeared to play variously the banjo, an old washboard, spoons, and guitar. They also appeared to wear costumes in keeping with the name of their group, for they were dressed in what appeared to be deliberately shabby clothing, and the next box that Isabelle opened contained various outfits that Ian Druitt must have worn: from faded dungarees to bib overalls, to boots, to work-worn T-shirts, threadbare work shirts, and various kinds of hats.

The kept newspaper turned out to be another copy of the *Ludlow Echo,* featuring Druitt's Man of the Year story. Havers read it thoroughly, as Isabelle had not, and she read out the deacon's volunteer life: member of the catch-sterilise-release feral cat group, leader of the Ludlow Boys' and Girls' Club, member of the Victim Volunteers Society, architect of the developing Street Pastors Programme, director of the choir of St. Laurence parish. He also seemed to participate in visiting shut-ins, the elderly, and those living in convalescent homes.

"Bloody hell," Havers concluded at the end of her recitation. "When did this bloke have time to do his deaconly duty?"

Isabelle knew as little about the job of church deacon as, apparently, did Havers. "Perhaps this was what constituted that duty."

"I s'pose." But Havers sounded doubtful.

Isabelle looked at her. The sergeant's eyes were narrowed speculatively, but when she saw that Isabelle's attention was on her, she managed to construct a perfectly blank expression. That, Isabelle thought, was not only irritating, it was also unhelpful. She said, "Stop that, Sergeant," although she immediately realised that she sounded like a mother speaking to her newly adolescent daughter who'd just discovered attitude.

Havers started. "What?"

"If you're thinking something, I'd appreciate knowing what it is."

"Sorry, guv. I was—"

"And *stop* apologising!"

"Sorry." She clapped her hand over her mouth.

Isabelle shot her an exasperated look. She said, "Let's get ourselves on the same page. We're here to sort this matter out. The sooner we do that, the sooner we can return to London. Now. What was it that you wanted to say?"

"Just that it all seems a bit much." Havers indicated the newspaper article, which included a series of interviews with individuals who had benefitted in one way or another from Ian Druitt's various activities and with individuals who'd worked alongside the deacon in those various activities. As one would expect, they constituted glowing reports of his profound influence upon the youth of the town, of his generosity of spirit, of his warmth and kindness. "It's like he's . . . you know that bit: 'protesting too much'?"

"What on earth do you mean?"

"Oh. Sor—whoops. It's that Shakespeare thing. The lady protesting too much and all that."

Isabelle sat back on her heels where she'd been kneeling next to one of the boxes. She scrutinised Havers closely. "Why is it that I think you've learned a fascinating skill set from DI Lynley? Do you two regularly apply Shakespeare to your enquiries?"

Havers chuckled. "He's just been trying to build my enthusiasm for the finer points of literature, guv. I expect he'll head into Dickens next. But only after I master Shakespeare. He deals just in the bloody bits, by the way. I mean plays where someone gets the chop. So far I've got *Hamlet* down. I keep blotting things when it comes to *Macbeth*, though."

Isabelle took a moment. There was something about Havers's eyes that suggested . . . "You're joking, aren't you?" Isabelle said.

"Well . . . yeah. I s'pose. A little."

"Why do I suspect that it has to do with not quite mastering

*Macbeth*? Why do I think you can probably quote *Macbeth* in your sleep?"

"Can't do that!" Havers said hastily. "I mean, not beyond the bloody dagger bit. Well, maybe I c'n get into murdering sleep and the damn'd spot, but that's about it."

"Ah." Isabelle turned back to the matter at hand and said, "Regarding the lady protesting?"

Havers indicated the article. "Just that it seems to me if someone's got to do all this volunteering, there's a reason for it, and could be the reason is all about appearances. That phone call to 999? The hypocrisy bit? All this public hoopla about Druitt being so . . . I don't know what to call it exactly."

"Unimpeachably good? Equally admirable?"

"Like he was doing every single thing that the Lord said a good Christian is meant to do. Like he kept a list and was ticking off his acts of goodness. It's too much, you ask me. It's like he had something to hide. So some bloke out there reads this article and thinks, 'Wait a bloody minute, mate. I'm not having this,' and makes the phone call 'cause the last thing he can cope with is seeing some monster get glory when what he ought to get is—"

"Arrested," Isabelle finished.

"Word gets out and he's not looking so Man of the Yearly."

"Agreed," Isabelle noted. "But we also can't discount the possibility that the phone call had nothing to do with hypocrisy but rather with revenge."

"But wouldn't revenge also key in to the paedophilia? 'You did this to my kid—or better yet, to me when I was ten years old—and I'm having you for dinner, mate.' That sort of thing."

"I see that, yes. And I tend to agree with you, Sergeant. Man of the Year, the newspaper article, and the phone call? They could be intimate friends, couldn't they?"

Havers looked quite pleased at this, but the last thing Isabelle wanted was the detective sergeant thinking that she could begin to have her own way in things. So she said, "But I hope *you* agree that revenge in this case wouldn't necessarily lead to murder. The ruin of a reputation would have been sufficient, and that could have been managed by an arrest, an investigation, a trial, and the attendant publicity, no matter the outcome."

"Oh, I see that," Havers said, although she didn't look the least abashed. "But there's still this to look into." She held up the diary that they'd had off Flora Bevans. "Column A," here she wiggled her hand with the diary in it, "wants matching up with Column B," here a gesture to indicate the newspaper article.

"Meaning?"

"Meaning there could be something in the diary that no one ever considered because no one ever saw it. And if we want Mr. Druitt to stay away from his solicitors, we probably ought to see if that's the case."

LUDLOW
SHROPSHIRE

Barbara Havers parted with Ardery, feeling that she'd actually managed to win a round. Between their mutual perusal of Druitt's belongings and their meeting up for drinks in the lounge before dinner, then, she leafed through the deacon's diary. She discovered that there was indeed something that wanted closer examination.

When she descended to the residents' lounge, however, she found that new guests had checked into Griffith Hall that day, and the presence of these newcomers swilling down champagne prevented any serious police conversation between herself and the DCS both during their preprandial nibbles and drinks—vodka martini for the guv and a half pint of ale for Barbara, which she would make last throughout the meal—and their dinner that would follow.

Although Ardery's mobile rang three times during nibbles, drinks, and dinner, she only glanced at it to ascertain the caller—twice with an expression of supreme distaste—and then let it go to message. During coffee back in the lounge, however, her mobile rang a fourth time and this call the DCS took, saying to Barbara, "Hillier," as she rose from the sofa and left the room.

Rather you than me was what Barbara thought. When it came to what they were doing in Shropshire, if the assistant commissioner was being true to character, he doubtless wanted them to smarm all over the locals and then make tracks.

Barbara had brought the IPCC file with her, so while Ardery was taking her call, she opened it. She searched for the part dealing with what she reckoned was the core element of the investigation into Ian Druitt's suicide: what PCSO Gary Ruddock had been doing during the time that the deacon hanged himself and what he had done upon finding Druitt motionless and strung up to a doorknob.

She saw that Ruddock's explanation of what had occurred that night had been confirmed by all parties: the owner of the Hart and Hind in Quality Square had agreed that some binge drinking had gone on that night; the owners of the other pubs in town indicated that they'd indeed received phone calls from the PCSO, asking them not to serve any inebriated youths as he wouldn't be available to help out if there was trouble; the PCSO's superior officer—a sergeant from the Neighbourhood Policing Team—had substantiated the details about the burglaries that made it necessary for Ruddock to make the arrest of Druitt. And the paramedics who had been sent once Gary Ruddock made his frantic call to 999 described the state of affairs when they'd reached the station: the body of Druitt supine on the floor—ligature removed from round his neck—and Ruddock performing CPR and shouting, "Come on, come on, you bastard!" as if the dead man could hear him. For it had been obvious to the paramedics on the scene that the man was dead, although they did everything they could to revive him. At the end of the day, all efforts were futile, and the death of the deacon sat firmly upon the PCSO's shoulders.

The death could have been prevented if Ian Druitt had been taken to Shrewsbury, where a duty sergeant manning the custody suite would have made sure that proper procedures had been followed: everything with the potential for self-harm removed from Druitt's person, a pair of custody visitors called in to ascertain that his detainment in the cells was on the up-and-up, a duty solicitor arranged for should the deacon not have a solicitor of his own. But none of that had occurred, which was why she—Barbara Havers of the Metropolitan Police—still had an itch that wanted scratching. So when Ardery returned to the lounge from her phone call and asked Peace on Earth to bring her a very large port wine, Barbara made the excuse of an early night in order, she said, to dip more deeply into Ian Druitt's diary. She was relieved when the DCS required nothing more of her.

Upstairs, she dropped her collection of folders onto her nunlike bed and ignored the diary altogether. She had an odd request that she needed to make, and she rang the reception desk in order to make it. Yes, she discovered after a pause on the part of reception, a broom *could* be left for her next to the front door of the hotel. It would take at least thirty minutes, as hotel guests were still being served their various after-dinner liquid substances, but if Ms. Havers could wait . . . ? Ms. Havers could, so she rang off and used the time to reconfirm her route on the town plan.

She needed to get out of the hotel without the DCS seeing her. While she reckoned that what she was doing was perfectly reasonable, she preferred that Ardery not know about it. She didn't want her to interpret *anything* as DS Barbara Havers going merrily her own way as she'd done in the past. To make everything look kosher, when Barbara proceeded down the stairs and towards the front door, she took with her a packet of Players and nothing else save her room key and a book of matches: just another resident of the nonsmoking hotel slipping outside to have a fag. A shoulder bag would make her look suspicious should the DCS see her. The broom was going to be bad enough.

Luck was with her, as she made it to the door without incident. There was no one about, and the broom was where it had been promised, leaning against the wall behind a coat tree. Barbara grabbed it and within seconds was out into the darkness. With the broom over her shoulder, she set off towards Castle Square.

Albeit late, it was a pleasant evening, so she wasn't the only one out and about. A few chatting students carrying books and wearing rucksacks appeared to be heading home after sessions of studying. A few individuals strolled along the path that followed the route of the castle walls. A coach had pulled up in front of the Ludlow Assembly Rooms in Mill Street and pensioners were being assisted up the coach steps to get inside it at the end of whatever performance they'd attended. As before, there was virtually no traffic, just a lone taxi parked at the top of Church Street.

In her earlier conversation with Gary Ruddock, his suggestion that they attempt to swivel the CCTV cameras by means of a broom had slipped her mind. But now she had the broom in hand and it was her intention to test both cameras: the one in the front of the police station that had been pointed in the direction of the steps up from the pavement and the one behind the station that had been pointed at the car park.

When she reached the station, she did a quick recce. As before when she'd been there after dark, there was a light on somewhere inside. As before, at the back of the building there was a panda car parked. This time, however, no one was having a kip inside of it. She got close just to make sure, and she tested the car's door handles, all of which were locked.

Since she was already at the back of the building, she used the broom to check the CCTV camera hanging above and to one side of the door. It was fixed firmly in its position, with no possibility of being swivelled. Because of this, she reckoned it would have a lens with an angle wide enough to take in the two steps to the door as well as the car park.

Onward to the front of the place, she thought. She was heading in that direction—along the side of the building and behind the shrubbery in cat burglar mode—when a patrol car glided by on the street, rounded the corner, and cruised into the car park behind the station. It disappeared from Barbara's view. In a moment, its engine was cut.

Barbara carefully retraced her steps, and with some caution she peered round the side of the building to see that the car was reversed into a parking bay across the car park and against its brick wall. It was at an angle that put it into the deepest shadow cast by a leafy tree in a nearby garden. She watched. She counted off a minute. No one got out of it. Nothing happened.

She was about to turn back to the front of the building, then, when the passenger door of the car swung open, shining a light briefly upon the occupants. PCSO Gary Ruddock was the driver. The passenger was a youngish woman, perhaps twenty or so, light-haired and not overly tall. She began to get out and her words, ". . . don't actually care about that," came to Barbara clearly. Whatever Gary Ruddock said in reply was unintelligible. However, it gave the young woman cause to hesitate, and during her hesitation the PCSO got out of the car and faced her over its roof. They engaged in something of a stare-down, in which he looked quite patient and in which she looked however she looked, because at that point Barbara couldn't see her face. Nothing more was said. But after some fifteen seconds, the young woman got back into the car, as did Gary Ruddock. Then, nothing. Absolutely nothing. Or absolutely something, but whatever it was, Barbara couldn't see. She had an imagination and the ability to count, though. In her book one plus one plus two made four: with the first one being the car, the second one being the darkness, and the last two being Ruddock and his companion. That equaled four, which equaled either a conversation in the dark about the state of the economy, a confession of malfeasance requiring deep shadow, or a round of tricky business of the sort that sometimes occurred when you put a car, the darkness, a man, and a woman together.

This, Barbara understood, could *well* have been what Gary Ruddock had been up to when the deacon was offing himself inside the station. If so, he certainly wouldn't want anyone to know it. At his own admission, Ruddock lived with an old bloke. The young woman probably lived with flatmates or with her parents. Assuming that she and Ruddock were eager to put the sausage into the roll—and not just engaging in earnest nighttime conversation—they would need privacy to carry it off. Despite its lack of comfortable furniture, inside the station would be perfect under some circumstances, but with the deacon there waiting for transport to Shrewsbury, it would have made things dicey. Why not have it off in a car as had been done since the invention of the automobile? Desperate times called for desperate measures, and truly, this particular setup wasn't desperate at all. Climb into the back seat, divest oneself of the appropriate bits of clothing, squirm thrust groan for five minutes or less, and the deed was done. Three minutes for foreplay on one side of the action, two minutes for a post-coital cuddle, thirty seconds to rearrange one's clothing, a quick trip in the car to drop the bird back to her cage, and that would be that.

Ruddock would return afterwards, discover what had happened while he and the girlfriend had been in the car park, see that the deacon was a goner, hurriedly make his phone calls to the pubs to cover his absence, ring 999, and act the part of a man desperately attempting to resuscitate a suicide—which wouldn't have been that much of an act considering the wretched mess he'd made of things—and all the time knowing that his career was finished if anyone discovered what a complete cock-up he'd made out of a simple arrest.

It could have happened that way. Ruddock was dependent upon the pub owners being able to confirm he'd rung them about shutting down, but after the fact, how would they be able to tell investigators the precise time he rang them? And if whatever they told investigators was within the range of Druitt's possible time of death as established by the forensic pathologist, he'd be cleared of responsibility. It would just have to stay a secret that he'd been in the car park doing whatever.

Barbara faded back against the building. She wondered exactly how long she was going to have to remain out of sight. She didn't fancy squatting in the darkness behind a shrub for an extended length of time, but she was going to have to as she also didn't fancy being seen in front of the station messing about with the CCTV camera when Ruddock and his passenger drove by in the car on their way home.

It was about a quarter hour before she heard the car start. She maintained her cat burglar position until she heard the car pass on the street below her. Then she made her way to the front of the building, where a motion detector light caught her in its beam as she approached both the door and the CCTV camera.

Standing below the camera, she gently placed the broom handle against its side. A bit of pressure from her end of the broom was enough to alter the camera's position. From taking in the steps up from the pavement, the camera's new position allowed it to encompass the front door and the intercom fixed to the left of it. Barbara was gratified. It meant that someone wishing to make an anonymous call would merely have had to do what she had just done: to come from the direction of the car park and to slide along the wall, hidden by the thriving shrubbery. As long as the wall sliding could continue out of sight of the CCTV camera that would have been directed at the front door, it would have been a simple matter to swivel it without being seen, so that it was altered to take in the steps. Once that was accomplished, the phone call could be made without the caller being photographed.

Of course, Barbara thought, that begged the question why the caller had not then moved the camera back to its original position, but the answer to that could go in several directions. Perhaps at that moment the PCSO or a patrol officer had arrived and the anonymous caller had been forced to scarper. Perhaps its position had been altered days in advance with no one being the wiser, and the plan was to put it back into the original position a few days after the call, only that had been forgotten in the aftermath of Druitt's suicide. Perhaps its position had never been on the front door at all but merely focused on part of the street and the steps. There was certainly more than one explanation here, and Barbara knew that the answer lay in having a look at what the CCTV camera had recorded over a period of time.

She needed to go through the reports again to see if the position of the station's cameras was mentioned. If it wasn't—and she was fairly certain it wasn't—she then had to convince the DCS to have a go with what the CCTV had recorded not only when the anonymous call had been made, but also what it had recorded prior to and after that call. *That* was definitely a step that needed to be taken.

# 7 MAY

LUDLOW
SHROPSHIRE

Isabelle had been a witness to Barbara Havers leaving the hotel on the previous night. She'd seen her from the doorway to the residents' lounge, where she'd just finished her second port, and she'd frowned because she knew what it could mean as soon as Havers disappeared with a broomstick balanced against her shoulder. Despite the hour, the detective sergeant was about to go her own way in the investigation.

As the door closed behind her, Isabelle's mobile had rung. It was the identity of the caller that pushed her into her next move. Sherlock Wainwright doubtless wished to guide her into what he would see as a more reasonable course of action against her former husband. She didn't want to talk to the solicitor, so she let the call go to message, and she followed Havers.

Outside at night for the first time in Ludlow, Isabelle caught the scents of the town: the subtle fragrance of flowers in the window boxes along the way, abruptly cut into by the stronger odour of marijuana. This came from an open window above her, along with rap music and loud conversation between two males.

Ahead of her, Havers turned into Castle Square. When Isabelle reached the corner, she saw the sergeant proceeding along the pavement on the square's south side. Shops here were long closed for the night, but streetlamps shone upon their interiors of books and tourist offerings and clothing in one of the town's charity shops. It was late enough that just a few people were out, although chatter and laughter from a hidden location across the square suggested there were still pubgoers looking in on their nightly establishments. Havers didn't head in their direction, though. Instead she continued from the square into King Street and along it to the Bull Ring, where she crossed over and disappeared into a pedestrian precinct that was badly lit.

It was here that Isabelle had considered that Havers might well have been out for a stroll, with the broomstick being carried for protection just in case. She thought of turning back then, but she could see that the end of the pedestrian precinct opened onto a more travelled route, and just as she recognised this, a police car passed and was lit by a streetlamp. The station, she decided, had to be nearby. And that had to be where Havers was going.

This suggested that, in reality, the sergeant was showing some initiative. The fact was that Isabelle had given Havers no orders about how to spend the rest of her evening. If she was on her way to the police station with a broomstick over her shoulder, she would be checking on the CCTV cameras. While it was true that this activity—depending upon the results of it—could elongate their time in Ludlow, it was also true that they'd come up with nothing to show that Ian Druitt's death was anything but a suicide. She reckoned the CCTV cameras would emphasise that. So she walked in Havers's wake long enough to verify that the police station was her destination. Then she turned back to make her way to the hotel.

Now, the next morning, she prepared herself to listen to Sherlock Wainwright's message, which she hadn't done on the previous night. Her preparation for this consisted of three capfuls of vodka, which she measured carefully into a tooth glass. She didn't need a drop more than three capfuls. They represented mental preparation.

Wainwright's message was merely a request for her to phone him because, he asserted, he had some very good news: Robert Ardery had offered a compromise and Wainwright believed it was going to please Isabelle very much.

When she rang him, she immediately asked what the compromise was. Wainright said, "I'm delighted you've phoned. Let me read it to you. I had it from your husband's solicitor late yester—"

"Former husband."

"Yes. Of course. Sorry. I had it from your former husband's solicitor last evening and I rang you at once."

"I'm afraid I'd gone to bed."

"Not a problem. There's no date indicated by which I was to respond. Shall I get on with it?"

She told him to do so. She wanted only the facts, however, not a reading of a document filled with legalese. He was succinct, then. Robert Ardery, he told her, had generously proposed that Isabelle be allowed to spend unsupervised personal time with the boys when she came to Auckland to visit them. He would allow them to stay weekends with her at any house, cottage, or flat she might rent. He would also allow them to stay weekends with her at her hotel. He was, Wainwright announced, thus broadening her options in New Zealand. He would even allow her to take them away from Auckland for three-night stays at various holiday locations of her choosing. These would, of course, need to be approved in advance by him, but as there were dozens, he didn't think this would be a problem. Naturally, these jaunts would have to take place during the boys' school holidays. He would want them at home with him at Christmas, but if Isabelle chose to visit New Zealand at that time, she would be welcome at family lunch.

Wainwright finished with, "Apparently the boys are quite excited at the prospect. Now, I've had a look at what New Zealand has to offer for holidays. The Coromandel Peninsula isn't far from Auckland, and the Bay of Islands—"

"No," Isabelle said.

There was a pause. During it, Isabelle heard a television go on suddenly in a nearby room, offering Sky News at a shattering volume before it was hastily lowered. Wainwright said, "But surely you see that coming up with a compromise like this paints Mr. Ardery in a very positive light. A court is going to see it that way."

She said, "I'm sure it does, especially to people who've never met him. But as I've more than met him, the answer remains the same. No."

"Please do think about this, Isabelle. Should your visits to New Zealand work well for you and for the boys, there's every possibility of revisiting the arrangement in two or three years."

Isabelle locked her jaw on what she wanted to say. Two or three years? After a pause in which she gathered what few resources of patience she possessed, she said, "We're finished with this conversation now, Mr. Wainwright. I leave you to carry on as before."

She cut off his "But his own solicitor has—" by ending the call because she had only one interest in this entire affair and that was to keep her sons in the same country in which she herself lived. If she had to drag her former husband through every court in the land to effect this, she intended to do so. And if Sherlock Wainwright could not bring himself round to seeing her determination, then Sherlock Wainwright was going to find himself kicked to the kerb.

In a fury, she punched Bob's number into her mobile. His wife answered. Isabelle didn't bother to identify herself. Sandra would know very well who was ringing at this hour in the morning. She said, "Let me speak to James and Laurence."

Sandra said, "Isabelle. Lovely to hear from you. I'm afraid they've already left for school."

"*Don't* you lie to me," Isabelle said. "It's seven in the morning! Put them on the phone at once or I swear to God, Sandra—"

"Why would I lie to you?" Sandra's voice was the virtual embodiment of reason. "You've every right to speak to them. I'm fully aware of that. Are *you* aware of what all this legal drama is doing to them, by the way?"

"This legal drama—as you call it—exists only because you and Bob are determined to separate me from them."

"Yes, I'm sure you see it that way. It's always about you, isn't it?"

"You *fucking*—"

"That's the just point, Isabelle." It was Bob's voice. The cow had handed the phone to him after her last remark, having provoked Isabelle into a rage that could then be demonstrated for her former husband. "There," he went on. "Just there. And it's something I don't want the boys exposed to."

"So what you've decided is that it will be quite a treat for the boys to be separated from their mother for most of their lives, eh? And to see her where? In an Auckland hotel? That's the compromise I've been offered?"

"You need to be reasonable," he said in his most unctuous tone. "I'm not allowing them to fly from Auckland to London to see you, if that's what you have in mind."

"What I have in mind is an injunction preventing you from taking them anywhere at all."

"That's not going to be remotely possible. I'm certain your solicitor has explained it to you. Now we can continue to pour money into the coffers of the legal system or you can face reality. It's up to you."

"I'm their *mother.* I gave birth to them. I raised them till they were—"

"We're not about to call what you did 'raising' James and Laurence," he broke in sharply. "If you stop just a moment to get beyond your rage at not having things your way, you'll see that what I'm offering you is far more than you've had in the past. All that's required of you is to purchase a ticket to Auckland as many times in a year as you'd like to come and to arrange a safe venue for them to stay with you at weekends when you're here. *And* I've given ground on allowing you to take them on holiday here as well. Not during their school term, but that's hardly unreasonable. Additionally, Sandra and I are happy to give over half of their summer holiday to you, again in Auckland and not, naturally, on Christmas Day. But if you're here in Auckland on Christmas Day, we're happy to have you for lunch, and should you wish to be with the boys on their birthday or at Easter, there won't be a problem with that. We'll have to pound out how much time each visit would comprise, but this does *not* have to be the problem you're making it."

"Oh, you're the bloody voice of reason, aren't you?" she said bitterly.

"I'm trying to do what's best for everyone."

"Why do you hate me so much?"

He fell silent for a moment and then in an altered voice he said, "I don't hate you. You merely see it as hate. But your thinking has been distorted by drink for so many years. . . . Isabelle, do you want me to recount how many times I asked you to get help?"

Her lips felt frozen. She could barely get the words out to say, "I deserve a relationship with my sons. They deserve a relationship with their mother. There's a bond between a mother and her children that can't be broken."

"They have a mother. I don't want to hurt you, Isabelle, but—"

"Don't you? What else is this supposed to be?"

"—you know it's the truth. Sandra has been a mother to them since they were less than two years old. You share a blood tie with them, but nothing more. That was the choice you made: to let everything save the blood tie go. If that's painful for you now, then all I can say is that this is something you might have considered when we divorced. I'm not to blame that you didn't."

"You bastard." She found it so difficult to speak that she wanted to rip the words from her own throat. "You'll never have done with punishing me, will you?"

"You're punishing yourself. But only you know why. I haven't a clue."

"Is that Mummy? Is it Mummy?"

Isabelle heard the words from the background and cried out, "She lied to me! Let me talk to them!"

"You're not in any condition to talk to either of the boys. When you are, you can ring again, and if they're here I'll let you speak to them both. I'm ringing off now, Isabelle. We've the school run to do."

She was left with her mobile in her hand and black silence coming out of it. Her nerves were screaming at her to do something. Her mind was doing much the same. Her heart was pounding and her palms itched so badly that she wanted to claw the flesh till all that was left was bones.

She picked up the bottle of vodka. She saw how badly her hand was shaking. Her fury was demanding that she act. She knew that while her options for acting were limited in this moment, a drink could at least stop the shaking and stop the terrible itching of her palms. But she put the bottle back on the bedside table. Staring at it, she counted the reasons: want, need, desire, hunger, safety, stillness, peace, oblivion. She quaked for it. She yearned for it as if it were a lover whose touch could lift her away from herself. After the two phone calls she'd just endured, she deserved this as well as needed it.

She didn't measure from the cap this time. She drank straight from the bottle.

LUDLOW
SHROPSHIRE

Isabelle encountered Peace on Earth enroute to breakfast. She was about to ask him to bring her a very large pot of coffee and one slice of toast when Barbara Havers popped out of the residents' lounge, where she had apparently been lying in wait. She wore on her face an expression that Isabelle could have well done without. Clearly, she was champing at the bit.

She said, "Guv, a minute?" and did not wait for a reply. She headed towards the hotel's front door and darted outside, casting a look over her shoulder that suggested she had something valuable to impart.

Isabelle saw nothing for it but to follow. Once outside, Havers led her towards the pavement. Across the street, a lone gardener was mowing the lawn that bordered the castle walls with a petrol-powered machine that sounded like a jet taking off. Isabelle longed for her coffee.

She noticed that clutched to her chest, Havers had the folders from the IPCC and DI Pajer. She launched into conversation in a tone of undue excitement, beginning with the announcement that she had a report to make and, she declared, one that suggested there was much more in Ludlow that wanted looking into.

"Indeed," was Isabelle's noncommittal response. She hoped Havers's recitation would not take long.

It was, apparently, a case of yes indeedy-o. For Havers went on to talk about what she deemed as "crucial points of interest" that she had uncovered during the night. Only one of the two CCTV cameras on the police station's exterior swivelled, she announced, while the other was in a fixed position. From reading the IPCC report another time, Havers had discovered that the complaints commission *had* taken note of this. She added that the IPCC had also reported that the nonswivelling camera—which was on the rear of the building—was not functional. This apparently was a monumental detail because while the sergeant was on her way to play with the camera at the front of the station, a police car driven by PCSO Gary Ruddock had pulled into the car park at the rear.

"And this is important for some reason?" Isabelle asked her. The jet engine lawn mower was working on her head. It had begun to pound. She needed coffee.

Apparently, this was important because of what the sergeant had witnessed: the PCSO and a young woman getting out of the car, having something of a stare-down, and then getting back into the car, which, by the way, Ruddock had parked in the deepest shadows of the police station's car park. Havers added, "Far as I know, there's only one reason why a bloke and a bird park in the dark and don't get out of the car, guv."

"But they did get out."

"For ten seconds. But then they were back in and in is where they stayed. You ask me, on the night in question, *that's* what Gary Ruddock got up to once he fetched Ian Druitt to the station. A little feel me-poke me-whatever in the car park with his girlfriend. Only it wasn't filmed because the camera back there doesn't work."

"Are you truly suggesting that Ruddock fetched Druitt to the station, left the station, went off for a young woman whom he also fetched to the station, had some sort of encounter with her in the patrol car, drove her back to wherever, and then returned to the station? How could anyone possibly be that stupid?"

This seemed to be what the sergeant was waiting for. She said, "No. Not quite. I don't think it happened that way." With something of a flourish, she removed from one of the folders a detailed tourist map of the town. She beckoned Isabelle to follow her over to a wall that separated the hotel car park from its garden and, handing over the folders, she unfolded the map and said, "Look at this, guv," a rather useless imperative since what else did she expect Isabelle to do? She pointed to a spot and said that here, in this location, was the police station, hardly startling news. Then she said, "And look here next. There's a route anyone can take to get from the river up to the police station, guv. It's more or less direct."

She showed it to Isabelle: a curving thoroughfare called Weeping Cross Lane that took one north from Temeside to Lower Galdeford Street, where the police station sat at the corner of Townsend Close. Now, Havers pointed out, if there were CCTV cameras anywhere along that route—

Isabelle stopped her with, "This is getting wildly out of hand, Sergeant." And when Havers merely looked at her blankly, Isabelle went on. "I have a feeling your next recommendation is going to be to have an actual search for those CCTV cameras. And if there *are* any, your next suggestion is going to be to have a look at all the recordings made on the night in question, should any be available all these months later. Why?"

"Because a young woman could have—"

"Sergeant, if a young woman *is* seen on film somewhere in Weeping Cross Lane, it can only *suggest* she was heading up from the river to meet Ruddock the night Druitt died. Surely you know as well as I that there's absolutely nothing to prove it."

"But there's something else, guv." Havers traded Isabelle the map for the filing folders and from one of them she took out a document that they'd found among Druitt's possession: the list of names, addresses, and phone numbers of everyone associated with the after-school children's club that Ian Druitt had established. One of the addresses was actually in Temeside. It belonged to someone called Finnegan Freeman.

"See," Havers said, "the idea of an eager female slipping in from somewhere to meet Ruddock got me looking at the map to see how she could've managed it. And the fact that one of the routes she could've used came from Temeside got me looking at the list of kids in the club, 'cause it sounded familiar. I mean the Temeside part of it. And there was the name and the address."

"We're back to paedophilia then?" Isabelle allowed herself to sound as weary as she felt. "And this is our victim, whose parent crept up from the river—"

"Oh no, not our victim." Havers indicated the list again and pointed out that Finnegan Freeman's name was the only one *without* parentheses following it, with those other parentheses containing the names of the parents of the boy or girl in question. "When I spoke to Reverend Spencer—remember?—he told me there was always an older kid who helped out at the club. I reckon this is him, this Finnegan Freeman, because no parents for him are on the list. That being the case *and* considering that the IPCC looked only at the film from the night Druitt died—"

"What else were they *supposed* to look at since he died at the station?" Isabelle asked. She was holding the map and she saw that a tremor was in her hand. She was quick to drop the map to her side.

"They *didn't* look at what got recorded from the night of the anonymous phone call," Havers said. "If we examine things with that phone call in mind, it seems to me that we can reckon whoever made the call wanted Druitt arrested and questioned. We agree on that, right?"

Isabelle made a somewhat royal "continue, please" gesture, a sort of rolling of her hand that Havers took as she intended it, for she plunged merrily on. "So what if the person who made that phone call wanted him arrested in order to get him into the station in order to give him the chop? What if that person had done his homework and knew that on certain nights Ruddock had the evening off from caring for the old gent he lives with and—"

"What old gent? Where the devil are you heading with this?"

"The old gent isn't important. Just a bloke Ruddock cares for in exchange for room and board and some cash. So what if someone knows that when he has some free time—which we can assume is on some kind of regular schedule—Ruddock takes his lady friend to the nick's car park for a bonk? And what if this someone also knows the lady friend, our bonkee. What if the two of them cooked up a deal in which the someone waited for an arrest to be made of Druitt—post the anonymous phone call that this someone had *already* made—and when this occurred the bonkee was sent to clear Ruddock out of the station in order to give the someone time to get to Druitt?"

Isabelle couldn't take her eyes off Havers, so convoluted did she find her scenario. She said, finally, "Sergeant." And then she breathed for a moment in-out and in-out and in again in order to say, "We can 'what if' this into next week. We can 'what if' this into next year."

"Right. I know. I understand. But the point is, guv, that the IPCC didn't look into this part of things because the IPCC didn't know about Ruddock and his lady friend in the car park."

"Because," Isabelle said and she dug into her lack of resources for a patience she did not possess, "the IPCC were here to look into a *suicide* in the police station and there was nothing in what they found—and there *is* nothing, and I mean absolutely nothing—that indicates this was a murder. That ought to tell you something, so why doesn't it?"

Havers was silent, although the left side of her mouth jumped in such a way that she must have been biting her cheek. This, admittedly, was fairly admirable in someone who had never before seemed to believe that controlling herself was a requirement of her line of work. The sergeant looked towards the hotel as if waiting for confirmation of her ideas, perhaps from Peace on Earth. She looked to the castle where, blessedly, the lawn mowing had ceased and the gardener was—unfortunately—adding petrol to fire it up again. Then she said carefully, "Due respect and all that, guv? Sometimes when there's nothing to be found as proof, it's because something's been missed or something's there in order to hide what isn't there."

"You're attempting to make a point, so make it."

"It's like I said: the CCTV recording on the night of the phone call was never looked at. And no one's talked to this Finnegan kid, who just happens to live nearby. I'm not saying either of these points mean anything. I'm just saying they *could* mean something and they were overlooked. And isn't that why we're here . . . more or less?"

God, Isabelle thought. They were never going to get out of Ludlow. They would be going at this into eternity when she needed to be back in London, where she could fight Bob and Sandra properly. But she knew the maddening sergeant was right. She might have been bending the facts like the limbs of a Chinese contortionist, but the basic truth was the basic truth. No one had spoken to this Finnegan Freeman and apparently no one had watched the film of the night of the anonymous phone call.

She couldn't avoid the thought, then, of Clive Druitt and the threats he'd made about his team of solicitors. He and they were out there somewhere, waiting for whatever report she and Havers came up with. To avoid a lawsuit and the kind of attendant rotten publicity that policing didn't need, she was going to have to make certain that every cobweb in every corner had been located, looked over, and swept away. And the cobweb that had been the thickest from the first was the one declaring Druitt a paedophile.

There was nothing for it. She had to agree. They were going to have to watch the film taken on the night of the phone call. They were also going to have to speak to Finnegan Freeman. But that did not turn out to be the worst of things. For Havers next picked up what Isabelle had not earlier noted: Druitt's diary.

"There's this as well," she happily announced.

ST. JULIAN'S WELL
LUDLOW
SHROPSHIRE

Rabiah Lomax had just stepped out of the shower when the phone began ringing. She decided to let it go to message and wrapped a bath towel round her. It was just the way she liked her bath towels: large, fluffy, warm from the towel rack, and as white as the soul of a virgin. She was sinking into the blissful enjoyment of the terry's embrace when she heard a woman's disembodied voice say ". . . of the Metropolitan Police," which gave her pause to reconsider her plan of not answering the call. She went into the bedroom where the nearest phone was, and said into it, "Metropolitan Police, is it?" assuming one of her fellow morning runners was having her on. Only today Rabiah had been salivating over that scrumptiously delicious black actor whose unusual name she could never recall. He was, at present, starring in a gritty police drama, and this caller would be one of the runners setting her up as a result of that post-run conversation. So she said, "D'you work with that black bloke with the odd name? Could you send him along as I've been the victim of a crime and I need him to comfort me."

The voice said, "I beg your pardon? This is Detective Chief Superintendent Isabelle Ardery of the Metropolitan Police. To whom am I speaking?"

Rabiah reconsidered. The voice *did* sound official.

"We need to speak to you if your surname is Lomax," the woman went on.

Well, no one she knew would beat a dead horse, so Rabiah said, "What's this about?"

"I assume your name is Lomax?"

"Of course it is. What was your name?"

The woman repeated it. Ardery, she said. Detective Chief Superintendent. Metropolitan Police. If Ms. Lomax would remain at home, the police would be with her directly. Would that be convenient? Within the next ten minutes?

A call from the police was hardly ever going to be convenient, but Rabiah didn't see that she had a choice, so she said a half hour would be preferable as she'd just returned from a run and wished to shower. She'd need to dress afterwards and all the et ceteras, so a half hour—no, let's make it an hour—would be sufficient. The Met officer said that would be fine and rang off directly she had Rabiah's address.

Naturally, Rabiah didn't need that much time since she'd already showered and she certainly didn't wear enough makeup to require more than two minutes at most to see to her face and another thirty seconds to comb her hair—most of that eaten up by trying to find a comb—but what she did need was time to phone her solicitor. She'd seen enough police dramas to understand the foolishness of *ever* talking to the coppers alone about anything without legal counsel.

She went for her personal phone directory and punched in the number of Aeschylus Kong. Years ago, she'd chosen him to write her will purely because of his name. Who could possibly resist the temptation of meeting someone so interestingly monikered?

She was put through to him as soon as she uttered *Police are coming*. In a moment she heard Aeschylus's reassuring tenor. It said, "Rabiah. How good that you have phoned in this most curious situation. It pleases me that you understand the way of wisdom regarding the police and phoning one's solicitor." He always sounded like a combination of an eighteenth-century gentleman, Confucius, and a fortune cookie. "I shall be there as soon as I can manage. In the meantime, should they arrive in advance of me, do not speak with them at all."

"Shall I leave them on the doorstep or let them in the house?"

"The doorstep is preferable but courtesy suggests entrance."

Confucius, she thought.

He went on with, "Entrance is safe as long as they understand that you will not be having a conversation with them prior to my arrival."

"Won't that look suspicious?"

"Of course. But have you anything to hide from the police?"

"Aside from the body beneath the patio?"

"Hmm. Yes. Well, if they come with shovels, do not allow them into the house."

She also liked him because he knew when a joke was a joke.

He told her he'd be there soon, and she went back to the bathroom to finish drying herself off. She ran a comb through her hair, vigorously rubbed her face with sunblock as always, threw some colour onto her skin, and went for something to wear. She generally wore tracksuits when she wasn't fancying herself up, and she wasn't about to fancy herself up for the police. So she chose her lime green one and reached for her sandals. She was putting them on when she saw that the nail varnish on several of her toes was chipped. She muttered "Oh blast," and went for the varnish remover. She absolutely loathed chipped varnish. She needed a pedicure, so she took a moment to ring her girl in Craven Arms for an appointment. Becky didn't like women wearing toenail varnish till June—she wanted everyone's nails to breathe from November onward, she claimed, although Rabiah didn't think toenails needed to breathe at all—but Rabiah didn't have time to argue with her on this subject, so she lied and said it was a manicure instead. They could have their toenail argument when she showed up.

She was energetically removing the remains of the varnish when her doorbell rang. It rang two more times before she got to it because it was out of the question that she would open it to the police only half varnished and chipped at that. When she finally jerked the door open, it was to see a tall blonde reaching to have another go with the bell while beside her stood a companion female who would barely have scraped five foot three on a good day.

They could have been anyone, Rabiah thought, since they weren't wearing uniforms. But police detectives on the telly didn't, did they, so there was no reason to suppose these two would.

The tall one said, "Ms. Lomax? I'm Detective Chief Superintendent Isabelle Ardery," and presented her identification while she tilted her head towards her companion and said she was Barbara Havers, although Rabiah did not catch her rank since she was examining Ardery's ID and trying to decide why the photo on it made her look ten years older than she appeared to be in person.

She handed the identification back to Ardery and considered how she had jumped to a conclusion that was clearly antifeminist. A woman had phoned, yes, but Rabiah had expected her to be the inferior officer to a man, and this despite having in her possession every season of *Prime Suspect* on DVD.

"Thank you for seeing us," Ardery said and waited for what she obviously expected: an invitation inside the house. This made Rabiah want to leave both of the detectives on her front step till Aeschylus arrived, but instead more than six decades of social breeding forced her to hold the door open and admit them.

She led them into the sitting room, where she informed them that her solicitor was on his way. Both of the women looked surprised. She said, "It's the telly. I can never work out why they don't ask to ring their solicitors if the police want to speak with them."

"Speeds things up if they don't," was the reply given by the shorter woman, Havers.

"How?" Rabiah asked in spite of herself.

"Moves the drama right along. They can get to a confession or a clue or whatever sooner if there's no solicitor."

Ardery said pleasantly to Rabiah, "Have you a clue for us?"

"Not when I don't know why you're here. I was heading to the kitchen. What appeals? Coffee, tea, mineral water, juice? It's grapefruit. I'm a victim to grapefruit in whatever form it comes, although I'm having a coffee just now. I've not had breakfast. I can forget that, but I must have my coffee."

The superintendent said, "Ah. Coffee takes more time, of course. Mineral water is fine for me," and the other woman agreed that mineral water was just the ticket for her as well.

Rabiah was assembling her tray of drinks when the doorbell sounded again. She went to admit Aeschylus Kong. He gave his usual formal greeting that was part bow from the waist and part handshake, his left hand over his right breast as if his heart had moved there during the night. He said, "Rabiah, if only everyone were as wise as you," and she told him where he would find the coppers. She asked him if he wanted a coffee.

He said a coffee would be splendid, black with one sugar. She returned to the kitchen as he joined the women from the Met. She could hear him introducing himself.

The higher-ranking officer, Ardery, did the honours for their side. The other officer, Rabiah overheard, was a detective sergeant.

When Rabiah returned to the sitting room with the tray of drinks, she saw that everyone was still standing as if in anticipation of her arrival. Aeschylus was looking out at the back garden, the woman called Havers was flipping through a Rockette scrapbook, and Ardery was examining one of the photos from the mantel of the fireplace. Rabiah couldn't see which one it was, but what she could see and did note was that the DCS handed it over to the other copper, who gave it a look, gave the DCS a look, then put the photo back on the fireplace mantel. When she did so, Rabiah saw it was the photo of *Volare, Cantare,* the consortium of pilots she was part of, standing in front of the glider they had purchased together. Considering the detective's interest, Rabiah wondered if the glider constituted stolen property.

When everyone had a coffee or mineral water, Aeschylus suggested that they all sit. He said to the police, "You have a wish to speak to my client, I understand," as he brushed his hand along his perfectly groomed head as if it wanted his attention.

"We're rather surprised that she felt she needed a solicitor," Ardery replied.

"That would be upon my advice, which I would give to any client who rang me and told me the police wished to speak to them. You must not, as a result, presume her guilty of anything."

"We don't," Ardery said. "I merely find it odd that, not knowing what the subject of our call was going to be, she would phone her solicitor."

Aeschylus made a movement of his hands, opening them briefly in a gesture that looked rather welcoming. He said, "What is it that we can do for you?"

"Your client is the only Lomax in the phone directory. She's listed as R. Lomax."

"*R* for Rabiah, yes," Aeschylus agreed. "Women should always use only their initials in any directory. On their bills as well. It's an issue of safety. Please go on, Superintendent."

Rabiah saw the other woman—Havers—take a notebook out of her shoulder bag along with a mechanical pencil. She was curious about why her words or those of Aeschylus Kong were going to be noted, but she didn't ask about it. If asking was going to be necessary, she had little doubt that her solicitor would do the job.

"Are you acquainted with Ian Druitt?" Ardery asked her.

Rabiah glanced at Aeschylus, who nodded, so she said, "He's the bloke who died at the police station a few months ago."

"Remember that, do you?" Havers asked the question, looking up from her notebook.

"It was in the newspaper for days and on television news," Rabiah said.

"Were you acquainted with him?" Ardery asked again.

"I'm not religious."

"So you know that he was a clergyman."

Rabiah was about to reply when Aeschylus touched her hand briefly and said, "The fact that he was a clergyman was also in the newspaper, Superintendent. And it was mentioned on regional news as well. I, too, who am also not religious nor a member of any congregation, know that he was a clergyman. All of that was made public knowledge at the time of the man's death."

"Of course." Ardery sounded not the least bothered by these revelations. "But what was not made public was the contents of the man's diary. The name Lomax was in it. Sergeant?"

Havers said, with a glance at an earlier page in her notebook, "Twenty-eighth of January through fifteenth of March. Seven times."

Rabiah didn't reply at once. She tried to consider every ramification of speaking. Then she made her decision. "That would have been about a family matter. I didn't think of him as a clergyman because it wasn't as a clergyman that I met with him."

"May I ask why you met with him?" Ardery asked.

"If you can explain the importance," Aeschylus said politely.

"The sergeant and I are here to follow up on two investigations into Mr. Druitt's death."

Rabiah liked the sound of this even less than she'd liked the sound of the police claiming to have seen *Lomax* seven times in the dead man's diary. She said, "To be frank, my two adult sons are substance abusers. One is in recovery and one is not. The one in recovery has been having a very bad time of it. His middle daughter died some eighteen months ago after a long illness. My son isn't coping well at all and I wanted—I needed, actually—to talk to someone about it. Mr. Druitt was recommended to me."

"Who did the recommending?" the DCS asked.

Rabiah was silent. This was exactly what happened when one talked to the coppers and said anything beyond either yes or no. She needed to keep her replies as simple as possible.

Outside the house a cat howled suddenly, one of those disconcerting preludes to a fight. Another cat responded. What followed was a mercifully brief spat of combined shrieking as the animals went after each other. Rabiah grimaced. She wondered if anyone would mind should she dart outside and shoo the felines off. But no one besides herself seemed to have noticed the noise.

"Ms. Lomax?" the DCS said.

"I'm trying to recall. One of my square-dancing group, I think. Or it could have been one of the people I train with."

"Train with?"

"I'm a runner."

"But you don't actually remember who it was?"

"Why don't you recall?"

They'd spoken at once, the detectives. Aeschylus stepped in. "My client's memory is germane to very little and certainly not to your purpose in coming to speak with her today. She has indicated why her surname appeared in Mr. Druitt's diary and I can attest to the death of her granddaughter, although that, too, has nothing to do with any question about who suggested Mr. Druitt as a sympathetic ear."

"Fair enough," Ardery said in reply, and then to Rabiah, "Where did you two meet when you had your conversations?"

Rabiah saw that Aeschylus was about to intervene again, but she also saw that they could go round and round forever, so she said, "That's easy enough to answer, Aeschylus," and then turned to the DCS and said, "It rather depended upon our schedules. Sometimes here, but more often in one café or another."

"I'm not sure what you mean. The day and the time are always the same."

"What she means," Aeschylus interjected, "is that while the day and the time are always the same, the place would alter due to whatever else she or Mr. Druitt had on that day."

"Busy, are you?" Havers was the one to ask the question.

"Quite," Rabiah said.

"Doing what?"

Aeschylus stood. He said, "Now we have gone entirely off topic. My client has explained why she met with Mr. Druitt, and if there is nothing more on that subject, I shall have to draw this meeting to a close. Do you mind if I do that, Rabiah?"

Rabiah did not.

Ardery locked eyeballs with Aeschylus. It was one of those moments when one person wants the other person to know who's *really* in charge. Then she said to Rabiah, "I believe you've explained things sufficiently." And to her colleague, "Sergeant Havers, have you a card with you?"

A few moments of strained silence passed while the sergeant excavated in her lumpy bag. She found a holder for her business cards and handed one of them over to her superior, who then handed it with some ceremony to Aeschylus Kong. She said, "If your client remembers anything pertinent from her sessions with Mr. Druitt, please ring my sergeant."

"What could possibly be pertinent?" Rabiah asked before she could stop herself, although she did take the card from Aeschylus.

"I'll let you decide that," the DCS said.

ST. JULIAN'S WELL
LUDLOW
SHROPSHIRE

The photo begged for an explanation. Barbara reckoned that the DCS would bring the matter up the nanosecond that Rabiah Lomax closed her front door upon them. There was more going on here than met the eye, and Ardery had to know it. Barbara gave her a quick look as they walked to the car. When they reached it and still Ardery hadn't said word one, Barbara took the plunge.

"What kind of a coincidence do we want to call the glider bit?"

Ardery clicked the vehicle's locking system and they got inside. "The photograph? I don't see calling it a coincidence at all."

Barbara chewed on this, saying nothing more till they were retracing their route to the centre of Ludlow. Then, "But it's too dead odd."

"We're not in London, Sergeant. The population's small. The fact that Nancy Scannell and Rabiah Lomax are both in a photograph with a glider has no real significance. Or do you wish to make it significant?"

"It seems like something we need to take on board as they both knew the dead bloke. I mean Rabiah Lomax and Nancy Scannell."

"Nancy Scannell did not know 'the dead bloke.' Nancy Scannell cut 'the dead bloke' open. If there's an important element I'm missing here, I'm intrigued to hear it because otherwise it seems to me that you're suggesting collusion on the part of Nancy Scannell—altering the facts as she saw them on the corpse—and Rabiah Lomax, based on Rabiah Lomax's appointments with Druitt."

"The IPCC report doesn't say a word about Lomax," Barbara said. "They missed the connection. So did DI Pajer. Her report doesn't mention it anywhere."

"Why would either report mention Lomax? They didn't have the diary. And even if they'd got their hands on it, there is no connection to be mentioned." Ardery's voice sounded edgy. The tone was a warning not to press this any further. "Everyone was investigating a suicide while in custody, sergeant. Full stop. Are you trying to build a case that Rabiah Lomax—for reasons unknown—got into the police station along with—let us assume—Nancy Scannell? The two of them then subdued Ian Druitt—also for reasons unknown—then strung him up by means of a doorknob and left him to die? Apart from there being no apparent motive and absolutely no evidence, how would they have accomplished this? Perhaps they're the ones who planned the burglaries that kept the patrol officers occupied? Perhaps one of them disguised her voice, made the phone call about paedophilia, contacted the others when Druitt was brought in, fed the PCSO a convenient sleeping draught obtained from the local crone practising witchcraft, and the rest is what happened after the PCSO downed it and passed out, allowing them to commit murder."

"He wouldn't've wanted anyone to know. There's that," Barbara said. "Ruddock *could've* let someone in that night and that person could've done the deed while he was conveniently out of the room making his pub phone calls."

"So now it's collusion on the part of Rabiah Lomax, Nancy Scannell, *and* the town's PCSO? All of this coming from a random photograph of a group of people grinning round a glider?"

Barbara heard the DCS's frustration, and she wanted to explain herself. She wanted to tell her that she and Lynley had always operated on the basis of anything being possible. Nothing was ever too outrageous to consider because the outrageous was always within reason when it came to murder. So was the unlikely. So was the unthinkable. So was the putatively inexplicable. Lynley was the fine cop he was because *nothing* was ever off the table. He had never been the kind of bloke whose priority was making an arrest so that he could go home to supper. It was looking more and more, though, as if Isabelle Ardery might be. Only . . . it wasn't going home to supper that she had on her mind. It was going home to something else. Barbara had already seen that. She could, even now, practically breathe it in with the air.

"And, by the way," Ardery continued, "are you now eschewing your previous theory about the PCSO, the woman he's bonking, and someone sneaking into the police station while said bonking is going on?"

"Guv," Havers said, "it's just that—"

"Really, Sergeant. This can't go on. I'm willing to speak with this

Finnegan Freeman—whoever the hell he is—but that's it. I've gone along with the issues you've raised, but this is as far as I'm going to go."

Barbara said, "It's only that when you showed me that photo, I thought—"

"May I remind you that it was your *thinking* that put you where you are today?" Ardery snapped.

Barbara knew where that remark was going to lead. She liked to believe that she also knew when it was time either to change direction or to reverse course altogether. So she said, "I s'pose I might be looking at things wrong way round," although she didn't believe this for a moment.

"I'm glad to hear that," Ardery said.

"There's still that anonymous call, though."

Ardery gave her a glare. "Your point being?"

"If we want to make sure this bloke—Clive Druitt—is satisfied that we've looked at every possible angle, it's prob'ly time to look at the CCTV footage on the phone call night." And before Ardery could respond, Barbara added, "I could do that while you talk to Finnegan Freeman, guv. How long would that take? Less than an hour, you ask me. And then we would've touched on every possible item that might send Clive Druitt running to his solicitors."

Ardery squeezed her temples. She had a look of a woman whose internal resources were being quickly depleted. She said, "Point taken. The CCTV film from the phone call night. Full stop. And I hope you take my meaning, Sergeant."

Barbara assured her that she did.

LUDLOW
SHROPSHIRE

When she rang the PCSO's mobile about the CCTV footage in question, Barbara found that Gary Ruddock had not yet begun his official day. Old Rob had taken a fall, he told her, and he was just returning to Ludlow from Accident and Emergency. He reckoned he could meet her at the police station in forty-five minutes. That was perfect as far as Barbara was concerned. There was a small detail she'd not mentioned to Ardery that she wished to check out.

To her way of thinking—which, admittedly, meant overlooking the DCS's way of thinking—if someone had given Ian Druitt the heave-ho into eternity, then that person was either the PCSO for reasons yet unknown, or it was a person—also yet unknown—who gained access to the station while the PCSO was engaged in something else. In this scenario, Barbara believed that the something else involved a car and a female, and she also believed that there had to be a way to prove this. So she set off for the station.

She went with the idea of someone—be it Ruddock's lady friend showing up for a bit of clothing removal in the back of a car or a killer with strangulation on his mind—gaining access to the police station via the route she'd pointed out to Ardery earlier. When she reached the station, she walked past it and along the street a short distance into Weeping Cross Lane. There, she paced slowly along, looking for the kinds of CCTV cameras that were ubiquitous in London. This was a commercial area of town, with businesses serving many interests: from van hire firms to equestrian needs. At least eight of them had CCTV cameras, Barbara found, which piqued her interest until she got close enough to see that not a single camera was pointed towards the street. That meant there was no joy to be had. But it also meant that anyone could come up from the river to the police station without being photographed along the way.

She proceeded to the end of Weeping Cross Lane and found herself in Temeside. Since the to-be-questioned Finnegan Freeman lived in one of the houses here, Barbara thought it might serve her purposes to sort out which one it was. She checked the address in her notes and headed in the direction of the Ludford Bridge. As she did so, she caught sight of Ardery's car pulling up onto the pavement in front of a house at the end of a terrace called Clifton Villas.

Barbara hesitated. She knew that Ardery didn't expect to see her in Temeside, so she gave thought to doing a rapid about-face and scurrying back into Weeping Cross Lane, where she could find a wheelie bin to hide behind, if necessary. But she needn't have worried. The DCS didn't get out of her car at once. Although she was facing Barbara from where she'd parked, she rested her head on the steering wheel for about a minute before she finally shoved the car door open. She ran her hand over her hair, looked at her wristwatch, and proceeded to the front door of the house. She was out of Barbara's sight at that point, as the house appeared to have a shallow porch. For her part, Barbara made tracks back to the police station, where she sat on the back step and wondered about all that she was witnessing in the DCS that she would have vastly preferred not to witness at all.

There had been something not right with Ardery earlier. It wasn't just that Barbara had waylaid her before she'd had a chance to eat her breakfast. She had a feeling from her colourless complexion that Ardery wouldn't have been able to hold down food anyway. Nor was it the fact that the DCS had not been able to have her morning coffee prior to their conversation. Instead it was what her right hand did when she took the map Barbara handed to her. It was how she dropped that right hand to her side when she couldn't stop its trembling. Barbara had concluded that the DCS was in a condition that might prevent her from noting a detail that needed noting. But she—Barbara Havers—wasn't in a position to point this out to anyone.

Some ten minutes after Barbara's return to the station, the PCSO drove into the car park. He gave her a friendly wave and strode to unlock the back door. She joined him, telling him about the movability of the camera in the front of the station as she followed him inside. She ended with, "So what I'm hoping is that it was in a different position the night the 999 phone call was made." This was only partially true. She had more on her mind than the 999 call. She led them in this direction by saying, "How's old Rob doing?"

"He was talking about having a fry-up when I left him. He only gets 'em once a week and his fall this morning prevented that. He was thinking I might do the honours, but there he got it wrong, poor bloke."

Ruddock led her along the corridor towards the front of the station, the overhead lights shedding their usual unappealing glare upon the lino and—she reckoned—upon her unwashed hair. She said, "Sounds like you're quite fond of him."

"Can't help liking a bloke his age who's still got so much life in him," Ruddock said.

"On the other hand," she pointed out, "living with a pensioner must get in the way sometimes."

"How d'you mean?" He shoved open the door to the reception cubicle where once someone had sat to greet both visitors and individuals wanting police help. It was a small area, barely large enough to contain both of them. A desk to one side of it held on its top an out-of-date computer terminal. Ruddock switched it on and waited while it groaned into action.

Barbara said, "Your love life and all that."

"Eh?" He turned back to her.

"Just thinking that it must make things rough—living with an old bloke like you do—if you want private time with someone."

He laughed, saying, "*If* I had a love life. With my wages, it's better not to. I s'pose I could offer a lady a lager and a pizza on payday, but that's about it. That being the case, I keep them more or less at arm's length. The ladies, I mean."

Barbara listed this under the heading *interesting factoid* in her mind. She wasn't sure what to make of it.

Behind him, the monitor came to life and within a few keystrokes, there was a split screen to view. One half of it was black—"Looks like that CCTV camera in the back isn't working, just like I thought," he said—and the other showed a slice of the street in front of the station, the steps leading up from the pavement, and a portion of the path leading to the door. Ruddock went at the keyboard and images flashed on the screen. What they took in remained the same with respect to the camera's position, although they documented a partial view of activities on the street as they flashed by: cars passing, mums pushing prams and pushchairs, joggers, and two different individuals coming up the steps towards the path and—one assumed—discovering that the station was unmanned. Then he stopped the images and they were at the night in question, for it turned out that the call had been made at night—hardly a surprise when one considered that it was anonymous—and there was nothing recorded save the night itself and the time, which was shortly after midnight. The image was what it had been from the start: a slice of street, the pavement, the steps, and part of the path to the door.

Barbara hadn't actually expected to see someone wearing a Hannibal Lecter mask as he—or she—gazed up at the camera before swivelling it away from a position taking in the front door. There was something else she'd come to check. She asked Ruddock to continue going back through time, which he did. Finally, the image altered, and the camera showed the area immediately round the front door. When she asked him to advance the image forward slowly through time, in the direction of the night Druitt died, she was able to capture a moment when the screen went to black. When it brightened to picture again, the camera documented what it had shown ever since the call had been made, which was not the front door but rather the route to get to it. Prior to the black screen, however, no matter how far back they went in the film, the focus of the camera remained on the door, which meant it also remained on the intercom.

She asked Ruddock how much time had elapsed between the alteration of the camera's position and the anonymous phone call. He examined the images connected to both and he told her six days. She said, "So our boy—or girl, for that matter—knew that the camera swivelled and did the job days in advance. That way anyone—like me—looking at the images from the phone call night would think the camera had always been looking out towards the street and not at the door where the intercom is." She pointed to the image frozen on the screen. "Shimmy along the station's wall once the camera's been moved to take in the steps up from the pavement and you're not on camera at all."

"But you would be filmed *moving* the camera's position whenever you moved it," he pointed out. "Unless . . ."

Obviously, the bloke was no dummy. He'd twigged that whoever had moved the camera had to have done it when it was completely nonfunctional. The only way to make it so was from inside the station. And it had to have been done quickly because the lapse during which the image was black had to be virtually unnoticeable were someone skimming back through the images to see if someone had been caught on camera making the anonymous call. Anyone doing the skimming would have seen that on the night of the phone call the camera was documenting the approach to the station from the pavement. It was only by going back six days in the images that one could see the camera's original position in addition to the moment of no image at all, during which that position had been altered.

Ruddock's consternation was playing out on his face. Barbara said, "This call to 999 about Druitt? It could've been made from anywhere, you know, and still have been anonymous. Someone wouldn't want to use their home phone or their mobile, 'course, but a call box somewhere? Providing there was no CCTV nearby? That would be no problemo."

"So why use the intercom?" he asked. "The whole bit with moving the camera. Why go to the trouble?"

She examined him. He examined her. It took him only a moment. "'Cause it *needed* to be made from the station," he murmured. "That was the only sure way to make me look guilty."

"Just that, yeah. So what's your enemy list look like, Gary?"

"Jesus. I didn't think I had one."

She thought about what she'd seen of his use of the car park at night, and she also considered asking him about the lady he was with back there. But she decided to hold that on another burner of the cooktop and instead she said, "In my experience, everyone has at least one."

He turned back to the image and studied it. Then he glanced at her. "But why not make the phone call straightaway once the camera was moved? Or why not move it back into position at some point?"

"Could be the mover got interrupted and didn't have time then. Could be after moving it, he wanted to make sure that a few days passed so that someone checking the film would think—without looking back far enough—that the camera had always been in the position it was in the night the phone call was made. Could also be the usual one, though."

"What's that, then?" he asked her.

She shrugged. "No one thinks of everything when it comes to a crime."

LUDLOW
SHROPSHIRE

When Isabelle first saw Finnegan Freeman, she hoped that he didn't represent what she had to look forward to as a mother of two boys, regardless of who had custody of them. He wore his hair in a style that featured dreadlocks on the right and a shaved skull on the left. This latter allowed the display of a disturbing tattoo showing a wild-looking woman screaming, complete with uvula displayed as well as overlong canines, one of which dripped blood.

The rest of Finnegan wasn't a picture, either. His clothes weren't entirely objectionable although they favoured excessively tattered jeans and an extremely threadbare flannel shirt. He wore sandals—perhaps in a bow to the spring weather—but his black-painted toenails did not delight. On his right ankle was a piece of braided leather, and a bulbous knot of the same material formed an earring that looked like an excrescence on his left lobe. He actually might not have been a bad-looking young man, but taken as a whole, he was something that might have been created by Munch.

She'd found him in what went for the sitting room of a house in Temeside. It sat at the end of a terrace of Edwardian vintage, if the tiles decorating the front porch were anything to go by. They featured sunflowers backed by dark green, a colour repeated on the front door of the establishment. The tiles had somehow remained in good condition. The same could not have been said of the door, which had been bashed repeatedly, possibly by careless removal men, and to which various transfers had been applied over time, most having apparently been placed by a fan of *The Wizard of Oz* in general and the flying monkeys in particular.

Isabelle had gained entrance to the house by helping herself to the doorknob upon a shout from within of, "It's unlocked, whoever you are." She found the owner of the shout in the sitting room. He was entertaining himself with a graphic novel while dining on what seemed to be a burrito, and he was doing so hunched over a coffee table of uncertain vintage and seated on a long chintz-covered sofa that looked to have come from someone's great-grandmother's attic.

The rest of the room's furniture consisted of three overlarge beanbags, one ladder-back chair, a floor lamp, a television, and a three-bar electric fire, the flex of which suggested real fire was imminent should it ever be used. It hadn't been, if the fireplace tools and the blackened condition of the small fireplace itself and its surrounding wall were anything to go by. A large sign on the mantel forbade the fireplace's use, but that had obviously been a small matter easily ignored by the house's inhabitants.

Finnegan Freeman had made it clear that indeed he *was* Finnegan Freeman when Isabelle enquired as to that person's whereabouts. He'd said, "Who wants to know and why?" and when she'd told him that the who of it was New Scotland Yard and the why of it was Ian Druitt, he was more than happy to say, "It's me, then," and he added, "My mum rang you, di'n't she?"

Isabelle said, "Why would your mother be ringing New Scotland Yard?"

"She's waiting for me to be enough out of order so she c'n drag me back home."

"Are you frequently out of order, then?"

He grinned and took in an enormous mouthful of burrito. He said while masticating, "She hates me having fun. It's just how she is."

Isabelle reassured him that his mother hadn't rung New Scotland Yard and that even had she done so, it wasn't within the purview of the Metropolitan Police to chase down misbehaving young people at the request of their parents.

He said, "Not misbehaving. Just having a bit of fun. She calls it me being defiant. Ha. I could *show* her defiance, I could, but she'd prob'ly have a stroke."

"I see." Isabelle told him then that Ian Druitt's death in the police station was what had brought her and another detective from the Met to fair Ludlow to engage in a look-see at the conclusions that had been arrived at by the Independent Police Complaints Commission.

At this, the young man set his burrito on the kitchen towel he'd been using as a plate. He eyed her as if measuring the level of her sincerity. Isabelle had the odd sensation of being evaluated by someone who was quite a bit more than his appearance and manner of speech indicated.

He said, "What've I got to do with that, then?"

"We found your name amongst his belongings. It heads the list of members of a children's club here in town. As yours was the only name without what appeared to be the accompanying names of parents, we assumed you were the young man who assisted Mr. Druitt."

"Quite a gumshoe, eh?" he said.

"So you did assist him. What did that consist of?"

Finnegan seemed, at that moment, to remember something vaguely resembling manners, for he slid along the sofa, patted one of its numerous lumps, and said, "Park it, 'f you want," by which she assumed he was extending an invitation for her to sit. She did so although the proximity to him brought with it an attendant odour of dirty socks, which was rather odd as he wasn't wearing any. She waited for illumination on the topic of what he did for Druitt's club.

He said, "I helped 'em with their school prep. I helped out with equipment for sport. I showed 'em how to use the Internet for school projects and the like. We did country walks sometimes. 'N I gave demonstrations."

"Demonstrations?" Isabelle hoped his demonstrations did not touch upon personal grooming or the world of fashion.

He held up his hands. They were, she saw, oddly small for someone his size. He said, "Karate. Kids always love that stuff."

"That makes you quite strong, I assume," Isabelle noted.

He shot her a look that said he knew where she was heading. "No crime being strong, far 's I know."

"Of course," Isabelle agreed. She shifted to Druitt, asking Finnegan's assessment of him. What was he like? she wanted to know.

"That's easy enough," Finnegan replied. "What he *wasn't* like was a bloke who killed himself, which's what I been saying to anyone who'll listen, only no one's been in'erested in my opinion."

"That's why I'm here, Finnegan."

"Finn," he told her.

"Sorry. Finn. I've come to hear your opinion."

"Why?"

"Because you worked with him at the children's club."

"You want to know did he mess about the young ones, that's what this is. You want to know did he plaster himself 'cause he was gonna get grilled 'bout that."

"I want to know whatever you care to tell me. Your opinion would be welcome on any matter related to Mr. Druitt."

"You sound like my mum."

"I have children of my own. Motherspeak gets into the blood. Do you have an opinion about Mr. Druitt?"

"I do," he said. "This is it: He was a good bloke. He cared 'bout every one of those kids in the club. Most of that lot? They got sent there for what he could do for them, which was, let me tell you, buckets more 'n their parents were doing. I never saw him—not once, mind—do a single thing to any little kid except maybe, 'n I'm only saying *maybe* since I never saw anything and it's not like I remember even this, 'cept maybe giving a little one a pat on the shoulder or the head or the like. Other 'n that, he didn't do a *single* thing. He was just nice to 'em. He was great."

She said, "I understand."

He huffed. "Good."

She went on with, "But child molestation is a process of seduction that generally unfolds over time. A child is groomed by his molester, positioning him to accept the molestation as part of the relationship."

Finnegan had reached for his burrito during his recitation, but now he threw it onto the kitchen towel with enough force that the towel slid across the coffee table and dumped the burrito onto the fitted carpet. This looked like something that hadn't been hoovered in a generation or two, so the resulting splat of beans, cheese, and whatever was of little matter. He said, "Did you even hear me?"

"I did. Of course. But, Finnegan, a man—"

"Finn!" he cried. "It's Finn Finn Finn!"

"Yes. Sorry. Finn. A man gets away with acts of abuse or molestation because he seems exactly as Mr. Druitt has been described: gentle, caring, committed, and all the rest. If he doesn't seem like that to prospective victims and their families—even to his mates—then he would never get on as an active paedophile in the first place. But I expect you know all this."

"What I *know*," he said, "is that he never stepped out of order wiff any 'f those little kids. They would've come to me if he did."

"And what about you?" she asked him.

He went instantly red. "I was *never* out of order wiff those kids! Are you accusing me of—"

"Sorry, no," Isabelle said, although she did wonder what Sergeant Havers might have dragged out of her Lynley-inspired Shakespearean knowledge to address the young man's reaction, not to mention his occasional lapse into some interesting form of guess-my-social-class lingo, as if he couldn't quite decide from which stratum of society he had sprung. "I was asking if Mr. Druitt was ever out of order with you."

If anything, Finnegan became redder still. "You listen if you can. He went out of his way to be nice to everyone. 'Specially to kids who were bullied. He knew what it was like, and he taught kids that bullies're people who need to feel big and the only way to stop their bullying is to take them on. Wiff words or wiff fists. Whatever it takes."

"Is that why you learned karate?"

"My dad put me onto it. I was bullied, yeah. But first time I showed what I could do? That put an end to that. And doing stuff to a kid like you're accusing Ian of doing . . . ? It's just another way to bully and Ian di'n't bully. He knew what it was like."

"So he was bullied," Isabelle said. "Or do you mean that he was sexually abused as a child? Did he reveal that to you?"

"No way!" Finnegan fairly shrieked the words.

"Which?" she said. "The revelation to you or the sexual abuse?"

"Both! And if you think he was and if you think he passed it on to the little ones, just ask 'em. You ask every one of 'em. You'll see that there's *nuffink* in it that he s'posedly messed wiff little kids."

When he paused for breath, the noise of someone clomping down the stairs sounded. A girl appeared in the doorway to the sitting room. She said, "Hey, Finn, I'm off to—" and then stopped at the sight of Isabelle. She switched to, "Sorry. I didn't know anyone else was here."

Isabelle found that difficult to believe since Finnegan's voice had been raised to a volume that couldn't have gone unnoticed. The rooms of the house were hardly soundproof.

The girl stepped into the room, as if courteously waiting for an introduction. She was college girl in appearance, with long hair that looked professionally streaked with blonde, petite but possessing a womanly body. She said, "I'm Dena Donaldson, but everyone calls me Ding."

Finnegan said, "Mind you be careful who you're introducing yourself to. This is a copper. All the way from Scotland Yard to wring the truth out of me."

Ding took in Isabelle much the way that Isabelle had taken her in. She said, "But you don't wear a uniform?" as if this were a critical detail.

"She's a *detective*," Finnegan told her. "You watch telly, right? They don't wear uniforms on telly. She's here about Ian."

"Mr. Druitt?"

"Any other Ian a copper might want to talk to me about? You've gone a bit thick. Drink too much last night?"

The girl didn't reply to this. Instead, she shrugged out of her rucksack and she placed it on the floor. She was wearing a bright fuchsia skirt that she smoothed in a gesture that might have been nervous or might have been intended to be read as nervous, and she adjusted the scarf that she'd fashioned as a cummerbund. Its tight print of clouds and flowers picked up the colour of the skirt along with the grey of her T-shirt.

Isabelle said, "Did you know Mr. Druitt?"

The girl looked startled. Her gaze darted from Finnegan to the fireplace to Isabelle. "How?" she asked.

"How *would* you have known him?" Isabelle clarified. "Or in what *manner* did you know him?"

"I'm not . . . I don't exactly . . . If you mean—"

"For Christ sake, Ding. Spit it out." Finnegan sounded like someone who knew the girl was buying time.

"I only heard about him," she told Isabelle. "From Finn mostly."

"Who else?"

"D'you mean who else did I know?"

"No." Isabelle found that, once again, her head had begun to pound. She was going to have to do something about it, soon. "You said 'Finn mostly' in reference to hearing about Mr. Druitt. From whom else did you hear about him?"

"Oh!" Ding crossed her arms beneath her breasts, a movement that made them more prominent. It had always left Isabelle incredulous when women did this sort of thing, suggesting that they'd made no progress at all as a sex. Flash some grapefruit, and one ruled the world. "I expect it was all from Finn. I don't think Brutus knew him."

"Brutus?" Isabelle said. "Is he someone who lives here as well?"

"Bruce Castle," Ding said. "Everyone calls him Brutus. It's . . . well . . . sort of a joke."

"'Cos he's a half pint," Finnegan said shortly.

"Like a boy?" Isabelle asked. "I mean, in size. Is he more like a boy?"

Finnegan took clear exception to this. "Ian didn't do *nothing* to anyone here or anywhere!" he declared hotly at the same moment as Ding said, "Brutus *wouldn't've* done . . . I mean, he wouldn't've let anyone mess him about, if that's what you're thinking."

"You know about the accusation of paedophilia, do you?"

"Yes. Well, yes." Ding sent a nervous glance in Finnegan's direction. "Everyone knows. I think Finn told me. Or maybe I heard Finn going at it on the phone with his mum. Maybe that was it. Is that it, Finn? Would that be how I found out? Or did I read it somewhere?"

"Hell if I know." Of a sudden, Finn sounded bored, perhaps determinedly so.

"D'you overhear a great deal in this house?" Isabelle asked the girl.

"It's smallish," Ding pointed out. "So one hears. . . . You don't even have to try, really. Which is why, you see . . . I mean it's not like Mr. Druitt visited here. We didn't really ever know him. By that, I mean Brutus and me. We didn't. It wasn't the same for Finn, of course."

"I'm not entirely sure what you'd like me to infer," Isabelle said.

"Infer? Nothing! Only that we don't have much to add anywhere. Me and Brutus, that is. I can't say about Finn."

Finn, Isabelle saw, was watching the girl. His expression seemed speculative at the same time as it bordered on hostile. "Don't you have somewhere you're s'posed to *be*, Ding?" he asked. "I mean, you were leaving, right?"

Ding picked up her rucksack and settled it back on her shoulders. She seemed unoffended by Finnegan's tone. She said, directing her final words to Isabelle, "I hope you get the information you need."

"From Finn, I assume?"

"Oh yes. Because like I said—"

"Yes. You and Brutus didn't even know Ian Druitt, did you."

LUDLOW
SHROPSHIRE

Ding took her bicycle as if she meant to ride it to her geography lecture. And she might actually have done this had she not been unnerved coming down the stairs to find a Scotland Yard detective in the sitting room. That—and the short stretch of conversation she'd had with the woman—put paid to all scholastic intentions. But for the next few minutes she needed to maintain the appearance of cycling off to the lecture, so she set off in the direction of Lower Broad Street. This, should she turn into it, would take her up to the narrow stretch of Silk Mill Lane and one of the college lecture halls. However, she didn't turn. Instead, once she was out of sight of the house, she coasted into the car park of the Persian carpet shop. Like every other Persian carpet shop in England, it was having a going-out-of-business sale. A large banner fixed across the front window declared this to be a fact. Although it was faded from however many years it had hung there, the shop owners had so far not twigged that this was a clue about the truth of their declaration of finality.

There was, as always, a pile of rugs outside of the shop. Ding stopped next to these, hopped off her bicycle, and began earnestly flipping up their corners as if in a hunt for the perfect one for her bedroom floor. Within moments, she was joined by the shop owner, who was not, as one might expect, Middle Eastern, but rather a Scot whose Glaswegian accent was virtually unintelligible. Had he been speaking Farsi, she would have stood a better chance of understanding him.

She told him she was just looking at what he had on offer and when he said whatever it was that he said, she replied with, "Not now, thank you." Mostly, she wanted to be off the street until the coast was clear to return to the house.

Ding knew that her answers had scarcely been believable. Her brain had started to whir insanely the moment Finn told her who the woman was. The *last* thing she'd expected when she'd come down the stairs so innocently was to find a police detective having a chat with Finn.

She stalled by means of the rug pile for ten minutes, perhaps more. This required her to engage the Scotsman in a conversation that seemed to have as its topic the reverse side of the carpets. Once again, she had no clue what he was actually telling her, but since he was gesturing and running his hands against the back and since she did catch hold of the words *hand* and *knot,* she nodded and told him, "Yes, I see." Fortunately, this appeared to be all that was required of her. After those ten minutes, she said, "Thanks awfully," and rolled her bicycle back to the street.

The police detective's car was gone. Ding was safe. It took less than one minute to pedal back to the house, where she dropped her bike in the front patch of concrete. Once inside, she closed the door as quietly as she could and hurried towards the stairs. But it was pointless. She heard Finn call out, "Hey, you," from the sitting room. She paused and saw that he was lounging as before on that ugly sofa they'd found in one of Ludlow's bazillion charity shops. He was picking something out of a burrito, wiping his fingers on the sofa's upholstery.

She said to him, "Someone might actually want to *sit* there, Finn?" in reference to the finger wiping, which appeared to be depositing streaks of bean juice—or whatever it was inside of a burrito—on the faded fabric.

He ignored the comment and said to her, "What was *that* supposed to be about?"

"What?"

"All the 'me and Brutus' shit. You were making it only too seriously obvious that you wanted the cop to keep her eyes on *me*."

"I don't know what you're talking about."

"That's the case, is it?" He inspected the bitten end of the burrito, seemed to find it sufficiently edible, and took a mouthful. "Sure as hell didn't seem like that to me."

He rose. The sofa retained the impression of his arse. It retained the impression of the cop's arse, for that matter. He approached her and said while chomping through his food with more noise than seemed to be required, "Got to tell you, Ding. I don't what you're on about these days."

"I'm 'on about' nothing." She headed for the stairs but he adroitly blocked her way. She said, "Let me go, Finn."

"What? I'm stopping you or something?"

"You're in my way."

"Don't like that, eh? Tell me this, then. What the *fuck* is going on?"

"Nothing. I just don't like someone thinking bad of me when I haven't done anything."

"Specially if that someone's a cop, eh? Now why's that? You hiding something?"

"No!"

"Well, let me tell you, that's not what it looked like to me."

"I can't help what it looked like to you," she said. "Now get out of my way."

Ding pushed past him and ran up the stairs. Behind her, she heard Finn say, "I'm not exactly stupid, Ding," which was the last thing she heard before she strode to her bedroom, closed the door, and locked it behind her.

She hurried to the small clothes cupboard, and she began removing its contents. She was in haste to get to what she wanted, but she didn't pull things out and drop them onto the floor as if in a scene from a film in which her depicted actions were meant to telegraph panic to the audience. Instead, she took them from the rod and placed them carefully on the bed.

Because of her family's circumstances, she'd been forced to purchase her own clothing for years. She'd done so by cobbling together funds from offering herself as a childminder, a shop assistant, a weed puller, a feeder and walker of dogs, a waterer of plants, and just about anything else she could come up with in her limited free time since she was twelve years old. So she treasured every shoe, skirt, pair of jeans, jersey, pullover, and boot that she possessed. She gave away nothing until it was threadbare. She simply couldn't afford to.

But now . . . She had to rid herself of two pieces that were dear to her heart. They were at the farthest reach of the cupboard, and she had to dig through her winter clothing in order to find them where she'd placed them together on a hanger. She'd buttoned her red wool coat over them and that was what she ultimately pulled out of the cupboard and carried to the bed. She undid the buttons and gazed at the hidden skirt and top. Before she could dwell on how much they had cost and how she would miss them, she scooped them up, and from the floor of the clothes cupboard she grabbed a carrier bag.

It was impossible for her to shove the skirt and the top inside the bag indifferently. She folded them neatly instead. Then she folded the bag itself upon the clothes, and this she put into her rucksack. For just a moment, she tried to tell herself that she really didn't need to do this, but the problem was that she couldn't depend on that being the case.

LUDLOW
SHROPSHIRE

Barbara Havers knew that she needed to get to the call centre in Shrewsbury. She wanted to listen to the message about Ian Druitt that led to his being taken to the Ludlow station on the night of his death. Although she'd read the transcript of that message in the IPCC's report—at this point she had the bloody thing memorised—she believed that there was still a chance that something in it had been missed by the previous investigators. It could be anything: from the pronunciation of a word that would prove peculiar to a single individual involved in the circumstances of Druitt's life to some kind of background noise that could be connected to a person they hadn't considered yet.

She knew quite well that when it came to listening to the call to

999, she was going beyond what she'd been told to do by the DCS. But she assured herself that she owed it to the dead man to leave no stone unturned if she could help it.

Shrewsbury was just a bit more than thirty miles north of Ludlow, and those miles were a direct route along the A49. Barbara felt certain she could make a dash up there and back within two hours with no one the wiser. But she required Gary Ruddock either to allow her to use the patrol car or to drive her to Shrewsbury himself. He said he would drive her.

He had managed to get them some ten miles along the way when her mobile rang. She dug it out of her bag and gave it a look although she was certain who the caller was. It was, and she let it go to message. She would tell Ardery that she hadn't heard it. In the loo was always a good excuse. She'd have to work a bit on the reason she didn't return the call, but she would come up with something by the time she saw the DCS.

Five minutes later, however, her mobile rang again. This time Ruddock glanced at her when she didn't answer it. She said, "Men," with a sigh and rolled her eyes.

Ruddock might have gone for that had his own mobile not rung some thirty seconds later. Without a look, he took the call, saying, "PCSO Ruddock, Ludlow," followed by a moment of silence as his caller spoke, after which he said, "Oh, aye. She's just here. I'm taking her up to Shrewsbury to—"

Barbara groaned. Ruddock listened to his caller. Then he handed the phone to Barbara, saying apologetically, "Your guv."

Before she spoke, Barbara wondered how the hell Ardery had come up with Ruddock's mobile number. But it wouldn't have been difficult, she realised. A phone call to West Mercia Headquarters would have taken care of that. She said in a rush that would give Ardery no time to wonder why Barbara hadn't answered her own mobile, "Guv, after looking at the CCTV film, it occurred to me that the logical next step was—"

"Were you given leave to take another step?" Ardery asked. "I recall uttering the words 'full stop.' What I don't recall is also telling you to take any further action. Sergeant, are you at all capable of recognising how an investigation is organised? It's from the top down, by the way, and not the opposite."

"Guv—"

"Have Ruddock turn the car round at once and return to Ludlow."

"—it's only that—"

"There *is* no 'Guv, it's only that,'" Ardery snapped. "There is only what I authorised you to do. And if you get it into your head that there is the *tiniest* possibility—getting tinier every moment—that I might agree to some additional action on your part, your next move is to speak to me about it and obtain my permission. Am I being clear? Or is there something about the chain of command that you're simply incapable of ever understanding?"

"You're being clear." Barbara's spirits could not have sunk much deeper. She had, at one point, given a stray thought to the ludicrous idea that she and Ardery were beginning to get on. What a howler, she thought. She said, "Will do as ordered, ma'am."

"How pleasant that sounds. When can I expect to see you?"

"We're maybe twenty minutes out from Ludlow."

"I'll expect you here in twenty-five, then. If it stretches to thirty, we'll have something to discuss. Do you understand?"

"Do." But Barbara hated to leave it like that, with her being disciplined by her superior in the presence of the PCSO. The embarrassment, the frustration, the sheer inability to make any point at all with Ardery, prompted her to pretend that the two of them had at least something to discuss beyond her apparent inability to adhere to Ardery's plans for the investigation. So she said, "How did you get on with Finnegan Freeman? Anything useful?"

"More of the same. According to him, Druitt was nothing short of the Second Coming. What an eyeful he was, however."

"Druitt or Freeman?"

"The latter. I feel for his parents."

"Got it," Barbara said and added, "See you soon."

To which Ardery replied, "Soon is what I'm depending upon, Sergeant," before she cut off the call.

Ruddock shot her a look, saying, "Progress somewhere at least?"

"Who the hell knows," Barbara told him. "We need to head back.

I've got twenty-five minutes to be in her presence. If I don't make it in time, one of us turns into a pumpkin."

LUDLOW
SHROPSHIRE

They made it back to Ludlow in exactly twenty-two minutes because the PCSO was good enough to put some speed into their journey. But Castle Square was so crowded with market stalls, shoppers, and tourists that the only way he could have deposited her in front of Griffith Hall would have been to drive on the pavement to reach Dinham Street at the other end of the square.

Ruddock barely had enough room to pull the car to the kerb. Directly in front of them, in addition to the lines of stalls, there were individuals who'd decided to transform the place into something of a car boot sale without the car boots. Their wares were spread on blankets. Some of them blocked access to the market.

"Damn," the PCSO said, and then to Barbara, "I have to run this lot off 'least twice each month. They're not meant to be in the market and don't they show up anyway."

As he shouldered open his car door and got out, Barbara did likewise. She saw a familiar form among those individuals flogging bits and bobs from their blankets. It was the old dosser and his dog, whom she'd seen on her first walkabout. She said to Ruddock, "Who is that bloke? The one with the Alsatian?"

Ruddock followed her gaze and said, "That'll be Harry."

"I saw him the other night. Sleeps rough?"

"He does," Ruddock said. "I keep hoping he'll move on to another town, but he seems dug in. He's not bothered you, has he?"

"I've not even spoken to him. Is he a fixture in town?"

"Oh, he is that." Ruddock nodded to her, then, and set off to deal with the blanket-goods floggers. Barbara was sorry she'd brought up Harry since Ruddock headed straight to him to make him the first of those who were ordered to clear out of Castle Square. Ruddock squatted and seemed polite enough, but Harry didn't look inclined to cooperate till Ruddock began picking up his items for sale and putting them into a neat pile.

She strode quickly in the direction of Griffith Hall, preparing herself mentally for her encounter with Ardery. By the time she went in the front door, she thought she might have come up with a way to get back into the DCS's good graces.

Ardery was waiting on the hotel's back terrace, an expanse of flagstones and urns of bright flowers overlooking a lawn that dipped in the direction of the distant river. She was seated at one of the outdoor tables, rapidly tapping something into her mobile. Considering that this could well be a message having to do with her aborted trip to Shrewsbury, Barbara wanted to interrupt the DCS before she hit send since there was only one person with whom Ardery would want to share information of Barbara's misdeeds.

She said heartily, "Guv. Here you are," and went to her, pulling out one of the other chairs at the table and plunking herself into it. She said, "You're right. I'm dead sorry. Sometimes I get too caught up in things. It won't happen again."

"It won't happen because we're finished here," Ardery told her.

Barbara tried to console herself with Ardery's use of the plural pronoun. She said, "There *is* this one bloke, though. He wants talking to. With your permission. I've seen him about and I've got his name and it's nowhere in the IPCC's reports."

Ardery set her mobile on the table. Barbara allowed herself a nanosecond to feel relief that she'd retarded the message's electronic flight to London and, doubtless, to AC Hillier's office. Now what she needed to do was position the DCS to forget about the message entirely.

"Who might this bloke be?" Ardery asked.

"He's called Harry. Last name unknown at present. He sleeps rough round town. What I'm thinking is that he might have information that could confirm the allegations about Ian Druitt. He could have seen something."

"Are you saying that this Harry Whoever might have seen Ian Druitt exploring children's bodies in a public location? You can't possibly want me to consider that, Sergeant. We've not uncovered a single detail that suggests Ian Druitt was a fool."

"This bloke, though, this Harry . . . ? He might've seen Druitt loading one of them into his car, guv. Or walking one of them . . . here or there."

"He also might have seen Father Christmas loading an elf into his sleigh. All we have is conjecture going in both directions about Ian Druitt: yes he was and no he wasn't. And that's not why we're here anyway."

"Due respect, guv," Barbara said evenly, "but there's been only one allegation that Ian Druitt was messing children about and that one was anonymous. From everyone else it's been no way, no how, and have you gone bonkers even to suggest it."

At this moment, Peace on Earth glided through the French windows that led from the terrace back into the hotel. He asked Barbara if she wanted anything. What Barbara wanted was a crowbar to pry open Ardery's mind so that it could take in what she was trying to tell her. But she reckoned that wasn't on offer. Since Ardery was having nothing, she was reluctant to go her own way, although the reality was that if there were any biscuits, teacakes, scones, or croissants languishing in the kitchen, she would have been dead chuffed to sink her gnashers into one or three. However, she went for what she presumed was the way of wisdom and said thanks, but no.

Ardery waited till the young man had vacated the terrace before she said, "Let me repeat this a final time: Whether Druitt was or was not a paedophile is not nor has it ever been why we're here. Yet you've continually attempted to guide this investigation into those waters instead of into the waters of his suicide and the subsequent enquiry, which is where we belong. *That's* the point: How did this happen, and how did the IPCC follow up on it. We could venture into why some officer at the call centre took the mad decision to have the man hauled into the nick ASAP instead of waiting till the proper patrol officers were free to do it. But the point is that the call centre officer did take that decision based on what the operator heard on the phone. The rest has been a massive cock-up in which a man killed himself rather than have his name, his reputation, and his entire life dragged through the mud."

"*If* he killed himself," Barbara said. "'Cause all along—and you have to admit it—what's looked like suicide could've been murder. With someone buzzing the call centre about paedophilia just as a means to get him into the station."

Ardery picked up her bag from the terrace and took a few moments to stow her mobile. She seemed to be buying time to garner patience. Finally, she said, "We aren't here to explore that, Sergeant. How many more times do I have to repeat this? Now, I've placated you and your concerns by interviewing Finnegan Freeman, from whom I gained absolutely nothing aside from a heated declaration of Ian Druitt's innocence—hardly unexpected, you'll agree—along with the limited entertainment of also speaking with his dizzy housemate, who kept referring to another housemate called Brutus, who she would love me to believe conveniently or otherwise knows nothing about anything."

"*Brutus*?"

"Bruce Castle, and that is *not* the point. The point is that this could go on forever, and we do not have the time, the luxury, or the funds to make it go on forever."

"I understand that, guv. Really. I do. But I still think—"

"For God's bloody sake, there is no 'I still think.' There is simply what happened on that night, what DI Pajer did in the aftermath, and what the IPCC did once the matter was turned over to them."

Barbara saw that the DCS was about to rise, and she knew she had to stop her because there was something else. It was only a small detail, but in any investigation the devil, as they say, was in those details. She said, "I'm on board with all that, guv. I've read and reread and counterread those reports. Which is why when I looked at the CCTV films with Ruddock, I realised that the IPCC watched the film for the phone call night and they watched the film for the murder night. But what they didn't watch was the film from six days *before* the phone call, because there's no mention of that in their report. And six days *before* the phone call, the film shows the camera was moved so that the caller could make the call later without being seen. My point is that if they missed that, they could've missed something else. Like something *in* the phone call, which is why I was heading up to Shrewsbury to listen to it."

"Did *they* listen to it? Did *they* find a single thing unusual in it? Yes to the first and no to the second. So what is it that you expect to hear since you already have the transcript of the call? A Greek chorus in the background identifying the caller? And even if the caller is identified—which, of course, he isn't—what does that prove?"

"I don't know. I admit that. But I did see Ruddock in the car park the other night making the big nasty with—"

"Stop that at once! Talk like a police officer!"

Barbara was hasty with her switching of gears. "I saw Ruddock with a girlfriend—which, by the way, he says he doesn't have in the first place, a girlfriend, that is—in a patrol car. Just like he was, mind you, the night we got here, because *that* night I saw what I thought was one of the patrol officers having a kip in the car but now I think it had to be Ruddock with the girl, because I could see this bloke leaning back in the seat looking *very* comfortable, and I reckon that means that she was doing a gob job on him." And when Ardery's face reflected outrage and she opened her mouth to speak, Barbara added in a flash, "I mean fellatio. She was performing fellatio."

"And this means what? That while Officer Ruddock was enjoying some young woman's sexual ministrations in the nick's car park on the night of Druitt's death, someone else got inside the place, murdered Druitt, and got back out without being seen and without—as we've *already* discussed, by the way—leaving a trace of evidence behind? Nothing suggests that. Nothing even hints at that. The man killed himself for whatever reason he had, the autopsy confirms that, and there's an end to it. We can play this game of he was or he wasn't, he did or he didn't into the next decade, but the reality is that sometimes people kill themselves for reasons we cannot work out: a deep depression they've been hiding, a spiritual crisis, a psychological wound, a sudden diagnosis of disease, a life change that they can't contend with, mental instability. And when that happens, no one—and especially the family—wants to believe it was a suicide because suicides result in everyone connected to that person having to examine *themselves* for a reason it happened, and believe me, no one wants to do that. People would often rather die than have to look at themselves when—"

Her sudden stop caused Barbara to say, "What?"

Ardery stood. She took up the strap of her shoulder bag. "Nothing," she said. "We're finished here. Be packed and ready to leave in the morning."

LUDLOW
SHROPSHIRE

"Barbara." Lynley's voice on the phone was at its most reasonable. He'd heard her straight through to the end of her tale without interruption, and his tone told her that he now had something thoughtful to say. She *hated* that. She wanted him to declare, "By God, I'll see to this at once, Sergeant." Pretty dim of her, she realised. *By God, I'll see to this at once, Sergeant* was hardly Lynley's style. He said, "I don't need to remind you why you're there, do I?"

She said, "I know why I'm here, sir. Believe me, Herself keeps making *sure* I know it. But the thing that—"

"If 'the thing that' is asking you to step out of order in any way," he cut in, still maintaining that tone of patience, "what you must ask yourself is whether that's truly necessary, because it seems to me that the moment you and the PCSO set off to Shrewsbury—"

"Sir, the call centre in Shrewsbury would have—"

"The *moment* you set off to Shrewsbury to listen to a recording, the transcript of which you already have, is the very moment you did just that."

"What?"

"Began to step out of order. We've been over this before, Barbara. If you continue on this path, you know where it's going to lead."

There were distant voices in the background. There was the sound of a phone ringing as well. There was the sudden interruption of Dorothea Harriman speaking from the doorway of Ardery's office, where Lynley was, at present, acting as guv. Barbara heard her say, "Acting Detective Chief—" before Lynley stopped her with, "Give me five minutes, Dee."

And then he said to Barbara, "We don't need to explore this another time, do we, Sergeant?"

Well, yes. They did need to do just that, Barbara thought. She said, "She keeps banging on about our brief, Inspector, which is bloody well blinding her to what's hanging in front of her eyes."

"And that is what? I ask because, from what you've told me, the only thing hanging before her eyes is doing what she was told to do by Hillier. Unless something new has occurred, she's under orders that she received from Hillier himself. Has anything new occurred? Anything indeed to warrant this phone call you've made to me?"

"I don't know," Barbara admitted. "But maybe. Could be. See, there's this CCTV camera that got its position moved and what I'm thinking is that if the IPCC report doesn't mention that—which it doesn't—then it's reasonable to conclude that the IPCC report might have missed something else."

"I venture to say that if that's the case, what they missed is not going to be on the recording of a phone call. Barbara, the IPCC will have gone over that call in every possible way. They will have interviewed every person connected even remotely to what happened up there. I'm going to make a leap here and assume that's what they did and you've been given every relevant report dealing with all of this."

"I've seen things that they didn't see, sir, because *what* I've seen has happened since their report was filed."

"But Barbara." Now Barbara could hear that Lynley was at last striving for patience: busy man, busy day, and why can't you just get on with things, Sergeant, without having to ring me for a pep talk that you shouldn't bloody need?

"Sir," she said.

"You're not there to reinvestigate, reinterpret, reevaluate, or any other re. You know why you're there and if Isabelle is telling you—"

"Isabelle, *Isabelle*," Barbara said before she could stuff a sock down her throat. Quickly, she added, "Sorry, sir." He didn't reply at once, so she added what, in her heart, she knew was the real reason behind her call to Lynley. "She's drinking, Inspector."

Silence met this. She let it hang there. She knew he was processing what she'd said. Finally, "What do you mean by drinking?"

She said, "What do you mean what do I mean? You *know* what I mean. Something's going on with her and she's trying to drink her way out of it. I'm sorry to tell you this, but it's a fact pure and simple."

"Rarely pure and never simple," he murmured.

"What?"

"Never mind. She's allowed a drink when she's not on duty, Barbara."

"Believe me, I'm not talking about a drink in the singular, sir. She's shooting it down—I'll wager she's got it in her room—and it's getting in the way of her being able to see things clearly."

"That's a very serious allegation."

"It's not an allegation. It's a sodding fact."

"Has she made an unreasonable demand of you? Has she avoided looking at the paperwork you've been given? Has she assigned you the bulk of the work while taking herself off duty?"

"No," she said. "But at the same time—"

"Then what is it that's concerning you, Barbara? Because it seems to me that what's concerning you is that you cannot bend her to your will."

"I just want to—"

"This isn't about what you want. Do you not see that what you're doing just now is exactly what put you in the tenuous position you find yourself in the first place?"

"I *know*. That's why I've rung you."

"To do what? To say what? Barbara, you must know my hands are tied."

"But—"

"What?"

You were lovers, she wanted to say. That means you have influence and I'm begging you to use it. But she could not say that because there was the fact of crossing lines and the other fact of crossing lines that one could never uncross. So she was silent.

He went on; he was reason itself. "There is no but. There is only doing what you were assigned to do. From everything you've said, it seems to me that Isabelle—that the DCS—is doing exactly what she was told to do and that's making certain the IPCC report is complete and unbiased so that she can give this information to Hillier, who can then pass it on to the MP who asked for the investigation, who can in turn explain to the father of the dead man that there is nothing more to be done and he has everyone's utter sympathy."

Still she was silent, finally at a loss as to how to argue her side in things.

He said, "Are you still there, Barbara?"

"Unfortunately."

"Please hear me. All you have to do at this point is merely to stay in order. Surely that can't be as difficult as you're making it."

"It's only that . . ." She could hear the defeat in her voice and she wanted to expunge it but she no longer knew how. "It's only that her drinking is out of hand, sir."

"Do you know that or do you think that?"

"I think it," she said.

"Could your thinking be at all influenced by what you want to do and what she's telling you directly not to do?" When she didn't reply, he said, "Barbara?" and she was forced to hear the kindness in his voice, that enduring quality about him that always declared the man to be a gent.

"S'pose," she said.

"So there it is, isn't it?"

"S'pose," she admitted. "Only . . . what's to do?"

"You know the answer to that. What's to do is to obey her orders and I believe you can do that for what remains of your time together."

She said heavily for the third time, "S'pose," and was once again the recipient of the man's infuriating compassion. He said, "You don't have to like this, Barbara. No one is asking that of you, least of all me. You must merely soldier on."

"Sir," she said. "Yes, sir."

But when they rang off, she *thunked* herself onto the nunnish bed in the nunnish room into which she'd been thrust by bloody *Isabelle*. She'd wanted Lynley to intercede, to take her part, to play the bridge over her sodding troubled waters, to do something anything who even bloody knew what, and she was mightily disappointed. At the very least, she wanted him to ring the DCS, making a suggestion that would allow her—Barbara Havers—to go exactly in the direction that she wished to go. Barbara knew this. She admitted it. She owned it. But she also desperately wanted him to understand that it was the DCS who was blotting things this time, and not Barbara Havers. That, however, was not going to happen, and now she could only do what she could do.

She went to the phone. She got herself connected to Ardery's room. She told the DCS that she would be skipping dinner. Dead knackered, she told her.

Very well, was the reply. Just be packed and ready for London in the morning.

LUDLOW
SHROPSHIRE

Isabelle had placed her suitcase on her bed, but she hadn't started to pack it yet. She was waiting for the ice she'd requested to be brought to her room, and she wasn't going to begin anything till she'd made herself a nightcap. She'd insisted upon a bucket of ice this time, not three or four cubes languishing dispiritedly in a cereal bowl. Surely, she'd said to the omnipresent Peace on Earth, the hotel has an ice bucket for champagne and the like. Yes? Good. That would do.

She'd had one nightcap already, downstairs in the residents' lounge cum hotel bar, and she wasn't planning on leaving the hotel. She was fully in control and unaffected by the wine she'd drunk over dinner and the brandy she'd had afterwards. Another vodka and tonic wouldn't hurt her.

When Peace showed his face with ice bucket in his hands, Isabelle thanked him briefly and went about her business. Yes, vodka and tonic would be just fine, she decided. It would sit on top of the earlier vodka, the wine, and the brandy, but these had already moved nicely through her system, soaked up by the food she'd eaten below in the dining room.

She made her drink. She took it to the sofa that her room provided her. She sat, she drank, and she thought about the investigation: how she saw it and how the maddening Havers appeared to be determined to see it.

It seemed to Isabelle that every one of the sergeant's concerns was either inconsequential or dismissible. Why were the Crown Prosecutors not called in? Because the police complaints commission had decided that there was no criminal conduct involved. With no criminal conduct the CPS had nothing to prosecute. Why did Ruddock not remain in the room with the deacon? Because no one had told him to do so and he was never informed that the deacon had been accused of anything. What he had been told—verified by the IPCC—was that patrol officers would turn up eventually to fetch the man to Shrewsbury. As to the CCTV camera's having been swivelled in advance of the phone call: What was the point of making an anonymous phone call if a film was taken with your mug caught front and centre?

They had, Isabelle concluded, gone far beyond what Hillier had sent them up to Shropshire to do. They'd tracked down the Lomax from the deacon's diary and they'd spoken to Finnegan Freeman from the deacon's list of children's club members. They'd met up with Reverend Spencer and had a chat with Flora Bevans. They'd even interviewed the forensic pathologist despite having her full report in their possession. They could carry on in the vein that Havers appeared to want, but that was *not* why they'd been sent.

She downed the rest of her drink and rose. She experienced a moment of dizziness. On her feet too quickly after having been seated. Must watch that.

She was crossing the room to deal with her belongings when her mobile rang. She went for it and glanced at the number. Her dander rose. She was sick and tired of having to deal with Bob, his coming life of bliss in New Zealand, and his intention of ripping her own sons farther away from her than he'd already done. She took the call and said into the phone, "What else do you want? A pound of flesh?" She slurred the last bit. She straightened her spine. She walked to the window and opened it as Sandra's voice said, "Ah. Is it vodka or have you moved on to whiskey?"

Isabelle let the fresh air hit her face. She said, "What do you want?"

"That's a telling question, wouldn't you say?"

"What. Do. You. Want. Sandra."

"I'd expect you'd see the number, take note of the time, and ask at once, 'Has something happened to one of the boys?' Or even to Bob, for that matter, once you heard my voice."

"Oh, you'd expect that, would you? I, apparently, have not yet attained your level of sainthood." The *s* was difficult.

"It's not sainthood, Isabelle. It's motherhood."

God, she was a bitch. "I'm not sure how you dare to say that when you know exactly what your husband"—Isabelle said the word like a sneer. She couldn't help it—"has done to deny me any sort of motherhood I might have otherwise had."

"It *is* always about you, isn't it?" Sandra said. "And you know quite well that this has been in the hands of the courts from the first."

"Oh right. Of course. Naturally." Isabelle crossed the room to the bed. There on the bedside table sat the vodka, along with tonic and the ice. Her tongue felt dry. She would not submit. She said, "What do you want, Sandra? Have your say and be done."

"Are you aware that you're slurring your words?" was Sandra's reply. "*Have* you been drinking? But then, why do I even ask that question? You're generally drinking, aren't you."

"I'm about to ring off, as apparently you can't hear me."

"You know you can't win this," Sandra said, finally changing her tack. "I want it to stop. It's tearing Bob apart. It's tearing the boys apart. Aren't you the least concerned about that?"

"Aren't *you* the least concerned that Bob's plan is to move them permanently away from their own mother? Oh, he's offered very *generous* terms of visitation as long as visitation takes place in New Zealand."

"I'm glad you put the emphasis where it belongs, on *generous*. He's offered to let them stay with you when you're in New Zealand; he's offered to let you take them on holiday with you when you're in New Zealand. What more do you want? Where is this going to end?"

"I want my sons within range of their mother. And this will end when I have exactly that."

"You can't possibly think that any court in the land—"

"You've already made that point."

"—is going to allow you to put a spanner into Bob's advancement in his career."

"I'm not putting a spanner anywhere. He can advance as high as he likes anywhere that he likes, including Mars. What he can't do is take my sons with him."

"*His* sons," Sandra hissed. "Who have grown up in *his* household from the day of your separation, and we both know why. So don't make me say it. It's going to come out in court, you know: the drinking, the abuse."

"I did *not* abuse—"

"How many teaspoons of vodka went into their bottles? Or was it tablespoons?"

"Don't you threaten me."

Sandra gave one of her classic sighs, illustrating how reasonable she was attempting to be with a madwoman. "I'm not trying to threaten you. I'm merely pointing out what's going to come up in court."

"Let it, then. It's his word against mine."

"The word of an alcoholic. Isabelle, you need to consider all of this. You need to think about whether you truly want it. I mean what's going to come out in court, which is not going to make you look or sound like a doting mother, no matter how your solicitor spins it. The route you're taking is going to do little more than amass fees from more and more solicitors."

"Which part of that is supposed to bother me? Put Bob on the phone."

"He's with the boys. I expect you know it's their bedtime, yes? He's supervising."

"They're nine years old. They don't need supervising."

"Well, no one suggests you know your own sons. I'd like you to think about what I've said. You can consider either part: the fees that you'll be paying for at least ten years or the ruin of your career that is going to come about once we lay out the truth in court. I'd think you'll probably concentrate on the career. It's always been more important to you than James and Laurence."

She cut the call directly she said the names of Isabelle's sons. Isabelle's body had turned to pure fury.

She punched to return the call. It went directly to message. She cut it off. She rang the number again. Again it was message. She rang a third time. Again, the message. She grabbed the vodka and dashed it into her glass.

The mobile rang. She grabbed it, answered, and shrieked, "Listen to me, you *fucking* little worm. If you think you can—"

"Is that DCS Ardery?"

The room began swimming. The voice was unmistakable. AC Hillier was ringing.

She dropped onto the bed. She said, "Yesh. Yes. Sorry. I fought . . . I thought . . ." Get a bloody *grip*, she told herself. "I jusht had . . . I just had a go-round with my ex and his wife. Sorry. I thought one of 'em was ringing."

There was a pause. It was far too long. She'd thought he'd rung off, but then he said, "I've had a phone call from Quentin Walker."

Isabelle tried to squeeze from her brain a visual that went with the name. She couldn't do it. She said, "Sir?"

"The MP from Birmingham. Clive Druitt's been on to him again. He's agitating about the CPS. He's insisting on a prosecution."

She wanted to say, So is Havers, but she didn't wish the fish from that kettle to go swimming in the waters of this conversation. She said, "We haven't found a reason the CPS would prosecute, sir. They could go for dereliction of duty, but as no one told the PCSO why the vicar . . . or the deacon . . . sorry . . . why he was being brought in, they don't have a case against him."

"We need to give them something. I mean the MP and Druitt. A crumb would do. Anything you've come up with."

Isabelle tried to consider this but an ache had blossomed behind her eyes, and she wanted nothing more than to sleep, drifting off in a haze, having vodka-induced dreams. She pressed her fingers into her eyeballs.

"Are you there, Superintendent?"

She'd been drifting. She'd felt her body relaxing in the way she loved it to relax. Nothing there, nothing on her mind, bliss itself just out of reach, but she *could* reach it, she could, she could.

She roused herself. "Yesh. Here. Yes, sir. Just thinking. We've got the dead man's diary, which the complaints commission didn't have before. But all it's got inside is days and days of appointments. We can trace them all, but that'll take some time, and I'm not sure that's where we want to go anyway. So far, everything points to suicide. Havers found that the position of a CCTV camera had been changed prior to an anonymous call being made, but that's it. The IPCC didn't catch that, but it's the only thing that they didn't catch."

"Hmm. Yes. I see," Hillier said. "That might do. Write a complete report when you get back to London. We'll present it to Walker to give to Druitt."

"Will do." In her room, Isabelle saluted. She caught sight of herself in the mirror. She must have been pulling at her hair while speaking with Sandra, she thought. It was tangled and looked filthy and she wondered when she'd last had a shower, as she couldn't recall.

"What about Havers?" Hillier said. "Anything yet?"

Isabelle rose, went to the mirror, examined herself more closely, saw the lines mapping outward from her eyes. She said, "There's nothing, sir. She was heading off to Shrewsbury at one point to listen to the tape of an anonymous phone call, but I called her back as I hadn't told her to do anything other than have a look at the CCTV films."

"Had you given her an order?" he asked sharply.

"Unfortunately, no. Not definitively."

Another pause. She could picture him shaking his head in disgust. But she couldn't help the fact that Havers was keeping herself in impeccable order other than the misstep of her decision about Shrewsbury.

Hillier said, "Well, we can't bake a pie with that, can we, Superintendent?"

"She's being wily, sir. I expect she's speaking with DI Lynley each night or each morning for a pep talk."

"Ah yes, Lynley," Hillier said. His tone suggested that he wouldn't mind sending Lynley off to Berwick-upon-Tweed as well. "Carry on then, Superintendent. I'll want to see you tomorrow afternoon."

LUDLOW
SHROPSHIRE

Barbara waited a good long while before she left the hotel. She had her bag and she had her fags, and no one could question her heading out for a smoke and to scare up something to eat after not having had dinner.

She had given thought to trekking over to Lower Galdeford Street, on the chance that PCSO Ruddock was having another go with his still unmentioned female companion in the car park of the police station in Townsend Close. But so far she'd made no progress arguing with Ardery over the issue of Ruddock, the patrol car, and his female companion in her attempts to stress what the PCSO's dereliction of duty might have meant in the death of Ian Druitt. Besides, everyone knew he'd not been in the room with Ian Druitt. He'd said as much, and he'd explained what he'd been doing. But if the truth was that he'd been laying some pipe in the back seat of a parked patrol car, that was a far more serious matter than merely making phone calls to pubs from another office in the building. For if Ruddock had been shagging his lady friend in the patrol car, someone easily could have slipped into the car park, then into the building to murder the deacon, staging it as a suicide and scarpering afterwards.

Of course, staging a suicide was the sticking point, according to Nancy Scannell's examination of the body. Still, Barbara couldn't remove from her mind the photo she'd seen of the forensic pathologist and her consortium of glider owners that Rabiah Lomax had displayed in her house. That *meant* something. Barbara could feel it down to the soles of her feet.

So she was still on the trail of what had really gone on beneath the surface of what everyone claimed had gone on the night of Ian Druitt's death. That trail just now was leading her the short distance across Castle Square and through the passage to Quality Square, where her plan was to duck into the Hart and Hind for a half pint of ale and a packet of crisps or a jacket potato if one was on offer. In the pub, she intended to engage in a bit of casual conversation with anyone besides the publican who might be able to confirm Ruddock's claim that binge drinking had truly been going on the night of Druitt's death, requiring him to make phone calls to the town's pubs. She wasn't entirely sure what it would mean when she had the information. It was, at least, something she could do.

He was a nice enough bloke, Ruddock. Barbara didn't want him to lose his job because of what had happened to Druitt. But even nice blokes make serious mistakes—she liked to think of herself as nice enough and she'd made a barrel of them—and it seemed to her that Ruddock wasn't being completely honest about the exact nature of the mistake he'd made.

Inside the pub, she sauntered to the bar. The place was virtually deserted.

There were two barmen. The older of them came to take her order. It would be a half pint of Joule's Pale Ale, she told him, and if they still had jacket potatoes like those listed on the blackboard, she'd have one of them as well. He told her the jacket potatoes had been in the warmer since noon and they had seen better culinary days at this point. She told him she didn't care and if he had something to stuff them with, all the better. He said that, for stuffing, they were down to what the kitchen had in tins and how did she feel about sweet corn and butter? She said, "Bring it on. I'm not a picky eater." His look-over of her suggested that he was only too aware of that.

He saw to her half pint and then disappeared into the back where, she presumed, the kitchen was. As he did this, two individuals descended the stairs at the back of the pub beyond the bar. They were a boy and a girl—college age—and they carried a key with an overlarge fob. The boy handed this over, in addition to two twenty-pound notes, to the younger barman, who placed the money in a receptacle behind the till and returned the key to a spot beneath the bar. Interesting, Barbara thought.

When the older of the barmen returned with her jacket potato and cutlery, she said to him, "Trying to evade the revenue men, or is it just something minor—for cash—you've got on the side?"

"What's that, then?"

"Two blissful individuals of an age not to have another location for achieving bliss have just handed over a room key and some cash."

"Ah." He gave her a wolfish grin. "Sometimes individuals like a bit of privacy. I provide it."

"By the hour, I expect."

"One does what one must to keep food on the table." He treated her to a more assessing look than he'd done before, saying, "You're the type to notice things, are you?"

"With those two, it was a case of seeing, no noticing required."

He laughed briefly, said, "Typical, that is," and went on to pull a pint for an older woman whose black beehive hairdo made her look like a refugee from the 1960s. He nodded at her, said, "Georgie still giving you grief there, Doreen?" and slid the pint in her direction.

"I'm here, ain't I?" was her reply.

"You show him the door, luv, and I'm your man."

She laughed in a horselike fashion, displaying a set of teeth so crooked that an orthodontist would have had heart palpitations. "'F you say so, Jack," was her reply before she took up the drink and returned to her table.

Jack scooped up a dampish-looking rag from beneath the bar and wiped from it the rings of moisture from the people who had not yet discovered the purpose of coasters, which lay about everywhere. He said to Barbara, "I don't know you, do I."

"Know all your customers, then?"

"Generally," he told her. "Good for business." He extended his hand to her and said, "Jack Korhonen."

"Barbara Havers," she replied. She tucked into the potato, which was, at least, steaming. The kitchen had been generous with the butter as well. The tinned sweet corn was tinned sweet corn, but with the butter added the entire concoction went down a treat once she threw on some salt, some pepper, some brown sauce, and a daub of mustard, and mooshed it all round. She said, "I asked here and there for a pub and got told this was the place to be."

"Expect that's due to the location. Near to the college? That brings in the drinkers better'n naked ladies dancing round poles."

"Not so many here tonight."

"Midweek. And we're closing soon."

The younger barman was cleaning off tables, carrying glassware to the bar. He brought a load over on a tray and he slid this to Jack, saying, "Things look finished for the night up above," with an eyebrow lifted to indicate—it seemed—the rooms upstairs. "One hundred twenty pounds. Slow evening."

"Probably time to change the sheets," Jack told him. They both laughed heartily at this. Then Jack turned to Barbara and said, "You didn't say what your business was in town. Can't be a holiday 'less you do your holidaying alone."

Well, the holidaying alone part would be true, Barbara thought, when she had time to take a holiday at all. She said, "Bit of a history buff," since Ludlow appeared to be crawling with it.

"History, is it?" Jack Korhonen said. "I expect you've come to the right place, then. History of what?"

"What?" she asked him.

"History of the universe, history of England, history of the Celts or the Angles or the Saxons? What sort of history?"

"Oh," she said. "Royal, particularly the Plantagenets."

"Real brawlers, that lot," he said with a nod.

"They liked their battles. I'll give you that."

"Which of 'em interest you?"

"Battles?"

"Plantagenets."

That one put her into serious waters. She thought she might be able to name a Plantagenet, just. She could go with Edward since she did know that history was positively littered with Edwards. But she reckoned Korhonen's next question would be which Edward, and if he asked that, she was going to be sunk. Not every Edward could have been a Plantagenet. Consider Edward VIII and the woman he loved. He was a . . . what? What the hell *was* he? A Windsor? Had they even begun using the name Windsor then? Or, for that matter, had he actually *been* an Edward *VIII*? Was she confusing him with Henry VIII, whom she absolutely *knew* was not a Plantagenet if both sides of the blanket were thoroughly examined. Lynley had a first in history from Oxford, and he'd made *that* much clear to her. Or had he? Perhaps he'd been speaking of Henry VII? And why the bloody hell didn't royalty branch out and try a few new names so history wasn't so difficult anyway? King Kevin would've been just the ticket.

She settled on saying, "Well, that's just the trouble, see. I haven't settled on which one of 'em. I'm having a thorough look at what's left of the castle though. Tomorrow morning. Inspiration. One never knows."

"Ah. Edward the Fifth, then. 'Course, it could also be the Fourth as he must've lived there for a bit when he was a boy, before he was the Fourth, of course. Mary Tudor as well."

Good God, she thought. She needed to direct him away from her putative reason for being in the town. She said, "I s'pose I ought to wring the brain of some college type for inspiration, eh? Recommend anyone?"

"Couldn't possibly. Assuming you mean a lecturer, I wouldn't know a college type if he shook my hand. Long as they're here to order drinks, they c'n be whatever they want to be. It's the great equaliser, I find, drinking is. Everyone from football hooligans to the royal family likes to have a tipple. Some of them like it too much."

"Bingeing? Colleges, unis, and bingeing always seem to go together."

He looked a little cagey at this. He began wiping the bar again and he went on to polish the taps. "On the odd occasion, true. Mostly we keep things under control."

"Not like in the cities, eh?"

"Like I said, we keep it under control. And if things start going down the toilet round here, I'm luckier than the rest. Someone living in Quality Square always calls the coppers and one comes by to sort things for me. The rest 'f them?"—a jerk of his thumb over his shoulder seemed to indicate the rest of the pubs across Ludlow—"They have to sort it on their own. We had a street pastors programme for a bit: slew of do-gooders in the streets at night, gathering kids being sick in the gutters, getting them to where they're meant to be. But that went tits up, so we're back to sweeping up our messes individually."

He set to taking the glasses from the tray that had been placed on the bar. Barbara wasn't sure how to get to the information she wanted: whether on the night of Druitt's death, Gary Ruddock had been phoned about binge drinking, which he then had to handle from the police station as best he could do. For it was one thing to confirm that he did indeed at times deal with the binge drinking. It was another to get specific with Jack Korhonen about one *particular* night without inadvertently tipping Ruddock to the fact she was checking a story that the IPCC had already checked.

She was about to take a stab in that general direction when Jack Korhonen said, "There's the man now," and Barbara turned to see that Gary Ruddock had entered the pub. It seemed that he was something of a regular, for Korhonen said, "You're later'n usual."

Ruddock strolled to the bar, saying, "Couldn't get Rob to the toilet in time. A shower was required afterwards."

"Better you than me," Korhonen said.

Ruddock said to Barbara, "Your guv cool down?"

Before she could reply, Korhonen said, "You two acquainted?"

Ruddock replied with, "Barbara Havers, she's Scotland Yard."

"Is she indeed?" Korhonen asked, a smile lifting the corners of his mouth. "Now that's a pretty detail that hadn't yet come out in our confab. Mostly, we were speaking of the Plantagenets."

"Heavy going, that," Gary Ruddock said.

Barbara decided it was time for her to make tracks. She said she was off and if she could get the bill . . . ? Korhonen said, "For Scotland Yard? It's on me, madam. Come back when you reckon you know which Plantagenet you want to study, eh? Might be I c'n help you. With something."

She said right, she would do that, and all the rest. Then to Ruddock, "We're off back to London in the morning. Thanks for your help."

"Anything else I can do?"

"I wouldn't say no to hearing the recording of that phone call, by hook or by crook, if you can help there in any way."

"Oh. Right. That." Ruddock nodded and seemed to consider this.

He said, "Could be . . . I might be able to arrange for it to be sent to you."

"What's this?" Korhonen asked.

Ruddock said, "There was a 999 call about that bloke, Ian Druitt. You know. The deacon. The bloke who—"

"Oh Christ. 'Course. Him."

"The sergeant and I were on our way to give a listen to the recording made when she got called back by her guv." Then he added to Barbara, "I can give it a go."

"Thanks," she said. "Much appreciated." She nodded at them both and left the pub. She'd got very little for her efforts, merely confirmation that binge drinking went on and that Gary Ruddock dealt with it. It was less than nothing, really. If Ruddock managed to get his mittens on the recorded phone call, there might be something in that. But there was nothing else to hang her hopes on.

Outside, bright lights shone on the tables, chairs, and furled umbrellas that constituted the pub's outdoor seating area, empty now of anyone. Beyond the short lane leading to that terrace, Quality Square opened. She could see how the noise from outdoor drinkers would be a real irritant to anyone living in the vicinity. The square was small, so noise would echo, and although it was mostly lined with shops, there were accommodations above each of them, in addition to two ancient dwellings. No doubt both the dwellings and the accommodations were occupied by people who didn't take lightly to pissed college kids conglomerating beneath their windows.

Barbara left the way she'd come, through the passage and into Castle Square. There, she was no longer alone. She saw the Alsatian first because he was at rest on the pavement a short distance away, in front of a cheese shop along Church Street, his head on his paws. In the shadows of the shop doorway, what looked like a heap of bedding was propped up. It moved lumpishly. An arm emerged. Harry had evidently found his spot for dossing, and Barbara decided to give conversation a go.

The Alsatian raised his head as she approached. A low growl issued from the dog's throat. Harry said, "Steady on, Pea," and changed his position slightly. He'd been leaning up against one wall of the entry since it was too narrow for him to recline. He patted the ground just next to his bedding—Barbara could tell it was a sleeping bag of indeterminate age and indeterminate cleanliness—and he brought forth a torch, which he shone up into her face. As if the torch were a command, Pea began to rise. The man said, "Stay back," and Barbara halted at once as she didn't fancy tangling with a dog looking like an extra from a film about Nazis.

The man said, "Oh. Sorry. I didn't mean you. I meant Sweet Pea. She worries about me rather too much. Down, Pea. She looks all right, girl."

The man's voice was a complete surprise. He sounded like a newsreader on the telly: all received pronunciation and the like, the kind of voice rarely heard in these days of displaying one's roots with pride. Barbara didn't know what she'd been expecting, but it wasn't this.

She said, "You're Harry."

"And my pleasure in speaking to you would be . . . ?"

"Barbara Havers," she said. "New Scotland Yard."

"Those are words I certainly never expected to hear." He set down the torch and began to remove himself from the bedding. She told him it was fine by her for him to remain where he was. If she could have a word, she'd be grateful, she told him.

"Certainly," he told her. "As long as this isn't a governmental programme to move individuals off the streets."

"Is there a programme to do that?"

"I haven't the least idea. But I recognise that this can always happen, political movements being what they are. Some people, I find—and particularly politicians—do so dislike the sight of anyone sleeping rough in city centres and towns. Which is why, frankly, I used to remain in the countryside. Mostly just beyond villages. One sometimes needs to take advantage of shops and post offices and banks and the like."

"But no longer?"

"I beg your pardon?"

"It's no longer the countryside for you?"

"Alas, no. I've become rather too old, and I require a bit more shelter."

He gestured to the recessed doorway. "And, to be frank, my sister likes to know she can contact me in an emergency, although what that emergency would be, I have never been able to ascertain. Please, though, you must allow me to rise. This feels decidedly awkward, and if I continue in this position, I'll only end up with a crick in my neck."

He didn't wait for permission. He struggled out of the sleeping bag and brushed himself off. He picked up the torch and stood. He was tall and rangy. Closer to him, Barbara could see that he was also shaved, and although his greying hair was too long, it was clean. He switched the torch off. "Saving the battery," he explained. "And you do look harmless."

"I like to think I am. Can we go somewhere to talk?" she asked him.

He smiled, as she could see from the dim light of a streetlamp some twenty yards away. "Claustrophobe, I'm afraid," he said regretfully. "It will have to be in the open air."

"That's why you sleep rough? A room with all the windows open won't do for you?"

"Unfortunately, no, although it did at one time. And aren't you a fine detective, Barbara Havers. Look at the information you've gleaned from me so quickly. What is your rank, by the way? I'd prefer to eschew the familiarity of referring to you by your given names."

"I'm a detective sergeant. The name's fine, by the way. Barbara, I mean."

"Not when one is brought up as I was. Detective Sergeant Havers, I'm Henry Rochester. Harry, as you've learned. How might a conversation with me be helpful to you?"

"I've seen you here and there in town, Mr. Rochester. Flogging things in the market as well."

"Please. Harry."

"Barbara, then."

"Very well. It's only fair, isn't it. Barbara. And yes, I do get round a bit. Mostly in the centre of town, as I like the atmosphere. Surrounded by history, you know. One can almost hear the phantom sounds of horses' hooves as the Yorks come galloping out of the castle."

Barbara wasn't about to go there again. Still, she said, "You're a historian?"

"I was once. But that was in the days when an open window would suffice, and I could operate within a classroom. History was my subject."

"Must be tough, letting all of that go."

"I find that acceptance of life's vicissitudes is the sole requirement for contentment. My material needs are small, and when they arise, they're taken care of nicely, as modern banking allows me to access my funds at cash points. Thanks to my father's fascination with various economical ways to dry one's hands in public, something of a fortune—if you'll pardon me for being so crude as to mention money—was amassed and then left to me and to my sister. Catherine would, of course, prefer that I live other than as I do, but she's able to force her concerns about me into submission. Thus, I go through life unburdened."

"And in the fresh air."

"And in the fresh air."

"Inclement weather isn't a problem? Winter either?"

"I am, fortunately, quite robust. I do have an acquaintance here in town who insists I take shelter sometimes in an area beneath his home that's entirely open to the air, and he also allows me to store my winter belongings there. Heavier clothing, heavier sleeping bag, and the like. Altogether, I consider myself most blessed."

They'd strolled together to Castle Square, where several benches allowed one to rest while viewing Ludlow Castle's crenellated walls, brightly lit as usual. Sweet Pea accompanied them, remaining at Harry Rochester's side and settling at his feet when he and Barbara sat.

"May I ask what brings you to Ludlow?" Harry said to her.

"The death at the police station in March. Have you heard about it?" Barbara had little hope Harry might know about Ian Druitt's death. She reckoned his newspaper reading was somewhat limited due to his life in the streets. The same went for his telly viewing, she supposed.

But he surprised her. "Oh yes. Poor man."

"Did you know Ian Druitt?" Barbara brought out her fags and offered one to Harry. He said thank you, no, as he'd given them up. But then he changed his mind and said a mere *one* couldn't hurt, could it. Barbara assured him that the time he spent in the fresh air no doubt negated the harm of the weed, and she repeated her question once she'd offered Harry her plastic lighter.

"Not to speak to him at any length greater than it took to refuse his offer of an anorak one night. I did see him about. But I tend to see everyone out and about at one point or another. Some of them I know, others I merely recognise."

"Sleeping rough like you are, no one tries to move you along? Town council asking someone to have a word?"

"You mean the police? No, that hasn't happened. You must know, I expect, that we have no regular police constables in the town. The police presence is confined only to Officer Ruddock."

"The PCSO," Barbara said. "You know him, then."

"As his job is to maintain order in the streets, I know who he is. But I couldn't say I actually know him."

"Does he attempt to move you along?"

"Only on the odd occasion when I've set up in a spot that causes someone to lodge a complaint. I do try to be careful about that, but there are times I misread a location. Restaurants, I find, do not take well to someone dossing in their doorways, even after hours."

"Any other spots he moves you away from?"

"Primary schools don't go down well. But I expect Mr. Ruddock mostly sees me as harmless as I actually am because it's generally 'Hallo there, Harry, hope you're staying out of trouble,' and that's it. Unless, of course, I find a few things that want selling in the market square. I do have to say that Officer Ruddock isn't pleased when I do that, as I have no license to be a vendor."

Barbara sucked in on her fag and nodded at this, saying, "I saw him having a word with you today. But why do you flog things in the market when you don't need the money?"

Harry flicked ash onto the cobbles, took another hit, then carefully ground the cigarette out beneath his shoe. He picked the dog-end up and put it into his pocket. "I do so hate to see anything go to waste," he told her.

For a moment she thought he meant the cigarette, but then she twigged he was referred to selling items in the market. "Clobber you find, you mean?"

"People are remarkable when it comes to what they throw away. I rescue it and sell it. Occasionally Officer Ruddock takes exception. He's an equal opportunity policeman, however. He rousts everyone else who's selling illegally as well."

"Sounds like he doesn't give anyone real aggro."

"He might do, but he's never to me. I find him a decent bloke with a tiresome job on his hands. I don't like to make it more difficult than it already is."

"Why tiresome?" she asked.

"I should say tiresome *looking*. To me, that is. Walking round neighbourhoods in town, checking locks on shop doors, collecting drunken college students in the street, driving them home when they're too inebriated to be on the road, let alone behind the wheel of a car."

"Did you see him on the night Ian Druitt died, by any chance? Officer Ruddock was asked to fetch him to the station, and they would have been coming from the church, St. Laurence's. This was in March."

Harry scratched his head. "That would be difficult for me to recall. Most nights look to me like other nights, and as a result, things blend together. Is there anything that might distinguish this particular night, aside from Mr. Druitt's death?"

Barbara thought about this. Harry Rochester was correct, of course. People did not generally recall what occurred on a given night in their lives unless they were creatures of such compulsive habit that any variation would throw them into hopeless disarray. There was a chance, however, that one small detail might help him. She said, "Does it help to know there was binge drinking going on? Officer Ruddock wasn't able to take care of it as he usually does, so it might well have gone on for some time."

Harry said, "Alas. Binge drinking is an unfortunate feature of life in Ludlow. It happens several times a month. Officer Ruddock generally deals with it, but I couldn't possibly tell you if there was a night he failed to do this."

"On this night, it probably would have gone on for a while because he would have had to take care of it by phone."

Harry mused on this, and then said, "I can't say how successful that might have been, to tell you the truth. Generally, he handles bingeing in person."

"Doing what?"

"Now that would be difficult for me to say exactly. I assume he begins by clearing the drinkers out of pubs, after which he moves them off the streets. But the only part of what he does that I've actually *seen* is when he loads one or two or more into his car and drives them home. At least I assume he's driving them home. I suppose he could be taking them to the police station to . . . what is the term? . . . to dry out. Truthfully, though, I have no way of knowing. There's the man now, though. You could ask him."

Barbara had been facing away from the passage into Quality Square as she talked to Harry. Now she pivoted and saw that Gary Ruddock had just emerged. He saw them and raised a hand in greeting, although he didn't approach.

He called out genially, "You two stay out of trouble," and walked to his car, which he'd left just beyond the entrance to West Mercia College. He climbed inside and drove into Dinham Street, which would, Barbara reckoned, put him onto the route to his home. She found herself wondering—post helping old Rob shower—what had brought him out on this night at all.

# 8 MAY

VICTORIA
LONDON

Isabelle Ardery was aiming for patience as she waited for the assistant commissioner to return from lunch. According to Judi-with-an-i, Sir David had gone to Marylebone, meeting a nameless political powerbroker for a discussion about broking political power. Judi was privy to no additional information. That the assistant commissioner was long past due she was willing to reveal. Traffic, doubtless, was its usual nightmare. She *had* suggested that Sir David might want to go by Underground. But, well, one knew Sir David.

Isabelle recognised the implied ellipsis at the end of the sentence. Yes, indeed, she thought. One could hardly visualise David Hillier besmirching any part of himself with a ride via public transport from St. James's Park station to Baker Street and back again. Since there was no direct route to Marylebone, he would assure himself that it was far better to have a car take him, no matter how late that rendered him.

She was prickling over much of her body. She knew what it would take to soothe her anxiety about the coming meeting with her superior officer, but she couldn't afford to do anything other than try to cope. The unexpected phone call from the assistant commissioner on the previous night might have seriously dented her professional reputation. She had to take care of that, and shortly after awakening that morning in Shropshire, she'd come up with the plan to do so.

She'd begun by dealing with the rest of the vodka. There had been merely three inches left—perhaps a bit more. She downed only half of it, and she'd poured the rest down the bathroom basin. She tossed the bottle in the rubbish, and she told herself that *that* was it. Being rung up on the previous night by Sir David Hillier had constituted exactly what she needed to put an end to all this drinking nonsense.

Shortly thereafter, Peace on Earth had knocked her up with the early morning coffee she'd ordered. She drank it all as she dressed, so by the time she met Barbara Havers turning in her room key at the front desk, she felt entirely herself.

The sergeant's first words to her were, "Got some news, guv," which did not constitute music to Isabelle's ears. She said in reply, "Keep it until we've negotiated our route to the motorway, Sergeant."

Havers opened her mouth, seemed to think better of whatever she intended to say, then shut it. She kept it shut till they reached the M5. Isabelle barely had time to accelerate before the DS began her recitation. They'd not had breakfast, so Isabelle had been in hope that Havers would hold her tongue and her flapping lips until they'd at least got to a Welcome Break, but such was not the case. The bloody woman spoke as if she, too, had downed a large cafetière of coffee the moment she'd rolled out of bed.

She recited as if ticking items off a list, including details and confirmations of alleged facts that she'd not been asked to confirm in the first place. Listening to all of it, Isabelle understood that once again the sergeant had gone walkabout during the previous night. Her excuse of "looking for something to eat, guv, after the kitchen was closed" was so ridiculous that Isabelle wanted to interrupt her by asking exactly how dim the sergeant thought she was.

Havers obviously did not want an interruption as she piled the information on, just below the speed of light. Yes, Ludlow had trouble with binge drinking among the young people; yes, the PCSO was frequently charged with dispersing binge drinkers; and "this is what's interesting," there was also an eyewitness account of the PCSO sometimes piling drinkers into his car for delivery to . . . wherever. Possibly to their parents, to the police station, to their accommodations, or to . . . the eyewitness couldn't say. He turned out to be an individual by the name of Harry Rochester, who slept rough in the town.

Isabelle interrupted the general flow with, "It's commendable that you've sought more confirmation for the PCSO's story, but I'm not seeing your point."

"It's this. What Harry *can't* confirm is that there was binge drinking going on the night when Druitt was arrested."

Isabelle would have closed her eyes to shut all of this off had she not been driving. As it was, she saw the sign that gave two miles as the distance to the Welcome Break, and she sent thanks heavenward for her deliverance. She said, "Let's stop for breakfast, Sergeant," and when Havers looked determined to carry on, she added, "Let's speak more after we've eaten."

Havers's enthusiasm about relating her various discoveries had not curbed her appetite, Isabelle discovered. Although there were more fashionable—not to mention nutritious—offerings like fruit, yoghurt, and nuts from a Caffè Nero, the sergeant went for the full English breakfast available cafeteria-style. For her part, Isabelle chose a latte and a banana from Caffè Nero, whereupon she joined the sergeant at a table and watched her tuck into watery scrambled eggs, sausage, grilled tomatoes, baked beans, mushrooms, toast, and a triangle of something that looked like breaded cardboard. She also had a pot of tea into which she dashed milk and several packets of sugar.

"Now," Havers said between mouthfuls, "what's interesting is that the IPCC never talked to Harry Rochester, guv. They didn't even know he was involved."

"I can't see that he *was* involved." Isabelle had taken to drinking lattes through a straw. It was so much easier than doing battle with a takeaway cup and its frustrating plastic top, she found. She took a pull of it, found it lukewarm, sighed, and thought about taking it back. Too much trouble, she decided, rather like Sergeant Havers. "From what you've just told me, Mr. Rochester's sole contribution to our knowledge is that, yes, binge drinking goes on in Ludlow."

"But, like I said, he doesn't remember if there was any drinking that night, guv."

"Can I point out that what a vagrant recalls or doesn't recall is hardly substantial because he *is* a vagrant?"

"This bloke's no vagrant," Havers countered. She waved her fork for emphasis, a slice of the sausage hanging perilously upon it. "He lives rough, true. But he's claustrophobic."

"Ah. Well. The fact that a claustrophobic individual who domiciles in doorways cannot recall whether there was binge drinking going on on a particular night more than two months ago is—"

"But the IPCC's report says that the Hart and Hind publican *did* confirm it. It also says that the other pubs in town confirm that Gary Ruddock rang them up like he said, leaving Ian Druitt time to string himself to a doorknob. But here's what's interesting, guv, the owner of the Hart and Hind has a little business going on on the side that he'd probably like Ruddock to turn a blind eye to—I'm talking about the rooms he lets out by the hour, it seems—so he's got reason to go along with whatever Ruddock asks him to say, right? And all those other pub owners Ruddock rang . . . ? When you think about it, they had no way of knowing there was bingeing going on that night in Quality Square. They only know what Ruddock *told* them was going on. What we have could mean—"

"Sergeant, stop." Isabelle pointed out to Havers what she had been pointing out every which way since they'd first arrived in Ludlow: what their job was. When she'd done so, she added, "Our part now is to get to London and to write the report that we've been asked to submit to Hillier to give to Quentin Walker, after which our part is to get back to our own work. I hope you see that, Sergeant."

"I do. Except—"

"I also hope you're about to say that you're planning to commence working on that report the moment we arrive in Victoria Street."

Havers averted her eyes. She looked down for a moment before she answered. "Yes, ma'am."

"I'm happy to hear it."

Isabelle had checked on Havers before coming over to Tower Block. The sergeant had been beavering away. Now her own part was to speak with the assistant commissioner, and she was relieved when he finally showed up, twenty minutes later than scheduled and with a meeting to attend in just ten more minutes.

He was speaking on his mobile as he came out of the lift, saying, "It's *parents'* day, Laura, not grandparents' day. Please inform Catherine that her father will not be attending as he has more important things to do than watching all the mummies engage in a pancake race . . . Of course I'm joking . . . No. I cannot be there . . . Darling, no. I'll see you tonight . . . Of course." He shoved the mobile into his jacket and said to Isabelle, "Seven grandchildren at school are six too many. Have you a report?"

He opened his office door and made a gesture for her to enter. He said to Judi-with-an-i, "I'll need to cancel Stanwood. Schedule something next week. First thing in the morning," before following Isabelle inside and shutting the door behind them. The fact that he made no offer of coffee, tea, or water indicated that he wasn't going to give her more than a few minutes.

She said to him, "Sergeant Havers is seeing to it, sir. I'll have it to you by the end of the day. Or tomorrow morning at the latest."

"Then why are you and I meeting?"

Isabelle readied herself. She needed to be apologetic but not submissive. "I wanted to apologise for last evening."

He hadn't told her to sit and he didn't himself sit. He merely stood at the corner of his desk and took her in and allowed her to take him in: a big man, full head of iron grey hair, always slightly florid of face, handsome without being the least bit pretty. He would seek to intimidate her. She would seek not to be intimidated.

"What about last evening?" he asked.

"I'd taken a sleeping pill. My former husband and I are in a dispute that's been weighing on my mind, and on the occasional night I have trouble sleeping. Your call last night awakened me. I'm terribly sorry."

He was silent. She reckoned he was comparing her story to what she'd actually said on the phone when she'd assumed Bob was ringing her. She knew that she hadn't sounded like someone coming groggily awake from sleep unless, of course, she'd been having a nightmare and assumed the phone call was part of that dream. Hardly likely. But she'd known the second she heard Hillier's voice that she was going to have to have this conversation with him.

She added, "I rarely have to use the pills. I'm afraid they're of the don't-take-if-operating-heavy-equipment variety. I've actually never spoken on the phone to anyone once I've taken a dose and . . . well, I hope you understand, sir."

Still, he was silent. Damn the man. He was generally readable, but that wasn't the case now. She could feel the backs of her knees dampening. She was, she told herself sternly, one hundred percent Isabelle Jacqueline Ardery now, and she fully intended to remain that way. There was enough on the line.

When he finally spoke, it was to say abruptly, "What are we giving to Walker? He's going to want something to hand over to this Druitt fellow in Birmingham. What's it going to be?"

"When Sergeant Havers completes the report, I'll give it a look," Isabelle told him. "If anything needs . . . further work on her part, I'll instruct the sergeant to do it. I met with Mr. Druitt, sir, and I didn't find him unreasonable. He's in great distress over his son, as you can imagine. But as no one can ever know another person entirely—particularly a child grown into an adult—I do think he'll see reason."

"Which is what?"

"That while his son might not have been what he was accused of being—a paedophile—the fact that he killed himself with no evidence to indicate there was anything like foul play suggests that he did have a reason to do it, even if we can't say exactly what that reason was. And Mr. Druitt must come to understand that it *was* suicide, and that it's actually no one's remit to find a reason for it. Neither the first investigating officer—DI Pajer—nor the IPCC were looking for a reason, nor were they expected to. They were investigating exactly what happened that night and in the aftermath. We can add to that that we're happy enough to turn our report over to the CPS—in fact I do suggest that, as our best next step if Druitt remains unhappy—but as neither the IPCC nor we have found a case to prosecute, the likelihood of the Druitt family getting a prosecution is very remote."

Hillier hadn't taken his eyes off her, which Isabelle felt was rather more intimidating than necessary. She and he were, after all, supposed to be on the same side. She decided she had said enough, and she would wait for his reply. Through his bank of office windows, she could see a flock of pigeons flying in magical unison against a true blue sky. Until he spoke, she would watch them.

Hillier finally said, "Yes. I like that. I think that will do very well."

"Thank you, sir," she replied. "And again, I'm terribly sorry—"

"Take them often, do you?"

It was the abruptness that warned her to have a care. She said, "Sorry?"

"Those . . . pills of yours. Do you take them often?"

"Rarely, sir. Hardly ever, in fact."

"Good. See that it stays that way. We'd hate to lose you to making a mistake with them one night."

"Of course, sir."

He went to the user side of his desk, an indication that their meeting was over. She thanked him for his time and turned to leave. She was at the door, her hand on the knob, when he spoke again.

"Keep on with Sergeant Havers, will you? There will be something. Just give her time."

"Yes, sir."

"And rope," he added. "Of course she'll need rope."

VICTORIA
LONDON

At least the journey back to London hadn't been as trying as the trip to Ludlow had been. Given, it had begun early, but Barbara had long ago set her mobile's alarm to play the final moments of the *1812 Overture* at a casual suggestion from DI Lynley, and it did the trick when required to do so, virtually catapulting her out of bed the moment the cannons began to fire. She was in her tiny bathroom when a knock on her door turned out to be Peace on Earth with a tray of early morning coffee. He'd just delivered one to "your companion," he said, and he reckoned she might do with one herself. It was on the house, he told her. He looked as sympathetic as a bloke with overlarge earlobes could look at half past five in the morning.

She'd been discouraged at first that there was to be no breakfast at the hotel prior to their departure. But then the Welcome Break had come along, as had DCS Ardery's invitation to get stuck in. She was glad she'd done so, because when they finally arrived in Victoria Street Ardery assigned her the task of writing a report that would prove fully acceptable to AC Hillier. She was to have it completed by four o'clock,

Ardery informed her. She added that she would be waiting to have a thorough look at it the moment Sergeant Havers had completed it and *before* the DS set off for home.

This, Barbara knew, was verbal shorthand for what she herself was meant to do. There were certain requirements attached to this piece of writing, and if they weren't met, she was going to have to alter the report until all parties were satisfied with it.

She'd got nowhere with her recommendation that listening to the 999 call ought to take precedence over writing a report that was to be presented to a member of Parliament and, potentially, to a grieving father. Ardery had maintained her position that a recorded call wasn't going to get them anywhere new. To this she'd added that she was "truly getting tired of hearing you bang on about it, Sergeant, since all you argue is that it must be listened to without presenting any clear reason for doing so. *Have* you a reason that I've missed in all the backing and forthing we've done on the topic?"

"It's just a feeling," was what Barbara had said with resignation. She set to on the report. Four o'clock was still four o'clock and she knew Ardery would show up at her desk at 4:03 if Sergeant Havers did not present herself and her report in the DCS's office at the prescribed hour.

She was industriously at it when her mobile rang. It was Gary Ruddock, telling her he'd managed to get the recording of the 999 call per her request. He'd sent it as an attachment in an email. Had she listened to it yet?

"I haven't," she told him. "I've been caught up with the bloody report for my superiors. But ta, Gary. I hope you didn't have to pull many strings."

"Only a few," he replied. "Let me know if there's something in the recording that strikes you, eh?"

She said she would do. She took a moment to check her email, figuring that Ardery wasn't going to pop up beside her like a funfair shooting game's target. She found his message first: *Hears the recording. You mite find something in it. Let me know if you need anthing esle.*

Bloody hell, she thought. No wonder the poor bloke couldn't go beyond the level of PCSO. She was surprised he'd made it that far.

She got onto the attachment and fished in her desk for a headset or earbuds. There were none to be found, which was no surprise. But Winston Nkata was her polar opposite when it came to being prepared for anything. He tossed her his.

She listened to the message. She had the transcript of it memorised, and she found that the message itself was word-for-word identical to it, as Ardery had pointed out to her that it would be. So she listened again. And then again. She wanted to recognise the voice, but the message was—no surprise, really—whispered. Still, she wanted a *gotcha!* moment, although she would have settled for a mere *aha!* or a mild *very interesting.* But there was sod all to hang even a hope on. The sibilant *s*'s present in the words of the caller could easily have been part of the intent to disguise the speaker's identity. At the end of the day, she had to admit that it could have been anyone standing at the doorway to the police station making the phone call: from the local dustman to Dracula.

Then she noticed.

As she was about to log off, she saw the date upon which the call had been made: nineteen days before the deacon had been taken to the police station. That detail had been mentioned nowhere, yet it suggested something that wanted noting. In the nineteen days between the phone call and the arrest of Ian Druitt, *something* had to have been going on, and what that something was had to have been an investigation giving enough cause to bring the man in. But if that was the case—and it certainly seemed logical to assume so—then why was there no evidence *anywhere* that some sort of preliminary look into Ian Druitt had occurred?

*This*, she told herself, was something. *This*, she assured herself, was a detail that DCS Ardery had to be told about. *This*, she concluded, shed light on everything that had happened in Ludlow, although the light it shed illuminated the fact that the deacon was probably exactly what the anonymous call declared him to be: a paedophile.

She was turning this over in her mind when Dorothea Harriman showed up at her desk, wearing one of her summery frocks, probably with the hope of encouraging the weather to behave. "Detective Sergeant Havers," she said. "How did it go?"

"Kept my nose clean, more or less," Barbara told her. "The occasional use of a handkerchief might have been necessary, but you're not hearing that story from me."

Dorothea tapped a stiletto-adorned foot. "I was actually referring to the practice sessions. Tell me you did them nightly."

"Like a trooper," Barbara lied.

"Good."

"Glad you approve."

"Because we've got only two weeks left till the audition for solos and small group performances." When Barbara looked at her blankly, Dorothea said, "The dance recital? July? Now, what *I* think is that you and I could do a two-person number. Or we could ask one of the Muslim girls to join us and make it three. I'm thinking Umaymah. She's definitely the most serious of that lot, and with a Cole Porter tune . . ."

Speaking of tunes, Barbara thought. Time to tune out. What she also thought was that when it came to tap dancing at a public performance, it would be done over or upon her dead body. As Dorothea rattled on, Barbara finally said, "Oh, see here, Dee, I'm nothing compared to the two of you. I'm less than zero. Negative ten or whatever. But you and Umaymah? You should have a go."

"Nonsense. You're more than enough for what I have in mind. If we use that Cole Porter number . . . 'Anything Goes.' You know it, right?"

"If Buddy Holly didn't sing it, I'm clueless."

"Well, never mind that. You're going to love it. And if you're worried about Umaymah being one of us, we can let Kaz decide. I'll come by for you tonight round half past, as usual, by the way."

This reminded Barbara, to her chagrin, that tonight was a dance class evening. She thanked her stars she had nothing with her suitable for class save her tap shoes, which were in her suitcase where she'd obediently stored them for carting up to Ludlow, where she'd avoided putting them on. She said, "Haven't the right clothes with me, Dee."

Dorothea fluttered her fingers. "Not a problem. I have an extra leotard. And don't tell me you can't possibly fit into it because just look at you, Detective Sergeant Havers. You've slimmed down so much that you're a mere . . . a mere whatever of what you used to be. Which do you prefer then, the red or the black?"

"Red," Barbara said with a sigh. "Matches my shoes."

Dorothea said she would see to it, then, and off she went on her stilettos. Barbara watched her go and wished for her to trip on something and break her kneecap on the way back to her realm.

No such luck.

VICTORIA
LONDON

Thomas Lynley was leaving for the day when Barbara Havers turned up at the side of the Healey Elliott in the underground car park. She was carrying a manila folder with her, and her expression told him that her report on the doings in Ludlow had been rejected.

He lowered the window. "Who was it?"

She said, "Ardery. The only saving grace is that I won't be able to go to a bloody tap-dancing lesson tonight because I'll be here doing this."

"Saving grace indeed. Get in, Sergeant."

"I'm not going anywhere, according to Ardery."

"Neither am I, apparently. But at least we can both sit." He switched off the Healey Elliott's engine as Havers rounded the car, opened the door, and plopped into the passenger's seat.

He said, "What's wrong with the report?"

He'd known, of course, that she'd been assigned to write it. She'd been hard at work upon it since she'd arrived in London with the DCS. He himself had brought her a sandwich and a cup of tea at half past three. She'd not left her desk save to use the ladies', not even slithering into the stairwell for a smoke.

"There was something the IPCC missed, sir. I put it in the report. I gave the report to the guv. She ordered that missing bit taken out."

"What was it?"

"A timeline issue, nineteen days, that they didn't make a note of or didn't notice in the first place."

"And your opinion?"

"That they didn't notice. I barely did myself. But what I reckoned is that there's also an investigation that someone in Shropshire did between the time of an anonymous call to 999 and the night that this bloke Druitt was arrested and died at the station. But if I put any of that in the report—that there's probably been an investigation of Druitt that the IPCC didn't get hold of—then it means this bloke's dad isn't going to be happy. And neither is Hillier."

"I see."

"So I can do what she's telling me to do: take the timeline issue out of my report. Or I can leave it in and send this along"—she lifted the folder containing the original report—"to the dead bloke's dad or to his MP. But if I take the information out . . . well, you know what it means. How many ways is *cover-up* spelled?"

"Christ."

"He's not available just now. You are. What should I do?"

Lynley hadn't the first idea what to tell her. She could read the future as well as he. If she deleted what Isabelle had ordered her to delete, she not only engaged in police malfeasance, she also stood in contravention to what she herself believed in. If she kept the information within the report and bypassed her superior officer by sending it onward to the dead man's father or his MP, she was finished at the Met and she might be finished in policing as well.

He said, "I can't possibly tell you what your decision should be. You know that."

"S'pose I do," she said.

"The only direction I can give you is to consider what the additional information might do for the dead man's father."

"You mean it might tell him his kid was a bona fide paedophile."

"I don't know," he said. "But let me ask you this: How did you come by this information?"

"That there must be a report somewhere? Because I asked Ruddock to get me the recording of the anonymous message if he could. He managed to get it and he sent it along. The date was on it and that date was *seriously* before anyone got round to ordering an arrest of the bloke."

"Had Isabelle asked you to listen to that recording?"

Havers shook her head. "She told me . . . well, she more or less ordered me not to, sir, since we have the transcript. But then Ruddock rang me and said he'd sent it and I reckoned five minutes away from writing the report wouldn't be so bad."

"In other words, you went against her orders?"

Havers was silent. Someone passed behind the Healey Elliott and Lynley caught a glimpse of their fellow officer, Philip Hale, on his way to his car. He was with Winston Nkata, and they were deep in conversation, so they didn't catch sight of Havers and him also in conversation, which was just as well.

She finally said, "I expect that's how it might look. Only—"

"Barbara, this could well be a case when there is no *only*. There is merely what you were ordered to do."

She nodded, but she was studying him as if she wanted something more, which he could not and would not give her. She said, "She keeps telling me—she *kept* telling me—that this and that weren't part of our brief."

"Was that the truth?"

"Reckon," she said.

"There you have it," was his conclusion.

But when, drooping of posture, she left him, he didn't head for Belsize Park, where he was expected at the home of Daidre Trahair. Instead, he sat in the car and thought. Ultimately, he rang Daidre, telling her something had come up and he would be late. Then he went for the lifts.

When he walked into Isabelle's office, he found her packing up to go home for the day, cleaning off her desktop by sweeping things into drawers and stowing a stack of files into a leather satchel. She looked up from what she was doing and said, "Ah. She's spoken to you. Of course, she would do. Let me be clear and save you the trouble of whatever you came to talk me into or out of. I've told her that I want the new report on my desk when I walk in tomorrow morning, and if she has to spend the night at her computer writing it, then that's exactly what she's going to do. So if you're here to interfere in some way, might I foreshorten our coming conversation by telling you that she has her orders, I have mine, and you have yours. That's how the system is meant to work, Tommy."

"And what, precisely, are my orders just now, guv?"

"To stay out of affairs that don't concern you." She finished with the folders and clipped the satchel closed. She was standing, so they were eye to eye as she was quite tall and, with heels of a mere two inches on her shoes, she matched him in height. "I realise that this isn't exactly part of your modus operandi, but on the remote possibility that it might become just that, I can be clearer if you request it."

"What happens to Barbara Havers does concern me," he told her. "We've worked together a good many years and I'd like to continue to do so. I don't want to see her transferred to the north for reasons having to do with her failure to obey an order requesting an obfuscation of the truth."

"Honestly, Tommy," Ardery said irritably. "Can we attempt to have a conversation in which you *don't* sound like an Oxford don? It's extremely off-putting, not to mention annoying. And anyway, I know why you use that tone and that manner of speech with me. But the real question is: what exactly is the social distance gaining you?"

Lynley had had enough conversations with Isabelle Ardery—both professional and personal—to recognise a verbal derailment when he heard one. He said, "Barbara believes that if she includes in her report what she sees as an important piece of information that was either missed, ignored, or deleted by someone at the IPCC—"

"Are you actually suggesting that someone at the complaints commission—with absolutely no reason to do so—would have *deliberately* left out a detail crucial to their own investigation? As I've tried to make clear to Sergeant Havers, Tommy, they were looking into the immediate circumstances surrounding the death of Mr. Druitt, full stop. They were not there to conduct an investigation into the reasons for his arrest, and because of this, it wasn't our remit to do that either. Sergeant Havers has had an impossibly difficult time seeing things that way. At the moment, I'm putting that down to her being more used to taking an active part in a murder investigation and not an investigation having to do with a report made by the IPCC.

I can, of course, adjust my thinking on this matter. Say the word. Is that what you would have me do?"

He had to admire her adroitness in shifting the focus onto him. He said, "Isn't it to everyone's benefit to get to the truth?"

"What truth exactly? Sergeant Havers and I went beyond our remit as it was. We spoke with the dead man's landlady, we looked into information we found in his diary, we tracked down a woman who'd met with him some half a dozen times before he died, I myself spoke to a college boy who assisted him at a children's club in town, and the sergeant questioned a pub owner as well as a vagrant who'd seen the sort of binge drinking that the PCSO was asked to handle by phone on that night. Barbara has read every report a dozen times, we've questioned the pathologist who performed the postmortem examination, and . . . Really, must I go on? Because it seems to me that what you're arguing—"

"Isabelle, I'm not arguing at all."

"—is that *unless* we can prove or disprove something that's impossible to prove or disprove without witnesses or corroborating evidence—and I'm speaking of the paedophilia here—then the entire investigation is at fault. I don't agree with that assessment. And *do* stop calling me Isabelle. Now, if you don't mind, it's been an extraordinarily long day and I'm going home."

He was quiet for a moment, considering whether the point had finally been reached when he would have to speak. He went to the office door and closed it.

She said, "We've completed our discussion, Inspector."

He replied with, "She knows how hard you hit it in Ludlow. She spoke to me about it while you were there."

She didn't speak. But he saw her fingers spread against her thigh, and the whiteness beneath her nails was an indication of how much pressure she was applying.

"You've got to see where this is going to lead," he told her, "and you can't avoid seeing where it's led already."

"First of all," she said with a deadly kind of quiet, "you are seriously out of order, Inspector. There is nothing in the moderate amount of drink I take that need concern you or anyone else. Second, I don't appreciate Sergeant Havers playing copper's nark. In her present position, that not only doesn't become her, it also endangers her."

"Which is why she expressed her concern only to me. May we sit for a moment, guv?" He indicated the two chairs in front of her desk.

"We may not. I think I've made myself clear that there's nothing more to talk about. If the sergeant wishes to draw a conclusion about me and pass it along to you and God knows who else—"

"She won't have done that."

"Which part? No, don't answer. She's already done the first part, hasn't she. She's spoken to you without bothering to give me the slightest indication of her uneasiness. Which, by the way, was quite simple for her to shrug off, apparently, as she was happy enough to take the opportunity of doing some drinking herself."

"For God's sake, Isabelle, what else was she supposed to do? You have her boxed in in such a way that any move she makes might well be enough to send her packing north. She was afraid to refuse the drinks. You must know that."

"And what *you* must know is that Barbara Havers richly deserves to be exactly where she is just now."

"Fine. Admitted. She was completely out of order last year. But what I also know is that you're quite adept at alteration in a conversation, moving from a subject you don't wish to discuss to a subject guaranteed to put the other person on the defensive."

"If Barbara Havers finds herself in a position of defence—"

"I'm bloody well *not* talking about Barbara Havers!"

Having spoken, Lynley felt immediately exasperated with himself. He'd long ago eschewed raising his voice once he'd learned how little distance volume ever went in making some sort of point with an addict. His own brother had taught him that. He took a moment for calm and then said, "Isabelle."

"Do *not*—"

"*Isabelle.* You stand to lose everything. You can't want that. You've lost your marriage, you've lost your—"

"Stop this instant."

"—sons, and if you keep on this path, you're going to lose your job as well. You're fighting battles on too many fronts and you've begun to unravel." He wished she would sit. He wished they both would sit. He wanted to be in a chair facing hers so that he could grasp her hand in order to let her know that he actually *did* see what she was going through. Ludicrously, he felt that if she could feel the touch of his hand and know a moment of human connection, it might somehow move her. He said, "I don't think you're able to see this because you can't afford to see it. If you see it, you'll have to admit it. If you admit it, you'll have to take action. And this will be real action, not action having to do with hiring solicitors to tilt at windmills for you."

For a moment, she said nothing at all, but a pulse rapidly hammered the vein in her temple. Then, "You are one of my largest regrets, Inspector. I must have been quite mad. You are, of course, very good in bed, as I'm sure many women have told you, but for you to take what was on my part a period of weakness and to use it to make these kinds of allegations against me . . . What will it be next? A threat to go to Hillier?"

"You aren't going to succeed in changing the subject, but I will acknowledge your attempt to do that by noting that, yes, we were lovers and you regret it. For my part, I say it wasn't the best of ideas, but we were both vulnerable at the time."

"I wasn't nor have I ever been vulnerable. And certainly not to you and your handsome ways."

"Accepted. Whatever you wish to make of it. But having been lovers isn't the point. Your drinking is the point. You're no longer doing it to escape whatever you were once wishing to escape when you first began. You're doing it now because you must. You think you can control it but you must see, after Ludlow, that you can't. You're going to need help. You *do* need help."

"Not yours."

"I'm not volunteering. But I'm also not standing aside and letting your alcoholism hurt or destroy the people around you. Handle the drinking any way you will, but keep clear of damaging Barbara Havers. Because if you do, Isabelle, if you have her transferred out of some sense of pique, then I *will* do something and you're not going to like what it is."

He turned to leave, but her next words stopped him.

"How *dare* you threaten me." He faced her once again and she went on, her voice icy. "Do you *know* what I could do with that last statement of yours if I chose to? Do you have any idea how much Hillier would love to be rid of you as well? Or do you, perhaps, believe that having a mouldy title attached to your name actually protects you in some way? Are you really thinking that Hillier *isn't* looking for a move to make against you because . . . what? He envies you your fine London townhouse and your rotting-from-the-rafters estate? He's ambitious for some other title besides his completely ridiculous knighthood and he believes that you—outranking him in the realm of the utterly meaningless—could put the crunch on his advancement to . . . What would it be? Baronet?"

"Isabelle, you must—"

"I must *nothing*. And certainly not upon your advice. You'd be very wise to believe me when I tell you that this sort of thing"—and here she gestured rudely round the office as if to indicate the conversation they'd been having—"is exactly what Hillier is waiting for: an unforgivable act of insubordination that clearly makes it impossible for you to remain employed by the Metropolitan Police. And a word from me . . . about what's gone on here . . . right here in this office . . . a word from me . . ."

Lynley could see how badly she was shaking. He knew she needed a drink. She looked so terrible that he very nearly told her to take the vodka from her desk please, an airline bottle, because he knew it was there and she ought to drink it down quickly now.

He said with his eyes on hers, "Isabelle. Guv. I'm speaking to you about this as a colleague, a fellow officer, and a friend, I hope. You're in pain. You're afraid. And you're not alone in that because nearly everyone round us is also afraid and probably in pain and also trying to do something about it. Including me, as you well know. But the choice you're making in order to cope is going to destroy the very things you're trying to protect. What I'm here to say is that I hope you know this and I hope you intend to do something about it."

There was nothing left for him to say to her. He waited to see if she would respond. When she didn't, he nodded and then he left her, shutting the door quietly behind him. He paused just beyond it. Once again, he waited. Then he heard the sound of her desk drawer opening, recognising the squeak of it because it was the desk that he, too, had occupied during the period when he acted as superintendent while the higher-ups decided who would replace the retired Malcolm Webberly.

It was the lowest drawer on the right. Generally, it took something of an effort to open it, as it did now for Isabelle. He continued to listen until he heard what he didn't want to hear. Something hit the top of her desk. Some ten to fifteen seconds passed and something else hit the top of her desk. She would, of course, sweep them both into her bag when she was finished.

He looked down at his shoes and considered everything for a moment. Then he went in search of Barbara Havers.

# PART II

Nothing fools you better
than the lie you tell yourself.

—Raymond Teller *of Penn & Teller*

# 15 MAY

WANDSWORTH
LONDON

Isabelle had spent the night on the sofa rather than in the bedroom, so when she awakened, her back ached, her neck was stiff and sore, and her head was throbbing. She awakened not because an alarm went off and not because the television—which had been blaring all night—suddenly disturbed her, but because she was powerfully thirsty and in need of the loo.

When she got to her feet, she saw that she was still in the clothes she'd worn to Maidstone for a dinner with her sons. This had taken place at a Pizza Hut because she'd been stupid enough to allow James and Laurence to choose their favourite spot for a meal. She'd been picturing something quite special, with the twins dressed to the nines, as she herself would be. What she hadn't pictured were queues of customers, plastic tables, sticky chairs, fluorescent lighting, and an argument over everything-on-it versus mushrooms-and-olives-only. What she also hadn't pictured was who else was present: Bob and Sandra, seated far enough away from the boys so as not to hear Isabelle's conversation with them but close enough to watch the interaction should things not go as swimmingly as they were intended to go.

A dinner out was, Isabelle had argued, the least Bob and Sandra could agree to. They'd won everything, they were leaving, her boys were lost to her. She wanted to talk to the twins about what happened next in their relationship with their own mum, she told Bob.

Things had not gone the distance into court. A very long and apparently very frank phone call from Bob's solicitor to Sherlock Wainwright had taken care of that. Cleverly, Bob had waited till "You've given me no choice, Isabelle," and when he'd reached that no-choice point, he'd laid out every additional fact he'd not yet given his solicitor. These facts his solicitor passed along to Sherlock Wainwright, who was not happy when he heard them and understood exactly how much Isabelle had not told him about the roots of her divorce.

He'd said over the phone, in the remonstrating tone of a school's head teacher, "So you can accept what your former husband is offering as the best arrangement you're going to get in the circumstances, or you can sack me and find another solicitor. But the reality is clear: it's going to come down to this again and again, no matter who represents you. I'm going to advise you to agree to Bob's terms. You'll be better off because what you don't spend on solicitors' fees in carrying this forward uselessly you can then spend on airline tickets to New Zealand."

She so wanted to continue to fight, but she knew that Bob had the upper hand. She'd given it to him, after all. For what did she have left, aside from the career he threatened to destroy if she didn't comply with his wishes? So she'd agreed, she'd requested a dinner with the twins, and thus they had all ended up at a Pizza Hut in Maidstone.

She could almost hear the conversation that Bob had had with the boys in order to influence their choice of dining establishment. "She says to choose your very, *very* favourite place," he would have said because he knew what their choice would be, and he also knew there would be no wine or lager and certainly no vodka available to Isabelle there.

The boys were nervous, despite apparently being quite at home in Pizza Hut. Laurence squirmed as if he'd outgrown his underpants, and James kept glancing across the room towards Bob and Sandra as if hoping for rescue. Isabelle had done her best to engage the twins in conversation: about what they were going to do together when she came to New Zealand to see them, about the school they were going to attend, about what they'd learned in advance about the country where they were going to live. No poisonous anything. Did they know that? Overrun with furry opossums, though. Had they seen a picture of one? Surfing, swimming with dolphins, and a special beach with a hot spring beneath it where you could dig a shallow pit and watch it quickly fill with warm water. Were they excited about going there?

Her every question was answered by Laurence while James kept ducking his head and shooting looks at Bob and Sandra. Finally, in exasperation, Isabelle slapped her hand on the tabletop and spoke to him sharply about attending to *her.* He burst into tears, at which point Sandra rushed over to him with a "Darling, darling, here's Mummy." Isabelle felt herself get so red hot that she thought the top of her head would explode. Sandra scooped James from his seat and told the boy that Mummy would take him home straightaway, and Isabelle knew that to protest would be to cause further trouble that she would pay for in the end.

Sandra left with a sobbing James in tow, Bob remained as if worried that Isabelle would cause a disturbance with Laurence at its centre, and Laurence himself—ever the peacekeeper—explained to Isabelle that James was only "a bit scared about starting school in New Zealand and being the slowest in the class and having the other kids laugh at him." To Isabelle's assertion that James was *not* slow, Laurence had replied with, "Fact is, Mum, he is."

They'd finished their meal rather hurriedly and Laurence had refused her offer of a sweet. She could tell that he was anxious to get home to James, and she might have been pleased to see this degree of fraternal affection and loyalty had the dinner not turned out to be such a balls-up. The very moment Laurence pushed his plate away from him, Bob was there at the table with a jovial "Ready-o, then?" to Laurence and a quiet "We'll take a taxi" to Isabelle's offer to drive them home.

When Laurence headed towards the door, Bob did have the grace to say to Isabelle, "Sorry about Sandra. She's a bit overprotective when it comes to the boys. She was out of her seat before I could stop her."

Isabelle found his regret difficult to swallow: an apology, of all things, from the very man who was in the midst of destroying her life. So she said, "Is this how you plan our future to look?"

He said, "Meaning?"

"Meaning I'm never to have private time with my sons. Meaning it's all to be arranged so that I remain a distant figure to them: no mother at all but instead some stranger who drops into their lives now and then merely to upset the flow."

Bob looked towards Laurence, who, Isabelle saw, was watching them anxiously, as if expecting them to come to blows. He turned back to her and said, "You can't see that you made a choice, can you?"

He didn't wait for a reply, instead moving to join Laurence and placing his hand on the boy's thin shoulder to lead him out to the street where they would find a taxi. For Isabelle's part, she returned to London. She felt as if a portion of her insides had been bitten out by an unseen ghoul, and she told herself that she deserved something in recompense for the disasters of the evening. She pulled the vodka from the freezer where she kept it, she poured herself three fingers of it, she added a splash of cranberry juice, and she carried both the bottle and the concoction to the sofa. There, she switched on the television, found a costume drama featuring tricorn hats, swarthy miners banging round underground stone tunnels, and some bloke with a naked chest and admirable pectorals scything wheat in a field. She sank onto the sofa and watched without watching and certainly without thinking. She drank until she could no longer think.

The television was still at an unmerciful volume when she awoke, this time to the morning news. She searched for the remote and finally found it inexplicably inside one of her shoes. She turned off the sound on the weather report and stumbled to the bathroom. There she grimaced at the condition of her hair and her makeup, examined her bloodshot eyes, and began to shed her clothes with one hand while with the other she looked for eye drops. When she found them, she also found that her hand was shaking too badly to put them in. She decided a shower was in order.

She stood beneath it and wondered what time it was and gave herself a mental shake for not having checked. Making short work of the shower—most of the time she simply stood beneath the water and allowed it to beat on her head and shoulders and down her back—she found her watch after something of a search, where she had apparently left it, which was inside the freezer where the vodka had come from. The vodka itself was still on the coffee table in front of the sofa, and she did her best not to look at it or think about it as she went to the bedroom for fresh clothing.

Clothed, she returned to the bathroom. Most of dealing with her face had to do with removing shine and adding colour. Not a problem at all, but then she came to her eyes, the need for the eye drops, the additional need for shadow and mascara, and her shaking hands, which had not stopped shaking since needing a shower was not what the shaking was about.

She decided that a bit of the hair of the dog was in order. It would set her to right, and she needed it anyway because she otherwise would not be able to make her appearance what it had to be for her working day. Beyond that, she deserved it as well. She'd had nothing at all to drink with James and Laurence on the previous night. If nothing else, she was absolutely owed.

CHALK FARM
LONDON

It was something of a relief to get back to Pop-Tarts, Barbara Havers decided. Those Ludlow breakfasts had been true artery cloggers. The eggs alone had been enough to do her in. Adding bacon, toast, great slashings of butter, jam, mushrooms, baked beans . . . It was a sodding miracle that she'd survived long enough to throw a chocolate fudge Pop-Tart into the toaster. She accompanied this with a large mug of PG Tips combined with a dash of milk and two lumps of sugar. Without the slightest twinge of guilt, she fired up her first fag of the day and experienced a moment of bliss. But she was going to need more of everything to wake herself up, she decided. Last night had been an epic experience: dinner after their tap-dancing class in the company of Kaz and Dorothea.

She'd tried to beg off once she saw that Kaz meant to accompany them. She reckoned that begging off was what she was meant to do. After all, Dorothea had come to the class dressed in something very like a Catwoman costume, and Barbara was certain that she wasn't the only member of the class to conclude that Dorothea's choice of clothing—tight in every right place with a neckline screaming *ooh la la*—was intended to attract the attention of their instructor.

But Dorothea insisted Barbara accompany her. She declared that they were a team—she and Barbara—and for this reason where one of them went, the other was intended to go. In this case, that meant to dinner. With Kaz.

It turned out that Dorothea had her reasons, these being the outcome of the audition for the July dance recital. She had made the cut—no surprise there—but, alas, Barbara had failed to impress, being instead assigned a place in a group number that she fully intended to miss. For her part, Dorothea had been given a partner in the person of the talented and determined Umaymah. Barbara's overwhelming relief at her own failure was something she'd done her best to hide. She'd said quite solemnly to Dorothea, with an effort at disappointment, "It's better this way," but Dorothea wasn't having that.

Hence, the dinner. Hence the ensuing conversation during which Dorothea pointed out to Kaz that her "choreography" called for rather more bumping and grinding than Umaymah's husband—not to mention her father, her brothers, and all her male relatives—was going to be happy about. Barbara shot her a "*What* choreography?" look, but Dorothea ignored her in favour of casting her blue-eyed gaze upon their instructor and then curving her lips in what could only be called a come-hither-darling-man smile.

Twice Barbara tried to leave them. It was only too obvious to her that, at least in Kaz's eyes, she was a fifth wheel on a lopsided cart. But Dorothea stopped her. She finally relented only when Barbara pointed out that preventing her from going to the ladies' was going to cause embarrassment to them all. Once released from the table at which Dorothea had cleverly sat her so close to the wall that she couldn't move without the cooperation of her dining companions and everyone at the next table, she made her escape. It was only when she was finally on the Tube that she sent Dorothea a text telling her, "My arches have fallen. Kaz wants you alone. Be a good girl." But still, she arrived home later than she would have liked, and unable to sleep due to the thought of *possibly* having to bump and grind in tap shoes while in the presence of other human beings, she finally picked up her battered copy of *Bartlett's Familiar Quotations* and turned to the Shakespeare section for more quotable quotes pertaining to murder. She'd been sticking with the tragedies, most recently working her way through *Othello* and wondering when she'd encounter a situation in which smoting someone thus could be talked about. She reckoned that taking the circumcised dog by the throat wasn't ever going to happen. Pondering all this, she'd at last fallen asleep. But it had seemed a matter of moments only before the *1812* cannons blasted her out of bed.

She was just wiping the remaining crumbs from her second Pop-Tart off her plate when her mobile rang. She'd left it on the table next to the daybed that nightly was transformed into the spot where she and Morpheus met up, and she gave it the eye and willed it to stop playing the opening bars to the *Twilight Zone* theme music. It finally did after ten rings but in fewer than five seconds the entire routine began again. Reckoning that this would only happen time and again until she got to work, Barbara heaved herself to her feet and went to answer it.

To her hello, she heard Dorothea Harriman's breathless voice saying, "Detective Sergeant Havers?"

"If you were expecting someone else, I hate to disappoint," Barbara told her. "So did the earth move?"

Dorothea responded in a whisper with, "Word of warning. She's in a twist."

"And we're speaking of?"

"Who else? Her nibs. She wants to see you the moment you step onto the premises."

"Any idea why?"

"It's to do with the assistant commissioner. That's all I know. Between you and me, that's all I *want* to know."

Barbara rang off. A command performance in the DCS's office immediately upon her arrival in Victoria Street did not sound like the manner in which she preferred to start her day. She cursed first and sighed second. Then she put another Pop-Tart into the toaster.

VICTORIA

LONDON

Barbara's options for getting to Victoria Street quickly from Chalk Farm were nonexistent. She had a choice between the enduring horrors of street traffic or suffering a ride on the notoriously unreliable Northern

Line. But at least with the Northern Line she'd be able to save on the congestion fee, so she got herself from Eton Villas to the Chalk Farm Tube station like an Olympic medalist in the fast walk competition.

The wait at the Underground station was bad. The crowd that grew on the platform was worse. The ride was worst of all, as the masses of people inside the carriages were a terrorist's dream. They ignored one another as per usual, jostling about like kittens struggling for a nursing position while also attempting to text, read their newspapers, listen to tinny-sounding music via earbuds, and in one case eat what smelled like a sardine sandwich.

Nearly an hour had passed by the time Barbara reached St. James's Park station. She dashed to the street and headed towards the looming grey mass of New Scotland Yard that rose like a barricaded monolith before her. There, she waited impatiently for the security hoo-ha to be completed: a labyrinth of queues, X-rays, more queues, and inspections that every year became more complicated. Finally, she reached the lifts.

She was charging towards Isabelle Ardery's office when the DCS opened the door and snapped at Dorothea, "I thought I told you she was to get here directly. So where the hell is she?" And then, before Dorothea could reply, Ardery spied Barbara and said, "Get in here," before she spun on a heel and went back inside.

Barbara exchanged a look with Dorothea. Dorothea murmured, "The assistant commissioner was waiting in her office when she got here. Closed doors and massive shouting."

Bloody bleeding *hell* was what Barbara thought.

She went inside the office, not knowing what to expect and fearing that she was about to come face-to-face with Hillier at his most Hillieresque. But the DCS was in the office alone, standing rigidly behind her desk. She barked, "Shut the goddamn door," and Barbara instantly did so.

As she crossed the room, Ardery took up a filing folder. "Sit," she told her. When Barbara took the chair in front of the DCS's desk, she was, apparently, close enough to satisfy because the DCS threw the folder directly at her. "You're finished," she said. "Sign it."

Barbara gaped at her. "What's going on?"

"Sign it and get the hell out of my office. Pack up your desk. If you take so much as a paper clip that doesn't belong to you personally—"

"Guv!" Barbara cried. "What's going on?"

"Don't you bloody say another word. Sign the paperwork and be glad it's only a transfer to the north and not what you deserve, which is to be given the sack, with me making certain that no police force on the planet would ever be willing to take you on, even as a cleaner. Do you understand me?"

"No!" Barbara could see that something terrible must have happened, but she hadn't the first clue what it might be. She went on with, "I did *everything.* Just like you said and you even said that I . . . you said . . . I didn't . . ." Barbara couldn't get her mind round what she wanted to say, so flummoxed was she by what was happening. She forced herself to get under control. She said at last, "If you want me to sign, you're going to have to tell me why. Because I know that Hillier was waiting for you, so I know that something has—"

"*Did* you hear me?" Ardery jerked open the centre drawer of her desk. She pulled out a handful of pens. She threw them at her. "You've crossed the last bloody line with me, in your entirely miserable career of crossing lines. You've stepped out of order for the last time you will *ever—*"

"No! What did I do? I didn't—"

"I said sign this!" Isabelle strode round the desk. She grabbed a pen up from the floor. Then she grabbed Barbara's hand and forced her fingers round it. She shoved Barbara's chair closer to the desk. "Now sign! Or is this just another order you intend to disobey? Because you know better, don't you, because you're some kind of omniscient policing god, because no matter what you're told to do or how you're told to do it or when you're told to do it or how anything is meant to be done, if you, Barbara Havers, don't happen to agree with it because it is not to your liking and your will, you don't intend to do it. Now sign!"

"But you're not . . . Stop it!" Barbara pushed her away. She started to rise. Isabelle pushed her back down. She shrieked, "I've had enough of you! Everyone here has had enough! Do you actually think you can bring the entire Metropolitan police force under a microscope and *not* be found out? Are you honestly that stupid?"

"Microscope? What's . . . ? Why won't you tell me?"

A voice entirely unexpected cut into this, saying, "Leave her, Isabelle. She did nothing."

They both swung round to see that Lynley had joined them. Ardery shouted, "Who gave you leave to enter this office? You get the hell back to where you belong. If you do not—this very instant—I'll see you hauled in front of—"

"Barbara didn't do it," Lynley said with that preternatural calm that seemed second nature to the bloke. "She doesn't know what you're talking about."

"Don't you dare run interference for her."

"You can put her on the rack and it won't make a difference, guv," he said. "I'm the one who sent it."

"Sent what?" Barbara cried. "Where? What?"

"The first report," Lynley said. "The one you were told to amend by the DCS. I sent it to Clive Druitt, who turned out to be a very easy man to locate. My guess is that he's been to see his MP and his MP has been to see Hillier and what's happened is that we've been accused of either a cover-up or a monumental lapse in judgement." And with a look at Ardery, "Which is it, guv?"

Her answer was an icily enraged, "You supercilious bastard. Who the hell do you think you are? Have you any idea at *all* what you've done?"

Instead of replying, Lynley said to Barbara, "Perhaps it's best if you leave us, Sergeant."

"You stay where you are," Ardery said. "I'm not finished with you."

Lynley had been standing by the door, but now he crossed the room to join them. He and Ardery were eyeball to eyeball. What ran between them would have kept a refrigerator operational for at least a month, Barbara reckoned. "As I said," Lynley explained in what sounded to Barbara like his most reasonable tone, "she had no idea. She gave me the report to read. She was concerned about having been told to exclude part of it. She wanted my opinion. I gave it."

"Oh, did you," Ardery said with a sneer. "And exactly what would Lord Asherton's high, mighty, and excessively lofty opinion have been?"

"He told me to do like you told me, guv," Barbara said hastily. "So I revised the report. You read the new one, didn't you? I left out the part about—"

"Get out! Both of you! Get out!"

As Ardery strode behind her desk again, Barbara decided she needed no further invitation from the DCS. She surged to her feet, found herself slipping on one of the pens that Ardery had thrown at her. She felt Lynley steady her. She made hasty tracks for the door and was heading for safer climes as behind her Lynley was saying, "You've got to see reason, Isabelle. If you can't—"

And as Barbara shut the door, Ardery broke into his words with, "You haven't the first clue what you've done! But that doesn't matter to you, does it? Nothing matters but how you see things, you insufferable piece of upper-class irrelevance."

The door shut now, Lynley's response was only a murmur that Barbara couldn't understand. Ardery's next comment was, on the other hand, delivered at maximum volume. "Don't you put that on me. Don't you bloody *ever.* You think nothing of intruding upon the lives of others because your own life . . . your own miserable life . . . who you are and what that's meant to every step you've ever wanted to take—"

Another murmur from Lynley, which was followed by, "I won't listen to another word of this. Get out before I ring for security. You heard me, didn't you? Have you gone deaf? I said get out!"

Barbara dashed away at this. En route, she saw that Dorothea had already done the same thing.

VICTORIA

LONDON

She escaped into the ladies' first. Her heart was still pounding so hard that she could feel it hammering against her eardrums. She needed a moment. Two. The entire morning. Whatever. She wished like the devil that she could have a fag but she didn't want to risk it, although on another day she might have done so, bellowing the smoke into the toilet and hoping that continually flushing would suffice to cover her crime, which she knew it would not. But now that seemed like professional suicide in a bowl with whitebait. So instead she ran the water in the basin and thought about dunking her head into its meagre flow.

She was fairly well staggered by what Lynley had done. It wasn't the first time he'd put his career out there on the chopping block, but it was definitely the first time he'd done so in such a way that could be interpreted as underhanded. Underhanded was not his style. He was more a bloke who threw down gauntlets in public. Barbara reckoned it came with the title, running through his noblesse oblige blood like he was the Scarlet Pimpernel. She couldn't imagine how the assistant commissioner was going to react when he learned that DI Lynley was behind the original report's being sent to Clive Druitt. Apoplexy came to mind, however.

By the time she got herself back to herself in the ladies' and had made it to her desk, the entire department was abuzz. Lynley had returned and was at his own desk, the door to his office open and the man himself looking as unruffled as she'd ever seen him. She shot a look at her fellow sergeant Winston Nkata, who cocked his head and shrugged. She went to Lynley.

He was about to pick up his phone, but he stopped when he saw her in the doorway. One raised eyebrow said, Yes, sergeant? in that mild manner she'd come to know. She said, "Sir. I don't . . . Why did you do it? This could . . . I mean . . . It's not like . . ."

He half smiled. "I don't think I've ever seen you at a loss for words."

"Then why?"

He lifted a hand and then dropped it. It was one of those born-to-the-purple gestures that he made every so often. It said, What else could I possibly have done? but as far she was concerned, he possibly could have done half a dozen other things. So she said, "Well?"

His reply was, "Everything needs to come into the light of day, Sergeant. That's all this is. Isabelle—the DCS—knows this at heart. Believe me. She does know this."

Barbara nodded. She understood. He wasn't talking merely about the two differing reports.

VICTORIA
LONDON

It was just after noon when Lynley received the message that he'd known would be coming. He was surprised it had taken so long, as he'd reckoned that once he'd reached his own office it would be merely a matter of minutes before Judi MacIntosh would be giving him the word from on high: a sort of angel Gabriel without the trumpet. As it was, however, things in Tower Block had apparently begun with the assistant commissioner being called upon the carpet inside the commissioner's office. According to Judi, who served them both and relayed the information to Lynley in a modified murmur suitable for the confessional, considerable conversation had taken place between the two men behind the closed door. So she'd thought it best to do Lynley the favour of pretending that he—Lynley—was actually not present in Victoria Block when, after his words with the commissioner, Hillier had barked a demand for DI Lynley's immediate appearance. She'd reckoned, she informed Lynley, that Sir David had needed about an hour to cool off, so she'd only just now informed the AC that Dorothea Harriman had finally announced Lynley's putative return. So, Judi said in conclusion, if she could *possibly* tell Hillier that Lynley wouldn't at all mind stepping over to Hillier's office . . . rather soon . . . ? Lynley said he would be there at once.

Isabelle would have given Hillier the word, of course. Her feet were doubtless being held to the flames, so Lynley couldn't blame her for wanting to pass the joy of the heat along to him. If Hillier was frothing at the mouth and ready to go for her throat—not to mix too many metaphors, Lynley thought wryly—there wasn't much else she could do save what she had done: track down the source of the report that had been sent to Clive Druitt.

He couldn't blame her. He couldn't even say she'd been in the wrong to tell Havers to eliminate from the official report the information that a gap between an anonymous phone call and an arrest suggested that an investigation into the allegations made against Ian Druitt had, might have, or should have occurred. That fact had not been germane to what had been Isabelle's assignment in Shropshire. But it had been germane to the overall issue of someone's death in custody, which was why Lynley believed it had needed to be included in Isabelle's report.

When Lynley entered the assistant commissioner's office, Hillier jerked his head at a chair, saying only, "Enlighten me, Inspector. I'm trying to work out which part of this entire manure pile we're walking through at the moment represents the worst of the bollocksing up that's gone on in the past several weeks. What's your opinion on the matter?"

Hillier was not a man to ask a subordinate's opinion about anything. He was more the type to set off the bomb first and question its accuracy later. Lynley knew that the assistant commissioner was, thus, waiting for the wrong answer to be issued so that he could take a subsequent action that he'd already decided upon. The difficult part was trying to suss out what that action was going to be. What fell upon his own head was not an anxious issue for Lynley. What fell upon Barbara's head was.

He said, "You've been told that I posted Barbara's initial report to Clive Druitt."

"Holmes, you amaze me," Hillier responded drily. His narrow-eyed expression did not alter with the words.

"I agreed with DS Havers."

"Are you telling me that posting this report was her idea?"

"I'm not. She didn't bring the matter up. She was concerned about being ordered to alter her report, and she wanted my advice. To give it, I read both the reports. It seemed clear that the nineteen-day gap between the anonymous call and the arrest of Ian Druitt suggested something that wanted looking into. That was the area of our agreement."

"Indeed." Hillier said the word not in acceptance but rather in assessment of Lynley's decision-making process.

"Barbara's thinking—and mine as well—was that the IPCC either noted the time gap and decided it wasn't relevant to their investigation or, what's more likely, they didn't notice the time gap at all. It seemed to me that leaving out that detail had the potential to make the situation far worse than it was already."

"Did it."

"What, sir?"

"Did it seem that way to you? And if it did, the real question is why you didn't speak to your immediate superior about all of this 'likely' business of yours, which apparently has been plaguing your otherwise tranquil mind."

Hillier folded his hands together on the top of his desk, displaying buffed fingernails and a gold signet ring. He regarded Lynley evenly. It came to Lynley suddenly how quiet it was inside the assistant commissioner's office when the door was closed. There was a churchlike silence within. The only sound breaking that silence when they themselves were not speaking was the siren of an emergency vehicle down in the street.

"She was the one who'd given the order, sir. She'd actually left Sergeant Havers no choice in the matter. A man has died in custody—"

"Does it astonish you that I already know this?" Hillier cut in sharply.

"—and it's my belief that the father of that man deserves a full account of what went on. Or, in this case, what did not go on, which was someone looking into the nineteen-day gap or even mentioning it. Putting that one detail into the report was all that was ever necessary."

Lynley could have gone further to point out that Isabelle's complete refusal to consider the detail important or at least to acknowledge its existence was worrying. But just as he did not want Barbara Havers to have to suffer for a decision that he had made, so also did he not want his actions to have consequences for Isabelle.

He wasn't reassured at all when Hillier shoved himself away from his desk and stood, looking out of the window behind it. From his own position, Lynley could see only the clear blue sky. Hillier would see more: the lushly green tops of the trees that rose above the buildings along Birdcage Walk.

Hillier said, "She's impressively cocked this up. You know that, of course."

"Sir, I disagree," Lynley said quickly. "From the first, she merely wanted to make every point clear so that in the event of solicitors becoming involved—"

"I'm not talking about Havers," Hillier cut in, "although God knows she's the bloody queen of creating cock-ups. And believe me, this has to be a first when it comes down to a question of who cocked up what. No, I'm talking about Ardery. This is down to her. Something's gone completely to hell with that woman, and we're going to get to the bottom of it."

Lynley wasn't enamoured of the plural pronoun and hoped Hillier was using the royal and oft political *we.* He said nothing, waiting for clarification.

"Christ, but I was an idiot to name her permanently to DCS. Sacking her now . . . what a bloody nightmare that would be. I'd throttle Malcolm if he were only here to present his neck."

Lynley followed this train of thought to its logical destination. Malcolm was Malcom Webberly, who formerly had occupied Isabelle's position. His sudden retirement after a hit-and-run accident and Lynley's refusal to take on Webberly's job permanently when it was offered to him had placed all of them in the position they occupied now. That position could only be described as precarious, and he felt a rush of alarm that his actions might be the cause of Isabelle's being sacked.

So he said, "Her point was well taken, though."

Hillier turned from the window. The light was behind him now, making his expressions more difficult to read. "Whose?" he asked.

"DCS Ardery's. In her eyes, she and Barbara were in Shropshire solely to look into the IPCC's report. Full stop. The doctored report—"

"Pray God don't use that term, Inspector. Things are bad enough as it is."

"The second report that Sergeant Havers wrote reflected that: what the DCS's initial orders were."

Hillier returned to his chair, sat, fingered a pen on his desk. He said, "You can't have it both ways. Either you're out of order for passing along that initial report or Ardery is out of order for having Havers revise it. Which do you choose?"

Clever trap, Lynley thought. He said, "It's a matter of two points of view, sir."

"That's your choice?"

"There isn't a choice. There is no choosing. There is merely reflecting the two points of view."

Hillier snorted derisively. "You're a pretty one, aren't you."

"Sir?"

"You've an answer for everything, including this, which has taken a member of Parliament to the Home Office to register a complaint in advance of God only knows what lawsuit, frivolous or otherwise. I've managed to buy us a ten-day reprieve, but after that . . . and with no satisfactory result . . . heads will roll. Do you understand?"

Lynley wasn't at all happy with where this appeared to be leading. "Satisfactory?" he asked. "What are we talking about?"

"We're talking about what you're going to do, Inspector. You didn't actually assume that you could project yourself into this situation without consequences."

Lynley then saw where this was going. He knew how well he deserved it. Still, he tried to forestall with, "Sir, I've had a holiday cancelled already because—"

Hillier laughed outright. "I'm meant to care about your holiday, am I?" He didn't wait for a reply. "You're going to Shropshire, Inspector Lynley. You're going to shovel this pile of manure back into the wheelbarrow it came from, and if you have to use a teaspoon to do it, that's what you're going to use. Is that clear? You're taking Sergeant Havers with you. If together you can't deal with this matter in the next eight days—allowing one for travel and one for report writing when you return—you'll both be answering for it. As will DCS Ardery. Am I being clear?"

There was nothing for it but what he said. "You are, sir."

"Delighted to know it. You may leave. And I don't want to hear from any of you until this matter is resolved. To my satisfaction, by the way. Certainly not to yours."

# 16 MAY

LUDLOW

SHROPSHIRE

There didn't seem to be a single area of her life that wasn't fractured. She was like a wall mirror hit by a stone, with a hundred fault lines cobwebbing out from a single point of contact. This made it so difficult to get up in the morning that there were times when Ding didn't get up at all. And the fact that her undoing had been effected by her own hand resulted in her not having the false respite of being able to blame someone else.

She'd made it clear to Brutus that more than one person could engage in the friends-with-privileges life. She'd done so with Finn. She'd been drunk and he'd been stoned and the whole encounter had been wretched to the absolute extreme. But—as she'd hoped—Brutus met Finn coming out of her bedroom the next morning and Finn's "Me too, Brucie" had required no further explanation since Finn was naked and he'd laughed and thrust his hips forward suggestively. And just in case Brutus didn't understand, he'd also asked, "Ding put out for *you* like that? Why the hell are you trying to get it some place else?"

That very night, then, Brutus had brought Allison Franklin home. He'd led her up the stairs, and she'd held back, giggling tittering whispering murmuring *whatevering* her faux reluctance even as she'd cast a triumphant glance into the sitting room where Ding was trying to get rid of the snow on the ancient television she'd brought back months ago from Cardew Hall. Finn was supposedly helping her, which was all about a running commentary having to do with girls, technology, and demands that she let him "see to it, for fuck's sake, Ding."

Ding heard the front door open, she heard it close, and then she heard Allison Franklin's breathless, "I *can't*, Bruce. Really. She's *here*, isn't she?" She tried to ignore this, but it was impossible, especially with Finn saying loudly, "Keep the orgasmic howling to a minimum, you lot, and we'll do the same," as Brutus led Allison towards the stairs.

Ding's eyes met Brutus's eyes. His expression was blank and she made hers indifferent. Up the stairs the two of them went. They didn't come down them till the following morning.

She hadn't expected this to be so excruciating. Distracting herself seemed like the only option. The easiest distraction available turned out to be the one that came knocking on her bedroom door nearly every night following the first one. Each time she let Finn in, and she did things to him that kept him coming back for more.

After the third time, Brutus confronted her. They weren't at home. She was in Castle Square on her way to a lecture. That, luckily, gave Brutus very little time to say what he wanted to say.

It was this: "I got to talk to you, okay?" And without pausing for her to reply because, obviously, he could see her face hardening and anyway even if he couldn't, he knew how reluctant she would be even to say hello, "You've made your point."

"What point?" She aimed for sounding arch. "I don't know what you're talking about. If it's me and Finn—"

"There isn't any you and Finn. Not like there's a you and me."

"*You've* got some bloody nerve."

"Come on, Ding. What you're doing with Finn . . . it isn't even who you are."

She wanted to shove him onto his bum at that. She wanted to kick his shins and do everything else an eight-year-old would do because Brutus knew her better than anyone, and she hated him for it.

"We're friends with privileges," she told him. "Me and Finn. And I can't see it's any of your business."

"Don't be an idiot, Ding. You know you're doing this to get at me. I fuck Allison, so you're fucking Finn. You wouldn't even be *doing* it with him if you didn't know Allison and I were doing it."

"Oh, that's how you see it? You're inside my head? Or is it just that what *you* do can't apply to anyone else?"

"It can apply wherever it wants to apply." He shifted his weight, and he ran the heel of his palm back through his tousled hair. He was, as always, dressed like a male model, so it was little wonder that it took no effort for him to pull girls. "It's just that . . . Look, it's not like I don't like you, Ding. I mean 'like you' as in really like you. I *do*. But the rest of it . . . ? The exclusive bit . . . ? I keep trying to tell you it's not how I'm made. I just need more."

"Oh, I got that," she told him. "I discovered it's not how I'm made either. I s'pose I owe you for that, don't I? There's lorries full of advantages in spreading the joy all round, and I wouldn't ever have worked that out if you hadn't shoved that cow Allison down my throat. Whoops. Not exactly right, is that? It's your tongue you were shoving down *her* throat, and the rest of you, you were shoving some place else."

He made an expression of distaste, saying, "See? Even that. It's not you. You're not like that. Let's call a truce."

"You don't *know* what I'm like." Her voice rose. "You want a 'truce' but what you really want is me just waiting, hanging about, hoping you get tired of *her* so you'll maybe come back and do me the favour of being your Temeside fuck so you don't have to go to the trouble of bringing Allison home."

"That's not true." Brutus blushed, however, so Ding knew how closely she'd hit the mark.

"Oh right," she said. "Which part of it, Brutus? No, don't even answer. The trouble isn't bringing Allison home to fuck, is it? The real problem is waving her off afterwards. You can't get rid of her the way you want to. Isn't that it?" She laughed. Even to her ears it sounded a little hysterical, but she felt the triumph of knowing she was correct. "Oh God, it must be a total nightmare! She's expecting to spend the night and *you're* expecting her to dress and be gone only you can't actually tell her that, can you? Thanks for the shag, darling, now if you don't mind . . . What a problem you've got!"

She expected him to stalk off after that, but he didn't do so. Instead he watched her and he waited till she was finished. Then he said, "You can't work out what that means, can you?"

"What?" she said. "What *what* means, Brucie?"

"That I stayed."

"Where?"

"With you. In your room. All night. In bed. I stayed because you're different, you're not one of the others. I stayed because I cared. I *care*."

But there was something not right in his voice. Ding could hear it, just the edge of something very close to panic, so bloody close. She knew then *exactly* why he was talking to her there in Castle Square. She bloody knew what he wanted from her and how he was lying in order to get it.

She kept her fury going for the rest of that day. She knew she would need it in order to do what she'd decided to do. When she arrived back at the house in Temeside, she went to her room. She dragged out of the cupboard what she'd tried and failed to toss into a wheelie bin nine days earlier. She'd got as far as holding the two articles over a pile of smelly rubbish, but she couldn't do it. She'd wanted to. She'd seen the necessity. But at the final moment, she'd stayed her own hand. She *could* keep them hidden away, she'd told herself. Surely, she'd be able to wear them again one day, wouldn't she?

Now she opened the carrier bag into which she'd folded the skirt and the spangly top. She removed them, spread them lovingly on the bed. Then she waited.

When Brutus came home, she heard his entrance because once again he brought that simpleton Allison with him. She could hear the murmurs and the quiet laughter—no giggling this time—and the pause for a prefatory snog in the corridor and then the door of his room and how it opened and closed and *that* was what she was anticipating.

She gathered up the clothing. She strode to his room. She didn't knock. She opened the door, threw the clothing inside, and said, "I *protected* you. So do what you bloody *want* with this."

Then she saw that Allison Franklin wasn't the girl Brutus had brought home this time. It was Francie Adamucci, all bright-eyed and on her knees, her hands in the act of unzipping his trousers.

"Ding!" Francie said with a laugh as she went about the business she'd been engaged in. "Want to join us?"

HINDLIP
HEREFORDSHIRE

Every tedious part of her earlier trip to West Mercia Headquarters was repeated. Barbara and Lynley began with the interminable wait at the distant reception building, made just long enough to challenge their patience. Then came the drive to the headquarters' main building, past all the CCTV cameras and through the expanse of open land. After that, there was a break in the action for something new as Lynley sought a parking bay that was suitably distant from all other vehicles. This was done, Barbara knew, to preserve the one-million-pound paint job—copper in colour and every inch of it polished lovingly by hand—on his motor. Following that, however, the former process resumed. They were made to wait in the reception hall while Chief Constable Wyatt proved to them that the Met was as unwelcome today as the Met had been before.

After ten minutes, however, Lynley put an end to the wait. Approaching the enormous reception counter, he said to one of the civilians there, "The chief constable has more than made his point. Now as my detective sergeant is quite familiar with the route to his office, you can let him know we're on our way up, or we can surprise him. It's entirely up to you. Sergeant?" He nodded towards the stairway.

Barbara beat a happy path there while, behind her, she heard first a protest and then a hasty phone call being made, after which a voice cheerfully called out, "Oh yes. Do go up. The chief constable is expecting you." At that point she was already at the top of the stairs with Lynley just behind her.

She went to the same grand doors she'd been through before. This time, one of them stood open and as she went through it, CC Patrick Wyatt was coming across the room in her direction. His face was granite.

He said, "See here—"

To which Lynley replied with, "We can agree at once, Chief Constable: You've no time for us. We've no time for you. Shall we get on with it or argue who's more affronted by this situation?"

Oooh, Barbara thought. He was using the Voice. He rarely did that because he knew that when it came to being a duck out of water, *he* was the duck and it didn't make any sense to emphasise that. But every so often, such emphasis was necessary and the Voice was required. Upon hearing it, the other paused in surprise. It was the pause that Lynley sought.

Into it, he said, "We're not here to make your people look bad, sir, and we're certainly not here because we volunteered. The IPCC overlooked a detail when they investigated your Ludlow situation, and our job is to get to the bottom of that. Our presence has nothing at all to do with your force and everything to do with the IPCC."

Well, Barbara thought, this wasn't *entirely* true, but it did the job of catching the CC off guard, adding to what the Voice had started: instead of putting him on a defensive footing, the CC was now at least partially disarmed.

"Go on." Wyatt made no move to usher them farther into the office. But his granite face altered just round the eyes and his head turned a fraction as he unconsciously presented them with more of his ear.

Lynley said, "May I?" but he didn't wait for permission to shut the door. He didn't ask to sit, as this would give the CC an opportunity to refuse him.

Barbara took careful note of the nature of this pissing contest. She kept her mouth shut because between herself and Lynley, she knew which one of them was the bull, and this particular shop was filled with the kind of porcelain she was only too expert at smashing to bits.

They needed to know, Lynley explained to Wyatt, exactly who did what and when during nineteen days that had stretched between the paedophile call made from the Ludlow police station and the arrest of the deacon of St. Laurence Church. Nineteen days comprised quite enough time for at least a cursory look into the allegations made against Ian Druitt, but the IPCC had made no mention of any look at all. What could Chief Constable Wyatt tell them about that period of nineteen days?

Learning that the Met was making a second incursion into his patch, the chief constable had apparently prepared himself for this meeting, but he had little enough information to share: The IPCC had mentioned nothing in their report about an investigation because there had been no investigation. Had the anonymous call constituted information about a possible murder, the matter would have been taken differently. But this was a single call about a clergyman who had only just been given a public award in Ludlow. The call centre operator had done exactly what was required: logged the call in. When the log was read by the officer on duty, that officer made a judgement that anyone would have made: It was a crank call phoned in by someone who either was jealous or had an axe to grind with Ian Druitt.

"But surely you're not saying paedophilia is something that goes disregarded," Lynley said.

"Of course not," Wyatt replied. "But absent the ghost of a whisper of wrongdoing other than a phone call made—by the way—to the wrong calling centre, which is another matter entirely, have you a suggestion as to what the force was supposed to do?"

Wyatt went on to tell them that the closest manned station—in Shrewsbury—*could* have brought Druitt in for questioning immediately, yes. But failing a lengthy investigation into what appeared to be a nasty crank phone call, such questioning would have consisted of "What do you have to say about this, sir?" to which Druitt would have replied "It's absolute rubbish." After that, *if* there was sufficient manpower—which there was not—officers *might* have begun the process of interviewing every man, woman, and child with whom the clergyman had come into contact in the years he'd been part of St. Laurence parish.

"But the fact is that we don't *have* the manpower," Wyatt concluded. "What we do have is a single murder squad in the area and they're responsible for assaults, rape, and every other violent crime that happens on their patch. We're meant to make due. So I hope you see why an anonymous message about a deacon from St. Laurence Church would fall rather low on the list."

They did, of course. But . . . there remained the small matter of the arrest of Ian Druitt nineteen days later. If there had been no investigation based on the message, why had he been arrested at all?

"You must admit," Lynley pointed out, "something more must have come up. What my sergeant was able to learn from the PCSO in Ludlow—"

"Gary Ruddock," Barbara added. Wyatt shot her a look. She was undeterred. "He told me he got the order from his sergeant. But his sergeant would've got the order from somewhere else, especially if there wasn't ever an investigation, right?"

"Have you any idea who gave that order to the PCSO's sergeant?" Lynley asked.

"I try not to micromanage, Inspector. I've told you what I can. Any more information will need to come from the PCSO's sergeant. Since she gave the order to pick up the clergyman, only she can tell you what prompted her to do so."

Her name? was Lynley's next question.

She was called Geraldine Gunderson and the Met officers could get the rest of her details from reception.

MUCH WENLOCK
SHROPSHIRE

Havers lit a cigarette as they walked from the main headquarters building to the Healey Elliott. She began sucking down the smoke like someone determined to enjoy her final moments before execution. "The more I learn about what's gone on, the less makes sense," she said from within a cloud of smoke. "Nineteen days without an investigation and then the bloke's arrested. You ask me, someone knows something, and I expect that someone is sitting behind us in that building." She jerked her thumb back over her shoulder. "And *whatever* it is, no one wants the Met to dig it up."

Lynley couldn't entirely disagree. *Irregular* didn't begin to describe the arrest and subsequent death of the deacon of St. Laurence Church, Ludlow. But as to the what, the who, and the why of it all, he had difficulty assigning any of those to West Mercia Headquarters.

He said, "I wouldn't want to be in the CC's position. The cutbacks he's coping with are bad enough. On top of that he's been saddled with a death in custody, which he assumes the IPCC have investigated and found unfortunate but not criminal. He thinks that's the end of it, then suddenly the Met turns up in the person of you and the DCS. He goes through that, thinks it's finished, and then he learns the Met's to arrive a second time. He digs up everything he can and tells us what he knows, but we still have questions that he can't answer. It's pressure on pressure. One can't blame him for wanting it to end."

They reached the car and stood on either side of it while Havers finished her fag. She said, "I'm chuffed you can be so philosophical, sir. Especially since you've lost your holiday in Cornwall for a second time."

He looked beyond her towards an activity ongoing that appeared to involve police cadets and riot gear, which was not an especially reassuring sight. He said, "Yes. Well. It wasn't shaping up to be the holiday of my dreams anyway."

"Things not going swimmingly in the relationship department?"

"Daidre's become something of an expert at coming up with excuses."

Havers tossed the fag on the ground and tramped on it. "What d'you reckon she thinks you have in mind, taking her to Cornwall: planning to dump her down one of those abandoned mines you lot have scattered round the countryside?"

"That could be what concerns her, I admit," Lynley said wryly. He unlocked the car. They both climbed in.

When they were buckled up and he'd turned on the ignition, Havers said, "As ever, sir, you've got your work cut out. I mean, it's not like I don't keep saying."

"You do. But I remain ever sanguine."

"One of your finer qualities. But can I just say . . . ?"

"Since you will anyway," Lynley noted.

"It's only that not everyone wants to end their days in Cornwall inside someone's ancestral home with three hundred rooms."

"Howenstow's hardly that, Barbara."

"P'rhaps not, but I expect you've got a whopping great gallery with a few hundred years of Lynleys hanging there looking like they smell something nasty."

"I'd hardly call it 'whopping great.'"

"Ha! I *knew* you lot would have a gallery."

Lynley cast her a look and knew she would read it as he intended, something she would undoubtedly call one of his "See here, Sergeant" expressions. He said to her, "It's not as if I'm proposing marriage, Barbara. But it's been over a year for us now, and I merely thought Daidre might at some point in time like to meet my mother. And the others, of course."

"Who would those be, the butler and the scullery maids?"

"We have only day help, Sergeant, and not even every day at that, unfortunately. Aside from the butler, of course, and while I'd very much like to apologise for his presence, he's nearly one hundred and fifty years old and no one quite remembers who hired him. To force him out into the street now in order not to offend someone's republican sensibilities seems rather like an act of cruelty."

"Very funny, sir. You can make a joke but what I'm saying is that she probably reckons it's some bloody test. For all you know, she thinks you want to see if she knows which of the twenty-five forks she's meant to use on her sausage and mash. Not that you'd let sausage and mash pollute your fine china, 'course."

"Not that I would," he noted.

"So, what then? You're planning to just soldier on in that department?"

"Soldiering on appears to be what I do best."

They left the grounds of West Mercia Headquarters with Havers using the huge *A-Z,* which Lynley preferred to any other method of navigation. He liked to have a sense of the countryside through which they were driving, something that a smartphone's GPS wouldn't ever give him. Havers groused about this as she would do, but she settled in. She managed to get them to the small town of Much Wenlock without a single wrong turn, although admittedly things got a bit iffy in Kidderminster's town centre, where she forced him to circle a roundabout three times since she couldn't take in the road signs quickly enough to make a directional decision. But they finally made it to their destination, finding themselves in another of the county's picturesque towns: a mediaeval place of half-timbered and timber-framed buildings begging for tourists to aim cameras in their direction, as well as a few ranges of perfectly proportioned Georgian homes. The age of the town was suggested by its ancient Guildhall, which stood upon enormous oak pillars and rested above what had once been the prison. It was a building of timber and plaster, of gables and mullioned windows, and beneath it the iron staples of a whipping post suggested justice that had been swift and bleak.

The address they had for Sergeant Geraldine Gunderson was, as one would expect in such a place where the postman was expected to know everyone by name, less than crystalline. It involved the number 3, the identifying location as The Farmhouse, and Nr the Priory, which completed the given information. The Priory was easy enough to find since it was an historic ruin and the routes to historic ruins were generally well marked so that the curious might investigate, but even then following the signs to it did not actually reveal any part of the great abbey itself, since it was sheltered not only by a stone wall but also by banks of limes and beeches and cedars that would have made it difficult for even Cromwell to find. But past it and down a secondary lane so narrow that Lynley winced at the danger to the Healey Elliott's wings, they came upon what was posted "The Farmhouse," which turned out to be quite a large building of ancient vintage, timber-framed and subdivided into respectably sized cottages. Conveniently, these were numbered, so all that was required was finding a space to park where the car would be most sheltered from passing tractors.

Once this was accomplished—with Havers going on in her usual fashion about the two hundred fifty yards they had to hike back to the farmhouse from the narrow lay-by that Lynley found—they made fairly easy contact with Sergeant Gunderson. Her part of the subdivided farmhouse was the most tumbledown, its appearance suggesting this state mostly because of an ill-kept garden in the front that had long ago waved the white flag to a wisteria never trained to do anything but choke each piece of vegetation that had tried to gain a foothold there. They tramped through this to the front door, where an iron knocker had rusted nearly through. There was no bell, so the knocker and a good few whacks on the unpainted wood were the only means of alerting someone that visitors had come to call.

A tall and harried-looking woman answered. She said, "You're the Met, I presume," and added, "Come this way, then. I'm in the midst . . . ," and she left them to enter, to close the door, and to follow her along a stone-floored corridor that took them into a dining room. There, a massive piece of bright green fabric had been thrown on a table, with part of it being attached to an elongated form made from chicken wire. A scissors, a stapler, and a roll of Sellotape were all being used to effect the fabric's attachment while the same implements had already been applied to a large piece of polystyrene shaped not unlike an Elizabethan ruff. It was now covered with a layer of bubble wrap while yellow fabric dotted in pink appeared to be waiting to cover this.

She said frankly, "Yes. Well. I'm *complete* crap at sewing, but didn't my eldest raise her hand and shout, 'My mummy will!' when the teacher asked who might be the Hookah-Smoking Caterpillar. Afternoon tea, this is. One of those blasted school fundraisers that they have every time one turns round. For this one—if you can believe it—the servers will be characters from *Alice in Wonderland*. Or perhaps it's *Through the Looking-Glass*. I have no clue there. I suppose I should be happy Miriam didn't raise her hand and volunteer me to bake tarts or whatever because the one thing I actually do worse than sewing is baking. But on the other hand, I could have bought the tarts. Where on earth could I buy a caterpillar costume? The hookah was simple. One can order them off the Internet. No surprise there but it *was* a surprise to discover that a caterpillar costume could not be had for love or money."

"You're Sergeant Gunderson," Lynley verified.

"Oh. Sorry. Of course. But it's Gerry, if you will."

Lynley introduced himself and Havers, and Gerry Gunderson said that she was happy enough to take a break from the wretched sewing exercise because she was close to losing her mind and even closer to *seriously* abusing her eldest daughter when she next walked through the front door. She offered them fresh lemonade. She warned them that "it's rather tart as I don't use much sugar," but both Lynley and Havers indicated that they were willing to have a go.

Gunderson then recommended that they sit outside "in the back of the place," as she put it, adding that since the day was fine and as long as they didn't mind chickens, they could all enjoy the good weather. They agreed to this as well, and she led them from the dining room through a neatly kept kitchen to a door leading out to the back of the cottage. There seven chickens pecked at the ground while two more roosted on a round wooden table whose chairs were tufted with years of lichen.

They were advised, "No worries. That won't come off on your clothing at this time of year, and I rather like it," regarding the lichen. The chickens were shooed away. Gunderson told them that she'd be with them presently, and in the meantime they were to enjoy . . . "whatever," she said with a wave of her hand. Lynley wasn't sure what she meant: the chickens, the lichen, the condition of the garden, which had mostly been taken over by the fowl, or the swelling of a hillside in the distance where a coppice of what seemed to be hornbeams had created a smallish woodland long gone without maintenance.

Gunderson wasn't away from them long enough for either of them to make a decision about what they intended to enjoy. She banged into the cottage and then banged out of the cottage. She carried a large baking pan in lieu of a tray. On it she'd assembled the offered lemonade.

Lynley considered Gunderson as she deposited the refreshments. There was virtually nothing English about her save her accent, which was English Midlands through and through. Otherwise, she looked foreign, with her olive skin, coal-coloured hair, and deeply brown eyes. She had a nose reminiscent of Italian noblemen.

She threw herself into a chair, watched them each take a sip of her lemonade, and said, "Well? Can you stand it?"

"Not bad at all," Havers replied.

Gunderson looked pleased at this, and Lynley took a sip of his. It turned out to be mostly water, for which he was grateful, considering Gunderson's remark about sugar. He then explained what they were doing in Shropshire.

Gunderson said, "Oh God. I know, I know. I don't need my memory jogged about what happened."

"Meaning?"

"Meaning the night in March that put all of us on this road. It's not likely I'll ever forget it, Inspector."

"Thomas," he said.

"Thomas," she agreed.

"What can you tell us about that night?" As Lynley asked the question, Havers removed her notebook and a pencil. She'd switched, Lynley saw, to the sort of pencil Nkata used: mechanical. He was duly impressed.

Gunderson went through the night for them. She confirmed what Havers had written in her report regarding the Shrewsbury patrol officers who were in the midst of dealing with a series of house and shop burglaries and were thus unavailable to fetch Ian Druitt from Ludlow. She also indicated that she knew nothing of any investigation that might have been done into the accusation of paedophilia prior to the order to fetch Druitt. She said she'd only learned—after the man had "offed himself in custody," as she put it—that this "rotten mess" had begun with an anonymous phone call. *That*, she told them, had been a real jaw-dropper for her. Essentially, she didn't know what anyone had been thinking and what the bloody hell had been going on.

She added, "Look, some of that's my fault. I've said that to my guv."

"How so?" Havers was the one to ask.

"My husband's in hospital. Colon cancer. He's going to survive but it's been hell. My mind occasionally goes elsewhere and it certainly might have done on that night. But all the same, my remit is merely to be responsible for the PCSOs in the area. I was told to pass on the order about Druitt to our Ludlow officer, and that's what I did. I didn't ask why as there was no reason to. Like you, I expect, I obey an order when it's given."

Lynley chose not disabuse her of her conclusion since Havers was not the only Met officer present who'd ignored an order in the past. Instead he asked her where the order to have the Ludlow PCSO fetch Ian Druitt had come from. He was surprised by her answer.

"From headquarters," she said.

He looked at Havers. She looked at him. Her expression answered his unspoken question. Headquarters giving anyone orders about anything had not been mentioned before this moment.

He said, "From whom, exactly?"

"The DCC," Gunderson replied.

"Deputy Chief Constable?" Havers clarified.

Lynley added, "We've met CC Wyatt but no one else connected to headquarters. He said nothing about a DCC."

Gunderson didn't seem to find this unusual. She lifted her lemonade, took a swig, and said, "Don't know a damn thing about that, do I? All I can tell you is the DCC rang me and gave me the word: have Ludlow's PCSO take a bloke called Ian Druitt to the local station and wait for the Shrewsbury officers to fetch him up to the custody suite there. That's what she wanted and that's what I did: I rang Gary Ruddock—that's the PCSO—and gave him the word."

"'She'?" Havers said.

"What?"

"You said 'she' in reference to the DCC," Lynley pointed out. "May we have her name?"

"Oh. Right. Sorry," Gerry Gunderson said. "She's called Freeman. Clover Freeman. I took the order from her."

MUCH WENLOCK
SHROPSHIRE

"Something's not right, sir." Havers paused just outside the door of Geraldine Gunderson's part of the ancient farmhouse. She did the depressingly expected: she fished in her shoulder bag to bring forth a packet of Players. She lit up.

Lynley wanted to ask her for the umpteenth time when she planned to kick the habit, as he was becoming quite concerned about the impact on her health. He refrained, however. She would only point out that the sanctimony of the former smoker was as bad as an erstwhile atheist's banging on about his moment of coming to Jesus. So instead he said, "Which part of it, aside from the sergeant's sewing skills?"

They proceeded through the mini jungle of wisteria and made it unscathed to a narrow lane, where a sudden *ker-wit, ker-wit* striking the air suggested partridges were nearby. Havers puffed away. She said,

"Oh, she's got her work cut out there. It wasn't looking like any caterpillar I've ever seen."

Lynley said dryly, casting a look in her direction. "So if it's not Sergeant Gunderson's sewing . . . ?"

"It's this: we were just slapped on the side of the head by a bloody interesting coincidence. The DCC Gunderson told us about? The one who rang her up with the order to fetch Ian Druitt to the police station?"

"Clover Freeman," Lynley said.

"Happens she's not the only Freeman the guv and I tripped over in Shropshire, sir." She took another lungful of smoke. This one was deeper than the others. Really, Lynley thought, she *desperately* needed to take the cure.

He said, "Who's the other?"

"I never met him. The guv did the honours. But he's called Finnegan Freeman, and he was a helper at this after-school kids' club that Druitt ran. Far as I know, when Ardery questioned him, he didn't say word one to her about having a relation in the police force."

"Perhaps she's not a relation. Freeman isn't an unusual name."

"Not like Stravinsky. Right."

He lifted an eyebrow. "Sergeant, you continue to impress."

"Couldn't hum a note. That came out of nowhere."

"Alas," he said. "But do go on."

"My point is, assuming his mum and this DCC Freeman are one and the same—or saying she's just his auntie or something or even his gran—it seems to me he would've mentioned it when DCS Ardery had a word with him. Deputy Chief Constable? That outranks Ardery by a long chalk. A London copper shows up at his door to have a word or two and why wouldn't he mention on the by and by that *he's* got his own copper up his sleeve?"

"Assuming they're related, would he have a reason to do that?"

"To shake Ardery up. To put her on the wrong foot. To get her worried about dealing rough with him. But he didn't do that and I wonder why." She was silent for a moment, examining the tip of her Player and rolling it between her fingers.

"Again, there might be no relation between them."

"Right. Unless there is. Unless, he *did* tell her and she didn't mention it to me for some reason."

Lynley knew Havers well enough to catch the underlying point she was making. He said, "Because she wanted to get back to London and she knew that a DCC related to someone she was speaking to made things more complicated? It threw a bone into the pack of dogs, so to speak."

"Not that I like the comparison much."

"Sorry," he said. "It was inadvertent. And more metaphor than simile if we want to get technical. As to DCS Ardery deliberately overlooking something that might be crucial . . . ?"

"It's possible, isn't it? If she was hot to get back to town and she told me about this Freeman thing, sir, she'd've known I'd want to shake that nut like a squirrel in a tree." And when he glanced in her direction, she added, "I know, I *know*. Squirrels don't shake nuts. But you catch my meaning."

"It's curious," was all that Lynley was willing to offer her. They reached the Healey Elliott and leaned against it while Havers finished up the fag. One side of the car bordered a hedge taller than Lynley. The other opened onto a field where ripening wheat grew so precisely laid out, it was as if the hand of God had applied shears to the height of it. A breeze rustled it. A deep blue sky banked with cumulus clouds hung above it in contrast to its golden hue.

Havers tossed the dog-end of the Player onto the ground at last and saw to it with the toe of her shoe. She said, "It looks like something more to me," and he knew she was referring to the issue of coincidence. "Say she's a relative of this kid Finnegan. If she is, could be she knew there might be some truth to what that anonymous call said about the paedophilia bit. Or at least that she *thought* there could be truth to it and she wanted to find out pronto because her son-nephew-grandson-whatever worked with the bloke and might end up involved."

Lynley considered this as he unlocked the car and they climbed inside. When he had the engine engaged, he said, "Or the son-nephew-grandson himself could have made the call."

"Right. And say this kid's a relation of hers. He stumbles on something," Havers said meditatively. "Something he sees. Something he hears."

"He witnesses something directly," Lynley offered.

"Or one of the kids in the after-school club tells him something. He can't believe it but he checks it out and he *has* to believe it then. But the last thing he wants is to be marked as a grass—what kid wants that and he's still a kid, according to Ardery—so he uses that intercom outside the nick in Ludlow and he does it anonymously. All he knows is that what's going on has to stop. But nothing happens . . . so then what? He tells his mum or his aunt or his gran or whoever this DCC Freeman might be and she sets the wheels in motion?"

"That does play out, doesn't it?"

"Except the guv said that he was hot, bothered, and righteous when the subject of Druitt diddling children came up. 'Course, that could have been all for show, I reckon, because he'd *have* to be heavy with the righteous protecting of Druitt so the gaff wouldn't be blown, the gaff being the fact that he was the person grassing up Druitt in the first place, eh?"

Lynley took all of this on board as he managed a three-point turn farther along the lane and then headed them back in the direction of the village. It seemed to him that it was time to track down DCC Clover Freeman in order to get her side of the tale that concluded with the death of an Anglican deacon.

While he drove, Havers tracked the DCC. She began with West Mercia Headquarters, reporting back to him that Clover Freeman had left for the day. She managed to get the DCC's mobile number off the chief constable's secretary after explaining it was a matter of some urgency that the Met coppers speak with her personally since they'd sorted out her involvement in the matter of the death of Ian Druitt. . . . Reaching those last five words was as far as she'd needed to go. Lynley murmured, "Nice work," as he followed the route into the village and pulled over when they were in view of the timber-framed Guildhall, where a woman with a selfie-stick was grinning into her mobile and, he reckoned, ruining an otherwise lovely picture of the town's most photographed building.

He listened idly to Havers's half of the conversation, which appeared to consist of a negotiation with the DCC, who seemed to think this matter of speaking with the Met officers could wait till tomorrow, especially since she herself was en route to her home.

Some back-and-forthing happened next, during which Havers was all courtesy with her *No, ma'ams* and *It's necessary, ma'ams* and *We can easily come to you, ma'ams.* The result was an agreement that, considering the hour, she and Lynley would come along to the DCC's home in Worcester, after having an early dinner themselves at some point. They would arrive at the DCC's home round half past eight. If the DCC would text her address . . . ? Thank you, ma'am.

When Havers ended the call, she said to Lynley, "She'll be waiting for us, but she won't be happy."

"I did get that impression," he told her.

WORCESTER
HEREFORDSHIRE

When Trevor Freeman returned from his walk with the Rambling Rogues, he took an evaluative look at his hiking boots. They wouldn't do, he decided. They were far too clean.

Along with his hiking sticks, he accomplished what needed to be accomplished in the back garden, where he used the hosepipe and the herbaceous border that was not a herbaceous border at all but rather a dug-up and eternally uncultivated rectangle of earth running along the fence. There, he created a nice pool of muck and stirred it about with one of his sticks, achieving a fine goo into which he plopped his boots. He wrestled them round a bit, and when they were sufficiently filthy, he returned to the front of the house, where he placed both boots and sticks in extremely plain sight.

Inside the house, he went for his mobile. He hadn't taken it with him while he was out with the Rambling Rogues because mobile phones were verboten. The group leader was allowed one, of course, but only for use in cases of emergency. Should one of the older members of the Rogues have a heart attack or a stroke, the club did not wish to see him languishing away for want of a device of communication.

When he took his mobile from the work top, Trevor saw that he'd missed four calls while he'd been gone. Three of them were from Clover. The fourth had come from Gaz Ruddock. Trevor went for Clover's first and was struck at once by what she asked him: Could Trev phone Gaz Ruddock? Would he invite him to dinner for tomorrow night? Trevor went on to her second: Had Trev managed to make contact with Gaz Ruddock yet? Was he coming for a meal? And finally: Why wasn't Trev returning her calls?

Trevor found all of this mystifying and, frankly, a little troubling. Why, he wondered, had Clover not merely phoned Gaz Ruddock herself? Since she had the time to ring her husband on three occasions while he'd been with the Rogues, why not just make the phone call she was asking him to make?

He pondered this as he opened the fridge and brought forth a bottle of fizzy water. He drank it down, tried to come up with an answer, failed to do so, felt a twinge of disquiet, but phoned the PCSO as requested. He caught Gaz at the market, picking up some staples along with the ingredients to put together spag bol for dinner that night. Before Trevor could extend the invitation that Clover wished him to extend, though, Gaz continued.

"Scotland Yard are up here again," he said. "I had the word from my sergeant this afternoon. It's the Druitt suicide. You know about it, Trev?"

A very odd question, Trevor thought. That Gaz hadn't been summarily sacked as a result of Druitt's death was owing entirely to Clover's intercession on behalf of the young man who'd quickly become her protégé while he was in training. Gaz surely knew that Clover would have told her husband about all of it. He said, "I'm not likely to be in the dark about that, Gaz."

"Oh, I didn't mean the . . . you know . . . the death? I meant did you know Scotland Yard're coming a second time. Did Clo tell you? I'm only wondering why she didn't ring me, see. I'd think she would do. She has to know about this, eh?"

"Haven't the least idea. I've not seen her. I can have her ring you when she gets home."

"I'd be that grateful. It's only just that—"

"It's only that you're worried. I know. It's reasonable."

"Rumour is there might be a lawsuit."

"Try not to think so far ahead. One day at a time. Clover's asked me to phone you about having dinner with us, by the way."

They made their arrangements for the dinner, and his duty done, Trevor set to rummaging through the fridge. He was the family cook—had been since the day of his marriage to a cop with a hellish schedule—and he sought whatever he could come up with for a decent stir-fry. He was sniffing a package of tofu and asking himself if tofu could go bad when his mobile rang.

He saw it was Clover and he answered with, "I expected you home long before now, Missus Freeman. I was hoping for a little bit of this and a bigger bit of that. Can I interest you?"

She answered him with, "Have you managed to reach Gaz? Why haven't you returned my calls?"

"What's all this with Gaz, Clover? He's in a twist about Scotland Yard planning another trip to Shropshire, by the way."

"They're not planning. They're here," was her reply. "Wyatt's in a *complete* state about it. Well, who can blame him? What a bucket of horseshit this is." Then she sighed and went on with, "Never mind. I'm in a mood. I'll be home soon. Shall I stop for takeaway? Or have you done the shop?"

Takeaway would save him, but he knew she was probably knackered and would prefer just to drive straight home. "No need," he said. "I'll manage something," although the truth was that he'd also had a look at the celery, which had turned out to be as limp as a eunuch's dick. The red and green peppers weren't much better and an onion was in the midst of turning an unappealing shade of purplish grey. "I'm concocting a healthy dinner to impress you. I'm concocting other things as well."

"Are you? We'll see about that. I've had one hell a day."

When they rang off, Trevor started the brown rice, a lot of it as the rest of the meal was going to need some serious help. Once he'd done that, he went for wine. Considering Clover's state, she would want a very large glass of it. From the cupboard beneath the stairs, he unearthed a bottle of Tempranillo. He uncorked it and decided it could breathe well enough in two large-bowled glasses. He poured them and reckoned his own didn't need to breathe at all.

He drank as he chopped all of the usable veg they had. He had bought himself an electric wok some time in the past, but so far he hadn't gone to the bother of learning how to use it. So a large pan was going to have to suit, and he sorted this out and doused its bottom with cooking oil. He was just about to peel the garlic when he heard a car door slam outside the house. He grabbed Clover's wine, made fast tracks for the front door, and opened it.

She was done up in that no-nonsense fashion she employed for workdays: hair a severe bun low on her neck, uniform uncreased even late in the day, stud earrings of gold and no other jewellery save her engagement and wedding rings. She did indeed look knackered, but as ever, she looked perfectly delicious to him.

He saw that she was examining his hiking sticks and boots as he'd intended. She raised her gaze from them to him. He extended the wineglass to her, and as she took it she said, "How far then?" When he said he'd done twelve miles, she hooted and returned with, "When pigs fly."

But still she kissed him there on the doorstep. She made the kiss last and he did nothing to end it. She said against his mouth, "Please feel me up properly. The neighbours would probably like a diversion."

He was very happy to cooperate. Despite the day she'd had, there appeared to be hope for what would follow.

She said, "You know, you're still the most delicious thing on two legs." And then she added with a laugh as her hand explored his crotch, "Hmm. Seems like three legs."

Trevor decided that sex as a prelude to dinner and conversation could be the answer. After an interlude in the bedroom or the sitting room or right there in the entry, Clover might be able to relax. But before he could engage in a move other than circling the tips of his fingers round her left nipple, she stirred in his arms and said, "Is something burning?"

God. He'd completely forgotten. He released Clover and said, "Fuck!" Then, "Got to go to the rescue. Won't be long till dinner. Sorry. About the . . . you know . . . the third leg and all."

"Just as well. I'm done in."

"P'rhaps later?"

"We'll see. Best take care of—" She sniffed the air. "Would that be rice?"

"You're very good," he told her.

He dashed to the kitchen where he discovered that while the bottom of the rice pan held a real blackened skin of the stuff, the rest was edible. So while Clover was, one hoped, up in the bedroom slipping into something seductive, comfortable, and suitable for quick removal, he saw to the rest of their meal.

He'd finished browning the tofu when Clover returned to him, wineglass in her hand. She topped up her Tempranillo and held the bottle out to him with a questioning look, but he shook his head. The glass and a half he'd downed had produced enough of a pleasant buzz.

She sat at the table. He could see she was restless: rearranging cutlery, folding paper napkins, realigning plates. It wasn't like her to be so fidgety. He said, "How bad is it?"

"This Scotland Yard business? I'm not drunk enough yet." She took up her wineglass but merely examined the garnet colour of the Spanish wine. She said shrewdly, "Did you really walk twelve miles?"

He knew he looked abashed as he replied, "No."

"One mark for honesty. Where did you go? Down the pub?"

"I was with the Rambling Rogues, all right. But there was . . . a shorter option today."

"Of . . . ?"

He chose this moment to attend to the browning tofu. When she said his name in that way she had that declared, *You'll be in trouble if you don't answer,* he said, "Three miles," and glanced in her direction.

She was casting her own gaze heavenward. "Oh for God's sake, Trev. You own a bloody fitness centre. If *you* can't find the time for a decent workout—"

"I know," he cut in. "And I intend to. Don't make your day worse by worrying about me. I'm fit. I'm giving up chips and beer."

"As before, with the pigs and their wings . . ."

They bantered with each other as he finished up with their dinner. It didn't take long till he carried the meal to the table, which sat in a small alcove that looked out at the back garden. In the month of May their lawn, at least, should have been thick and lush, but it seemed that they never had the time to deal with it properly. The sole attempt at making something special out of the entire space had been to throw fourteen different packets of seeds on the ground and to hope for the best. That hadn't turned out half bad since they *did* have flowers here and there, those that survived through some sort of Darwinian process.

He said to her, "As to Scotland Yard?"

"Still not drunk enough. Tell me about your day."

There wasn't much to tell when one ran an fitness centre. Spinning classes, hot yoga, swimming, Zumba, weight training: these didn't offer intriguing topics of conversation unless an old codger took on too much activity and an ambulance needed to be called. Occasionally one of the trainers ran afoul of propriety and had to be dealt with—hands off the lovely young mothers attempting to get back into condition, please—but that was it.

He said, "Very little to report. Went out with the Rogues, saw many trees, frightened half a dozen deer, observed rabbits, counted magpies. Aside from doing the wages at the centre and chatting to Gaz, that was it. I do think he wants you to ring and give him reassurance about Scotland Yard turning up again."

She was, he saw, not digging into her food. She'd removed her hair from the severity of its bun and she ran her hand through it, back from her forehead. She said, "I expect he does. But I don't know how much more I can do for him, Trev. The real issue is going to be Finnegan anyway."

Trevor frowned. He saw that she clocked his expression because she went on to say, "They're probably going to speak to him again, the Met."

"Ah. Well, Druitt and Finn were mates, after all."

"But they weren't, not really. Ian Druitt was someone Finnegan *thought* he knew. And nothing anyone can say to him has been enough to convince him he didn't actually know Druitt at all."

"Anyone?"

"What?"

"You said nothing anyone can say. But I expect you mean nothing you could say."

"I do tend to know more about the darker side of mankind than Finnegan does."

"I wouldn't disagree with that. On the other hand, the boy *was* rather involved in that club. He wasn't just going through the motions. He had a real interest for once. So he would have seen things from the inside, wouldn't he?"

"I think it's rather that he would have seen exactly what he was intended to see. This passion he has about Druitt's innocence in all matters . . . ? It's quite mad, Trev. God. I wish he'd never met the man."

Trevor had gone back to his food but now he looked up from it. He said nothing but he didn't need to. She read him well, as she always had done.

"Yes, yes. I know," she said. "I was the one who wanted him involved in a social programme. I was the one who made it a condition of this college experience he was so desperate to have. I was the one who approved his choice of the after-school club *as* the social programme. I see, I see, I see it all. But he was meant merely to volunteer in an activity in Ludlow. That was it. Full stop. He *wasn't* meant to make it a life interest."

"He's hardly done that," Trevor pointed out.

"Oh, I don't know. It's all gone straight to hell. My intention was just to keep him occupied so when he had free time, he'd have something other than . . . I don't know . . . drinking, drugs, sexual profligacy, *whatever* to tempt him . . . and look how it's all come out. Every which way it's a mess when all along the only thing I want is to get him through life without his ending up in gaol."

Trevor deliberately made no reply to this because he wanted her to hear her own words. From them, he wanted her to understand for once what she was declaring about their son. It was no lie that Finnegan had been a challenge straight out of the womb, but he was not a criminal type nor had he ever been. A bit wild, yes. Rather more ungovernable, yes. Sometimes defiant. But never with any intention of doing wrong.

After a moment of silence, she said in a completely altered tone, "All right. I see what you want me to see. This isn't about Finnegan. It probably never was. And I admit I'm out of sorts. It's the pressure, Trev. If the work of the West Mercia police force is under scrutiny, it means we're all under scrutiny and Gaz Ruddock's work in particular is under scrutiny. Again. I suppose my concern is that Finnegan not make things worse with wild declarations about Druitt that cause everything to turn out badly."

"For who?" Trevor found himself asking this question with some care because there seemed to be waters here that he'd not known existed before this conversation.

She said, "For Gaz, I suppose. This is—essentially—the fourth time he's been looked at. He might be sacked."

"He might well be. But that would be down to him, wouldn't it?"

"Well, it's hardly fair to ask him to go through this yet *another* time."

"Is it a question of fairness?" Trevor reached for his wineglass but didn't drink until he'd said, "To be honest, Clover, I'd no idea that what happens to Gaz Ruddock worries you."

"Of course it worries me. Why wouldn't it worry me? I took him *on*, Trevor. I told myself I saw something in him that warranted my interest and I made him special, my personal project, my protégé. And he's done splendidly until this . . . this Druitt thing. He's never put a foot wrong. So I don't want him to lose his job, and beyond that . . ."

Trevor could tell she was hesitating because she'd either just realised something or because she was venturing near to something she didn't want him to know.

He said, "What?"

Still, nothing. She looked at her wineglass. She turned its stem in her fingers. She drank.

"Clover? What?"

"It's this. If he looks bad, then I look bad. I don't want that and I expect, in my position, you wouldn't want it either."

"And that's all, is it?"

"What else would it be?"

Trevor said after a moment of hesitation, "I suppose that's the real question." He knew his next remark was iffy, he recognised that it was going to stir up those waters that he'd only just realised might be there, but he needed to take a step closer to those waters, so he said, "I've not thought of this before but . . . what's Gaz Ruddock actually *to* you, Clover?"

She stared at him for what seemed like a minute but was probably not. She finally responded with, "What on earth are you asking me?"

"Nothing more than the words I spoke: What's Gaz Ruddock to you? Is he something more than someone whose cause you took up because you told yourself you 'saw something' in him?"

"I believe I've already explained myself."

"Have you? Completely, I mean."

"What exactly are you implying?"

"I'm just asking you a question. It seems you're in a state about Gaz Ruddock so it's logical for me to ask about him. Isn't it?"

"Is it?" she asked. "We see things differently." She placed her napkin on the table, crossed her cutlery on the plate. "I think we're finished here," she told him. "The Scotland Yard officers are arriving soon. You might want to explore your concerns with them."

WORCESTER
HEREFORDSHIRE

The DCC lived in a newish housing estate where detached brick houses had both garages and driveways, and front gardens grew lawns that were bordered with colourful flower beds. The Freeman home was identical to the others but in possession only of a sad-looking lawn.

Upon ringing the bell, they were admitted into the house not by the DCC but by a man who introduced himself as Trevor Freeman, the DCC's husband. He was a sharp-featured bloke with a shaved skull where the shadow of stubble indicated a deeply receding hairline. He was tall, just an inch shorter than Lynley, but he carried too much weight round his middle like a lot of men his age, which appeared to be somewhere in his late forties or early fifties. That, Lynley thought, probably eliminated Clover Freeman as gran. So if there was a relationship between her and one Finnegan Freeman, it would probably be mother or aunt.

Clover, Trevor Freeman told them, was just putting together a tray of coffees. If they'd take a seat in the lounge, she'd be with them directly. He indicated an open doorway to their right, where a fireplace held unlit artificial coals and where on the wall a very large flat-screen television with the sound muted was broadcasting *Withnail and I.*

They entered, and Trevor Freeman followed. They saw at once that one of the walls had been dedicated to family photos. The couple apparently had only one child, as pictures of a boy throughout the years were arranged, as artfully as these things can be, round a large wedding picture of the late-twentysomething Freemans: Trevor with fine-looking curly hair and his wife appearing suitably radiant. Unexpectedly, the photo brought to Lynley's mind his own wedding day and Helen and, fleetingly, how it had felt the moment they were made husband and wife: that stab through the heart that was his being's way of saying yes to something he had not recognised till he'd nearly lost her to someone else. And then he'd lost her anyway. But that did not bear thinking about.

Havers was saying, "This is your boy, eh?"

Trevor Freeman was replying with, "Yes, right. That's Finn, that is."

"He's nice-looking," Havers noted.

"He was that. Then he shaved off half his hair and had his skull tattooed. I can't say it did much for the overall look of him."

"Ouch," Havers said. "But at least he can cover it when he grows the hair back. Presumably."

He rubbed his own bald head, saying, "Long as he doesn't inherit this."

Havers looked among the other photos, saying, "He's your only one?"

"We wanted more, but it didn't happen. Might still, of course."

"How old's he, then?"

"Just nineteen. He lives in Ludlow. He's at the college."

"We're hoping he finds something useful to do with his life while he's there. I'm Clover Freeman."

They swung round from the pictures. The deputy chief constable stood in the doorway, bearing a tray that held a large coffee press as well as mugs and the rest of the paraphernalia of coffee drinking. Her husband quickly took this from her, which allowed her to offer her hand first to Lynley and then to Havers. Each of them introduced themselves. She suggested they sit, and she poured them each a cup of coffee, along with one for herself. There was no fourth mug, and she clarified why when she said to her husband, "Trev, if you've something else to do, there's no need for you to be here, I expect," and she turned for verification to Lynley, adding, "Is there, Inspector?"

Trevor said, "You've not come about Finn, have you?" as if their answer was going to dictate whatever he did next.

Lynley said pleasantly, "Not that I know. Should we have done?"

Clover said, "I can't see why."

"Then I'll leave you lot to it," was Trevor Freeman's conclusion, and he did just that. A moment later they could hear him climbing the stairs. A moment after that, a television programme blared, but its volume was immediately lowered.

All of this gave Lynley the time to study Clover Freeman, now that it had been established that she was the mother of the Finnegan whom Havers had referenced and whom Isabelle had interviewed. She wasn't tall, but she was in admirable physical condition as evidenced by the singlet-style top she wore, which showed the firm arms and developed shoulders of someone who trained with weights. Her cropped leggings completed the picture of her fitness. She was muscle and sinew without a hint of flab anywhere.

Once they'd all seen to their coffees, she said to them, "How can I help you? Chief Constable Wyatt told me you'd be coming to headquarters. I'm sorry I couldn't be there when you spoke with him earlier."

Lynley nodded at Havers to give her the lead. She said, "Our guv—DCS Ardery—she took your Finnegan through the paces the first time we were here. He never once said his mum's a cop. He also never said his mum was the one who gave the order to pick up his pal Ian Druitt."

Clo Freeman looked from Havers to Lynley and back to Havers. She said, "Am I meant to comment on that?"

Lynley said, "We're trying to clarify all the relationships we're coming across."

"There certainly can't be many."

"This one," Havers pointed out, "you, your son, Ian Druitt, Geraldine Gunderson, and I s'pose we ought to add Gary Ruddock . . . It's the one that's got us wondering the most."

"Why?"

Havers shrugged. "It's a case of turning over a rock in Ian Druitt's death and discovering another relationship lying in wait."

The DCC picked up a spoon and stirred her coffee. She said, "I see. Well, I have one actual relationship here: with my son. He had a relationship with Mr. Druitt. I never met the man. Everything else is either chain of command or what led up to Mr. Druitt's suicide."

Lynley saw that a Q & A about relationships could quickly become merely a disagreement about how three individual police officers saw things relative to Ian Druitt's death. He said, "We're back in Shropshire because Sergeant Havers discovered there was a stretch of nineteen days between an anonymous call and the death of Ian Druitt. But the IPCC's report makes no mention of that or of what went on during those nineteen days. We know from our conversation today with your CC that there was no enquiry made into the paedophilia allegations during that time gap. Since you were the one who brought the nineteen days to an end, we're hoping you can tell us why."

She'd been listening carefully, her gazed fixed on Lynley as he spoke. She replied with, "That's quite simple to explain. I knew nothing about an anonymous call prior to that day."

"How'd you learn about it, then?" Havers had taken out her notebook, Lynley saw. So, apparently, had DCC Freeman, and her expression was not one that welcomed the fact.

Freeman frowned and said after a moment, "I got the word at the training centre, as I recall. We had quite a large meeting there—it's on the headquarters' grounds—and at some point word started going round. A deacon of the church, paedophilia."

"Do you recall how you yourself heard the word?" Lynley asked.

"I'm very sorry. There was a great deal going on that day. What I can tell you for certain is that I became aware that a number of individuals were talking about an allegation against this man Ian Druitt. I wish I could be more specific than that."

"Why'd you have Druitt fetched in for questioning, then?" Havers asked. "Is that typical when a tip is rung in? I mean, it's obvious that a tip having to do with an ongoing investigation would be passed along straightaway to the officers in charge, but this wasn't about an ongoing case at all, far as I've been able to suss out."

"That's true," Freeman said. "But this was a tip about a possible paedophile that had been ignored, and I didn't like that: either as deputy chief constable or as a mother."

"So you rang Gunderson and told her to haul him in."

"That would be the short version. I ordered her to see to it that someone brought him in."

"How long was this after you heard about the accusation?" Lynley asked.

"As I've said, I rang her that same evening and told her to have someone fetch the man to the station and that's what she did. But you must have paperwork from the Met's earlier visit that explains all this."

"If you'll refresh our memories," Lynley said politely.

Freeman's expression altered. It was one of those momentary things: muscles tightening quickly round the eyes, something one might miss altogether if one were not watching for every reaction. This particular reaction told Lynley that the DCC fully understood that neither his mind nor Havers's mind needed refreshing, that he was only asking her to go over old material in order to rattle her.

"For example," he said, "why didn't you just ring the Shrewsbury station and tell them to handle it?"

"I did do," she replied. "But there was no one available as they had a situation going on, so I rang Gerry Gunderson. She's in charge of the PCSOs in that area. I asked her to have the Ludlow PCSO do the job."

"Why the rush?" Lynley asked. "If the Shrewsbury officers were busy, surely this was something that could have waited till they were available."

"Indeed, it could have done," she admitted. "I'm at fault for what happened. Finnegan, you see"—and here she nodded at the wall of photos—"worked with Mr. Druitt. If there was the slightest chance of *anything* . . ." She picked up her mug and cradled it between her hands. She looked as uncomfortable as she no doubt felt when she went on, saying, "I wanted Finnegan away from Druitt if there was the slightest chance that any part of this paedophilia allegation was true. So I wanted Mr. Druitt questioned thoroughly." She took a sip from her mug and set it back on the coffee table. She said frankly, "I overreacted, Inspector. Druitt, Finnegan, paedophilia, a children's club, a tip that Druitt was messing children about. I wanted to know what the actual situation was, because of my son." She tilted her head in the direction her husband had taken and added, "Trev would be only too happy to tell you that this wasn't the first time my focus was on Finnegan. Only this time it ended terribly."

Havers said, "Gary Ruddock's told me he left Mr. Druitt on his own in the Ludlow station because he was dealing with other events in town."

"He's not telling you he left the station, is he?"

"Sorry. No. Just that he left Mr. Druitt by himself."

"That's what I understand happened," the DCC concurred. "I was told it was a binge drinking matter. But I assume you know this already. I can't imagine you didn't learn it the first time you were here."

"It's the nineteen-day gap that brought us back here," Lynley reminded her.

Havers added, "Well, that and Clive Druitt, the dead bloke's dad. No one wants the publicity that'll go with a lawsuit if he files one."

"I'm desperately sorry about it all," Freeman said. "The ultimate responsibility for *when* it occurred is mine. I know that. Believe me, if I could turn back time . . ."

"Like the song says," Havers agreed.

LUDLOW
SHROPSHIRE

Barbara Havers knew she had to work not to loathe Clover Freeman. The DCC had more than ten years on her, but she looked like a bloody Olympian. Barbara's inclination was to find her either deeply suspicious or downright guilty of something, although the truth was that the only real thing she appeared to be guilty of was seeing to her health and well-being through working out on the athletic equipment that Barbara had espied within a conservatory that opened off the Freeman sitting room. Bloody woman was probably a sodding vegetarian as well, Barbara thought.

She made no mention of this as she and the inspector headed back to Shropshire, wending their way to Griffith Hall, which once again would be her lodgings. Instead, she dwelt on one aspect only of what they'd been told by the DCC, and that was her admission of being an overprotective mother. The way she saw it, Barbara explained to Lynley, Clover Freeman's overprotecting her son could mean one of two things in a situation of alleged paedophilia. Either the DCC was attempting to run interference in case there was truth to the allegation and she hadn't wanted Finnegan hanging round the bloke, or she was worried Finnegan himself might be involved in some way.

"He watches Druitt for a while and decides to join in for a round or two of grope and poke," was how she put it. When Lynley gave her one of his dry glances, she said quickly, "Sorry." And then after a moment to think more about it, "Or *he's* the one messing the little ones about. He gets caught at it and he has to do something, so he makes the call accusing Druitt. He doesn't live far from the Ludlow station, as it turns out."

After a few minutes of silent and—she presumed—meditative driving on Lynley's part, he said, "I see those are possibilities, as unpleasant as they sound."

Then they were silent again. It was now growing dark. North of London as they were—despite the distance not being overly great—the days were longer. Not many structures, less to block the sun, she reckoned. More open land and rolling hills, the panoramas broken by coppices planted long ago.

Finally, Lynley said, "This issue of paedophilia, Barbara . . ." and he paused. He looked reflective and she wondered why till he went on with, "I knew someone from Eton who was so inclined."

"A teacher?"

"No. An old Etonian. He claimed he'd never acted upon it but he had photos. They were hidden, but in the course of an investigation, I came across them." He glanced at her and she was surprised to see that for the first time in her memory of him, the inspector looked not only uncomfortable but also troubled.

She said, "Christ. John Corntel. You *covered* for him? Did you never think . . . He could be out there right now. Like, this very moment. Like, doing what he only was looking at before. Jesus on the Cross, sir."

"I know," he said. "I'm not proud of what I did. He keeps in touch with me. He says he's clear of it, but the truth is God only knows."

"So what is this?" she asked. "Confession time? Might've come sooner, considering all the rubbish you're holding on me."

"It's given me some sleepless nights, Barbara. I'm fully aware of how much I might be responsible for. Among other things I'm responsible for."

She knew what that last bit meant: Helen's death. He should have borne nothing at all on his shoulders for what had happened to his wife, but he refused to see that. Yet Barbara didn't go there in conversation, considering what he'd just told her. What he'd done was an abrogation of responsibility so profound on his part that it left her reeling. It also left her seeing him more fully as a human being, which she had to admit was how he had always seen her.

They were negotiating Leominster before he spoke again, seeking a route to the A49, which would take them up to Ludlow. "What all of that brought to my mind was the idea of photographs. Was there anything among Druitt's belongings that suggested paedophilia to you?"

"Photos of naked little kids? Child porn? Nothing like that, if you're talking about *actual* photos and the like. But isn't that gen'rally done with the Internet anyway?"

"That's where the trails are, yes. Did Ian Druitt possess a computer? A laptop? A tablet?"

"We never came across one," Barbara told him. "Considering that he wouldn't've been rolling in dosh, that's not too strange, is it?"

"What about Clive Druitt?"

"D'you mean did he hand one over? If that's what you're asking, the answer is no. 'Course, he could've just kept one he came across, couldn't he? He might've needed one. Except . . . he's probably not hurting for it, so why wouldn't he just buy one? Why keep his son's?"

"If there was something on it," Lynley pointed out.

"He would've had to check. And that means he would've had to know he ought to be looking for something. That doesn't seem likely, you ask me."

"The woman he lived with? His landlady? What was her name?"

"Flora Bevans. I s'pose she could've kept a laptop or a tablet although I don't know if she would've handed it over to Druitt as she'd need it herself."

"He could have done his searches on his mobile," Lynley said.

"Except . . ."

"Good God. Are you telling me there wasn't even a mobile?" Lynley looked over at her. He'd made the turn onto the A49 and now they were on a straight path to Ludlow. He went on with, "That doesn't make sense. He didn't live at the vicarage. The vicar would need a way to contact him. Even if he had a landline where he lived, how convenient would that be? He'd have to keep dashing home to pick up messages or someone would have to keep taking them for him. I can't see it. There must be a mobile somewhere. We need to find it."

Barbara saw the logic in this and was embarrassed that in going through Ian Druitt's belongings, it hadn't occurred to her to ask a single question about the technology the deacon might have used. She said, "I reckon Mr. Spencer's the one to ask first, Inspector. The vicar. He doesn't have an oar in this race, if you know what I mean. I expect he'll tell us the truth straightaway: computer, laptop, tablet, mobile, and what-you-will."

"We'll speak to him tomorrow morning, then."

It was late when they finally reached Griffith Hall. Lynley manoeuvred his treasured motor through the narrow gate to the car park and found a place for it suitably distant from any other vehicle as well as from the random passerby who might lay a finger upon it. They collected their belongings, and in very short order Peace on Earth was welcoming Barbara back to Ludlow and introducing himself and his ear gauges to DI Lynley.

"I've put you back in your original rooms," he told them helpfully. He said to Barbara, "I can show you the way if you don't remember . . . ? Or if you need help with the bags?"

Barbara wanted to say it wasn't likely she would forget either the way to or the luxury offered by her room. She said to Peace, "I expect we can manage. Follow me, Inspector," and she went for the stairs.

When they reached her room first, as they'd done before, Lynley politely swung the door open. He said, "Ah," before he placed his own bag on the floor.

She said, "Oh, Inspector, this one's mine. You're meant to take the other."

He said, "I can cope, Sergeant. It's only a place to sleep."

"Are you sure? I mean . . . DCS Ardery had a different room. A bigger one. This one . . . To be honest, I think she more or less wanted me to suffer."

"When the Met is paying, we all suffer, Sergeant. Shall I help you with your belongings?"

"I can manage," she told him. "You'd never find your way back once we get there. It's all corridors, stairs, and fire doors from this point on. But . . . are you *sure* you don't want the room that DCS Ardery was given?"

"How different could they possibly be?" he asked.

"Well . . . there is that," she said.

# 17 MAY

LUDLOW
SHROPSHIRE

As soon as Barbara saw DI Lynley wince as he politely rose from the breakfast table, she knew that she should have insisted. On the previous night, she'd taken a quick tour of the suite—she didn't know what else to call it—that Ardery had been given on their earlier stay, and sheer guilt had compelled her to retrace her route to Lynley's room directly, her bag in her grasp. Of course she *wanted* the Ardery room. It wasn't likely she'd ever be able to afford to stay in those kinds of digs with her own money anytime soon. But she knew that she didn't belong there.

Lynley had answered the door with his toothbrush in hand. It held a quite thick linear glob of toothpaste. His dentist, she thought, would have been proud. He blinked and said, "Sergeant? Something wrong?"

She replied with, "We have to switch rooms, Inspector."

"Must we? Why?"

"You'll know when you see it. You haven't unpacked, have you? I mean, aside from the toothpaste. And I s'pose the dental floss if you're a good boy and I reckon you are when it comes to your oral hygiene."

"I'm delighted you've noticed."

"Right. Anyway, collect your clobber and I'll show you the way." She plopped her own bag on the floor and shoved it into his room with her foot.

He said, "Again, why?"

"Why do we have to switch rooms? Because the other's more grand. It's more suited to your . . . your worshipfulness or whatever."

"Don't be absurd, Sergeant," was his reaction. "We're both of us using the rooms for sleeping. We're not here for anything else. At least, I'm not. And if you are—perhaps meeting up with some dashing devil in tap shoes that I've not learned about from Dee Harriman—then you're best to remain where you are. I shall see you in the morning."

She reckoned he'd regret it, and when she saw the wince, she knew she'd been right. But he refused to speak of how he slept—or didn't sleep—and once they were finished with their breakfast, they got on to the vicar.

They found him just coming out of St. Laurence Church, perhaps in the aftermath of a morning service, as he was in the company of several elderly women carrying similarly shaped and bound books in their hands. Rather a depressingly small congregation, but as it was midweek, perhaps that was the reason, Barbara thought.

As Christopher Spencer bade the women farewell, he caught sight of Barbara and Lynley. He walked to join them just the other side of the wrought-iron fence that marked the grounds of the church.

"Sergeant Havers," he said in a friendly fashion. "Are you still in town or have you returned?"

Barbara was pleased he remembered her name, although since he was probably charged with recalling the identities of his parishioners, she expected he'd long ago come up with a way to keep people's names in his head. She said, "Returned," and she introduced him to Lynley. Then she said, "We're hoping to have a word with you if you have time."

"Of course. Would you like to come to the vicarage with me? I can't offer you anything save coffee, although I can probably dig up a digestive of dubious freshness."

Barbara demurred, as did Lynley. She said to Spencer, "We'll only need a moment."

"Shall we, then?" He indicated the door of the church, saying regretfully, "It's perfectly private inside if you'd like to talk there. Morning services aren't well attended any longer. Nor, actually, are Sunday services unless a terrorist attack sends people to church."

They indicated that inside the church was fine with them, so Spencer led the way, taking them to what he called St. John's Chapel.

Barbara recognised it from the last time she'd been here: its great stained-glass Perpendicular window unforgettable because it had escaped destruction.

Spencer spoke first, saying, "You must be back because of Ian. I'm not sure what I can tell you beyond what I told you at our last encounter."

Lynley took up the issue. "Matters turn out to be not quite settled with regard to his death. We'll be prowling round a bit more."

"Are you starting your prowling with me?"

"We did some yesterday."

"Did my name come up?"

"Only in that there are a few questions that weren't asked first time round."

"I see. Well, I'm not sure what help I can be, but I'm completely happy to have a go."

Lynley thanked him in that urbane way he had. He nodded at Barbara. She said, "Last time I was here, Mr. Druitt's dad handed over the deacon's possessions to my guv. We sorted through them and they all seemed on the up and up and logical, if you know what I mean."

"Logically the belongings of a man of God, I presume." Spencer pushed his spectacles up the bridge of his nose. They immediately began to slide south again.

"Right," Barbara said. "But me and the inspector here . . . ? We're thinking that there might be a few things that got left out and we wanted to check with you. He lived with you and your wife for a bit, didn't he?"

"For a bit, yes. But I assure you that neither Constance nor I would have kept something belonging to Ian. We would have noticed at once that he'd left it behind. It would have been returned to him. As for our children and grandchildren—"

Barbara hastened to reassure him that they were not there to accuse one of his offspring of kleptomania. She said, "We're only wondering if you might have seen him with any of the missing items. Actually, we're not sure they're missing at all because he might not ever have had them in the first place."

"I see. What are these items?"

"A mobile phone, a PC, a tablet, or even a desktop computer."

Spencer nodded and took no time before he replied with, "When he was with us, he used the computer at the vicarage. It's a bit of a beast—I mean quite large and rather out of date—but it serves our needs. I'm assuming he picked up his email on it and otherwise used it to contact the various individuals he met with. Of course, I can't speak of what he had at his other lodgings. He might have purchased something when he began to live elsewhere. When he was with Constance and me, though, he had no other device aside from our computer. At least I never saw anything in his possession."

"Not even a mobile?"

"Oh sorry. I wasn't including a mobile in that. Yes, indeed, he had a mobile. One of those smarty phones or whatever they're called."

Barbara cast Lynley a *bingo!* look. She said, "There wasn't a mobile with the lumber we had off his dad. Flora Bevans—that's the woman he had a room from—didn't have one belonging to him, either. Can you think where his mobile might be?"

Spencer said as he glanced between Barbara and Lynley, "That's quite odd, isn't it. I can't think why it wasn't amongst his things, unless it simply got left out somehow. Was it perhaps taken into evidence when he died? I ask because he was *very* good about keeping it with him, so he would have had it that night. There was always someone trying to contact him. He was needed here, then needed there, and he didn't like people to ring and not be able to reach him. I mean, by phoning the vicarage or his lodgings."

They were all silent for a moment considering this. Lynley said reflectively, "As I recall from the paperwork, he was taken from this church, wasn't he? He was doing a service or dressing for a service or just finishing a service?"

Spencer smiled. "Of course. The vestry. He would have left it there when he put on his vestments. Force of habit, and he wouldn't have wanted the distraction of it buzzing or going off or whatever during prayers. Do come with me."

Spencer led them out of the chapel and back into the nave. They walked up the middle aisle and into the chancel, where a heavy oak door set deeply into the church's stone interior took them into the vestry. There, Spencer flipped on a set of bright overhead lights, which shone down upon closed cupboards as well as a bank of drawers and locked glass-fronted cabinets. These last held the requisite items for a church service: chalices, patens, crosses, and the like. The rest was kept in the cupboards and the drawers.

"Now," Spencer said to them. "It must be here somewhere. I suggest the drawers rather than the cupboards. Those hold cassocks, surplices, and the chasubles. The larger vestments. The cassocks have pockets but it isn't likely he would have put his mobile into a cassock he intended to wear for the service, is it? Let's check the drawers."

The wider drawers held, Barbara saw, the starched white dressings for the altar. Further down the row of them, seasonal banners appeared to be stored. There was nothing else in any of them, but on either side of these was a row of narrower drawers holding neatly folded stoles, candles, printed histories of the church, postcards to sell, and as it turned out, a mobile phone and a set of keys.

"Here we are, my friends," Christopher Spencer said. "This must be Ian's because it isn't mine. And these would be his car keys as well."

Of course, Barbara thought. Ian Druitt would have had a bloody car! He wouldn't have taken public transport into town from Flora Bevans' home, and he certainly wouldn't want to rely on public transport to get him to his various commitments. It was one more thing she hadn't thought to bring up with Ardery, and she was furiously embarrassed about this fact. She looked at Lynley to measure the level of his irritation with her and the guv, but he merely looked thoughtful.

He said to Spencer, "Any idea where his car might be?"

Spencer pulled at his upper lip before saying, "It's restricted parking in the immediate area. Residents, deliveries, that sort of thing, although here and there one can find two-hour spots. I'd think Ian generally used one of the car parks because he would have been here longer than two hours, you see." He gave the subject a bit more thought before adding, "There're two that would have worked for him. One's behind the college—West Mercia College, just off Castle Square?—and another is quite near the library. That's on the other side of Corve Street—up from the Bull Ring?—and it's easy enough to reach the church from there. However," and here Spencer looked, if anything, deeply apologetic as he said, "the trouble is that he would have been towed by now. They wouldn't have used the clamp. They generally don't."

"Might his father have come for it, with an extra set of keys?" Lynley asked.

"It's possible. Providing he knew where to find it, of course."

"He hasn't asked you about it?"

Spencer shook his head. "Only you have."

"D'you know what kind of motor he drove?" Barbara asked him.

"Oh Lord. I'm so sorry. I'm wretched at cars. I saw it but didn't think to register what it was, aside from blue. And it was old. That's all I can tell you."

LUDLOW
SHROPSHIRE

Before they left the vicar, Lynley told the man that he and Havers might have to take his desktop computer for a forensic specialist to have a go with. He explained that, since Ian Druitt had use of the computer during the time he lived with the Spencers, he may have left some sort of trail upon it that would assist them in their investigation. Spencer looked concerned when he heard the word *trail* but he didn't ask what sort of trail Lynley meant, and he assured them that he would be ready to hand over the computer if that was required of him.

They went on their way. Their first objective was to find a charger for Druitt's mobile, which was at this point dead. Lynley reckoned that the hotel would have a supply of chargers for hapless residents who showed up without theirs, so he and Havers began to retrace their steps in that direction.

At this hour, the market stalls were up and running. It appeared to be clothing, bedding, and bric-a-brac day. Lynley was surprised to see that the affair caught Barbara's interest, less surprised when she said, "There's Harry, Inspector," and led him not to one of the stalls but rather to a line of five individuals offering wares from blankets they'd laid out on the cobbles that edged the square's east end.

Harry, Lynley saw, was a late-middle-aged bloke accompanied by an intimidating Alsatian. The man wore clean but otherwise wrinkled clothes: a pair of trousers that seemed too short for him and a golf shirt with *St. Andrews* embroidered on its left breast. He had Birkenstock sandals on his feet and a droopy straw hat to protect him from the sun. He swept this off when he spied Barbara approaching him, and he got to his feet and made an antique bow. The Alsatian did likewise, minus the bow, plus some considerable tail wagging. She was apparently called Sweet Pea, Lynley heard, and she was friendly as a kitten, according to Havers.

"What're you flogging today?" Havers asked the man. "And how long do you expect to sit here before the PCSO runs you off again?"

"How I do try to win over Officer Ruddock," Harry said in a voice that came very close to the real Voice and was something of a shock to Lynley. "I find it a source of profound sadness to be at such odds with the man. I honestly don't intend it."

"So why d'you do it?"

"One does so hate to see the waste that occurs in modern society."

Lynley saw that he was referring to the items he had on offer upon his blanket. These consisted of a pair of tarnished grape scissors, two leather dog leads, four porcelain cups without saucers, two sandwich plates in very good condition, an ancient slide ruler, a protractor, a compass, and a Swatch. There were also three cardigans, neatly folded.

"Additionally, of course," Harry went on, "there's the prospect of conversation with people walking by, which I very much enjoy. That doesn't happen whilst one merely sits on the pavement and plays one's flute in front of a shop, you see. I've noticed over time that people tend to avoid someone who appears to sleep rough. I expect it's due to their belief that something might be asked of them and they won't know how to cope. And, of course, Sweet Pea doesn't help matters. Aside from yourself, Sergeant, no one else has ever approached me when I'm in a doorway. Who is your companion, if I might ask?"

"DI Lynley," she said. "Also from the Met, like me."

"Might one enquire what you and DI Lynley are doing in Ludlow?"

"Just now we're looking for a phone charger. We've managed to come up with Ian Druitt's mobile."

"Have you indeed? Is this something of a coup?"

"We won't know till we charge the phone. You don't have one, do you?"

"A phone, yes. Long ago I caved in to my sister's anxiety about my sleeping habits and other elements of my lifestyle. I have no charger, though, being without the means to use one. My banker charges mine whenever I hand it over to him for an hour or two, however."

Another surprise. One could hardly picture this scarecrow of a man having a banker. He let Havers continue.

"Any interesting business going on round town that you care to share?" she asked him. "Binge drinking and the like? Riots in the square? Cheesemongers deciding to go on strike?"

Unconsciously, Harry lifted his golf shirt and scratched his fish-flesh stomach. He said, "They're setting up for the annual Shakespeare Festival on the castle grounds, but I doubt that's what you mean, although someone did break a leg when she fell through the platform's trapdoor yesterday. Hadn't been fastened properly. Let me see, what else . . . Ah. Two days ago we had a tour coach fail in front of the concert hall, and thirty-eight elderly women in twinsets and brogues were left waiting on the kerb three hours for a replacement. One would think elderly women—having seen so much of life—would have had more patience with the problem. But there was a great deal of walking stick waving and at least one Zimmer was shaken in a threatening manner. Officer Ruddock had to have a chat with them. If he hadn't done, a blue-haired riot might well have broken out."

"Has he had to roust drinkers from round the Hart and Hind since I've been gone?"

"Not that I'm aware of, but of course it's possible, young people being who they are and the college nearby."

"He's not popped anyone into the patrol car, then?"

Harry gazed at her and then at Lynley. His eyes, Lynley saw, were intelligent and frank. He said, "I hope the poor lad isn't in trouble. He's quite a decent bloke even though he won't allow us lot"—he gestured to his companion vendors on their blankets—"to do our bit here. But that's on the demand of the mayor and the town council. No one blames him for following their orders."

Lynley wasn't sure where Havers was going with this. He wondered if she had a plan for the conversation. It seemed she did, at least in some respect, because after another few words between her and Harry, she told him good-bye, advised him to keep an eye out on the goings-on round Ludlow, and handed him her card so that he could phone her if anything interesting popped into his head.

As they headed back towards Griffith Hall, she said to Lynley, "He sees a lot, that bloke. He told me a bit about the PCSO carting drunken college types to wherever, and I'd already seen him—Ruddock, this is—doing whatever-it-was with a young woman inside his patrol car at night. He's said he has no girlfriend or partner—Ruddock, this is—so he's had me wondering. Like I told the guv, if he was out in the nick's car park making surreptitious nasties with some young thing in his car, anyone could have got inside the place to do away with Druitt. And Ruddock would hardly want someone to know that's how it happened."

When they walked into the entry of Griffith Hall, a young man who actually was *not* Peace on Earth held a hand up to stop them as he completed a phone call, after which he said, "You've had a message," to Havers, and he handed over a folded piece of foolscap, which the sergeant unfolded and read, saying to Lynley, "The PCSO stopped by. If we need him for anything, we're to ring. He's ready to help." She looked up from the paper and added, "I expect you'll want to meet him, sir."

"I will," Lynley told her.

The receptionist then said to them both, "There's a gentleman waiting for you in the residents' lounge. I did tell him I wasn't sure when you would return, but he wished to wait."

The gentleman turned out to be Clive Druitt. He rose from midmorning coffee as they joined him, saying, "Are you the Met officers? My MP told me two were on their way."

He told them he'd brought Ian's belongings with him just in case they wished to go through them another time. The other officer—"that woman," as he called her, and Lynley could see Havers's hackles rising at the term—had assured him that she and a sergeant had gone through everything once, but he had a "feeling about that one," he did. Earlier when he'd met her near Kidderminster, her breath . . . Well, never mind. She's off the case now?

Lynley's "Not exactly" didn't do much to reassure the older man. But he had no wish to hear anything about Isabelle's breath because he knew quite well where that could lead between him and Havers and he didn't want to go there. Instead, he thanked Clive Druitt for making the trip and he asked—as he'd done before—whether his son had possessed a PC, tablet, or desktop computer.

"Ian?" Clive Druitt said with a short laugh. "Not bloody likely. He was hopeless with technology. He did have a desktop computer years ago, but he drove it into the ground when he figured he'd delete a few items that he wasn't using. Ended up deleting the entire operating system. That was it as far as he was concerned."

"No email account, Facebook page, LinkedIn, or whatever?" Havers asked.

"He would have done all that on his mobile. Which wasn't amongst his things, by the way. I'd like to know what happened to it."

"We have it," Lynley told the man. Peace on Earth appeared at this juncture, offering midmorning coffee, fizzy water, orange juice. "Just someone to carry these boxes up to my room," Lynley told the young man.

"Best put them in my room, Inspector," Havers said. "More space if we mean to have another go with them."

"I damn well hope you do," Clive Druitt said. "I hope you mean to have another go with everything. I want *nothing* swept under the carpet this time."

"We aren't certain that happened earlier," Lynley replied. Before Druitt could argue the point, Lynley told the man he'd like to have the birth dates of every member of the immediate Druitt family as well as the phone number of each. He explained that there was probably going to be a code to unlock Ian's phone and, people being people, there was every chance that the deacon had used numbers that came from one of those sources.

Druitt asked when he needed those numbers. Lynley politely told him now, if he didn't mind. Havers took out her notebook and mechanical pencil, her expression becoming immediately fascinated with whatever Druitt intended to reveal. His revelations included a phone call to his wife, as it seemed he knew only the birth date of their first child and he was even a bit unsure about that. Fortunately, his wife was not, and he repeated the numbers as she gave them to him so that Havers could make note of them. He listened to his wife for a moment after the recitation was completed and then he told Havers that Ian had been awfully fond of his great-aunt Uma, and here were the relevant numbers for Aunt Uma as well.

Once he'd rung off with his wife, he said sharply, "What're you after with Ian's phone?" to Lynley.

"It's all procedure. We'll be putting in a request for his phone records as well, but what you've given us might give us a leg up in advance of getting them."

"My son was a clean liver," Druitt said. "Anything different you're told about him is a lie."

He took up a quite large padded manila envelope then, and he handed it to Lynley. It contained, Lynley saw, a billfold, a Bible, the Book of Common Prayer, an address book, and a sheaf of bills that Ian Druitt's father had paid after his death. Havers fashioned a receipt to give him and when she handed it over, Druitt rose, saying, "If there's nothing else I can do for you . . ."

There was one thing, Lynley told him. They were attempting to find Ian's car, but while they had the keys to it, they didn't have the make, model, or year. Could Mr. Druitt help them with that? Did *he* have the car, by any chance?

He did not. But he told them how to identify it: It was a Hillman, vintage 1962, light blue in colour, and there was considerable rust on the rear wings round the wheel wells. Period transfers decorated the rear window, celebrating the Kinks, mostly, but there were several enthusing over the Stones as well. He didn't know the number plates, but there couldn't have been too many vehicles like it in town.

And then, taking his own car keys from his pocket, he ended with, "Someone murdered Ian. As I stand in front of you and swear to it: Someone murdered my son."

Lynley said as gently as he could manage, "It's very difficult to fake a suicide by hanging."

"Someone," Druitt asserted, "managed to do it."

LUDLOW

SHROPSHIRE

Brutus hadn't even created an excuse. That made it worse. Yes, Ding had been having it off with Finn, and yes, Finn was one of their housemates. But it wasn't as if Finn and Brutus were friends.

Ding totally knew that Brutus had *selected* Francie. Probably, he'd even tracked her down, challenging himself with: "Let's see if the dish with the big ones'll get it on with me." But the other part was: "If this is how you want it, Ding, see how it can be?" which was also pure Brutus. And *that* was seriously unfair, because he just didn't *get* it. But not getting it didn't excuse him, because when he brought Francie back to the house when they could have gone to Francie's home or to her car or even to somewhere on the banks of the Teme, Ding knew that Brutus was sending her a message. Fine and all right, was the conclusion she came to. If that's how Brutus wanted things to be, then that's how things were going to be. But they weren't going to be that way with her *friends*, no matter what he thought.

She wanted to have a word with Francie. She knew it would be easy enough since between spontaneous rounds of bonking anything with the right equipment when the mood was upon her, Francie was a creature of habit. So once Ding had cooled off sufficiently to put behind her the sight of Francie on her knees at Brutus's crotch, Ding knew where to find her: at the life drawing class.

This was tucked at the back of the Palmers' Hall Campus in Mill Street, one of the three areas in town where classrooms and lecture halls were located. Here the art studios shared space with the photography classrooms and digital printing labs along with the areas set aside for media studies. The bottom half of the windows for life drawing were papered, as was the window in the door. This was, Ding knew, to afford models a modicum of privacy from anyone wishing to peer inside.

When Ding opened the door, the instructor approached her, hands held palm upward in a universal *halt* gesture. Ding said to the rather imposing woman, who wore a medical lab coat splodged with paint and smudged with charcoal, that she needed to have a word with Francie Adamucci. The instructor said, "She's occupied. You'll have to wait for a break. And do your waiting outside, please. This is a private class."

"She won't mind. It's important."

"I'll mind."

"It's fine with me, Ms. Maxwell," Francie called out from the dais upon which she stood in three-quarters profile, absolutely naked, a wreath on her head and a shallow basket of fruit balanced against one hip. "I know her. It's fine with me if she wants to stay." She neither moved her head nor altered her pose as she spoke, as if with the wish of demonstrating that Ding's intrusion into her session of nude modeling would not affect her.

Ms. Maxwell said, "As long as she doesn't distract you."

"She won't," Francie said. "Will you, Ding?"

Ding assured the instructor that she would be brief and be gone, and she was given leave to approach the model. She realised when she reached Francie, however, that this might not be the best of times since she wanted to be eyeball to eyeball with her friend and that wouldn't happen while Francie was modelling. Plus, seeing Francie naked was disheartening. She was voluptuous, a complete contrast to Ding, who had all the right parts, just not like these.

Unlike a lot of modern girls, Francie didn't strip herself of her pubes. Her bush was trimmed neatly to the shape of a shield, but there was none of the excessive waxing that turned young women into little girls, underwear models, or porn stars. Instead, Francie announced that if some bloke didn't like the look of a real woman, then to hell with him. She wasn't about to do things to her body in order to appeal to some juvenile's wet dream fantasy. She did draw the line at body hair elsewhere, however. Hairy armpits and hairy legs? Even hairy toes? Hairs on the nipples? She wouldn't have that. There was being a *real* woman and there was *being* a real woman, she would say. Whatever *that* meant.

Ding got as close to the dais as she could. She said in a quiet tone, "I just want to know if it was him or you."

Francie didn't pretend to misunderstand. "The idea, d'you mean?"

"We'll start with whose idea it was and we'll go from there."

"It didn't *mean* anything," Francie said. "Brutus is a cutie but it's not like . . . I mean, I don't *want* him, Ding. He's . . . what? Is he even eighteen years old? What would I want with an eighteen-year-old?"

"You're not saying, though, are you?" Ding hissed.

"Huh? What'm I not saying?"

"Whose idea it was. That's what I want to know first."

"Idea? All right. Let me think." Francie's brow furrowed for a moment as she thought about what had occurred in Brutus's room, or at least she pretended to think about it. She finally said, "It's that . . . I'm not sure."

"Oh, that's rich, that is. I'm expected to believe that?"

"Well, you *know* me, don't you?" When Ding made no reply to this, Francie sighed and said, "All right. I'll try." And then after a moment of putative trying, "He was on the river kayaking."

"Alone?"

"He had some random girl with him. No clue who she was."

"What did she look like?"

"*I* don't know. It's not like I studied them or anything. Maybe she was sort of round in the shoulders. Oh yes. I *do* remember she had a terrible haircut. She was wearing a tank top—I remember that as well—and *truly* hideous running shorts from what I could see of them when she got out of the kayak. Baggy in the arse. And the color? Appalling. Like mushy peas gone bad."

Ding rolled her eyes. Trust Francie to note the girl's haircut and her wearing apparel. "Get on with it, then," she told her.

"I was on Ludford Bridge. I was crossing over from home, and I heard someone call out my name and there they were: Brutus and Baggy Arse. She had on those specs that change colours in the sun?

And, oh yeah, she was wearing this necklacey thing, something super large, like it was an Olympic medal or something?"

"Allison Franklin," Ding said. The description was fair enough to know.

"Whatever," Francie said. "So like I said, I heard someone yelling hello and I waved and said something like, 'You're looking all muscly and scrumptious' or whatever."

"Do you ever let up?" Ding asked her.

"I don't *mean* anything." Francie gave her a quick glance that earned her a sharp word from Ms. Maxwell. "I *didn't* mean anything. It was just something to say. Only Brutus? He took it like an invitation or something because he asked me to wait. He said he wanted to talk to me about our biology lab."

"You aren't studying biology. Neither is he."

"Which is why I reckoned he was sending me some kind of message. Like maybe he wanted to give this girl the chuck and I was meant to help him do it by playing along. And who could blame him with those hideous shorts she had on. Some girls need to be super careful what they show to the world, you know? Anyway, turned out I was right. Brutus gave her some tongue and a hand on the arse when they got out of the kayaks, p'rhaps to show her he was all hers or something. No clue there. Then off she went so he and I could study biology in a serious way. Only it wasn't *that* kind of biology, obviously."

Ding was beginning to feel hot. The room was warm anyway because of Francie's nudity—her nipples were nonetheless erect—and she could see that some of the art students were sweating. As for her, the heat came from her outrage because she could feel it like a coal in her stomach. She said more loudly than she intended, "So it was his idea? Your idea? *Whose,* for God's sake?"

Francie gave her a look then. She asked Ms. Maxwell if they could have a brief break. The basket of fruit was getting heavy, she said. Five minutes? Ten?

Ms. Maxwell agreed to five and Francie set down the basket and stepped off the dais. There was a cover-up for her to put on, a striped seersucker affair with a belt. She didn't bother with it, remaining nude instead. She walked Ding over to one side of the room, where various cubbies held canvases, drawing pads, and other accoutrements of drawing and painting.

"Look," Francie said, "you *always* said you and Brutus aren't exclusive. So I didn't think it mattered."

"Whose idea," Ding snapped.

"Probably both of us. Ding, I don't *know*."

"Then tell me what happened. Exactly."

Francie shifted her weight. One smooth hip jutted out. Unselfconsciously, she scratched her pubes. She said, "I think I asked him what was with the biology bit? He said something like he just felt like he wanted something different. He gave me that grin of his—let's face it, he's rather adorable even if he *is* too young for my taste—and I said different what or how or who? He gave me another one of those grins and he did that thing when he brushes his hair back and sort of looks at you like—"

"I know his routine," Ding told her. "Finish up."

"So we went to the house. We had a spliff and a snog. That's it."

"Oh, come *on*." Ding's voice rose. Three nearby male artists looked up from their work. She whispered, "You were on your knees and that wasn't about praying for world peace."

"Well, of course I was going to blow him," Francie said. "But it wasn't serious. We were there and he was . . . he was that Brutus person he can be, and it seemed like—"

Francie stopped suddenly. Ding's eyes had filled. She was furious with herself for reacting in *any* way, let alone for being upset.

Francie said, "Ding! OMG. It's not like the two of you have ever been exclusive, is it? And it didn't *mean* anything. It was only a bit of fun, it was only sex, him and me and twenty minutes if it was even that long."

"You mean . . ." Ding's lips were so dry she thought they might split as she went on to say, "You mean that after I slammed the door on you two, you actually . . . You went *on*? Like, you're caught in the act but that didn't *matter*?"

"But why should it? And we'd gone up there to . . . I don't know what to say. Dingie, you've told me about the lads at Cardew Hall. That delivery bloke with the jars for your mum? That other one in the back of the church over Easter? And what about the one doing the roof of the stables? Wasn't any of that true?"

"That's not the point," Ding said. "You knew me and Brutus . . . and we live together, Francie."

"But not like in *living* together. And I didn't think it would bother you. Really. Do you think I would've done it . . . And we *didn't* do it all the way like that. Not to finish because he couldn't. Not in my mouth, that is. So I had to—"

"Stop it!" Ding shrieked then, and her hands flew up as if on their own accord to cover her ears.

"I'm sorry! I'm sorry!" Francie cried. "If I'd known he actually meant something to you . . ."

"He doesn't. I thought he did, but he *doesn't*."

Francie looked away in the direction of the door. Ms. Maxwell was striding purposefully towards them. She said in a rush, "I didn't *mean* anything by it. And what I said about the threesome? It was just what popped into my head. But I saw your face and I knew straightway that you were upset only I didn't know exactly why because of all the blokes at Cardew Hall and . . . *Are* there any other blokes, Ding? Is it just Brutus? Because if it is, I'll want to die right here because I wouldn't've meant ever to hurt you. It was me being stupid. That's all it was."

"Ladies, if we can draw this tête-à-tête to a conclusion . . ." Ms. Maxwell's voice was heavy with meaning.

"Ding. Dingie . . ." was the last Ding heard as she rushed for the door. She was beginning to cry and she didn't know why and she didn't want even to hazard a guess about where the tears were coming from. For the truth was that she had never misled Francie about the various blokes at Cardew Hall and what she'd done with them and where. There were more, even, than she'd ever told Francie. But the additional truth was that Brutus had always meant something more to her. Only, she knew who he was and she knew what he was and she didn't know what to do about either.

LUDLOW
SHROPSHIRE

Lynley took on the search for Ian Druitt's Hillman while Havers remained at the hotel with his mobile phone, a charger provided—as they had hoped—by reception, and a list of the birthdays and the phone numbers of all members of his immediate family, to include Aunt Uma as well. For his part, Lynley decided to begin with the close environs of St. Laurence Church on the remote chance that Ian Druitt had managed to park nearby, in a place that was not marked by any restrictions.

He set off from the hotel and headed towards Castle Square once again. He found it quite crowded now. Three nearby tour coaches had recently deposited their loads of visitors at the top of Mill Street, and a number of them had invaded the market for a look at the bric-a-brac stalls.

Rather than attempt to work his way through the throng, Lynley kept to the pavement and only crossed the square at its east end. There he saw that Harry Rochester and his fellow floggers were in the process of being moved along by the town's PCSO. This would be Gary Ruddock, he reckoned: a solid-looking bloke of some six feet tall with a thick but fatless waist and round face. He appeared a bit older than Lynley had anticipated. He'd assumed the officer would be round twenty-one or so, but this man looked closer to thirty. He and Harry Rochester were in conversation. It didn't look either unpleasant or aggressive.

Lynley didn't approach them but instead crossed over the square behind them and entered the environs of St. Laurence Church. The route took him down one of the town's cobbled streets—little more than the width of the ancient carts that would have been used by merchants who served the castle's inhabitants—and deposited him in College Street, opposite the church. Midway along its route, he saw the first of the available parking spots. But he also saw the restrictions posted as Mr. Spencer had indicated: The parking in the street was reserved for residents; visitors were restricted to two hours only and would be towed thereafter. The street itself was residential, a mixture of plaster-fronted and redbrick buildings heading northwards into Linney Street. Here, too, were residences, of slightly later vintage than those near the church, overlooking the River Corve. Here, too, the parking was restricted and the signage indicated again what would happen to violators of the restrictions. Had Ian Druitt parked anywhere in the immediate vicinity of the church, then, his Hillman would have been towed away, possibly the very same night that he died.

Before ringing the phone number given on the warning signs, Lynley decided to check the closest car park to be certain. His town plan showed it behind West Mercia College, accessed on the north side of Castle Square. A short walk on a pleasant day, he thought.

Returning to the square put him once again on the edge of the market, where he saw that the blanket floggers had now dispersed. The PCSO he caught sight of at the far west end of the square, where a small white caravan stood. From this, various types of grilled sausages were filling the air with the idea of lunch.

Ruddock was in conversation with a man who appeared to be the caravan's owner, and he was indicating some sort of instructions about the placement of a sandwich board that listed the food options and their prices. It was apparently blocking access to West Mercia College's grounds, because when the officer walked on, the sign was moved, although the bloke moving it didn't look especially happy about having to do so.

Lynley turned away to seek out the car park, which was easy to find behind the college buildings. As there was a Pay and Display machine, he reckoned the Hillman would have been removed long ago had it been here in the first place. Nonetheless, he thought it best to check. The car park was crowded—students' vehicles, he supposed—but as it wasn't an enormous area, it didn't take him more than ten minutes to walk it. There was nothing there as old as a 1962 Hillman, although a Volkswagen camper van in wretched condition came fairly close.

The phone number for the towing service was, as before, posted in several locations. Rather than going on to check the car park near the town's library, Lynley decided to ring the service for the location of whatever impound facility they used. He had luck with this, for there was one impound yard only, and he was told he could find it two miles to Ludlow's northeast on the A4117 beyond Rockgreen. He would recognise the place by the large, revolving pink elephant in front of it. God knew why the yard owners had chosen that device, but no one looking for the place ever got lost.

Lynley rang the impound yard next as there was no point in trekking out to it—even to see the revolving pink elephant—if the Hillman wasn't there. But a conversation with the telephone receptionist, followed by an interminable wait during which he spied two college students exchanging cash for a small plastic bag of what was doubtless an illegal substance, gave him the information he was looking for. Yes, they had a 1962 Hillman in the impound yard. Was he the owner?

No, Lynley told them. He was the police. The owner was dead and they were seeking his vehicle.

Who's paying the fine, then? There's a towing charge and an impound charge, you know.

Lynley said he would pay it. It was easier than going through the legal manoeuvres necessary to wrench the vehicle from the impound yard's grasp without paying.

As the location was out of town and since he wanted to take possession of the vehicle, Lynley rang for a taxi to cart him there. He waited at the top of Mill Street, and soon enough the taxi showed up, driven by a grandmotherly sort with the vehicle's radio playing classic—but mercifully soft—rock 'n' roll.

They wound through the town, the driver informing him there was no direct route to Rockgreen. Thus he was more or less a victim to "Where the Boys Are" followed by "Judy's Turn to Cry" followed by "Johnny Angel."

The revolving pink elephant came into view in the midst of "Tell Laura I Love Her." Lynley paid the driver and wondered how he'd managed to escape such teenage angst. But then, he'd had larger things to concern him when he was sixteen years old: a dying father, a mother having an affair with his cancer specialist, a lost soul of a younger brother, and his own confusion and grief.

Inside the impound yard, he went to a caravan that appeared to serve both as living accommodation and as an office for the owners of the place: a couple in the vicinity of seventy wearing matching boiler suits with their names embroidered upon them. He was Totally Roger and she was The Absolute Lucinda, who seemed to do double duty as the receptionist. Lynley showed his warrant card, told the couple what he was after, explaining once again that the owner of the Hillman—one Ian Druitt—had died in March. The name meant nothing to either Totally Roger or The Absolute Lucinda, but the fact that Lynley was a Met officer did. They went round a bit in the area of "So what'd he *do*, this bloke?" (Roger) and "Were you lot after him?" (Lucinda), and they seemed reluctant to part with the vehicle unless some kind of additional proof could be offered that DI Lynley was indeed authorised to relieve them of it. Lynley wondered at the fact that they would even want to keep the ancient vehicle on their premises, but he reckoned that they had few enough chances to make the police dance round for them, so he indicated that he *could* get formal authorisation to take the vehicle, but it was likely that doing so was going to rob them of two months' payment for having stored it if they went that route.

That decided matters in a quick fashion, and after The Absolute Lucinda ran Lynley's credit card through its paces, Totally Roger showed him the way to the Hillman. The wily couple had already moved it to the end of one of the rows of vehicles. They'd known they were on the losing side of the situation, and they'd decided to play it for what they could get.

Lynley thanked Roger and looked the vehicle over when the man left him to it. He saw that the Hillman's tyres were virtually threadbare and there was quite a dent in the front right wing, but otherwise the car was exactly as Clive Druitt had described it: old, rusting round the wheel wells, and decorated with 1960s transfers on its rear window. The original owner had been a concertgoer, it appeared. He'd memorialised his attendance at various musical venues, but Clive Druitt had been correct: the Kinks were first in that person's heart, followed by the Stones.

Lynley unlocked the vehicle and swung open the driver's door. By its condition, he saw the upholstery was as original as the rest of the vehicle appeared to be. It needed repairing or replacing. Seams were split on the driver's seat and the upper part of the back seat's cushion bore a lot of damage from the sun.

Lynley sat inside and tried the ignition. The Hillman, unburdened by modern electronics that wore on a car's battery, started without difficulty. He drove it to one side of the impound yard, shut it off, and began a more thorough look through it.

He began with the boot, where he discovered that Ian Druitt was not exactly neat in his automotive habits. Aside from the tools to change a tyre (although there was no spare tyre at all), Druitt had a collection of ratty-looking wool blankets stored inside. On top of these and to the side, five tins of motor oil suggested that the Hillman burned more than its fair share. Three more tins were empty and waiting for someone to discard them. Smashed into the back of the boot was an ancient pullover, and beneath it a sticky roller for removing lint sprouted a very thick beard of animal fur. This was explained by the presence of two humane traps, both of which were marked with tags that read "Feral Cat Rescue" with a phone number beneath it.

There was nothing else inside the boot save dust and dirt, so he went next to the car's interior. Ian Druitt, he saw, had used the Hillman as a mobile office of sorts. On the backseat, Lynley found manila filing folders in a cardboard container designed for this purpose. They were arranged in no particular order, and among them he discovered receipts for maintenance work done on the vehicle over the years; handbills for Hangdog Hillbillies—the whimsical looking musical group that, according to Havers's report, he had been part of; Internet searches for street pastors programmes in larger cities and towns in the UK; another Internet search on victim volunteers programmes; a record dating back ten years of petrol purchases, including the day of purchase and the cost of purchase and the mileage on the vehicle at the time; a collection of sermons given by various notable Anglican leaders; and a book of the collected poetry of William Butler Yeats with a place mark at "The Second Coming." Beneath this box was a large UK *A-Z* circa twenty years earlier, with dog-eared pages attesting to its use. He flipped through this but there was nothing unusual about it: no X marking a spot that indicated a special destination that Druitt had had in mind.

Oddly, the floor of the backseat held a galvanised washtub, and placed so it leaned at an angle from the floor to the ceiling of the vehicle was a broomstick with no actual broom straw but rather with a heavy string attached to it. Lynley frowned at this and wondered for a moment, until he understood this was the deacon's contribution to Hangdog Hillbillies: a washtub bass.

He flipped the passenger seat back into position, sat in it, and opened the glove box. Here he discovered that Druitt had worn prescription sunglasses, which he carefully kept in a leather case. There were also folded documents attesting to his ownership of the vehicle and his possession of insurance. An RAC membership card had been pushed to the back, and a brochure for National Trust Properties indicated that he might have been interested in the nation's religious, architectural, or aristocratic history. What was most interesting, though, was the first indication they'd had that the man might have been sexually active. A container of condoms was part of the glove box's contents. When Lynley opened it, he saw that half of the original twenty were missing.

LUDLOW
SHROPSHIRE

The one thing Barbara knew for certain at the end of her first hour with Ian Druitt's mobile phone was that the UK would have fallen to Nazi Germany had she been sent to do anything at Bletchley Park. In DI Lynley's absence she'd used every birthday, trying to unlock the device. She'd done them forwards, then she'd done them backwards. She'd also mixed them up, a spontaneous idea that resulted in her complete confusion. She went from there to the street addresses Clive Druitt had provided her, and still there was no joy to be had. To keep the bloody thing from locking up on her, she'd shut it down and rebooted it after each third attempt, but ultimately she called it quits. She'd then turned to Ian Druitt's engagement diary, and she'd worked backwards from the deacon's death in order to compare the names in the diary with Ludlow's telephone directory in an attempt to ring every person whose surname indicated an appointment had been at least made, if not kept, by or with the deacon.

Not every name was in the local directory. She reckoned the individuals who went along with the names were either domiciled in another part of Shropshire or they were simply ex-directory. Those people she'd managed to track down, however, seemed open enough about their connection to Ian Druitt. It ate up several hours, but Barbara was able to unearth a few details that, while not necessarily intriguing, at least added to their knowledge of Druitt's movements in the weeks before he died.

When Lynley arrived back from his search for Druitt's auto, she was outside of the hotel at the far end of the car park, giving herself a smoking break. It was with some amusement that she greeted the sight of the detective inspector rumbling onto the premises in a rattling Hillman. The only time she'd ever seen him in such an automotive disaster was on the very few occasions when she'd been able to entice him into her Mini. That he'd pollute the seams of his bespoke suit by exposing them to the interior of Druitt's motor was a particularly enjoyable sight.

He parked near her and climbed from the vehicle. She said to him, "That's the motor, eh? It sounds worse than mine, and I didn't think that was possible."

"Its interior is remarkably similar as well," he told her. "Save the empty takeaway cartons, of course. The deacon appears to have taken his meals at home."

"Or he used rubbish bins."

"There is that." Lynley hoisted a few items out of the car.

"Find anything of an evidentiary nature?" she asked.

"A fully lived life, but not much else." He said he'd leave her to her habit, and told her that he would wait for her in the residents' lounge.

She sucked down the rest of the fag quickly. When she went inside, he was laying manila folders out on a coffee table and telling Peace on Earth—who seemed to be rather too curious as he hovered round the room—that a cup of tea would be the very thing, lapsang souchong if they had it, Assam if they didn't.

"Earl Grey?" Peace on Earth asked hopefully.

That would be fine, Lynley told him. To Havers, he said, "Sergeant? Earl Grey? Or will that wash away the less-than-salubrious effects of your cigarette?"

"Amusing," she said. "I like PG Tips," she told Peace on Earth. "But I'll swill Earl Grey if I have to."

When the young man went off to see to the tea, Lynley asked about Barbara's progress with the smartphone. She said it had been more or less a white flag exercise for her. On the other hand, she told him, she did have something of a success with the deacon's appointment diary and the Ludlow telephone directory.

She'd stowed her notebook inside her bag while she was out indulging her habit, so she excavated for it, flipped it open, picked a piece of tobacco off her tongue, and began. She'd spoken to two sets of parents of children in the after-school club, she said, because Druitt apparently scheduled meetings with parents—as noted in his diary—before a child's first attendance at a gathering of the club.

"They loved him to bits," she told Lynley. "Far as they were concerned, not a hint of anything going on 'cept guidance, school prep, outdoor activities, games, and the like."

Druitt had also met with an individual from Birmingham, she went on. This was a woman who had begun an effective street pastors programme there to help the city cope with young people out in the streets late at night. "Clubbing, binge drinking, drugs," she said. "The regular thing. Only now, they have a sobering-up centre for them. The street pastors go out, gather 'em up, and bring 'em back to where they serve up soup and coffee and tea and sandwiches and whatever else. The deacon was trying to set up a system like that here. I expect Gary Ruddock was on board with that—we'll need to have a word there—because he was the one having to do it all and probably would've been dead chuffed to have some helpers."

She pointed out the name MacMurra, which appeared several times in the lead-up to Ian Druitt's death. This, she said, was one Declan MacMurra and the relationship there had to do with cats.

"Catch, neuter, and release?" Lynley said. "There're traps in the boot of Druitt's car."

"MacMurra's, those are," Barbara told him. "He asked me about 'em when I phoned. Big cat lover, he is."

She went on with Randy, Blake, and Stu, the sole Christian names in the diary. These were members of Hangdog Hillbillies, as it turned out. She only worked this out when she was looking through one of Clive Druitt's delivered boxes. There was a handbill with the names of the other musicians: Randy on banjo, Blake on guitar, Stu on percussion. No surnames, though, so she couldn't track them down, although she reckoned she and Lynley could go to one of their venues where they'd probably find someone who knew their full names if that was necessary.

*Spencers* in the diary was obvious, as Druitt had written it on the dinner hour three times. Two other names turned out to be individuals whom the deacon had checked on in the custody suite at the Shrewsbury station.

Lynley picked up one of the manila folders at this. It had been among several others that he'd removed from the carton he'd brought in from Druitt's Hillman. He said, "He has information here about the Independent Custody Visiting programme."

"Everyone told me last time I was here that the bloke was a volunteering machine."

"Anything else from the names in the diary?"

"Three are shut-ins who belong to the parish. One was in hospital at the time. Four are victims of crimes. Not big stuff, this. Petty crimes, although one was a mugging that involved a head wound."

"That's another volunteer programme he's got information about," Lynley told her. He fingered through the folders and handed her one. "Victim volunteers," he said. As she opened it and gave the contents a look, he added, "It *is* curious, though."

"What is?"

"Even by the standards of a man of God, it does seem like an extraordinary amount of volunteering."

"That's what me and the guv thought first time through." Barbara reflected on everything she'd learned on her earlier trip to the town and added, "Mr. Spencer told me Druitt couldn't manage to pass the tests to become a full priest or whatever they're called, sir. He took it five times and it was still no go, owing to his nerves. Could be this"—she gestured at what they had before them—"was his answer to not being able to serve God and his fellow man the way he wanted to serve."

Lynley nodded, but he looked thoughtful. He said, "There were condoms in the car as well. A box of twenty. Ten were left. What does that suggest to you?"

"He could've been handing them out to the lads round town. I mean the older boys, sir. That's more or less in character, don't you think?"

"Anything else?"

"The obvious. He had a lady friend somewhere and was being careful. Odd though."

"That he had a lady friend?"

She shook her head. "That we haven't run into her name. Or even a whisper about her. On the other hand . . ." She lifted the deacon's diary and said, "Here's something, sir. There's this Lomax person. A woman."

"You suspect the condoms have to do with her?"

"Not hardly. Unless he liked grannies. The guv and I met her. She looks round seventy."

"So where does she take you?"

"She's in his diary seven times, she is. She told me and the guv she was meeting with Druitt 'cause her family was in a crisis and she needed to talk to someone about it."

"Is that unreasonable? He's a clergyman, after all."

"Yeah, but she told us herself she wasn't religious and she was vague when it came to how she connected with him in the first place. Plus there's this, sir: Druitt didn't counsel anyone. I mean, *all* the people I've talked to so far? Every single one of them? They said he was a lovely bloke and all the rest but none of them went to him to get themselves counselled, spiritually or otherwise. And the Lomax woman? She had a solicitor there when we talked to her. You ask me, there's something in that needing another look."

"Let's see about looking, then," Lynley said.

ST. JULIAN'S WELL
LUDLOW
SHROPSHIRE

When Rabiah Lomax opened the door and found Officer Dowdy—whose name she could not recall—and her companion, Mr. Well Dressed, standing on her front step, she gave brief thought to ringing Aeschylus, but she didn't do so. She had other things that she needed to see to on this evening and primary among them was ringing the members of the Maintenance and Repairs Committee to lasso the lot of them into a meeting. Sending for Aeschylus would require her to wait for Aeschylus. She decided it would be far easier to handle these two herself and shoo them on their way.

Officer Dowdy was the one to speak, saying to her, "Mrs. Lomax, can we have a word, please? This is DI Lynley. Sorry, but we're back in the traces. We'd like to confirm a bit of this and that with you. D'you want to ring your solicitor?"

That was an interesting twist, Rabiah thought as she racked her brains for the woman's name. When did coppers ever begin with an invitation to bring on the legal advocates? Certainly not on any telly programme she'd ever seen. Usually, they wanted the opposite. She said, "I'm sorry, but I can't remember your name."

"Barbara Havers," Dowdy said. "Can we have a word?"

"Has something happened?"

"Should something have happened?"

"I hardly know. I certainly don't have any further information to give you about Mr. Druitt. Is that why you've come?"

In pear-shaped tones that matched his clothing, which, while beautifully made, also screamed worn-by-a-retainer-for-a-year to make the items look suitably lived-in, the detective inspector said, "Sergeant

Havers and I have been asked to look into something related to Mr. Druitt's death."

"Didn't you lot do that once already? I don't know what I could add to what I've already told you."

Sergeant Havers said, "You did give us a bit of information, right. But then something more came up and here we are. Can we come in?"

Rabiah looked behind herself, almost as a reflex since she couldn't have said why she did it. She said, "I suppose," and she didn't attempt to make her voice sound friendly.

She stepped back to give them entry. She made no offer of refreshments, and she wasn't happy when Sergeant Havers asked her for a glass of water. The other officer made the same request, which made her immediately suspicious, as this smacked of an advance plan of some kind. She wanted to tell them that they could take themselves off to a shop and purchase a bottle of water each, but she reckoned it might start all of them off on the wrong foot. So she went to fetch the water—two glasses, each half full—and she joined them in the sitting room. She was just in time to see the sergeant returning a framed photo to the fireplace mantel. A glance told her what it was: once again the photo of the glider pilots' consortium jauntily standing in front of the craft they'd purchased.

"Here we are, then." Rabiah handed each of them a glass. Neither drank. They were, she decided, trying to unnerve her. She was determined not to be unnerved. "How can I help you this time round?"

The detective inspector gave the merest of nods at the sergeant. If Rabiah hadn't been directing her gaze to him as the superior officer, she wouldn't have caught it at all, so slight a movement it was. The sergeant said, "Right, then. We've spent a bit of time contacting everyone in Mr. Druitt's diary. That would be the diary that has your name in it. Now we haven't made contact with every *single* name—he was one busy bloke—but a pattern's emerged and we'd like to ask you about it."

"I doubt I can shed any light on a pattern in someone's diary, Sergeant."

"P'rhaps yes, p'rhaps no," she said cheerfully. "Turns out Mr. Druitt had his fingers in a massive pile of social-responsibility pies. Also turns out that the individuals he saw—the names we ran down from his diary, I mean—all fit into one or another of these pies." She used her own fingers as she named them, and Rabiah could tell she was doing it to make a point. "We've got the children's club kiddos and their parents, a street pastors programme, a crime victims programme, the custody visitors programme that took him up to Shrewsbury to make certain the cells were all squeaky clean, the church choir, and the Neighbourhood Watch where he lived. We've also got meetings with the mayor and with three town councillors."

Rabiah tried to look interested in this information. She could feel a pencil line of perspiration breaking out along her hairline, though. She said, "I'm not sure what your point is or indeed why you've come calling. Have you been here for days interviewing everyone in Mr. Druitt's dairy?"

"Good question, that," Sergeant Havers acknowledged with a jaunty single-finger salute from her forehead. "I did this bit by phone since every name—'cept the mayor and the town councillors—was only in the diary once."

"Your point still escapes me," Rabiah said.

"It's this: When we were here last—me and my main guv, DCS Ardery, this was—you told us that you and the deacon met because you were talking over a family situation."

"That's correct. That's what I said and that's what we did."

"Right. But the odd thing we came up with is that Mr. Druitt didn't ever meet with anyone about family problems. I guess you could argue, 'course, that family problems're why some of the little ones prob'ly got sent to the children's club, eh? But all of this made me wonder if there's anything about your explanation that you want to change?" She finally paused to take a sip of her water. The other officer, Rabiah noticed, still had not touched his.

"What explanation is this?" Rabiah asked. Her voice sounded too faint. That wouldn't do.

"The explanation telling me and my guv—DCS Ardery, like I said—that you and Mr. Druitt were talking about your family. Seven times talking about your family."

Rabiah knew it was time for her to come up with something more specific and she wished desperately that she'd made notes of what she'd told them initially. But she hadn't done, so she had no choice save to bluff her way forward and get them out of her life. She said, "Mr. Druitt and I spoke about my elder son."

"Makes you special, that," the sergeant said, "you being the only person he counselled."

"I suppose it does make me special," Rabiah countered. And after a pause during which she recognised that the police were waiting for something more from her, which she was perfectly determined not to give them, "Is there anything else, then?"

"P'rhaps you c'n tell us what you spoke about regarding your son?"

Surely, Rabiah thought, the woman had it in her notes. She wanted to tell her to bloody look through them but she wanted them gone from her house more. She said, "I did tell you. It was a family situation."

"And there're so many," the sergeant said. She looked solemn and anticipatory at the same time. "What was this one?"

"I don't see how it's the business of the police," she said.

"Oh, it's not at all. Except, 'course, the bloke you talked to about your family situation turned up dead."

"Are you implying there's a connection? As I've said, I spoke to him about my son David."

"He would be the one whose daughter died?"

"No. That's Tim," she said before she understood what had just occurred.

The sergeant nodded. "Got it," she said. "Only last time we were here you told us it was that one—the one whose daughter died—who was being talked about. A user, he is. Drugs? Alcohol? What you will?"

Rabiah said, "Both of my sons are users, Sergeant. One is recovering and one is not. I probably talked to Mr. Druitt about both of them during those seven meetings he and I had since Tim's daughter had died and David's wife and children had recently left him. One doesn't cease being involved in one's children's lives simply because the children are grown. You'll understand that at some point if you don't understand it now." She rose then and settled her hands on her hips. "Is there anything else I can help you with?"

The sergeant looked at the inspector. He'd remained watchful and unnervingly silent, but all the time he'd kept his gaze on Rabiah. Despite a smallish scar that marked his upper lip, he was a handsome man, quiet and solemn in just the way she'd always thought a man should be: seen, admired, perhaps flirted with, and without opinions that wanted declaration.

He finally spoke the first words he'd uttered since coming into the house: "Nothing else just yet," he said.

ST. JULIAN'S WELL
LUDLOW
SHROPSHIRE

Lynley could tell when Havers was about to start pulling on the bit. There were generally two signs. The first was her gait, which altered from her usual saunter to something akin to a charge, heading into the wind when there was no wind. The second was her expression, which could either telegraph the triumph of *gotcha!* or the absolute knowledge of what had to be done next to make *gotcha!* a proximate certainty. As they headed towards his car, she was demonstrating both gait and expression.

"You saw her, right?" Her voice was low, and she looked round furtively, as if expecting someone with a recording device to jump out of a nearby window box.

"I did. But I'm uncertain where the coincidence takes us."

She halted in the middle of the street. "How about to the fact that it's *not* a coincidence?"

He glanced back at the house: well kept, tidy, nothing sinister about it, a house like the others in the street. He said, "Rabiah Lomax and Clover Freeman are in a photo together, posing along with eight or ten individuals in front of a glider, which I assume they all pilot. I'm presuming they're a club of some sort?"

Havers ignored the question because, as it turned out, she had a piece of information that she was determined to give him. "Yes, yes, but forget Rabiah Lomax. It's not about her. It's about the other."

"Clover Freeman."

"Nancy Scannell."

"Who?"

"Nancy Scannell, sir. She's in the same picture. *With* Clover Freeman. *And* Mrs. Lomax. She's one of the pilots. She's also the forensic pathologist who did the autopsy on Ian Druitt. She's who called his death a suicide. So *do* you see now?"

What Lynley saw was that Havers could well be too excited by half. In fact, he saw that Nancy Scannell's membership—if it could be called that—in the glider group was less coincidence than the coincidence of Clover Freeman and Rabiah Lomax both being members. He said, "Barbara, think about it. How is this significant? It makes perfect sense that two individuals who are professionally acquainted might discover a commonality between them. Is there a gliding airfield round here?"

"Up on the Long Mynd, yeah. And when we went up there—me and the guv—we went to talk to Nancy Scannell. That's where she wanted to meet us 'cause she was helping someone launch a glider that day. And then later we discovered that Rabiah Lomax was part of the same glider group. They all own the glider *together.* Which, you ask me, is totally coincidental in a seriously *non*coincidental way."

"Nonsense," Lynley argued. "I doubt there's more than one airfield for gliding in Shropshire. So if there's a local centre for the sport, it's even more likely that these two women—professionally related, Barbara—would discover they share a mutual interest in gliding. They might well have run into each other at the airfield. Or there could have been a notice on a bulletin board asking for interested parties to contact someone about purchasing a glider together. They could have discussed the idea of ownership. Or they could have hit upon it separately, only to discover at the first meeting of potential owners that they both are pilots and that they both wanted to be part of the group. My point is that there are a number of explanations, and none of them can actually be labelled *suspicious.*"

"But my point is—"

"The point is that it's just that: a point of interest. Something to be noted for now, but that's all. It may be useful, but it may be a wild hare, and I trust you know better than to follow it simply because you can apply a label to it."

She looked away from him and he could see from the set of her face that she was prepared to argue the point a few more rounds. He stopped her with, "Check your phone. Let's see if Ruddock has tried to make contact."

They'd rung the PCSO before setting off from the hotel, but the call had gone directly to message. Havers had asked him to ring as soon as he could. She hadn't told him why.

During their conversation with Rabiah Lomax, however, she'd put the mobile on mute. She brought it out now as directed.

She said to Lynley, "Nothing yet. So don't you think we ought to—"

"What I think is that we need to take care not to get ahead of ourselves. One thing at a time, Sergeant."

"Time," she said. "Isn't that just it? Isn't that exactly what we don't have?"

"We're not at the point of desperation, Barbara."

Her expression, however, suggested otherwise.

# 18 MAY

WORCESTER
HEREFORDSHIRE

Trevor Freeman woke into darkness feeling like a man put into suspended animation for a hundred-year journey into space. For a moment he wished that he actually were inside one of those science fiction capsules because regaining consciousness brought into his head a score of mental images that he could have done without. They got the better of him quickly, and just as quickly he tried to dismiss them, but to no avail. They took their strength from their very sources. Two of these were overheard snippets of conversation on the previous evening. The other rose from his own stupid, unquenchable, libidinous behaviour.

Gaz Ruddock had joined them for dinner as invited by Trevor at his wife's request. But the unsatisfactory conversation he'd earlier had with Clover, touching on the topic of the PCSO and the convoluted nature of how the dinner invitation had to be extended to the young man, had roused Trevor's suspicions. As a result, he'd become hypersensitive to everything, both during the meal and afterwards. They'd had their steak, potatoes, salad, and pudding on the patio, and from start to finish each word, action, tone of voice, and glance seemed supercharged to him.

Clover's choice of apparel hadn't helped. Round him, she always dressed with an understated sexiness, but for some reason she'd decided to bypass understatement altogether in her selection of cropped trousers showing off the best ankles in Christendom, sandals—one of which she continuously swung from her big toe—and a top fashioned to fall off her shoulder. Perhaps in a declaration that she'd had to dress hastily, she hadn't put on a bra. So her nipples made a perky statement on her chest that it would have taken a blind man to ignore.

Of course, she'd taken care to have an excuse for this clothing, hadn't she. She was clever that way. He'd been in the kitchen flipping steaks in the marinade when he'd heard her return from work. She'd joined him briefly, saying that she would be available to help out, once she'd changed from uniform into something more comfortable. He was having a look at the baking potatoes in the oven when she called from above, "Trev, can you possibly help me?" and since he had the marinade doing its bit and the potatoes were fine and all that was left was the salad, he went up to see what Clover needed.

He'd found her in their bedroom, where she had altered herself to a nun. He realised that the costume must have been in the package on their doorstep that he'd found upon returning home for the day. It had also contained the costume for a priest, he reckoned, since she'd laid this out on the bed for him to get into prior to carrying on with what she obviously had in mind: He would be the Catholic priest seduced by the nun. Or she would be the pious nun seduced by the priest in the midst of her prayers. That one seemed more likely as she'd also fashioned a prie-dieu by dragging the ottoman over to a chest of drawers. She was kneeling upon it as she fingered her beads.

She'd turned as he entered the room. She wore on her face the expression of a young Madonna. She held out her hand to him and made clear what the coming event was meant to be, saying, "Father, will you hear my confession?"

He'd had not a moment's hesitation about his desire to play along. Nonetheless, there was something of a problem: the factor of time. He said, "I would do, gladly."

She glanced at the bed, where his priest togs lay. "Do you need to put on your garments, Father?"

"That I do and again, gladly. Unfortunately, you've forgotten. Gaz is coming to dinner."

She was Clover in an instant. "Damn. I saw the package and completely forgot." Then she laughed. "Well, I must be quick, then. I did think the randy priest would be the one to orchestrate things, but never mind. Come over here, darling. See what Sister Mary Rosary Beads has in mind for you."

"You're the naughty one, aren't you."

"Always. Come along, Father Freeman."

He'd laughed. "Clover, truly. There's no time."

"Oh yes, there is. You'd be surprised what I can accomplish in—"

The doorbell had gone then, and he'd said, "I expect twenty seconds is beyond even your talents, girl. It'll have to wait and I hope it does." He crossed to her, bent and kissed her, easing his hand between her legs to caress her and then dodging as she reached for his zip. He went off and answered the door. He'd welcomed Gaz Ruddock into their house.

Her proposed encounter should have been sufficient to occupy his mind for the evening until such a time as they could don their respective costumes. Indeed, those moments in the bedroom might well have sufficed to make him blind to everything else save his own anticipation, had he not overheard Gaz saying to Clover, "We can always have a go if"—a remark that he cut off abruptly as Trevor had come out of the house onto the patio with their after-pudding coffees. And then Gaz switched quickly to a compliment on the meal and a stated wish that he could man a barbecue like Trev.

Trevor, however, hadn't been easily thrown off the track of what he'd heard so he said, "And what're you having a go at, you two?" as pleasantly as he could manage.

"This Scotland Yard business," had been Clover's reply. "You know how he can be if he's pushed."

"Who?"

"Finnegan. Who else?"

He'd taken a deliberate moment to let the question hang there before he said, "I don't know. Perhaps you ought to tell me."

It had to be said that Clover looked mildly surprised at this but she went on with, "If the Met want a second round with him, they'll be rougher. I'd like to be there if they show up. Failing that, I'd like Gaz to be there."

It would have been nice to name this exchange a deliberate dodging of the question, but he couldn't do so as it made perfect sense. He told himself it was only his desire for Clover that was making him so attuned to anything smacking of someone else's desire. He might have held on to that thought straight into the night had he not also heard the softly spoken good-bye Clover had offered Gaz as he'd departed. "We'll speak later" begged the questions: What exactly would they speak about? Why the secrecy? Why the murmur to ensure her husband did not hear?

These were the queries first on his mind, then, when she shut the door on the PCSO and her gaze fell upon her husband, whom she'd obviously not expected to be standing so close behind her. But before he could ask for answers, she excused herself with a "Darling, I've got to run upstairs for a moment," and off she went.

From there, it had been such a simple matter for Clover, hadn't it? He'd been gathering the barbecue implements for cleaning when she returned to him, outside on the patio. She'd donned the nun's costume another time, but with a difference. As she slid into his presence, she was wearing only the veil and the wimple with the rosary beads fastened round her waist.

His first thought was, *Christ! The neighbours . . . !* as he looked round for eyes eagerly watching from the windows overlooking their back garden. But he had no chance to remonstrate, for Clover came towards him, and she declared, "Sister Mary Rosary Beads has something *very* special for you," as she put her hands on the waist of his jeans.

Although it was an utter lie because already he felt the belly heat within him, he said, "I'm that done in, Clover. It'll have to be another night."

"Surely not," she said, and her fingers moved to lower his zip.

He pointed out that Gaz had stayed later than Trevor expected him to.

She said piously, "You know the will of God must always come first, Trev."

"Must it?" he said as her cool, smooth fingers moved against his flesh.

"It must." She mounted the patio table. She crooked her finger. She spread her legs. "Come along," she whispered. "God's will be done."

Which it was, of course. Which she had known it *would* be because when it came to Clover, he was weak as a dying fish with a hook in its mouth. And not only there had God's will been done but later again in the bedroom where, after the washing-up in the kitchen, he'd found her as she'd been earlier in the evening, a nun at her beads. This time she was fully clothed in the costume and she became all surprise and fear to see that a stranger had somehow broken into her cell, where she was solemnly praying.

He was—damn him—only too happy to find her thus and to play the stranger come to take her against her virginal will, which her terrified "Who are you? What are you doing here?" told him he was meant to be. Afterwards, they'd collapsed together and had fallen asleep.

That was the thing about Clover. He'd allowed her to know him better than anyone, and what she knew best was that he'd remained like a randy sixteen-year-old boy when it came to her, and most of the reason for this had to do with her crazy sex games. Clover knew that the single simplest way to derail him, distract him, and deny him access to her scheming mind was to give him access to her perfect body.

Now in the early morning, he stirred in their bed. His body smelled rank, even to himself. A shower was called for, but instead he dressed in tracksuit and trainers and descended the stairs. He could hear the rapid whirring of Clover's stationary bicycle in the conservatory. She was going at a clip that he could not possibly have maintained.

That was another thing about her: the importance she gave to staying in condition. Prior to the past few days, he had always assumed her reasons had to do with her father, whose sedentary life as a psychoanalyst and whose personal habits as a heavy drinker and heavier smoker had resulted in his premature death at fifty-four years old. She'd always claimed that she had no intention of following in her father's footsteps, and while Trevor had admired her single-minded dedication to staying fit—it was, after all, how they'd first met, back in the days when he, too, was a fitness aficionado instead of employing other individuals to be—he could see it as something that served another purpose entirely: keeping her body youthful, tight, and firm in all the right places. And not necessarily for him.

He went into the conservatory where the early morning's darkness was just about to give way to dawn. It was still night enough that he could see his reflection in the glass, a little haggard, a little more dumpy, growing jowls where a jaw should be solid and strong. Clover didn't notice him as she was concentrating on her aerobic workout, dripping sweat onto the towels that she'd laid at the base of the stationary bike. She was wearing headphones.

He crossed in front of her and sat on the bench that was part of her stationary gym. She looked up and he could see that he'd startled her as he was generally abed till seven. She removed the headphones and continued to pump apace. He had no doubt that the woman possessed the heart of a twenty-year-old.

A buzzer sounded, calling an end to her aerobic session. She went into her cool-down period, breathing hard and pumping now at a slower pace. She sat straight up and said the obvious. "You're out of bed early. I didn't wake you, did I?"

"Bugger that for a lark. I was in a coma. I thought you might've given me something."

"I did give you something. Two somethings. You seemed to enjoy them as much as I did. Want more? That can be arranged."

He knew he was supposed to leer at this, rising from the bench and going to her in order to slide his hand up her thigh. If he went for it, they would end up where she wanted them to be and he would end up yet another time in the position of telling himself that she was one in a million, which made him one in a million when it came to luck and why the bloody hell couldn't he just enjoy his life with her without rocking any boats. But so soon after their two encounters on the previous night, this offer of hers was more than just Clover having yet another itch that could only be scratched in a single manner.

Trevor could see from her expression that she had concluded something was wrong. He should have slept in as he would have done in other circumstances.

She spoke first. He understood from this that she recognised the necessity of getting the advantage. Still, what she said surprised him: "I have a confession to make. Will you hear me out?"

He was at once wary. "What sort of confession?"

"The sex was deliberate last evening. I *did* want you. But it's not fair if I pretend that I didn't have something else on my mind."

Trevor had hardly thought she'd go straight to the point. He wasn't sure what to make of it, which was what he said to her.

In reply, she said, "It's just that I didn't want to get onto Finnegan with you last evening."

Another surprise. He frowned, saying, "What about Finn, exactly?"

She was slowing up on the stationary bike, and she reached for her water bottle and drank half its contents. "You're not going to approve."

"I'm listening."

She drew a long breath, then blew it out quickly, saying, "I have an arrangement with Gaz. You weren't ever to know, but I can tell . . . You can't hide things from me, and I could see last night that you were closing in on it. Trev . . . You and I . . . It's just that we've never seen eye to eye on Finnegan, have we. And now he's in Ludlow with all sorts of freedoms he didn't have here and what with that scheme to go to Spain that he cooked up last Christmas . . . You see, I had to consider . . . Well, you *know* him, Trevor."

What Trevor knew was that it was completely unlike her to look for words, which told him something was up and he wasn't going to like it. He said, "Why don't you tell me directly what you want to tell me."

She slowed her pedalling even more, but she didn't look as if she was ready to dismount. She said, "It's this. I've asked Gaz to keep an eye out."

"What do you mean?"

"I've asked him to watch over Finnegan. I've asked him to let me know if he . . . if Finnegan . . . well, if he goes off track. You know how he can be. That reckless part of him? And what with the freedom to drink as much as he likes and to smoke weed—because you can't possibly think he isn't doing both in Ludlow—and with access now to other substances that kids his age use . . . I've been worried. And because I knew Gaz from the training centre and I could see he was eager to do well whenever an officer asked him to do something . . . I thought he might be willing to keep Finnegan on his radar, even to look in on him now and again."

Trevor said nothing as he digested this. He could see that she was trying to read his expression just as he was trying to read hers.

She seemed to reach a conclusion, because she went on hurriedly with, "I should have told you about the arrangement before now, but I knew you'd disapprove. I reckoned that Gaz could do everything on the . . . on the sly, if you will. Finnegan wouldn't know and neither would you. It would look like Gaz was just being friendly. But then with this Ian Druitt situation, it's all become something of a mess, and I don't want a mess between you and me. So I'm confessing."

Frustration had always cramped his gut when it came to Clover and their son. It did so now. Trevor said, "The real problem isn't Finn. It's your inability to sit with the uncertainty of will he or won't he. He's been showing you since he was six years old what happens when you insist on walking this path, Clover, but it's done no good."

"Darling, I admit I should have told you what I arranged when he got established in Ludlow, but I knew you'd argue against it."

"I'd argue against it because you keep making moves that are guaranteed to rile him, not to mention drive him towards the very things you want to keep him away from: excessive drink, drugs, too many parties, whatever."

"I don't agree. And anyway, we go at things differently, you and I. We always have done."

"Christ, Clover." He rubbed his face and then his bare skull. "We can go at being parents as a result of our past or we can go at it with knowledge of our past. Which of those two d'you reckon describes this thing you've got going with Finn?"

"This thing? What thing? You sound like my father. This isn't *about* him. And it's not about my mother. Or your father and mother and siblings gathered round the dinner table making happy families, which is what I know you wanted, and I'm *sorry* I wasn't able to give that to you, all right?"

Now that, he thought, was a very clever move, but he wasn't about to head in that direction. He said, "Agreed. Completely. It isn't about anyone except the two of us, how we see Finn, and how Gaz Ruddock fits into the picture."

"*What* picture? I have Gaz keeping an eye out, full stop."

"Really? There's nothing more? Are you saying that this request of yours to Gaz comes out of absolutely nothing?"

"This 'request of mine' comes out of the fact that Gaz is out and about all day in Ludlow. He sees things. He hears things. So how difficult could it possibly be for him to let me know how Finnegan's coping? This entire experience is new to Finnegan: being away from home, living with mates from the college, being exposed to choices he's never had before. I've been concerned, and to be honest, I can't understand why you haven't been. Or why you've never been."

"Because you can't keep watch over a child every second. If you try to wrap him in cotton wool—"

"I'm not doing that." She got off the bike then. She took up one of the towels on the floor and wiped herself energetically with it. She said, "Why can't you see that I'm only trying to be there for him as best I can? Oh never mind. I don't want to talk about this as if I'm some sort of mentally defective individual who can't stop herself from intruding on her child's life. If you believe that your place just now is to tell Finnegan what his mother has organised—for his own good—then go ahead."

That said, she took up the other towel and her water bottle and left him sitting where he was. It was time for her weight training after her aerobics, but she'd apparently determined that weights were better left forgotten this morning.

He decided he needed coffee. He went to the kitchen to make it. It was only when he heard the roar of the shower upstairs that he saw how Clover had derailed the conversation he'd intended them to have. Her bringing Finnegan into things was what had done it.

How bloody clever the woman was. He'd learned nothing at all that she hadn't decided in advance he was meant to know.

LUDLOW
SHROPSHIRE

Lynley had just finished his morning shower when he heard his mobile ringing. He had hopes that Daidre was phoning him, but he saw that it was Isabelle. He wasn't quite ready for whatever the DCS had in store in the way of conversation at seven o'clock, so he let it go to message and returned to the bathroom—such as it was—to shave.

His ingrained inclination to be ever the gentleman, allowing Barbara Havers to have the room Isabelle had taken, had cost him this time. His bed was so abominable that he'd removed the mattress from its frame on the previous night, and had slept upon it on the floor. The bathroom was suitable only for a munchkin, with a shower that was actually smaller than a telephone booth. There was a single oval mirror above the basin and nothing reflective at all in the bedroom, unless one counted the antique television set, which could, he supposed, be used in a pinch if the picture was off, the curtains were closed, and the weak overhead light was on. The resulting shadowy image might then be helpful, but only as far as a silhouette could carry things.

He was wiping steam from the mirror when his mobile sounded another time. Another time he went to check it. Daidre, he saw, and he felt a rush of gratification.

When he answered, she said, "I suppose I ought to ask first if Barbara is practising her tap dancing as ordered."

"As I've given her what is apparently the larger room, she ought to have space to do it. Whether she has the will remains to be seen."

"Should I ring Dorothea and recommend a pep talk?"

"You know Barbara and pep talks. I think it's best to let Dee be surprised when she sees Barbara in action. We can only hope her tap shoes will be flashing. If tap shoes flash, that is. I'm uncertain of that part. I will say that my anticipation is building, however, although I'm keeping mum on what actually comprises my anticipation."

"You're very cruel."

"'I must be cruel only to be kind,' although I don't think Ophelia much appreciated the thought. How are you, darling? Are you at the zoo or still at home?"

There was a pause. It was the *darling.* But he'd given her space with the follow-up question and she seized upon that. "Home, Tommy. But I think I must go to Cornwall."

Now *there* was irony, Lynley thought, although he knew she certainly didn't mean that she planned to drop by Howenstow to press palms with his family. He said, "Has something happened?"

"Well, yes." He heard her sigh. He wondered where in her flat she was at the moment, and he decided that she was in the kitchen that she'd remodelled, standing at the French windows overlooking the weed-choked ruin of a garden. She'd have made herself a cappuccino, no sweetener added. It would be on the kitchen's island and she'd be turning just now to drink it. She'd be dressed—not for work but for the drive to Cornwall, so what she wore would be comfortable for the journey—and her sandy hair would be drawn back from her face. The lenses of her specs would be newly cleaned, the smudges from yesterday carefully removed.

She said, "Gwynder rang last night. It's nearly time if I want to say good-bye."

"Do you?"

"That's just it. I said good-bye so long ago that this part seems extraneous."

"Yes. I can see how that might be the case."

"The difficult bit for me is trying to work out whether my reluctance to see her one last time is due to bitterness, anger, or a complete lack of grief."

"Perhaps it's all of that. Or none of that. Perhaps it's just natural reluctance. She wasn't actually a mother to you. She gave birth to you, but largely that was where things ended. For all of you, your brother and sister as well."

"I so want to be like Gwynder. I want to see our mother as someone who did the best she could do, but it's only that I've always had the worst time believing it."

"I doubt anyone who knows the circumstances would disagree, let alone cast stones if you decide not to go."

"It's my name, though. I mean my real name, Tommy. The one she gave me, as if she knew how it would all work out."

"Edrek, yes," he said. It meant *regret*. It—like her birth in a lay-by in Cornwall, like her childhood in a caravan along a stream in which her father believed he could make his livelihood finding tin—was part of the past she'd been lifted out of when she and her siblings had been taken from their parents. It had been a case of complete neglect: no schooling, no healthcare, the environment unkempt, the clothing filthy, the hair matted and infested with lice, even the teeth in their mouths loose and beginning to rot. He wanted to tell her that she owed them nothing, despite the fact that her mother was dying. But then there was her name—Edrek—and what she might feel if she did not make this final effort to release the past.

"I do wish you were here," she said.

"Why is that? I'm not much good in the counselling department."

"But you're very good in the being-with-me department. I'd ask you to go with me. Just to be there."

"Ah. Well, at this moment it can't be helped. I've rather made my bed, and unless I sort out this matter, my next likely bit of employment will be walking a beat in Penzance. Or alongside Barbara in Berwick-upon-Tweed. So whatever you decide, you must go it alone. I'll be with you in spirit, though. But let me say that these sorts of things—the things that hang over us—it does seem best to put them at rest if the opportunity comes up to do so. This may be it. I hate to say that, but there you have it. I hope you're not sorry you rang."

There was a pause, quite a long one. For a moment he thought they might have been cut off. He finally said her name.

She said, "Oh. Yes, yes. I'm still here. I was just considering."

"Whether to go?"

"Not at all. I'm going to Cornwall."

"Then . . . ?"

"I was considering whether I'd ever be sorry that I rang you, Tommy."

"Dare I ask?"

"I wouldn't be. Sorry, that is. No matter how this present thing works out."

They rang off then, and Lynley remained where he was for a moment, sitting on the room's only chair at the narrow table that served as a desk. He examined his heart and its steady beating and he wondered what it meant in one's life: making a decision to love again after terrible loss.

He was still holding his mobile, so when it rang another time he answered without looking to see that it was Isabelle phoning this time.

She said with no preamble, "Is there more?"

He didn't ask what she meant, and he didn't sugarcoat the matter, which he might have done had he not just spoken to Daidre and heard her wish that he be with her on her journey to Cornwall, which, of course, he could not be. So he said bluntly, "Ian Druitt had a mobile. He had a car as well. We've come up with both. We've also come up with the fact that West Mercia's deputy chief constable is mother of the boy you interviewed. She and the forensic pathologist who examined Druitt's body belong to the same gliding group, by the way. Apparently, they own a glider together. The deputy chief constable—she's called Clover Freeman—rang the PCSO's sergeant and gave the order to fetch Ian Druitt for questioning. All of this leads to a single point: Barbara was on the right track when she wrote the report that you ordered her to change."

Isabelle was silent, perhaps evaluating what this meant. The fact that she might be doing so made Lynley's hackles rise. He said, "What the *hell* were you thinking telling Barbara to alter that report? You were sent up here to—"

"Don't you dare tell me my job," she snapped.

"—look into what the IPCC made of their investigation into a custody death, and that's exactly what Barbara was trying to do. We have nineteen days between an anonymous call that led to an arrest and the arrest itself, and during those nineteen days, Isabelle, there was, we have learned, *no* investigation done into Druitt, which means there was no apparent reason for his arrest. That's where Barbara was trying to head, so why the hell did you stop her?"

"We weren't in Ludlow to do anything more than look at what the IPCC did in their investigation after Druitt died—not *before* he died—and that's exactly what we did. The rest is irrelevant."

"Are you goddamn mad?"

"How dare you speak to me like that? Who the hell do you think—"

"That horse isn't nearly high enough, Isabelle. I suggest you dismount. And while you're doing that, consider this. Clive Druitt came to the hotel to meet with us. He knew you'd been drinking when he spoke to you. He could smell it on you. Since he mentioned it to me, you can't possibly think he didn't also mention it to his MP. And what his MP did with the information . . ." He let her consider that as well.

She finally said, "Now this," in a near whisper, to which she added in an altered tone, "'What's it going take,' eh? You're thinking that, aren't you, Tommy?"

He didn't bother to deny anything because indeed he'd been thinking along those exact lines. At the same time, though, he felt the compassion of someone who has watched this sort of thing play out before. "Isabelle, listen to me. You're not the first person and you won't be the last," he said. "If it were easy, people placed into your position—having lost nearly everything—would just stop. *You'd* just stop because you love your sons and because you've lost both them and your marriage at your own doing. It's very possible that now you stand to lose your job as well. At some level, you see this. But the monster still has you and unless you shake it off your back—no matter how the hell you do it—you're going to die. Do you understand that? Even remotely?"

"Don't be dramatic with me, Tommy. I'm not that far gone. You see me as standing on the brink, but that's not what this is. It's not where I am."

He raised his gaze to the ceiling, to the heavens, to whatever being existed who could possibly get through to her. From his experience within his own family, though, he understood that the only person who would be able to reach Isabelle Ardery was going to be Isabelle Ardery. And then it would happen only when she'd had enough of the cock-up she'd made of her life.

He said, "We're speaking with the PCSO this morning, I hope. We tried to arrange it yesterday, but we weren't able to make contact. Barbara left him a voice mail, but other than a note he left for her at reception, that was it. We're taking a stab with Finnegan Freeman as well. What did you make of him?"

"He plays at working-class-boy-making-good—he's quite adept with the accent—and he has the gruesome habit of talking with his mouth full. Of burrito, when I saw him. He's a strong advocate for Ian Druitt's innocence in all things."

"It's interesting, then, isn't it: that he knew Druitt and that Druitt's arrest was called for by his own mother."

The DCS was quiet for a moment. Lynley knew that she fully

understood how much she had missed because of her haste to be finished with Ludlow. There was no point in underscoring that another time. She finally said, "Good hunting then, Tommy. You might be able to get more from the PCSO. Barbara was right. I do see that."

That, he decided, was the first hopeful thing he'd heard from her. They rang off then. It was time to get down to the business of the day.

LUDLOW
SHROPSHIRE

Rabiah Lomax had long ago learned that a morning run cleared her head for whatever she had to face that day. She'd developed the habit during the trying adolescent years of her two sons. Up before dawn, out in the early morning streets, she was able to dismiss her concerns about David's drinking—always claimed on his part to be "experimental" only—and Tim's dabbling with marijuana. She could tell herself that this was *her* time, that she would get back to her sons and their difficulties later.

When she left the house on the morning following the second call upon her by the Metropolitan Police, she altered her normal route. Generally she included the Breadwalk in her run, an earthen slice through the forest that carved beneath the ancient limes and alders, marking a route high above the River Teme. This path stretched from Lower Dinham Street all the way to the Ludford Bridge and on many mornings it afforded one a pleasing view of the dawn breaking over the town's ancient rooftops. But this day she needed Temeside to be part of her route, so she headed in that direction from St. Julian's Well.

She wanted to look at the house where Dena Donaldson lived. She'd had a phone conversation with her granddaughter on the previous evening, and as things turned out, Ding had unexpectedly become a part of it.

Rabiah didn't like lying. She had always adhered to the philosophy: tell the truth because there's less one must remember that way. Out of necessity, however, she'd lied to the Metropolitan Police upon their first visit because it was the simpler thing to do given the circumstances. But to have now lied to the Metropolitan Police a second time was something that she could see as having the potential to fill her life and the lives of her family with unexpected sinkholes.

So after looking at the possible alternatives she could choose from once the police had left her, she knew that she had to ring Missa. She hadn't done the first time round because it hadn't seemed necessary. Besides, there had existed in her family an atmosphere of letting sleeping dogs lie for quite some time, and Rabiah had gone along with it, hoping for the best and telling herself that it was not her place to intervene in the lives of her adult children, their spouses, and their offspring.

But upon reviewing the two visits she'd had from the Met—what they said, what she said, what they asked, and how she answered—she altered the hands-off approach she'd long taken with her boys and their families. When it was late enough for Missa to be in her bedroom and out of earshot of her parents, Rabiah punched in the number of the girl's mobile.

She went directly at it with her granddaughter: "Tell me about the appointments you had with Ian Druitt, Missa."

There was a considerable pause. During it, Rabiah heard a wannabe 1940s crooner singing in the background. She wondered if a talent programme was playing on telly. Evidently, Missa was watching it on her own, because the sound went off and then she said, "What are you talking about, Gran?"

"I've had two encounters with detectives from the Metropolitan Police on the subject of Ian Druitt. I'd like to avoid having any additional conversations with them, although I know that might not be possible."

"Do you mean the *London* police?"

"That's exactly who I mean. The first time they were here, I had Aeschylus hold my hand and do the talking. This time, I went it alone. They're hunting down a Lomax who met with the deacon of St. Laurence Church—this is Ian Druitt, as I expect you know—and while I declared that Lomax to be myself—"

"Why did you do that? Did you know him, Gran?"

"—I'm uneasy having done so. Not so much because I don't wish to lie to the police—although I *don't* wish to lie to the police—but because I dislike lying blindfolded. Now. What did you and Mr. Druitt meet about? If I'm to keep lying, I'd like to know what I'm dealing with."

There was another pause. Its length did not suggest that Missa's next words were entirely reliable. "Gran, I never met with Mr. Druitt at all."

"Then why would our surname be in his diary seven times?"

"*Seven* times? I don't have any reason to meet any deacon of any church one time, let alone seven. Someone must have done it using our name."

"Would there be *any* reason in the world for that?" Even as she asked the question, however, Rabiah could herself come up with a list of answers. It began ominously with *lest someone find out.*

"Probably," was Missa's answer. It hung there for a bit before she added, "Gran, it has to be Ding."

"Why on earth . . . ?"

"She must've been talking to him about how to cope with Brutus. Bruce Castle? He's her . . . well, sort of her boyfriend? They seem to lurch from crisis to crisis. At least that's how it was when I was in Ludlow. Or could be she was talking to Mr. Druitt about wanting to make some changes in her life and not knowing how to do it. I don't expect she meant anything by it, though. I mean: to cause any trouble by using our name."

"I don't like anyone using our name, no matter how *or* why," Rabiah told her. "I intend to speak to Ding about this."

Missa said quickly, "Gran, please don't do that."

"Whyever not?"

"It's just that she's had *such* a rotten time of it because of Brutus. He cheats on her and he expects her to be fine with that and she's not at all but she's been pretending and now if she's finally got up her courage to end things with him . . . I wouldn't want the fact that she used our name to be the thing that makes her back off from tossing Brutus from her life. You see?"

The fact was, Rabiah didn't see. It was one thing staying out of the lives of her sons and their families. It was quite another if someone *not* of the family was asking her to do the same while putting her family in a bad position.

Now, she crossed the river where dawn cast a glow upon the water. On its placid surface a lone swan floated. It preened its feathers before rising up to unsettle its wings. Incredible, the size and aspect of the bird, Rabiah thought. Swans looked so gentle, so placid, so accepting. And then in an instant, they altered.

Lights were beginning to come on in the houses along Temeside. But at the house where Dena Donaldson lived, all was still, and what Rabiah could see of the interior through the front bay window looked full of shadows. She paused there and considered Ding: what she knew about her already and what she'd learned from Missa on the previous night.

She wanted to feel sorry for the girl with her cheating boyfriend and his expectations that she should be happy to accept however little he was willing to toss her way. And at one level, Rabiah did feel sorry for her. But she also decided to ignore Missa's wishes in the matter. Rabiah *would* talk to Dena Donaldson. She was far from satisfied that she'd gotten to the heart of Lomax times seven in a dead man's diary.

LUDLOW
SHROPSHIRE

Ding had spent a restless night. Her conversation with Francie Adamucci had asked her to examine herself and to reach a conclusion about why she was so bloody overwrought about Brutus being with *anyone* when she—Dena Donaldson—had spent the last five years and counting doing practically the same thing in Much Wenlock, and with any bloke who looked at her twice. *It's who I am* didn't work as a rationale for the way she'd been going at life, though. That might have done the trick for Brutus, but it went nowhere when it came to her because *it's who I am* suggested *it's who I'll always be,* and setting herself up as Shropshire's foremost fuck machine was not what Ding had ever entertained as a lifetime ambition. One wouldn't know that from what she'd done on the previous night, however.

She'd gone out alone. She'd told herself that she needed a break from struggling with a paper she owed her tutor, but as she'd only written a single sentence of that paper, she moved straight off the idea of a respite from essay writing and from there she went to telling herself that the air would do her good because the room was stuffy and a brisk walk would help her organise her thoughts.

Reality turned out to be somewhat different, as her brisk walk took her directly to the Hart and Hind, where she had not been—on her own, that is—since she'd run off from Jack Korhonen and room 2 upstairs from the pub. She wouldn't have approached the bar itself had anyone known to her been inside the place. But no one had been, which meant that if she wanted a drink, she had to give her order to one of them: Jack or his nephew.

She would easily have managed ordering herself a lager and making that all she did—aside from drinking it down—had the nephew remained behind the bar. But as she approached, Jack said, "Let me handle this, Peter. You see to the glassware," which took the nephew off to clear tables.

At that point, Jack said to her, "You best be explicit with what you want this time round. We don't need to misunderstand each other again, do we?"

She said, "I don't know what you're talking about."

He said, "Let me put it this way, then. Are you here to wet your whistle or to wet something else?"

"That's incredibly rude."

"Isn't it just. But rude works a treat for me, darling. Only question is does rude work for you? See, first time I saw you in here—months and months ago, this was—I reckoned you as a match for me. I thought, she's a hot one, she is. It'll only be a matter of weeks before she gives me the signal."

"Well, it wasn't weeks, was it?"

"True. It took a wee bit more time, but there it was all the same. You wet, me hard. And the rest."

"You're not a gentleman, you know."

"On that, we see eye to eye. Is it a gentleman you want, coming in here alone, or is it something a bit more thrilling? Or is the truth that you're a tease like before and when it comes to the rest of it, there's something not quite right in your head?"

"There's *nothing* wrong with me *or* my head."

"Proof is in the pudding, as they say. Could be the way I see you is different to how you see yourself."

"I'm fine, I'm just *fine*."

He nodded. "So you say. But 'f I were you? I'd want to prove it. See, girls your age? Oftentimes, they don't know what they're about. They get themselves into situations, don't they, and all of a sudden the picture they thought they were going to paint isn't the one they find themselves painting. When that happens . . . ? Well, you know. Off they scurry into the night."

Ding knew damn well what he was talking about. But that was then and this was now and things were *not* what they had been. She said, "You think that, Jack Korhonen, you just give me one of those keys. We can get this straightened out fast enough."

Jack turned to the Korhonen nephew who, to Ding's embarrassment, had been close enough to hear the exchange. Jack said to him, "What d'you think, Peter, my lad? Should I give Little Missy here another chance?"

"You don't want to, I will," Peter replied as he hoisted a plastic bin of glasses onto the bar.

"Can't have that," his uncle told him. He reached behind the till, handed one of the room keys to Ding, and said, "Five minutes, darling. Be ready this time."

So she was: every thread removed from her body, standing in front of the window with her back to the glass and her face in the shadows. She found she wasn't the least bit nervous. When it came to proving to herself who she was, Dena Donaldson was never nervous.

When Jack came into the room, she walked to him. His hair was longish and thick, and she grabbed onto it with one hand and pulled his head to her mouth. As he kissed her, she felt for his dick. Hard already. Good, she thought. She would make it harder. She would make him want it in ways he'd never wanted it before and they would do it in ways he'd never done it before. So she set upon that course and she saw it through, and if the publican knew nothing else about Dena

Donaldson by two in the morning, what he was absolutely sure of was that Dena Donaldson was not a tease.

She went home sore. She staggered into the house and up the stairs, thinking she would be comatose in thirty seconds after all that had passed. But instead of that, she was left with, What's wrong with you, Ding? She could fuck till she dropped from the face of the planet, but she could see that would not come close to answering the question.

When she could no longer put it off, Ding groaned and rolled to the edge of her bed. She stuck her legs out and contemplated getting up and having a shower and perhaps going to a lecture. She was on her way to committing herself to those actions when her mobile rang.

It was on the bedside table, so she answered it without checking to see who was ringing her. When she heard the voice, the name, and the occupation, though, she wished she'd let the call go to a message she could easily ignore.

"Is that Dena Donaldson?" a woman's voice asked. "This is Greta Yates, the college counsellor. You're going to need to come to my office. If you have an interest in remaining here at West Mercia College, that is. Have you that interest?"

Ding hadn't, actually. But she had less interest in being rusticated. So she said yes, yes, yes, indeed. When did Ms. Yates want to see her?

LUDLOW

SHROPSHIRE

Barbara told Lynley they could walk to the police station easily enough, but it was his decision to drive. Who knew where their conversation with Gary Ruddock might lead them? was his reason. If they needed to track down someone or something once they spoke with the PCSO, it would save time to have the car available.

When they left the hotel at half past eight, Barbara directed Lynley to the police station, realising as she did so that the required route via car instead of on foot would take them directly past the house in which Finnegan Freeman lived. She pointed it out as they cruised past. She also brought Lynley into the picture of what she'd discovered about someone's being able to access the police station on foot—or by bicycle—from this location.

Unlike the DCS, Lynley nodded thoughtfully as he took this on board. He said, "Good work, Barbara. That bit of information could turn out quite useful."

When they reached the station on the corner of Townsend Close and Lower Galdeford, they found the PCSO waiting for them, leaning against his patrol car in the car park. He held up a takeaway coffee in a form of greeting, and he came to be introduced to Lynley as soon as they'd parked.

"I expect you'd like to see inside the place," he said, indicating the unmanned police station.

Lynley said that having a look inside would be welcome, especially having a look at the office where Ian Druitt died. Ruddock said it was ready and waiting. The door, he told him, was already unlocked. Barbara could show him where the office was. He reckoned they might like to make their inspection without himself lurking in the background.

Although there wasn't much to see, Barbara appreciated this, as it would allow a more open conversation between Lynley and herself. So she led the way with Lynley following and Ruddock having a seat on the back steps, where he put on his sunglasses against the sunlight of what was clearly going to be a beautiful spring day.

Barbara took Lynley to the office in which the deacon had died. As before there was little enough to see: the desk with its battered rolling chair tucked into the kneehole, an empty bulletin board, bits of tape still stuck to the walls where maps had probably once hung, the coat cupboard, and the doorknob that had served the purpose of ending Ian Druitt's life. She told him what she herself had been told by Dr. Scannell: how suicide was managed in this way through the pressure exerted on the jugular veins, resulting in venous congestion, resulting in unconsciousness and death. Lynley observed as she spoke. He pulled out the rolling desk chair, but there appeared to be nothing untoward about it. He prowled the room, eyeing everything from the dust on the windowsills to the scuff marks on the lino.

When they left the office, she took him to see the rest as well:

the former lunchroom, the monitors behind the reception counter upon which the CCTV cameras could display their documentation of anyone's coming and going, the computers used by patrol officers who came and went from the station during their duty hours, the other offices in which someone might have been lying in wait. She ended with taking him outside to show him how easily the position of the CCTV camera could be altered above the station's main entrance.

Their tour completed, they rejoined Gary Ruddock, who quickly rose from the back steps and dusted off the seat of his trousers. "Helpful at all?" he asked.

"Everything helps, I find," Lynley replied. He leaned against the brick wall of the station, his gaze on the car park. Barbara waited to see what sort of conversation Lynley had in mind to have with Gary Ruddock post their inspection of the police building. Lynley said, "I've had a look through Druitt's motor. How well did you know him?"

"Not especially well at all. I knew him to nod at in the street, saying hello and that sort of thing. And, 'course, I knew where to find him. I mean that he was connected to St. Laurence Church."

"That's it, then?"

"Pretty much, it is." Ruddock joined Lynley in gazing at the car park. Then he added, "Is there something you reckon I ought to have known about him? Like . . . did you find something inside his car?"

"Interesting question. Why do you ask?"

"Well, I don't expect the bloke was dealing drugs on the side or anything, but as there was that phone call 'bout paedophilia . . ."

"Do you mean pornographic photos or the like? No, there was nothing along those lines. Although . . . No one's mentioned a relationship Druitt might have had, but he's got a box of condoms in his glove box. I may well be stereotyping him, but the condoms do seem rather unexpected in the car of an unmarried church deacon."

"I expect he was giving them to young people," Ruddock said. "He was round them a good bit, through the church and whatever else."

"He did know the Freeman boy," Barbara pointed out. "The DCC herself told us that: how Finnegan helped out Druitt at the children's club. Did you know about that, Gary?"

He nodded. "Could be the condoms were for him, then. Or, like I said, for other lads his age. Kids get up to things, and I can see a churchman worrying about that."

"That makes sense if they weren't Druitt's," Lynley noted.

"How old is the Freeman boy?" Barbara asked. She answered her own question with, "Eighteen? Nineteen? I suppose Druitt could've learned from him that he and a girlfriend were up to the usual, only just like a lot of kids, he wasn't using protection so it could have turned into a case of *whoops*. And Druitt was trying to prevent this."

Ruddock didn't respond. His silence of a sudden seemed strange to Barbara. She rued that he'd donned sunglasses. She couldn't tell if he was thinking this over or thinking of a way he could avoid thinking this over. In either case, she didn't see what the actual need for silence might have been, aside from the fact that he didn't want to get onto Finnegan Freeman since there was a known connection between Finn Freeman and the dead man, and the boy's mother was a high-ranking official in the same police force as Gary Ruddock.

"On a stretch," she finally said, "it could also be that the allegations against Druitt were true. That he was messing about the children but wearing a condom to keep things tidy, if you know what I mean."

"There's that as well," Lynley said. "As unpleasant as the painted picture is, I might add, Sergeant."

"That anonymous message did bang in the direction of paedophilia," Ruddock said.

"Hmm, yes. Although one has some trouble with the idea of your garden paedophile using protection. Everything considered, it seems more likely that Druitt was handing out the condoms to older boys. Or he had a relationship with someone and we might want to suss out who that person is."

"But . . . Can I ask?" Ruddock seemed hesitant but plunged on when Lynley nodded. "Where does that lead you? I mean, the condoms and why Druitt even had them."

"To be honest, it probably leads nowhere," Lynley said. "But it's something to follow up on, and in the absence of anything else, I always like seeing where things will take us."

BURWAY
SHROPSHIRE

They decided to speak with Flora Bevans. Where there was evidence—in the form of the condoms—suggesting present lovers, former lovers, married lovers, vengeful spouses, arguments, conflicts, tears, and any one of the passions and the deadly sins, logic dictated it be investigated. If Gary Ruddock could only speculate about Druitt's possession of the condoms, perhaps Flora Bevans could do more.

While Lynley set a course out of town, Barbara combed through the notes she'd taken of the conversations she'd had with the individuals attached to those names in Druitt's diary that she had been able to track down. There hadn't been a ghost of a suggestion anywhere that the man had a relationship with anyone save his God, but then she hadn't questioned any of these people on that actual topic. She was probably going to have to deal with them all again should Flora Bevans be unable to give them happiness on the subject of condoms.

The Bevans' Beauties van was in the driveway when they arrived, suggesting the florist was at home. To Barbara's leaning upon the bell, the woman herself answered the door, her mobile phone pressed to her ear, and a finger already raised to tell her visitors she would be with them when she could. Her eyebrows lifted in surprise when she saw Barbara, and she said into her phone, "Hang on just a moment," and then to Barbara, "I didn't think I'd be seeing you again," to which Barbara replied, "This is DI Lynley. Can we have a word?"

Flora opened wide the door, saying, "Come in, come in. I'm just finishing up with an order." She retreated towards the back of the house, saying into the phone, "You see, the size of the urn is more important than it would seem upon first consideration. If it overwhelms where it's placed . . ."

Barbara and Lynley had remained in the entry, and Lynley murmured, "Cremations?" to her.

She frowned and said, "What?"

He said, "Urns. Cremations."

"Oh. She does plantings, sir. Big pots and the like. Huge pots actually. For people's front steps and, I reckon, for their back gardens as well. And inside their houses. And wherever."

Flora Bevans joined them then, saying, "Sorry. I've been talked into a garden wedding, all the pots and urns to be fixtures in the garden afterwards, which means the bride must be pleased with the colours, the mother of the bride must be able to work with the colours afterwards as it *is* her garden, and the mother of the groom has—apparently—already chosen her kit for the affair and the flowers must not clash with that nor must they clash with the gown of the chief attendant, who is apparently going to be dressed in fuchsia. Appalling choice even for a summer wedding, but there you have it. Now. You've returned and I have a feeling this hasn't to do with your ordering up a few urns for your terrace. Sorry. I cannot remember your name."

Barbara reintroduced herself and then Lynley.

"Is this about poor Ian?" Flora asked. "Do you want to see his room again?"

Barbara said to her, "We've come to talk to you about condoms, actually."

"Good heavens. Do come in. You have me in the dither of intrigue." She ushered them into a sitting room, saying, "Please, sit. Shove those magazines onto the floor, Inspector. May I get you something? Tea, coffee, water? Oh! I didn't see Jeffrey there. Excuse me. Let me post him elsewhere."

Jeffrey turned out to be a cat with fur that virtually matched the sofa's upholstery. He was curled into a corner of it, and he looked up just before Barbara planted her bum on top of him. His expression indicated that he wasn't pleased to see any of them. He protested with something between a meow and a trill as Flora gathered him up. But as posting him elsewhere consisted of placing him on the top of the largest cat tree that Barbara had ever seen, in order to give him a view of the street, he didn't seem entirely unforgiving that his nap had been interrupted.

Both Barbara and Lynley demurred on refreshments, so all of them sat. Flora said, "I don't know how much help I can be. Condoms. Heavens, am I blushing just to say the word?"

"They were in Ian Druitt's car," Lynley told her.

"Were they indeed? Was he being naughty?"

"Or careful," Barbara pointed out.

"Of course, of course. But how can I help you with Ian and his condoms?"

"Possession of them indicates use," Lynley said.

Flora chewed on this one and its implications. Barbara said, "What the inspector means is were you and Ian Druitt lovers?"

"Good gracious, no. I did tell you and the other officer that between us there was simply no frisson, did I not? I doubt he looked upon me as anything other than his landlady. For my part, I never gave a thought to him as anything—perhaps I should say any*one*—I would want in my bed. I don't mean to imply there was anything wrong with him, mind. He was quite a lovely chap. But the truth is that aside from there being no chemistry between us, sex with one's lodger does bring up the dicey issue of what next? Does one still expect to have the rent paid on time? Was this a one-off or can one expect a repeat performance and if so, when? So if Ian was carrying condoms about with him, I was not his intended . . . hmm . . . beneficiary?"

"Did he ever mention any other 'beneficiary' to you?" Lynley asked.

"Even clothed as someone you might not have suspected was a 'beneficiary' at all?" Barbara added.

"Well, that's rather difficult, isn't it," Flora said. "Ian knew so *many* people. Not only through the parish and the church but also through all his activities. Really, it could have been anyone."

"Male and female?" Lynley asked.

"Goodness. I have absolutely no idea. But if he was engaged with someone—you know what I mean—then he was the absolute soul of discretion. He never mentioned a name or received a phone call or even a letter or a card in the post. And when I packed up his things after his most unfortunate death, I surely would have seen something—a pressed flower? a theatre stub? one half of a cinema ticket?—to indicate he had a lover."

"A married woman?" Lynley asked Flora Bevans.

"I suppose that *could* be the case," she said. "Although again, Inspector, there was no sign."

"Someone underage?" Barbara offered.

"Oh dear. One hates even to *think* of Ian in that capacity: a man of God and a young girl. I always felt completely safe with him in the house, you know."

"No one's suggesting that he was engaged in criminal behaviour," Lynley reassured her.

"Well . . . except for the paedophilia thing, sir," Barbara said.

"Yes, of course."

"Oh, I can barely stand to talk about that. I don't believe it. I can't picture Ian doing *anything* of the sort. I do wish I could be more help to you. But from everything I saw and heard and overheard—well, the house *is* small, as you can see—regarding Ian, I can give you nothing save the fact that he seemed to be a complete man of God. I hope I'm not wrong." She sighed, put her hands on her thighs, and stood. "I *am* sorry not to be of more help," she concluded. "You've trekked all this way out here for nothing."

Barbara dug round in her bag for a card to give the florist, and she handed it over with the usual remark about ringing if anything came to her mind. She and Lynley stood as well. They were heading towards the front door when it occurred to Barbara that Flora Bevans might be able to aid them with something else. She asked the florist whether Ian Druitt had known the date of her birth. He'd lived with her for some years, after all.

Flora responded with, "What an odd question. But yes, he did know," and when Barbara asked her for it, she told her.

Before the florist could enquire about why the police wanted her birthday, Barbara flipped her notebook closed and said, "Thanks. I'll remember to send you a card."

They were out in the street before she tried the relevant numbers on Ian Druitt's locked phone. She smiled and looked up from the phone to Lynley.

"Bingo," she said.

BROMFIELD
SHROPSHIRE

Since they were on the Bromfield Road, they drove from Flora Bevans' house into Bromfield itself, where a secondary road near the post office took them to what one could reliably find in any village in the country: a pub. The journey took all of eight minutes, two of which were spent overshooting the lane upon which the pub was established and thereby requiring Lynley to find the rough tractor entrance to a farmer's field, where he could execute a three-point turn. During all of this, Havers devilled with Druitt's mobile phone, which, of course, had not been used since the night of his death.

She finally said to him, "Treasure trove, sir. God bless smartphones. As the song says, 'We're in the money.' Where did it come from, that song, by the way?"

"The larger question is where you might have heard it," Lynley pointed out to her. "It's not 1950s rock 'n' roll, after all."

"It can, however, be tap-danced to," she informed him.

"Ah. As to that, Daidre wished me to enquire how it's going. The tap dancing, that is."

"*Daidre*? Why the bloody hell . . . ?"

"She's one of the intrigued, Sergeant. As am I, I hope you recall. How *is* it all going? I ask because daily I fear a phone call from Dee Harriman. I'll need something to report in order to remain in her good graces."

"Tell her I'm a dead cert when it comes to the heel drop, but the Irish is slaying me. Umaymah remains the better bet if Dee doesn't want egg on her tap shoes on the night in question."

"Remind me when it is, Sergeant Havers."

"In your dreams, Inspector Lynley. Not a bloody chance."

The pub, they discovered, was not only the local watering hole but also a gathering spot for an ambitious male knitting group that appeared to be taking instruction from a pensioner who looked as if he'd spent most of his life on the sea, so weathered was his skin. They seemed to be working all on the same kind of project. This could have been an extremely long sock or a rather short scarf. It was difficult to tell, although the colours chosen by the knitters suggested something of a military nature. Their lesson was accompanied by a good amount of libation. It appeared to be adding a great deal to their enjoyment, if the noise was anything to go by.

As Lynley and Havers took a table, the sergeant pulled her notebook from her bag once again. She said to him, "Did you know these lovely gizmos"—and here she waved the mobile in the air—"keep a record of your calls directly on 'em for a couple of months back without you having to ask anyone to send them to you? Calls made and calls received and calls missed and messages left. And since, as we know, this particular mobile hasn't been used since the night Ian Druitt died, we're sitting pretty. Or at least prettier than we would have been with an older-type phone. Anyway, if you'd put on your country pub persona and fetch me a lemonade from the bar, sir, I'll see what's what with the *whos*, the *whys*, and the *howevers*."

"Anything else?" he asked her before turning towards the bar.

"I wouldn't say no to a packet of something edible. Salt-and-vinegar crisps if they have 'em. Pork rinds'll do in a pinch. There's the lad."

Lynley shuddered but did her bidding. In the minutes that it took him to get the attention of the publican, purchase a lemonade, a packet of crisps, and a cup of coffee—which extended the wait since the coffee had to be made—and return to their table, Havers was able to go through the first few weeks of Ian Druitt's phone calls. She was using her notes to compare the phone numbers with those she'd compiled from the deacon's various church and volunteer activities as listed in his diary. She was onto the fourth week as Lynley set his purchases upon the table.

"Ta," she said to him. "Dig into the crisps if you've a mind, Inspector."

"I shall pass," he told her.

"Could you do the honours anyway?"

He opened the bag and handed it over to her. She unceremoniously dumped its contents onto the tabletop, oblivious to germs, bacteria, social diseases, and the remains of meals. She tucked in directly. Lynley reckoned that, at this point in her life, Havers had an immune system worthy of advanced scientific study.

As she munched, she reported on her findings. "We've got Mr. Spencer, a woman I spoke to earlier from the Neighbourhood Watch programme, Flora Bevans, the two crime victims listed in his diary, his dad, and the bloke who heads up the feral cat catch-and-release group. There're some other calls to and from numbers I don't have in my notes, and I'll ring them and see what's what when I've finished with the first of the two months we've got."

Lynley nodded as he stirred some questionable-looking sugar into his coffee, trying to avoid the bits that were clotted together from wet spoons having previously been dipped into the bowl. He said, "So far, then, there's not a lot of joy to be had?"

"Could be the case, sir. *But* there's something missing and there's also another phone number that I wouldn't expect to be here."

"Indeed? Continue."

She shoved a handful of crisps into her mouth, munched, and washed them down with a gulp of lemonade. She said, "First, unless one of these phone numbers is attached to Rabiah Lomax's mobile—assuming she has one—there's no phone call either received or made that deals with her. That's curious, you ask me, since she had those sessions with Druitt and one would think she'd need to ring him about an appointment."

"It could be that she contacted him prior to this two-month period you've got on his phone, Barbara. If she did that in order to set up her first appointment, there wouldn't be a reason to ring him again, would there?"

"I s'pose," Havers agreed, "assuming that at the end of each appointment, she set up the next right there in his presence. On the other hand, could be she's been lying to us."

"It does remain a disagreeable fact of our employment that someone is usually lying about something. What else, then?"

"Gary Ruddock."

"What about him?"

"In the weeks I've looked at so far, Druitt rang him five times. And during that same period on his end, Ruddock rang Druitt three times."

"Did he indeed?"

"I reckon we ought to take *that* one on board and stow it with the baggage since he claimed barely to know the bloke." She reached for another palmful of crisps and munched happily. "Seemed to me, sir, Ruddock went dead quiet when the Freeman kid was brought up. I wonder if he was hoping we'd move off that topic before he had to address it."

"Or to answer questions about him. The boy, I mean."

"Right."

"There's something not quite as it should be in what he said about Druitt, then."

"Ruddock? Too right. And here's what it is for me, Inspector: One phone call between him and Druitt . . . ? Okay, whatever, it could be dismissable. But *eight*? That's dressed in neon lights, that is."

"We can't discount Druitt and the victim volunteer bit, however. It stands to reason that Ruddock might well have put him in touch with several victims of crimes."

"He might have done, but there would've had to be a real crime spree in Ludlow since the calls back and forth span something like . . ." She referred to the phone. "Eleven days."

He nodded thoughtfully. "Could be it's to do with the boy, then. Finnegan."

"The guv thought he was a piece of work. Could be he was up to something and Druitt knew what it was. Or Ruddock knew what it was and told Druitt to keep an eye out on the sly."

"Drug dealing, housebreaking, muggings, graffiti, tagging, street fights—"

"We know he was into karate."

"—chopping watermelons in half with his index finger?"

She raised her eyes heavenward. "Whatever, sir. But I got to say it: There's things about this bloke—the PCSO—that're starting to make me feel like a dormouse's running round my insides. There's these dodgy bits we keep coming across, starting with when the DCS and I were here."

"Elucidating that point . . . ?"

She ticked items off an imaginary list on the tabletop. "The CCTV camera in front of the station being shut down long enough to have its position moved; whatever Ruddock might've been doing with a girl in his patrol car on the night Druitt died; Ruddock claiming he has no relationship with a female when he clearly has something going on with her of the patrol car; Ruddock saying he left Druitt alone in that office while he was making phone calls to pubs; and now Ruddock not mentioning he and Druitt spoke by mobile. *And* there's prob'ly more. I'm thinking we've not got all there is to be had from Gary Ruddock, sir. You ask me, we need thumbscrews."

"You might well be right," Lynley said. "But it seems that at the moment we have only one available to us."

"One thumbscrew? What is it, then?"

"The PCSO's mobile phone. Since Druitt's mobile is something of a revelation, Ruddock's might be the same."

Havers thought about this before saying, "We could go for his phone records. But that'd take days, wouldn't it, assuming we could warm the cockles of some magistrate's heart enough to get a warrant for virtually no reason. And even *with* a warrant, it'll still take even more days to get the records, right? So do we have enough time from Hillier to be going that route?"

"You won't find me arguing that we do. I daresay we'll have to go at this directly. And more creatively. Since the constable has announced himself eager to help in any way he can, I suggest we take him up on his offer."

Havers shot him an incredulous look. "You're saying we ask him to hand over his phone?"

"I am. When you think about it, how can he refuse? If we structure our conversation with him correctly, our request to look at his phone will be inevitable. Indeed, he might well offer it to us without our even having to make the request."

She took a moment to consider this before she said, "You're a bloody wily one when you want to be, Inspector."

"I like to think *wily* is my middle name."

"I'm on board, then." She flipped her notebook closed and returned it to her bag. She put the mobile with the notebook. Then she wiped the salt-and-vinegar crisp crumbs from the table onto her hand.

For a horrifying moment, Lynley thought she might actually consume them as she'd done the crisps: from the unhygienic surface of the table. She caught his expression and said, "Please. I draw the line *somewhere*, Inspector."

He said, "Thank God," as she added, "I just don't do my line-drawing here," and licked the crumbs from her palm.

LUDLOW
SHROPSHIRE

While Barbara liked Lynley's proposed direct approach to putting their maulers on Gary Ruddock's mobile, she wasn't sure how well it was going to work. The PCSO didn't know that they were in possession of the dead man's smartphone, of course, so that was to their advantage. On the other hand, since Ruddock had already indicated that he knew there was a connection between Finnegan Freeman and Ian Druitt, she didn't really see how going over a record of his phone calls to and from the man was going to serve the purpose of dealing with all the bits that were looking dodgy about the bloke.

A quick call to the PCSO told them that he was not in the police station at the moment. Although he sounded just a bit surprised to hear that the Met detectives wished to speak with him again, he was otherwise cooperative. He told Barbara that, at present, he was at the mobile home centre just outside Ludlow Business Park. One of the vehicles had been broken into. Did they want to meet him there? It was just off the A49. Or he could meet them back at the station. Unfortunately, it was locked or he'd tell them just to wait inside till he got there.

They chose the station, and Ruddock said he'd meet them there as soon as he could. He reckoned an hour would do it since he needed to finish up at the mobile home centre.

While Lynley drove them back into Ludlow and then to the nick, Barbara used the time to continue ringing the numbers registered on Ian Druitt's phone. She continued this as they waited for the PCSO's arrival, and the time allowed her to discover Druitt's connections with the head teachers from three nearby primary schools, all of whom were recommending youngsters for the children's club; requests he'd made to parents of children in that club for transportation to a gymnastics exhibition; communications with the parish organist; a request for a change in the choral music made by one of the choir members. She was also able to track down various calls he'd made to his father, his mother, and three of his siblings about a celebration of his paternal grandmother's ninety-fifth birthday. Several other numbers went directly to automated voice mail when she rang them, giving her no option but to request a return call from whoever it was who owned the phone.

When she finished her work with the mobile, Lynley told her that he had a conversational plan for Gary Ruddock that would make the PCSO's handing over his mobile to them inevitable. In the final moments before Ruddock's arrival, he explained it to her, and when Ruddock at last drove into the car park, they set upon that task.

Barbara said to the PCSO as they joined him, "Can we sit and have a natter, Gary? We've come across a few new details, me and the inspector."

"'Course," Ruddock said. "I'm that happy to help," and he took them into the former lunchroom, where he and Barbara had sat before. He told them to hang on a moment so that he could fetch another chair. This one turned out to be a desk chair that he rolled down the corridor.

Lynley was the one to tell him that they were in possession of Ian Druitt's smartphone. He'd left it in the vestry, Lynley said, the night that Ruddock had gone to St. Laurence Church to fetch him to the police station. Ruddock nodded. He waited for more.

"We charged it up," Barbara said, "and once we finally worked out the proper code to unlock the bloody thing—"

"Thanks to Barbara's efforts," Lynley added.

"Ta, sir," she said. "I do my best." And then to Ruddock, "Like I said, once we got the thing operational, we started looking through the calls. Into and out of the phone, I mean."

Lynley said, "Since it hadn't been used since March, it had a record of the calls for the last two months of the deacon's life."

Ruddock surprised them with, "My own number would've been there. He and I went back and forth a bit."

"I recognised your number," Barbara told him. "We have him ringing you and you ringing him."

"We're speaking to everyone attached to the phone calls, clarifying why they phoned him and vice versa," Lynley said.

"So you'd want to know about the calls between us, me and Druitt, I wager." He looked from Barbara to Lynley back to Barbara.

"That'd be the case," she agreed.

"Can I have a look at the phone?" he asked, and Barbara handed it over to him. He said, "Goes back a bit, this does."

"That'd be because it's not been used since he died," Barbara said.

He nodded thoughtfully. He also seemed to consider what or how much he wanted to reveal. Finally he said, "Well . . . it's nothing to do with what happened. See, he was ringing me about Finn Freeman."

"The deputy chief constable's son," Lynley said.

"Druitt had some concerns about him. Truth to tell, there's always the odd concern when it comes to Finn. He's done something of a job with his looks, and he makes himself seem real rough round the edges. It's mostly an act, but he puts people off. I think Druitt was more watchful with him than he might've been with another lad had another lad been his helper at the club."

"Was he waiting for him to be out of order in some way?"

"Prob'ly. He rang wanting to know if Finn had ever been in any trouble in town. Aside from drinking too much, he hadn't been, which was what I told him."

"He rang more than once, though. Can we assume he wasn't reassured?"

"Way I recall, it was like he had a feeling about Finn and he was looking for someone to support it or p'rhaps to explain it away. I didn't have even a sprat to give him. The boy smokes weed now and again, but so do the rest of them. He drinks as well, but he's never been in any trouble round here. That's what I told Druitt. Eventually, though, he rang asking how to contact Finn's parents. He wouldn't tell me what it was about, just that he needed to speak with them and he didn't want the boy to know, so he couldn't ask him directly how to contact them. Somehow he knew Finn's mum was a police officer—I reckon Finn told him or told the kids in the club—and he wanted to know from me did I know how he could contact her without it getting back to Finn."

"Ringing his parents suggests it was something fairly serious," Lynley said. "Did he give you any idea at all what was going on?"

"I asked," Ruddock said. "But all he said was 'I can't be sure' and something like how he didn't want to judge the boy wrong. I got the impression he was worried about Finn's . . . well, I guess you'd call it his impact on the club's children and he was hoping to get some information about him from his parents."

"What sort of information?"

"No clue, really," Ruddock said. "It could've been about anything, I s'pose. Like did they ever see him pinch coins from the collection plate? Or had he been badly injured as a boy and in need of pain medications? Or had he ever had a behaviour change with no way to account for it? What I'm saying here is that those're *my* speculations, because aside from saying he wanted to have a word with the parents and did I know how to contact his mum since she's a copper, he didn't tell me much of anything."

"Finn Freeman's been something of a recurring theme, we're finding," Lynley said.

"Along the lines of all-roads-leading-to him," Barbara put in.

"I wish I could tell you more," Ruddock said. "But that's the extent of it."

"Do you recognise any of the other numbers registered on Ian Druitt's messages and phone calls?" Lynley asked. He nodded at the phone that was still in Ruddock's hand.

Ruddock cooperatively gave all this a look, but his expression was one of regret. He clarified this with, "I got to say: I'm dead rotten at this. Way I do things with my own phone? I just find the name on my list and tap it. I c'n barely remember my own number, let alone anyone else's. I mix them up, see. I put them backwards and the like."

Barbara remembered that, from the first, Ruddock had been in the open about his learning difficulties. She gave Lynley a fractional nod. A silence grew. Lynley and she did their best presentation of being deep in thought: Barbara with her arms crossed and her lips pursed as she gazed upon the hideous grey lino, he with a bent index finger touching the scar on his upper lip and his brow furrowed as he looked out of the window above the table at which they were sitting.

After a good thirty seconds of this, Lynley said, "There *is* one point we've come across. You might be able to help with it."

"I'm that happy to," Ruddock said.

"It has to do with the night Mr. Druitt died. You've told my sergeant that you spent some time away from him making phone calls to the town's pubs once you learned about the bingeing going on. And during that period of making calls to the pubs, Mr. Druitt hanged himself."

"I've been that sorry from—"

"Understood. But in looking at the number of pubs in Ludlow and considering the time required to ring them all about shutting down for the night—"

"It was just about not serving college-age drinkers, sir," Barbara put in.

"Yes. Of course. Not serving young drinkers." And to Ruddock, "My sergeant and I have begun to wonder why it took you the amount of time you've said it took to make those calls. Barbara?"

She made much of going back over her notes. "Nearly ninety minutes, sir."

"So we've begun to ask ourselves what else might have happened during that time."

"Nothing." But there was colour in Ruddock's cheeks that had not been there before.

Barbara did the leaning forward this time. She said, "Gary, when I was here first time round, I popped by the station one night. It was . . . I dunno . . . round half past ten? There were no lights on, but there was a patrol car in the back, in the car park."

"Generally, there is," he said.

"This patrol car was in the shadows. It was as far from the building as it could be. I know that doesn't mean anything in the normal course of events but on this night—when I was here, I mean—a young woman got out of that patrol car. Then you did. Then you and she had something of a stare-down. Then the two of you got back in. And stayed there."

Ruddock said nothing. He was perfectly still.

"So," Barbara said, using the word as a full stop before she went on with, "males and females inside a car parked deep in the shadows at night. What does that suggest to you?"

He began to reply but Barbara wasn't finished so she said quickly, "Now, what I remember is you telling me that you didn't have anyone in your life of a girlfriend nature. If that's the case—"

"I *had* to lie to you." Colour was climbing up his neck, turning his skin into a burning bruise. "If I said the truth, you would've gone to her. I couldn't have that. I'm sorry about it all. I know everything's my fault. I know what happened with the deacon is down to me, but I couldn't just announce . . . No one could in my position."

This bore some sorting through. Barbara glanced at Lynley to see what he was making of it. He said to the constable, "I'm assuming you mean that on the night Druitt died, in addition to making the phone calls to the pubs, you also had—"

"Sex," Barbara put in, knowing Lynley's inclination to use polite euphemisms, gent that he was. "A prong in the pudding, as it were. In the car park inside the patrol car."

Ruddock averted his gaze. "It'd already been arranged. Her and me. This was before I was told to fetch him. And even then, no one *told* me what was going on with Mr. Druitt. The paedophile thing. I was just told to bring him in and wait for the patrol officers. So I expected . . . What I *didn't* expect was what happened."

"You left him unattended." Lynley waited for Ruddock to nod, then he said, "Which gave him time to hang himself."

"Or gave someone else time to fake his suicide," Barbara added, and when Ruddock quickly turned to her, she added, "You do see how that could've happened, eh? You and whoever she is, out in the shadows going at it like ferrets and someone gaining access to the station, someone who knew you and the nameless female would be doing just what you were doing . . . ?"

"No!" Ruddock cried. "It couldn't have! Not that way."

"You understand we'll need her name," Lynley told him.

"We're ticking boxes here, Gary," Barbara added, "and whoever she is, she's one of them."

"It's nothing to do with her," he said hotly. "She doesn't know . . . she *didn't* know Druitt."

"Perhaps that's the case, but she'll need to confirm that," Lynley said.

"She'll also, when you come down to it, be providing you with an alibi, Gary."

That stopped him exactly where they wanted him, Barbara saw, directly on the edge of the precipice. He could plunge over or he could retreat. He was running out of options.

He said hoarsely, "I can't have her dragged into this. She's married. What's happened is down to me. I was derelict in duty. No one else was."

"Then we're going to need your mobile, Gary," Barbara told him. "We're going to have to search for her. You do see that, don't you? It's easier for all of us if you hand it over. There's less official involvement that way. It stays between us. If we have to go the route of a warrant, then, well, everyone knows, eh?"

They were at it. It all came down to what the PCSO wanted and did not want others to know, particularly his superior officers. Barbara and Lynley were relying on the fact that Ruddock's self-interest would supersede everything else.

It did. Ruddock handed over his mobile.

"You do know that if she's on here, we're going to find her," Lynley told him. "So is there anything you want to tell us in advance before we begin checking on your calls?"

Ruddock said, "She's not on there."

"We'll be determining that, of course," Lynley said. "Is there anyone on here you want to tell us about before we work it out on our own?"

Ruddock considered this, directing his gaze to the window. When he finally looked back at them, it was impossible to tell if he'd decided to lie or had been dwelling on the ramifications of what he was about to say. "There's calls you'll see to and from Trev Freeman."

"The DCC's husband," Barbara clarified.

"He asked me to keep an eye on Finn. He's been a handful at home. Trev thought if I was . . . well, sort of a big brother to him . . . because, see, Trev and Clo—"

"You seem closer than normal to the DCC." Barbara couldn't imagine calling the guv *Isabelle,* and trying *Dave* on Hillier would doubtless get her booted down the nearest stairway.

"Oh, I wouldn't ever call her by her first name in company or the like. It's just that . . . Look, she took me under her wing a bit. She introduced me to her family, particularly to Finn. I liked him and he liked me."

"Got it," Barbara said. And then to Lynley, "Sir?"

He nodded. "I think we have what we need." He rose to leave and then added, "But it is surprising, nonetheless," he said.

"What's that?" Ruddock asked him.

"How so much that we've learned takes us to this boy Finnegan Freeman."

They left him then, his mobile phone in their possession. As they climbed back into the Healey Elliott, Barbara said, "I wager he's racing to the landline as fast as he can, ringing every number he can remember. There's going to be some he knows by heart."

"Perhaps," Lynley said. "But I don't actually doubt him when it comes to the phone, Barbara. Don't you find that technology is eliminating brainpower in virtually every area of life? Why memorise a number, why even write it in an actual address book or diary when one can merely tap a name on a smartphone and—"

"Bob's your whatever," Havers finished. "Right. I get it."

"Thus technology doth make numbskulls of us all."

Barbara offered him an instructive look. "Inspector, do you *ever* plan to advance into the current year? Or decade? Or even century?"

"Something Helen asked me often enough," he said, smiling. "Although since she never quite managed to work out how the microwave operated, I think she'd forgive me the sin of Luddism."

"Hmph," was Barbara's reply.

"The real point is that we have his phone." He lowered the Healey Elliott's window but did not start its engine. He went on with, "Let me ask you, Sergeant. Did you believe the bit about the calls to and from Trevor Freeman?"

"About the son, Finnegan? The entire watching-over of the son?" And when Lynley nodded, she went on with, "He could well want watching over, sir. The guv found him something of a piece of work, I can tell you that."

"Then you and I shall have a word and see how we find him."

WORCESTER

HEREFORDSHIRE

Trevor Freeman had to admit that he and his wife had begun their relationship as a veritable cliché. She'd been a young detective constable employed in the city, newly out of training, ambitious to climb upwards in the police hierarchy. She'd been equally ambitious to remain in top physical condition, and in this cause she'd taken on a personal trainer. He'd been that trainer.

From the first, he'd found her compelling. So often he'd discovered that, given a few weeks of intense conditioning, both men and women began making excuses for their inattention and sloth. But not Clover. She showed up at the gym where he was employed, she did the work, she grunted, she sweated, and she didn't worry how any of this affected her looks. This, of course, made her immediately intriguing to him.

He had pursued her: inviting her for a cup of coffee after a training session, offering her a drink at the local, suggesting a meal together. But nothing worked. He was considering just moving on when his sister-in-law invited him to a small drinks party to which she said she'd also invited a woman who, she thought, would be a good match for him. Someone she'd met at a charity run, she said.

He'd gone, and there she was. Clover. The woman his sister-in-law had met, the good match for him, the female whose interests were so similar to his own. They'd both been astonished to see the other, they both had laughed, the situation had to be explained. Then Clover had agreed to share a dinner with him after the drinks party.

There, however, she'd put paid to the idea of the two of them acting on what was an obvious attraction between them. She said before they even took up their menus, "This isn't going to lead to sex. I've gone that route before, but I've moved on from it. I thought it best to mention that at once so we know where we stand with each other."

She'd sounded so matter of fact about it that he'd been completely done in by what he'd seen as her breathtaking honesty, an honesty she'd held true to throughout their marriage. But now there was Gaz Ruddock to think about. Now there was the "we'll speak later" that Trevor had overheard. And he damn well could have had "we'll speak later" sorted a quarter hour after he'd heard those words had he managed to keep his bloody wits about him, but he kept getting sidelined by his dick.

He was in his office in Freeman Athletics thinking of this when his desk phone rang. He'd just decided to descend to the weight machines. There one of his trainers was in the act of getting friendly with a woman far too vulnerable to him. She'd lost four stone and was enough out of condition to make a young stud's advances welcome if he was subtle enough. Boyd was an expert at being subtle, and Trevor wasn't about to have that.

The phone stopped him before he could make his move, though. He turned from the window and saw that it was his private line. Clover or Finn, he thought.

But it was Gaz. He said, "I've tried to get through to Clo, but she's not answering her mobile, and she's not in her office. Can you pass along a message to her, Trev?"

Trevor instantly realised that an opportunity had fallen into his lap like a gift. He said, "Does the message concern what you and Clover planned to speak about later?" He didn't stop to consider how to frame the question more carefully.

There was something of a silence before Gaz said, "Sorry?"

"Last night," Trevor told him. "As you were leaving."

Another silence during which, Trevor reckoned, the wheels of Gaz's mind were probably turning to come up with something that would suffice as a reasonable excuse for what had been said. "Oh that," came finally. "It was Scotland Yard. That's why I'm ringing. They've been here twice today, and I thought Clo would want to know."

"So this isn't actually about what you planned to speak of later?" Trevor pressed him. He wanted to pin the young man down. Clover might be nearly impossible to converse with when she had something she wished to hide, but the one thing that Gaz Ruddock wasn't was Clover Freeman.

Gaz said, "Look. C'n I just say . . . Mostly it's due to Finn. Clo asked me to . . . I s'pose I'd call it to *engage* Finn in some way now that Ian Druitt's gone and there's no after-school club for Finn to volunteer at. 'Course, there probably *will* be another club . . . I mean . . . Eventually there will be, eh? But for now, there's not . . . I mean, not till someone from the community takes over . . . or another deacon gets assigned to St. Laurence Church or whatever. So she's wondered how well Finn's going to do without something extra to occupy him."

Trevor didn't like the idea of having an indirect sort of conversation with Gaz. He said, "I know all about your arrangement, Gaz."

Gaz went for a show of confusion. "What arrangement's this?"

"The one Clover set up last autumn, to have you look in on Finn and report back to her. So is that why you're ringing? Have you something to pass along about my son?"

"Oh." Trevor heard the young man blow out a breath. It sounded like relief. "Not one hundred percent exactly. But truth to tell you, it's good to hear that you know about what Clo asked me to do. I expect she told you last night? I could tell you knew something was going on."

"That I could, Gaz. Want to explain what else is going on?"

"I don't understand."

"I reckon you understand well enough. I'm curious about why you're ringing me instead of just leaving a message for my wife on her mobile. What's that about? Seems to me that it's about looking innocent."

"Of what? What're you on about, Trev?"

Trevor looked out of the window again. He saw that Boyd had now joined his middle-aged client on the bench for pressing weights. Both of them were straddling it, facing each other, legs spread. Christ. He needed to put a stop to what was going on inside Boyd's head, but at the moment, he had something more important that he had to cope with. He said—his gaze still boring into Boyd's skull in order to get his attention—"What I'm on about is 'let's speak later.' What I'm on about is getting to the truth, which I intend to get to before I pass any messages along to my wife."

"Trev." Gaz sounded like someone making an appeal. "I swear to God I don't know what you mean. I'm ringing because I reckoned Clo would want to know that Scotland Yard were here to talk to me about Druitt, since there was a relationship between Druitt and Finn."

"What the *hell*? Gaz, do you want to tell me what's actually going on?"

"It's just that since Clo asked me to keep the eye on Finn, I thought . . . all things being equal . . ." He paused as if to gather courage or to collect his thoughts. When he went on, he did so in something of a rush. "Trev, listen. Druitt rang me about Finn a few times, and I let Clo know. I also told the two from Scotland Yard. I more or less had to because they had his mobile—Druitt's—and they could see he rang me and, obviously, they wanted to know why. And now they've taken mine as well, which is another reason why I'm ringing you."

"*Your* mobile? What do they want with it?"

"They're checking everything."

"And exactly what constitutes everything?"

"Turns out Clo was using your mobile on occasion when she rang me about Finn. Least that's what I worked out when I saw how many calls came to me from *your* mobile, which I'd never noticed before. So what it is, is this." There was another pause that did seem suspiciously like a working up of courage. "I ended up telling them—the Met detectives—that I've been keeping an eye on Finn and that you were the one who asked me to do it and you were ringing me from your mobile to see how things were going. So now they'll be tracking you down since your number'll be in my mobile's records. I told 'em as much, but they're going to want to confirm. It's what they do. So what I'm hoping is you'll say you were the one asking me to watch Finn. Otherwise, Clo gets put into the mix and what's the point in that?"

Protection was what this was all about, Trevor realised, and he read that hidden agenda like an article above the fold in a broadsheet. Protection of Clover was on Gaz's mind, and there was going to be a fascinating reason for that. But there was nothing to be gained by trying to delve for more information from the PCSO, so he gave lip service to going along with Gaz's request. But he didn't plan to do it without managing some kind of confrontation with his wife.

HINDLIP
HEREFORDSHIRE

Prior to setting off for Hindlip, Trevor took a look at his mobile's history of calls made and calls received. He didn't know how long these intimate conversations between Clover and Gaz had been going on—that complete history was not available to him—but what he could see with just a glance was that six had occurred during the first visit of the Metropolitan Police, either late at night or during the early hours of the morning. Of course, he thought. His mobile would have been unavailable to her at any other time unless he was charging it somewhere within her reach.

When he arrived at the main building of the police headquarters, Trevor learned that Clover was not in her office but rather at the training facility for the policing area's PCSOs. She was leading a discussion on the topic of Options for Community Safety, her secretary told him. Did he want to walk over to the centre and catch the end of it or would he rather wait here?

Trevor said he'd listen in on the discussion Clover was leading. He knew where the training centre was. He set off at once.

His choice of bearding her at work was deliberate. Clover was far too adept at misdirecting him and he was far too weak when it came to the sort of misdirection she employed. Their discussion had to be on territory where she couldn't rely on her ability to trigger his animal nature.

The training centre was beyond the chapel at the far end of the administration building. It was an institutional structure that offered an unappealing contrast to the older great house in which Clover, the chief constable, and the heads of various departments had their offices. Access to it required nothing more than opening the door. Once inside, it was a simple matter to find the hall in which the PCSOs in training were attending to the sage words of the officers on the panel at the front of the room.

Trevor took up a position at the back of the hall, standing at the closed double doors with his head cocked in interest as he watched his wife. When she glanced in his direction, she did not react other than to curve her lips in the smallest of smiles. She was surprised, however, and never a fool, she would immediately know that something was up. She just wouldn't know what it was since her presence here in the training session indicated why she'd been unavailable to Gaz. Even had she been within his reach, though, Trevor doubted that Gaz would have rung her even from a landline, as he wouldn't have wanted to risk further contact between them should he be intent upon protecting her.

The meeting's conclusion released the PCSOs to depart for the day. Clover's fellow panelists exchanged a few words as they gathered up folders and other materials. Then they, too, were leaving while Clover herself remained at the front of the room, stuffing her belongings into a briefcase.

Trevor joined her and went straight to it. "You've been using my mobile to ring Gaz. I wouldn't've known, but he rang me. He's had to hand his phone over to the London detectives."

"Hello to you as well," she said. "It was a surprise to look up and find my handsome husband listening. How long have you been here? The subject must have bored you to tears."

"Gaz made a request I thought best to run by you. He's asked me to confirm with the Met that I was the one who asked him to keep watch over Finn. He'd like me to say that the relevant phone calls to and from my phone dealt with my request and his subsequent reports as to Finn's activities. In other words, in case I'm not being completely clear, he's asking me to lie. For him and, apparently, for you, since if I tell the London coppers I haven't a clue about a mass of phone calls to and from Gaz Ruddock on my mobile, they're going to want to know who else uses it. You're following me, Clover, aren't you?"

She ran a manicured fingernail along one of the seams of her briefcase. He wanted to force some kind of response, but when it came, it wasn't what he was looking for. "I can see what you think. 'How clever she's been to use my mobile to arrange their trysts'—or whatever you want to call them—'since, really, when does someone check his *own* mobile to see what calls are going out from it? Or coming into it, for that matter.' We're heading to that, aren't we, with the image of me running my fingers over Gaz's lovely, toned pectorals, the two of us all hot and bothered and ready for it in God knows whatever location we've managed to find."

He was meant to deny that, but he saw that the issue of "We'll speak later," which he'd intended to bring up with her, was going to end up becoming another way to avoid a different sort of conversation. Instead of what was actually going on—and this appeared to have Finn sitting directly at the centre of it—he was intended to snatch at the image she'd presented to him, his mind arrested by the image's correlation to what he'd overheard. He was then intended to be led by the nose into making *that* the subject of an ensuing discussion. It was a vintage Clover Freeman move.

"If you share Gaz's hope that I'll lie to the police, should they show up again on our doorstep, Clover, then you'll need to complete the picture of what's going on, because that's what it's going to take."

She was silent again as somewhere outside dogs began barking. Dinnertime, he reckoned. She finally said, "All right. Here it is. I'll make it bald, as I presume you want the facts as plainly and simply stated as I can make them."

"You're right about that."

"Fine. Ian Druitt had some concerns about Finnegan. They

developed over time and he finally rang Gaz to talk them over as he knew Gaz and Finnegan were friendly."

"What sort of concerns?"

"The kind that begin with 'He's a nice enough boy but I'm worried that I'm seeing something I ought not to be seeing.' Gaz rang me once Druitt spoke to him. It was a question of what we were going to do about it."

"About what? Stop dancing round this, Clover. You said you were going to make it bald, so do it."

"Finnegan and drink, Finnegan and marijuana, Finnegan and his rather salty language, and Finnegan not behaving round the children quite as he ought to have been behaving."

"What the hell is that supposed to mean? Are you saying that Finn was . . . what? Supplying children with beer and wine? Selling them weed? Leading them astray by . . ." The implication took his breath away. "Wait. Was Finn supposedly *doing* something to those children? Is that what you're telling me?"

"I don't know *what* I'm telling you. I'm giving you the information I was given. You wanted to know, so I'm letting you know."

"I don't bloody believe it."

"Neither did I."

"*Did*? Not *do*?"

"Stop playing with words. I'm telling you what Druitt was concerned about. I'm telling you why Gaz and I rang each other. He was tasked—by me—with keeping an eye on Finnegan and now here was this suggestion on the part of Druitt that Finnegan was misbehaving in a way that could get him into the kind of trouble that could haunt him for the rest of his life no matter what it was. Drink, drugs, sexual misconduct. I didn't know. I still don't know. But what I did know was that I couldn't have that happen: Finnegan in trouble. And I *especially* couldn't have that happen as I was the one who put Finnegan into the position of being round those children in the first place. As far as I was concerned—as far as I *am* concerned—what actually happened is that Finnegan witnessed something between Druitt and a child, that Druitt realised this and made a preemptive strike. He turned in Finnegan to Gaz before Finnegan could do the same to him."

"And *then* what?"

"Then Gaz told me. I wanted Finnegan away from Druitt as quickly as possible, but bloody-minded as he's ever been, Finnegan refused to leave the children. Can you see how *that* looks? He said he was helping them, he liked Druitt, he even got to show off his karate skills, and on and on. So he had to be told at least part of the truth, which—Finnegan being Finnegan—he did not for an instant believe."

"Which 'part of the truth'?"

"Just that Druitt had spoken to Gaz about having some concerns how Finnegan was interacting with the children. I kept it vague because it needed to be vague."

"Why would that be, Clover? Why not tell him what was going on so that he could at least defend himself?"

"Listen to your own words, for heaven's sake. *Think* about what goes for 'defending himself' when it comes to Finnegan. I was worried that he might lose his temper, he might act out in a way that could result in trouble for him."

"So you must have been thinking—"

"I wasn't thinking anything but getting our son away from Ian Druitt and his after-school club. But then, Druitt won some *bloody* award and a phone call was made anonymously accusing Druitt of child molestation and—"

"My God, you think Finn made that call, don't you. Getting his own after Druitt spoke to Gaz."

"I don't think anything. I don't *know* anything. But when I finally heard about that call to 999, it was something that couldn't be ignored, so Druitt had to be brought in for questioning."

Trevor took this last bit in with a growing sense of horror. Puzzle pieces began to fit together in ways he did not dream he would ever have to look upon. He forced himself to say, "So Druitt had to be eliminated."

She grasped her throat. "What in God's name do you take me for? Of *course* he didn't need to 'be eliminated.' But whatever was going on in that club had to be looked at because if it wasn't, *Finnegan* was going to be looked at. You *know* how he is and how he reacts and how simple it is to trigger his temper. When his temper goes, he's nothing but reaction incarnate, completely devoid of the ability to think. I didn't want to put him in that position then and I don't want to put him in that position now. I can't take that chance." She lifted her briefcase from the table at which the panel had been sitting. He could see that as far as she was concerned, their conversation had reached its conclusion.

But not for him. He said, "Exactly what the hell does that mean, you 'can't take the chance'?"

"I don't want the Met talking to him. I don't want them even looking at him. Not because he's done anything at all but because—"

"He'll think you set them on him." Trevor felt staggered by what she was saying about truth and lies and crime and its aftermath. "Christ, Clover. This isn't *about* what Finn thinks of you. Don't you see that? This is about a possible crime. If Finn did nothing to anyone, he has nothing to worry about."

"You can't possibly be that naïve." She stalked up the aisle towards the doors to the hall. When she reached the exit, she spun back to him. "You haven't the first idea how the police work, so let me enlighten you. If they speak with Finnegan and he says anything to pique their interest, they will *not* let up. They'll move from Druitt's 'concerns' about him directly to Druitt's suicide and they'll be on their way to deciding it wasn't suicide at all. It was murder and here's their suspect because he has motive and from there it's a hop and skip to his having opportunity. *Do* you understand that, Trevor?"

"You believe he's done that as well." Trevor could scarcely get the words out, so aghast he was at Clover's thinking. "You believe that Finn—"

"I don't believe *anything*," she said. "I don't have all the facts. I never had them. All I know is what was said: the back and forth of it all. All I ever knew was that Finnegan spent time with those children. So *will* you just look at the larger implications here? I'm his mother—for the love of God—and my first job in life is to *be* his mother. Everything else falls into line but that line forms after Finnegan's well-being. And nothing, Trev, takes precedence over that."

He let that one weigh down the air for a bit. He strode up the aisle to join her by the exit. He removed his mobile from his pocket as he walked. He gestured with it as he said, "Just to be certain I'm on board with everything, you want me to lie to the police as well, should they come calling on me about Gaz's mobile and my own. You and he expect me to tell those detectives that Gaz and I were speaking about child-minding Finn, about *my* request that Finn be child-minded and *his* reports on how the child-minding was going. Would that be how it is, Clover?" She didn't reply, although her face was fixed enough to give him her answer. He said, "You two must be thick as planks to think the Met are going to swallow that and walk away without having a word with Finn."

"Then tell them what you wish," she replied. "Tell them everything I've just told you. Tell them my objective: to keep Finnegan from ruining his life through his own bloody-mindedness. And then start praying that when they go to speak with him, he'll be able to hold his own against them."

# 19 MAY

LUDLOW
SHROPSHIRE

Ding had briefly considered skipping her appointment with the college counsellor because she couldn't see that anything positive might come from it. The truth was she'd completely lost the will to haul herself to her lectures, and when it came to her tutorials, she'd been hit-and-miss for ages. Her tutor had tracked her down several times. The poor man had even attempted his version of reading her the riot act. So, really, it was no surprise that Greta Yates had now insisted on an intimate little chat. The only real surprise was that it had taken the counsellor so long to get round to giving Ding the order. Thus Ding made her way up to Castle Square campus at the appropriate time.

She hadn't slept well, but that was how things were now. She did the job with Finn, shared a spliff afterwards, tossed him out of her room, locked her door against his "Hey! Don't be that way!" when he expected a thanks-for-the-weed in the form of letting him spray her tonsils again, and then hoped for sleep. It finally arrived but on a train so slow it was after three A.M. before the voices in her head stopped shouting and allowed her a respite in the form of restless dreams.

Greta Yates turned out to be a ginormous woman with a chesty way of breathing and a voice that suggested she wasn't able to get enough oxygen. The trip from her office door, where she'd called out Ding's name into the waiting area, back to her desk chair brought enough blood to her face that Ding feared the woman would start bleeding from her eyeballs. She sank into her chair, then pulled a box of tissues from a drawer in her desk. This she plopped onto a stack of folders so tall that Ding wondered what they represented: her workload or a lack of organisational skills.

The tissues turned out to be for Ms. Yates's use. She blotted her face with two of them and blew her nose on a third. Then she folded her hands—displaying a huge emerald ring that was either totally phony or a testimony to serious family wealth—and she favoured Ding with a look-over. Her first words stated the conclusion she'd reached:

"Parties, pubs, or a boyfriend? I've seen that you don't live at home. Have you lived away from your parents before now?"

The mention of parents in the plural grounded Ding in an excuse. While it wasn't the truth, it also wasn't a lie. And it took absolutely no effort on her part to summon tears when she spoke of it.

It was her dad, she said. She felt her chin quivering. It was an accident, she said. It happened at home. They had a putrid, petrified wreck of a house near Much Wenlock, and all of them were meant to work on making it liveable for the family. She herself went home at the weekends to help with the project. The wiring was being replaced and her dad was upstairs. . . . A long hesitation, she found, was the very thing to build not only suspense but the dread of being fairly certain what was to come.

It was the electricity, Ding said, because although she knew the story was false without knowing *why* she knew the story was false, it remained the fiction that her mum clung to just as she had done the first time, when Ding had recovered enough to say, "But, Mummy, what was he *doing*?"

Ms. Yates was all sympathy at once. She was all "I'm very sorry. When did this happen? Why wasn't your tutor advised?"

It had happened fourteen years in the past, but Ding could hardly tell her that. So she said, "Round Easter."

"Have you spoken to anyone about it?"

Ding shook her head. "We keep things rather close, my family."

"But you surely can see from what's happened with your performance here at the college that you mustn't hold these things inside."

She did see that, Ding told her. But it was too difficult at present. It felt so raw. She simply could not speak of it. But she knew she had to because, obviously, she wasn't coping well and her work at the college was showing this. She understood that. She really did.

"You now know I'm here," Greta Yates said. "If you need to talk, please do stop by."

Considering everything on the woman's desk, Ding couldn't see how Ms. Yates would have time to do anything but give cursory comfort, cursory advice, or cursory warnings about the consequences of one's failure to attend lectures and tutorials. And what did it matter anyway, because everyone lied—including herself—and as a result there was no comfort available anywhere.

So Ding thanked the counsellor and explained that, while she had been in a terrible funk, she was coming out of it. She could *feel* the difference in her. She thought it had to do with the arrival of spring and what spring meant: hope, rebirth, rejuvenation, blah blah blah.

"Will you be able to get back to your studies?" Ms. Yates asked. Her voice was warm enough but it still managed to be monitory.

Yes, Ding told her. Dena Donaldson would now be able to get back to her studies. Ms. Yates could expect that without a doubt.

"Sometimes," Ding said, "it's still difficult but I do think I'm through the very worst of it." And she wanted to believe her own declaration even as she knew it was just another lie.

LUDLOW
SHROPSHIRE

Rather than stopping immediately in Temeside when they left the hotel, Havers directed Lynley back to the police station first. She had something she wanted him to see, she told him. When he had the car in gear, she directed him first to Broad Street, where they dropped down to the river. From there, they cruised east to Temeside till they came to Weeping Cross Lane. A left turn and they were less than one minute by car from the nick. She pointed out that the businesses along the route were set back far enough from the road that no one driving, biking, walking, rollerblading, or hopping along on a pop stick would be caught doing so by a CCTV camera on a building.

"In other words," she concluded as Lynley pulled into Townsend Close, "you've got a nice quick route from the house where Finnegan Freeman lives. I made the walk myself, sir. I reckoned then—and I reckon now—it's an interesting detail."

"It's even more interesting now we know what Ruddock was up to in the car park when Druitt died."

"It would've been a simple matter for someone to get to the station using that route. No one would think twice if they saw someone walking or biking in that street. It leads up to town, it leads to the rail station, it leads to Tesco. You name it, sir. And it would've been another simple matter to get past the patrol car—unseen—and into the station. *Then* it would've been a short stroll down the corridor to the office where Druitt was stowed."

Lynley followed the direction of her gaze, which was on the station's car park. "Let's learn what's what with Finnegan Freeman," was his conclusion, to which he added, "And there's something else we might want to toss round."

"What's that, sir?"

"DCC Freeman and Ruddock." Lynley reversed and they returned to Lower Galdeford. They cruised back along Weeping Cross Lane and from there to the river. "If Trevor Freeman feels he can make a request of Ruddock involving Finnegan, then Ruddock obviously knows Trevor well. Why not the DCC in addition to Trevor? And perhaps those two know each other well enough to get up to unofficial business together."

"I can see them as lovers," Havers said. "She's got to be less than twenty years older than he is, and those years don't count for much when you're as fit as she is. Which makes rolling round naked—"

"With a young PCSO—"

"—something we can't cross off the list. She could be using the husband's phone to set things up."

"As you say, nothing can be discounted."

They reached the home where Finnegan Freeman lived, a very short distance from Weeping Cross Lane. They parked farther along, and mostly on the pavement, before walking back to the house, where they rapped on the door then rang the bell.

The door was opened by a young man dressed so dapperly that he looked like a model for menswear. He was accompanied by a girl with mounds of tumbling dark hair. Their fingers were twined together as if their intention had been to leave the house and not to answer the door. That indeed turned out to be the case.

He said, "Oh. Sorry. Can I help you? We were just heading out."

Lynley showed his identification and introduced Havers. Before he could explain why they'd come, the boy said, "You lot must want Finn."

"Why do you say that?" Lynley asked him.

"'Cause if there're coppers at the door, fact is they don't ever want anyone else."

"And you are?"

"Bruce Castle," he told them. "I live here as well. This is Monica."

"Jordan," she added.

"She *doesn't* live here," Castle said. "Come inside. I'll see about Finn."

He left the door gaping open and walked to the foot of a stairway close by, yelling, "Freeman! You're wanted by the filth again." Then he said to Lynley with an apologetic shrug of his shoulders, "Sorry. Slipped out. Too much telly." And then once more in the direction of the upper floor, "Freeman! Pull it out of her and get down here, wanker!" which caused his companion, Monica, to giggle nervously.

No answer to Bruce Castle's shouts. Finn Freeman was either comatose or not at home. Castle turned to them and said, "You lot want me to . . . I don't know . . . tell Finn he's wanted? Have him ring you? Let you know if he shows his face?"

Lynley took out a card and handed it over. Havers did the same, for good measure. Castle shoved the cards into the breast pocket of his tailored shirt and told them they could always wait if they wished. Or they could come back. They could even surprise Finn if they had a mind to. "Door's never locked," he informed them with a casual shrug. "So have at him if you want. Morning's generally best. The earlier the better."

Then he was off, towing Monica along, leaving the door gaping open behind them.

"We could turn over the furniture," Havers said. When she glanced into the sitting room, she added, "Such as it is. Which it isn't. Bloody hell. How do people live like this? The place's a rubbish tip."

"It's the resiliency of youth," Lynley answered. "We'll come back. As Mr. Castle just informed us, I expect early morning will do the trick."

They shut the front door behind them. As Havers headed to the street, Lynley checked to see if Bruce Castle had spoken the truth. He had done. The door was easily opened. That was to their advantage if they wanted to rouse Finnegan Freeman at dawn.

LUDLOW

SHROPSHIRE

Ding was trudging along Temeside with the house in sight when she saw Brutus. She didn't know the name of the girl who accompanied him, but she could tell by her expression that she was yet another of Brutus's mindless conquests. Ding found, oddly, that she wasn't bothered. Put up against having to face Greta Yates and experiencing yet another round of having to manufacture believable tales, Brutus leaving the house with whoever she was traipsing along behind him didn't seem to matter.

Brutus, remaining true to form, of course, thought she was going to care mightily. He, of course, thought she was going to cause a scene. Ding couldn't blame him as that had been their routine, but instead of the usual, she said to him, "Just tell me Finn has actually gone to a lecture for once and I'll be happy." Before he could reply, she said to the girl with him, "I'm Dena. Ding, actually. I've got the room next door to Brutus."

"Monica," the girl said, with quite a pretty smile. She'd worn braces. Her teeth were way too seriously perfect.

It was clear that Brutus didn't quite know what to make of this. He said, "You just getting home, Ding?" and his tone was suspicious, as if what he thought was that this was yet another game in which Dena Donaldson made yet another ridiculous attempt to stimulate him to raging jealousy.

She said, "Had to have a chat with the counsellor." She ran her hand through her hair, which she realised she'd not brushed before leaving the house earlier. "I'm knackered. I need some sleep. Tell me no one's home."

"No one's home," he said.

"Except the police, Bru," Monica said. "They're still inside." She looked over her shoulder and added, "Oh. There they are. I guess they decided not to wait."

"More cops wanting a word with Finn," Brutus told Ding. He peered at her closely, as if attempting to read her in an entirely new way. "You sure you're okay?"

She was, Ding thought, more or less. One thing was certain, though: She did not want coppers to be part of her day.

There were two of them: a blondish man dressed the way she expected Brutus would have dressed if he were ten inches taller and twenty years older, and a rumpled-looking woman with short, shaggy hair that appeared as uncombed and unbrushed as Ding's hair was. She said to Brutus, "Who are they, then?" and he removed two cards from his pocket and handed them to her.

"You can give these to Finn when you see him. No clue what they want to talk to him about, but it's probably Druitt again since that's what it was last time."

Ding looked at the card and took in the fact that the two officers were detectives and that once again someone from London had been sent to Ludlow. She said to Brutus, "If I see Finn, I'll tell him."

"Why wouldn't you see him?" Brutus sounded suspicious. How odd, she thought. He still thinks I'm playing a game.

She said to him. "Just now, I don't much feel like seeing anyone. Nice to meet you, Monica." Which, really, was all she wanted to say.

She saw that the cops were looking her way. She reckoned they'd caught sight of Brutus handing over their cards to her. That would mean a deduction on their part that she was also someone who knew Finn Freeman and was thus worth talking to. But she didn't want to talk to cops. She'd managed not to the first time they'd been in Ludlow and she intended to manage not to this time round as well.

She was considering the best way to avoid them when her circumstances underwent an alteration. For just as she was about to head in the direction of Lower Broad Street with the pretence of sauntering to a lecture at the college, which would take her away from the position the cops had adopted on the pavement as if waiting for her, Rabiah Lomax not only drove by, but she also honked. She gave Ding a signal with her hand that unmistakably telegraphed *Wait right there.* She parked not far from the weir, got out, and called, "Dena Donaldson, I want a word," which of course got the cops' attention.

They looked over to where Mrs. Lomax was slamming shut her car door. Then they looked from Mrs. Lomax to Ding. Then they looked at each other.

None of this, Ding reckoned, was going to do her the least bit of good.

LUDLOW
SHROPSHIRE

Rabiah saw the Scotland Yard detectives a moment after she called out to Ding. She didn't have time to develop any theories about what they were doing at the building where Ding lived or about what they might conclude seeing Rabiah Lomax in the same location. The only activity that she had time or the inclination to engage in was whatever activity it was going to take to keep Dena Donaldson from doing a runner.

That she wanted to was clear. She gave a quick glance round, and half a turn in the direction of the Ludford Bridge. She called, "You and I need to have a talk, Ding. Come here at once. And as for you two"—this she added towards the two detectives who were already crossing the street in her direction—"I've got no time to have another confab with the Met. My attorney is called Aeschylus Kong. He's in the directory. Ring him and ask for an appointment if we need to speak to each other again."

Ding hung back. The detectives did not. When they reached her, Rabiah said, "What *is* it about having family difficulties that you lot don't understand?" And then, "Ding, you heard me. Go into the house and I'll be there presently. Do *not* even think about doing a runner. I can chase you down and am happy to do it."

Ding apparently took her seriously as well she might since she knew Rabiah was a marathon winner while Ding herself probably wouldn't have made it one hundred yards without needing to catch her breath. So she grabbed at the chance to scurry to the house, looking neither at Rabiah nor at the cops.

The male—Rabiah remembered his name, Lynley—said to her, "This won't take longer than a minute or two, Mrs. Lomax."

The female—God, what *was* her name?—said, "We've got Ian Druitt's mobile, Mrs. Lomax. You had seven appointments with him but there's not a single call to or from you on his mobile's records."

"What about it?" she snapped. "Do you not see I've no time for this rubbish?"

"It seems you would have needed to arrange your appointments," Lynley said. "Will you tell us how you managed that without ringing him?"

"Oh, don't be absurd," she said. "I have no idea what number I rang to speak with him. For all I know, I rang the vicarage. I didn't have any other number, least of all his mobile's."

"Are you saying—"

"What I'm saying is that I have a family situation I'm dealing with at present. So I've more important things to do than providing you with instant answers to whatever questions you decide to ask me. Now, as I've said, he's called Aeschylus Kong. Your sergeant here has already met him."

That said, she left them and plunged across the street, where she strode to Ding's front door and didn't bother with the bell or knocking.

She found the girl in what went for the sitting room, which was sparsely furnished and looked as if it hadn't been hoovered, dusted, or had its uneaten crusts of pizza, empty yoghurt cartons, and balled-up crisp packets removed since the beginning of autumn term. It also smelled disgustingly of boys' shoes and underwear. Rabiah couldn't begin to comprehend how Ding lived in such a place.

The girl was sitting on a chintz sofa that was stained with substances that Rabiah didn't wish to identify. She had her knees together and her legs splayed out from them at angles. She looked like a schoolgirl who knew very well she was in for a dressing-down.

"Just *what* the bloody hell is going on?" Rabiah demanded. "That's what I want to know and that's what you're going to tell me. I've spoken to Missa."

Ding touched her upper lip with her tongue. "Oh. Is this to do with Missa?"

"You know damn well it's to do with Missa. So let me repeat the initial question: What the bloody hell is going on?"

Ding shook her head, her expression perplexed. "Really, Mrs. Lomax? I don't know what you mean."

"Then let me clarify. I've got cops sniffing round my family. Missa claims that the reason for this is spelled D-e-n-a. I didn't hand you over to them just now because I want to get to the truth. Either Missa is lying or you're lying or you both are lying. But in any case, we've reached the finish line when it comes to all that. Do you want to talk to me or to them? Make up your mind before I lose patience with you."

Ding placed one of her hands flat on the filthy sofa. The other she kept balled in her lap. She said, "What're we supposed to be lying about?"

"The deacon. The one who died. He had our surname in his diary and that's proving quite titillating for the police."

"Is that why they know you?"

"Don't try to misdirect me. You had seven meetings with him. You used our name. We're going to talk about that and *then* you're going to tell the police, who will exit stage left from my life."

"No way," Ding said.

"Don't argue with me. Just take a moment to thank God I didn't turn you over to them three minutes ago."

"I didn't mean . . . Mrs. Lomax, I never used your name for anything. I never talked to the deacon. I didn't even know who he was. If Missa told you that . . ." The girl didn't seem to want to finish the sentence.

Rabiah did it for her. "Missa lied," she said. "Is that what you wish to tell me? And exactly *what* bloody reason would she have for lying?"

"I don't know. I don't even know why she was talking to him."

"Don't you take me for a fool. I know something about friendship between women and what I know is that very good friends—let's go so far as to call them best friends—do not have secrets from each other. What I also know is that you and my granddaughter were best friends. And then all of a sudden she wanted to leave Ludlow and that was that. And now I discover that she might have had a very good reason for wanting to leave, with that reason sitting in this room, guilty of using our surname in God-knows-*what* scheme that she had going on."

"That isn't true!" Ding protested. "I never did anything. And I keep getting accused . . . and I don't know . . ." Unaccountably, she began to weep. "*Nothing* works and now there's *Monica* and every single night he keeps wanting more and it's like I can't ever stop even if I want to."

Rabiah knew hysteria when she saw it. She said, "Good Lord, child. What's happening here?"

"You talk to Missa if you want to know," Ding cried. "If anyone's lying about anything, it's her."

LUDLOW
SHROPSHIRE

Barbara Havers did not want to get anything wrong, so she hesitated once they'd exchanged words with Rabiah Lomax. She knew she had to take massive care in how she relayed her information to Lynley because she wasn't entirely certain it was accurate. Lynley wouldn't act hastily once he heard what she had to say—he never did that—but the fact remained that one false move on their part might put the wind up.

When Lynley said, "There's another coincidence for you, Sergeant," she replied with, "What's that, sir?"

He looked rather surprised that she needed to ask, saying, "Do you find it at all odd that Rabiah Lomax has just turned up at the home of Finnegan Freeman?"

She said, "Oh that."

"What do you expect it's about? She's not there to sign him up for scouting, I daresay."

"What I reckon is that we've got too many bloody coincidences at this point for them to be coincidences."

"I don't disagree."

"She wants talking to again."

"Hmm. Yes. Although since she's now hauling in her solicitor, I doubt we'll manage much information from her. Did you hear what she said to the girl?"

Barbara nodded. He'd given her the entrée she needed, so she decided to use it. "As to that, sir, there's something else."

Since they'd been nearly across the street when they'd accosted Rabiah Lomax, they'd walked the rest of the way to the river and were looking over the water at a family of swans, which allowed Barbara to access her Players and light up. Lynley automatically moved upwind.

She sucked in some smoke. "That girl Mrs. Lomax was talking to? Dena Donaldson, right? She called her Ding? I'm not one hundred percent on this 'cause it's been ten days or so and it was dark. But that girl Ding . . . ?"

"What about her, aside from the name. It reminds me vaguely of my mother's, by the way. Her name is Dorothy but she's always been called Daze. I've never thought to ask why."

"Why would you since you call her Mummy? Or Mother. Or Mater. Or whatever you lot call your *madre*s. . . . Anyway, that girl Ding? I think I've seen her before."

"Hardly earthquake material, Sergeant, Ludlow's centre not being particularly large. Unless, of course, it's the where and when of seeing her that's the important bit. Where was it?"

"In the car park behind the police station."

Lynley turned his gaze from the river to her. "Indeed?"

"She was the one who got out of Gary Ruddock's patrol car, sir. It was at night so, like I said, I can't be one hundred percent on this, but she sure as hell looks like her."

Lynley gazed from Barbara to the house into which the girl and Rabiah Lomax had disappeared. His expression was speculative.

Barbara warmed to her topic. "He's gone wobbly whenever it comes to the women in his life, Inspector. First, he told me he doesn't have a woman. Then he tells us he does but she's married and he's more or less love-bound or whatever to protect her. And *now* there's this girl. And we see her going into a house—presumably where she lives—which is also the house where Finnegan Freeman lives, which is also the house that sits seriously near a quick route to the police station. And that smells like three-day-old fish, wouldn't you say?"

"It's certainly not fragrant," Lynley noted. He went on to point out, "However, as you said, it was night when you caught a glimpse of her."

"And it was shadowy where he'd parked. I'll give you that, so I could be mistaken. But when she got out of the car, the light inside it went on, as per usual. Then he got out. He said a few words. Then she got back in. It was like first she decided to give him the romantic heave-ho, but then he said something that made her reconsider. So she climbed back in and he did as well and the rest is whatever they got up to after that."

"The question," Lynley said, "is whether Ruddock is lying about the married woman or whether he's having more than one relationship. In either case, the fact that he told you from the start that he had no one in his life . . . How did that come up, Sergeant?"

Barbara thought back to recapture the moment. She said, "A tattoo. It's uppercase C-A-T, for Catherine. I asked him was he an animal lover, but he said Cat was his mum and he'd grown up in some dodgy cult in Ireland where the babies got taken early from their mums and they lived totally separate from them so they had to have tattoos so the boy babies didn't have sex with their own mums later on. Or with their sisters. It gave me the shivers, that story. P'rhaps I should've checked it out, but I reckoned I needed to do . . . well, whatever the guv told me. You know."

Lynley seemed to take all of this in with an unexpected lack of surprise. He turned from the river, crossed his arms, and leaned against the wall that separated them from one of the weirs. He said, "Poor Oedipus. Had he only had the same. It would have saved him from so much trouble. But, of course, they thought they'd dispatched him, didn't they?"

Barbara was used to his literary and historical musings. She let this one pass. She dropped her cigarette to the ground and put it out with her shoe. He eyed it, eyed her, and she sighed. She picked up the dog-end and stripped it, allowing the unsmoked flakes of tobacco to float away on the breeze.

"What I'm thinking is this," she said to him. When he nodded, she went on, "If the PCSO is involved with that girl, then someone besides the girl herself and the PCSO is going to know it."

"How do you arrive at that?" Lynley asked her.

"The simplest way, sir. If I saw them together, someone else has to have seen them together as well. At some time. In some place. We just need to find that person, and I've a good idea where to look."

BLISTS HILL VICTORIAN TOWN
SHROPSHIRE

Since motorways had never sliced a hideous incision into the Shropshire countryside, there were very few direct routes to anywhere, and that was certainly the case with the route to Blists Hill Victorian Town. The place lay just west of Ironbridge, which itself had been built along the River Severn, leaving it unfortunately exposed to the river's periodic flooding. Blists Hill, on the other hand, stood at a much higher elevation, reached through a thick woodland of oaks, chestnuts, and sycamores that unfurled their fresh spring leaves in such a way that sunlight dappled the road. The inspiration of an enterprising individual who had seen a unique use for brick blast furnaces, an abandoned mine shaft, and an ingenious inclined plane that had once lifted boats from the river to the Shropshire Canal, Blists Hill had been created as a tourist attraction and an educational centre. It featured an entire town circa 1900.

It was here that Rabiah drove once she left Ding in Temeside. She hadn't been to the place in years, and on her arrival she saw from the crowded conditions in the car park that it hadn't lost its popularity as a destination for day trippers and pensioners as well as an opportunity for schoolchildren to see in person what their teachers droned on about at the front of their classrooms.

Rabiah joined the queue to purchase a ticket. While she could have phoned ahead and arranged for her granddaughter to meet her and sign her onto the property as a guest, she wished for the element of surprise. So she handed over the exorbitant amount required—had they never heard of *decent* concessions for pensioners? she wondered—and she accepted a street plan of the place although she didn't actually need one.

Rabiah knew where to find Missa. She'd heard from the girl's mother instantly once Missa had informed her that, despite having been talked into giving West Mercia College another chance after the Christmas holiday, she'd made her final decision and was adamant about it. College and uni were not for her.

"She's decided candle making is a fine career," Yasmina had declared bitterly over the phone. "Can you not talk some sense into her, Mum?"

At least it was a step up from the fish and chips shop, Rabiah had wanted to point out, but a lighthearted response would not have been helpful in the situation. So Rabiah had attempted to reassure her daughter-in-law that all young people went through stages and this, no doubt, was one of them. But Yasmina hadn't believed that for a moment, and Rabiah could not fault her for this since Yasmina herself had never gone through a single stage other than the one that had taken her to her goal of practising paediatric medicine. While it was true that an unplanned pregnancy had slowed her progress, that was all it had done. So for Yasmina's own daughter to eschew a formal education in favour of a life dipping wicks into tallow was inconceivable. "Something's happened to her thinking," Yasmina had told her. "She says it has nothing to do with Justin, but I don't believe her. *He's* brought her back here somehow. He's said something. He's done something. He's threatened to . . . Oh, I don't know. Please talk some sense into her, Mum, because Timothy and I have tried and we've got nowhere."

Rabiah had done her part, but it had come to nothing. At the time, though, she'd had little knowledge at her fingertips. Now, at least, she had Missa's claim versus Ding's claim and the certainty that something was being hidden from her.

Since Blists Hill featured demonstrations of late-Victorian life in a factory town, various craftspeople plied their "trades" in purpose-built locations. Hence the streets accommodated tinsmiths, harness makers, ironworkers, and blacksmiths, as well as grocers, bakers, butchers, and bankers, all in suitable buildings. Among them was the candle maker's shop, at the midway point of the main thoroughfare.

The shop was illuminated only by sunlight coming from two windows and the open door. When Rabiah entered, she became one of ten observers who were listening to Missa's explanation of the process. It looked deadly tedious, the sort of activity that Rabiah would have lasted one eight-hour workday doing: the attachment of long wicks to narrow dipping boards, the immersing of those wicks into a rectangular vat of tallow, the wait for the wicks to dry, the second, third, fourth, and what had to be one thousandth dipping in order to build up tallow on the wick to have enough to burn. If there was a more boring activity on the face of the planet, Rabiah could not have said what it might be.

She worked her way into a position from which she would be seen once Missa looked up from her work. Her granddaughter was garbed in a cotton gown of the period, which was covered by a heavy pinafore apron to protect her costume from dripping wax. She was explaining to the observers that the candlemaker's job was generally done by a man, since most women of the period would have been teachers or shop assistants or wives and mums. When one of the watching children said, "Miss, c'n I ask you a question?" Missa looked up and saw Rabiah. Rabiah was relieved to be greeted with a delighted smile. She pointed to her watch and made a movement that simulated having a cup of tea, and her granddaughter nodded. Rabiah took heart from this.

Instead of the refreshment pavilion, though, Rabiah went first to the blacksmith's shop. There, she saw that Justin Goodayle, Missa's longtime boyfriend, was completing a demonstration of horseshoe making. There wasn't a horse present to be shoed, but there was a roaring fire inside the forge as well as all the tools needed to make just about anything out of the pieces of iron that lay about the smithy. Some items, she saw, had already been fashioned. In addition to horseshoes, the business ends of rakes, hoes, shovels, and pitchforks sat in display cases and hung from the wall. Additionally, iron hooks of various sizes formed a jumbled pile upon the floor.

Rabiah waited as Justin's small audience moved off to another location. He saw her then and said hello, over the noise from the forge. Like Missa, he looked quite pleased to see her.

"I'm having a break." He removed his heavy leather apron and a pair of anachronistic safety glasses. His flannel shirt bore perspiration rings, and his face was damp with sweat. Rivulets of this ran from his forehead down his cheeks and into his neatly trimmed beard. He removed a kerchief from his pocket and wiped his face.

He'd always been a nice-looking boy, Rabiah thought, and he'd grown into a very handsome young man. He had a wealth of beautiful chestnut hair that he wore long and tied back, perhaps in the fashion of a Victorian-era blacksmith, his brown eyes were deeply dark and soulful, and his expression was utterly appealing. He was big and burly, as one would expect of a blacksmith, with muscular arms and a broad chest. She imagined the local girls found him quite swoonworthy.

She said, "If it's your break, c'n an old lady buy you a cup of tea?"

"No old lady round here that I can see," was his reply. "But if the handsome woman talking to me would like to treat me to a cuppa, I wouldn't say no."

"Flatterer," she said. "You must be negotiating for a scone as well."

"I was thinking cake," he admitted.

She laughed as he joined her. He was careful about seeing to it that the smithy was secured, and he offered her his arm in a gentlemanly fashion as they walked to the refreshment pavilion. It sat just opposite a Victorian fairground, and once they'd secured their tea and a slice of lemon sponge for Justin, they found a table within viewing distance of the stalls serving as games of chance where, for a Victorian tuppence, children could try their luck in order to win sweets, muslin bags of marbles, and garishly painted figures rendered in plaster.

"So." Rabiah lifted her cup of tea. "Are you pleased to have Missa home again?"

"I am that." Justin dug into his cake.

"It must be nice for you, then, having her put away college and uni for a simpler life."

"I wasn't ever against her going to uni," he said with a glance at her. "Whatever Missa wants is what I want for her. But I won't lie. I'm that glad she's given it up. She wanted to back in December, you know. But she got talked out of it by her mum."

"Yasmina told me at the time," Rabiah said. "To be honest, none of us were ever sure why she wanted to give up on it."

"She told me she couldn't cope with the science course. I s'pose it's difficult for some people, eh? But a science course is no real matter to her future, is it. I'll be supporting us and there'll be our kids and she'll want to be at home with them anyway."

"You two have plans, then," Rabiah noted. "Missa's not told me. Do her parents know?"

"What?"

"The plans. You, Missa, children . . . ?"

"Oh. Well, not yet. I mean . . . We've been together so long, me and Missa, that her mum and dad won't be surprised, will they? Meantime, I've got more saving to do. I mean us to have our own place. Not *before* we marry, 'course. We wouldn't do that. Missa wouldn't ever . . . Well, she's not one for that sort of thing. Before marriage, I mean. Her mum's made sure. Not that I think it's a *bad* thing, mind you. Not to, I mean. But Yasmina—Dr. Lomax—told her about it all. You probably know that, eh? So Missa's always said there won't be any of it till afterwards."

Rabiah took a moment to sort through this. Justin was an open book, but he often communicated in ways that only he understood. She said, to clarify, "You mean no sex before marriage because of what happened to Yasmina and my Tim?"

Justin squirmed a bit and shot her a glance. "Missa says the wedding night's meant to be special. She says a white wedding is a white wedding. I've got to respect that, don't I?" He squinted in the sunlight and directed his attention to a young couple passing by, their hands in the back pockets of each other's jeans. They paused and locked lips. Justin looked away. "Don't much like it," he admitted. "I'm red-blooded as the next one. Sometimes me and Missa . . . Well, none of that. It'll all happen soon enough, and I can wait."

"There are other girls, of course," Rabiah pointed out. "Happy to have a roll in the hay or whatever it's called these days. In the mean-time, I mean. Sex with no strings? A hookup and handshake . . . ?"

Justin looked appalled. "You mean doing it for . . . for *relief* or the like? Oh, I'd never do that, Missus Lomax. I'm no cheater. Besides, now Missa's back home, it won't be much longer. I've got my savings and something I'm doing on the side that's bringing in money."

"Have you a second job, then?" Rabiah asked.

"Starting my own business," Justin told her. "I don't like to say because it's early yet, but it's doing the kind of work I always did best." He held up his hands. They were nicked, calloused, and bore scars from burns that probably had occurred at the smithy. "These're my best tools. Long's I have these in working order, I c'n do just about anything."

"Granny, it's such a treat to see you!"

Rabiah looked up to see that Missa had come into the pavilion and had purchased a flapjack. She kissed Rabiah on the top of her head and joined them at their table, where she divided the flapjack in half and handed a share to Justin. She said, "What a mad day! I've had to spend most of my time keeping ten-year-old boys away from the tal-low vat. What about you, Justie? Any of the kids trying to stick their hands in the forge?"

"Only every one of them." He had finished his cake and tea, and he glanced at a wristwatch that he took from his pocket. He rose, then, took up the flapjack portion, wrapped it in a paper napkin, and said, "Half past, then?" to Missa in a message that she apparently understood.

She said, "Gran, you're going to see Mum and Dad, aren't you? Sati as well? I could go home with you if you're still here at closing."

Rabiah wanted to speak with Missa's mother alone, so she said, "I'll be long gone by then, love. There's only so much Victoriana that a woman my age can take. You're better with Justin."

He looked pleased. He bent to Missa as if to kiss her, and she tilted her head to give him her cheek. He hesitated, then kissed her in the manner she wished. He nodded at Rabiah in a farewell and he left the pavilion. Not, Rabiah noticed, without receiving the admiring glances of one girl at the till and two others in Victorian garb having their afternoon cups of tea. Missa appeared oblivious to this.

"What're you *doing* here?" She offered Rabiah a fond smile.

"I've come to see you."

"Really?" Missa used both hands to slide her sleek bobbed hair behind her ears. It was, as always, shiny with health, which relieved Rabiah although she could not have said exactly why. "Why've you come to see me? Not that it isn't a treat that you're here." Missa added this last hastily, but Rabiah could tell that she was suspicious. If her grandmother had driven up from Ludlow to see her particularly, there would be a reason and chances were she wasn't going to like it.

"Justin seems as devoted as ever," Rabiah noted. Outside in the Victorian fairgrounds, a period roundabout began its slow spin, with calliope music accompanying it.

Missa fingered her portion of the flapjack she'd bought, but she didn't take a bite. "Hmm," was her reply.

"He was talking about his savings and what he intends to do with them," Rabiah told her. "And about a business he's developing that involves his hands. It's hush-hush, apparently, but its purpose seems to involve buying a home."

"Well it was *always* stupid for everyone to think he'd just stay with his mum and dad forever and be content as the one to take care of them. That's what they thought, you know. His dad was always saying, 'Justie's our dumb one. He'll keep at home so when we get doddery, there he'll be.' Like Justin wouldn't be bothered by the label *dumb one*. Like he didn't want a life of his own."

"Oh, decidedly he means to have a life. Do you know about this business he's got on the side? Has he told you about it?"

"Just that he's saving," Missa said. "I don't know anything about a business."

"You might want to ask. Or have a talk with him. Or . . . something."

Missa looked up, wide-eyed. "Why?"

"Don't be obtuse, Missa. You know very well he intends the two of you to marry, have children, walk hand in hand into your dotage. If that's what you want, fine. If that's *not* what you want . . . Which is it? You were meant to be taking a break from each other when you first came to Ludlow. You told me as much last September. Where are you with each other now? I mean, according to you. I've already heard according to Justin."

"We're not anywhere different, Gran," Missa replied. "We're just like we've always been."

Rabiah eyed her. "Really, Missa. You're not simple-minded."

Missa cocked her head to one side. She had a way of looking at one that made it easy to assume an offence had been given. But Rabiah wasn't going to back away. This wasn't exactly the confrontation she'd intended to have with her granddaughter, but it would do for now.

"I wonder how he's going to react if you tell him that it isn't your intention to settle down in Ironbridge, have his babies, change their nappies, launder his clothing, and perhaps grow organic veggies in an allotment somewhere."

"You're not being very nice when you talk like that," Missa pointed out.

"Are you being nice?"

"I don't know what you mean."

"Rubbish. You know very well what I mean. Here you are—according to him—stressing virginity, no sex before, and all the rest, which I assume means no hand—"

"Granny!"

"—no mouth, no back door—and . . . Oh God. What is it?"

Missa's eyes had filled. Rabiah saw she had gone too far.

"Oh dear, I'm sorry," Rabiah said.

Missa made no reply, but she looked away.

"Missa, is there something that's happened between you and Justin that—"

"I just want to *be,* Gran. Why can no one let me just *be*?"

"All right," Rabiah said. "Forgive me, dear. I've not come all this way to do anything at all with regard to you and Justin."

"Why *have* you come, then?"

"Because Ding and I had a talk today. After two visits from the Metropolitan Police, you must have known I'd have a word with the girl before I set them upon her like a pack of dogs."

Missa moved her gaze to Rabiah, and her expression remained as open and frank as it always was. "What did she say?"

"I caught her by surprise. It would have been wise had you rung her directly you and I spoke, since she hadn't a clue what she was supposed to be doing or saying to me once I confronted her about using our name when she spoke with Mr. Druitt. Had you given her the word, she would have had time to cook up something. She might have had any number of stories about her seven appointments with a clergyman. For my part, I would have believed her at once had she told me she was using our name to meet with Mr. Druitt for a reason that needed to be untraceable to her. As it was, though, she denied seeing him at all. When I pressed her . . . Perhaps the best way to describe her reaction is to say she simply fell apart."

"She'd been caught in a lie," Missa pointed out.

"I think it's rather she'd been caught without time to *create* a lie. At the end, all she was able to do was to instruct me to talk to you. So here I am. What you need to know is that while Ding and I were in the midst of our initial words to each other, we were in the street. And so, unfortunately, were the detectives from New Scotland Yard. *Why* they were there, I couldn't tell you. *That* they were there suggests Ding is in their sights now. When I last spoke to them, they wanted to know why my phone number wasn't registered on Mr. Druitt's mobile. I like to think I'm in line for a BAFTA with my explanation to them, but now they've seen me with Ding, I rather doubt it. What would you like to tell me, Missa? I ask because you *will* tell me something and I suggest you choose the truth."

Having said that, Rabiah waited. Doing so, she was forced to consider the idea of Missa's speaking to a member of the clergy seven times prior to leaving Ludlow. Rabiah had to admit that the girl had certainly been under pressure from her mother not to leave the college when she'd first wanted to do so in December, and Rabiah herself had called the idea completely mad. Doubtless her friends and instructors at West Mercia College had joined in the chorus of disapproval. But once she'd cooperatively returned to the college after the Christmas holiday and *still* wanted out of the place, it did rather make sense that Missa would have sought someone with whom she could talk rationally about the matter. She would want someone with no chips in the game, and didn't a clergyman fit into that role like a foot into a shoe? Of course he did. Beyond that, didn't Missa have a right to privacy as she made her decision? Of course she did. And really, who the hell could blame her?

"Mr. Druitt rang me," Missa told her.

Well, this was certainly *not* the direction Rabiah had thought the conversation would take. "The clergyman rang *you*?"

"He said he'd been told I needed someone to talk to about leaving college. I expect my tutor put him onto me. He disapproved, you see. Just like everyone else."

"Druitt disapproved?" What a tangle this was, Rabiah thought.

"My tutor disapproved. I'd explained to him that I was intending to leave, and he thought I was rushing things."

"So he put a *clergyman* onto you?"

"That's what happened. I expect he thought I might be able to sort everything out better with a . . . I don't know. With a man of God?"

"As you're here now, Mr. Druitt must have supported the idea of leaving college. Did he?" Rabiah made the question casual because the fact remained that the man had *killed* himself. And Missa had left Ludlow soon afterwards. "The police are going to trace you, Missa."

"But you said you told them that you were the one who met with Mr. Druitt."

"True. But Ding isn't about to do you that favour. And they're going to want to speak to her, after catching me with her today."

"All right. I see that. But what I don't see is how any of that has to do with his suicide."

"I expect among other things they'll want to know what your relationship was with the man prior to his death. Are you prepared to talk about it?"

Missa's hand drew into a fist that crumpled her paper napkin as she took this in. She said, "My relationship with him?"

"If anything happened between you."

"I don't understand. What could have happened?"

"Missa, *I* don't know. But our surname appears in the man's diary often enough to cause suspicion in the eyes of the police. Since they're in Ludlow because of his suicide, it stands to reason that they might also be in Ludlow to look into what led up to it."

"That can't have anything to do with me. We only ever talked about college and uni."

"Then if you're asked, that's what you'll tell them. Of course, that begs the question: why didn't you simply tell me that when I phoned and asked you about it?" Rabiah waited. There was more here. She could see that much in Missa's tense body. She went on with some care although her exasperation with the girl was mounting. "And if there is some *other* reason, Missa, you should tell the police what it is . . . if, as I said, they come to call upon you."

"There isn't some other reason," Missa told her. "There's just the fact that I've finally become *myself*, Gran. I've become who I am, and I don't want to keep defending my decisions. I can't explain it any more than that."

She rose then. She said that her break was finished, and she was meant to get back to her candle making. Everything was fine, *she* was fine, life was fine, she said. Her grandmother needn't have lied to the police to keep them away from her. If they wanted to ask her questions about Mr. Druitt, she would tell them whatever she could.

"He didn't do a thing except try to help me make my decision," she said. "I needed someone to be there for me, and he was that person, Gran."

COALBROOKDALE
SHROPSHIRE

At their clinic, Yasmina Lomax had been trying daily to keep her gaze away from where her husband worked in the pharmacy. Most of the time, she was so busy with her young patients and their parents that she was successful in this endeavour. In this way she could tell herself that Timothy wasn't stealing opiates. She could conclude that since he'd beaten back his need for drink directly Missa was born, she had nothing further to worry about. She could also assure herself that, with time, he would find his way back to her just as she would, with time, find her way back to him. If they didn't manage to do that, she couldn't imagine what life was going to be like. Prior to Janna's death it had been difficult enough.

They'd been too young when they'd met. She'd been utterly inexperienced, the child of parents whose arranged marriage had worked out well and who were thus convinced that applying this same traditional approach to their daughter's future was wise. Yasmina had at first acquiesced to their plan, accompanying them on one trip to India, where a cousin had revealed to her the nature of her own arranged marriage to an older man who'd already raped and beaten his way through one wife and was raping and beating his way through her. Her parents' reassurance that this was an anomaly in the world of arranged marriages did very little to soothe Yasmina's fears. But since they promised that no marriage would take place prior to their daughter's completing her university studies, her anxiety about her future lifted.

She hadn't intended to become involved with any young man at university. Her focus had been on her studies. And studying was exactly what she'd been doing when she first met Timothy Lomax, with his goofy, slightly sticking-out ears, his curly hair, and his blazing smile that made one not notice anything else but how attractive he was, even with those ears.

He'd come from a uni drinks party. She'd been studying in a café, nursing a cup of tea long gone cold. He'd been slightly drunk and he admitted this to her, adding that if he hadn't had several too many drinks he wouldn't have had the courage to approach her at all. "You're gorgeous," he told her. "Gorgeous is a bit off-putting to an ordinary bloke like me."

She didn't have the experience to ask if this was a line he used to acquaint himself with young women he fancied, although she did wonder it much later. But by that time, she was in love with him, or she was in whatever state it is when the brain stops functioning and the body takes over, riding roughshod over one's future plans in the urgency of satisfying lust. Indeed, she didn't know what lust was as she'd never felt it. So she'd called her obsession with his body and with what his body could do to her body by the only word she could come up with: love. That was what was used in films, wasn't it? Whatever else could it be?

They'd had four lucky months before she'd fallen pregnant. He'd used protection, but it wasn't fail-safe. Beyond that, there was just one time when exigency overcame common sense—no condoms at hand and really, how on earth could she become pregnant if they didn't actually complete the act in the traditional fashion—and the rest was permanent estrangement from her family. The arrival of Missa and later Janna and Sati made losing her natal family less painful, and Rabiah's kindness and support had got them through the thornier times created by having three small children and two careers.

Things began to get difficult, however, no matter Rabiah's helpful presence. Yasmina found herself far too busy with her practice and with her growing girls to consider the degree to which she and her husband began merely to go through the motions with each other. She assured herself that she was doing her best, since even when she was exhausted by her life she persevered in being her husband's lover because it was another wifely duty that had fallen upon her with her hasty marriage. After all, she'd grown up learning that a woman's lot in life was defined by the two chromosomes that made her just that: a woman. So she accepted that she was to cook the meals, keep the house neat, bathe and feed and see to the various needs of the children, do the weekly shop, use the iron to press the wrinkles from her husband's shirts. And when he reached out for her thigh in the darkness or caressed her breast to awaken her in the early morning, she cooperated and hoped that it would soon be over so that she could simply just sleep. This was enough, she told herself. Timothy had to be satisfied with what she could give.

And then Janna. And how one's imperfect world crashes around one when a child becomes critically ill. And how one begins to think—no matter one's religious or spiritual upbringing—about being punished by God for not being enough. Not enough of a mother. Not enough of a wife. Not enough of anything, really.

All the ways relating to how she and Timothy managed their marriage came to a halt as they faced what was growing like a tentacled monster within their daughter's skull. The fact that Timothy did not believe in disease as punishment did nothing to ameliorate Yasmina's anguish. He wouldn't hear any talk of the many ways in which she—a paediatrician, for God's sake—had failed their daughter. Ultimately, he would not hear any talk of anything at all.

He'd begun with the opiates during Janna's illness. The excuse was his need to sleep, although the truth was his need to escape from what they both knew lay directly in their path, which was the soul-destroying grief of losing their child. The diagnosis had carried within it the seed of truth, although Janna's team of specialists had tried, as they would do, to put the best possible face upon it. Five years if we fight this aggressively, they said. Eighteen months if we do not. But in any case, terminal. Always terminal no matter the youth and prior health of the person stricken. So terribly, terribly, terribly sorry.

People believe, she thought, that they will emerge from the nightmare of losing a child and somehow find their way back to at least a semblance of who they had been before. And perhaps that was the case for some, but it had not been the case for her. She did her best. She wanted only what was good for her two remaining children, and she managed to direct her waking moments to fulfilling her obligations as a physician and as a mother. But she had nothing left when it came to her husband.

And now Missa. And the alteration in her that illustrated to her mother that there was more than one way to lose a child. But loss of many kinds had hardened Yasmina's resolve, so when it came to Missa, she wasn't about to accept it. She could see how the girl's future was going to play out if she—Yasmina, her mother—did nothing to force the issue of her fractured decision making out into the open.

Timothy opposed her. "She needs to find her way through this, and you can't find it for her, no matter how much you want to," he said. But if nothing was done to stop it, Missa's "way" was going to lead her directly to becoming exactly what Yasmina saw in the clinic every day: a too-young mother with a very big belly, a runny-nosed child in a pushchair, and another holding on to her skirt. "That's who she'll be if she ends up with Justin Goodayle," Yasmina said to her husband. "You don't want to admit it because you like the boy. I like him as well, but *not* as a husband for our daughter." His response was, "Keep this up, Yas, and you'll drive her straight into marriage with Justin."

Yet why would that be the case? Yasmina wondered. All she'd *ever* wanted for her girls was that their paths into wholesome careers not be like her own: made excruciating through the loss of her nuclear family and difficult through unexpected pregnancy. At least, she thought, they didn't have *that* to concern themselves with . . . unless Missa had got herself pregnant during her months at West Mercia College, unless Missa had had an abortion, unless Missa was now pining for the baby . . . or perhaps she was still carrying the baby . . . or if not that then—

Yasmina knew she was driving herself mad by spending too much time inside her head. So when she left the clinic, she stopped at the market in Buildwas Road and spent half an hour pushing a shopping trolley up and down aisles with the hope that whatever she put into it could transform itself into a meal that she might prepare for the family's dinner.

The supermarket was not far from New Road, where the Lomaxes lived. Their sturdy brick house with its double-glazed windows backed into a hillside overgrown with ivy and shrubbery. Its length followed the course of the narrow lane. This climbed in the direction of the town church, above a well-travelled riverside street called the Wharfage, which was the main route between Ironbridge and its neighboring village Coalbrookdale. The Lomax house looked down upon the Wharfage and upon the River Severn that flowed to its south.

They had the luxury of a garage, but when Yasmina arrived home, she saw that her mother-in-law's car was blocking access to it. She squeezed her vehicle as far off the roadway as she could get it, after which she wrestled the carrier bags from the backseat. She wasn't in the best frame of mind by the time she got into the house.

Rabiah, she saw, was at the kitchen table with Sati, and they appeared to be working on Sati's school prep. This was an additional irritant. "She's meant to do that on her own," Yasmina said to her mother-in-law.

Rabiah's response was a mild, "You need a lovely long bath and a cup of tea, my dear. I'll see to things down here. Use bubbles, please."

"What I need is to start dinner, Mum, and what Sati needs is to do her school prep by herself."

Rabiah rose from the table and gave Yasmina an affectionate pat on the shoulder before she took the carrier bags from her. "She can't do it if she doesn't understand it in the first place. What's the point of having a pensioned maths teacher for a gran if I can't help her?"

"She's only *explaining* things to me," Sati said. "You let Missa explain things, Mummy."

"That's because Missa can be counted on not to give you the answers," Yasmina said. "I'm going to ask to see your work, my girl. And it had better be in your writing and not your grandmother's."

"Scoot along," Rabiah told her, clearly unoffended. "I'm putting the kettle on. What d'you have here? Ah. Lamb. Perfect for kebabs and how fortunate is that since kebabs are virtually the only thing I know how to make."

"You do goose at Christmas, Granny," Sati pointed out. "You do roast beef as well. *And* turkey."

"Holiday meals are simple," Rabiah said. "It's the daily business that defeats me, which is why I stick with tomato soup and soldiers. Lentil soup as well, I suppose, when I feel like going wild. At any rate, finish your prep and you can help me while your mum has a soak in the tub. And I do mean it, Yasmina. I'll bring you your cuppa and if you're not in the tub with mounds of bubbles, I shall be quite annoyed."

Yasmina knew when her mother-in-law had become the unmovable object. Since she hadn't considered what to do with the lamb and the other items she'd purchased, it was nothing to her to have Rabiah turn them into kebabs. Besides, a bath sounded quite lovely. A bath, a cup of tea, silence, and peace.

She had sunk into the bubbles when she discovered that while she would have the bath and the tea, what she would not have was the rest of it. Rabiah knocked on the bathroom door and when Yasmina told her to enter, in she came bearing not one but two mugs. She handed one mug to Yasmina, kept the other, and settled herself on the loo's seat.

"Ah." Yasmina didn't trouble to hide the weariness in her voice. "As I feared."

"Well, you can't have thought I just stopped by to help Sati with her school prep. We need to talk, you and I. Some London coppers have been sent up to Ludlow to have another look into the death of that deacon fellow. D'you know who I mean? He was a suicide while in police custody."

Yasmina sipped her tea. It was too weak, a characteristic of Rabiah's lack of skill at teabag dousing. The only cure for this had always been to have Yorkshire Tea on hand. Boiling water, approximately two seconds, and the brew was so strong that one's teeth stood in danger of losing their enamel. Anything else in Rabiah's hands was more like drinking slightly darkened water.

"You can't have come up here to tell me about the London police, Mum," Yasmina said. "And yes, I remember the 'deacon fellow.' It was everywhere, that story."

"What wasn't everywhere was the name Lomax associated with the man," Rabiah told her. "And since that particular *Lomax* did not belong to me, I concluded it belonged to Missa. Has she told you that she knew him? No? Let me carry it further. *Lomax* was in the deacon's diary seven times. So she had regular meetings with him. And, by the way, this is the second visit I've had from New Scotland Yard, so something's going on and I daresay it's serious. I've fended them off for now but I doubt they're going to remain fended."

Yasmina wanted to rise from the water at all of this, but natural modesty prevented her, as her mother-in-law had known it would do. Rabiah's suggestion of bubble bath had been inspired. Yasmina was covered by the foam and hence a prisoner of this conversation. All she could do was stare at Rabiah: that distinguished unlined face of hers, those frank brown eyes, the sinewy body of a distance runner. All she could think was that Missa had been lying to her for months upon months and that *every* time Yasmina thought she'd got to the root of what was on her daughter's mind, she discovered she knew nothing at all.

"You've spoken to Missa?" Yasmina said.

"I stopped at that Victorian place first, before coming here. I spoke to Justin, and I spoke to her. *He* tells me he was never against her going to college and uni, by the way. I get the impression he thinks his cooperation with the college and uni thing constitutes your—what do they call it? that quasi-religious word? Oh yes. Your imprimatur on future nuptials between Missa and him."

"What did Missa tell you?"

"About rendezvousing with this clergyman? At first she tried to claim it was her friend Ding using our surname. Once we worked our way through that little tale, she told me that someone put him onto speaking to her about leaving college. She thinks it was her tutor. She says, like you, her tutor was opposed to her leaving and when the clergyman—Druitt, that's the name—contacted her, she reckoned the tutor had arranged it. Had he?"

Yasmina knew what Rabiah was asking her. She also knew that Rabiah would not approve. But the truth lay in between what Yasmina had done and what subsequently occurred, so she told it. "I did speak to her tutor, Mum. Missa's story kept changing. I had no choice."

"What story? About why she wanted to leave the college?"

"First she told me it was Sati and what she called Sati's 'need' for her at home because of Janna's—" *Still*, she could not utter those words. She attempted to cover her inability to make that agonising death final by carefully setting her tea to one side. She reached for the soap as if intending to wash. "That was at Christmas, and Timothy and I quashed it. But after she returned to Ludlow to give college another try, she claimed something had gone wrong in her brain. She said she couldn't concentrate. She believed she'd developed dyslexia or attention deficit disorder because none of her science coursework made sense to her any longer. She said she was going to fail. I told her that one does not *develop* a brain disorder unless one has had a head injury. She didn't want to hear that, naturally. All she wanted was to come home. So I spoke to her tutor. And yes, I already know, Mum.

Missa would have hated my interfering. So I asked him not to tell her that I'd contacted him, but it didn't matter. Missa had already spoken to him about leaving and he was as concerned as I was."

There was a pristine washing flannel on top of a stack of freshly laundered towels, and Rabiah handed this to her and said, "So he . . . what? Rang the vicar?"

"He told me that he'd contacted a college counsellor. I was worried she wouldn't get to Missa in time to keep her there, so I asked her name and I rang her myself. I left a message. Twice, this was. That was all. She never phoned back."

Rabiah nodded. Wisely, she made the next connection by saying, "Does Tim know about all this?"

Yasmina didn't like what was implied by the questions. She said, "I don't keep secrets from Timothy," and couldn't stop herself from adding the bitter words, "although he thinks he's getting much better at keeping secrets from me, Rabiah."

*Rabiah* instead of *Mum* sent the message that if her mother-in-law wanted to go in this next direction, Yasmina was willing to do so, but it would not be an easy conversation. Rabiah said, "We can't discuss whatever Tim's up to just now. This octopus he's carrying round on his shoulders . . . ? He must face it and you can't force him to do that."

"Believe me, things have progressed much further than a tumble from the wagon," Yasmina told her. "But don't worry. We shall continue to muddle along till someone somewhere counts up their pills and begins to ask questions." And then when she saw the stricken look on Rabiah's face, she added, "I'm sorry. Mum, I'm *sorry.* But it was just that your question . . . No, let me answer it. I told Timothy what I intended to do: that I would be phoning Missa's tutor. He told me I was interfering. And when she did leave the college in March, he put it down to me. I forced her hand, he said. If I'd've just let her find her way, she would have found it on her own. Everything would have come right in the end."

"Now that's a fairy tale," Rabiah said.

"If it is, Timothy's the one writing it," Yasmina told her.

ALLINGTON
KENT

The drive to Kent was as deadly as Isabelle Ardery had assumed it would be, considering the time of day and Kent's proximity to London, and although she'd known it would be difficult for her, the traffic turned out to be more than her nerves had bargained for. Ultimately, she pulled into a lay-by. There she attempted to calm herself. She chose deep breathing, trying to free her mind of its snarl of thoughts, which were taking her in every possible direction: from the dog's dinner she'd made of her time in Ludlow to the dog's dinner she'd made of her marriage to the dog's dinner she was making of her life. She sat motionless, putting her will into her skin in order to keep it from crawling up her bones in the direction of her vocal cords, which would require her to scream. She gripped the steering wheel and watched the traffic crawl by.

She should have taken the train. It would have been packed, but at least it would have got her to Maidstone without exposing her to every single one of her weaknesses. Just now, she couldn't afford to be exposed to any of them. She wanted her wits about her because she needed to get out to Bob's house while she actually had his agreement to see and speak to the boys alone. True, she would have to see them in the back garden of Bob and Sandra's house in case James became "overwhelmed" again, as Bob had put it. But Isabelle was willing to accept this condition because it was essential to her that she be allowed to talk to the twins.

She'd had a fortifying drink before leaving the Met. After she'd downed it, she'd gone to the ladies', where brushing, flossing, and gargling—and then doing it all a second time—had resulted in her not being able to catch the scent of anything on her breath save mint when she cupped her hands and exhaled into them. She'd also chewed mint gum and sucked on mint breath lozenges as she drove. But the ghastly traffic had taken its toll. There in the lay-by she sat in her car and felt the longing, the abject need, and the growing inability to think of anything else no matter how she tried.

She had it with her. It was there in the glove box as always. She also had with her the toothpaste, the toothbrush, and the mouthwash. This meant, as she well knew, that she *could*—

She told herself that she would not. She pulled out of the lay-by when there was an opening in the traffic and set off again. Twenty minutes later, however, she saw the sign for a Welcome Break. As it was growing ever later, she followed the route into the car park, and there she pulled into a parking bay and placed a call to Bob from her mobile. It was very brief and he was quite nice about everything. She told him traffic was far worse than she'd imagined it would be, so she wouldn't be in Allington when she thought she would. That was quite fine, he told her. One certainly couldn't do much about traffic, eh?

The phone call finished, she stared at the Welcome Break's main building. It was a large one, and she knew that there would be various options for food inside, as well as coffee sellers. But either coffee or tea would only make her nerves worse. She settled on looking for something to eat.

Inwardly, though, she rolled her eyes at the idea of food, coffee, tea, and her nerves. When it came to nerves, after all, how long would it *really* take to settle them? She had what she needed there in the car and after two—or perhaps three—airline bottles of vodka . . . No. Not three. She was not that far gone. Two would be fine because two would do what it took to stop her hands from shaking because shaking hands would frighten the boys, especially if the shaking became worse than—she held them up in front of her—it was at present.

As quickly as she could manage it, she downed two of the small bottles of vodka. She let them settle into her and reached to close the glove box upon the third. But at the final moment, she took that one into the palm of her hand as well. She drank it down. The relief was enormous.

Since she did have with her the rest of what she needed, she locked up the car and went into the building, where she found the ladies'. There, she repeated the brushing, flossing, and gargling that had served her purposes at New Scotland Yard.

Her business completed, she went into a smallish M & S food hall, and there she purchased a muffin to serve as her dinner. This she ate on the way back to her car. She felt one hundred percent better.

Bob and Sandra lived not far from the lock on the River Medway, and when Isabelle pulled in front of their large, cantilevered and tile-cladded cottage, she did her best not to compare it to her own basement lodgings south of the Thames. There, she was fixed between HM Wandsworth Prison and Wandsworth Cemetery. Here they were fixed beside an orchard of fruit trees, in a home shaded by an enormous hornbeam, with a river offering a pleasant vista for them to enjoy from their back garden.

The flagstone path she followed to the front door was swept neatly, with beds of yellow, white, and pink primroses on either side of it. She surreptitiously checked her breath when she got to the porch, and she smoothed her hair, which allowed her to discover that somewhere along the way she'd managed to lose one of her earrings, not an easy thing to do as her ears were pierced. Quickly, she removed the other before ringing the bell above a wrought-iron stand that held a fern so lush that it looked edible.

Laurence answered the door, crying, "Mum!" and "Mum's here, James," over his shoulder. His father appeared behind him in an instant, saying, "Ah, here you are," as he did his best—she saw—not to look as if he were checking her for signs of inebriation.

Sandra showed up as well, before Isabelle had walked more than six feet into the house. Isabelle greeted her in a friendly fashion, but she couldn't help looking round for James. Laurence called out to his brother once again, and James finally showed his face by peering round the doorway to the dining room where for some reason he'd decided to lurk. Before Isabelle could speak to him, Sandra said, "Come say hello to your mum, darling," and held out her hand to the boy. James joined her then, and she put her arm round his thin shoulders, bending to murmur something to him that Isabelle couldn't hear.

She did her best not to feel indignation, but what she truly wanted was to grab her son—*her* son, not Sandra's—and do some of her own murmuring into his ear, although what she would murmur was something she couldn't come up with. Instead, she said to him, "Hello, darling. Laurence and I are going to chat to each other in the garden. Will you come?" When he made no reply, she schooled herself to feel nothing. She said only, "Well, if you decide you want to, do come outside."

Bob gave a look to each of the women before saying to Isabelle, "It's just this way," as if she didn't know where the garden was. But she followed him cooperatively, one of her hands holding Laurence's, saying to the boy, "Are you getting excited about New Zealand?" She'd seen the packing boxes when they walked through the sitting room towards the garden door. They were still in a flattened shape, but soon enough Sandra would no doubt be gleefully shoving her Spode into them, having finally managed to achieve the triumph of fully co-opting Isabelle's boys as her own.

Bob took them across a perfect lawn to a grape arbour under which sat a table and chairs. Isabelle noted that he would be able to watch her from inside the house. Just another indignity she had to ignore. She knew he would push her as far as he could, probing for the point at which she would break. Since she had no intention of breaking, she said, "This is lovely. Thank you, Bob," and was surprised to hear him murmur, "I'll see what I can do with James," before he went back to the house.

Laurence was happily going on about New Zealand, the school he would be attending along with James, and the fact that the worst bit was that "we won't have summer hols, though, Mum. I mean, *this* year we won't have 'em. See, it's upside down in New Zealand. They have summer hols in the winter. I mean it's *their* winter. I mean *our* summer is *their* winter so they've already had their holiday and we'll miss ours. I don't like that bit at *all*."

"But the school sounds nice, does it? You'll enjoy the school?"

"Dad says I will." He looked over his shoulder at the house and confided, "I don't know about James, though, Mum. He's being *such* a baby. More than usual cos he's pretty much always a baby."

"Sometimes things that are easy for one person aren't easy for another," she said.

"*I* just think he's being *stupid*." Laurence kicked a leg of the table.

The house's garden door opened again and Sandra came out. She was carrying a tray, and James was reluctantly trudging along in her wake, his head so far down that his hair fell forward in a veil and his chin rested upon his chest. Sandra called out to Isabelle cheerfully, "I thought ice cream might be nice in this fine weather."

When she put the tray on the table, Isabelle saw that she'd dished up three bowls of strawberry ice cream with chocolate sauce and nuts poured over it and a cherry sitting at the top of the mound. She'd even inserted a wafer biscuit that erupted jauntily from one side. Clearly, she was tempting James to remain with his mother and his brother. She said to Isabelle in a low voice, "I thought this might help," and then to James himself, "Come along, James. You certainly don't want to miss ice cream."

Laurence's whoop of joy helped. James eased onto one of the chairs—the farthest from Isabelle, she noted—and he went at the ice cream with his spoon clutched into his fist. Isabelle stopped herself from telling him to use the spoon properly as he was quite old enough to know how to hold a spoon, and anyway, she'd *seen* him hold a spoon before and she knew very well that what he was doing was all for show. Instead, she tucked in, pronounced the ice cream delicious, and waited for Sandra to leave them.

"Are you excited as well?" she asked James, when Sandra took herself off to regions unknown but very probably near a window. "New Zealand's going to be quite an adventure for you. Laurence says school has already been arranged. You'll miss regular summer hols, but think of it, darling: Christmas in the summer instead of the winter. Won't that be fun? You can go to the beach. You can have a barbecue. How different it will be!"

James still had not looked directly at her. Compared to his brother, his behavior had always been more retired, but this seemed extreme and Isabelle felt punished by him, which did not seem the least bit fair.

She said, "James, is it me you're unhappy with? Or is it something else? Is the idea of going off to New Zealand—"

A rambunctious dog suddenly appeared out of absolute nowhere. It charged wildly to the table as if it had materialised from another world. It was large, it was pure black, and it was thoroughly excited, becoming all wagging tail and flopping ears and leaping attempts to join them, if not on the table then at least in their chairs. It barked joyously. It ran round in circles. It hurled itself at their bowls of ice cream. It particularly hurled itself at James.

The boy screamed. King Kong might have leapt into their midst. James flew out of his seat and began running madly towards the river. This, of course, to the dog meant that James wished to have a game of chase. So the dog yelped happily as it tore after the boy. James shouted, "No! No! Dad! Mummy! *Mum*my!" as Bob burst from the house.

"Oliver won't hurt you," Bob called. "James! Stop running! He thinks you're playing."

But James kept on. He shot from the riverbank to the orchard and circled the trees, and Isabelle could see he'd begun to cry. His terror of the animal was absolutely real. She got to her feet and set off in his direction.

Sandra raced outside, calling to him. She held out her arms. She shouted, "Bob, catch that wretched beast," and she said to Isabelle, "We'll handle this. Stay right there. James, James, it will be fine. Your dad's getting him. See? Look at your dad. And here's Mr. Horton come to fetch him home."

The dog, at this point, had James backed into one of the apple trees. He was in the play position that anyone who knew dogs would recognise but apparently James did not, for he kept shrieking, "Get him away! Mummy, get him *away*!" When Bob finally reached him, the child was a sodden heap of emotion. He'd curled himself into a hedgehog roll. Isabelle could hear him sobbing from across the garden.

"I am *so* blasted sorry," Mr. Horton said. "Sandra, Bob, I only opened the front door and there he went. We're working day and night on his training but . . . Oliver! Enough! Come!"

Bob had reached the dog at this point, and Oliver was thrilled with another potential playfellow. It was no real trouble to grab on to his collar, and it was equally easy to draw him away from James and hand him over to his master.

Sandra, in the meantime, had reached James and scooped him up off the ground like a toddler. She was murmuring to him and smoothing his hair and, to Isabelle's way of seeing things, generally treating him like a two-year-old.

During all of this, Laurence hadn't moved. He'd continued with his ice cream and had watched all of the activity like someone enjoying a television programme. When Isabelle returned to the table, he said frankly, "It happens all the time, Mum. Oliver likes the river and he gets out and comes over here and then he sees us and wants to play. James doesn't *get* that. Really, he's such a wanker."

"Laurence, that's not very nice," Isabelle said.

"James, you are such a wanker!" Laurence called out to his brother. Bob had joined Sandra. He'd taken James from her and, cradling his head with his hand, he was carrying him back to the garden table. He said to Laurence, "Enough of that."

"But he is, he *is*," Laurence declared. "Mum, he even looks under his bed every night to make sure there's no monsters before he'll get into it and *I'm* even right there in the same room! I don't look under my bed, do I? No. But he does cos he's a wanker. Wanker wanker wanker who's even afraid of a stupid dog!"

"Enough!" Bob pointed sternly at the boy. "What part of that do you not understand?"

"Bob, should I . . ." It was Sandra now, having trotted along behind Bob like an obedient sheepdog.

"No," he said to her. And then, "James, the dog's gone. I'm going to set you down with your mother and brother. You can finish your ice cream. Mr. Horton's taken care of Oliver."

"An' if you don't eat it, *I* will, James," Laurence announced. "'N fact . . ." He reached over, grabbed his brother's ice cream, and began to dig in.

"Laurence, *that* is absolutely enough!" Isabelle spoke without even thinking what was and was not appropriate. "You are *not* your brother, so you can't possibly know what he's thinking or going through or fearing or anything else, for that matter. I don't want to hear you *ever* calling him a wanker again. And stop eating that ice cream this instant."

There was something of a shocked silence at this. Isabelle's heart was thudding. Laurence had the ice cream spoon halfway to his mouth, James had raised his head from his father's shoulder, Bob was staring at her transfixed, and Sandra's jaw had dropped. She snapped it closed.

Isabelle saw how far she'd just gone. She regretted it instantly, for everything that it revealed about her inability to cope. But then, Bob's mouth moved in what might actually have been a small smile and Laurence dropped the spoon back into his brother's treat and pushed the bowl back to where James had been sitting. Bob set James down, kissed the top of his head, and turned from the table. He took Sandra's arm and they went towards the house, leaving Isabelle alone with the boys.

She said quietly, "I spoke a bit sharply to you, Laurence. I do apologise. But I can't have you teasing your brother like that. It's not fair. And to be honest, it's not very handsome of you when it comes down to it."

He looked from her to James back to her again. He said, "Sorry, Mum."

She said, "It's not me you ought to be saying sorry to, is it?"

To James, then, he said, "Sorry, James. But I do so wish . . . Oh sorry, just sorry."

James was looking only at his ice cream, which he had not returned to. He was caught up in *whatever* a nine-year-old-boy might be caught up in at the end of such an episode, and Isabelle hardly knew what that might be. But she did see how very different the boys were to each other, despite being identical twins. She also saw that if James Ardery was a fearful child, she was very much part of the process that had made him so.

She said to him, "There's not the slightest thing wrong with being afraid, James. Of dogs, of monsters under the bed, of creatures in the wardrobe, of snakes in the bushes, of anything at all."

He didn't reply. He didn't look up. Laurence snorted and she shot him a look. She went on.

"The difficult part of coping with fears is facing them and walking through them. But the case is this: that's the only way to dismiss them. And if we are never able to dismiss this fear or that fear—no matter what it is—then they tend to get larger. Do you know why I know this, James? Do you know why I know this better than everything else I might *ever* know?"

He shook his head. Laurence, she saw, had stopped eating his ice cream and was watching her warily.

"Because in my life, darling, I have been absolute crap at facing my own fears. That's why you live with Dad and Sandra and not with me. That's why what I did was take the first opportunity I had to run away from Maidstone and go to London. And here's what I know now after all these years of running. If you run, your fears run with you. And they stay with you till you turn to face them."

"But you're a cop!" Laurence protested. "Cops aren't 'fraid. Don't cops have to be *not* afraid?"

"If I were afraid of the bad sort of people I come across, that would be true," she said to Laurence. "But in my case, I'm afraid of who I will be if I ever face my fears in the first place."

Laurence frowned. James looked up. He, too, seemed perplexed. But he also looked like a boy who was sorting through various ideas in his head, so Isabelle waited.

He said, "D'you mean you're afraid of being *afraid*, Mum?"

"That," she said, reaching for his wrist, closing her hand round it, and feeling its fragility for the first time, "is exactly what I mean. So here is what I did with all those fears: I tried to drink them down."

"Like medicine?"

"No. Like a potion you take when you want to forget. I used vodka and I used it too often and when your dad asked me to stop, I couldn't do it. I couldn't do it because I was far too afraid at that point even to try. So I lost him and I lost you and now I'm losing you more. Which hurts very much. So I'm saying that the end of being afraid is losing. One loses everything from happy experiences in life to the people who should be part of those happy experiences. That's not something I want for you, James. And it's not something I want for Laurence either."

James said, "Laurence isn't ever afraid."

Laurence said, stirring his ice cream into a goo and not looking at his brother, "Thing is . . . I am, James."

"Of what?" James clearly did not believe that Laurence could possibly fear anything.

"Leaving here and never coming back and . . ." His lips trembled and he swiped at his ice cream angrily.

"And what?" James asked him.

"And never seeing Mum again, that's what." He began to cry.

Isabelle felt as if her lungs were collapsing. She wanted to speak. She could not do so.

# 20 MAY

WANDSWORTH
LONDON

What had she feared the most? Not losing her husband, since it had been her incalculably insane belief that, like so many men, he lacked the nerve to go it on his own after having had a wife at his beck and call, and this despite the fact that being at anyone's beck and call was the last behaviour in her limited uxorial skill set that she ever engaged in. Nor had she feared the loss of her children. She was their mother, she fed them, she changed their nappies even when those nappies were at their most disgusting, which, frankly, was most days. She bathed them, she put dangerous items out of their reach, she purchased temporary gates to keep them from tumbling down the stairs. Nor had she feared losing her job since, despite being a wife and a mother, she still managed what she'd always been able to manage: maintaining that air of competence and cool professionalism no matter what was going on at home. No. She had feared none of these things. What she had feared most was running out of vodka.

Driving home from her encounter with James and Laurence, Isabelle had felt what she knew was absolutely essential for her to feel: the great, gaping, guilt-ridden, never-to-be-filled chasm that she had created in her life. She owned her sons' fears. She owned their pain. She had bought and paid for every anxiety they had about leaving the home they'd always known and being taken off to another country where they would have to face all those things children face in a new environment: from a school where they would be expected to make new friends to an upside down year where summer was winter and winter was summer. And what she knew was that there were very few words she could utter to reassure them.

When she arrived home from her journey to Kent, the last thing she felt she could face was descending the wrought-iron steps to her basement flat, with its bleak silence an illustration of consequences she had disregarded. So once she'd parked and locked the car, she set off in the direction of Trinity Road. It was her intention to walk until she could walk no more.

She didn't mean to go into the off-licence. She hadn't the first thought of even finding one. But find one she did, and the worst of it was, she came across it not fifteen minutes into her walk.

She told herself that her need was merely to purchase a bottle of water. She was thirsty and if she was going to walk until she could walk no more, she needed to remain hydrated. So in she went, and she kept her eyes fixed on the lights inside a cooler in the back of the shop. She allowed herself to see one thing only: the plastic bottles of water inside that cooler.

She felt triumphant as she grabbed one, carried it to the till, placed it on the counter, and looked in her bag for her coin purse. But when the shop assistant said, "Oh, hullo! I live just opposite you. You're the policewoman, aren't you? At least that's what my mum says and she's *such* a nosy parker, she knows what's going on in every house in the street," Isabelle had to look up. She saw a twentysomething girl with—of all bizarre things—a colourful crab tattooed on her neck and then just over her shoulder the lines and shelves of bottles. She smiled automatically as one does and she told the girl that yes, she was a policewoman, but she didn't think she knew the girl's mum and the girl laughed and said, "Oh, you wouldn't. You'd never even see her since all she does is stand behind the curtains and give them a twitch occasionally. Anyway, that'll be ninety p, unless you'd like something else."

Which was how she'd ended up buying two bottles of Grey Goose vodka. And because above all her life was about don't tell me what to do, don't lecture me, don't point anything out because by God I'll fight you and you will regret it, she ended her evening walk just there. She went back to her flat. She placed one of the two bottles of vodka into the freezer compartment of her fridge, and the other bottle she opened.

She awakened when a car alarm went off in the street nearby. Her initial thought was that it was still evening because dim daylight was filtering into her flat from the street above. But then she saw that her glass was overturned on the coffee table in front of the sofa on which she lay and so was the bottle of Grey Goose, which, she swore, she had left in the kitchen but which now swam in a pool of extremely expensive vodka that was contained by the raised edge of the coffee table.

Her mouth felt contaminated. She was aware of profound thirst. She swung her legs off the sofa and saw, then, that she'd removed her trousers and that her bikini underwear clung only to one leg.

For a blighted moment she wondered if she'd let someone into the flat at some point. But then she hit upon a dim memory of using the loo and thinking it was so much easier just to leave the trousers in a pile on the floor and then to giggle at the absurdity of staggering back to the kitchen for who knows what number of martini it must have been. Only . . . how could she possibly have been that drunk when it was only . . . what? . . . an hour past the time she'd first entered the flat?

She looked at her watch, which she still wore, thank God. She saw that it was just after five. She frowned then because she realised this meant that either her watch had stopped—which it clearly hadn't as the second hand was still in motion—or time had somehow gone backwards or it was actually the next morning. In any case, what she needed to do was go back to sleep for two hours, since rising from the sofa seemed completely impossible at the moment. But before that, she decided, she could ring her own office in order to leave a message for Dorothea Harriman. She would tell her that she was ill. After all, her head was muzzy and when had she last taken a sick day anyway?

She couldn't remember and she doubted Dee Harriman was keeping track.

LUDLOW
SHROPSHIRE

Considering the hour, Lynley was impressed to find Barbara Havers waiting outside for him. She'd apparently taken a decision to give her hair a trim at some point during the previous night. When he gave it a look—admittedly askance—she said, "I reckon I needed a second mirror to see the back and sides. Live and learn," to which he replied, "An admirable motto, although asymmetry has its own appeal."

She made a gesture towards the castle ruins across the street, saying, "Ever notice how much we like our heaps of stone, sir? I wager we're the only country in the world that has telly programmes about this or that pile of rubble, eh?"

"Havers, I'm duly impressed," he replied. "Has your television viewing undergone a change?"

"Not hardly," she said. "Just got a new battery for the remote."

"My hopes are summarily dashed."

"Oh, I know this one's got to do with the Plantagenets, sir. Last time I was here that bloke Harry was going on about the Yorks riding out from the castle, and I know they're part of that clan. He didn't say which of 'em, though. And as I'd already gone all to smash with the Edwards, I didn't want to enter into any more royal discussions, if you know what I mean."

"Ah. Yes. Well, you could have named quite a number of Edwards, as Ludlow was batted back and forth amongst the group like an historical tennis ball. Ultimately, of course, it ended up in the lap of the usurper. Like everything else, including the privilege of defining the narrative, as things turned out."

"Sir?"

"Henry Tudor. History is written by the winners, Sergeant. Shall we be off?"

Aside from a single milk float doing its duty, there was no one out on the streets at this early hour. It was a matter of minutes only to reach the house in which Finnegan Freeman lived. At the front door Lynley rang the bell. When no one answered, he gave the door a decent banging. When that proved insufficient unto the day, he tried the knob.

The door was unlocked, and inside the building all was silent. The air bore the scent of burnt eggs, sort of a charcoal-fading-to-sulphur odour, the source of which turned out to be a pan sitting on the lowest step of the stairway. This held what appeared to be petrified scrambled eggs covered by a skin of Fairy Liquid.

Havers went towards the back of the place, where a door indicated the kitchen was. She shook her head at Lynley to indicate no one was inside busily seeing to the bacon and toast. She held up a finger and entered the room, and he heard the sound of cupboards opening and shutting. Knowing Havers, he understood that anything was possible—including her deciding to cook herself a meal—but she emerged soon enough with two lids from cooking pots, and he saw her intention at once. He glanced into the sitting room to verify its emptiness, and they headed for the stairs, careful not to upset the egg pan and spill its contents onto the floor.

Above, there were three bedrooms and a family bathroom only. Again, there was no one about. The first door they tried was locked, but the second was not. Lynley swung it open quietly, saw the figure sprawled out on the bed, and heard Havers murmur next to him, "Not exactly Prince Charming, is he."

True. Finnegan Freeman was not an attractive sleeper. His mouth hung open, he snored faintly, and the underpants he had on looked as if they could do with a day's soak in bleach.

Softly, Havers walked across the room as Lynley followed her inside. With the window closed, the air was hot and it smelled of sweat and copious emissions of a gaseous nature. He watched as Havers took up a position. She looked towards him with eyebrows raised. He nodded. She set to with the lids, shouting "Wakey-wakey-wakey!"

That did it. Finnegan rolled off the bed. He landed in a karate pose. He yelled, "Eeee-yah!" and switched to another pose, a sight to see in his underwear.

Havers lowered the lids, saying, "Bloody hell, that's all you've got?"

Lynley had his warrant card out. He said, "DI Thomas Lynley.

New Scotland Yard. We rang the bell but no one answered. The door wasn't locked, by the way."

"You lot need to watch that," Havers added. "Not that it looks like you have anything to steal but you'd hate to come home and find Goldilocks in your bed. Or maybe not."

Finnegan was still in something of a crouch. He rose from this as he snarled, "She sent you! She fucking sent you!"

"Goldilocks?" Havers asked. "No. We tend to go our own way, me and the inspector, here. So whoever 'she' is—and I reckon it's your mum, the DCC—she didn't do any sending of anyone anywhere. D'you want to get dressed?"

"I'm not going with you lot *anywhere*."

"This is just a natter, Finn. We can do it here with you in your smalls and all of us lined up on the bed like the see-no-evil monkeys, *or* we can toddle down to the kitchen or the sitting room and chunter there. Kitchen's my recommendation as you might like a cuppa and I'm happy to be mother."

"I want my privacy. I'm getting dressed."

"I'll remain with him, Sergeant," Lynley said. "If you'll replace the cookery items and put the kettle on . . . ?"

She nodded and left them. Lynley saw a chair in the corner of the room and brought it to the door, which he closed. He sat.

"I got to have a piss," Finn said to him.

"Dress first, please. Let's not make this difficult, Finnegan."

"It's Finn," the boy said.

"Finn. Shall I sort out clothing for you?"

"Oh yeah. Like I need you to do that." He scooped up clothing from the floor. Jeans and a T-shirt, which he donned without ceremony. He approached Lynley with, "Now you want to get out of the way?" and Lynley accommodated him although he did follow the boy to the bathroom. On his way there, Finn yelled, "Coppers are here, you lot! Hide the pickings from last night's break-ins."

He went into the bathroom, leaving the door open to the entertaining sight of him peeing forcefully and accompanying this with an explosive passage of gas. Finished, he left the toilet unflushed and his hands unwashed. Lynley made a mental note not to shake with him at the end of their colloquy.

Finn shoved past him, saying, "You're breaking the law, you are. Don't think I don't know it. And I know my rights 's well. You can't just walk into someone's house like you did. This is just like breaking and entering, this is. This is like kidnapping. This is like . . . this is like. . . . What d'you lot do at night? Watch telly to see how cops're meant to act? Why didn't you kick in the door, then, just like some stupid private eye. You think you can intimidate anyone, anytime, anywhere, and they're not going to step up and do something straight back at you. Well, you are so fucking wrong when it comes to me. I know how things're meant to work."

"I expect you do. Shall we go to the kitchen?"

One of the other bedroom doors opened. Bruce Castle, Lynley thought. That had been the boy's name. Behind him lurked the same girl from the previous day: Monica-who-doesn't-live-here. She was biting on the side of her index finger.

Bruce said, "Freeman, when're going to sort out this thing you have happening with all the coppers in your life? What's going on round here is getting annoying."

"Sod you and whoever the hell *she* is. And where the fuck is Ding?" He strode to the last of the doors and banged upon it. "You got someone in there, Ding? He doing it better than me or Brucie?"

Lynley took the boy by the arm, saying, "You've made all the necessary points, Finnegan."

Finn jerked away. "It's *Finn.* And you touch me again, I'll break your collarbone."

"Interesting skeletal choice," Lynley noted. "Are you ready for your tea now?"

Finn shot him what Lynley reckoned went for his best withering look and led the way to the stairs. These he banged down with grumblings suitable to the moment. In the kitchen, they found Havers, who had sorted out three mugs and a box of PG Tips. She said, "Milk's gone bad but there's something resembling sugar."

"I didn't say you lot could have our tea, did I?" Finn demanded. "I know my rights. You don't just bloody get to help yourself to—"

"We'll all use the same teabag," Havers told him. "I could go next door and borrow some water for the kettle as well, but I expect you'd like us to be gone, so why don't you start cooperating?"

He threw himself into one of the three chairs that served as a table in a corner of the room. Above it hung a bulletin board, pinned to it a schedule of cleaning duties meant to be fulfilled by the housemates. It was, obviously, something that the group of them ignored. This was especially true in the kitchen, where the sink was full of used and unrinsed crockery, the cooker resembled a science experiment gone badly wrong, cupboards gaped open, and work tops held an assemblage of tins and boxes and bags.

The kettle clicked off and Havers did the honours with the single teabag, as promised. She brought the mugs to the table. Finn said, "I want sugar, I do," and Havers handed him a bowl of something grey and solid, chunks of which he had to pry out with a teaspoon.

"So what d'you want?" Finn said to them. Surprisingly, he did not slurp his tea, although Lynley had steeled himself to hear the boy's lips flapping against the liquid. "I c'n give you exackly five minutes. I've a lecture to go to and you can't make me skip it. And don't think you can trap me because you can't. I'm not stupid, you know. And anyway, I know my—"

"Rights. Yes. You've made that clear. We can't hold you here, although something tells me that there isn't actually a lecture at this hour in the morning."

"Early bird and the worms, sir," Havers noted.

"Hmm. Yes. But I rather doubt that applies here."

"What do you *want*?" Finn demanded. "She sent you, right?"

"Your mum?" Havers said.

"Who bloody else."

"Why would she send us?" Lynley asked.

"You ask *her*. Like you think I would know?"

"She didn't send us. That's not how it works. We'd like to speak with you about Ian Druitt."

"Why do I keep having to talk about Ian? I've *said* what I've said and there's nothing to add. He was a good bloke, he was nice to everyone, he never put a finger on any of those kids. All of that was a bloody lie and no wonder someone reported him on the sly like he did because *no* one'd put his face in the light and say it about Ian. No one."

"Interesting that you know the anonymous call came from a man," Havers said.

"What? You think it was *me* made the call? I don't even know who you're s'posed to ring if you want to tell rubbish like that."

"That's interesting, that is, since your mum's a copper," Havers noted.

"Like I'd tell *her* if I thought bad about Ian, which I didn't and I don't and I never will."

"What if Ian thought 'bad' about you?" Havers said.

The boy lifted his tea. He *did* slurp then. "What's that mean when it's on the news?"

"There were apparently some concerns about you," Lynley told him.

"Turns out," Havers added, "Mr. Druitt wanted to speak to your parents."

"No fucking way," Finn said. "Ian didn't even know my parents. He didn't even meet them, ever."

"We're on board with that," Havers said. "He was asking round for their phone numbers."

"Who told you that shit?"

Havers held up her hands in a *whoa* gesture, saying, "Privileged information, that. But I can guarantee—and so can the inspector here—that he wanted a word and the subject was you."

"That's rubbish. If Ian had a problem with me, he would've talked to me directly. That's how he was. And he *didn't* have a problem with me, 'cause I did exactly what I was meant to do. I was meant to help the kids with this and with that when they came to the meetings and that's what I did. I was meant to show them the Internet for school prep and how they could use it and that's what I did. I was meant to organise games for them and make them teams for competitions and the like and that's what I did."

"Nice. Right. All the rest. But it seems Ian Druitt wasn't concerned with what you were *meant* to do. Seems he was concerned with what you might've been doing that you weren't meant to do."

"Like what? Selling drugs? Talking up weed? Giving them E? What about teaching 'em how to crawl through doggy doors so we could rip off houses together?"

"All interesting possibilities," Havers acknowledged. "Which seems the likeliest to you?"

"The word Mr. Druitt used was *impact*," Lynley said. "He expressed concern over the impact you were having on the children."

"Far as I know, I was meant to have an impact," Finn said.

"Could be yes, could be no," Havers said. "Could also be that when Mr. Druitt said *impact*, he was using a . . . what's the fancy word, sir?"

"Euphemism," Lynley replied.

"Right. That's it. There being all sorts of impacts, if you know what I mean," Havers said to the boy.

Finn was silent. Outside, Havers's early birds went about their business with the worms, cheeping brightly as they did so. A car started with a roar as someone used its engine ill, possibly thinking this was actually good for it. Finn looked from Havers to Lynley and back to Havers. He slouched further in his chair, put his hands round his mug of tea, and said, "Why don't you spit out what it is you got to say so I can toss you from the premises?"

"If Mr. Druitt developed concerns about your interactions with the children in the club," Lynley said, "that's what he may have wanted to speak to your parents about."

"So?"

"So there's more than one kind of interaction," Havers said. "There's the kind you've already described: where you play big brother to a collection of nippers who look at you and think you're the next King Arthur. And then there's the kind you might prefer no one to see or to know about. And if someone saw *those* interactions, that could be unpleasant all the way round."

"I don't even know what you're on about," Finn said.

Havers said, "Here's what it is, Finn. We've got this web of facts and figures and who knew what and who did what and what happened next. And we keep getting led back to the centre of the web, where the spider is. And that spider keeps looking exactly like you."

"We've also learned that your father asked the PCSO here in town to keep an eye on you," Lynley told him. "So it looks as if he—your father, that is—had his own concerns."

"No way." Finn licked his lips. His tongue looked grey. His gaze shifted to Havers. Then back to Lynley. He looked like a boy whose bravado had suddenly been stripped from his body.

"Which part no way?" Havers asked. "Because I expect you can see what it looks like from our perspective." She gestured aimlessly to her right, saying, "I also expect you know how easy it is to tiptoe up Weeping Cross Lane—practically outside your front door this is—and from there to the nick with no one the wiser, 'specially at night. You can saunter right into the car park, you can, and not be caught on CCTV, since it doesn't work. You can even go in the back door of the station. And if Gary Ruddock is doing what he sometimes is doing with his lady friend in a patrol car—"

"Gaz doesn't even have a girlfriend. He whinges about that often enough."

"—then you can pretty much do anything at the police station, including ringing the call centre—"

"I told you! I got no idea about that stupid anonymous whatever-it-was about Ian and it wasn't true anyways!"

"—or even locating Mr. Druitt one night last March and giving him the chop since Mr. Druitt might have seen something he wasn't supposed to see."

"*What*? No way! Who spun all this for you? Was it Gaz? 'Cause if it was, he was lying. Or Ian was lying. Or some little kids who got their feelings hurt by me and I don't even know it is lying. But here's what it is: I don't have to talk to you anymore and I'm not going to. You got *that*? Because this is all rubbish and I'm not listening to it and *whatever* anyone's said about me is a filthy lie."

He shoved his chair back with a scrape on the lino that it wouldn't soon recover from, and stamped out of the room. At first it looked as if he intended to do a runner when he opened the front door. But then he shouted, "You lot get out! I know what you're doing and I'm not playing. Get out!"

When neither of them moved from where they were in the kitchen doorway, he slammed the front door closed so forcefully that the windows shook in the kitchen. He pounded up the stairs and did the same to his bedroom door.

"That's some protest." Havers started to head for the front door herself when above them, a door opened, footsteps padded on the landing, and then a girl's voice said, "Finn? Are they gone?" Gentle knocking on his door. "You in there, Finn? What did they want?"

Havers looked at Lynley. He held up his hand. They waited. Silence and then the girl herself came down the stairs. She saw them and stopped dead. She wore a thin cotton nightdress that she clutched virginally at her throat. Dena Donaldson. She began to turn to go back up the stairs.

Lynley said, "If we could have a word, Dena."

"Why?"

"For the sake of curiosity."

"About what?"

"Rabiah Lomax."

She remained where she was. She looked at them in turn. She said, "I haven't done anything. I don't see why I need to talk to you."

"You don't need to. We're merely requesting. You can deny the request."

"Which," Havers added, "would make us wonder why."

"A great many things are centring on this house," Lynley said. "You might be able to clarify at least one of them, and we'd be in your debt."

Dena didn't look as if she were anywhere close to being on board with that idea, but she came slowly down the stairs. She was not a tall girl, Lynley noted. She was shapely, however, and quite pretty as well, although at the moment her face was pinched.

She joined them and said, "All right. What do you want me to clarify?"

"Thank you," Lynley said. "You can clarify your relationship to Rabiah Lomax."

"Why?"

"Because she appears to be on the periphery of what we're here looking into."

"That's got nothing to do with me."

"Accepted."

She said nothing to this. Havers said, "So if you wouldn't mind . . . ?"

"I know Missa. Her granddaughter. Missus Lomax came over here yesterday 'cause she had a message for me from her, from Missa."

"Odd that it couldn't have been given by phone," Havers noted.

"Missa had a necklace off me. She forgot to give it back. Mrs. Lomax brought it."

"Was it a message or the necklace?" Lynley asked.

"What? It couldn't've been both?"

"What was the message?" Havers asked.

Dena cocked her head and observed the sergeant. She said, "I don't think I have to tell you that. It was personal, and I don't expect it has anything to do with why you're here. She had a boyfriend, she broke up with him, they're back together. That's all I'm saying."

"What about you?" Havers said. "You have a boyfriend 's well?"

"Not at present."

"Not even Gary Ruddock?"

"Who?"

"The PCSO. I saw you with him one night at the police station. In a car, actually. What was that about?"

Dena's gaze flitted from Havers to Lynley back to Havers. She said, "I don't even know that bloke. *All* I know is he comes round the Hart and Hind whenever there's the tiniest complaint about the noise because everyone round there goes to bed, like, at half past seven. But there's no way I would be in a patrol car with him. Okay? So I've answered your questions and if you don't mind, I'm going back upstairs. I've got a—"

"Lecture, right," Havers said. "The whole boiling kettle of you are real scholars, aren't you?"

They watched the girl go back up the stairs and heard a door shut. The roar of water into the bathtub began a moment later.

Havers said to Lynley, "Swear to God that was the girl with Ruddock, sir."

Lynley said, "It's impossible to be certain, Sergeant. At night. The car in the shadows anyway."

"Right. Except for one thing."

He glanced at her. She looked oddly happy. "What's that?" he asked her.

"I never mentioned a *patrol* car. She's the one who said it was."

He directed his gaze up the stairway again. He nodded thoughtfully. "We'll need someone to confirm," he said.

"Right. I know who can probably do it. We just need to find him."

WORCESTER
HEREFORDSHIRE

Trevor Freeman hadn't the first clue who would be ringing him at such an hour of the morning. It wasn't even half past six. But then he saw the name of the caller on his mobile's screen, and his skin jumped uneasily. He pushed away the bedcovers, grabbed his phone, said, "Finn? You all right?" In answer, he heard what sounded like a combination of shouting and sobbing.

He could understand nothing. He said, "Slow down. I can't understand you. What's happened? Has there been an accident? For God's sake, Finn, take a breath. Are you sitting? No? Sit down. Find a place. Sit *down*. I'm here. Just put yourself in order."

He waited. He heard noises: snuffling, shuffling, heavy breathing like a runner's, and then the story. It came from his son in fits and starts but he got the gist of it easily enough: New Scotland Yard, the same detectives who'd come to Worcester to speak with Clover, something to do with pots and pans and his bedroom, and then the claim, the accusation, the grilling, the whatever the hell you wanted to call it and it was easy enough—wasn't it easy—when it did not involve your son. By the end of Finn's fractured recitation of the facts, Trevor felt a claw grab his lungs. He got himself together enough to calm the boy, which was mostly an attempt to reassure him that his father was going to handle this.

"Dad, he lied. He *lied*."

Trevor didn't know if he meant Gaz Ruddock or Ian Druitt. He said, "I'll see to it, Finn. You're not to do anything. Do you understand?"

"That whole bit about the kids . . . I only ever did what I was meant to, Dad . . . I wouldn't . . . Why would anyone say . . . And now they think . . . and they've got it in their heads I went to the police station . . . I didn't do *anything*, not a fucking thing."

"Let me handle this, Finn. Will you trust me to do that?"

"What? *What*?"

"Just wait. Don't do anything. I'll be in touch."

"I want to fucking—"

"Right. I know. I'd feel the same. But keep your distance. Trust me."

When he rang off, he could feel that the claw twisting a path to his bowels. Dimly he heard the radio below in the kitchen. Morning news was playing. She was still at home. But of course she would be. Twenty-five minutes after the hour. She would not have left for work yet. He started for the bedroom door, realised he was naked, and searched round for his shorts on the floor. As he was doing this, the radio snapped off, footsteps followed, and then the sound of the front door opening and closing and he understood she had left the house.

He dashed to the window. But her back was to him and she was inside the car before he had the presence of mind to bang on the glass. Then he grabbed up his shorts, pulling them on and racing down the stairs, but she was gone before he got the front door open because ever the security buff, she had double-locked it and the key wasn't on its hook.

She'd hidden it from him! She'd expected this. She'd known it was coming, and she wasn't intending to be there to face the consequences of what she was bringing down upon them all.

He ransacked the single drawer in the entry table that served the purpose of holding their day's post till they could get to it. The key wasn't there. Then into the kitchen and shoving things round the work top. Then at last the table, where the key lay in the basket of paper table napkins and God, he hadn't put it there, he *swore* it, she had to have done it. He grabbed it and made for the door and ran outside to the street, where his car was parked.

It was when he tried to insert the key that he saw how badly his hands were shaking. So were his knees and so were his arms and what *was* it that was causing him to quake like a child alone in the dark: anger, fear, terror, anxiety, despair . . . Could one shake from despair?

He set off after her. She was a creature of habit. Weren't they all when it came to the routes they took to their jobs? It wasn't a time for a leisurely drive. It was a case of get there the fastest and easiest way, which, in Clover's case, meant the A38.

When he reached that road, he switched on his hazard lights. He used the horn. There was one dual carriageway on the route and when he came upon it, he pulled into the right lane and pressed the pedal to the floor. He'd caught her up within five miles as she was driving sensibly, not at all like him. She pulled over at the first opportunity. It wasn't a lay-by, just a broader than normal stretch of verge edged by poplars. There, they both got out of their cars, he with his mobile, which he waved at her, she looking puzzled as well she would since there he was shirtless, shoeless, wearing only his shorts, the cool morning air making his bollocks shrink.

She said, "I have it in my bag, Trev. That must be yours. You should've just rung me, and you would have known."

"It's all gone to hell," he told her. "*Whatever* the two of you are up to, it's all gone to hell."

She blanched at his tone. "What's going on? You're scaring me."

"What's going on is our son. He's just phoned me. I've never heard him in the state he's in."

"Is he . . . Did he . . . ?"

"Those two London detectives appeared at his bedside like the ghost of whatever Christmas you want it to be. They woke him out of a sound sleep, dragged him into the kitchen, and grilled him."

"My God." She looked at the phone he still was holding. Then she looked beyond him at the traffic that continued to whizz by far too close to where they were standing, and she drew him between their two cars. "What did he say? Where is he? He wasn't arrested, was he?"

"When I could understand him between the shrieks and sobs—"

"He's at home, isn't he? He hasn't been arrested, has he?"

"The cops came to talk to him about what he's been up to with the six-year-olds or eight-year-olds or *however* old they are in that fucking after-school club that you *bloody* insisted he take on as a social duty. Your London coppers—"

"They are *not* my coppers."

"—have apparently concluded that Druitt's concerns about Finn must have had to do with Finn and children. So what I want to know is, did you know this from the first?"

"Know what? That the London police were going to—"

"Bollocks to the London police. Did you know that Druitt's phone calls to Gaz were about Finn's behaviour round the children? Is *this* what everything's been about between you two?"

"I've *tried* to explain it to you, Trevor. This is about the Met, start to finish. I know how they think and I know how they work. The first time round when they were in Ludlow, I tried to tell Finnegan that he wasn't to speak to them without someone there, but he wouldn't listen and now here we are. This is *exactly* what I feared."

"What? That the cops would decide our son's a child molester?"

"Of course not! It was the Metropolitan Police, full stop. I never wanted him to face them alone for *any* reason but he wouldn't see the importance of that. He thought he would be a match for them, for whatever they had to ask him, because he thought it was all about Ian Druitt and children. And it *was* about that and about the IPCC investigation and I bloody well thought we were through with it all. Yet here they are again and—"

"He thinks you set them on him, you and Gaz. Now why would he think that, Clover?"

"Stop being ridiculous. Look, you're shivering. Can we at least get into one of the cars if we're going to go at it?"

"Don't do your usual."

"Which is *what*?"

"Which is trying to position me where you want me to be. Which, as we both goddamn know, you're expert at doing."

She raised her hands as if she wanted to make them into fists or pull her hair out or seek guidance from the heavens. She said, "Trevor, *why* would I set the Met on our son? I've spent his life trying to protect him from himself, so why at this goddamn eleventh hour would I decide the effort's just too much trouble and have at him, London, because I give up?"

"Because that makes one hell of an excellent smokescreen," he said. "Especially if you know there isn't a shred of evidence against him, so it won't matter what happens to him in the short term since you're looking at the long run."

She took this in with a slow inhalation. She was, he knew, either garnering inner reserves of calm or merely trying to look like someone garnering inner reserves of calm. She said, "You say directly what you're implying."

"There are things you don't want anyone knowing—including me—and this is one hell of a good way to accomplish that."

"'Things'? What things?"

"You tell me, Clover. I'm sick and tired of being played for a fool."

"That's what you think?"

"That's what I think."

She stepped towards him. She spoke directly into his face. "You listen to me," she hissed. "I didn't want him at West Mercia College, but I agreed to it. I didn't want him in accommodation, but I agreed to it. Yes, I've had doubts that he can ever manage his life on his own, but I went along with what he wanted and what you wanted. And now just look where we are. God knows *what* he's said to those Met detectives. God knows *what* they think. I would like you—just for once, Trevor—to see that what's going on just now has nothing to do with my relationship with our son or my relationship with anyone on the planet. If you want to stand there and accuse me of interfering in Finnegan's life, you might also want to take a look at your *own* bloody focus on every interaction he and I have ever had. And that probably includes how I changed his nappies. We've been at loggerheads over him since the day he was born, and I suggest you look at *that*. I also suggest you look at where we are now because of it. Now I'm going to work to see what can be done about all of this because you and I can at least agree on one bloody thing regarding Finnegan's life."

"Which is what?" he demanded.

"Which is that there isn't a shred of evidence that Finnegan did anything to anyone at any time. That's what needs to be dealt with first. As to the rest of it"—she gestured between the two of them—"we shall have to deal with that later."

She turned then and strode back to her car. She'd left it running, so it was a simple matter for her to drive off and leave him standing there, unsure which of them had scored how many points.

LUDLOW
SHROPSHIRE

Barbara Havers had expected to engage in something of a search through the centre of town to find Harry Rochester. She was surprised, therefore, to see him crossing the Ludford Bridge as she and Lynley were heading in the direction of Broad Street's climb up to the mediaeval heart of the town. She pointed him out to Lynley, who pulled over to the kerb, saying, "You take this, Sergeant. I don't think it needs both of us."

When she climbed out of the car and called out to the dosser, he gave her a jaunty wave with his flute. He called back, "This is early hours for you, isn't it, Barbara?"

"You, too," she said. "Can I have a word?"

"Certainly."

They met at the foot of the bridge on the Ludlow side. Barbara greeted Sweet Pea, who was, as always, obediently at Harry Rochester's thigh. The Alsatian's tail wagged when Barbara said her name, but she waited at her master's side to be greeted.

"Are you already so early at work?" Harry said to Barbara.

"I'm generally engaged with a pillow in a meaningful way at this hour, but we had something needed doing early. Where're you coming from? You and Sweet Pea having an early morning stroll?"

"Yes and no," he said. "We spent the night above the river."

"Get tossed from the centre of town?"

"No, no. When the weather improves, Pea and I sometimes like a bit of nature on the occasional evening. There's something of an open area along the Breadwalk with quite a nice view of the castle. And it has the added benefit of being off the path far enough that I can leave my belongings there—such as they are—and go about my day unburdened. Or I can pick them up in the evening and choose a spot lower down on the bank. On this side of the river, of course, as there's too much of a bluff on the other." He vaguely indicated an area beyond the Charlton Arms. "Are you familiar with the Breadwalk?" he said, settling in for a natter. "People from town take exercise there. Strolling, biking, running, walking their dogs. It's a very good route between the bottom of Dinham Street and here."

"A shortcut?"

"Yes. And what I find fascinating is its history. It's called the Breadwalk because the workers who used it in ages past were paid not in coin but in bread. This was to keep them from drinking down their wages on their way home and arriving there with no food for their families. Not a bad idea, when you consider man's weakness for the drink."

"But a bit annoying if one has a plan to put something away for one's golden years, eh?"

"Well, yes, there is that little problem, isn't there, although I'm not certain anyone actually lived long enough to have golden years in those days. Would you like to accompany us, Sergeant? Pea and I were heading up to Castle Square."

"With something to flog?"

"Alas, not today. We're interested in the stalls as it's a food market morning and we're feeling peckish. And—which is particularly interesting to Pea, here—the sausage caravan will be present. It's early for them to be selling yet, but we'd like to pay a very quick visit to the Spar to pick up a few supplies of a personal grooming nature being held for me at the till. I wouldn't say no to finding a copy of the *Guardian* as well, although the news is always a day old and bad anyway, so one does occasionally ask oneself what the point is. But one feels the need now and then and today I feel the need."

"Premonition?"

"I hope not, as my premonitions are generally disaster laden: earthquakes, tsunamis, hurricanes, tornadoes, entire towns falling into the sea. That sort of thing. Are you with the inspector?"

"He's back in the car." She gestured in the direction from which she'd walked to meet Harry at the bridge. "Want a ride up to the square, then?"

"I couldn't possibly cope with being inside a car. I can barely manage thirty seconds inside the Spar to pay for my purchases. Can I help you in some way, Barbara? I ask because while I'm quite pleased with the early morning greeting, when it comes from a member of the police force, one tends to think there might a secondary agenda."

"Wise way to look at things. It's to do with the PCSO, actually." Barbara reminded Harry of what he'd told her: seeing Gary Ruddock with various young people, squiring them home or to the police station or to wherever it was he took them when they were causing aggro late at night in the town. Did Harry remember telling her that?

Indeed he did, he told her.

She asked him if he thought he would recognise any of them if he saw them again, but not in the company of the PCSO. To that, he told her that he wasn't at all sure. When he'd seen Mr. Ruddock with young people, it was often at night, it was generally quite late, or if not late it was usually dark. Unless they passed under a streetlamp, he wouldn't have got a good look at them. So he couldn't swear with any degree of certainty about anything. Plus, there was the difficulty of seeing young people all round the town anyway, and especially in the vicinity of Castle Square, with its access to West Mercia College. Thus it would be difficult for him, seeing a young person after the fact, to say that he or she was also someone he'd seen previously in the company of Gary Ruddock. Did the sergeant understand what he meant?

She did, naturally. But, "Would you be willing to have a go anyway?"

"Certainly. Should I ring you if I happen to see a familiar face?"

Barbara told him that, no, she had something different in mind. Now that the weather was improving—although England being England, it would probably all go to hell with the advent of

June—would he be willing to meet her and the inspector at the Hart and Hind this evening?

He would indeed be willing, he told her, as long as he could meet her and the inspector outside even in the event of a cloudburst and as long as he could also remain in the company of Sweet Pea.

Barbara agreed to this. So they set a time and said their farewells. Barbara returned to Lynley. He'd got out of the car, she saw, and was contemplating the weir. A female mallard and her ducklings were tranquilly paddling there.

Lynley said, "He's out and about early, isn't he?"

"Says he likes a change of scenery when the weather allows it."

Lynley nodded but looked thoughtful. After a moment, he said, "That's quite good to know, isn't it. It makes him available for all sorts of things: to act, to be acted upon, to be a witness to action."

"That's what I thought, sir." She told Lynley about the plan she'd laid with Harry Rochester: the Hart and Hind, that evening, fingers crossed about who might turn up. She was just concluding when her mobile phone rang. She had to do a bit of excavating, but she found it before it went to message.

It turned out to be Flora Bevans, yet another early riser. She said she'd had a thought, one she'd tossed round in her head to decide if it had any value at all. "I certainly don't want to muddy the waters," she said. "But I've recalled something having to do with Ian that I failed to tell you earlier."

Barbara gave a thumbs-up to Lynley. She said, "Any information is helpful," and waited for what that information was.

"It has to do with my sister, actually," Flora Bevans said. "As you're in town—at least I assume you're in town—"

"Standing right by the Ludford Bridge admiring the waterfowl."

"Oh yes. It's quite lovely, isn't it, that bridge, with those wonderful spars for pedestrians. I'm quite fond of it."

"And your sister . . . ?"

Flora didn't assume Barbara was enquiring about her sister's affection or lack thereof for the bridge. She said, "This was several months ago. Greta rang me and asked if Ian might be willing to speak to one of the students at the college. I can't remember whether it was a male or female student—I'm not sure I ever knew in the first place, frankly—but what I do remember is that Greta asked me if I'd pass along a message to Ian to phone her so that she could explain as it seemed rather an urgent matter."

"Is she connected to the college in some way?" Barbara asked.

"Oh. Sorry. I've left that part out, haven't I? She's a counsellor at West Mercia College, the only one there is, actually."

"So this was about . . . what? Something she couldn't handle herself? Beyond her expertise or whatever?"

"I expect it was more to do with her workload. She's fully qualified for the job she does but getting to things is the issue since there is one of her and . . . I actually have no idea how many students there are, but it's got to be hundreds, hasn't it. On the other hand, if the student was in some kind of spiritual crisis, Ian would have been better as a counsellor since Greta gave up religion as an adolescent. At any rate, I thought you ought to know about it as it had to with Ian. Shall I give you her number? I'm sure she'd be happy to talk to you."

Barbara told her that yes, indeed, Greta's number would be appreciated. And if anything else popped into Flora Bevans's mind, she wasn't to hesitate, day or night.

"I hope you find it marginally helpful," Flora Bevans said.

"Everything is," Barbara assured her. She rang off and related the information to Lynley. He agreed it wanted looking into.

"After breakfast?" he suggested.

She was happy to hear this. "You know me, sir. Last thing I'd ever say no to is a meal."

ST. JULIAN'S WELL
LUDLOW
SHROPSHIRE

When she'd volunteered for the duty, Rabiah Lomax hadn't given the slightest thought to the fact that chairing the Maintenance and Repairs Committee of *Volare, Cantare* might be quite a time devourer. Why would it be? The beauty of a glider was the fact that in comparison to a motorised plane, there was very little to maintain or repair. But her taking up the position of chair was soon followed by one of the club member's forgetting to engage the undercarriage prior to landing, and who would pay for the subsequent damage to the plane was the hottest topic they'd come upon in years. Obviously, one group asserted, the pilot ought to pay. Unfair, another group declared, as their dues were supposed to cover *something* besides drinks and nibbles at their monthly meetings in Church Stretton, weren't they, and by the way, what about their insurance? A fortuitous occurrence, announced the third, since really shouldn't they start thinking of purchasing an entirely new glider anyway? Every year more bells and whistles were added to gliders in the form of safety features and technical components. Theirs was a virtual antique, and this was a moment they could seize, making use of it to benefit everyone. Thus the Maintenance and Repairs Committee were tasked with making a recommendation and the club members were tasked with agreeing to it. Thus each proponent of a solution to the problem had sent a representative to be part of the meeting on this particular morning. Rabiah was only too glad she'd insisted on a relatively early start because it looked as if Dennis Crook and Ngaio Marsh Stewart (whose mother had obviously had a thing for Roderick Alleyn) would prefer to resort to fisticuffs in the street rather than compromise.

They'd just reached the point of Ngaio's "See here, my good man"—always an indication that more was to come and it wasn't likely that the more would be pleasant—when the doorbell sounded. Rabiah excused herself, rather thankful to have an escape from the rising tension, although when she saw who'd come calling upon her, she was equally thankful to have an excuse not to let them into the house.

"I'm quite sorry," she said, "but I've got something on at the moment." Detective Inspector Lynley, she reminded herself, was the man. The woman was Sergeant Havers. "It's a committee meeting, and I'm the chair."

"We're happy to wait," Lynley replied.

"Love to listen in as well," Havers added.

"Unfortunately, there's not enough seating. And the topic is nothing that will please, I guarantee you. An argument over the purchase or repair of a glider."

"Sounds exciting to me," Havers said. "What about you, sir?"

"Indeed," from Lynley. "But if there's no room for us—"

"I'll ring you when we've finished."

"—we can easily wait in the kitchen. Or your garden. Or we can speak here on the pavement if you'd like to step outside."

"We've had a word with Greta Yates at West Mercia College, Mrs. Lomax," Havers said, in a tone far less friendly than that which was carried on her earlier words. "Turns out that in a roundabout fashion, she put Ian Druitt—the deacon? I reckon you remember him—into contact with a girl called Melissa, surname Lomax. To me and the inspector here . . . ? We were thinking that what we have is one of two things. Either one hell of a coincidence with two Lomaxes being counselled by a bloke who turns up dead in the local nick, or one Lomax being counselled by the bloke while the other Lomax tells tales to the coppers who're trying to work out what the hell happened to him."

Lynley said, "Do you care to shed any light on this, Mrs. Lomax? Ms. Yates was good enough to give us Melissa Lomax's details—"

"That means we can track her down," the sergeant added politely.

"—but we thought you might wish to illuminate the matter."

"You don't need to, 'course," the sergeant went on, "but things keep getting curiouser and curiouser, if you know what I mean, since Dena Donaldson *also* has a connection to your granddaughter and we're wondering what that's all about when it's tucked up in bed. Turns out that Melissa's mobile number matches one that Mr. Druitt phoned on two occasions, by the way. I've rung it myself, but all I get is one of those automated messages. The owner of the phone—that would be Melissa, I reckon—hasn't returned my call."

Rabiah had felt the sweat on the backs of her knees the moment Greta Yates's name had been spoken. She was determined, however, not to be cowed. She needed to buy herself some time, though, and she tried to use the committee meeting once again to do so. It was a complicated matter they were dealing with, it was going to take more time than they wanted to wait about, surely. She would ring them—

"As I said, we're quite happy to wait. You might want to ring your solicitor as well."

"Since spinning tales for the rozzers is never quite the idea," Havers added.

Rabiah saw no other choice. She said, "If you'll wait in the kitchen . . . And I'd be grateful if you didn't introduce yourself to anyone as the police."

"I'm fine with that," Havers said. "What about you, sir? Good at posing as a roofer, are you? Or a plumber since we'll be in the kitchen?"

"If only I'd thought to bring my spanner."

Rabiah hustled them into the house. She rejoined the subcommittee meeting, where it had been decided in her absence that the only solution was going to be bringing the matter to the entire club for a vote. The committee could recommend nothing, it seemed. The three factions could reach no compromise.

By the time she'd shut the door on the last of them, Rabiah had made her decision about what she wanted to say. She went into the kitchen—astonished when the man actually stood politely, something she hadn't seen from a male in years—and she began before they could pose a question.

"When you first came to speak with me, my main concern was the protection of my granddaughter. The lives of her entire family—of *my* entire family—have undergone an upheaval. Missa's younger sister died over a year ago after a long illness. Missa wanted to leave West Mercia College and return home to be a support to her youngest sister. Sati—her youngest sister—wanted it, but no one else thought it was a good idea. Missa first brought it up over the Christmas holiday but was talked into returning to the college. It was clear she wasn't happy about it, but none of us knew she was seeing Mr. Druitt for support. And I certainly didn't know when you lot first came calling. I wanted to speak with Missa before I turned her over to you. I'm sure you would have done the same had you found yourself in a similar position."

"Perhaps she was seeing the deacon for another reason," Lynley said.

"She's not a liar," Rabiah said. "Things have been difficult for everyone since Janna's death, and things were terrible enough leading up to it. She had very good reason to want to speak with someone."

"Except since Greta Yates turned her name over to Ian Druitt, it's not like your granddaughter sought him out herself," Havers noted.

"Regardless of how she got there, what can Missa's seeing him possibly have to do with his death?"

"We have no answer for that," Lynley told her.

"But we're working at it," Havers added. "See, it's turning out that everyone's connected to everyone else: We speak to you about Ian Druitt, we see you speaking to Dena Donaldson, Dena Donaldson lives in the same house as Finnegan Freeman, Finnegan Freeman assisted Ian Druitt with his after-school club, Ian Druitt had meetings with your granddaughter, your granddaughter is a close friend of Dena Donaldson."

"The number of connections is rather remarkable," Lynley said.

"I can explain where I fit easily enough," Rabiah countered. Now her armpits were dampening as well. "There was a misunderstanding I was clarifying with Dena. I'd assumed that she was using our name because *she* was meeting with Ian Druitt."

"Why did you assume that?" Havers asked.

"It seemed logical as she and Missa were close friends."

Lynley was watching her, his expression frankly appraising. Rabiah noticed his eyes, which were brown. Odd in a blond, she thought. There was a tight little silence among them. In it, a car drove by, that irritating rap music pounding from its open window. Lynley finally said, "Might we return to the possibility of your granddaughter seeing the deacon for an altogether different reason from the one she's given you?"

Good Lord, Rabiah thought, the man spoke courteously. Her defences immediately rose. She said, "We're not a spiritual family, if that's what you mean. I can't imagine Missa meeting with him to discuss Jesus, the Trinity, afterlife, or any other topic associated with religion."

"There were condoms in Mr. Druitt's car. An open box with a number of them missing."

"You're suggesting a sexual relationship between Missa and the man? No. It's unthinkable. Missa has a longtime boyfriend in Ironbridge, and even if that were not the case, she's put great store in being a virgin when she marries. Old-fashioned, I know, but there you have it."

"Sometimes girls do that," Havers said. "I mean sometimes they say they intend to stay pure or whatever . . . until they don't, if you know what I mean."

"That she found the deacon compelling and decided to sleep with him? That's hardly in character."

Lynley said, "We're going to have to speak with her. You do see that, I hope."

Rabiah did see it, only too well. But speaking to Missa was the last thing she wanted because the waters of her family were troubled enough already. She said, "Please don't. She has nothing to tell you. This poor man who died . . . ? It's nothing to do with her. How can I get you to see that?"

And of course, she knew the answer to her question even as she voiced it.

LUDLOW
SHROPSHIRE

Yasmina Lomax believed that the real source of her daughter's troubles sprang from the death of her younger sister. From being witness not only to Janna's death but also to the potential dissolution of her parents' marriage as a result of that death had sprung Missa's determination to alter her own life. But she'd chosen a way to do this that was going to be self-defeating. It was because of this that Yasmina had attempted to speak with Missa that morning. It was because of this that she cancelled her appointments at the clinic and made the journey to Ludlow.

With Missa, Yasmina had got nowhere. She had risen early—grateful for once that Timothy had drugged himself into a state from which his alarm failed to awaken him—and she'd gone to her daughter's bedroom. She'd opened the door softly and paused there, taking in Missa's sleeping form and then the room itself. She wondered why she'd failed to find it odd that the room was unchanged from Missa's childhood: beloved children's books tucked into their shelves; dolls in their respective positions on top of a chest beneath the window; a stuffed bear long ago given the silly name Eeshy Beeshy for reasons no one remembered; the jewellery box atop the chest of drawers, which, when opened, displayed a plastic ballerina dancing on a mirror to "Lara's Theme," that musical paean to doomed love, always sending out the message that giving into passion would lead to disaster.

Yasmina opened the jewellery box, the tinny music played, and from behind her she heard Missa stir in her bed and say, "Mum? What time is it?"

Yasmina closed the box, turned, and answered with, "We must speak, you and I. Will you come to the kitchen and have some tea or shall we speak here?"

Missa flipped onto her back. For a moment she looked only at the ceiling and Yasmina wondered if it would be the girl's intention not to speak at all. But then she sat up, took a sip from the glass of water on her bedside table, and said, "Here, then."

Yasmina drew the chair from the kneehole of Missa's desk and carried it to the bedside. She said, "Your grandmother told me about the London police coming to question her. She also told me about the conversation you and she had." She fancied seeing a hardness coming into Missa's expression. She went on. "One doesn't generally need to speak to a churchman about leaving college, Missa. So I want you to tell me what's really going on."

Missa looked away from Yasmina towards the window as if wishing she could join the chattering birds outside. She remained wordless.

Yasmina said, "I don't understand why you've come to think you can't talk to me. Something has happened. I can see that. Something besides wanting to leave college took you to see that man. But why you—"

"Why don't you tell me what *you* think has happened?" Missa cut in sharply. "Because what I can see from this side of things is that you refuse to accept that I'm not like you. I want something different in my life to what you've had and you can't cope with that."

Yasmina felt slapped by the reply. "That isn't true."

"No? Just look at the fact that you can't leave this alone. Here you are wanting to 'talk about it'"—she made air quotes round the final three words—"when I tried to tell you ages ago that what *I* want for myself isn't what *you* want for me and is never going to be what you want for me."

"Tell me now, then. What is it that you want?"

"Why should I tell you *again*? Have you actually forgotten? Right, then. Let's do this one more time. What I want is to be someone's wife, to be a mum, to have a simple life supporting the man I love and the children we have together. And since you can't entertain that idea in your head for one second, something *has* to be wrong with me. What's wrong with me, Mum, is that I needed the courage to be who I am and not who you want me to be. That's why I talked to Mr. Druitt, all right?"

"To build up your courage to speak to your own mother? You met with this man not once, not twice, but seven times to build up this courage?"

"Yes! And look how you're reacting. You're searching for some deep reason that I wanted to leave college when there *is* no deeper reason than the one that I gave you. Or at least that I tried to give you back in December when you wouldn't listen."

"I *did* listen."

"You heard. You didn't listen. Because all you said was that it was too soon, I needed to go back, I had to at least finish college even if uni wasn't for me. Don't you remember that? And I went back, didn't I? That's what I did because that's what I *always* do. No matter how I might feel about something, that's what I do: what *you* want. Or that's what I always did. So I talked to him—the deacon—seven times because I have no one here to talk to and no one who'll listen without jumping in and trying to make me into someone I'm not."

"And who is that?"

"I've said! I've just now said and even *that's* not good enough. You're not listening because you never listen when you've set something up in your mind."

"I am listening now. I'm trying to learn. I want to know how I've failed to such a degree that you had to seek out this deacon . . . *Did* you seek him out?"

"What difference does it make? No. I didn't. He found me and I'm grateful he did because he helped me understand things. He helped me see what was right for me to do and I've done it. And now I want to be left alone. All right? Leave me alone."

With that, she'd drawn the bedcovers up round her neck and turned her back. And Yasmina had given her the peace she wanted.

But things were not over between them, and it was the belief that there was more here than met the eye that took Yasmina from Ironbridge into Ludlow, where she drove to Broad Street, found an available parking spot, and walked the remaining distance to Castle Square. She wound through the market stalls and went beneath the arch on the square's northwest side. Upon it the words WEST MERCIA COLLEGE glittered in the sunlight of a beautiful spring day.

She discovered that the college counsellor, Greta Yates, was not in her office as she'd left to attend a meeting. She was welcome to wait, she was told, but there was no guarantee that Ms. Yates would have time to see her as her diary was generally filled. Yasmina decided she would take her chances. The matter was critical, she explained.

Forty minutes passed before the arrival of Greta Yates occurred. When she first came through the door, Yasmina found herself slipping into physician mode, bearing witness to what was in the process of killing the other woman: high blood pressure, weight, and type 2 diabetes. She was breathing heavily, her face was suffused with blood, and a sheen of perspiration spread across her brow. Once Yasmina managed to get into Greta Yates's office—which did not as take long as she'd been led to believe—she added the woman's workload to the list.

The state of the office suggested a burglary had recently occurred, one that required the criminals to dump everything from the room to the top of her desk and onto the floor surrounding it: filing folders, computer printouts, brochures, university pamphlets, books, and more. From her desk, Greta Yates brought forth a box of tissues. She took one, blotted her face with it, and then said to Yasmina, "These are unusual circumstances. This is the second time today that someone's been to see me about your daughter, Mrs. Lomax."

Yasmina didn't make the correction from Mrs. to Dr., as she would have under other conditions. The fact that someone else had been there to talk to the student counsellor about Missa was far more important. "Someone else?" she said.

"Two officers from New Scotland Yard."

Yasmina tried to get her head round this, as it meant either Rabiah had changed her mind and revealed to the police that there was a connection between Missa and Mr. Druitt or the police had some other reason for speaking to Greta Yates about her daughter. She tried to appear more confused than anxiety ridden about what was going on. She said, "I hope you don't mind telling me what their concern was. Missa's not in trouble with the police, is she?"

Greta Yates waved a plump and negating hand, one finger of which was dressed with an impressively large green stone. "Good heavens, no. They came to see me because I'd asked my sister if she would give a message to Mr. Druitt."

This was hardly making sense. "A message about Missa?"

"About meeting with Missa. You see"—she gestured round her office at the piles of material everywhere—"Melissa's tutor requested that I speak with her because she'd begun doing poorly in her studies. She'd done quite well during autumn term, but then she began to . . . the best expression would be slack off. Her tutor had had a private meeting with her and he wished me to do the same because she told him she wanted to leave the college and he had the impression something was wrong. Considering her age, he reckoned it was boy troubles, and she might want to talk it out with me."

"Did she tell him that?"

"She told him only that she wanted to leave college. But it was strange to him because, as I said, she'd done quite well autumn term."

"What did she say to you?"

"Well, that's just it. Her tutor had counselling sessions in mind. Sessions in the plural. And in a perfect world I *could* actually get round to counselling as that's what I trained to do. But in this world I can do little more than work through piles and piles of rubbish like this—please don't quote me on that—in an attempt to keep my head above water." Again she indicated the papers and files. "However," she added as Yasmina was about to speak, "I knew that my sister had a lodger who was a clergyman. She'd told me he had a degree in social work, so I asked her if he might be willing to have a go. He rang me and I gave him Missa's details. According to the police this morning, she did have a number of meetings with him."

"She's left college anyway. She won't speak of it other than to say that university is not for her so there's little point in her attendance here. But I don't believe her."

Greta did not look unsympathetic. "I understand your concern. Most parents would feel as you do. But what I've learned from years of working with young people is that there's a point when parental intervention is more a hindrance than a help."

"He's dead, you know. The clergyman. That has something to do with why the London police are here, evidently."

"Flora—my sister—did tell me he'd died. She said it was suicide." Greta was silent for a moment, looking across the room at a cluttered bulletin board but not seeming to see it. She said, "You aren't thinking your daughter had anything to do with that, are you?"

"I don't know what to think. She won't clarify anything. I speak to her. She shutters her face. She's a different person. I don't know why." Anxiety was rising within her. Yasmina could feel it shimmering behind her eyes. Missa, college, a dead clergyman, the future, the past, Janna's death, Timothy's drug use . . . Everything was swarming in her head and she had to make someone see that a crucial moment had been reached, and this crucial moment had to be explored or cracked open or smashed to bits or reversed or *something* because she didn't know what to do any longer and she needed someone to step in and take charge.

Greta said as if in answer to her roiling mind, "This has to be dealt with, obviously. Can you bring Missa here to Ludlow?"

"She'll refuse. She and I . . . at the moment . . ."

"Of course. Is there someone else who might get her here?"

Yasmina thought about this. There *was* someone, but he would have to be convinced to act against his own interests.

Greta went on. "If you can get her to me, I'll meet with her happily. Something may well have put her off college, and I believe I can get to the bottom of it. When I do, I'd like to offer her a return so that she can finish up the work from this term and then go on fresh next autumn." She leaned forward and clasped her hands in what seemed to be a gesture of sincerity. She added, "But please do understand, Mrs. Lomax, often all it takes is a period of time for young people to develop a bit more maturity so that they can see more clearly where they're heading and what the result is going to be if they continue to head there. Would I be correct if I said that it's been quite difficult for you to give her this period of time?"

"You would be, yes," Yasmina replied.

"Then your course seems clear, doesn't it? Find the person who can convince her to see me. Let that person do it. And then—as difficult as it is—be patient. We *will* sort this out."

WORCESTER
HEREFORDSHIRE

For the first time in only the devil knew how long, Trevor Freeman not only needed a workout, but he also wanted one. He reckoned if he drove himself hard enough he would be able to banish from his head the phone call he'd received from his son, the subsequent conversation he'd had with his wife, and the choices he now faced.

When he arrived at Freeman Athletics, he went straight to the treadmill. From there, he went to the free weights. From there he went to the stationary gym. From there he went back to the treadmill. His sweat dripped onto the floor round him, and one of the trainers set aside working with a client and came over to him for a word. Back off before you give yourself a heart attack, was what she said. What he thought was that a heart attack, the emergency services, and a stay in hospital might not be a bad idea.

Then the police arrived. He was surprised to see them, as he couldn't understand how they'd managed to track him down unless they'd gone to the house, found him not at home, and spoken to one of the neighbours. Also, he wondered why hadn't they just phoned him? Why trek all the way to Worcester?

But he answered his own questions once he saw their faces and the manner in which each of them made a study of him. Of course they wouldn't want to have a phone conversation. They would want to scrutinise his every twitch as he answered their questions.

When they asked to talk to him privately, he led the way to his office. He knew he was reeking, so he shut the door on the three of them. If they wanted to question him, they could also damn well breathe in the stench of his dripping body.

He said to the male officer, "I've had a phone call from my son. You talk to him again without my being there, and you'll be dealt with by your superiors. And what do you lot call it anyway, bursting into a boy's bedroom when he's sleeping and scaring the hell out of him?"

"He's been difficult to find at home," the man said. Lynley, Trevor thought. His name was Lynley.

The woman—a sergeant, he remembered—added, "We did knock and ring the bell. You might advise him to lock up at night. God knows who'll end up in bed with him if he doesn't secure the premises."

Lynley said, "I conclude he was disturbed by our call upon him?"

"If that's what you want to name it: your 'call upon him.' And how the hell do you expect him to feel?"

"He rang you and not his mum?" the sergeant said. "Odd that, since she's a copper. Odd, too, that he didn't ring the PCSO since he lives in the area."

"Your finding things 'odd' is your concern, not mine."

"It's just that we've been wondering—me and the inspector here—how the PCSO fits into the lives of the Freeman family."

"He's a decent lad. My wife took an interest, which is actually part of her job. And I don't see what this has to do with the two of you entering my son's bedroom at dawn."

"Don't think I'd call the PCSO a *lad*. What about you, sir?" she asked Lynley.

"He's rather old for that," Lynley agreed.

"What the hell difference does it make how old he is?" Trevor demanded. He couldn't work out what they wanted from him, nor could he see how they'd got him on the defensive so quickly when being on the defensive was exactly where he'd intended *them* to be. He said, "The training centre for support officers is on the grounds of police headquarters, where my wife works. Finn and I met Gaz Ruddock through her."

"Bring him home, did she?" Havers asked.

"My wife wanted our son to meet him. She thought he'd be a good influence. Like a big brother as Finn has no siblings. Things went from there."

"Where?" Havers asked.

"What?"

"Where did things go to from there?"

"You already know the answer to that. Aren't you wasting your time at this point?"

Lynley spoke. "If you wouldn't mind humouring us."

"Since we like to keep our facts from getting all knotted up," the sergeant added.

"The PCSO," Lynley went on, "told us—as you undoubtedly know—that the two of you developed a plan for him to keep an eye on your son in Ludlow."

"Clover's idea," Trevor said. "She didn't want to ask Gaz herself. She thought he might feel pressured to do it if she was the one making the request. Because of their relative positions."

"Which positions would those be, exactly?" from the sergeant.

Trevor was glad that his face was undoubtedly flushed from the workout because he could feel his reaction to the double entendre rising tidelike beneath his skin. "The obvious one. She outranks Gaz by quite some distance. She didn't want him to think he was required to do her any favours, so she brought it up with me. I thought it was a good idea, so I did the asking." So there it was, he thought. He'd done it. White, black, or any other colour, he'd lied as he'd been requested to lie. He didn't like to think what this suggested about him or his relationship with his wife.

"Why?" Lynley asked.

"I just told you."

Havers said, "He doesn't mean why were you the one to ask. He means why did you and your wife believe he needed watching over in the first place. You must have been worried about something."

"I'd call it cautious, not worried. Finn's always been a handful, and his mum's gut told her that he might not do well in Ludlow with unrestricted freedom as he's never had that. She's tried to structure how he uses his free time."

"At his age," Lynley said, "I expect that would rather chafe."

"What would?"

"What the inspector means," Havers clarified once again, "is that most boys Finn's age wouldn't much like their mums either organising their time *or* assigning someone to play their shadow."

"Gaz doesn't do that. He just keeps an eye out."

"Is that what Ian Druitt was meant to do as well?" Lynley asked.

Trevor didn't like the way they manoeuvred him from point to point. He felt batted between them like a shuttlecock. He took control back, saying, "That rubbish you said to Finn this morning? About Druitt having 'concerns' about him or whatever it was? Wherever the hell you got that idea, it's complete bollocks."

"Which part of it? Mr. Druitt having concerns about your son or Mr. Druitt expressing those concerns."

"Either one. Both. Finn's a good lad. No one will tell you any different."

"Yet evidently, Mr. Druitt wanted to tell *you* different," Havers said. "We got told he was trying to get in touch with you, asking how to do that."

"He didn't get in touch, so whatever he wanted to speak about—and I assume you mean these 'concerns' he was meant to have—must have been taken care of. He was reassured or whatever."

Lynley nodded thoughtfully. "It's the whatever that we're trying to deal with, Mr. Freeman."

"Meaning what, exactly?"

"Meaning that Mr. Druitt was dead before he could speak to you," Lynley said.

Sergeant Havers added, "And that's one of those things that the coppers like to look into, bollocks or not."

MUCH WENLOCK
SHROPSHIRE

Cardew Hall wouldn't be open daily to visitors until the first of June, so Ding knew her arrival there was going to be unexpected, which was exactly what she wanted it to be. Unexpected and, if she could manage it, unacknowledged and unknown. She wasn't entirely clear in her head why all of this needed to be the case. She just felt it in her body, which was drifting between tense and downright ill. There was, naturally, more than one reason for this.

The Hall and its surrounds had always been some sort of vortex for her because it was in this location and farther along the road in Much Wenlock that she'd begun her journey of fucking boys the very moment she could manage it. She'd told herself for a long time that she did it for a lark, that she did it for the story she could tell her mates later, that she did it because she felt the urge. But the truth was she did it for none of those reasons. The larger truth was that she didn't know *why* she did it except that it felt like violently spitting into some bloke's face and *that* was something she wanted to do all the time. And *why* she wanted to spit and more—to claw, to bite, to punch—the very moment some bloke took possession of her body . . . ? This was something she *had* to learn because, if nothing else, the experiment in fucking that she had been engaged in for years needed to reach a conclusion. So when she'd attended her two lectures for the day, keeping her promise to Greta Yates, she took the bus that would eventually deposit her in the vicinity of Cardew Hall.

She reckoned her mum would be in the vast old kitchen, making batch upon batch of the Cardew Hall jams and chutneys that were offered to tourists to purchase after their visits to the Hall. Her stepfather would be busy as well, checking the public rooms for burnt-out lightbulbs, for slut's wool missed by the weekly cleaners, and for furniture wanting polishing. If she was careful not to be seen or heard, she could have the place more or less to herself: time alone to investigate, cogitate, and meditate.

From where the bus stopped, it took her twenty minutes to trudge to the grounds of the Hall. There, she saw, nearly everything was in bloom, so that the gardens and their beds were awash in colour, from the yellow primroses that edged the herbaceous borders to the purple iris that formed a casual backdrop and softened the effect of the stone boundary walls.

From the drive, she could also see the slate roof of St. James Church, the parish church but also the lord-of-the-manor church. It was where Ding's ancestors with their piles of money had nodded regally to their retainers—poor sods—as they serenely floated down the aisle to their special pew. That pew still had the family name upon it. Not Donaldson, of course, since the family name in question was her mother's and not her dad's.

That thought stopped her: her dad. Not the surname but the fact of him. Another thought seemed to accompany *dad*, resting just on the edge of her consciousness. She hesitated, her gaze on the church's tower, and tried to trick that thought out of her memory. But what came was only a feeling of hollowness and, along with it, a kind of quivering just beneath her skin that suggested . . . fear? Yes, it *was* fear.

She needed to get out of the sight of that church, she decided, although when she did so by walking round the ancient building that was her home, she really felt no different. She went to the back, to the cellar door, which was accessed by stone steps so old that they bore the indentations of hundreds of years of other people's feet upon them.

Once inside, she was in a stone-floored corridor, dimly lit by weak overhead bulbs that hung from flexes. The prominent features of the place were the damp, cobwebs, and dust so thick that the beams in the walls looked grey rather than what they would be if one ran a finger along them: black from having been fashioned from English oaks and taken from various parts of ancient ships.

This corridor led to the vast underbelly of Cardew Hall, to its working innards. These consisted of places the public never saw: the kitchen, the larder, the pantry, the scullery, the wine cellar, the root cellar, the laundry where in times past young girls "born into service," as the expression had it, had worn their hands raw with the washing.

Ding paused in the semi-darkness and listened. A radio was on, which meant that her mother was in the kitchen, as Ding had suspected would be the case. She could smell the fragrance of cooking fruit as well. That was a very good thing, since such cooking would require her mother's close attention and thus keep her out of Ding's way.

Then she heard her stepfather's voice. He, too, was in the kitchen, which Ding hadn't expected, talking either to her mum or into his mobile. The sound of him—and why *was* this? why?—did what it always did to her. First were the shivers. Then the fury started.

She didn't understand why she had this reaction to Stephen, who had always treated her kindly, and she was sick to the bone of not understanding those things that, surely, she was meant to understand if she was ever to put a full stop to how she'd been carrying on her life. And now she wanted an end to it because the fact of Jack Korhonen had brought her up short: she'd never once done it with someone old enough to be her dad.

It was the thought of her dad that took her to the steps at the far end of the corridor, those that would lead up to the traditional green baize door with its baize so tattered at this point that it might have been nibbled upon by mice and it probably had been, since, really, what could possibly be better than felt to line a mouse's nest? And God knew there were mice nests aplenty in Cardew Hall, along with birds' nests in the chimneys, and that's what she knew of a sudden—just there!—the nest of hair from which the penis emerged, but *why* was that important and *why* could she barely cope with seeing it and *why* did she force herself over and over to see it, to touch it, to take it into her mouth if that's what he wanted because wasn't that what he always wanted and didn't they all always want it and didn't it come down to that in the end: the penis and what was done with it and because of it and God God God what was *wrong* with her?

Before she realised she was doing so, she was up the stairs and into the body of the house and then up a second set of stairs, wide with panelled walls from which dim light from the landing window illuminated dusty paintings of nameless ancestors. Then she was in a shadowy corridor, panelled like the stairway walls, and she was standing in front of a broad door. It was locked, as it always was locked, because no one wanted to go inside because no one, it seemed, wanted to remember, although what it was that no one wanted to remember she could not have said. But what she knew in this moment of shivering torso and quaking hands was that she had to get inside that room.

She knew where the key was. It came to her that she'd always known, because in her mind's eye she was crouched in a corner in the shadows and once the police had come and gone she had seen her mother lock that door and put the key at the very top of a tridarn so tall that she could barely reach it and so, of course, Ding would never find it only she'd seen she'd seen she'd seen from the shadows that that was where the key had gone to and all along her mum had not shed a tear not a single tear and what was *wrong* with her?

The tridarn was still there. Nothing was ever moved in Cardew Hall and nothing this large ever would be. But petite as she was, Ding could not reach the top of it. She needed something to stand on, so she went to her mum and stepdad's room and there she fetched one of those ancient stools: the kind with carvings and banged-up stretchers that people breathlessly took to the *Antiques Roadshow* only to learn it was worth twenty-five quid.

She dragged it from the bedroom to the corridor and over to the tridarn. There, she mounted it and hoisted herself high. She felt round the top of the tridarn in the dust and the grime, along the edges and into the centre till she found the key.

Her bowels were loosening as she got down from the stool and approached the door with the key in her hand. She *had* to do it. For she understood now that whatever was behind the door was something terrible and she had to know exactly what it was because it seemed to her that it was the only thing left that was capable of explaining to her why she was the way she was and why she would continue to *be* that way if she didn't open that door and step into the room behind it.

The key was a burning brand in her palm. Hastily, then, she stuck it into the keyhole and turned it to release the lock. Her heart was thudding, so she took a moment, and she shut her eyes tight, not to blind her vision but to force the tears to go somewhere besides down her cheeks. This was stupid, she told herself. It was just a room. What was she expecting to find inside? Dancing skeletons? Jack the Ripper? Poltergeists tossing the furniture round?

She made herself do it. She swung the door open, and although her limbs were shaking so badly she wasn't sure she could even move forward, she managed it. Eyes open, arms at her side, feet rising and falling on a scarred wooden floor and then upon an old Persian carpet . . .

Ding saw it was a bedroom like any other, save for the fact that it was musty with lack of use, with lack of fresh air, with lack of dusting and hoovering. It was dark inside because the heavy curtains were closed, but still she could see the shapes of furniture. Her breath began to come faster, though, as she took it all in: a chest of drawers a heavy chair an armoire a bed with four posters a dressing table and suddenly she knew she hadn't been meant to go inside this room then either but she *did* go inside and why was it why except now yes she remembered it was the dog but had there ever *been* a dog? yes there had been and was he inside the room? no he hadn't been had he but he was upstairs where he wasn't allowed and he was in the dropdown position her dad had taught him and when she went to him and tried to take him away because *no one* was supposed to bother her father when he was in that room the dog bared his teeth which he never ever did because he knew he wasn't supposed to show his teeth then he whined some more and that was why she opened the door because she knew the dog wanted no he needed to go inside that room just the way she had done but what was it what was it about this room?

"Ding! My God! I thought I heard something."

Ding swung round. There stood her mother in the doorway with fingers on her lips and an expression on her face that told Ding something was there, there just at the edge of her own consciousness.

Her mother extended her hand and said, "You gave me such a fright. What're you doing here? Come out of there."

Yes! It was the gesture. It was the words combined with the gesture. *What are you doing here come out of there* and Ding remembered. All of it. She said, "It wasn't an accident. You told me it was. You said he was working in the house and there was something he was doing with electricity because of the flex. It *was* a flex and you thought I would believe—" It suddenly felt as if something deadly was flowing from her along with her words, a foul effluent that would drown them both.

"You lied to me," she cried. "You lied to me you lied to me and you kept lying."

"Ding, come *out* of there. Now. Please."

And then behind her mother in the doorway Ding saw her stepfather and in a flash it was so much worse because she remembered him her father's old school friend her father's best friend and he was there as well just after it happened no he was there *when* it happened and why was he there? What was he doing there? Why had he come?

"You killed him!" she cried. "I remember! He was . . ." She looked round the room and found it she found it she pointed to one of the two posters at the end of the bed. It was thick and carved and constructed of that same heavy and unbreakable oak that so much of the house had been made from and that was where he had hanged himself. "The flex . . . that flex . . . it was round his *neck* and he was . . . Mum, he was naked and he was *dead*."

Her mother entered the room, then. She said over her shoulder to her husband, "Stephen, let me handle this. Let me—"

"Lie." Ding wept. "Stephen let me lie is what you mean. Stephen let me lie let me tell her something so she won't ever know what I did what *we* did because both of you did it both of you planned it you wanted to be together didn't you so—"

"Stop it! Stephen, for God's sake, *leave* us."

"She needs to know what happened," Ding's stepfather said.

"Yes, all right, I realise that. Now go! Ding, come out of this room."

Oh she would, she would. She would come out, and then she did so, brushing past her mother and her stepfather, hurtling down the corridor in the direction of the wide stairway that would take her to the main entrance hall below and then to the door and finally she was out in the air because she had to get away only she could hear her mother calling for her to stop just stop but she would not listen she would not and there was the church and its graveyard but the road the road was in the opposite direction and she had to get to the road at once because there she could find the bus that would take her to—

"He killed himself, Dena! He didn't mean to. It was an accident. But he killed himself."

She spun round. "You're lying because that's what you do you always lie you lie and lie and you always have and I hate you!"

But she was finished running, and she knew it. She sank onto the uncut grass next to a grave marker so old and worn that nothing remained upon it save the indication by its presence that someone long forgotten lay buried beneath it. When her mother reached her, she did not protest. When her mother dropped onto the grass next to her, she did not try to get away.

Her mother did not speak at first. She seemed to be waiting. Ding reckoned she was waiting for courage. Or perhaps she was waiting only for calm.

After a bit she said, "Ding, you were four years old and just barely that. I couldn't tell you because there was no way to explain to a four-year-old what her father had been doing in that room and that what he'd been doing had caused his death. How could you ever have understood that he used that room for . . . that when he wanted . . . It was auto-eroticism. That's how he died. Do you know what that is? Well, you must because children know things these days that they never would have known before this bloody age of information. I didn't know what he was doing in there. All I knew was that we weren't meant to go into that room when the door was closed because, he said, he'd be reading and he wanted to be able to read in peace for an hour or so, that was all he said. Just a bit of time to relax. Earlier, this was before you were even born, I'd caught him at it but not there in that room because it was before I inherited the house. He told me he'd read about it in one of his novels and he'd been curious and it was *only* that one time and he could see how dangerous it was. He swore he would never do it again. He was lying, of course, because that's what people do. You were right in that, Dena, people lie. And I lied to you because I didn't know how to explain to a four-year-old girl who'd just come upon her dead, naked, strung-up father that he'd done this to himself because he wanted . . . he just *had* to have . . . it was all about him and his pleasure and he didn't *think* about us. So there he was in the middle of a Saturday afternoon naked with a flex round his neck, hanging from a bedpost, with his face contorted and his eyes his eyes and yes you are absolutely right I did not tell you because the last thing I ever wanted was that you would remember how he died much less why he died like that."

Ding's hand had risen to cover her mouth. Her mother had long since begun to weep. She herself saw the past in a series of images, pushed so far back into her memory that she wondered if they were real at all: the uniforms of the police; someone carrying . . . what? a medical bag? figures passing along the corridor; the black garb of a priest; an ambulance trolley rolling along the corridor; the long, dark, zippered bag; the dog barking at all the intruders and all the confusion; her mother weeping; questions being asked and answers being given; and a woman coming into her room and sitting on the edge of the bed and she had been the paediatrician hadn't she and she was saying over her shoulder *Children this young* and to Ding herself *Let's see if we can help you sleep a little, sweetheart* because it had been a nightmare, hadn't it, that she'd awakened from terrified and if she went to sleep when she next awoke it would all be as if it had never happened.

She understood. Not why her father had done that to himself, not why her mother had lied to her for years upon years, but why she herself had taken the route she'd taken, the one that was gaining her nothing and would continue to do so should she remain upon it.

COALBROOKDALE
SHROPSHIRE

Timothy was still at work in the pharmacy when Yasmina returned to the clinic late that afternoon. She found him counting out a prescription for antibiotics for an elderly gentleman sent from Broseley's chemist, who'd apparently run out of the drug. Once the pills were ready, Timothy did what he'd always done: carefully explain how they were meant to be taken. When he'd made certain the old gent understood, he clasped the man's shoulder and said, "You're going to mind me, aren't you?" to which the reply was a gruff, "Got a feeling you'll chase me down 'f I don't."

Timothy promised that he would do just that, squeezed the man's shoulder, and sent him on his way, which was out to a minivan where someone who looked like his daughter was waiting. Then Timothy turned to Yasmina.

"Did you play the truant today?" His tone was friendly, and he was smiling the same smile that had at first beguiled her all those years ago. "Where'd you get off to? The cinema? A shopping trip?"

"I went to Ludlow."

The smile disappeared. Caution came onto his features. "Everything fine with Mum?"

"I went to the college," she told him.

It took a moment before he said, "Yasmina . . . ," in a tone that established its position on the border between warning and resignation. He went to lock the front doors to the pharmacy. He returned and began to deal with the till, opening its drawer and removing from it the tray that contained notes and coins. He set this to one side and looked at her. "You must know that approach isn't going to work."

"How can you say that when you have no idea why I went there?"

He removed the notes from the tray, and from beneath the counter he brought out the leather zip pouch in which he deposited the money at night. He put the notes inside it and then added the coins, saying, "I'm not a fool. If you went to the college, it has to do with Missa."

"You're right, of course." She smoothed her hand along the counter. It wanted a good dusting and she wondered if she would have to speak to the cleaners about it or, more probably, do the work herself as she'd already spoken to them twice about the cavalier attitude they had towards doing anything more than casually mopping the floor.

"Yasmina, you *must* be able to see by now that what you're doing is going to drive her away. It's basic human psychology."

"What I'm doing is trying to keep her from ending up as someone she never intended to be in the first place and will hate becoming."

Timothy sighed. The money taken care of, he went to the drugs next. From the cabinet shelves he moved the opiates into the plastic baskets in which they were stored for depositing—along with the money—in the pharmacy's safe. He said, "That's just the problem.

You act like someone who can see the future when you can barely understand the present."

"What I *understand* is my purpose as her mum, which is to help her set a course for her life. If you won't recognise that as your purpose as her father, you put me into the position of having to do the entire job alone."

He let the implied accusation sit there. Yasmina thought his silence meant that he was thinking over what she'd said. But then he replied with, "It's not my purpose or any part of my purpose to insist Missa do what she clearly doesn't want to do."

"You seem to have forgotten that she *wanted* college. She *wanted* university. She had plans for her life and now she has none. Doesn't that seem strange to you?"

"It doesn't, because I don't agree with that picture of things in the first place." He went into the back where the safe was. The sounds from the interior indicated he was securing the money and the opiates. In a moment he returned. He'd removed his lab coat, she saw, and now he stood before her. He was closer to her then than he'd been in months—save when he was sleeping—and she saw how drawn he looked, how the last years had aged him. Lines incised a path from his nose to the corners of his mouth and from there they etched downward to his chin. His hair was fast becoming more salt than pepper, and his eyes were no longer bright and engaged. They seemed to beg for the moment when he would take something pinched from the pharmacy to ease his way into oblivion. He couldn't possibly want to engage with her just now, but he did so.

"Missa *has* plans," he said. "They may have changed from what they were originally, but you know what they are. You just don't want to accept them."

"No one changes to this degree. It doesn't happen, not without a cause."

"But she *has* changed, and there's a logic to it. She tried college, and she found it to be not what she wanted. She decided she needed to take another route, which she told us last December. She wanted out and she wanted to be home. But you couldn't accept that."

"It wasn't a matter of accepting. It was a matter of clarifying. At her age—"

"I don't understand why you're telling yourself such rubbish," Timothy cut in. "Or why you're rewriting your history with Missa. The facts remain the facts. You insisted she return to Ludlow after the Christmas holiday in order to give it another go. She's always been a cooperative girl—and you and I might look at *that* at some point—so she did as you told her. But if you want the truth from where I'm standing now and where I was standing then, you browbeat her into cooperating, Yasmina."

Yasmina felt the insult as a suffusion of heat. "*This* is how you remember things?"

"It's how things were."

"Really? Has your brain become so addled because of what you're ingesting every night that you can't recall any basic facts about what's happening inside your own family?"

"Don't go there, Yasmina."

She saw the tension in the muscles of his arms where they crossed against his chest. She said, "No. It's time we spoke of this. Night after night you've been drugging yourself with what you've stolen from this pharmacy. You can't see what's in front of your face *begging* to be seen because when you're not drugged you end up with memories of Janna, and you can't—"

"Yas, I'm telling you." His right hand made a gesture telling her to stop.

"—allow yourself to live through what the rest of us are living through because it's hell, yes, that's what it is and that's what it was. And look at *me*, Timothy, the doctor, the bloody paediatrician, for the love of God, who didn't see it, who didn't catch it, who didn't know what to think when her own child wasn't well because to think and to recognise and to know what it meant . . . ? God, I would *love* to drug myself. Day and night I would but *then* what happens? What's happened already, there's your answer. Your eldest daughter is falling apart while you declare she must 'be who she would like to be,' *whatever* that means, because that absolves you of responsibility, doesn't it? That allows you to drug yourself."

"I'm not listening to this." He walked to the switch for the overhead lights.

She followed him. "I'm beyond caring what you do, but I will *not* give up on Missa."

He swung back to her. "Which means what exactly?"

She said, "Greta Yates is the counsellor at West Mercia College. She's asked to have an opportunity to have a conversation with Missa so that she can understand what's gone wrong. She's also said it's a simple enough thing for her to catch up with the work since she left, but they need to get to the bottom of why she left in the first place so they can help her."

His gaze fixed on her. "Do you ever listen to what I tell you?"

"My first thought was that if you and I spoke to Missa together and presented . . ." She was finding it difficult to speak. She paused, told herself that she *could* do this, and then went on. "If you and I presented a united front—merely on the subject of Missa having a conversation with the college counsellor—she would do it."

"Yasmina, I'm having no part in this."

"Yes, indeed, she would do it, especially if she knows it's merely a conversation with no expectations."

"Stop it, Yas."

"And I believe that Justin would be willing to make sure she got to Ludlow to keep an appointment there, especially if we approach it correctly. So I intend to speak to him as well. I've already had an initial word. I'm to meet with him, and I thought if you went with me—"

"The world *isn't* malleable," he said. "I'm not going to be part of your attempt to mould it."

"Which I take to mean you've no interest in learning anything about what constitutes the *why* of life."

He barked a short, unpleasant laugh. "Whatever you say, Yasmina."

So she was left to alter the plan and do the rest on her own.

Upon ringing Justin earlier from Ludlow, she'd been surprised when he explained that their meeting would have to take place on the site of the Jackfield Tile Museum. This stood in the hamlet of Jackfield itself, on the opposite side of the River Severn from

Ironbridge, just southeast of the town's eponymous bridge. The tile museum was a complex of buildings tucked to the east of an enclave of houses, on the upper part of a wooded acclivity that had long protected it from the periodic flooding of the river's banks. Some tiles were still made here, hand painted here, and fired here, memorialising the heyday of Victorian and Edwardian decorative arts. The museum itself contained thousands of other tiles—the real thing—from those that together might form a scene of domestic life to those that stood alone to add beauty to a fireplace, a floor, a porch, or a piece of furniture.

But there were more buildings than there was present-day use for when it came to making tiles, and some of them were let out for other purposes. Yasmina discovered that Justin Goodayle had taken one of these buildings, and he was waiting for her in front of it at their appointed meeting time.

A young woman was with him, her paint-splodged pinafore apron indicating that she was part of the tile making that still went on in the location. She was chatting Justin up with a fair amount of industry, from what Yasmina could see. Her flirting should have been obvious to Justin, but he seemed immune to her smile, her light touch on his arm, and the way she played with tendrils of her autumn-hued hair that escaped from the kerchief that held it away from her face.

Justin waved happily as he saw Yasmina, and when she parked her car and joined him and his companion, he introduced the girl as Heather Hawkes. She dimpled and said she had to be off. She added, "Think about it, Jus. Missa's invited as well."

"I'll speak with her," was his reply. "She's not much for crowd scenes, though."

"Come on your own then."

"P'rhaps. We'll see."

This seemed to please her. As she twirled and headed in the direction of the tile works' paint shop, Yasmina said to Justin, "She'll depend upon it, that one."

He smiled sweetly, that honest Justin smile of his that told Yamina he wasn't sure what she meant. So she said, "She'd be quite happy to have you to herself, that girl."

"Oh, I don't think so, Dr. Lomax. Me and Missa, we went to school with Heather's sister. I've known Heather since she was in nappies. Come with me. I've got summat to show you before you and me talk."

He walked to the huge double doors of the brick building in front of which he'd been standing with Heather. As he did so, he dug in the pocket of his jeans and pulled out a set of keys. One of them fitted the shiny Chubb lock on the double doors. He swung them wide so that Yasmina could see what was inside.

It was a surprising setup, illuminated by a skylight high in the ceiling and by banks of fluorescent tubes that Justin switched on. One of these hung above a scarred workbench that sat along one of the walls. An array of tools were neatly arranged above it, and along the back of it large tins were labelled for various kinds of nails and screws. A rank of rolled papers sat at one end of this table, some of them tightly bound with elastic bands and others loosely formed into tubes. At the far end of the area stood several kinds of electric saws and to one side a stand on wheels where various sorts of hand tools hung. On the opposite wall from the workbench, shelves held tins of paint and brushes and rollers, with more fluorescent lights above them.

The scent in the air mixed sawdust and fresh paint, and it seemed to relate to what was in the centre of a very large working area. This was a wooden structure fashioned not unlike an extremely high-end garden shed. Painted blue with pristinely white trim, it featured French windows in the front of it as a means of gaining entry. Over them hung a miniature trellis suitable, Yasmina reckoned, for wisteria, grapes, or climbing roses.

"What d'you think?" Justin's eagerness made him seem even younger than he was.

"It's extraordinary." Yasmina approached it, wondering who on earth would ever want such a fanciful structure for stowing a lawn mower and bags of potting soil.

"Here, let me show you the rest." He passed her and swung the French windows open. "This is my demonstration model. It's meant for show. See for yourself."

She saw that the structure contained a neatly made full-size bed, along with a small table and two chairs. Above the table on the wall was a hanging rack for plates and cups and on the table an electric kettle stood. From the ceiling hung a brass chandelier. From the wall on either side of the bed, brass anglepoise lights for reading had been fitted.

It was beautifully done, Yasmina thought. She had no idea what it was for, however. She said, "It's lovely. What's it called? I mean, does it have a name?"

"You mean like 'Shady Bower' or summat?"

She smiled. "I mean like garden shed."

"Oh! This one's meant to be for glamping, but they've other uses as well."

"Glamping?"

She walked through the French windows and stood at the foot of the bed. The headboard was fashioned from wrought iron and painted the same white as the exterior trim, while the interior of the place was painted a soothing shade of yellow and the counterpane on the bed was speckled with flowers of the same hue.

She turned to him. "This is extraordinary, Justin. I'd no idea . . ." She didn't add what she'd been thinking: she'd had no idea he was so good at something. But, then, why wouldn't he be?

"Most people don't know about it." It seemed he'd let her *no idea* refer to glamping. "It's a step above camping. Or p'rhaps three steps above. See, camping means that someone shows up at a site—say a farmer's paddock in the Lake District?—either dragging a caravan behind the car or getting ready to set up a tent. It rains or it blows and the tent gets knocked about. But one of these is steady and sturdy, and it's already there when the campers arrive. It's called a pod. It's generally on wheels so town councils and English Heritage and whatever can't say the farmer's put a permanent structure where one's not allowed."

She said, "You mean he can move it here or there, in the paddock or wherever."

Justin nodded. He went on to enthuse about how a pod could be fitted with electricity and even be plumbed if it was allowed to stay in one place. Each was big enough to accommodate two adults and, should fold-out cots be added to the pod, two children as well.

"They can be used for everything, the pods," he continued. "I've done one for a lady who's made it her painting studio, and another's being used as a miniature tea house in a good-size garden. They do a fine job as beach huts as well—'course, they're a little high end for that but you can see what I mean—and they can be used as shelters if the weather gets rough. A gent outside of Shrewsbury wanted one to make his fishing ties in and to stow his gear, and I built that one half-timbered. Here. Let me show you."

She followed him to the workbench upon which the rolls of paper lay. He took one of the loose ones, unrolled it, and weighed it down with the tins that held the nails and screws. She saw that this was a detailed drawing of one of his little buildings, only this one looked like a miniature barn, and it was accessed by a Dutch door that, in the drawing, hung half open.

"I had no idea your talents stretched to this," Yasmina said. "I mean, of course, I know about how well you do with blacksmithing, but working with wood like this . . . I'm very impressed."

He ducked his head in pleasure. "I won't ever set the world on fire with my brain, but I've got ideas that my hands can bring off easy as anything. Mum's always said that following one's talent is the ticket, so that's really all I've done. The others? I mean my brother and sisters? They're the clever ones. 'Justie's our dumb one,' Dad would say, but Mum said once I worked out what I was meant to do, she'd see I had the means to do it."

"How long have you been at this?"

"Near three years. I'm working on saving for me and Missa. Once I get enough money together . . ." He looked suddenly bashful. "You know."

Yasmina was grateful that he'd given her an entrée into the talk she needed to have with him. She said, "Missa can also contribute to the life you have together, Justin."

"'Course," he agreed. "And she will 'cause we both want a family and we mean to start at that straight off. Not an over-the-top family, mind you. But p'rhaps three little ones. Three's a good number. We've talked about it, her and me. Mostly the *when* of it, mind. When's a good time for both of us, is what we've asked each other. Now Missa's settled back into Blists Hill and now I've got this business here off the ground *and* I've got my blacksmithing as well, any time is a good time is the way I see it. Mum agrees. She says have your babies while you're young enough to chase them round. And then when they're grown and on their own, you'll still have the rest of your life in front of you to do what you want with. Missa thinks Mum is right."

He spoke with such openness that Yasmina had a moment in which she reconsidered: not the end—for really, there could be only one—but instead the means. Justin was a very nice boy. Indeed, he was a very decent young man. He worshipped Missa. But a marriage between them was both unthinkable and unwise. She knew, however, that she couldn't tell him that. For that would be to court his refusal to help her—Yasmina—in what she needed him to do.

She said with an attempt at seeming to think things over, "I do see your point. It's a very good one." Justin beamed at this, so she hastened to add, "But another point to consider is making certain both of you have careers so that should something happen to either of you, you'll have a source of income to fall back upon."

He beamed a little less. "Like what? I'm not sure what you mean, is what I'm saying."

"You have your blacksmithing and now this business you're starting, but Missa ought to have something as well."

"Oh. I intend her to keep the books for me as we go along and the business grows. She can do those while the little ones nap and later on while they're in school. That way she'll be at home for them."

"But if something happens to you . . . ? Missa won't be able to build the pods. And she's not a blacksmith. What she'll be is a mum and a housekeeper for you and perhaps a candlemaker at the Victorian Town, but you must ask yourself if that's actually enough to support your children, you, and herself should you be in need of her becoming the main breadwinner."

He frowned, apparently sorting this out. "But why would she need to do that, Dr. Lomax? Long as I've got my hands—"

"We never know what the future will bring. I mean, we don't know what might happen to us. A sudden illness, a physical condition that we weren't expecting, an accident. That's what I'm talking about."

Justin looked down at his hands. He was silent longer than Yasmina expected. She wondered if he was trying to sort through what she'd said in order to have some clarity, but he greatly surprised her with what he said next. "You want her to go back to the college. And then on to uni."

"There's a counsellor in Ludlow who wants to speak with her, Justin. I talked to her earlier today. She told me that her job is to get to the bottom of things when a student decides to leave the college, but Missa—this woman told me—bypassed that step altogether. She'd like to guide her through it, and if at the end she's satisfied that Missa has taken a decision in her own best interests, then that's that."

He looked up then. Not for the first time, she thought what a shame it was that he was so slow, as if good looks and intelligence ought naturally to go together. He said, "You want me to talk her into speaking with this counsellor person, eh?"

"I do, Justin. I want you to take her to see the counsellor as well. I want you to be in the meeting with them. I believe with all my heart that Missa is meant for more than keeping your books and having babies and making candles on the side. And Justin . . . my dear . . . I think you believe that as well."

Slowly, he rolled the sketch back up into the loose tube it had formed. He placed it carefully where it had been along with some others. He said, "She won't want to go to Ludlow."

"I agree. She won't. But I believe you can talk to her about it, and she'll listen to you if you use the right approach."

"What's that, then?" He turned from the workbench and leaned against it, his hands thrust into the pockets of his jeans.

Yasmina had already thought this through. "Tell her that I've come to you. Tell her that I've asked you to do this. Tell her that nothing is ever going to sway me from my belief in her future as a professional woman like myself."

"How's that meant to get her on board?"

"Because you'll also tell her that the *only* way she'll be able to get me to let this subject die is for her to speak to Greta Yates, the counsellor at the college. You're to tell her that she's to insist—to me, I mean—that *you're* going to take her to Ludlow, and that she's to insist that *you* attend the meeting with her when she speaks with Ms. Yates.

You're to tell her that you agree with every decision she's made in her life including her decision to leave West Mercia College, but after having me browbeat you for an hour, you've decided that the only way to get me away from both of you is to meet with the counsellor so that she—Missa—can tell her personally why she left the college and why she doesn't wish to return."

He drew his eyebrows together. Yasmina was forced to wonder whether he would be capable of carrying this off. She reckoned he might need a crib to refer to. She told herself, however, that she had to have faith in him since she was about to offer him the world.

She said, "And when you're in this meeting, Justin, I want you to be persuaded that Missa's returning to the college in preparation for university is actually a very sensible plan. Indeed, it's what you want her to do so that she'll always have a way to take care of herself and your children should anything happen to you. And once you've done this and once she's agreed to return to the college, I want you to set a date."

"For what?"

"For your marriage, my dear," she said gently. "It can't happen at once, of course. But the moment she completes her education, the very week she receives her final degree, there'll be a wedding. A lovely one with all the trimmings, after which you may take her off on a honeymoon somewhere quite wonderful. And after that, you may invest in a house suitable for raising the children you intend to have together."

He shook his head. He scuffed one of his boot-shod feet against the rough floor of the building. He said, "I'm saving my money. But all that . . . it's not something . . . not for a while at least."

She put her hand on his arm. "You misunderstand, my dear. The house and honeymoon are our wedding gifts to you. Her father's and mine."

His head lifted quickly and his expression, she saw, was quite apprehensive as he said, "Oh, I couldn't ever, Dr. Lomax. It wouldn't be right. I'm the man and the man is expected . . . and it would lower me in her eyes. I wouldn't ever want that."

She squeezed his arm and smiled at him with great affection because she *did* feel real affection for him. She said, "I don't believe anything would ever lower you in Missa's eyes. But you and I don't need to work out every detail just now. What I want to know at the moment is . . . may I ring Greta Yates and make an appointment with her? For Missa and you and what we've discussed?"

"Missa's not going to want to do this," he said reluctantly, but far less decisively than before.

"That remains to be seen. It will all depend on your approach. Will you think about doing this for me? And for her and for your future?"

He seemed to consider all this. He might, she thought, be working out in his head exactly what he was going to say to Missa. Finally, he said to her, "When, then?"

"Your conversation with Missa? Going to Ludlow?"

"Both," he said.

"As soon as is ever possible."

QUALITY SQUARE
LUDLOW
SHROPSHIRE

There was always a chance that Dena Donaldson wasn't going to turn up at the Hart and Hind that evening, but barring waiting outside the house in Temeside with Harry Rochester in the hope that she would eventually present herself, the pub seemed to Barbara Havers the best option. As they approached Castle Square, Lynley said, "If there's bad blood between Harry Rochester and the PCSO, this could be a futile activity, Barbara. You do know that."

"Do," she said. "But no matter which direction we head, I end up going back to the fact that right from the start Gaz Ruddock either massaged the truth when he had no reason to or he left out details that he knew were important. And the more we've looked at the bloke, the more he's left out details we've eventually come up with. Some woman he's involved with, some girl he's bonking, a college boy he's meant to watch over, Finnegan Freeman, his mum, his dad, his housemate. Way I see it, we need something to lay before this bloke that's going to cause him to start talking frankly. I'm willing to try anything to get us there, including involving Ludlow's number one dosser in the project."

Harry Rochester had not yet arrived when they reached the Hart and Hind, dodging a boisterous Frisbee event in Quality Square itself. As the evening was pleasant, a fair number of drinkers were outside on the terrace in front of the place. There was plenty going on, but the serious action appeared to be at a table where a curious form of chess was being played. Two teams were battling, young men against young women, with fifteen seconds allowed between changing players and making moves as well. The match seemed to include a form of stripping off one's kit. If a chess piece was taken, the player who caused its loss had to remove an article of clothing. Five players to the team and the girls were beating the trousers off the boys, literally.

Barbara ducked inside the pub. There weren't as many drinkers inside as out, so it took less than twenty seconds for her to see they'd won a packet with her plan. Dena Donaldson was tossing back something in a pint glass along with one of her mates. Perfect. All that was required was sending Harry Rochester inside for a quick recce. If he recognised Dena as a girl he'd seen with Gaz Ruddock, they were in the clover, one step closer to getting to the truth of what had gone on the night Druitt died.

Unfortunately, she did not take into account Harry's advanced claustrophobia. What were thirty seconds inside a pub? More than he could handle, as things developed.

When she returned to Lynley, it was to see that Harry had arrived, Sweet Pea at his side. He'd brought along his gear for dossing as well, and he explained that since they'd required his presence in the centre of town this late in the evening, he'd fetched his clobber from the other side of the river and would use Ludlow's outdoor accommodations—as he fashioned the term—somewhere in the immediate vicinity.

"Let's go inside," Barbara told both Lynley and Harry

simultaneously. "This'll take less than a minute. Have a look round and if you see any girl who's been with Ruddock. Just memorise what she's wearing and—"

"Inside?" Harry's entire throat jumped with the gulp he took. "I couldn't possibly . . ."

"We'll be just out here. Or, if you want, I can go inside with you and hang onto your hand."

"No, no," Harry said. "You don't understand. I simply can't."

"You go in the bank to have a word with your banker, right? This can't be much different from that."

"He comes out."

"He . . . what?"

"He comes out. I ring him with my mobile and he comes out onto the pavement. I haven't actually been inside a building . . . well, it's been years. Aside from the Spar and, as I said earlier, they know what I want so they have it ready for me at the till."

"What about if you get sick? Don't you go to a doctor's surgery?"

"I'm blessed with remarkable health."

"But we need you to—"

Here Lynley intervened. "We'll wait for girls to come out." He looked at his pocket watch. Harry, Barbara noted, appeared damned impressed that Lynley actually sported a pocket watch, another of his anachronistic quirks. "The pub closes soon enough," Lynley added. "This can't take any more than an hour."

Harry looked relieved. They found places somewhat out of the main area of the terrace so that when Dena Donaldson emerged, they would be able to see her without her noticing them. In the meantime, they watched the progression of the chess game. The boys, Barbara thought, had obviously come to the event unprepared. They wore far too few items of clothing. Two of them were down to their smalls, while none of the girls were showing any flesh at all. Barbara wondered what happened at checkmate. She wasn't sure she wanted to be a witness.

It looked as if that wasn't going to be a worry because as she shifted her gaze from chess to the pub's door, Dena Donaldson emerged.

Barbara shot Lynley a look. Dena was alone so there shouldn't be the slightest problem that Harry would not see her or would confuse her with a companion. She waited. Dena walked into the light shed by one of the overhanging bulbs that crisscrossed the terrace. Someone called her name, and she swung round, which placed her fully into view. She was joined by yet another girl. They set off together in the direction of Quality Square, earnestly in conversation.

"Ah," Harry said. "Yes. I've seen that one."

Perfect, Barbara thought.

On Harry's other side, though, Lynley said, "Which one?"

"The blonde."

"They're both blonde, Harry," Barbara noted.

"Oh sorry. Of course. The taller one," he said.

"But—"

"Are you certain?" Lynley asked the man.

"As much as I can be, given that it was night when I saw them."

Barbara wanted to shake the bloke. This wasn't the result she wanted. This wasn't the result she'd expected. This wasn't the bloody result they needed. Not with Harry Rochester overlooking Dena Donaldson in favour of someone else.

"The other girl?" she said. It was worth a try. "The other blonde? The shorter one? What about her? You got a good look at her face, didn't you?"

"I did indeed. I've seen her about. That's not much, though, is it? I've seen most people about."

"But not with Gary Ruddock?"

He shook his head. "With some boys from the college and with other girls, but not with Ruddock, as I recall." He looked sorrowfully at her. "Was she the one you were hoping I'd point out to you? I'm terribly sorry. I do want to help."

"You have." Lynley's tone was a model of reassurance, although Barbara wanted to strangle the dosser. Lynley said with meaning, "Sergeant? Shall we be on our way? Shall we leave Mr. Rochester to find his spot for the night?"

She knew what Lynley's objective was. They needed to follow the taller girl and they needed to do it now.

LUDLOW
SHROPSHIRE

Lynley's intention to follow the girl proved to be entirely unnecessary. Whatever she and Dena Donaldson had needed to discuss had evidently been discussed, for less than a minute after she'd disappeared round the corner into Quality Square proper with Dena, the other girl returned and went back inside the pub.

Seeing her, Harry Rochester said, "Shall I stay, then?" although he didn't sound happy with the prospect.

Lynley said it wasn't necessary. But what was necessary, he said, would be for Sergeant Havers to wait outside for him. He could tell she wasn't pleased with this, but she would know the reason. The publican understood that she was a cop. He didn't know that about Lynley.

Once inside, Lynley saw that the girl was at the bar. She appeared to be trying to get a free drink out of the publican. He waited for her to buy or beg whatever she intended to imbibe. He waited for her to carry it to a table. Neither happened. He approached the bar.

"May I have a word?" he said to the girl and he added, "What are you drinking?" as lubrication.

She turned halfway and seemed to size him up. "Aren't you gorgeous," she said. "I *was* drinking lager, but I'd actually prefer gin and tonic."

Lynley nodded to the publican who managed a blustering guffaw, as if he'd seen this kind of operation on the girl's part before, as he probably had.

"Aren't you drinking as well?" the girl said to Lynley. She lowered her gaze briefly, either to take in his trousers or to show off her eyelashes, which were quite long and seemed to be real, but who really knew? "I don't much like drinking alone. I'm Francie. What's your name?"

"Thomas Lynley," he said. And in a lower voice, "New Scotland Yard. I need a word with you."

She looked up. Her blue eyes widened, but it seemed more mockery than surprise. She said, "I don't think I've broken any laws recently. But if I have, can I depend that you'll be the arresting officer?" She held out her wrists and added coyly, "Or can I do something else for you?" And then to the publican, "Jack, d'you think I'll look good in handcuffs? This Scotland Yard gentleman wants to take me away. Are you jealous?"

Jack put his gaze squarely on Lynley and said, "*Again* with you lot? First we have Scotland Yard round one, and now we have Scotland Yard round two. You with that woman 'studying up on the Plantagenets,' are you?"

"D'you already have a partner for tonight, then?" Francie asked Lynley. "What a shame."

She had her gin, two ice cubes, a slice of lime, and a small can of tonic. She opened this last, poured in a dollop, took a drink and said with a smile, "I'm . . . let's call it *ready*, officer."

Glass in hand, she sauntered towards the door. She waited for Lynley to follow, which he did. Then outside, Barbara Havers joined them. Francie looked her over, looked back at Lynley, offered a half smile that was probably meant to be knowing, and said, "Now where shall we chat?"

Lynley didn't want to chance being seen by Gary Ruddock should the PCSO stop by the pub, and he cast a look at Havers. She said, "St. Laurence's not far, sir. It has that churchyard . . . ?" Lynley nodded at her and she led the way.

Francie said, "You plan to question me in a *graveyard*? What sort of police work happens in a graveyard?"

"Digging up corpses, generally," Havers said over her shoulder. "But I reckon we'll let that one go tonight as there aren't any graves. Anyway, we'd like to have a word and not be seen having a word. We can do it somewhere else. Live at home, do you? On your own? With a flatmate? What?"

"The graveyard's fine," Francie said shortly, which was answer enough as to where she lived. The girl's parents would ask questions that she probably didn't want asked should she show up at home with two detectives from New Scotland Yard.

The churchyard wasn't dark, but it was private. One of the larger yews provided deep shadows, but otherwise the location was lit by streetlamps along two of its sides. Havers made for the tree, and Francie tripped along in her wake. Lynley brought up the rear.

"All right." Francie took a position that offered her the most darkness and also the tree trunk to lean against, in a position that thrust her chest outwards. "What d'you want?"

What they wanted, first, was to understand the nature of her relationship with Dena Donaldson.

"Is she in trouble?" The girl sounded far more interested than worried. She took a sip of her drink and watched Lynley over the rim of the glass. Havers she ignored.

"Interesting that you would make that leap," Lynley said to her.

"What other leap am I supposed to make when the police want me to talk about someone? You're checking her out for some reason and it can't be that she's applied for a job with you lot."

"Perceptive," Lynley said.

Havers added, "We've had a word with her. We'd like to confirm what she had to say."

"We just now saw you with her," Lynley added. "You appear to be acquainted so you seemed a good place to start."

"What do you mean 'confirm what she had to say'?" Francie took a moment to mull this over when they didn't reply. She shifted her weight, putting her hand on her hip. "Hey, is she making up some randomly weird story about me? Because if she is, let me tell you, *everything* started with her catching me blowing Brutus. Before that, we were super good friends, her and me. When she caught us, I explained to her that no *way* would I have been with Brutus if I'd known she was even *minorly* serious about him. And why would I have *ever* thought that anyway, because the entire world knows how much he sleeps around, and she *is* part of the world last time I looked. So it didn't mean anything that I was in his room and . . . Look, like I said, I explained it all to her. I *keep* explaining. How it all happened that I ended up with him, which will *not* ever be repeated. Which I *also* told her till I was blue in the face. So if she's trying to get me into trouble, which I wouldn't put past her because she's so . . . I don't know . . . it's like she's twitchy about everything these days."

"Sounds all tangled up," Havers noted. "If I'm following: what's going on involves you, Brutus, Dena, and various body parts, yes? A bit of looking for love in all the wrong places, as the song goes."

Lynley said, "While all of this is a fascinating study in human relationships, whatever has gone on among the three of you—Dena, Brutus, and you—isn't what we wish to speak to you about. We're far more interested in what's gone on between you and the PCSO here in town. Dena has made a claim that—"

"What? That I'm blowing *him* as well? She's trying to get me into trouble, isn't she? Because of Brutus. All because of that stupid Brutus. Or is it Ruddock she's trying to get into trouble? Ha. Let me tell you, carloads of people would be thrilled to bits about that."

"Why would that be?" Lynley asked.

Francie took another sip of her drink. Her eyes narrowed as she speculated. "You two ask round if you want an answer to that. I'm not about to be your Ludlow snout. I have enough troubles already. Meantime, you should look into Ding's relationship with Gaz Ruddock instead of trotting me out here in the middle of the night for a little chat. In a bloody *graveyard*, no less."

Havers said, "Trouble is you've been identified."

"As *what*?"

"As a woman who's been seen with the PCSO. Inside his car."

"Who supposedly saw me, then? And when? Never mind. Don't even bother to tell me because whoever said that is bloody well lying."

"According to our observer, you were in his patrol car being carted somewhere. What would that be about?"

"You mean someone's actually saying I was *arrested*? I've never even broken a law. You can check on your computers or iPhones or wherever you lot keep your information. Frances Adamucci. A-d-a-m-u-c-c-i. Middle name Sophia."

"No one's suggesting you were arrested," Lynley pointed out.

Havers added, "What you were up to indicates that arrest was the last thing on anyone's mind: yours, the PCSO's, your guardian angel, the Archbishop of Canterbury."

"What we've come to understand," Lynley added, "is that the PCSO has been quite good about handling complaints that deal with the binge drinking that goes on in town. We've also learned that he's loaded drinkers into his vehicle and taken them away. And a final thing we know is that he has a relationship with someone that he wants to keep quiet, especially in light of the death that took place in the local police station. Now which of those categories of relationships with the PCSO is the one you fall into?"

"*Now* you're saying that I killed someone?"

"That wasn't one of the categories," Havers pointed out.

Francie stamped her foot. She was, Lynley noted, careful not to spill any of her drink. "I don't have to place myself in *any* category, and I'm not going to."

"Ultimately, you may want to," Lynley said, "if only to keep yourself clear of suspicion."

"Suspicion of *what*?"

"Accessory to murder."

"What the hell? What's going *on*? I didn't do anything and I've never done anything. Ding's gone totally round the bend if she's—"

"This isn't about Ding," Lynley told her. "She's told us nothing about you and the PCSO."

"Then who said it? You tell me who."

"We can't give you the name," Lynley said. "But we can tell you that you were identified this very night as having been seen with the PCSO inside his patrol car. We can also tell you that we didn't at all expect you to be the person identified."

"I have never ever *been* in that patrol car except when he's carted us home because we were drunk in Quality Square."

"Who is 'us,' then?" Havers asked.

"Me and Chelsea and we've always been together when it happened and that is *it*. So whoever told you anything else is lying or has rotten eyesight or wants to get me stitched up for something."

"Why would that be?"

"Probably because I gave whoever-it-was's boyfriend a blow job, which is what happened with Ding, all right? So if she's behind this . . . I already said. I didn't even *know* he was her boyfriend! I just knew they did it occasionally. But so does everyone else. There's no strings attached and everyone knows it's just for a laugh. And if Ding's *not* behind this, then you lot better look at whoever it is told you the tale in the first place because I'm telling you right now that person's winding you up and there's probably a real interesting reason why. Which is what you ought to be concentrating on instead of taking me into bloody *graveyards*. You ask anyone over in the Hart and Hind if I ever been alone with Ruddock. You ask anyone drinking outside. You ask anyone in Castle Square. You ask anyone anywhere on the planet. Meantime, why aren't you lot doing something about Ruddock instead of harassing me?"

"You'll need to be more direct," Lynley said. "Is there something about the PCSO that we need to know?"

"You want an answer to *that*, you talk to someone else. Like Ding. *Or* you talk to him. But no way do you keep talking to me."

Having said this, she brushed past them both and headed back the way they'd come. Havers said to Lynley. "On the vehemence scale, that bird's climbing the charts."

"I don't know whether to believe her or not."

"I don't know whether to believe anyone. But seems to me we're onto Harry Rochester next. We either got to have his eyesight tested or we got to find out what's going on with *him*."

"Christ." Lynley blew out a breath. "It does go on and on, doesn't it?"

"Want me to get on it, then?"

He shook his head. "I expect whatever background information we need on Mr. Rochester isn't something we're going to dig up in Ludlow. I'll phone London in the morning."

# 21 MAY

IRONBRIDGE
SHROPSHIRE

As usual, Yasmina rose before the rest of the family. Early light was filtering through the closed curtains, and she could hear the tree pipits' high-pitched calling, which always announced their yearly arrival. They liked the woodsy hillside that rose behind the Lomax home, and while their singing was pleasant, its ear-splitting conclusion generally served as a wake-up call, whether one wished to have such a thing or not.

The birds didn't bother Timothy. They had done at one time, so he'd taken to wearing earplugs in order to sleep longer than the tree pipits wished him to do. But his need for something to block their noise had disappeared with his use of his "sleeping aids." Now, if Yasmina didn't do something to awaken him, he could easily sleep till one or two in the afternoon.

She found that Timothy's drug-induced slumber didn't bother her this morning. Her mood had shifted once she'd brought Justin Goodayle on board with the strategy she'd devised to get Missa back on course.

She went down the stairs in the silent house. She would have her morning tea at the table in the kitchen that looked out on the hillside. There, a rock rose thrived in one of the sunny spots, creating a haze of pink flowers against deeply green leaves. They didn't last long—that was their tragedy—but while they decorated the bush they were hard to look away from and Yasmina found that in those quiet minutes of tea and flowers, she could—

"Good morning, Mum."

Yasmina turned quickly towards the sitting room at Missa's greeting. She saw that her daughter was seated in an armchair with two suitcases on one side of it and three large cardboard boxes on the other. These latter bore a red-lettered advert for breakfast cereal, and the inane first thought that popped into Yasmina's head was the fact that Missa didn't eat cereal but rather yoghurt and fruit for breakfast.

After that, the notion came to her that Missa had actually arrived at her own conclusion, one that told her she didn't belong in Ironbridge but rather back in Ludlow. Following rapidly—in the way scenarios jump into the stream of ideas one has—was the startling possibility that Missa had spoken to Greta Yates on her own and was returning to Ludlow to study independently at her grandmother's house to catch up with everything she'd missed during the time she'd been gone so that she could take her exams at the end of the current term.

Yasmina tried to effect surprise, which wasn't difficult since she'd hardly expected such a quick result. But both surprise and triumph faded when she truly took in the expression on her daughter's face. Not exactly sullen, but rather unmoving, as if Missa had sat there for hours dwelling on thoughts that had turned her features into concrete.

Yasmina gestured to the suitcases and boxes. "Goodness. What's this, my dear?"

"I'm waiting for Justin," Missa said. "He and I spoke last night."

Yasmina became aware of cool air on her ankles and she wondered if she'd left the kitchen window open last night. She thought she might have done. She'd had so much on her mind. "I'm not certain . . ." she began, but couldn't come up with what ought to follow.

"We've spoken to his parents," Missa said. "Well, to his mum, actually. It was Justin who spoke to her. That was the important part. His dad is easy about everything, but mums . . . They can be rather difficult. Can't they."

Yasmina wondered what Justin's parents had to do with Missa's return to Ludlow, but she didn't ask. She had to say something in order to elicit more information, though, so she said, "I don't quite understand. The boxes . . . the suitcases . . . Are you going somewhere?"

Missa didn't reply, and Yasmina felt herself being inspected in a way she'd never experienced from her daughter before. Something insidious seemed to be creeping across the sitting room carpet towards her, seeping from Missa in a lava flow. Yasmina wanted suddenly to stop it or at least to try to redirect it, but she had no words that would not lead directly to those boxes and suitcases and Justin and his parents and what it all meant.

"You don't really know Justin," Missa said. "You think you do. I can see why. He seems so . . . You'd use the word *simple,* wouldn't you. Simple in his mind, simple in his actions, simple in his thoughts."

"That's not true, Missa. Justin has always been the loveliest—"

"Let's set all that aside." Missa's voice altered, becoming quite sharp. "He told me, Mum. *A* to *Z,* start to finish, whatever you want to call it. The Big Plan. The Course Objective. You didn't think he would, but that's because you see him just like everyone else in your world: clay. He's not. He's iron. But more than that, he's real. He's shown you that from the first. But instead of real you saw simple, like I said. You reckoned you could use him and—"

"Missa, I did not!"

"—*and* I'd never work it out. What you didn't reckon was that for him the truth is more important than what he might want or—in this case—what he might be offered."

Yasmina wanted to stop her. There was, she noted, an odd new scent in the air. Medicinal, it seemed. She didn't like it. She would have to speak to their cleaner. Her house smelled vaguely like a swimming pool. They couldn't have that. She said, "I'm not sure what you're talking about, Missa."

"Oh my God," Missa said. "Oh my *God*, Mum. Just now, just here, in this sitting room, I'm *telling* you that last night Justin explained the Big Plan. Oh, he started out exactly how you intended: telling me that you were badgering him to speak to me about West Mercia College, that the only way he could manage to get you to leave him be, he reckoned, was for me to go to the college to meet with the counsellor, that he would take me there and all the rest. Only . . . he couldn't, you see. Not like you thought he would, because what he knew was that the second I got into the car with him to go to Ludlow, I'd see it on his face anyway. So he told me the truth."

"Missa, surely you see the importance of—"

Missa surged to her feet. "I. Do. Not." Her voice was loud. She would awaken Sati. Things would fall apart from there.

Yasmina said, "Please. We can talk about this when you're—"

"We're *not* talking. We are *finished* talking because talking to you is all about *me* listening to you and then trying to talk to you and then crumbling and never once saying . . . telling you . . . and I'm done with that. I am done, done, done!"

"Stop shrieking. You're going to wake your sister. Or your father."

"And that will be bad, *won't* it, Mum? They might actually see what you've been up to. They might see who you are and what you want and how the only thing that has *ever* for a moment mattered to you is what things look like, not how they are. And if they see that, you're finished, aren't you? Finished the way this family is finished, only you can't see it and you won't admit it and I'm not part of it any longer. All right? Do you hear me? *Do* you?" She grabbed up a framed picture that stood on the table next to her armchair and she smashed it on the floor. "I am not part of this fucking charade! I'm not! I won't be! I—"

"Stop it at once! Stop that language and stop this hysteria."

"I won't!" she cried. "I goddamn bloody fucking won't!"

And that was on a scream. And that did it.

Sati came dashing down the stairs. She saw Yasmina and Missa facing off, and she saw the suitcases and the boxes. She began to wail. "Missa, no! No! No! I want to go! I want to go with you! Please!" She ran towards Missa, but Yasmina caught her arm.

"Sati, go to your room," she hissed. "Go. At once. Go!" She shoved the girl towards the stairway.

"Stop that!" Missa shrieked. "Leave her alone!"

"Missa!" Sati cried.

"Don't worry," Missa called to her. "I'll come for you. It won't be long. Sati, don't worry."

Yasmina whirled towards her. "Sati's going nowhere, and neither are you. Go to your room at once. Take those suitcases with you. We'll deal with the rest when your father—"

"You don't know anything! You don't know me and you never bloody will because . . . because . . ." She began to weep like Sati, but wilder and with an anguish that made Yasmina grow cold to the roots of her hair.

She said, "Missa, my God," but her daughter shoved past her.

That was when the doorbell rang. It was, of course, Justin. Missa did, of course, throw herself into the young man's arms. He spoke, of course, as he always spoke, saying, "Steady on, Miss. It's good. With my mum *and* my dad, like I said it would be."

Yasmina said, "She's meant to stay here," which was all Missa needed. She dashed out of the house and into the street where, doubtless, Justin's car stood waiting.

Justin remained where he was, clearly torn between going after Missa to offer comfort and fetching her belongings, which he was obviously meant to do. It was, after all, part of the plan he and Missa had concocted during their conversation on the previous night.

He said, "Dr. Lomax . . . I couldn't. I had to tell her and then she said she didn't care about any of it. The wedding, the house, the honeymoon, or whatever." And here he blushed in that Justin way and said, "I don't mean we won't marry. We will, 'course. It's what we both want. And we'll wait till we do. For the rest, I mean. No worries there. Mum says Missa can use my sisters' bedroom. They're long gone, see, and . . . well . . ."

He was good enough not to mention the tears that were coursing down Yasmina's cheeks. He saw them, naturally. He even patted her on the shoulder as he went for Missa's two suitcases. He would return in a moment for the boxes. It was all so easily accomplished when one made a plan.

And then they were gone. But there was Sati to be dealt with and her hysterical weeping, which Yasmina could hear even from behind the girl's closed bedroom door. Only, as she got to the top of the stairs, she saw that Sati had not gone to her room at all but rather to rouse her father, to get him to intervene.

"Mummy, he won't wake up!" The girl sobbed as she pulled on Timothy's arm and cried, "Daddy! Daddy!"

Yasmina ran to the bed. She pulled Sati away. She said, "Wait in your room."

"But he won't . . . What's wrong with him? Mummy, what's *wrong*?"

Yasmina bent over him. His colour was very bad. His respiration was stertorous, but it was there. She said his name loudly. No response. Then she shouted it while behind her she heard Sati sink to the floor, crying "No . . . nooooo . . ."

Yasmina pulled the covers off her husband. She climbed onto the bed and straddled his body. She made a fist. Fiercely, she began to rub the centre of his chest. She used the weight of her body to put as much pressure into the rubbing as she could.

Behind her, Sati cried, "Mummy, what's wrong with him? I'll ring 999. Should I ring 999?"

"No, *no*!" Yasmina gasped. And then to her husband, "Timothy, for God's sake. Timothy! Timothy!" She could not have him taken to A & E. If that happened, it would all come to light: his usage, his cadging pills from his patients, his full addiction. She said to Sati, "It's all right, darling. He's just having trouble. . . . He'll be all right. See? Sati, look. He's coming round now . . ."

And he was, thank God. His eyelids fluttered. He closed them. She slapped him. Hard. He opened them. She jerked him to a sitting position, then to his feet. She said, "See, Sati? He's up. He'll be fine. He took a pill last night to help him sleep. I'm taking him into the bathroom now. We'll need to be private but he's all right. See?"

Sati looked stricken. Yasmina felt fury whipping through her body. It seemed to give her superhuman strength. She reckoned she could carry Timothy if she had to but she didn't have to. He said, "Sati," although his head hung low. "I'll be . . . ," and he sagged into Yasmina.

But he'd said enough, so Sati backed into the corridor, her fists bunched beneath her chin as Yasmina got Timothy into the bathroom. She glanced back at her daughter before she shut the door. "I'm so sorry," Yasmina said. "Sati, darling, I'm so sorry."

LUDLOW
SHROPSHIRE

She was provoking in at least half a dozen ways, but Lynley knew that when it came to her considerations about a case, Barbara Havers could be absolutely trusted. So when they'd carried on their post-churchyard conversation as they walked back to Griffith Hall on the previous night, he'd listened to what she had to say once they were in agreement over the various screws, bolts, and spanners that were being thrown into the workings of their investigation.

She'd begun with, "Trouble is, she's too tall, sir."

"Francie A-d-a-m-u-c-c-i, as she terms herself?"

"The very same. They're both blonde and they've both got that college-girl-in-need-of-a-decent-hairstyle thing going on—" to which he lifted an eyebrow and she went on with, "All right, I know. Who'm I to talk, eh? But you know what I mean. All these girls're walking round like refugees from the 1960s. All they need is wreaths of flowers and tickets to San Francisco or whatever. My point is that *despite* both of them being blonde, that's where the resemblance ends. Their body types are completely different. The girl I saw with Ruddock was short. I could compare her height to the door of the car since she was standing next to it. This girl Francie . . . ? Willowy, tall, bosomy, whatever. You know what I mean: your basic nightmare for the rest of womankind. Now, I know it was dark, but when the girl I saw got out of the car, the light went on and I clocked her face and it wasn't that girl." At which point she'd jerked her thumb in the direction from which they'd walked. "And anyway, there's the fact of the *patrol* car in the first place."

"That Dena Donaldson brought up the patrol car when you'd only said a car, full stop."

"That means something. And *what* it means is that she's been with Ruddock. So you ask me, someone's not giving us all the facts. Dena, Francie A-d-a-m etcetera, or even Harry Rochester, who might've seen Dena but who's now pretending he saw Francie for some reason. You see that, don't you?"

What Lynley saw was that time was running out and soon Hillier was going to be demanding a result that wouldn't put the lot of them into the water boiling in the Home Secretary's office. So he said before they'd reached the hotel, "When it comes to giving us all the facts, Sergeant, I daresay it's more than one someone. I'll ring Nkata in the morning."

Which he did, as soon as he was certain the other detective sergeant would be at his desk. When he heard Nkata's distinctive voice—that blend of West African and the Caribbean via Brixton—he said, "Might I call upon your research skills, Winston? We've a bit of a muddle up here."

"Say what," was Winston's friendly reply.

Lynley gave him a list of names, at the top of which was Harry Rochester and at the bottom of which was Christopher Spencer, the inclusion of whom was largely the result of desperation. At the end, Nkata whistled. "Tha's goin to require some time. What am I lookin for?"

"Anything in their pasts that seems dodgy. Just now we're most interested in Harry Rochester, but if any of the rest of them have sneezed without covering their mouths, let us know. Can you fit this in today?"

"Can do. I got a bit of other research goin on but that'll—" He stopped because, as Lynley heard, someone was speaking to him. He said to that person, "Yeah. It is. He jus' gave me a bell," and then into the phone again, "Dee Harriman wants a word, Inspector."

When he heard her voice saying, "This is like divine intervention, Detective Inspector Lynley," Lynley responded with what he considered great loyalty, "As far as I can tell from her general level of exhaustion in the morning, Barbara's practising nightly, Dee. Or perhaps she's doing it before breakfast. I admit to not asking her *exactly* when she's channelling Ginger Rogers. But she's apparently wearing her metatarsals—or is it her phalanges?—down to the bone. But wait. Do forgive me. In either case those *are* bones, aren't they. At any rate, she's intent upon turning in a stellar performance at the dance recital. And do make sure I have the date in my diary because despite her every threat, I intend to be there."

Dee said, "I fully expect you, so if you're joking . . ."

"I dare not joke about an opportunity to see Sergeant Havers in tap shoes, believe me."

She laughed and said, "It's going to be brilliant. You'll see. *She's* going to be brilliant. But that's not why I wanted to have a word."

"Ah. The divine intervention meant what, then?"

There was a moment's pause. Then Dee spoke *sotto voce* and it seemed she'd moved away from Nkata's desk or at least turned her back on the DS. She said, "She rang in again. Ill, she said. She's never ill, Detective Inspector. What should I do?"

"DCS Ardery."

"Who else?"

"Perhaps it's better to say she's never been ill before now, Dee." He made his voice easy, but worry tightened his fingers on his mobile. "And now she is."

"What should I do? You haven't said."

"Have you spoken to her?"

"She left a message. Again. But someone's going to ring her—at any moment, Detective Inspector—or someone's going to ring *me* and ask about her. And I don't quite know what to say. Or what I should do. Perhaps if you rang her? I'm that concerned, you see. You're going to say that I shouldn't be or that it's not down to me if she's ill or whatever, but if you could hear how she sounds on the phone. And it seems to me . . . You know. I mean, am I meant to come out and tell you what I think, Detective Inspector Lynley?"

"What is it you think?"

"You *know.* I know that you know because there've been times when voices carry even if the door is shut and I don't intend to eavesdrop and it's not like I'm even doing it at all, and I've also seen you waiting outside her office door and listening and—"

"Dee."

"Sir?"

Lynley considered what he wanted to tell her. Dee Harriman's loyalties ran deep and in all directions, including towards Isabelle Ardery. Because of this, Lynley knew she meant well. He said, "We're without power here."

"Right. Yes. But I thought if she knew that other people know . . .

I mean . . . Although I s'pose she knows that at least you know, doesn't she?"

"And what good do you see that doing?"

In her pause, he heard other voices in the background. The day was in full swing in London. Dee wasn't wrong in her concern, as someone was going to have to take matters in hand eventually. But it wasn't going to be Thomas Lynley. It couldn't be. Nor could it be Dorothea Harriman. She said, "None, I s'pose. So I . . . do what, exactly?"

"You know the answer to that."

"God, I'm not meant to *report* her, am I?"

"You're meant to do your job," he told her. "She's left you a message that tells you she's ill. You believe she isn't, and you may well be right. But as you don't know and as she hasn't told you—"

"She's not going to tell me she's having a morning after or she's currently too addled to show her face round here!"

"—all you can to is merely report what you've been told, if and when you're asked."

"And if I'm not asked?"

"I think you know the answer to that."

"But this can't go on, Detective Inspector."

"It won't go on. These things never do."

They rang off then. Lynley had been sitting on the edge of his prison-cell bed as he made the call, and now he looked down at his shoes. They wanted a serious polishing, he noted. Unfortunately, he'd brought no polish with him although even if he had done, he doubted he'd do a job on them acceptable to Charlie Denton. He considered ringing him, just to enquire how the Mamet was going. And then he considered ringing Daidre. But she had deep concerns of her own: her birth parents and her siblings and her mother's final journey. Still, he wondered what it meant that he hadn't heard from her, that—thrust back into a world she'd believed she'd left forever—she was now confronting her worst memories without him. He was forced to ask himself why she didn't need him in a moment like this. He went on to ask himself the obvious: Did people actually need each other at all?

He couldn't answer that question, so he didn't try.

LUDLOW
SHROPSHIRE

When Ding awakened, she was alone in her bed as she'd been all night. This constituted one of the very few times she'd been alone in however long it had been because she couldn't actually remember, but it must have been two weeks after autumn term had begun, since that was when she first hooked up with Brutus. And although he'd begun doing it with other girls within five weeks or so from the start of term, he'd ended up in her bed nonetheless, save for the nights when she'd refused him from sheer outrage that he was so . . . so completely Brutus about everything.

She'd also not had sex with Finn or with anyone on the previous day or during the previous night. That was certainly not impressive, but what *was* impressive was that she'd been able to go to sleep and then wake up without being in a twist about it. In the past, she would've become instantly consumed with the question of who she was going to "be with" next as if "being with" someone—which, let's face it, was always a euphemism for fucking them—had something to do with who she really was.

She still had very little idea of that: who she really was. But at least she could now trace a path from the child she'd been to the adolescent and then the young adult she'd become. In this, she saw that she'd always been running. She hadn't known why, but she'd always felt like someone quite desperate to get to a destination that she couldn't identify. And because she couldn't identify the destination she was actually seeking—let alone recognise it when she arrived—she'd ended up seeking the one that was most familiar to her over and over again, even if she hadn't known why it was familiar to her in the first place.

When she saw her father's naked dead body, she thought, she must have decided at some level that everything he was in that terrible moment had to do with that thing between his legs. In that moment of seeing him dead and naked, she must have reached a conclusion of some kind, because that was the only way she could explain to herself the disgust she'd felt each time some bloke let her know how important it was to him to have her do something—anything really—that involved his penis.

So, she thought as she lay in bed with her gaze upon her bedroom ceiling, if that was the case, where was her true fury coming from, especially the fury she felt towards Brutus and the various girls he'd snogged with, bonked, or been blown by since she'd known him? She'd held *them* in contempt as well, but where did that come from and what did it mean?

She considered this and the answer dawned on her slowly but oh so visually that she knew at once what it was about. She could see their faces when they were with him: Allison, Monica, Francie. She could see what played on their features and she knew what it was: enjoyment, pleasure, whatever you wanted to call it. But it was something she herself could not feel. That's what it was. Allison giggling, Monica looking like a satisfied cat, Francie inviting her to join in the fun because it *was* fun to Francie and it always had been, whereas to Ding . . . She'd fucked them or sucked them or wanked them while waiting, just waiting, for when she could tell herself that only she saw what a miserable creature the male of Homo sapiens was.

She got out of bed. She rooted round in a drawer till she found clothing she could have worn for yoga but instead wore to slop round the house. Once she'd donned it, she left her room. Finn's door was closed. Brutus's was also. She approached the latter and knocked.

"Bru?" she called. "Can I have a word?" She heard a bit of muffled conversation but that was it, so she said, "It's not a big thing, Bru. No worries, 'kay?"

That seemed to do it. She heard bedsprings creak, and then in a moment Brutus opened the door. The fact that he sheltered the inside of his room from her view told her that he probably had a new girl with him. He slid into the corridor and shut the door behind him, saying, "Yeah? What?"

He sounded wary. He gave a look in the direction of Finn's room and then back at her. She saw he'd put on boxer shorts but nothing else.

"Can I talk to you?" she said. "It won't take long. Can you come to my room for a minute?"

"You and me aren't—"

"It's not about us," she cut in quickly. "We both know that there isn't an us anyway. But I got to ask you something and it's better inside." She tilted her head towards her bedroom.

He said with an obvious attempt at patience, "Ding, I explained things over and over. There's no more ways to explain it to you."

"It's not *about* that. There's one thing you never tried to explain because I never asked and that's what I want to talk about. But like I said, it won't take long."

He sighed and said, "Okay, but wait a second."

He ducked back into his room—more like a slither so he could get in without opening the door more than ten inches—and in a moment Ding could hear the murmur of voices, his and a girl's. She felt the hurt of the unnamed girl's presence, but she understood that what she felt was not about Brutus but rather about herself, which it had been from the first.

When he came out again, he was wearing jeans and a T-shirt. He followed her to her room and remained inside by the door.

She said, "It's not like I'm going to jump you or anything."

He said, "I know, but I needed to tell her . . ."

"Got it." She realised as she spoke that it didn't matter. Who the girl was, why she was there, what they'd done together . . . none of it truly and actually mattered. She said, "It's okay and everything, Bru. I get it now. We're not so different, you and me. We come at things different, but that's all it is."

"Right." If anything, he looked even warier.

She said, "Anyway, it's not about that. I got to ask you something about last year, in December, that night it snowed bad and we got so pissed at the Hart and Hind."

He frowned. "It snowed lots of nights. And we got pissed lots of nights."

"Right, but it's that night we went to the Hart and Hind with the plan, you and me. We drank cider instead of lager. It's that night, Brutus." She waited for recognition to dawn. When it didn't, she said, "Only the thing was that we didn't plan it to be as bad as it got. Finn was there as well. But he was drinking Guinness while the rest of us stuck with cider and you remember how we got wrecked? We didn't intend to—you and me, at least—but that's what happened."

He nodded slowly. "I remember. Yeah. That was dead stupid, wasn't it?"

"It was worse than stupid. It was really bad. I mean it got really bad. It's why things've been like they've been."

"What things? Ding, you're not making any sense."

"I haven't said anything to anyone. But now I need to know. My mind's been totally destroyed for ages and I'm trying to straighten it out so what I want to know is where you were. See, I woke up that night and you weren't here, and like you said, you always spent the night with me if we . . . you know . . . if we did it at night and not during the day or whatever. Only that night I woke up and you weren't here and you never came back. Where were you?"

He still looked confused, as if wondering why all these months later she would want to know something so meaningless. But he said, "I was hugging the loo."

"What?"

"I got up to pee. Only . . . I was bloody dizzy and then I started feeling like I was going to sick up on the floor. I made it to the loo and we got seriously acquainted—me and it—and I must've blacked out because I remember thinking I'd just rest a sec on the bathroom floor in front of the loo and next thing I knew, Finn was pissing over my head only it wasn't completely over my head. You know Finn. Anyway, he holds the drink better 'n I do and he wasn't drinking cider in the first place."

Ding raised her fingers to her lips. "The bathroom," she said. "You were in the bathroom that night when I woke up?"

"Till Finn showed, yeah. But by then it was light outside and I went to my room and that was it. Ding, what the hell's going on?"

She shook her head because she wasn't sure. She thought she had been. But the ground had shifted, and she had to think what she was meant to do.

LUDLOW
SHROPSHIRE

"Straight from the first—when I was here with the DCS—that bloke's laid out half-truths, sir. He's left out details and he's painted things this way first and that way later. Then it's been 'Oh, did I forget to mention my assortment of phone calls to the husband of the deputy chief constable and to Ian Druitt as well? And oh, yes indeedy-o, I'm acquainted with Finnegan Freeman and did I not ever mention that Mr. Druitt had concerns about him? *And* I'm also rather more than acquainted with a girl who just happens to live in the same house with Finnegan.'"

Barbara and Lynley had taken themselves onto the hotel terrace, where the coolness of the morning precluded anyone deciding to breakfast al fresco. Nor were they doing so. But daily more visitors were arriving in Ludlow, and daily Griffith Hall was housing them. Lynley had quietly told Barbara about his phone call to Nkata, and she wanted him to ring the DS another time and add Gary Ruddock to his list. Once she'd begun to argue this point, Lynley had taken her out to the terrace. Now they stood above the lawn and out of view of both the breakfast room and the lounge. Two gardeners were working among the shrubbery and the flowers, but they were at a distance, so the conversation between Barbara and her superior could go unheard.

Lynley was being too meditative by half. He appeared to be inspecting the work of the gardeners as if comparing it to whatever maintenance went on at the massive property in the Lord Asherton side of his life. She wanted him to swing into action, although she herself couldn't have said what that action was going to be. She said, "Sir . . . ? Earth to Inspector Lynley? Ludlow on the line."

He stirred. "I don't disagree in the least with the list of curiosities to which—"

"*Curiosities*?"

"—you're referring. But the fact remains that despite everything we've seen and heard—some of which is admittedly questionable—"

"*Questionable*?"

"—I think you'll agree that absolutely nothing amounts to a motive for anyone doing anything, *and*"—he raised his hand to keep her from interrupting again—"while I agree that motiveless suicide is on the list as well as motiveless murder *and* motiveless anything else, you must admit that that's damned strange, despite the nature of what's occurred."

"Those nineteen days, you mean."

"Among other things, but yes."

"So . . . ?" she tried to sound encouraging.

"We know there's more here than meets the eye, which is another reason to see what Nkata can dig up. But the problem remains what it was from the first, Barbara. We have no witness to anything save Officer Ruddock fetching binge drinkers somewhere, probably to their respective homes. And I don't need to mention that we have no conclusive evidence of anything else."

"And isn't *that* curious? Not Ruddock and the bingers. I mean having no witness to those other things, such as having a witness via film to whoever made the phone call that got Ian Druitt carted to the nick in the first place. Isn't it just too bloody convenient that the camera's position was switched so it wouldn't record the anonymous caller? And isn't it even more convenient that the camera itself was turned off for twenty seconds, which happens to be quite enough time for someone to get outside and move the camera's position and get back inside to turn it back on? Who the hell would you say is the likeliest suspect here?"

"Again, you won't find me disagreeing, although we have to take on board the fact that dozens of people have access to that station and those dozens include virtually every individual serving on the West Mercia police force. What time was that phone call made?"

"Round midnight."

"So do you actually see Officer Ruddock—who could have done the camera switching and the phone call at any time—getting up in the dead of night to trek over to the station to do it when all he really had to do was make sure he was alone in the station, which he apparently is most of the time, and then to do what needed to be done with the camera and the anonymous call?"

"Unless," she said, "he wants to make it look like he's being framed."

"There's that, admittedly," he noted. "But my point is that, there again, we've nothing at all that leads us to that conclusion."

"So we've come on a fool's errand? Is that it?"

Out on the lawn, one of the gardeners had started a mower and was now heading towards them. The other had begun spraying something on a climbing rose that was spilling blooms over the farthest corner of the garden wall. Lynley directed her off the terrace and towards Ludlow Castle, but they paused on the pavement across the street from the ruins to continue their discussion.

He said, "I'm not positing that. But you know what the problem is as well as I do: it's impossible to commit the perfect murder. There's always going to be evidence at some point unless somehow the murder manages to pose convincingly as a death so natural that there's no question about it. That being the case—I'm talking about the possibility of carrying out the perfect murder—if there *is* no evidence that this was murder, then the conclusion is the one originally reached. As regrettable as it seems, it was suicide."

"You actually believe that?"

"Barbara, I agree that the PCSO looks questionable. But the operative word—as you well know—is *looks*. And unless we come up with something beyond how things look, we're left with a great deal of finger-pointing and nothing else. And we're also left with being recalled to London, which I daresay is going to happen sooner rather than later."

She kicked at a small clump of weeds that was growing from a crack between the pavement stones. She muttered "Whatever" as she did so, but then she was struck by a sudden thought, so she looked up and said, "We're also left with manoeuvring, sir."

"Believe me, I haven't discounted that. But I'm not convinced we're at that point yet."

Over at the castle, someone was on the closest battlement arranging a flag that unfurled to advertise the coming Shakespeare Festival on the castle grounds. *Titus Andronicus* was on the menu. Lynley glanced at this and said, "Good Lord."

Barbara said, "What?"

"Rape, chopping off hands, cutting a tongue from a mouth, baking dead men into pies. You've not got there yet?"

"I'm only doing tragedies. Is that one of them?"

"That it's being produced at all, yes."

Barbara laughed in spite of herself. She said, "What about Francie Adamucci, then? She made it clear she wants Ruddock looked at. Could be that's at the bottom of what's been going on round here. Ruddock, drunken college students, trips to the nick for some of them . . . or at least trips to the nick's car park. Could be our Gaz doesn't have any special bird he's bonking and is 'too noble' to name. Could be he's collecting the bingers, taking them home, but each time saving one at the end to take to the car park instead."

"Why would she—I assume you mean that the one he takes to the car park is female—go with him?"

"Could be she doesn't want to be carted home for some reason. Trouble with Mummy and Dad comes to mind straight off, although I suppose it could be trouble with a tutor at the college, trouble with a housemate, trouble with anyone about anything. And could be that the trouble's avoided with a little bit of whatever our Gaz happens to fancy inside the patrol car."

"Where does that take us, Barbara?"

"To the first explanation of what's questionable about him. Everything else has been iffy but straightforward: meeting some woman he doesn't want to name for the sake of 'honour'—and didn't that have a nice ring to it—having it on with her the night Druitt died, dereliction of duty, and Gaz falling on his sword like Sir Lancelot and whatever."

"Lancelot didn't—"

"Oh, I bloody know that. Point is, he paints himself as nobility made flesh when all along could be he's forcing college girls to have sex with him when they're drunk. And that's not so straightforward. True that we need one of those girls to go on record. But in the meantime, back to manoeuvring, I say we let him think one of them has."

"And if we do that, where does it get us?"

Barbara considered it: where the possibility of Ruddock, drunken college girls, and the nick's car park could lead. Then she had it. She said, "Holy hell in a bun, sir! It gets us to a college girl spilling the beans to a man of God! It gets us to that man of God deciding that 'having a word' with Ruddock about what he's been up to is in order. It gets us to Ruddock deciding to do something about it before Druitt takes his 'word having' to another level, such as to Ruddock's superiors. We've got that Lomax girl meeting with Druitt, sir."

"You can't be suggesting it would take her *seven* sessions with Druitt to get round to telling him that Ruddock is having his way with young women in his patrol car."

"But if she's one of the girls—"

"Just think about it, Barbara. Isn't the solution to being 'one of the girls' merely to stop binge drinking? Or to binge indoors if bingeing's on the agenda?"

"*If* that's how and why he's collecting them, sir."

"And *if* he's 'collecting' them in the first place, because no one's being forthright about that."

"Harry Rochester is."

"Harry Rochester merely saw the PCSO with young people—some of them young women—who seemed to be drunk, full stop. You do see the problem, don't you?"

She looked to the castle again. On the battlements another banner was being unfurled. *The Importance of Being Earnest.* Lynley saw this as well, and murmured, "Hardly an antidote to the other, but at least it's a start." And then to her, "Well?"

She knew he wasn't referring to Oscar Wilde. She said, "We're dead in the water without proof."

"Even if we like the scenario of Ruddock and a college girl, we're overlooking any number of salient details to get there."

"I see that," she admitted. "Like where do the Freemans fit in, like why the phone calls between Druitt and Ruddock, like why's Ruddock been asked to keep an eye on Finnegan and is that even relevant, like why the gap in time to bring Druitt in for questioning once the anonymous paedophilia message happened. Like . . . What, sir?" Lynley had snapped his fingers.

He answered her with, "We've been absolute *fools*, Barbara."

"About what? Why?"

"About the nineteen days and what they've been telling us."

"Which is what?"

"That *Ruddock* had to be the one to make the arrest of Druitt. And that could only happen if the Shrewsbury patrol officers—whose job it otherwise would have been—were involved elsewhere. And *that* took nineteen days to occur."

"So Ruddock was *waiting* for those blokes to be involved somewhere else . . . like dealing with a string of burglaries?"

Lynley shook his head. "Not at all," he said. "Follow the breadcrumbs, Barbara. It's never been Ruddock who was doing the waiting."

LUDLOW
SHROPSHIRE

On the previous night, Trevor had done something that he'd not done in years. He'd gone down the pub and had too much to drink. Clo hadn't been at home for dinner, ringing to tell him she had a late meeting, so he'd decided the hell with making himself a meal, and at the pub he ordered fried scampi and peas with a hearty pile of chips. He swilled a pint of lager to wash the meal down, and when he'd finished it, he ordered another. Ultimately, he'd had four. He topped off his evening with two fingers of Jameson, after which he went home to find Clover in the kitchen, opening several days' post.

When he walked in, she gave him a look and said, "I hope someone drove you home."

He went to the table and stood before her. He gave her a mock salute. "Good little soldier checking in," he told her. "Scotland Yard showed up and I told them the tale. All's right in the world."

"I don't much like you when you're drunk, Trev. If you want to talk about this—"

"Didn't say that, did I?" And he took himself off to bed. He went to Finn's bedroom. There on the single bed he'd spent the night.

In the morning she was already gone when he rose, which he'd reckoned was just as well. He had things to see to and he didn't want one of them to be another attempt at wrenching information from his wife.

He drove straight to Ludlow. His conversation with Gaz Ruddock didn't need to be a long one, he decided, but it needed to happen. So once he arrived in town, he rang the PCSO's mobile to locate him. He'd appreciate a word, was how Trevor put it. He added the information that he was in Ludlow so he could easily meet up with the PCSO where and when Gaz could.

Gaz sounded surprised that Trevor was there in town, but he didn't ask for an explanation. Instead, he said that he was doing his usual walkabout, having a stroll from the superstore on Station Drive. He'd be taking in the railway station, and heading on past the library to the Bull Ring. Did Trevor want to meet him along the way?

That would be fine, Trevor told him. He was just at the police station and the Bull Ring wasn't far from there. He would see Gaz soon.

Their conversation could have been handled over the phone, but Trevor wanted to see Gaz in person. So once their plan to meet was laid, he set off up Lower Galdeford in the direction of Tower Street. This would take him to the Bull Ring, where just beyond it stood Ludlow's pictorial claim to fame, the fanciful multigabled, multilevel, multiwindowed structure called the Feathers Inn.

As usual, the inn was doing its bit as the subject of photographs, for its balcony displayed containers trailing vines and flowers and its leaded diamond panes caught the sunlight. Here was where Trevor saw Gaz Ruddock, posing cooperatively with a group of tourists. It was likely—although he wasn't clothed and helmeted as such—they assumed he was a traditional and now nonexistent English bobby on the beat.

Gaz saw him and grinned, giving a shrug that asked: What can one do? Trevor waited till the picture taking was completed, at which juncture the tourists moved off to follow their flag-bearing leader, fixing earphones on their heads. He joined Gaz and said, "Where next?" to which the PCSO said, "Mill Street by way of Brand Lane and Bell Lane, but that can wait if you fancy something. Coffee or whatever. But at the Bull"—he gestured across to that hostlery with its inn yard into which coaches once had set down their passengers—"not here."

Trevor didn't want anything to eat or to drink, but he also wanted to be able to see Gaz's face as he spoke to him. That couldn't be accomplished if they were walking side by side, so he agreed. The Bull was fine.

The hour was such that the only people in the bar area were a college-professor type—at least by his garb—and three younger people whom Trevor took for students. They were huddled in a far corner, engaged in an avid conversation. They didn't even take note of anyone else entering the place.

Trevor demurred on the coffee, but Ruddock fetched himself one. While he was doing so, Trevor decided upon a table where the light was best. There were stools, not chairs, so it wasn't going to be a comfortable spot to perch, but he didn't intend to be there long.

"Finn's well?" Gaz set his coffee on the table and dumped milk into it. He stirred it carefully, as if with concern that he might slosh the brew out of the cup should he apply the spoon too energetically.

"Not as well as I'd like. Scotland Yard burst in on him yesterday morning."

Gaz frowned. "They've got bees in their knickers, that lot. You want me to have a word with Finn? I can let him know he's not the only person they're paying calls on so he's not to worry."

Trevor studied Gaz. He had such an innocent face. It was either his natural expression, not to mention his very nature, or he'd become quite good at projecting it. He would need the earnestness, naturally. That had served him well at the training school and would be even more necessary to his future after the death at the Ludlow station. But it could also serve interests other than professional. Trevor didn't want to forget that for a moment.

He said, "You won't need to do that. Finn's handling it. He was a bit cut up when they showed up in his bedroom—"

"What the *hell*?"

"Right. It was a definite shocker and designed to be that way. But Finn's past it now. I told him I'd have a word, and I intend to do."

"Does Clo know about this?"

"Why d'you ask?"

Gaz drew his eyebrows together. He seemed surprised at the question, as if the answer should be obvious. "She outranks the two who came. Seems like she could do something about it if they show up in her son's bedroom. Like give a bell to London or whatever."

"Ah," Trevor said. "Yes. She does have that power. I'm surprised you were never put off by that. Most blokes in your position would take quite some patch of time to get to know a superior officer, but that wasn't a problem for you."

"I got to know them all, is what it is, Trev. I mean all the higher-ups who gave courses at the training centre."

"You definitely got to know Clover," Trevor remarked. "Least that's what all the phone calls from my mobile suggest. You went back and forth a lot, you two."

"Like I told you, it was Finn."

"Yes. Like you told me." Trevor gave him what he intended to be an avuncular look. He wasn't sure it was coming off as such because he didn't feel the least avuncular at the moment. But it was time to put the full stop in place, so he said, "We can call that off now, Gaz."

"What?"

"Your watching over Finn and reporting back to his mum."

"Does Clo not want me to do it any longer?"

"I'm sure she does. If she could, she'd have someone watching over Finn into his dotage. I'm the one putting an end to things. Finn's doing fine, so you can let him sort out his life on his own."

Gaz looked at his coffee. A muscle moved slightly, at the back of his jaw. He finally said, "If that's how you want it, Trev."

"It's definitely how I want it," Trevor told him. "Finn wants it as well. And I'm sure once I tell Clover, she'll agree it's for the best. No lad—well, I should actually say no young man, shouldn't I?—wants his mum assigning him a guardian angel. Or a guardian. Or a guard. As for the rest, let's keep things as they are. You're something of a friend of the family at this point, after all."

Gaz looked up. "I hope I am. You're that important to me, Trev. All of you."

Trevor smiled. "Beyond everything else, Gaz . . . ? I know that we are."

LUDLOW
SHROPSHIRE

Ding walked in the direction of the Ludford Bridge, her footsteps not quite as quick as they should have been, considering she was on her way to a tutorial and knowing that even if she jogged there, she was going to be late and Greta Yates was probably going to hear about it. But she couldn't make herself go at a faster pace because she was caught up in a combination of thought and memory, reaching conclusions that made her more uneasy than she'd been in months. She finally understood that she'd been taken in by Finn Freeman. So had everyone else.

The truth was that despite using him to "get at" Brutus, she'd actually not given much thought to Finn aside from his inept approach as a lover. But now she saw that Finn's ineptness had always been a clue to who he was, and she'd missed it. So she understood what she wasn't intended to understand or even to know. The problem was, she hadn't the first clue what to do about it.

She was considering this as she crossed the Ludford Bridge in the direction of the Charlton Arms. The Breadwalk was her chosen route, rising a good distance above the river just beyond the free house. This would take her quickly to Dinham Street, where her tutor held sessions with students in a former chapel that was now his house.

She was scurrying along when she heard her name called. It came from in front of her, and she saw that the caller was Chelsea Lloyd, of all people. Since as far as she knew Chelsea never got out of bed before ten in the morning and had made sure all of her lectures and tutorials reflected this, Ding knew something was up. Chelsea hurried towards her.

"Thank goodness," she said. "I was waiting outside Mr. MacMurra's house. Did you know there was a bloke sleeping rough under it? It's got this open area that was part of a crypt or something and—"

"Were you waiting for me? Why?" Ding cut in. "I'm late so I got to walk fast, Chels."

"Oh, right. Sorry." Chelsea hurried along at Ding's side. "Francie wanted me to talk to you. She told me she tried to explain the Brutus thing but that you didn't want to understand. God, are you in good shape or what? Can you slow down? I can barely breathe. Anyway, she's ever so sorry about Brutus, Ding. It's just how she is, you know? She just larks about, doesn't she? And it's not like you ever gave us a clue that Brutus meant something to you more than . . . you know."

"He doesn't."

"Oh. *Can* we slow down?"

"I'm already late, Chels. And I'm in trouble with the college anyway so I got to get there. Was Brutus what she wanted you to talk to me about? Because if it is, you can tell her he doesn't mean anything to me. He did, obviously, but now he doesn't. The coast is clear or whatever."

"Can I tell her you don't want to scratch her eyes out any longer?"

"You can tell her whatever you want. Was that the message?"

"Whoof." Chelsea was breathing hard. "I got to take up jogging or something. Anyway, no that wasn't. I mean it wasn't the message." She had to drop behind when the path narrowed, shrubs and weeds growing thickly in an area that allowed more sun, but she didn't stop talking. "She wants you to know the cops pinned her down last night. It was about Gaz Ruddock. They told her she got pointed out as someone who'd been seen with him."

"So? That doesn't exactly surprise me. It's not like she hasn't been with practically *everyone*, let's face it."

"Right. Yeah." Chelsea hustled to catch Ding up. The river below them glittered in the sunlight. Birds soared out of the trees in the direction of the bridge, chirruping happily. "But she hasn't ever been with him like *you've* been with him. If you know what I mean. He tried it with her, but you know Francie. Nothing puts the frighteners on her. And anyway, her parents know about everything she does: the drinking and the blokes and doing stuff with them. They've sort of washed their hair of her. So really, where did he think that was going to get him except, obviously, he doesn't know her. Or he didn't know her. And anyway that was, when? Last October?"

Ding did slow up then. Indeed, she stopped for a moment. Hand on her hip, she asked, "Is there a point to this, Chels?"

"Well . . . there is. See, thing is that the last thing in the world Francie wants to be is anyone's bit of fun. I know. I know. You know that already. But the thing is, the cops kept pressing her and she rather . . . She lost it a bit."

Ding resumed her pace. No matter what this inane conversation was about, she needed to get to her tutorial. She said, "Okay. Got it. She lost it."

"Right. And *when* she lost it . . . she sort of told the cops to talk to *you* if they wanted the real story on Gaz Ruddock."

Ding's legs went to jelly. She turned to Chelsea. "Why did she *say* that? Chelsea, that puts me straight *in* things, it does."

"Like I said, she lost it. She got caught up in stuff. And that's what cops do, don't they? They get you caught up. Look, she feels dead awful that she even mentioned your name to them, but she wanted you to know. And she *did* say something like how we'd all be dead chuffed if someone did *something* about Ruddock. And that sort of misdirects, doesn't it? I mean, it takes them away from thinking about you. They probably don't even remember she said your name, right? And it's not like she made something up or anything."

Strength returned to her legs and Ding swung back to the path, saying, "That just makes me feel *so* much better, knowing she didn't make something up."

"She's sorry, Ding. Really, she's sorry. She asked me to tell you as soon as I could, which, you see, is what I'm doing. She wanted to warn you and to give you a chance."

"For *what*, exactly?"

"*I* don't know. But I think she wanted to give you a chance to plan what to say. About Gaz Ruddock and everything else."

LUDLOW
SHROPSHIRE

When Lynley knocked upon the door to the room that Barbara Havers had been assigned, the last thing he expected to hear from the sergeant as she opened it was "I'm sorry. Really. I did *try* to hand it off to you, Inspector. Remember?" before she admitted him.

As she stepped back from the door, he saw the cause of her embarrassment. A sitting room, a sofa, two chairs, a coffee table, and beyond that a bedroom with an en suite into which, he guessed, since he could not see it at the moment, his entire room could have fit. He took all this in and said to her, "You do know you now have absolutely no excuse for not practising, Sergeant."

"Oh God, don't *tell* her. Here. Look." She dumped an overnight case onto the sofa and excavated through its contents to bring forth a pair of red tap shoes. "See?"

"I'm unconvinced. They look remarkably unworn."

"They aren't! I swear. Every night I've been at it. Whoever's below me . . . ? I expect they think woodpeckers have invaded the building." She threw the shoes in the general direction of the rest of her belongings and said, "I've cleared the bed."

"I rest reassured. Let's see what we have."

Lynley reached for his spectacles in his jacket pocket. On the bed he divided in half the reports and the photographs. Together, he and Havers began to lay them out. He remarked as they did so, "I think what we've failed to see is that this was about getting individuals—in the plural, mind you—out of the way. One of them needed to be got out of the way permanently—"

"Druitt."

"—while the other, Ruddock, needed to be temporarily out of commission in whatever way that could be made to happen. The IPCC looked at Druitt's suicide that night in the Ludlow station and at what occurred in the aftermath to deal with the death. Your investigation with Isabelle—with the DCS—looked at that as well as delving round Ian Druitt's life and times to see if someone might have wanted to eliminate him: anonymous phone calls, allegations of paedophilia, diaries, meetings with various people. You asked yourselves what he did, whom he knew, what he knew, and why he needed to be done away with if, in reality, he wasn't actually a suicide. You and I have taken things further but not far enough, because what we haven't considered is both of them together: Ruddock and Druitt."

"Druitt needing to be brought into the station," Havers said, "but only if it could be managed that Ruddock was the one who brought him in."

"Yes. Because the point was to keep Druitt in *Ludlow*, which couldn't happen if any of the Shrewsbury officers fetched him to the custody suite there."

"So once the paedophile message gets sent, someone starts monitoring things, waiting for the right moment for an arrest, and nineteen days later, there's Uncle Bob. Ruddock does what he's told to do, to fetch Ian Druitt, and then he's got out of the way as well." Havers was staring down at the photos that they'd laid beneath all of the documents. "But how?" she asked. "We know he made phone calls to the local pubs, but that was pure chance: that he'd need to do it. And calling round to the pubs isn't going to take long enough for someone else to sneak in and kill Druitt anyway. Unless, of course, those phone calls were a fly in the ointment, something he had to take care of before the main event of poke-grab-and-whatever in the car park. But with who?"

Lynley looked at her, an eyebrow raised, waiting for her to work it out, which she did quickly. "Someone who's made an arrangement with him, along the lines of tonight's-our-night-so-be-ready-for-me-you-big-hunk-of-manflesh. So she clears the way and Druitt's alone while she and Ruddock are panting and heaving in the car, giving someone else a chance to kill him." She tapped her lip, frowning and then going on with, "But that means that Ruddock . . ."

"He's left in a position he can't possibly defend, believing that Druitt killed himself while he, Ruddock, was outside in the patrol car—"

"Bonking someone he can't want anyone to know he's bonking. Which means as far as the night Druitt died is concerned, our bloke Ruddock's been telling the truth. He's just not giving us the name of the woman involved. Bloody hell, sir. He's not falling on his sword to be a gentleman, is he? He's falling on his sword because he probably worked it all out directly it happened. And if he makes a wrong move now, which is pretty much a move in any direction, isn't it, he's done for. Because he knows what happened and he also knows there's not a shred of evidence for it."

"So it's easier for the PCSO just to go along and agree it was a suicide. I daresay he was in a panic enough when he rang 999 because at first he probably thought it *was* a suicide until he put everything together."

"But now everything's falling apart. No wonder he's been making all those calls to Worcester."

"No wonder indeed."

Havers looked at the items on the bed, then back at him. "But where the hell does that take us, sir? We've not moved an inch. We don't have evidence."

Lynley picked up two of the photos and held them side by side. He said, "That's not quite it, Barbara. We do have evidence. It's here somewhere. We just have to find it."

WANDSWORTH
LONDON

Isabelle hadn't intended to take another day. Of course, she hadn't actually intended to take the previous day, either. But things had got away from her, as happened occasionally in life. In her case, one thing had simply led to another until going into work was out of the question and leaving a message declaring illness was the only available alternative.

Upon first rising from bed, she'd felt herself fully recovered from all previous physical difficulties. It was far earlier than her normal time to be up and about, and she considered this a positive sign. She'd gone to the kitchen and started the water for coffee, pausing first to pour her morning orange juice dressed with just a touch of vodka. She downed this, but afterwards she felt, oddly, not quite one hundred percent. It was, she reckoned, a case of not having had a decent meal in at least forty-eight hours.

With this on her mind, she decided an egg was in order. She'd always enjoyed a soft-boiled egg accompanied by granary bread, lightly toasted. So she took a pot and an egg and did her bit with them on the cooktop. The bread was a tiny problem in that mould had established a foothold on one side of it, but she merely cut that off and popped it into the toaster. By that time, the water for her coffee had boiled and as she'd already done her bit with the coffee beans, she saw to that next. She paused then. Another orange juice sounded good. It tasted just a bit off to her, so she helped it out with another splash of vodka. And then a lovely cup of coffee.

She'd been doing quite well with it all. She'd been doing positively grand. She'd forgotten to time the egg, but a glance at the kitchen clock told her it had probably been in the water long enough and anyway the bread was toasted and buttered and waiting.

It was the egg that did her in. When she tapped it round the top and lifted the shell, she saw that she'd miscalculated. The egg was so undercooked that dipping her spoon into it brought forth only a slithering mess. At the sight of this, her insides did a flip-flop that not even a large bite of toast—quickly taken and just as quickly chewed and swallowed—could cope with. Everything rose. Orange juice, coffee, toast. She ran to the bathroom and began vomiting.

What followed was a headache, which she hadn't had upon waking but which, after sicking up her aborted breakfast, she had in throbbing, blinding spades. It wasn't something two, four, or twenty paracetamol would be able to cure. But she was determined to get past it on willpower alone in order to get herself to work that day. She needed a lie-down first, though. So she staggered to her bed and lowered herself, whispering that this was mind over matter and the matter in question was merely a collection of blood vessels inside her brain. She turned on her side and clutched a pillow to her stomach. Ten minutes, she thought.

But that didn't do it, and Isabelle knew there was only one way out of her physical ailments. It involved vodka.

She told herself that *surely* she was enough of a woman to master this situation. It took an effort of will to get into the kitchen, but she managed it. She calculated that a mere few shots of Grey Goose would not lead to another day of oblivion. So she had them.

When the phone call came, it awakened her. She saw the time. More than two hours had passed. Her first thoughts took her to the Met, Dorothea Harriman, Hillier, and Judi-with-an-i, despite the fact that she was not yet terribly late for work. She swung to a sitting position, felt her stomach heave, and grabbed her mobile.

It wasn't anyone from New Scotland Yard, however. It was Bob. He said, "No need to panic, Isabelle, but something's happened to Laurence."

She pressed her fingers to her temples. She knew that she had to sound normal. She said, "Wha's go . . . ing on?"

A pause. Then, "He's taken something of a tumble at school, and we've brought him to A & E. At least, I've brought him. Sandra's with James. He was rather upset, as you can imagine."

"A & E? God. Is he broken?" That wasn't at all what she meant. She clutched one hand beneath her chin as if this would make her words come out properly.

Another pause. This one was longer before Bob said, "He's managed to give himself a hairline fracture of the skull. He was going at things a bit rough—well, he's a boy after all—and he fell from one of the flint-stone walls on the edge of the property where he wasn't meant to be in the first place. He was unconscious—"

"Oh Christ."

"—but that was brief. They rang for an ambulance and here we are."

What to say or do when her words weren't coming out correctly and she could barely move from her bed? She said, "Sh'll I . . . ?"

He said, "He's going to be fine. We're meant to watch him closely over the next several weeks and definitely keep him quiet, but there's nothing they can do beyond let his skull heal up."

"Oh God."

"The thing is, Isabelle, he's asking for you. He's got himself into quite a state about it—very unlike Laurence, I know, as one would expect this more of James—but he's calling for you. At first I thought he meant Sandra, of course—"

Of *course*? she thought.

"—because he was asking for Mummy, which is generally what both boys call her, as you know. But when she came to A & E, he made it perfectly clear that he wants you."

She was meant to jump to her feet. She was meant to go to him at once. Nothing was meant to stop her. She knew that just as she knew she was fully incapable of doing anything at all. She said, "Oh. Bob . . . I'm so . . . Can you say him . . . tell him . . ."

"You've been drinking, haven't you?" he asked sharply. "Are you at work? No. You can't be. Of course you can't be."

"I haven't. I'm ill. I think it's flu. I've been sick and now my head—"

"Isabelle, stop it. Just bloody *stop* it."

"Please. Please tell . . . I'm going to be there. Please tell him Mummy'll come to him as soon as she's able."

"And when might that be?" He didn't wait for a reply and, clearly, he didn't want one. "I'm not making excuses for you. He's not stupid. Neither is James."

"Bob. *Bob.* Least put him on the phone."

"Have you any idea what you sound like? I've no intention of allowing him to hear you like this."

"But tell him—"

"I'm telling him nothing. Get yourself together, Isabelle. When you finally do, you can tell him yourself."

He rang off and she was left calling out his name, asking for Laurence, asking for James, declaring she was well and fit and on her way even as she knew she could no more drive to Kent than could she fly there. She sank back onto the bed. She would, she would, she would, she told herself. She just needed rest, another day . . .

She rang the Met and was able to leave a message because thankfully Dorothea either wasn't there yet or was not at her desk. Then, because she could do nothing else, she went to the kitchen. She staggered there. Her head was thundering and her limbs were quaking. Upset, she thought. Worried, she thought. Laurence there in A & E with a fractured skull, crying for his mummy and of *course* she was beside herself with concern, which was all this was.

When she took up the vodka, her reason for doing so was clear. She needed it to soothe the worries, to make herself ready to go to her son, to be whole for once instead of someone who had to pretend every second of the day that—

No. No. That was not it. She would eat. No. She would drink. No. Coffee would help her and then she could get on with life as it was *meant* to be lived, which was not how she'd been living it.

She drank from the bottle another time and she told herself that was it. That was all she would have. But the worries got to her and the fact that she couldn't go to him when she was meant to go to him because she was, after all, the mother who loved him, who'd borne him, who'd changed those nappies and fed him from her breast, and did Sandra do that, did she even know what it was to have a child—two children—growing inside and then clawing their way out with so much pain and suffering and the only way ever to deal with the pain and with the suffering and with everything else that ate at her like some alien imbedded in her soul . . . She had reasons, not excuses, and there were a thousand of them and no one could take them from her and no one ever would.

She was conscious when the bell went on her door. She was in the sitting room and she hadn't dressed and it was true she'd been drinking but she was fully conscious. Still, she knew she couldn't answer that bell. Nor could she answer the knocking that followed a third ring.

Then it came to her that it was Bob. Of course it was Bob. He was showing mercy and he'd come to fetch her. All she needed was a very quick shower and she would be ready and she'd swear to him anything he wanted her to swear to, just to show her gratitude for coming into London to take her to their son.

Only. She made it to the door, and by the grace of God she did not open it. But it had been fixed with a fish-eye peephole, and when she looked through it what came upon her was a horror she never expected to feel, not with her life under her own command as it had been for so very long. For standing there in all her workplace finery was Dorothea Harriman, and as she called out Isabelle's rank in her habitual fashion, she didn't look like someone who intended to stop knocking anytime soon.

LUDLOW
SHROPSHIRE

They studied the photographs of Ian Druitt's dead body every which way to Saturday night and beyond. Barbara decided she could have drawn both the body and the scene of death from memory, when Lynley finally called a halt to things. He took up two photos, put the rest into the folder in which they'd been stored, and removed his specs. He said, "We need some air. Come along, although you'll have to lead as I've no idea how we actually reached this room."

She did the honours, snatching up her shoulder bag and snaking her way down stairs, through fire doors, and along corridors. When they reached the lobby at last, Peace on Earth was behind reception and he took them in with a glance that, to Barbara, looked like a knowing one. Man-woman-hotel, in addition to several hours' disappearance of man and woman into the depths of said hotel, apparently led to a single conclusion in his experience. That, she thought, was a bloody good laugh. She almost told Lynley but she wasn't sure his delicate sensibilities could handle the horror of it. So she let him lead the way out of the hotel.

He walked in the direction of the castle. She had a sinking feeling that her knowledge of kings, queens, and battles royal was about to undergo an expansion. She headed him off by saying, "It's the Plantagenets, sir, the whole bleeding kettle of them. I can't keep them straight."

He paused and turned to her. "What are you talking about, Sergeant?"

"That." Here she pointed at the castle. "That's where we're going, isn't it? The dungeon, the keep, the bailey, the whatever?"

He looked from her, to the castle, back to her. He said, "Havers, often I wonder what in God's name you actually take me for. Although"—and here she could see he was attempting not to smile—"I'm impressed with your knowledge of castles."

"Don't be. It comes from romance novels. Damsels in the dungeon having their bodices ripped and the like. Plus I've got *The Princess Bride* on video. 'My name is Inigo Montoya' and all that. I could probably quote the whole film."

"Ah. I'm nonetheless quite impressed. As before, however, come along."

He did cross the street to the castle, but he chose a bench at the base of the castle wall. There were people round and about, but most of them were walking dogs or airing toddlers in pushchairs. They offered something to look at besides the range of buildings across the street.

Lynley handed her one of the photos he'd brought with him. "What occurs to you, Sergeant?"

She studied it. The crime scene photographer had documented every inch of the office in which Druitt had died, and this particular photo took in a corner of it. There, a yellow plastic chair of the stackable variety lay on its side. Above it was an empty bulletin board with lighter patches on it where notices and such had hung. Next to it was the office window. Only part of this was visible and its venetian blinds were tilted upwards.

"The blinds," she said. "No one outside the room could see in. But didn't we already talk about this? As an item to pin something on someone, there's no value at all. Anyone could have put them in that position."

"Completely true. Anything else?"

She looked closer to see if there was something she'd missed, like . . . She wasn't sure what, although a declaration of someone's guilt scratched into the lino would have gone down a treat. She said, "Since there's just the chair and the bulletin board . . ."

"Yes. What strikes you?"

"About?"

"The chair."

"You mean that it's overturned?"

"I mean that it's in the room at all. The other piece of furniture was a desk, as you recall."

"Right. But no one'd put Druitt into an office to hold him but not give the bloke a chair."

"Agreed."

"So you mean . . ." She looked back at the picture and then at Lynley. "You mean *this* chair, don't you?" She turned the photo round to another angle. She could feel Lynley watching her and she knew there had to be something he'd seen, but looking for blood or hairs or fibres or anything else was getting her nowhere since, aside from blood—which wasn't present anyway—the rest wouldn't be visible in a photograph.

She thought back to her visits to the Ludlow nick, both with Lynley and earlier without him. When she did so, she understood what he was asking her to see and she felt chagrinned that she hadn't caught it immediately. "When you and I met with Ruddock," she said as she recalled the PCSO's actions that day, "we met in the old lunchroom, where he and I met the first time I was there. But there weren't three chairs so he had to get another for you."

"Indeed," Lynley said.

"He *rolled* a chair in there for you. That's what you're getting at, aren't you, sir? But what's that mean? The desk chair could have come from anywhere."

Lynley took the picture from her and studied it, saying, "It could have done, yes. And it's not the desk chair itself—that particular chair Ruddock offered me—that's of interest here, Barbara. It's the lack of desk chair in this office or this picture."

"I see that, but it could've been removed, just like Ruddock removed the chair from wherever to give to you."

"I daresay it *was* removed," Lynley said. "The question we might ask ourselves is why it was replaced with this other?"

"We could do," Barbara said. "But that's thin on the ground, isn't it? I mean, the other's more comfortable—the one on rollers—but who wants a potential paedophile to be comfortable anyway?"

"I don't disagree. There's that to be argued, a case of 'Let's not make this easy on him,' but that presupposes the PCSO knew why he was fetching Ian Druitt to the station, and we've learned he didn't know the reason."

"Or he *says* he didn't know."

"There's that as well." He put the photo back into the folder and he brought out the other he'd taken from Barbara's room. This, Barbara saw, was of Druitt's supine body, the ligature removed and lying on the floor post the PCSO's attempt to save him. Barbara looked from the photo to Lynley and back to the photo. She was about to ask him what was next when he told her, "Let's arrange to speak to the pathologist, Sergeant. If we missed something—as we did when it comes to the chair—she might have done also."

COALBROOKDALE
SHROPSHIRE

Sati had been persuaded to set off to school. Once Timothy was on his feet and leaning against the wall of the shower with the water hitting his head, Yasmina had gone to her youngest child and had assured her that Daddy was fine and that mothers and daughters sometimes argued, which was what she'd witnessed with Missa before she left with Justin. These things happened on occasion, and Sati was not to worry because Yasmina would speak to Missa that very afternoon and bring her home. As for her father, he'd only been asleep, darling, and it was a complicated matter to rouse him because he'd taken a pill last night.

So Sati had reluctantly gone off to school, clutching her Hello Kitty lunch box. That had left Yasmina able to deal with Timothy. She returned to the bathroom.

"You could have died," were her first words to her husband. "How much more do you want to put us through? Sati has watched her older sister die, she's just watched Missa leave this house with her belongings, and now this. You. Virtually unconscious with your wife beating on your body to bring you round. I might have had to use the naloxone, and she might have seen me do it. Is that what you want? Is that where we're heading?"

"We're already there," had been his mumbled reply.

She'd wanted to jump into the shower, to grab on to his curling steely hair and beat his head against the tiles on the wall. Instead she cried, "You're cursing us. No wonder Missa can't stand to be here. No *wonder* she's left."

He opened his eyes at this, raising his head and putting his bloodshot gaze upon her. "At least she has the courage to do something, Yas. That's more than I can say for the rest of us."

Which made her wonder if she'd ever known him. Which made her watch him at the clinic during the day with the window between them, just waiting for the moment when he'd cadge more pills. But she could not remain and monitor all his movements because she had to keep her promise to Sati. So she cancelled her last four appointments for the day.

The penultimate place she wished to head was to Blists Hill Victorian Town. But the ultimate place was to the home of Justin Goodayle's family, so she got into her car and drove out of Coalbrookdale.

Yasmina went directly to the candlemaker's shop. But there she found another young woman in Missa's place, explaining to a small contingent of tourists how candles had been fashioned in the days of the Victorians. When she looked in her direction, Yasmina mouthed "Missa?" The girl paused to reenter the present century, saying, "Hi, Dr. Lomax. She's at the fish and chips shop. Mary Reid got ill and Missa's the only one on the grounds just now who knows how to work the fryer properly."

Yasmina retraced her steps to one of main streets of the town. The shop she was looking for advertised itself easily enough with the tempting scent of frying food and a sign that read FRIED FISH AND CHIPPED POTATOES. ONLY THE FINEST BEEF DRIPPING USED. Inside the place, Missa had her back to the shop counter on which a line of paper cones stood waiting for chips and four customers stood waiting for the cones. Missa was offering them no explanation about her work. What could one actually say about immersing chipped potatoes into hot oil?

When she turned and saw Yasmina waiting among the others,

Missa gave no outward reaction. She merely filled the cones as requested and added to them two orders of the battered cod. The customers left happily, and Yasmina approached the counter. She ordered a cone of chips and when given them, she said to her daughter, "When will you be free, Missa? I'd like to have a word."

"We've said everything possible on every subject," Missa said.

"Nevertheless. When are you free? I doubt you would be very happy to have me lurking in the shop waiting for you."

Missa pressed her lips together as she considered this, finally saying, "My final break is in twenty minutes. If you want to wait, that's fine. You can always look up Justin for a private word in the meantime. I know you like to do that."

Yasmina refused to be drawn into defending herself. She said, "I'll wait at the carousel, my dear," and with her cone of chips in her hand, she left the shop. She dropped the wretched stuff into a rubbish bin as soon as she saw one.

The carousel wasn't far from the big refreshment pavilion, and there were benches nearby where parents could sit and watch their children on the antique ponies. Yasmina found a seat on one and took in what comprised the Victorian funfair.

There were five stalls featuring games of chance, but the carousel was the fair's most popular feature for families having a day out with small children. There weren't a great number enjoying the galloping ponies on this day, but those that were waved and laughed as they rose and fell with the cheerful music while watchful parents and grandparents stood nearby.

Taking this in, Yasmina's vision blurred. Her own daughters had ridden those ponies. They, too, had laughed and waved. Missa especially had loved the carousel, had loved the entire Victorian town. Yasmina had encouraged this love with picture books and paper dolls. She merely hadn't ever thought that Victoriana in this particular fashion would end up as her daughter's life work.

She waited patiently. She told herself she would listen to Missa instead of arguing with her or attempting to cajole her. She *wanted* to do this, she told herself. For if she didn't manage some sort of peace with her daughter here and now, there would be no resolution to anything.

When Missa at last arrived, she plopped down onto the bench. She, too, took in the carousel.

"How you loved it," Yasmina remarked. "You used to tell me that you would be in charge of that carousel one day. Do you remember?"

"We've beaten Blists Hill to death as a subject," was Missa's tart reply.

"I'm not here to talk about Blists Hill."

"So what is it that you've come to say? That you're sorry you promised rubbish weddings and rubbish honeymoons and rubbish dream cottages? Is that why you're here? Linda was impressed, by the way. She didn't know you and Dad have access to those kinds of funds."

"That's what you call her now? No longer Mrs. Goodayle, is it?"

Missa brushed a nonexistent hair off her face. "We've discussed whether it's going to be *Mum* after Justie and I marry, but that doesn't feel right to either of us. She said Linda's fine. She prefers it to 'Mother Goodayle' or 'Mother Linda,' which she said would make her feel like someone in a convent."

Yasmina had no wish to extend further a conversation on the topic of Missa's future with the Goodayle clan. She said, "I was wrong in what I did. I apologise. I'm here to ask you to come back home. Sati is terribly upset by what's happened."

"Which part of what happened? The part where she knows you've tried to use Justin to get me to do your bidding or the part where I called a halt to it all?"

"This thing . . . your leaving as you've done . . . this isn't good for her to see at her age. I believe you understand that, Missa."

"Not *good*?" Missa's face settled into that hardness that Yasmina found so disturbing. She said, "We're not setting a bad example, if that's what you're worried about, Mum. You can tell Sati I have my own bedroom. I'm not sleeping with Justin." She looked away, at the carousel and the laughing children. She took a moment before she went on with, "I still want what I always wanted, what you *made* me want, matter of fact. White wedding, virginity, pure as the wool of an Easter lamb."

Yasmina said, "Sati's lost Janna. She's—"

"We've *all* lost Janna."

"—twelve years old. You mean everything to her."

Missa gave a short laugh. "What I mean to Sati isn't important to you, Mum."

"That's not true."

"Whatever you say. Anyway, me living with the Goodayles? This is only till we have our own place, me and Justin. We're going to look for a cottage to let. We're thinking about one above the river. In Jackfield. It has only one bedroom, but we think it might do for now. Of course, Justie will sleep on the sofa till the 'blessed' day arrives. No worries, like always, Mum. We'll get a bigger place eventually, but that'll take time. Justie's business is going well but so far his output only pays for supplies, the cost of letting the building at the tile museum, and a bit of extra. Once he's able to hire a helper, production will increase. That person won't have as much talent as Justin, of course, but whoever it is can help with the work that's not so detailed." She looked directly at Yasmina. "You never thought of him as someone with talent, did you?"

"Sati is my concern now," Yasmina said. "I understand that you will do what you will do. Everyone has made that perfectly clear to me. But Sati needs you. That's all this is: something I'm asking you to do for Sati."

"Tell Sati that if we take the cottage, she can come to us," Missa said. "It won't be long and then she'll be free."

"Have we come to that, Missa? Is this truly what you want to say to your mother?"

Missa shook her head. It was one of those maddening movements that declared Yasmina's questions to be exactly what Missa had come to expect. It was also one of those maddening movements that Yasmina wanted to strike out against. *When*, she wondered, had her daughter begun this change of personality? More, why had she begun it?

"You would think that, Mum," Missa said. "You take everything as an insult. But all I did was state a fact."

Yasmina looked away from her then, at the endless spinning of the carousel and the children who were so enchanted by the fantasy ride it gave them upon the backs of its artificial ponies. "Then there's nothing else to be said, my dearest."

"Stop calling me that. I'm not your dearest."

Yasmina turned back to her. "Of course you are. Despite all this, you remain my child, my dearest child. This . . . this thing between us now, it will pass. Perhaps not exactly as I wish it to—"

"Not *exactly*, Mum? What *exactly* does 'not exactly' look like to you? We're going to get married. I know you'll still try anything you can think of to stop us, but we *will* get married. Can you understand that?"

"Missa." Everything Yasmina was feeling created a pressure against her chest. So great was it that for an instant she wondered if her heart was failing. "I understand. There isn't a point to my resisting any longer. I *see* that. But will you tell me why the urgency of it all? That's what I cannot understand. The urgency, the rush, as if you feel you must prove something, as if there's a need for haste."

"We want it like that," she said. "We want it soon. We want it *now*. Because it's been decided. Because I've decided. Not for you, not for Dad, not for Sati or Granny or even for Justin. *I've* decided for once, and I've decided for *me*." She stood then, and Yasmina saw with surprise that Missa appeared to be struggling not to weep. She saw it in the difficulty she had with what she said next. "It's what I want and it's what I'm doing. That's all it is."

But it wasn't. It absolutely wasn't. Yasmina knew it and she could see it. And then the sudden clarity came to her. Yasmina said, so close to a whisper that she wasn't sure her daughter could hear her, "You're engaged in a punishment. Aren't you?"

"Not everything in life is about you," was her reply.

"No, no. You misconstrue," Yasmina said. "I don't mean you're punishing me. I mean you're punishing yourself. I just don't know why. But it's the truth, isn't it?"

"And not every truth is yours, either," she responded.

WANDSWORTH

LONDON

She hadn't stayed long. One glance had been enough to tell her exactly what the detective chief inspector's spate of illness was all about. She'd come to Wandsworth with—God help us—soup and sandwiches purchased on the way. She'd said, thrusting them towards Isabelle, "We're all . . . We're . . . We hope you feel better soon."

Isabelle had felt the accusation of spying rise to her tongue. She felt *you're a little copper's nark, aren't you* looking for a way into the air. She had little doubt that while Dorothea Harriman might keep mum about what she'd discovered when she was anywhere near the officers currently under Isabelle's command, she would never keep mum round the one officer whom Isabelle wanted least to know about her condition.

When she'd managed to clear Harriman off the premises, she poured the soup straight down the drain. The sandwiches she stuffed into the rubbish. She didn't need either, nor did she want the concern they represented.

She'd phoned Bob repeatedly throughout the rest of the day. He'd not responded. She'd had to attempt getting Sandra to speak to her, which she finally accomplished round six o'clock. She'd only made herself one fortifying drink in the intervening hours. She had no intention of missing another day of work because she *was* the master of her basest desires.

Sandra answered her mobile with, "Please stop ringing me, Isabelle. I'm answering this once to let you know I'll not answer again. If you want to deal with anyone at all, you'll deal with Bob, not me."

"How is Laurence?"

"Resting and recovering. He wasn't particularly happy to know his mother would not be able to drive to see him, but Bob managed to get him past it well enough."

"Did he give him my message?"

"I don't know what your message was and I certainly didn't think to ask Bob if you sent any fond words to your own child."

"Is that Mummy? Is that Mummy? Can I talk to Mummy?"

James's voice was so filled with hope that it made a rent in the fabric with which Isabelle girded herself. She said, "Let me talk to James, please."

"Bob has told me—"

"I'm sure he has. I'd like to speak to him anyway."

"I don't think so, Isabelle. Darling, isn't that film still in the DVD player? You know which one. We were watching it last night."

"I want to talk to my mum. I want to tell her about Laurence."

"She knows all about Laurence, James."

"Don't punish him like this," Isabelle said. "I don't blame you for wanting to hurt me. But James has done nothing except have the misfortune of being born my son. Let me talk to him. Please."

That appeared to get through to Bob's wife because after a moment James's voice came over the phone saying, "Are you coming to Maidstone, Mum? When're you *coming*?"

"As soon as I can, darling."

"Is Laurence going to get well?"

"Of course he is. You're not meant to worry."

"Dad's worried. I can tell."

"Oh, that's all right, James. Parents always worry. We even worry when you tie your shoes in case they're not done properly and you trip over your laces. But if you *want* to worry, make it twin-brother worry."

"I don't know what that is."

"It's the worry about how you'll make Laurence feel extra special when he comes home."

There was a silence. She could picture his face, screwed up in concentration as he worked on this. Finally, he said, "It's just that I don't know how to do that."

"Well, let's see. Do you have something special that you know he likes?"

"You mean something to *give* to him?"

"Maybe something you haven't exactly wanted to share with him."

"My brontosaurus? We went to the museum—the natural history one?—and Dad said we could each have a dinosaur and Laurence chose the T. rex. But that's what everyone chooses, so I chose the brontosaurus. We took 'em to school but everyone wanted to know about mine because they already knew about T. rexes. Well, everyone does, don't they? Because of films. No one could believe that the brontosauruses were gentle so I got asked lots of questions while no one asked Laurence anything and he was annoyed. I could share my brontosaurus with him. For a while, I mean. I wouldn't want it to be permanent."

"So you could share it for a while," Isabelle said. "That would be quite nice, James. You could have it waiting on his bed when he gets home."

"'Course," he said, and he sounded thoughtful. "I *could* give it to him, couldn't I, Mum? I *could* make it a forever present. That would make it truly special."

"That's completely up to you, James. Whatever you decide."

"When're you coming here, then?"

"As soon as I absolutely positively can."

"Tonight?"

"I'm not able tonight, darling. But soon, I promise. Very soon."

A moment later, Sandra was back on the phone, saying, "I hope you didn't promise him anything. You've done that a thousand times before now, and the broken promises—"

"I said I'm coming and I'm coming," Isabelle cut in. "James knows it and you can pass it along to Laurence as well."

"And have you a message for Bob?" Sandra's voice had taken on an unpleasant archness.

Isabelle wanted to say, Tell him he didn't exactly hit the wife jackpot in either of his marriages, but she refrained. She said, "Please ask him to ring me when he gets home. I'm concerned about Laurence."

"Oh, I'm sure you are," was Sandra's reply before she ended their conversation.

Isabelle sat on the sofa from where she'd made the call, staring as she'd done before at the hideous unpainted concrete wall outside that acted to retain the earth and the pavement above it. She thought about what Sandra had said and she acknowledged it for the truth it was: She had broken promises to the boys. We'll do this together. We'll do that together. I'll come for a Sunday afternoon in fair weather and we'll take a boat on the river. We'll prowl round Leeds Castle. We'll go to Rye for the day. She was a veritable catalogue of broken promises. She'd given her word and gone against it left, right, and centre. She'd done this not only to her boys, but to Bob and Sandra and to her colleagues as well. Worst of all, she'd broken nearly every promise she'd made to herself. One drink only tonight, Isabelle. Oh all right, then only two. Don't put those bottles into your bag. For God's sake don't store them inside your desk. The list was long. It was probably endless.

A walk, she thought. She would take a walk. That was the best way to start keeping the promise she made to herself at the moment that she would not drink tonight or tomorrow morning.

Once outside in the evening air, she made for Heathfield Road. To get there, she had to walk along the grim southeastern boundary walls of Wandsworth Prison. From there she was onto Magdalen Road and it was there the thirst first came upon her. She told it no. No now and not tonight. She picked up the pace till she was on Trinity Road with its shops and newsagents and occasional cafés and an off-licence that she frequented.

The urge was as great as her thirst, but she said no again. She crossed the road and hurried north to where she would have access to Wandsworth Common. There were trees to walk beneath, there were spots where the occasional spontaneous football match was played. There was once a baseball game going on, although she'd been told it wasn't baseball but softball, which was apparently a different thing.

She set off on the first path she came to. She was walking briskly. The evening was mild and there were people about who were greatly enjoying it. A young couple was having a picnic on the lawn; a family had launched three small sailboats on one of the ponds; at a nearby bench two girls sat side by side gazing with fascination at their smartphones; on another bench, an elderly woman with stockings making ripples on her ankles was pulling crumpled bread from a bag and feeding pigeons.

That was Isabelle Ardery in her seventies, Isabelle thought. Alone in a society where people were never alone, left to feed birds because there was simply nothing else open to her.

Then, "Granny! Gran!" and two little girls came running to the woman, their parents not far behind them. The husband called, "Mum! Pigeons will eat all of Somerset if they're given the chance. Feed the swans instead."

The woman scooped up her granddaughters. They covered her face with kisses. She kissed them back. They laughed together.

So it wouldn't even be that, Isabelle thought. She had to get away from this place before despair overtook her and did not let go.

She walked. Farther and faster and without looking to see where she was. She was terrified that she'd notice another off-licence if she paid attention to her surroundings. If that happened, she was lost indeed.

She was taken aback when she saw that she'd walked as far as the Thames, as she hadn't even set out in the river's direction. She was even more taken aback when she saw that the bridge spanning it was not the Wandsworth Bridge. For a moment, she was clueless, till a bookshop with which she was familiar told her she was on Putney High Street, which meant the bridge was Putney Bridge, carrying motorists, cyclists, and pedestrians towards Parsons Green on the north side of the river.

She couldn't stop. She knew if she did so, the danger would be as enormous as the need. So she headed towards the bridge, and she only slowed when she saw that she was coming to a church and when she knew that she could not walk any farther as pure exhaustion from the day was upon her.

A sign outside gave the time for services. Evensong was being held. Isabelle reached a decision from among the two possibilities available to her: drink or pray. She understood that she was in a physical state from which God could not deliver her. But there were so few choices available just now. She grasped at the straw she knew evensong was.

The service had already begun when she entered. There were very few people present. In these days of secularism with people attending church only for Christmas, Easter, marriages, and funerals, Isabelle wondered if priests became discouraged. She would become so, she knew.

She entered a pew. She sat. Others were kneeling and she realised what an odd duck she was in this place, as she'd not been inside a church since the twins' christening. She dimly heard the priest intoning some kind of prayer. She came in on, ". . . like lost sheep. We have followed too much the devices and desires of our own hearts; we have offended against thy holy laws; we have left undone those things which we ought to have done; And . . ." She closed her ears. She would not listen. There was no God. There was nothing at all. Just the vast emptiness of space in which everyone floated trying to find a place where *alone* was not as terrible as it seemed since death was alone and death was where they were all heading anyway and "We have done those things which we ought not to have done." She closed her eyes. She brought her fist to her mouth. Then, "Spare thou those, O God, who confess their faults." She couldn't listen because she couldn't bear to hear.

She opened her eyes and saw the priest in his vestments and it seemed that he was looking directly into her heart. This wasn't possible since she was so far back in the nave but she could feel his gaze boring into her and it wasn't him at all but then who was it God or her conscience or an accusation.

She pulled one of the handmade kneeling pillows from the back of the pew in front of her. She dropped it onto the floor. The words went on and they sought to teach her. But teaching her wasn't what she needed although it appeared to be what she was offered.

She struggled for a moment to slide off the bench. No one else was kneeling at this point in the service, but it didn't matter. She needed to kneel because if she didn't kneel she was going to leave the church quickly and just as quickly she was going to find a drink. It was the only thing left to her. If there was going to be any rescue, it was going to have to come from her.

But these people didn't think so, this small congregation praying along with the priest. They believed something else entirely. And she wanted to believe in something because she could no longer believe in herself.

She murmured, "Oh please oh please oh please." Upon the third *please* she began to weep.

# 22 MAY

LUDLOW
SHROPSHIRE

The first phone call came from the assistant commissioner, and Lynley knew better than to let it go to voice mail. Hillier's good morning consisted of: "Where the hell are we after six days?" Lynley decided not to point out to the AC that, technically, it was only five or, at most, five and a half days since one of them had been nearly taken up with driving to Shropshire via West Mercia Police Headquarters. Before he could formulate an answer of any kind, however, Hillier went on. "I've had Quentin Walker phoning me for an update. He's making noises about the Home Office, although God knows what he thinks that fool of a Home Secretary is going to do about moving things along in the desired direction, whatever the hell that is. So where are you with this, and what have you and the redoubtable Sergeant Havers accomplished?"

Lynley could picture Hillier's florid face taking on even more colour as he spoke. That the man was tense was historical fact. That he'd not yet had a stroke was something of a miracle. He replied with, "We're narrowing things, sir."

"What the hell does that mean?"

"We think the Ludlow PCSO might be someone's dupe."

"*What* someone?"

Lynley didn't want to say the deputy chief constable for fear Hillier would experience apoplexy. So he went with, "We're not at the point of questioning anyone, sir. But we're having a much closer look at the crime scene today and we're meeting with the forensic pathologist."

"So the death *is* suspicious? Am I meant to tell Walker that?"

"It might be suspicious."

"What the dickens is 'might be' supposed to buy me, Inspector?"

"I reckon it's supposed to tell you not to say anything to the MP if you can possibly avoid it."

"Do I take from that advice the uplifting information that 'suspicious death' *isn't* going to discourage Clive Druitt from getting out his chequebook and ringing his legal team?"

"Just now it could well do the opposite."

"You know where that leaves me, don't you? I'm left with saying, 'They're moving things ahead and I'll be in touch.'"

"I'm afraid that's the situation, sir."

"Christ. I'm sorry I rang you." On his end, Hillier cut the call. From the incoming number, Lynley knew the AC had made it from his mobile, which had, unfortunately, robbed Hillier of the ability to bang down the receiver, as he no doubt would have liked to do.

Lynley had just finished shaving when the second phone call came through. He'd let go hoping to hear from Daidre, so he was unsurprised to see that it was Nkata ringing him.

"Clean as a newborn," were Nkata's first words.

"Have you ever witnessed a birth?"

"Haven't, 'nspector."

"Nor have I, just photos. *Clean* wouldn't be my word of choice."

"Got it. Right. But you know what I mean. Rochester, Henry Geoffrey, commonly called Harry? He's 'xactly who he says he is: professor of history who had to let it go. Panic attacks in the lecture halls, windows wide open in the dead of winter, all the rest. Only thing iffy is a loitering charge, but that went by the wayside long time back."

"That's it, then? Nothing involving him and students male or female or in between?"

"Not an itch to scratch. I did unearth why he's got this problem in the first place, though."

"The claustrophobia?"

"Yeah. It's a rough one, 's well."

Lynley walked to the window and opened the curtain. In the

morning light, he could see part of the castle. He noted that the banner announcing *Titus Andronicus* had lettering in which the uppercase letters both transformed into pools of blood beneath them. At least the audience would be forewarned, he thought.

He said, "Is it relevant to what we're dealing with here?"

"Prob'ly not." Nkata went on to tell him: A father who was a genius when it came to electrical engineering; that father's belief in his genius being passed on to his son; an expectation that the *type* of genius would manifest in an identical fashion; when it did not, frustration attended by the determination that the son's lack of aptitude in science was actually a case of malingering. "Turns out his dad decides the way to show the kid th'importance of electricity is to give him total darkness. Where they lived, he could only find what he wanted by putting him in a clothes cupboard when his marks in science weren't what Dad thought they should be. Tha's where he spent midterms and holidays. Up till he went to university, but by then damage was done."

Lynley heard all this with a hardening of his spirit. "Someday I'll get to the bottom of what's actually wrong with people's thinking, Winston."

"Good luck with tha', sir," was Nkata's reply.

"How did you learn all this?"

"The clothes cupboard? Tracked down the sister. Point is, like I said, he's got no paddle in this partic'lar canoe, 'n a manner of speaking. Nothin to hide and less to prove."

As in all the hotel rooms, there was an electric kettle, and Lynley set it to boil water for a cup of early morning tea as they continued to speak. He said, "Have you the time for another, then?"

"I c'n work it in here and there. Who's on?" he replied.

"Gary Ruddock, the PCSO. Apparently, he has a background that might be illuminating, according to what he told Barbara when she was here earlier. A cult in Donegal. I've no idea whether it's worthwhile to have a go with that, but Hillier rang me earlier and should he ring again as he's likely to do, having something to give him would probably save him from self-defenestration."

"Sir?"

"Throwing himself out of his office window."

Nkata laughed. "I'm on it, then. Be in touch." And he rang off.

Before the third call hit his mobile, Lynley was able to dress, descend the stairs, and have breakfast with Havers, who swore on the life of her pet cat—an animal that Lynley knew very well she did not possess—that she'd spent an hour practising in order to overwhelm Dorothea Harriman with her dancing expertise. When that third call came, they were on their way to the police station. As he was driving, Lynley took the phone from the breast pocket of his jacket and handed it to Barbara.

She looked at its screen. "It's herself," she said. "You want . . . ?"

He didn't. Isabelle Ardery was the last person he wished to speak to, as there was no depending upon what kind of condition she was in. He said, "Let it go to message. We can listen to it later."

"My thought as well," she replied.

They'd told Ruddock that another look at the office in which Ian Druitt hanged himself was in order. The PCSO had seemed surprised by this request, but he'd agreed to meet them at the station in advance of his regular walkabout. He was there when they arrived, although instead of waiting for them in the car park, he'd left the station door open for them. They found him in the former lunchroom, tinkering with an old microwave.

"Sounds like you're making progress," were his first words to them. "Now if I could do the same with this bloody thing . . ." He placed his hand on top of the old oven. "Thing's an antique, more or less, but sometimes it still does the job," he said.

Lynley said they'd just have a quick look at the office where Druitt died and then they'd be on their way.

"You know where it is," Ruddock said. He didn't appear to feel the need to go with them.

The office was as it had been before, although not as it had been in the photos. A rolling desk chair was in place of the plastic chair that had been in the office the night Druitt died. That was, however, the only change.

The bulletin boards gave them no additional information, nor did a waste-paper basket or the small gouges in the walls where frames had hung. There were marks on the lino where other furniture had once stood, but the shape of the marks suggested filing cabinets, possibly two sets of bookshelves, potentially a credenza as well. Other than that, the fact that the lino had seen hard use was not surprising, considering the age of the building. Havers remarked, "Looks like someone else was doing their dancing practice round this place, you ask me."

"Ah, you see? You're not alone."

He was examining the venetian blinds when she said, "We didn't see this first time we were here, for what it's worth, sir," although she sounded far less than hopeful.

Lynley turned to find that she was squatting at the desk's kneehole, having pulled the rolling chair away from it. He went to see what she'd found. Scuff marks, he saw, of the sort that rubber-heeled shoes would make over time when one pushes back from a desk. He looked from them to her.

She said, "All right. I know. Could be someone gave up fags and was beating his feet on the floor. Did you do that, by the way?"

"When I gave them up?" he said. "No. I gnawed on my fingernails for two years."

"See? There you go, sir. I'm sticking with them, I am. Wreaking havoc on my manicure is *not* going to happen."

She stood. They went to the cupboard door from whose knob the deacon had strung himself. It was sturdy, not the type of knob that would have been made loose by having to hold the weight of a man. From there, they surveyed the room again.

"Dead men and tales," Havers said with a sigh.

"Would that were not the case," Lynley said.

They returned to the lunchroom. Ruddock had the back of the microwave removed. He looked up from his work and appeared to register something on one of their faces because he said, "No luck, then?"

"We're not certain," Lynley told him. "There's something that could be odd."

Ruddock set his screwdriver to one side. "What's that, then?"

Lynley told him about the photos taken by SOCO in the immediate aftermath of the deacon's death. "What can you tell us about the chair?"

he asked Ruddock, going on to explain: the overturned chair, the fact that it was a plastic one, the additional fact that it was not a desk chair, and that—come to think of it—it probably wouldn't have been a suitable height for someone working at the desk at all.

After a moment for thought, Ruddock shook his head. "I never thought anything about that chair. It was what was in the office when I put him there. I mean, he had to sit on something and that was in the room. There wasn't anything else. I know how it got overturned, though. I had to stretch him out on the floor for CPR. I shoved the desk out of the way and the chair probably toppled. I was . . . Well, I suppose I panicked."

Considering that he'd already confessed to what he'd been doing out in the car park, this was hardly surprising. But there was still that issue of the woman he'd been with.

Lynley said to him, "Gary, we've a witness to your having college-age girls with you at night. In your patrol car, this is. Can you tell us about that?"

The PCSO seemed to hesitate. Then he said, "I expect that's to do with the drinking. When they're pissed enough, it's always seemed dangerous for them to be out in the streets on their own. I stow them in the car and get them back where they belong. Doesn't happen every time I'm dealing with bingers, but it does happen, so I'm not surprised someone saw me with them."

"This would be a *her*, not a *them*," Barbara pointed out.

"Well, I deliver 'em home one by one," he said, "so I'd end up with one—a *her* or *him*—at the end since most of the students round here live with their parents or in small accommodation like a bedsit or a room that's let in someone's home."

"Is this part of the job?" Lynley asked him. "Asked to do this by the town council or the mayor?"

"Just seems sensible. A way to avoid future trouble. Plus, it helps nip things in the bud. With the drink, I mean. I don't like to see the kids heading down that rabbit hole, if you know what I mean. It's easy to do at that age, and I reckon if their parents see them blotto often enough, they're going to do something about it. It's not part of my job, though. Obviously."

"Is Dena Donaldson one of the drinkers?" Lynley asked.

"Oh, she is, that one. She's called Ding, by the way. She's one of the kids who lives in accommodation instead of with her parents. She's got a real problem with the drink, she does, and last thing she wants is me telling tales to her mum and dad. I keep her in order by making sure she knows that I'm one hair away from carting her home to them."

"You've been seen with her in the car park here," Lynley said. "At night, this is."

"Not surprising, that. I've brought her here more 'n once to have a word. It's not like I *want* to drag the girl to her parents' house, what with the distance as they don't live local *and* with trying to be a decent cop . . . I mean helpful the way local constables've always been? So I've brought her here for a lecture on what's going to happen if she doesn't bloody stop it all, like she's probably going to die, if you know what I mean. And while things've improved—I mean she's let up a bit—sometimes the drink gets away from her. And there we go again."

"That sounds like something beyond the call of duty," Havers pointed out.

"When the kids drink, they cause problems. Town residents make an issue of it. They get on the phone and there you have it. I'd like to put a stop to it all, and I'm doing what I can."

"Like Mr. Druitt."

He cocked his head, as if unsure what the reference meant.

Havers said, "He wanted a street pastors programme here. Picking up the kids when they're pissed and giving them coffee and soup and whatever? He didn't manage to get far with that, though."

"That's only part of the shame of his dying, you ask me," Ruddock said.

CHURCH STRETTON
SHROPSHIRE

Along with the vast highland moors of the Long Mynd, the volcanic rolling Stretton Hills created a valley into which the Victorian town of Church Stretton sat. It resembled what it once had been: a nineteenth-century health resort where ailing individuals once had come to take the mineral waters of the area. Over more than a century, however, the town had greatly altered, morphing from a spa for the sickly into a centre for the hale and hearty. With rucksacks on their backs and collapsible hiking sticks in their hands, these enthusiastic individuals now climbed the heights of the Long Mynd, looking for the views that stretched well into Wales.

When Barbara Havers saw the country walkers gathered in the streets, she said irritably, "Better them than me. What's *happened* to people? Where are the good old days?"

"True," Lynley said and she could hear the sardonic tone he employed. "Those good old days of gout and tuberculosis were far better, Sergeant."

"Don't you start," she warned him. "What'm I looking for again?"

"It's called Mane Event. M-a-n-e."

"I hate clever names 's well. Have I mentioned that?"

"Do you need a cigarette? Is that what this is about?"

"It's about *him*, it is. She was with him, sir. That girl. Dena, Ding, whoever."

"He didn't deny it, Havers. And it does seem we know the reason why. If, of course, he's telling the truth."

"So is he lying about the other? The married one, or whatever she is?"

"Possibly. His mind must be whirling now, though."

"All those phone calls to Trevor Freeman, sir? They could be a good way to hide the fact that he was bonking the wife and using the husband's phone to make arrangements. How many people check their *own* phones for calls that've come in to someone else? Would you think of that? I wouldn't. 'Course, you have Denton to worry about, eh? Him making and getting calls on your mobile from New York. Broadway on the line and all that. Or Hollywood."

"There's always Hollywood to consider," Lynley agreed. "There it is, by the way."

"The Mane Event? Sorry, sir. Got distracted."

When they walked into the place, Barbara decided that to call it a hair salon would be stretching things. While it did contain two chairs suitable for cuts and colouring, having more than one stylist working at once would certainly turn a workday into a battle of elbows. The salon barely contained the client and stylist it currently held.

This was where Nancy Scannell had said she would meet them for their conversation. Lynley had told her that a hair salon wouldn't actually make the top ten on his list of choices for the coming interview, but she had explained it was this or waiting till after her court appearance later that day. As it was, she'd practically had to sell her firstborn child in order to set up this appointment. Getting in to see Dusty often took weeks. Not everyone could cut hair that curled like hers. And it was time for her summer do.

The do was doing when they arrived. The forensic pathologist was in the chair, Dusty was fluttering round with two pairs of scissors and a comb between her teeth like a flamenco dancer with a rose. Hair was flying hither and yon. It seemed that Nancy Scannell had decided to go short, and Dusty was dead chuffed to accommodate her. She also wanted to colour it, they learned, once the comb was removed from between her lips. Scannell had apparently said no, but Dusty was after a compromise that involved "just a wee streak of magenta, then. Nothing outrageous. You'll love it. You'll look ever so 'with it.'" The pathologist wasn't having this, however. She liked the grey in her hair, she said. She'd certainly earned it during her marriage and the less said about *that*, the better.

Dusty gave Barbara and Lynley a glance, most of her attention on Barbara's own hair. The stylist said, "What've you *done* to yourself? Did you use a paring knife?"

"Nail scissors," Barbara told her.

"Can't help you, 'm afraid. Too dead short. You'll have to come back when it's grown out more."

"I'll make a note of that in my diary," Barbara said. Then to the pathologist, "This is DI Lynley, Dr. Scannell."

"So I thought," she said. "Let's get to it."

"Here?" Lynley, Barbara reckoned, had probably assumed that, while they had arranged to meet the pathologist at her hair salon, they would certainly decamp for their conversation elsewhere.

"How it has to be if you want it today," Scannell said. Then she added to Dusty, "Have the earbuds?"

"Oh. Right. Hang on, then." Dusty fished in a nearby drawer and brought forth the earbuds, which she then plugged into a mobile phone, apparently accessing music to prevent eavesdropping. Within seconds her head was moving to a beat. It made no difference to her expertise with the scissors, it seemed, for onward she went, clipping and sculpting and assessing the style as the rest of them chatted.

"We've been to the office in the station where Ian Druitt died," Lynley told the forensic pathologist. "We've been through your report. We've also studied the autopsy pictures. How confident are you that Druitt was a suicide?"

She asked him to hand the pictures over, saying, "It's been a good many months." Barbara saw Dusty's expression become intrigued as she sneaked a glance at the SOCO shots over the pathologist's shoulder. Then she averted her gaze and was all business once again.

Scannell said, "The religious thing he used? It made the scene and the body trickier than normal." She indicated the red stole on the floor near to the body. "Fabric doesn't mark the skin the way another sort of ligature would in a suicide: a leather or canvas belt, a length of robe, a flex of some kind. This thing . . . what's it called? I knew at one time but my memory's getting more cluttered every year."

"A stole," Lynley said.

"Ah. Right. Anyway, it marked the skin . . . Here, you can see in the photos from the autopsy . . . the petechiae are just visible. The bruising is faint, but it climbs the neck at the angle indicating self-harm. I told your sergeant this when she was last here, at the gliding centre this was, not at the salon."

"Was the body strung up when you saw it?"

"The officer made it a wretched scene to gain much from. He'd done CPR on the man—one can hardly blame him for that—so of course he had to get him off the doorknob and he had to remove the stole from his throat. But had he not done, there really wouldn't have been a different conclusion. Faking a death by suicide nearly always gets discovered." She looked up at them from the chair. "And I take it that's what you're trying to do with this: discover something. I wish you luck with that, but I still stand by my original report of suicide. Enough signs were there to declare it: from the contortions of the face to the bulging eyes to, as I said, the petechiae. Not every possible sign, naturally, but *every* possible indicator in an unexplained death is rarely present, as doubtless you already know."

"We've read your report," Lynley said. "We can agree that the face and the neck are particularly indicative of suicide in the fashion he committed it. The abrasions round the wrists appear to be consistent with the PCSO's account of the arrest when he used them and why he took them off once they had reached the station. But since all of the signs of suicide weren't there, what else might have been?"

Scannell handed the photos and reports back to them. She tapped Dusty's arm to get her attention, then pointed to a spot on her head where part of her masses of hair, in her opinion, still apparently needed work. She said to Lynley, "With this kind of suicide—the doorknob bit, I mean—the legs often convulse. Considering where he was, there also might have been some kind of marking on the floor from those convulsions, which there wasn't. Of course, his legs might not have convulsed or he could have been wearing shoes that don't leave marks in the first place—most trainers won't mar a floor—but the lack of marks in and of themselves doesn't mean much when everything else is in order."

Barbara heard this with a sudden surge of energy. She said, "Sir . . . ?" to Lynley, but he was already with her.

"Do you mean scuff marks?" he asked Dr. Scannell.

"Yes. They could also be at the site of this kind of suicide. But as I said, convulsions aren't guaranteed—if you'll pardon the word—and they *could* have happened as part of the suicide, without leaving evidence of themselves."

Barbara looked at Lynley. He looked at her. Scannell caught the exchange between them, reflected in the mirror. She said, "What is it?"

Lynley said, "If the man was sitting in a chair, could someone standing above and behind him carry out a crime—a murder—and have it successfully pose as suicide?"

She said slowly after a moment of reflection, "That would probably put the stole in the right position to leave marks that encouraged a conclusion of suicide, yes. But I can't see it happening in that location—the office—without a mark on the floor indicating a struggle. And I certainly can't imagine the poor man sitting there and allowing himself to be done away with. Even with the handcuffs still on him, surely he would have kicked and writhed."

"Thus marking the floor," Lynley said.

"Thus *scuffing* the floor," Barbara added.

"Marking, scuffing, scoring, whatever." Nancy Scannell nodded before saying, "Sorry," to Dusty, who rapped her neatly on the shoulder for the movement. "Yes, I'd say that with that scenario, there would be scuffing on the floor."

Bingo, huzzah, and all the rest, Barbara thought. They were back in business.

WORCESTER

HEREFORDSHIRE

It had been an easy matter to switch mobiles with Clover. They charged their phones every night and, as they had identical phones with the same unlocking code in the event one of them needed to use the other's phone in a pinch, all that was necessary was to make the switch, after first seeing to it that the wallpaper on his phone was the same as hers. That part was easy as well since Clover wasn't a person to be bothered with selecting some personal and sentimental photo of baby, dog, cat to serve as a backdrop to the very few apps she took the trouble to sign up for. So finding the identical photo of rolling ocean waves in his own smartphone's offered wallpapers took less than thirty seconds.

Trevor reckoned she'd work it all out at some point during her day, but he also reckoned that he had enough time to do the snooping that his previous day's conversation with Gaz Ruddock suggested wanted doing. For Gaz didn't produce falsehoods as well as he thought he did.

Immediately after that conversation with the PCSO, Trevor had made a far closer examination of the calls into and out of his own phone. He had easy access to two months' worth of calls since the phone stored them, and what the list told him was that from March 22 until May 16, calls to Gaz Ruddock and from Gaz Ruddock had been going out and coming in regularly. Like those he'd discovered on his earlier and more cursory examination of the mobile, these calls had been made or had come in at night or very early in the morning. There were days when this occurred only once. There were days when this occurred as many as four times.

So after looking at what was available on his phone, he'd wanted to know more. While it was true that both Clover and Gaz had already claimed that their calls concerned their secret plan to keep a watch over what Finn got up to in Ludlow, the question was what sort of "watching over" warranted the number of conversations they'd apparently had. Trevor wanted some answers, and he began to assemble them by ringing his mobile's provider. He gave all the appropriate numbers and code words, telling the faceless and nameless voice at the other end that he wanted to check a few calls that a wayward child of his might have made. Then it was only a matter of waiting for the information to be sent to him.

The interesting bit was obvious once he had those records. The extensive nature of the Clover-and-Gaz communications via Trevor's own phone had begun on the first of March. Prior to that and no matter how far back in time he went with the records, there was nothing on his phone to or from Gaz.

It seemed damned odd that, for someone meant to be watching over Finn, Gaz hadn't called Trevor's phone regularly to report to Clover until the late winter. That meant that prior to late winter, he'd either been ringing Clover directly on her own phone, or he'd not been keeping an eye on Finn at all.

Trevor wanted to make his own determination about that, which was what had led him to make the switch with his wife's phone. Once he studied her mobile's history and once he'd gone through the same process he'd used with his own phone to see even further back in time, he knew he couldn't wait till the evening to speak to Clover. So he rang his own mobile number and when she answered, he said, "Sorry. We've done a switch with our phones, love," in the most casual tone he could manage. "Must've happened when we took them from their chargers."

"Have we?" she asked. "So that's why mine's not been ringing. I thought I'd finally got lucky enough to have a day without disturbances. Usually they start round half past seven and don't stop. *Has* my phone rung, by the way?"

"Once I saw it was yours, I've been letting it go to message. But there've been enough calls that I realised I ought to let you know about the mix-up. Shall I play them, then? The messages, I mean."

"Don't do that."

Was her response rather hasty? he wondered. He said, "Want me to bring it to you? I've nothing on at the gym till later. Or we can meet halfway if you're able."

"I've one bloody meeting after another."

"I'll bring it to you, then."

"That seems like such a bother, Trev."

"It's no trouble. Sh'll I set off, then?"

She said that if he *would* bring the mobile to Hindlip, she'd be ever so grateful. She'd meet him down at the reception building at the edge of the property. That way he'd have no need of going through the routine of sitting there waiting to be admitted. He agreed to this, although he knew that meeting her at that great distance from the administration building also served the purpose of allowing her conversation with her husband—should there be one—to be private.

When he arrived at police headquarters, she was waiting for him. She emerged from the reception building, lifting her hand in a wave. She carried his mobile in it. He lowered the passenger window once he'd parked. When she came to the car, he said, "Get in."

She looked surprised, although his tone hadn't been unfriendly. She said, "I've only a few minutes, Trev."

He said, "This won't take more than that."

When she was seated inside the car, she handed over his phone. He hung onto hers. She didn't fail to notice. She cocked her head curiously.

He said, "This business with the phones." When she made no reply, he went on. "It was deliberate. I switched them."

He looked over at her. Her expression hadn't altered. Nor had she moved. She said, "Ah."

"Are you going to ask me why?"

"I assume you've come here to tell me. I must say, though, I don't know why this couldn't have waited till I got home."

That was bravado in action. Trevor wondered why he'd never noticed the degree to which his wife could dissemble. He should have done. She'd been going at the sex games for years, and in every scenario, her performance had been utterly genuine, which was what had made it so arousing. Schoolgirl, nun, whore, railway ticket agent, deliverer of the post, yoga teacher, hotel maid . . . Clover didn't pretend. She *became*. He was going to have to watch her now like a specimen under a microscope.

"I went along with the lie to the Met as ordered," he said. "But it made me want to know a bit more about all these phone calls to and from Gaz. I don't think you can blame me for that. If I'm going to lie to the police, it's good to have at least a partial idea of what the truth is. Otherwise, it all gets difficult. Keeping everything straight, I mean. But you know this, don't you, as you're a cop."

"Have we not already dealt with this?"

"We have, in part. But you know how curiosity works on a person. Could be it's because I'm married to a copper like I am, but what happened is that my head started working on those calls and I reckoned the best way to get it to *stop* working was to take a closer look at 'em. I mean, Jesus, Clover, it was like a perpetual motion machine was banging on inside the old bean."

Her eyes narrowed. She wasn't fooled by his casual tone, and he didn't actually expect her to be. She said, "Yes. That does make sense. A lot has been asked of you."

"I'm glad you see it that way. So you're likely to be on board with my looking at all these calls to and from Gaz, trying to work out why there've been so many on my phone."

"When Finnegan—"

"Oh, I've got all that. I've put an end to it, by the way, this 'watching over Finn' business that you and Gaz have going on." He made air quotes, and she did not fail to pick up on them.

She said, "Are we going back to that other, then? Me hot and bothered to get Gaz between my legs and Gaz all hot and bothered to be there? The two of us planning our trysts by using your phone?"

"I'm not saying that, am I, Clover? But here's what it is: I'm beginning to think you *want* me to say it."

"I don't *want* you to say anything except what's on your mind."

"That being the case, what's Finn done that you don't want me to know about?"

She looked away from him. A car had just pulled up to the reception kiosk. She studied it as if searching for a detail she'd been ordered to be on the lookout for. A middle-aged woman got out, carrying a handbag the size of which was going to warrant extreme examination. Were this a prison, she'd have a Victoria sponge inside of it and inside the sponge she'd have a crowbar.

Clover sighed heavily. "I don't know what else to say to you, Trev. We seem to keep going round and round. I've nothing more to give you on the subject."

"Try thinking back to the beginning of March."

She turned back to him. She looked genuinely puzzled. He went on.

"That's when the night-time phone calls from Gaz started coming in on my mobile and going out from it. So if you and he are having natters about Finn, there's been at least one each night on my phone since the beginning of March. Now if all these conversations between you and Gaz are called for, and if the reason's Finn, I want to know what he's done, and I want to know it now."

She grasped the handle of the door, saying as she lifted it, "I don't know what you're accusing me of or who you actually think I am, but I think we've said enough, Trevor."

"Not quite. We haven't talked about your phone yet."

"I don't see where that's going to get us."

"That's what you actually believe? I ask because there're *eight* calls between you and Gaz Ruddock on your phone, Clover, made on the twenty-sixth and the twenty-seventh of February. Then they stop altogether and start up on my phone. So the way I look at it, either something happened prior to or on the twenty-sixth or you and Gaz came to some sort of arrangement that meant no more ringing each other unless you had access to my mobile."

She gave a disgusted shake of her head. "Yes. All right. Have it as you like. We've been going at it as often as possible. I need a younger man because you're not enough. Is that what you want to hear?"

"What I want to hear is the truth. If Finn's done something, I want to know what it is."

"*What* on earth could he possibly have done?"

"Druitt had his concerns, right? Drugs. Alcohol, children, whatever. Is that what's been going on?"

"For God's sake, Trevor, for all you and I know, that's complete rubbish. Do I need to remind you that we have only Gaz's word that Ian Druitt wanted to speak with us at all?"

"Are you saying that *Gaz* wants Finn stitched up for something?"

"I don't know! *All* I know is that life in Ludlow hasn't gone as well for Finnegan as he'd like us to believe. He's been drinking too much and smoking weed and missing lectures and tutorials. He may well have gone on to heavier drugs. Gaz was letting me know about everything as it developed. Then when Ian Druitt died, he began to think . . . *whatever* it was that he thought, because I wouldn't let him even say it, all right? But I had to take his calls because of Finnegan. *Now* do you see the position I've been in?"

He'd been holding back his final piece of information because he didn't want to think about it, let alone to bring it up. But he saw that he had to do so now. "There were three calls on the night that bloke died, Clover. I checked the dates."

"*What* are you talking about?"

"A call from you to Gaz and two calls from Gaz to you. That same night Ian Druitt died."

She stared at him. She did open the door then. He thought she meant to get out without another word, but he was wrong.

She said, "So you're suggesting, I take it, that Ian Druitt wasn't a suicide at all, that he died either at my hand or by my orders. Yes?" She waited. When he said nothing, she went on. "What do you take me for, Trev?"

The reply came to him absolutely unbidden. "I don't know," he said, "and that's the devil of it, Clover."

LUDLOW
SHROPSHIRE

"I *knew* he was dirty," were Havers's words as they parked in Temeside, two wheels and most of the Healey Elliott on the pavement. They waited for a moment to let traffic pass before they crossed over the street.

"I don't think we can go quite that far, Barbara," Lynley replied. "He's soiled, perhaps. Dirty, however? We're not there yet."

"Come on, Inspector. The scuff marks, the chairs, the handcuffs on and the handcuffs off, anonymous phone calls, CCTV cameras that get shut off for twenty seconds and then have their positions switched, college girls being carted round town for what*ever* reason, pubs being rung, women being bonked . . . What more do we need?"

"For a start we need to consider the nineteen days that elapsed between that phone call and the death of Ian Druitt. Then we must consider what it means that those nineteen days were brought to an end by Finnegan Freeman's mother. After that, we must consider what that detail means."

"All right. I'll see your point if I have to. It means *Finnegan's* in it. Or his mum. Or his dad. Or Ruddock. But in any case, someone in the DCC's circle."

"Which is why we need to know who, if anyone at all, was with Ruddock in the car park on the night of the murder."

"P'rhaps it was Colonel Mustard with the sodding candlestick," she muttered.

Lynley chuckled. "I'm glad you see my point." He glanced at his pocket watch. The day was getting on. Hillier wanted a result, soon. If this went to the Home Secretary's desk, there was going to be a problem that none of them were going to want to deal with. When his mobile rang, his first thought was that his mind had been read in

London. He gave it a look and saw he wasn't far off wrong. It was Ardery.

He didn't want to get into a conversation with her just now. He knew he ought to answer because of everything he'd learned from Dee Harriman about Isabelle's condition. But the fact was that he needed to keep his mind on the matter in hand, which was complicated enough already without any intrusion from the DCS. He let it go to message. Havers saw him do it.

He said, "The DCS again."

She said, "Better you than me," which was when her own mobile rang. She gave it a look and then said, "Bloody hell. Should I . . . ?"

They could hardly both avoid the DCS. He said, "Assess her condition."

"What should I say about you?"

"I've gone wherever I've gone and you'll give me the message when you see me."

"And where've you gone?"

"Sergeant, it's unlike you to fail in the area of creative alternatives at this eleventh hour. If by any chance she's ringing about the case—which she probably is—let her know we're closing in."

From there, he heard Barbara's end of the conversation only, which consisted of, "Guv? . . . Just about to have . . . Huh? He's out and about . . . Got started early. Like I was saying, we're wanting a chat with whoever happens to be at home in Temeside. Either Finn Freeman or his housemate—that girl Dena?—will . . . Oh. No. Sorry. Manner of speaking. It's only me . . . He's gone to—" She apparently saw the problem with a specific place and the possibility of being out of range and hence unable to take Isabelle's call because she quickly switched to, "He's tracking down the forensic woman again for . . . Hang on, guv. We've already done that twice, me and the inspector . . . Okay. Right. I'll have another look. I can do it later and give you a ring, okay? . . . Will do, ma'am."

She rang off and shot him an aggrieved look. "She sounds like she's had fifteen cups of coffee. She wants us looking at the SOCO photos another time. *And* to ring her while we're doing it. You ask me, she's trying to tiptoe out of cow dung without her shoe soles stinking."

"It costs us little enough to cooperate. I'll ring her later."

"Look at you," Havers said with a scowl as she shoved her mobile back into her bag. "D'you *ever* get tired of being the gent?"

"It's beat into one from childbirth, Sergeant. Ah. We appear to have arrived just in time." He gestured towards the house, where the girl Ding had opened the front door. She wore a rucksack, and she headed straight for a bicycle. She fiddled with its lock, which appeared to be stiff. When they got closer to her, they could hear her muttering, "Oh, come on, come *on*."

"Would you like help?" Lynley enquired.

The girl swung round. She did a back step at the sight of them. She said, "Finn's not here."

"Which is fine," Havers told her, "as you're the person we want to have a word with."

The girl was instantly suspicious. Her gaze darted between them like a bird hopping between two branches.

"I know Francie Adamucci put me into it, if that's why you want to talk to me," she said. "It might help you to know Francie'll bonk *anyone*."

"This actually won't take long," Lynley told the girl. "And you're right, by the way. Francie Adamucci did mention you. The PCSO confirmed her words, but we'd be interested in hearing your side of things."

"They're both liars and I don't have—"

"Time. Right. Who does?" Havers asked.

"I was going to say I don't have to talk to you. Anyway, I'm expected at home."

"This would be the home where your parents are?" Havers went on. "This would be the place you don't want Gary Ruddock carting you to?"

"Who said that?" she demanded.

"The man himself. He says it has to do with your problem."

"*What* problem?"

"If you'll allow us a few minutes, we'll explain," Lynley said.

She stalked back to the door and shoved it open with some emphasis. She walked into the house but made certain they knew from her posture that she wasn't intending to move an inch from the entry, although they could drag her into the sitting room should they choose to demonstrate the degree of police brutality she no doubt expected from the likes of them. She put her weight on one hip and her hand on the other. The stance said, "*What*?" better than she could have done.

"We've more than one person who's seen you with PCSO Ruddock," Lynley began.

She cut in at once with, "You've got more'n one person lying, then."

"We're not here to ask you for particulars," Lynley said.

"Between you 'n' me?" Havers put in, "we'd rather not know 'em. Top, bottom, whatever. Your secrets are safe."

"I *never*—"

"Wrong. You did."

The girl looked close to tears, which seemed at odds with her defiance. There was something more going on here, Lynley thought. He said, "Ding, you're not in trouble. But we have several people so far who've seen you with PCSO Ruddock, and Sergeant Havers here is one of them. What we want to know is whether you were with him in the patrol car on the night that the deacon—Ian Druitt—died at the police station. Whatever your relationship is with Gary Ruddock isn't our concern, but—"

Ding burst into tears. She covered her face with her hands. Within moments, she was weeping as if no power on earth could contain her grief. Havers murmured, "Bloody hell," as Lynley went to the girl.

"What's happened, Ding?" he said to her quietly. "You must see that it's time to tell us."

Havers decamped at once to the kitchen. The water ran. The kettle was filled. It was the English answer to everything, Lynley thought.

Ding began to slide down the wall, but Lynley caught her. As her weeping turned to sobbing, he gently removed the rucksack from her back and put his arm around her shoulder. "You're quite fine," he said. "Is anyone else here?" And when she shook her head wordlessly, he said, "Were you with him?"

"No . . ." She wailed the word.

He led her in the direction of the kitchen, saying, "Ding, it's down to you to help us understand—"

"Yes, but no," she cried. "*No.*"

Havers had a chair out from the table. She'd found tea mugs and tea from their earlier visit and she had them ready. She seemed to understand where Lynley did not. She said, "You mean yes you've been with him, but no, not on the night that the deacon died?"

The girl nodded. Havers handed her a kitchen towel at the same moment as Lynley was bringing out one of his pristine handkerchiefs. Ding took the kitchen towel and crushed it against her face.

"I . . . don't . . . want . . . ," she said, and then she drew in a breath and went on with, "He knows. I don't want . . . to go home."

"He told us you don't want to go home to your parents," Lynley said. "He said it's to do with your drinking, that you don't want your parents to know about it. He's picked you up more than once amongst the bingers. Is that not the truth?"

She wasn't pretty when she wept. Hardly anyone was. Her skin became blotchy, her nose turned red, and her lips moved spasmodically. She managed to say, "It's *more* than that. The rest of them don't care what he says and they don't need to, but I do, and it's why it happens. It started with the bingeing and I said okay because if my mum knew how bad it was she would make me live at home not here and I couldn't I couldn't only I didn't know why only now I do. He figured that. The first part. That I couldn't. So he said we can have a deal you and me and here's what it will take, at the police station in the car park, and I said I would do whatever because you don't know how much I didn't want to be at home so I did whatever and then he would take me home not to my parents but here to Temeside."

The water had boiled. Havers brought mugs to the table. Lynley was sorting through Ding's declarations, one item at a time, but the sergeant made a leap that, perhaps, only a woman could make, considering what they'd heard. She said, "You performed sex favours for him when he caught you bingeing. If you hadn't done, he would've carted you home to your parents drunk."

She nodded, weeping anew.

"And the other girls?" Lynley asked.

"Some. I don't know. Not Francie, see, because she wouldn't care pins what her parents said because she lives at home anyway and they don't . . . Well, they travel lots and she does what she wants and they let her and they know they can't . . . I don't know . . . tie her up or something?"

Lynley nodded. The girl had eye makeup down her cheeks and she'd even got some on her forehead as well and he had a sudden urge to clean off her skin, a desire that he knew had more to do with protection than anything else. He said, "But you've kept bingeing?"

She shook her head. "Hardly ever but it's not . . . It stopped mattering. To him, I mean. It ended up not having to do with bingeing at all. He . . . he picks me up when he's *decided* I've been bingeing. Sometimes I'm walking back to Temeside from the library and he . . . There he is and I don't want to go home and he knows it. I was afraid all the time when it started because it was like I'd finally escaped only I didn't know what I'd escaped from anyway and I thought what's it really matter when I'm doing these other blokes and I can't live there I *can't*."

"Can you be certain you weren't with him the night Ian Druitt died?" Lynley asked. For if her claims about Ruddock were true, how could the girl actually know when she'd been with him and when she'd not, unless she'd kept some sort of record? Lynley gave her the exact date.

"I *wasn't*," she said. "If someone was, it wasn't me."

"How can you be so sure?" Havers asked.

"That's my mum's birthday," she said. "I was at home. In Much Wenlock. You c'n ask Francie or Chelsea 'cause that was before Francie . . . We were friends then. They went home with me."

IRONBRIDGE
SHROPSHIRE

Yasmina didn't bother with a shopping trolley because she didn't need one. Inside the market, she picked up a basket instead. There would be three of them having dinner, but she couldn't face preparing an actual meal so she planned to search for ready-made items that she could remove from containers and present to Tim and to Sati as if she'd made them herself.

She looked at what was on offer. The difficulty was that she wasn't hungry and that, for her, eating was now something she was doing for medicinal purposes only. Other than that, it was to set an example for Sati. See, Mummy is eating and you must also do so, darling.

Quiche, she thought. Perhaps lasagna. Haddock and peas. Plaice and chips. It was just so difficult when one didn't feel hunger.

"It's Dr. Lomax, isn't it?"

Yasmina looked up. An attractive woman with cornflower eyes and a tartan jacket over slim trousers was smiling tentatively at her. Yasmina frowned as she failed to place her.

"It's Selina Osborne," she said. "Missa was my pupil in fourth form."

"Oh my goodness, yes. Of course," Yasmina said, although the truth was she couldn't remember the woman's face at all. "I didn't recognise you at first."

"It's my hair," she said. "New colour, new style. How are you? I imagine you're quite pleased and excited about Missa and Justin."

Yasmina couldn't track this. *Excited* would be the last descriptive term she'd use when it came to her frame of mind. "I'm not quite certain . . . ?"

Selina gave a light laugh. "Oh. Sorry. I saw the announcement in the registry office when Toby and I went to post our own engagement." She showed her ring, blushing as she did so. "It's second time round for us both so I really didn't want a ring, but he insisted. We're planning on just the registry office, but I expect you've got something else in mind for Missa and Justin, haven't you. I remember them both so well, especially Justin with that lovely face of his always so serious and all that hair falling into his eyes. One could tell from the first that it was only Missa he would ever care for. And now here they are posting the banns for their marriage." She laughed again and placed her hand on her chest, adding, "I can't tell you how old that makes me feel."

Yasmina nodded. She said faintly, "Oh yes. I expect it does."

"Do give them my best, won't you? Tell her Mrs. Osborne—soon to be Mrs. Joyce—sends her very good wishes."

"I will indeed," Yasmina said.

When Selina Osborne walked off, happily pushing her trolley,

Yasmina turned to the foodstuff and blindly picked up packages, not caring what they were. She wanted to believe there was some mistake. She couldn't accept that things had come to this when all along she had recognised the likelihood of things coming exactly to this. Timothy had predicted it, Rabiah had tried in her way to warn against it, but Yasmina had not wanted to hear.

There was nothing for it but to turn to the one person who truly might be able to see the ludicrousness of an early marriage between Justin and Missa, the one person who surely would have a concern equal to her own. So she carried her selections to the till and after she'd made the purchase, she drove to the Museum of the Gorge.

The museum stood on the bank of the River Severn. It was a former foundry whose original architect had disguised the massive building's use by including in its brick construction a series of gables, a crenellated roofline at the east and west ends, and smokestacks disguised with additional crenellation to suggest a castle rather than an ironworks. Additionally, facing in the direction of Ironbridge proper, a large bay with Perpendicular diamond-paned windows gave the building a churchlike appearance, as if the architect hadn't quite been able to decide what would work best to assure the townspeople that neither the air they breathed nor the water they drank was of questionable nature as a result of having a foundry in their immediate vicinity. The railway tracks leading directly into the building defeated its disguise, however, as did its position just above the river and near enough to it to have been flooded so many times that its continued existence was something of a miracle.

It was minutes from the closing hour, and there were only three vehicles in the car park. Yasmina went inside and asked the ticket seller for Linda Goodayle, since Justin's mum, as Yasmina well knew, was the director of the museum. She also knew that it was a source of pride to the Goodayle clan that Linda had begun as a ticket seller years earlier, when the museum was a mere shadow of the impressive educational facility it was today. She'd risen through the ranks exactly as her husband had done at Blists Hill Victorian Town. Despite their lack of university degrees or even any form of college, they were doers, movers, and shakers, the Goodayles.

After a moment on the phone, the ticket seller told her that the museum's director was finishing a few things up and would be with her presently. She could have a look round if she wished. There was a new diorama that might be of interest. Yasmina said that she would wait outside enjoying the afternoon sun. The ticket seller gave an indifferent shrug and went back to whatever she'd been doing on her computer.

Outside, Yasmina walked to the wall at the edge of the car park. The river was at a healthy level, she saw, its lower banks knotted with bluebells that tangled with golden saxifrage. As the bank climbed upwards, wild grasses grew thickly, among which wolfsbane raised its hooded heads. Opposite where she stood, willows and alders offered their fresh spring leaves to the sunlight. May had always been her favourite month of the year. But this particular May was one she wished she had experienced in a coma.

"Dr. Lomax . . . ?"

Yasmina turned. She recognised Linda Goodayle, of course, as they'd known each other for years. She also recognised what it meant that Linda had not used her given name. She said, "Please. Yasmina. May I speak with you, Linda? It's urgent."

Linda observed her with an expression that seemed devoid of all sentiment. She said, "Yeah. I expect it is. Your lot don't much like su'prises."

Yasmina wasn't fool enough to think there was nothing behind Linda's choice of distinct accent. She was using it as an implication from which Yasmina was meant to infer, *Our backgrounds are different and don't I know how you feel about mine.*

Yasmina felt her teeth dig into her lips. This wasn't how they were meant to begin. Somehow, Linda Goodayle had quickly managed to get the upper hand.

"But there's always su'prises in life, innit?" Linda dug round in her bag and brought out a packet of chewing gum. It was, Yasmina saw, a nicotine gum of the sort people used when they were trying to give up smoking. She realised that she hadn't known Linda smoked in the first place, and she wondered if this lack of knowledge on her part marked her as a social snob.

"So this speaking you want to do, Yas*mina*. It's 'bout my Justin, innit?" Linda popped a piece of the gum into her mouth and shoved its wrapper into the pocket of the hip-length cardigan she was wearing. "What I mean, 'course, is my Justin and your Missa. Tha's why you've stopped to have a little word with me."

Please oh *please* stop speaking like that, was what Yasmina wanted to say, because of the disadvantage Linda was causing her. But she knew that going in that direction would result in a conversation about class and any social differences that existed between their respective children and to whatever Linda believed that Yasmina thought about those differences. But the matter between them had *nothing* to do with class, although the Goodayles would probably never think that was the case.

"You must know they've registered to marry," Yasmina said. "The banns are posted."

Linda's face hardened at this direct approach. "Not living under a rock like some people, happens I do know," she said. "Got to say that I did wonder how long it would take you to get the information, as I don't see you running to the registry office every day to keep tabs on the goings-on round here. But you managed it quick enough."

"One of their former teachers told me just now. She wanted to congratulate me."

"I bet that one su'prised you, eh? You must've thought condolences were more the order of things."

"Linda, please. I *know* it's what they want. I know it's . . . It seems to me it's what everyone wants." Linda opened her mouth to answer this, but Yasmina went quickly on, saying, "And I'm not opposed to it."

"Tha's not what I've heard."

"It's only that I don't wish them to marry so *young*. When people are too young and they marry—"

"You must think I'm thick." Linda popped her gum loudly. That had to be deliberate, like her accent, like her choice of words. When she went on, however, she had utterly dropped the working-class game she was playing. She said, "I expect you think dimness runs in our family. This bit . . . whatever it is that you claim to feel or believe . . . It has nothing to do with their ages. It would be the same for you if Justin was twenty-eight and Missa was twenty-six. It's really to do with what you think of Justin."

"That's not true. He's a wonderful boy. He's always been important to our family and to Missa. My objections—"

"That's what this is, isn't it? Your *objections*. We're down to it now. Here comes the list."

"I've never denied wanting Missa to attend university," Yasmina said. "She has a very good brain—"

"Which Justin does not, according to you?"

"—and I would be remiss if I didn't encourage her to use it. Just as you would have been remiss not to encourage Justin as *you* did. He told me about that when he showed me what he's been doing with building those little . . . those little houses of his."

"Pods," Linda said sharply. "He's building something called pods. Quite successful he is at it, by the way. Which isn't a surprise to me, as I always believed his strength was in using his hands."

"Yes. I so agree. Just as Missa's strength is her brain."

"But this is where you and I part ways."

"How? Why? You can't think that Missa—"

"What I *think*," Linda said, "is that children are meant to discover their own strengths. They aren't meant to have their strengths thrust on them because their parents have some sort of plan in mind. You call your intentions for Missa's life your 'dreams' for her, don't you. But they've never been that: what you've got in mind. They've been your plans: whatever's on the path that *you've* decided is the one she'll take. And I bet you decided on *that* the day she was born."

"That isn't true. Missa herself fully intended to go to uni. She fully intended a future in science. *She* wanted these things, and then she didn't want them. She's thrown away her future and she won't tell me why."

Linda looked away from her, as if she wanted *thrown away her future* to echo round the car park for a bit. She had put her attention on a garishly painted purple building across the street from the museum, where a woman sold crystals, various rocks from round the world, and badly made silver jewellery. She was just closing shop for the day, a process that involved removing candles and folding up a gold lamé cloth that covered a small table outside the front door.

Yasmina added, "And now she's told Sati that when she and Justin marry, Sati may live with them in their house. You must see that can't be allowed to happen."

Linda turned back to her. She walked to the wall and spat out the gum. She said, "Would this be the house you told Justin you would purchase for them if he could talk Missa into returning to college and then going on to uni? Is that the house, Yasmina? And 'course, he believed you, didn't he? As he would do, not because he's dim like you think, but because he's honest. He appears to people exactly who he is, and he reckons other people are just the same. Only he's wrong, isn't he, especially when it comes to you, his future mother-in-law."

"Linda, please. You *can't* want them to do this."

"My kids' lives aren't *about* what I want. My kids' lives are about making their own decisions and getting the consequences and coping with those. You think my Justin isn't good enough for Missa—"

"I'm not saying that. I've *never* said that."

"—and it could be you're right as rain. And maybe that's what my Justin's meant to learn: that he's not the bloke for someone like Missa no matter how he feels about her. But there's this as well: it could be Missa's not good enough for him. It could be that, at heart, she's just like her mum, not able to believe in Justin's talent and in his goodness. Perhaps like you she really thinks, underneath it all, that stringing together a mass of uni degrees is more important than being who you are every single day. I don't know. Neither do you. But what I suppose is this, Yasmina: we'll all find out eventually."

She nodded sharply. She walked away, in the direction of her car, an ages-old Audi in a special parking bay marked *Director.* Yasmina was left with nothing to say and was about to go to her own vehicle when Linda turned back to her.

"So I won't intercede for you," she said. "That's what you've come to ask me to do, isn't it? All else has failed and now it's down to Justin's parents. Stop this madness, return Missa to her mother where she belongs. I won't do that. I wouldn't have done it to one of my own children and I certainly won't do it to one of yours."

Yasmina remained where she was as Linda reversed the Audi and then left the car park. She felt a numbness that kept her rooted to the spot. It was impossible for her to believe that any mother would allow events to unfold in the life of her child as events were unfolding in Linda's own son's life. The future was rolling out in front of all of them with the speed of a bullet train and no one wanted to lift a finger to alter its course.

When she finally left the car park and drove along the River Severn, she saw nothing of it. The hillside that rose to her left and contained the homes of the town might not have been there at all, and the great brick factories that had once produced the iron for the goods sent all over England might have disintegrated into nothing. All she saw was the future and what it could have been and what it would be now.

Sati, she decided, was her only hope. When she arrived home, she saw that Timothy was already there. She hoped that nothing played upon her face. He would not approve of her speaking to Linda Goodayle any more than he'd approved of a single thing she'd done to help Missa through this difficult time.

She gathered up her groceries and her shoulder bag. She forced her expression to pleasant and went inside the house, finding at once that her concerns about Timothy's reading her were unfounded. While Sati was at the kitchen table dutifully struggling with her maths prep, Timothy was not with her. Having a lie-down was the information Sati passed along in a subdued voice. He said he was done in from the day. He said to tell Mummy that he wouldn't want dinner. He said sorry but he needed rest.

Yasmina knew what *rest* equated to. She felt the urge to run upstairs. But how much, she asked herself, was one woman expected to cope with, and wasn't there a moment when that woman had to take life's hurdles one at a time and in order of importance?

"Well, you and I shall have our dinner together, then." Yasmina put her carrier bag on the work top and smiled at her daughter. She said, "What a good girl you are, Sati. Is your prep going well?"

Sati shook her head. Slowly, she sucked her lower lip into her mouth, pulling it so tight that she disfigured her chin. It was a most unattractive habit that she needed to shed. Yasmina didn't mention it, however. Instead, she went to the table, stood at her daughter's shoulder, and gazed at her schoolwork.

"Oh dear," she said as she took in the mess of it. Rubbings, scratchings, and an area that looked as if it had been wept upon. "It really shouldn't be this difficult. You have such an excellent mind. You merely have to be taught how to use it."

"I don't understand it," Sati said. "I never will. I won't ever need it either so I don't know why—"

"But of course you'll need it, Sati. It's the basis of so many things: science, technology, business."

"Not poetry. Not writing. Not art."

"But even then . . . Well of course you don't want writing to be what you'll do with your *professional* life. I suppose if you teach . . . but why would you want to teach with a fine mind like yours? We'll find you a tutor."

Sati gazed at her wordlessly. She was twelve years old but her eyes looked ancient.

Yasmina emptied her carrier bag to see what she'd grabbed in the supermarket. Chilli con carne, swede with cheddar, corned beef crispbakes, spaghetti carbonara. She announced with a laugh that it would be dinner surprises all the way round, which she knew Sati would like *especially*.

"Missa c'n help me," Sati murmured, her gaze on the papers in front of her. "She says she will."

"Of course," Yasmina said. "But when she's back in college, it'll be difficult for her. But, as I said, not to worry. There'll be a tutor, and while we look for one, there will be Gran to help you. We'll set about the tutor tomorrow, shall we? I saw Mrs. Osborne in the market only just now. Do you remember her? I'll ring her and she'll know someone. Why don't you finish up there and help me with our dinner? Afterwards, we'll watch telly, shall we?"

Sati nodded. She closed her books and gathered them up. She took them to her bedroom, always the child who did as she was told to do.

Yasmina had the table set and was reading the instructions on the containers of the bizarre meal she'd bought when Sati returned.

Yasmina chatted to her about what a silly dinner they were going to have. She gaily talked about how she simply didn't know *what* she'd been thinking as she picked up this and that, her mind obviously flitting about on other things: a celebrity marriage, a celebrity divorce, reading over lunch about a silly American woman on a trip into the Rocky Mountains who had thought her anti-bear spray was intended to be sprayed upon her children to keep the bears away! But it was meant to be used if a bear came near, to be sprayed at the bear! Her children ended up in casualty, Sati. Can you imagine the condition they must have been in?

Sati appeared to be engaged by the story. How mad it was to think someone would assume anti-bear spray was like mosquito spray! On the other hand, it *did* rather make sense, didn't it, Mum? Well, yes, but only if the spray had said on its label bear *repellent*, darling. Which, naturally, was rather different. What did Sati wish to watch on the telly, by the way? Did she want to look at *Radio Times* to see what was on? She could choose. They would curl up together and perhaps have a chocolate ice each. That would be lovely, wouldn't it?

When the meal was heated, Yasmina placed everything on the table, going to the effort of removing items from their containers and scooping them into serving dishes. She patted Sati's chair and spooned chilli into her bowl. Onto her plate went some swede, some spaghetti carbonara.

"I'm not really hungry, Mum," Sati said, standing behind her chair and looking down at the food.

"Of course you are," Yasmina said. "We both must eat. Sit, sit, my darling. And afterwards—"

"Mum—"

"No, no, sit, sit. Just eat a little. Do that for me, won't you, Sati?"

Sati sighed. She pulled the chair out and dropped onto it. She picked up a spoon and, when she toyed with her chilli and ultimately put a teaspoonful of it into her mouth, Yasmina did not scold her or urge her to have more. She picked up her own spoon and dug into the bowl and tried to ignore the unpleasant mixture of scents from the different foods on the table.

She chatted to her daughter: this, that, the other. Reality television, a royal faux pas, an increase in bullying, a decrease in bullying. Whatever came into her mind. And then, finally, she ventured where she knew she had to go.

She said, "Sati darling, I must tell you something that I learned today from Mrs. Osborne." Yasmina waited for a sign of interest. When it did not come, she ventured on anyway. "This was in the supermarket, when I saw her, as I've said. I'm going to tell you what I learned from her, and then I must ask a favour of you."

Sati looked at her with those ancient eyes. She was such a pretty girl, Yasmina thought. Every handsome feature that her parents possessed had managed to blend together in her. It was as if Missa and Janna had been experiments in blending this and that while Sati was the finished product, perfected after the first two tries. At twelve she was a child to be admired. At twenty she would cause people to stop and stare. Women would envy. Men would desire. And Yasmina's job with this, her youngest child, was to make certain Sati understood how fleeting it was: Beauty was temporal, wisdom was not.

"What?" Sati asked. "What favour, Mum?"

"Let me tell you first what I learned from Mrs. Osborne." Yasmina then revealed what she had been told: the registry office and the intended marriage of Missa to Justin Goodayle. "Mrs. Osborne was there with her fiancé to register *their* marriage, you see. And the banns were posted . . . Missa and Justin . . . to be married. Do you understand?"

As Yasmina had been speaking, Sati had dropped her gaze to her bowl of chilli. She'd lifted a fork and moved the swede with cheddar here and there on her plate. But now she lifted her head, looked directly at Yasmina, and said quite unexpectedly, "I'm not stupid, Mum."

Yasmina gave a laugh. It was too obviously forced, but she couldn't help that. There was something different in Sati's tone. She'd insulted her daughter without meaning to do so.

"I'm *sorry*, darling Sati," she said. "I didn't intend that. I suppose what I meant is that registering as they've done means it's to happen soon. It's perfectly legal, of course. They're both of age. But I think we ought to consider that this might not be the best for either of them." She paused to gather her thoughts and to consider the best direction to take. She went with, "Sati, here's what it is. A marriage when one is so young is nearly always doomed to fail, and I can't bear Missa going through such a thing as a failed marriage. Can you? I think—no, I am convinced—that Missa will listen to an appeal from you. She knows you miss her. She knows you need her. I want you to speak with her. Do you understand? I would like you to meet with her at the Goodayles' home or to see her at Blists Hill—I'm happy to drive you there—and when you do, I want you to ask her to come home. Tell her the truth: Mum is sorry for the mess she made of West Mercia College and Mum apologises with all her heart and you—Sati—need her to be with you, which she will not be if she marries—"

"She told me I can come to live with them," Sati said abruptly.

Yasmina took up her glass and drank some water. "Darling, surely if they *do* take the cottage in Jackfield—"

"This was before all that, Mum. She told me that when she and Justin are married, I can live with them if I want to. They won't be living in a little cottage. They'll find a bigger one. She said there will be a room for me—not the spare room but my own bedroom—and I can live with them."

Yasmina found that her mouth was dry. So were her lips. Even her palms felt completely desiccated. She said, "Sati, darling girl, you aren't of an age to live anywhere but with your mum and dad."

"She said she'll tell me exactly when the wedding's going to be so I can go to it. And after that, she and Justin will come for me and I'll live with them."

It dawned on Yasmina that she'd missed a quite salient point as her daughter was speaking. She said, "You already *knew* they'd registered to marry?"

"She told me they were going to. They both told me. They asked did I want to come with them to the registry office but I said no as you would be angry if I did that and they said it was quite all right if you were angry and if I was frightened of you, Justin would come for me. I said I wasn't frightened but I didn't want to upset you more so I would wait. But then when they have everything ready I would live with them."

Yasmina sank against the back of her chair. "Why did you not tell me any of this?"

"I knew you'd say no."

"I don't mean about living with them. I assure you that is not going to happen. I mean . . . the registry office, the marriage, their intention . . ." Yasmina reached for Sati's arm. Her fingers closed over it in a grip that made the girl cry out. "This is her future!" Yasmina hissed. "Do you not understand that? This isn't a game. This isn't a way to slap Mum in the face. This is her life, you stupid girl. And you *knew*. You knew all along."

Sati pulled away. "You're hurting me, Mum!"

"*Nothing* like I shall be hurting you later. What's the matter with you? Where is your sense? I could have been there waiting. I could have stopped it. I could have—"

"That's what she said!" Sati's eyes filled. "She said you would do anything. She said you hate her. She said you hate Justin. She said you hate *anyone* who doesn't do what you want them to do."

"I do not—"

"You're hurting me! Your nails . . . Stop it. Mum, *stop* it." She began to cry. "I won't stay here. I won't stay with you. Janna is gone and Missa is gone and I have *no* one because I'm not anything and I'm going to live with Missa and Justin and you can't stop me because if you try and if you do I'll run away and you'll never find me and I'll go to London and I'll live on the street and—"

Yasmina hit her so hard that Sati's head flew back. It took a moment before she realised that she'd not slapped her as she'd intended, but rather she'd punched her. She said, "Oh Sati . . . My God . . . Sati, my dear daughter . . ."

But in speaking, she'd also released her grip on the girl. Sati jumped to her feet. She ran for the door. Yasmina called after her with a desperation born of regret and sorrow and utter knowledge.

The slamming door told her the damage was done.

ST. JULIAN'S WELL
LUDLOW
SHROPSHIRE

When the doorbell sounded, Rabiah Lomax's first thought was that the police had returned for more questioning of her. If the telly was anything to go by, they knew that the unexpected call at an off-duty hour—especially after ten o'clock at night—was certain to produce better results than they'd managed to amass on an earlier go.

When she opened her door, however, she came face-to-face with her younger son. The fact that he had a carrier bag into which he'd apparently thrown a few garments did not bode well. Nor did his expression, which was so cut up that Rabiah knew immediately that something terrible had occurred.

She stepped back from the door. Timothy entered. He said nothing at first, merely going into the sitting room, dropping onto the sofa, and letting the carrier bag fall from his fingers.

"Sati as well," were his initial words, which drove a stake of fear straight through Rabiah's midsection. She sat upon the closest piece of furniture at hand, which was an ottoman.

Timothy rubbed his hand over his face, and from where Rabiah sat she could hear the *scritch* of his palm against whiskers. When he looked at her, she could see that his eyes were bloodshot, so she experienced another stake of fear that he'd been drinking. But he'd managed to drive all the way from Ironbridge, she realised, and he wasn't acting the least bit drunk. There were the pills as well, but he also wasn't acting drugged.

"She's driven Sati off as well," he said. "I went after her once I came downstairs. I'd just gone to have a lie-down, nothing more, and she probably thought that I'd taken something that would keep me dead to the world. I hadn't, so I heard their voices and then the door slamming. Hard, this was. The door, I mean. The windows in the bedroom actually shook. Why does that happen? Are houses not built well any longer?"

"What's going on, Tim?" Rabiah asked. "You're frightening me."

"Could I have a glass of water, Mum? Tap water's fine but if you have fizzy . . . Oh, fuck me. Why am I even thinking of what *I* prefer?"

Because you're a user was what she could have told him, and that's fairly close to the number one indication: me, me, me, more me. But she said, "Of course," and she fetched him what she had, which was an open bottle of Pellegrino. He drank from that.

She said, "What's happened?"

"Missa left us yesterday morning. Sati left us round dinnertime today."

"What do you mean, *left*?"

"I reckoned she'd gone to a mate's house at first, so that's where I started. I ended up at Justin's, which of course made sense since Missa's there. For now this is, according to what I've been able to sort out. Just till after the wedding, when Sati intends to live with them. Missa and Justin, this is." He spoke dully and when he was finished Rabiah could see why his eyes were bloodshot, as they filled with tears. She wanted to feel whatever pain he was going through, in order to take it from him. Only she found unexpectedly that she herself was feeling no pain at all. Rather, what she felt was fury. Not only at him, but at the whole boiling lot of them.

"I can't cope with her any longer," he said. "I managed through . . . through Janna, but I can't . . . It's like she's started to believe . . . Only it's not, is it? It's not that she's *started* to believe anything. It's that she always believed and I didn't want to see it. I tried to talk to her at first. I tried to tell her that everything she did would make life go wrong. But she wouldn't ever see that. It was her duty, she would say. Just like her parents said to her. Mould, shape, chisel, pound. Whatever it takes to fit them into the hole you've prepared for them. You would think her own experience would've been enough to tell her that she'd got being a mother the wrong way round. But it turned out that her own experience made her that much more determined that the girls would profit by her mistakes. That's how she sees it. A mistake. Herself, me, how we got together, all of it. Fine and all right, then. I've tried. I'm finished."

Rabiah knew that the only possible way she was going to be able to stop herself from flying off the ottoman and shaking Timothy by his shoulders till his teeth rattled was to make him tell the story from start to finish, although she had worked out much of it during his rambling. She said, "I'm trying to follow what's happened. Yasmina's done something. It's ended up with the lot of you leaving."

That was enough to get him talking: Yasmina's plan for Justin to cajole Missa about college and uni, Missa's very quick discovery of the plan, Missa leaving, the two of them deciding then—or really, perhaps they'd already done it but who knew at this point—to post banns for their marriage, Yasmina's discovery of this, her conversation with Linda Goodayle, the outcome of that conversation, and Yasmina's next manoeuvre to involve Sati in the whole miserable mess.

"She was in a state when I went downstairs," Tim said. "Missa getting married quickly and her father doing nothing to stop it so that she—Yasmina—would find herself in a position of having to beg Linda Goodayle to help and then that didn't work because for God's sake why should it, she was onto Sati. What else was there left to do but blame me? Janna's death, Missa's decisions about her life, Sati running off because her mother punched her in the face."

"*Punched*?"

"That's what she told me, but she was hysterical by then."

"Sati? You were able to talk to her?"

"Yasmina, not Sati. And then it was go out there and find her, damn you, instead of drugging yourself like a useless addict under a bridge. Go. Go! And I did, Mum. God, how I did. I grabbed some clothes and my shaving kit and I went, just like she wanted."

"Are you saying that you *didn't* look for Sati? You've already told me that—"

"I did. Like I said. I meant to bring her here with me, but she wouldn't leave Missa and Missa wouldn't leave Justin and Justin wasn't about to agree to anyone going anywhere once he had a look at Sati's face. Do you know what it looks like when a twelve-year-old girl is punched in the face, Mum?" He raised his gaze to take in the ceiling. Then he dropped it to her again. "God, I am so sick and tired of not being able to do *anything* to protect them from her."

That, Rabiah decided, was that. She rose so quickly she was like a runner who'd just heard the pistol. "*That*," she said. "is the bloody goddamn limit to what's gone on in this family."

He clasped his hands together as if in prayer and said, "Oh Mum, thank God you see, because there's no possible way—"

"I am *not* talking about Yasmina," she snapped. She approached the sofa and stood above him. "I am not talking about Missa or Sati or our poor Janna. I'm talking about you. What in the name of God is wrong with you? Oh, never mind. Never *mind*! It's exactly what's wrong with your brother, and it killed your grandfather, so why the *hell* not you, eh? From the moment you reckoned just one little time without protection and how could she possibly come up pregnant in only one time and anyway I'll pull out, won't I, that's what I'll do . . . From that very moment of gross stupidity, you've taken the easiest route every single time, and I've gone along and been there to help make things easier and neither of us is doing that now. Do you hear me? Do you *begin* to understand me? You may have reached your limit with Yasmina, but I have reached my limit with you. You're no more moving in with me, Timothy—and do not dare tell me that's not the master plan here—than you're moving to Tahiti. You're growing up, and you're doing it directly, because I have no intention of taking the responsibilities of your life and putting them on my shoulders. If Yasmina went wrong with the girls—and I'm not saying she didn't—then where the dickens did you go right? She's had to bring those girls up by herself. This doesn't make what she'd done sensible or even excusable. But it does make what she's done reasonable, given the hand she dealt herself when she was foolish enough to take up with you."

That she'd astonished him was beyond doubt. But as far as she was concerned, he stood six inches from the edge of a precipice and a fall was going to mean he'd failed in the very same way his brother had done, losing everything for the simple reason that he could not man up—God, she was thinking like a telly psychologist at this bloody point!—and take charge of himself. Easier just to talk oneself into believing that one was owed: the drink, the drug, the food, the sex, the bloody sodding *whatever*. If one didn't do that, one might actually have do something else. And by God that would take effort, wouldn't it. Because life took effort and it was time he learnt that.

"Stop gawping at me," she snapped. "Close your mouth, sit up straight, and stop blaming anyone but yourself. You may stay with me one night, Timothy, and only because it's late. Tomorrow morning you will deal with this like a husband and a father and a man, and just in case you're thinking you *won't* do that because what's the point and you've tried and tried and you haven't been able to get through to Yasmina and boo hoo hoo, I shall be with you. Not to take your part, by the way. But to make certain there *is* a part in the first place. Now get into the spare room and I do not wish to see your face till morning."

For a moment, she thought she might have gone too far with him. But then he said the most unexpected: "Thank you, Mum," after which he took himself to the spare room with his carrier bag of clothing and he closed the door.

# 23 MAY

LUDLOW
SHROPSHIRE

In Lynley's experience dirty in one way generally meant dirty in another, and after their conversation with Dena Donaldson, he'd come on board with Barbara Havers's conclusion that the PCSO was dirty, at least with regard to the college-age girls in Ludlow. The difficulty was that they had no substantial proof of this. While it was true that Harry Rochester had more than once witnessed Ruddock loading bingers into his patrol car and while it was equally true that the dosser claimed he had seen Francie Adamucci alone with him, that was the limit of what they had on the PCSO, which no prosecutor on earth was going to take to the bank and make a deposit with.

They also had Barbara's sighting of Ruddock and Dena in the car park of the police station at night, but there again it was something that took them no great distance. What Barbara had seen, just like what Harry had seen, was not evidentiary. While the two girls might claim that the PCSO was forcing them into sex acts, Ruddock could claim with equal credibility that those were false accusations based on a girl's desire for vengeance as he did his job and cleared the streets. Going back through the various times when he'd had to do exactly that was going to support his claim while doing nothing at all to support what the girls might say about him. So while Thomas Lynley and Barbara Havers had a clearer picture of Gary Ruddock and how he was using his position as Ludlow's PCSO, they had nothing irrefutable.

He rang Nkata as his first action of the day once he was up, showered, shaved, dressed and had a cup of hotel-room morning tea in hand, hotel-room morning coffee being something that he could not face. He sat on the bed, punched in the numbers of the DS's mobile, and said when he heard his voice, "What do we have, because God knows we need something."

"That kind of day already?" Nkata enquired.

"Merely girding myself," he replied.

Nkata started with West Mercia Police Headquarters, where Ruddock had received his training as a PCSO. He'd tracked down several of Ruddock's instructors and their reports about him declared that "the bloke was earnest and dedicated," Nkata told him. Apparently, he'd been eager to work his way into the regular force—despite the ongoing cutbacks—and he saw this as a route that would take him there. He was cleverer than most—

"Hang on," Lynley said. "We've been told he's got some learning troubles. Is that not the case?"

Nkata replied with, "I mean clever in a different way, 'nspector."

It turned out that at the training centre, Ruddock had learned to compensate for his difficulties by rubbing any elbow that belonged to a higher-up in the organisation. This got his name recognised and his mug known, Nkata told Lynley. "From what I c'n tell, guv, he was practic'ly guaranteed a placement at the end of the day. As PCSO, I mean, because the cutbacks were coming fast when he was in training."

This was interesting but it spoke of little save a young man who'd wisely learned how to compensate for his difficulties. "Anything else?" Lynley asked.

"His background tells an in'erestin story."

"The cult in Donegal, I presume." Lynley had made his tea in one of the ubiquitous hotel tin pots, and he poured himself a refill.

"Right," Nkata said. "Tha's where it gets in'erestin. Did he mention to Barb the place got broke up by the Garda? This was 'bout ten years ago."

"What was going on?"

"Massive sex abuse. Cult leaders claimed it was God's dictate written in the holy book. Increase and multiply and fill the earth and they were only following God's instructions, see. Only nobody had a choice in the matter and that included boys as well as girls. If a boy looked like he was a grand candidate in the increasing and multiplying department, he got taken to this place called the Palace of God's Will which, from what I've read, wasn't 'xactly palatial."

"I wouldn't wager against that," Lynley said.

"There he'd be told to do the business on whichever female'd been selected for him. Didn't matter ages either. For boys, this gen'rally started when they were round twelve years old. For girls, it was soon as they were old enough to have a kid without dying in the process. The lucky girls were the ones slow to develop. The others . . . ? Youngest gave birth when she was eleven."

"Christ. I don't remember any of this, Winston. Was it in the papers at the time?"

"Prob'ly, but as it was in the Republic and not the north, it wouldn't've been as big a story here. And anyway, where were you and what were you doing ten years ago? I was trying to extricate myself from the Warriors, so what was happenin in other countries didn't matter that much to me."

"What happened to all the children involved?"

"Went into care if they were underage. How old would your boy've been?"

"Sixteen, I think. He told Barbara he ran off when he was fifteen."

"Prob'ly did. I come up with a blank on him for a bit of time. When he shows up out of the ether, he's in Belfast in the building trade. Eighteen then. He goes from there to England by way of Wales, where he did carpentry. But he's not ever got into trouble, 'nspector. He might not've told Barb all the details 'bout the cult—like the Palace of God's Will and all that—but from what you gave me, he checks out."

Which, Lynley thought as he rang off, did not make the man not complicit in other ways. But with Winston's search, they'd got no further and they'd certainly not got close to being able to back Ruddock into a corner with regard to the claims being made about his behaviour with young women.

When the room phone rang, he picked it up absently, assuming Winston was ringing with something he'd forgotten. He said, "There's more?" and was instantly jarred by Isabelle Ardery's sharp voice.

"Are you avoiding my calls, Tommy?" she demanded. "Why the hell haven't you rung me back?"

She sounded completely normal, which was something of a relief. She sounded completely normal, which was also something of a worry. He replied with, "Sorry, guv. We've been on the run up here."

"When I ring you, Inspector, you're to ring me back. I remain your senior officer. And if you have just added 'for now' to what I said, I caution you not to do that."

"I hadn't at all, guv," he said.

"I'm very glad to hear that. Get out the suicide photos, please."

"At the moment, I don't actually have them. They're in Sergeant Hav—"

"Well, bloody well get them. When you have them in hand—which I will give you exactly ten minutes to accomplish—ring me at once. And put yourself in a place where your side of our next conversation will not be overheard. Am I being clear?"

"Do you mean by Sergeant Havers as well?" he asked.

"Don't be ridiculous. I'm not so stupid as to believe you wouldn't report every word we speak directly back to her anyway. Now get those photos and ring me back."

IRONBRIDGE
SHROPSHIRE

Rabiah had forced her son to get up at dawn. She could have done with an extra two hours' lie-in, but that was one of the many things that were not going to be an option today. So was the idea of either of them—Yasmina or Timothy—going to work. They were going to remain at home if she had to tie both of them to kitchen chairs. This would not be a problem for Timothy as, doubtless, he'd failed to show up at the pharmacy on any fixed schedule in months. Yasmina was another matter, as she would have to cancel patients. But she *was* going to do that. This was, Rabiah reckoned, a last-ditch effort.

She'd readied herself as if to do battle when she went to awaken her younger son. The information he'd brought her last night had been so gobsmacking that she'd not checked either his pockets or the carrier bag when he'd shown up on her doorstep. For all she knew he'd drugged himself, which meant he would not be easy to awaken. No matter, as she took a jug of water with her as the only weapon she could devise. But he was sitting up in bed. True, his eyes were closed, but he wasn't sleeping, as he opened them the moment he heard the door's movement.

He saw the jug and said, "I left without them. I was in a rush or I would have brought them, believe me. I didn't sleep."

"Nor did I. Get up. We're going to Ironbridge."

"Mum—"

"Do you think I *want* to get into the middle of this? Do you actually think I believe I have even one answer regarding the massive mess you've made of your life?"

"If you don't have answers, what's the point?"

"The point is that *you* have the answers, you ninny. You and Yasmina have the answers and you're taking a look at them today."

"She isn't going to want to do that."

"Do you *also* think that I care in the least what Yasmina wants? Get up, get dressed, and get in the car. You're driving to Ironbridge and I'm following you there."

She gave him a quarter hour, since he requested a shower. While he was taking it, she gathered up the clothing he'd tossed on the floor, and she put it into the carrier bag. This she took to the front door. It would make the only statement necessary to explain how willing she was *not* to have Timothy run off from his troubles and ask to take up lodging with her.

He didn't mention the bag when he was dressed. Lucky for him, she thought, that he'd carried clothing into the bathroom or he'd be driving to Ironbridge in his pyjamas, which was also just absolutely fine with her.

At that hour, there was no traffic aside from one articulated lorry outside of Bridgnorth attempting to negotiate a way into the heart of the upper town. Before and after that, it was only a matter of not hitting some confused animal that might wander into the road as they sped along chasing the growing daylight.

Rabiah went into the house alone when they reached Ironbridge, after informing Timothy that he was to wait just outside the front door. She heard sounds from the kitchen suggesting that Yasmina, too, was up and about. As her daughter-in-law was not in sight, Rabiah then roughly motioned Timothy inside and murmured that he would remain in the entry until his presence was required.

In the kitchen, Rabiah found Yasmina with Sati's Hello Kitty lunch box gaping. She was in the midst of cutting the crusts off a sandwich she'd apparently made for the girl. She appeared to be accompanying this with an apple, a snack packet of fig bars, and another packet of crisps along with a carton of juice with straw attached.

Yasmina swung round when Rabiah said, "You don't expect her to eat all that after yesterday, do you?"

Yasmina recovered quickly from the surprise of her mother-in-law's sudden appearance in her kitchen at six in the morning. She turned back to what she'd been doing and said, "Timothy told you, I see. I'm taking this to Sati's school. I want to apologise to her."

"Aren't you getting ahead of yourself?"

Yasmina looked over her shoulder without reply.

Rabiah went on with, "You're presupposing. First, that she's even going to show up at school today with evidence on her face of having been punched by her mother. Second that she will want to have a conversation with you if she *is* there."

"Be that as it may," Yasmina said with curious dignity, all things considered, "I must do this, Mum."

Rabiah stepped forward. She reached round the other woman and snapped the lunch box closed. "What you *must* do if we've arrived at the point of musts is this: You must sit the hell down, either here or elsewhere. The three of us are having a conversation."

"You must know that Sati has left."

"I'm not talking about Sati." Rabiah called out, "Timothy? You're wanted."

He came round from the entry. In doing so, Rabiah was reminded of him as a boy and saw how little things had actually changed. He had that hangdog expression about him, caught out for doing whatever he'd done that he knew he wasn't supposed to do but had done anyway, and now hoping for some kind of reprieve if he managed to look pathetic enough. This had worked at one time and Rabiah was outraged at herself that she'd allowed it.

When he joined them in the kitchen, she said, "I'm not here to sort out your marriage. You're going to do that if you want to do that. But I *am* here to tell you that you're not to leave this house until you next hear from me, because my concern is Missa and Sati, not the two of you. I'm leaving here now to speak to them. If I have any luck at all, I might be able to bring one of them or, God willing, both of them, home. And we three know bloody well at this point that that's not about to happen if either of you tag along."

"Mum," Timothy said. "Let me come. I've done nothing—"

"For God's sake, do *not* try to tell me you've done nothing to cause this. I'm not here to look for causes of anything and neither should you be. I'm here because at this moment we are still a family and I intend us to remain a family. Anything else is unthinkable, and if you two are not on board with that, I suggest you get on board. A hell of a lot is going to have to go on in this house besides apologising. Apologies mean sod all if they aren't accompanied by change. Do either of you come anywhere close to understanding what I'm talking about? Don't bother to answer. Just give me the Goodayles' goddamn address and remain in this house till you hear from me."

Neither of them argued. Yasmina produced the address and handed it over. Rabiah left them.

The Goodayles' home did not prove difficult to find. They lived high enough above the town to be almost part of Woodside. To reach it, Rabiah drove through the area where the magnates had lived during the industrial revolution, owners of the local factories that had fashioned everything from decorative iron doorstops to delicate china teapots. They'd occupied large Georgian homes of brick, which had fallen into disrepair during the last century and were slowly being restored to their classical beauties now. The Goodayles did not live in one of these but rather beyond them and higher still. It was yet another area that had fallen upon hard times, but again some of these homes were in the process of restoration. The home of the Goodayles was not one of them.

Their house, like so many others nearby, was constructed of Broseley brick. It featured a garden in the front, unlike the houses lower down on the hillside that nosed directly onto the street. When Rabiah parked and clambered out of the car to head towards the front door, she saw that the garden had been set up as a battle site. Plaster gnomes wearing handmade Highland kilts had apparently been facing off against their British enemies, also plaster gnomes, but these in their regulation gnome kit although accentuated by smallish Union Jacks set up behind them and both plastic muskets and rubber swords at their feet. Several of the soldiers had, alas, suffered at the hands of Highland warriors. Two were headless, and one was missing an arm.

In spite of herself, Rabiah smiled. The Goodayles, as she recalled, had five children, and the eldest was at least a decade older than Justin. There had obviously been grandchildren at play here. Actively imaginative grandchildren, it seemed.

When she gave the door a good pounding, it was Sati who opened it. She carried a bowl of cereal and a spoon, and she had a splash of milk on her chin. At the sight of Rabiah, her eyes became the size of penny coins. She apparently didn't know what to say because her mouth opened, then closed, and she sucked in on her lip before looking over her shoulder into the body of the house.

Rabiah said, "Ask your gran inside first. Give her a hug second. That'll do for now."

Sati stepped back, eyes still huge. There was no place to put the cereal bowl save on the floor, which she did so that she could obey the direct order. The fact that she would do this made Rabiah's regret stir inside of her. The Lomax daughters had needed to fight to be individuals, and mostly they'd failed. Why had she not seen it before this moment?

She hugged the little girl and kissed the top of her head. She tilted her face up and looked at the bruising. She said, "Your mum's very upset about this. She wants you to come home long enough for her to say sorry."

Sati's great dark eyes grew bright, but she didn't let any tears escape. "Missa says—"

"No need, Sati. I'm not here to talk you into going home. It's Missa

I've come to have a word with. When and if you go home? That's up to you. Understood?"

Sati picked up her cereal bowl. Her answer was a whispered, "All right."

"Maths still giving you difficulty?"

She nodded again.

"We'll need to sort that. Meantime, fetch Missa for me, there's my lovely girl. Tell her I want a word and it's not about either of you going home to your mum."

"'Kay," was her reply, along with a shy smile that made Rabiah's heart give a twist. Then she was gone up the stairs and Rabiah found her way to the sitting room.

It was—like the garden outside—kitted out for the grandkids' enjoyment. There were dozens of toys, but all of them were neatly stored in boxes with labels bearing each child's name. There was also a shelf of board games and, from a doorway leading into a dining room, a bouncy baby swing was hanging. There were pictures everywhere: grandchildren, marriages, christenings, university graduations. There was also a display case designed for collectibles, into which a number of infant handprints and footprints had been rendered in clay and several bronzed baby shoes were interspersed among them.

"Missus Lomax, is it?"

Rabiah swung round. The woman who greeted her was late middle-aged and dressed neatly in a tartan skirt, tailored blouse, and waistcoat. This would be Linda Goodayle. She didn't bear an expression of welcome, but Rabiah reckoned Justin's mum assumed that Missa's gran had shown up on her doorstep as an emissary of the family.

"It's Rabiah," she said. "Sorry to barge in like this. I've come to speak with Missa. Her mum didn't send me, by the way. It's nothing to do with . . ." She wasn't sure how to put it, so she gestured round the room and said, ". . . anything, actually, aside from Ludlow."

"She's not going back, if that's why you've come. She's tried to make that clear to her parents. But it's done no good."

"Completely understandable," Rabiah said. "What I mean is that Missa's old enough to know her own mind. I might not agree with what her mind's telling her, but I'm fully on board with the idea of the girl having a mind in the first place."

She heard, then, the clatter of footsteps on the stairs, and Justin appeared in the doorway. She was struck by the size of him, which was less noticeable when he was in his milieu at the Victorian blacksmith's shop. Like his mother, he was dressed for his workday and his hair was tied back in traditional fashion.

He said, "If you're here to talk her out of it, it's no go, Missus Lomax."

Rabiah drew a blank at that. "Out of what?" she asked him. "D'you mean living here? That's not why I've come."

"I mean the wedding," he said. "Me and Missa. Next month."

Rabiah was moderately horrified at the idea that Missa would marry *anyone* in just a month's time considering the chaos in her family. She wondered if that had been what she'd been discussing with Druitt. She found the voice to say, "Congratulations then. I'd not yet been told when. Just that it was intended."

"Mum doesn't want it," Missa said. She'd come in perfect silence down the stairs, and she stood behind Justin. Unlike the young man and his mother, she'd apparently been roused from bed by her sister, since she was in a dressing gown and slippers and her hair was still tousled from sleep. "So if you've come to have a go at that, you can turn round and leave, Gran."

Rabiah waved her off, a pooh-pooh motion that she hoped would disarm not only the girl but also Justin and his mother. "Give us a hug, for God's sake," she said. "You can marry who you want, when you want, as far as I'm concerned. I'll be cross if I'm not invited, though."

Missa didn't look convinced, but she did come into the sitting room and she did allow herself to be hugged and she did hug Rabiah in return. That was step one, in Rabiah's mind. Step two was being rid of Justin and his mother so that she and Missa could speak privately. She cared not one whit about being presumptuous. She said, "Might I have a cup of coffee, Justin?"

He and his mother exchanged a look. Something meaningful passed between them. Linda Goodayle said, with an attempt at sounding welcoming at this hour of the morning, "Of course. I'll see to it. Do make yourself comfortable."

That handled Linda, but Justin looked immobile, so Rabiah went at him directly, saying, "Justin, I need to speak with Missa alone. I'm not here to discuss the two of you, however, so you've no need to worry about that."

Missa looked towards the young man, and he waited for her decision. She said after a moment, "Gran's not going to talk me out of anything, Justie. She's also not going to talk me *into* anything. It's fine. No worries. Tell Sati for me, okay?"

He left them, but Rabiah could tell he was reluctant to do so. She waited till she heard his footsteps on the stairs before she quickly said to Missa, "This isn't about Sati. This isn't about your mother. Or your father. Who they are, what they've done, the whole bit of it. This is about me, and this is about you."

Missa appeared confused by this, as well she might. Rabiah and the girl had always been close, so that there was a me and you that needed talking about would be a perplexing issue.

Rabiah went on. "I've had the London police at my home three times now, Missa, and three times I've lied to them. As far as I can tell, there isn't a person in this family who *doesn't* lie—save Sati, perhaps, as she might be too young to have mastered the art—but that's about to stop. No, don't speak a word. I've been willing to believe that your seven encounters with Ian Druitt were about gathering some kind of support for leaving West Mercia College. I understand that you would need *someone's* support to do this, as you certainly weren't getting it from anyone else. But what I do not understand is why you apparently believed that your own grandmother would be unwilling to support your wishes. Moreover, what I do not understand is why you suddenly took the decision to leave at all. Please don't respond, dear. I see you would like to but I'm not finished. You lived with me in my own house and we were not exactly strangers to each other, were we? So what I knew then and what I know now is that you loved the college, you were doing brilliantly, you liked your tutor, and you enjoyed your courses. And then suddenly . . . you didn't."

"It became too difficult, Gran," Missa said. "But no one—"

"Cease, please. Someone like you does not go from performing brilliantly to finding oneself unable to perform at all. Therefore . . . there's something gone on between those two points in your life. Now, from all her dancing round with the truth when I spoke to her, I reckon Ding Donaldson knows what's going on. But she's loyal to you so . . . What is it?"

Missa had laughed shortly, a bitter sound. She looked away from her grandmother. Rabiah said, "What? You must tell me what. The London police have your details. They know where to find you."

"Not these details," Missa said. "They don't have *these* details. You can tell them where I am, of course, but—"

"That's exactly what I intend to do if you don't speak to me honestly. I mean it, Missa. They're dealing with a suicide that they apparently believe is *not* a suicide, and if you think they're not intent on putting everyone through it to get to the bottom of what happened, you're being very naïve. Your innocence has always been appealing but . . . Missa, *what*?"

The girl had begun to weep soundlessly. She covered her mouth as if this would stop up the tears, and when this didn't work, she dug her fingernails into her skin deeply. Rabiah got up and went to her. She embraced the girl and said into the side of her head. "Missa, what? Please. You must tell me."

"It was the cider," she said.

"Cider? What on earth . . . ? Cider?"

"I drank it and drank it. I didn't think cider *did* anything, but then I was drunk. It was all of a sudden and I couldn't go home. You'd see me just like Dad and Uncle David and I couldn't do it. I *couldn't,* Gran."

LUDLOW

SHROPSHIRE

The sharp knock on her door was followed by Inspector Lynley's mellifluous baritone saying, "Barbara? I'm sorry but I must get you up. Isabelle's phoned and—"

Isabelle, Isabelle, Barbara thought with an inward scoff. She said, "Right. Coming," and rolled out of bed. She was approaching the door when she realised she was wearing one of her slogan-bearing T-shirts, which she'd purchased in the largest size possible so that she could don it for sleeping. It was guaranteed not to amuse one's superior officer: *And yet, despite the look on my face, you're still speaking.* She called out, "Let me get decent."

He responded with, "Of course. But I *have* seen the Buddy Holly pyjamas before now, if you recall. Cornwall? Casvelyn? I wore blue and you wore Buddy Holly? Is this sounding familiar?"

"I think you were wearing a white towel, sir. Having just performed your morning whatevers." She was rapidly pulling on a pair of drawstring trousers.

He spoke again. "Was I? What a horrifying thought. I mean myself in a towel in a shared-bathroom situation. It hardly bears thinking about. Listen, Barbara, the guv is waiting for me to ring her back. She's not happy that we both ignored her calls yesterday. I only need the SOCO photographs, if that's of help. You can slide them under the door if you like."

Barbara wasn't about to do that. She wanted to be in on whatever the DCS had in her head. She decided not to worry about the T-shirt as a search through the pile of her clothing had produced only two more of a similar ilk. So she went to the door and opened it.

Lynley was, of course, fully and nattily dressed. She saw him read the slogan on the T-shirt. He said, "Ah. You've eschewed Buddy Holly."

"Sorry," she said. "I didn't expect you turning up like this."

"I wouldn't have, had she not been in a state. The guv, that is. And don't concern yourself about the T-shirt. I've seen far worse on your chest since you and I began keeping company." He frowned, then and went on with, "Sorry. That didn't come out quite as I intended. May I . . . ?" He was referring to entering. She would have barged right into his room if their positions were reversed, but Lynley was not a man for barging.

She held the door open. She'd left the files on the coffee table, so he went to the sofa. For her part, she scurried to her clothes pile and dug through it more deeply to find an appropriate top. She took this into the bathroom, where she divested herself of the T-shirt, found her bra where she'd left it dangling on a hook meant for a dressing gown, and once she had it on, she pulled a jersey over her head. When she left the bathroom more suitably attired, she found that Lynley had donned his spectacles and was on his mobile. She also found that he'd put it onto its speaker capability so that she could hear whatever Isabelle Ardery had to say.

She was in the midst of ". . . only of the body and what's nearby." The DCS waited on her end while Lynley sorted through the SOCO pictures and pulled from them every one that depicted Ian Druitt's body in situ. These he lay out on the coffee table. "I have them," he said.

"Is there one with the ligature in it?"

He said, "It wasn't a ligature, guv. It was—"

"I know what it was, Tommy. Call it whatever you like but find a picture that shows it and tell me what you see."

Barbara joined Lynley on the sofa. They exchanged a look. But Lynley did as he was asked and found a photo that showed both Druitt's body and the stole he had used to hang himself. It lay like a sprawled snake soaking up the sun.

He said, "Got it, guv."

She said, "Tell me what colour it is."

"The stole? It's red."

"There you have it," Ardery said.

Barbara had no clue what they "had." Ardery was continuing, however.

"I was in a church last night—"

Eyebrows lifted on both their parts.

"—near the river. I'd gone for a walk, ended up close to Putney Bridge, and there was a church holding evensong. It was all quite formal: the choir, the priest, the praying and the singing."

Barbara rolled her eyes at the idea that Ardery was getting religion. But Lynley seemed to understand that she was heading towards something.

"It was the priest, Tommy," Ardery said. "The priest or deacon or whatever he was. I saw him but it didn't register at first. Everything he was wearing was green."

Barbara had never been a churchgoer—even at Christmas, Easter, or during national tragedies. She was not a believer. But Lynley did not have a full chapel on his property for nothing. Not only were his ancestors and members of his more immediate family buried there, but services were held there as well. And he was part of a line of Asherton earls who'd been setting examples for the underlings for something like three hundred years.

Which was why she wasn't entirely surprised when he said, "My God. It was Lent when he died. He would have been wearing purple."

The DCS said, "It never occurred to me that the colour might have made a difference, but I was curious, so I went home and had a look online. Red is the one most rarely used, Tommy. Pentecost, saints' days, confirmation, ordination. I had a further look and it wasn't a saint's day."

"And prior to Easter, it wasn't Pentecost either," Lynley said. "I should have seen that in the photos, guv."

"No matter," Isabelle said. "We've got him, I daresay."

"It looks that way," was Lynley's reply.

He rang off then and looked at Barbara. His expression was speculative, but Barbara felt speculation was not in order now.

She said, "It's like we always say, sir."

"What's that, Sergeant?"

"No one thinks of everything."

IRONBRIDGE
SHROPSHIRE

Yasmina heard him upstairs. He was banging doors and drawers and cupboards as if he were a burglar searching for valuables. When she found him, he'd gone into the bathroom. This was strange, as it seemed to her that he would have gone there first.

She knew what he was after, naturally. He didn't know just yet that when he hadn't returned home on the previous night, she'd taken action. But he was fast reaching that conclusion if his frantic search through a drawer that held first-aid supplies was anything to go by. This must be his second time through the bathroom, then, she realised. He would have done the medicine cabinet earlier before going on to the other rooms and at last returning here.

"I threw them away," she said from the doorway.

"Well of bloody goddamn *course* you did. What else should I possibly have expected?"

He pushed past her and went to their bed. He sank down, head in his hands, palms on his skull. He grabbed his own hair and jerked it back and forth. He finally looked up and said, "Can you never leave *anything* alone?"

"I'm sorry about Sati," she said. "When I hit her—"

"You mean when you punched her, Yasmina. You do not mean 'hit her' because that isn't what happened. Hitting her would have been bad enough, hitting your child because she doesn't want to do what you would have her do. But punching her? Do you have any idea what can come of that? Or are you relying on her making up a story when the head teacher asks her what happened to her face? He'll do that, you know. It's what he's actually meant to do. Will she say she ran into a door? I expect that one's *never* been used before by a child terrified of being taken into care." He laughed wildly, got off the bed, and walked to the window. His posture suggested he wanted to drive his fist through the glass, but he swung round on her instead and she flinched.

She said, "Timothy, Sati wouldn't—"

"Shut up for once. All Sati has to say is what actually happened to her and *no* one is going to believe any story that you cook up to explain how our daughter ended up with her face beaten in."

She advanced on him but remained out of his reach. "I didn't beat in her face! I didn't intend to hit her at all!"

"It's rote. You're just like your father. What you did to Sati? That would have been his reaction."

This was something . . . but it *wasn't* true. She said, "I'm trying . . . Timothy, all my life I've tried to—"

"Don't begin to say you've tried to do your best or any other rubbish you might want to trot out as an excuse for what's happened. And I'll do you a favour and do the same. Here's what it is, Yasmina: You haven't tried and I can't blame you because neither have I. I could have stopped you or laid down the law or made threats or whatever else a man's meant to do to bring sanity into his home and I didn't because you made it simple for me to step aside. So that's what I did and, believe me, I do not fucking want to have to face that."

"I want my children back," Yasmina said. "I'm meant to protect them."

"From *what*, exactly?"

"Bad things," she said as she sought an answer that would encompass what she felt when she considered their children. "Ruining their lives, making mistakes. That's my job. But you won't see that. And really, why should you? It's easier to blame me for everything when all I've ever wanted is what's best for us all."

"Determined by *who*? No, don't answer. I already know. So does Missa. So does Sati, now." He headed for the bedroom door.

She stepped in front of him. "You can't say that I—"

He pushed her aside. "You haven't been listening because that's your stock-in-trade. I've already *told* you I'm to blame as well. You were just doing what had been done to you. I don't have that excuse."

He left the room, but she followed him. Down the stairs he went with her on his tail. She said, "What was 'done to me,' as you put it, was seeing to it that I was educated well, that I found a course in life. If it constitutes some kind of failure that I want to do the same for my children, then I'm guilty."

He was at the bottom of the stairs and he turned, a fist clenched on the rail. "I swear to God, you don't see anything. Your family rejected you, Yasmina. Not a single one of them has spoken to you in twenty years. And why? Because you made one mistake. You got pregnant. . . . No. That's not fair. I *made* you pregnant, and they were completely unwilling to see that one mistake might not ruin an entire life."

"It made life more difficult. I don't want life to be difficult for my daughters."

"Really?" he asked. "How's that working for you, then?"

She made no reply. How could she, when she saw at last that they were going round and round and would continue to do so?

"You're going to end up with nothing, Yasmina," he told her. "Me, though? I'm not going there with you."

He headed for the door. She said, "Your mum told us—"

"Stop it," he cut in. "Just bloody stop it."

Which was when the front door opened. Rabiah entered. Missa was behind her.

"Thank *God*," Yasmina cried, dashing down the rest of the stairs. But then she saw, and she asked, "Why have you not brought Sati with you?"

"Sati's not meant to hear." Rabiah drew Missa into the entry and closed the door.

Yasmina felt a distinct prickling of dread worse than anything she'd felt since just before receiving Janna's fatal diagnosis. She could see from her face that Missa had been weeping. She could see on Rabiah's face that whatever Sati was not meant to hear was going to be said by Missa.

Suddenly Yasmina did not want to listen. What swept over her was a tsunami of knowledge that told her one clear thing: Whatever had been on her daughter's mind for months had nothing to do with Ironbridge, Justin Goodayle, or marriage.

Rabiah led Missa into the sitting room. She sat next to her on the sofa and told Yasmina and Timothy to sit as well. Yasmina took one of the wingback chairs. Timothy came into the room, but he remained standing.

"I got badly drunk on cider." Missa directed her words down to her lap, where she'd clenched her fists together.

The tsunami of knowledge altered to one of relief. *This* was what Missa hadn't wanted to talk about! She'd known how upset her parents would be that she'd got drunk because she'd also known her uncle's history, her father's history, and her great-grandfather's history. She had been told from the first how dangerous drinking was in their family and she had always been fully on board with the facts of how dangerous drinking could become for her. Yasmina said, "Missa, darling, darling. You've *no* cause for—"

Rabiah snapped, "Let her go on," in a tone so harsh that Yasmina backed deeply into her chair.

Missa looked at her grandmother. Rabiah nodded. Yasmina wanted desperately to tell her that *nothing* could ever alter her parents' love for her, that all she'd done was what children do as they grow up. They experiment just as she had done and that was the *only* thing that had happened.

"I didn't know what cider would do, so when he kept ordering me another and another, I drank it because of how good it tasted. At first I was only a little light-headed, but that didn't seem to matter because it was . . . well, it was fun and I thought about breaking out of who I always am and at least *trying* something new because you know how I've always hated to do that. And then I was terribly drunk, only I don't even remember that part of it, that's how drunk I was. I don't remember much of anything except that . . ."

Even across the room from her in a wingback chair, Yasmina could sense Missa's tension. Rabiah smoothed the girl's hair behind her ear. She murmured something Yasmina couldn't catch.

Missa drew a shallow breath. She lowered her head. "I slept on the sofa. I don't even remember how I got there. I only remember that when I woke up it was completely dark in the room. And he . . ." She raised one of her clenched fists and pressed it beneath her right eye. "He was on top of me. I couldn't move. I couldn't even breathe. And then . . ." Her shoulders shook. Yasmina could tell that not only was she weeping but also that she didn't want her parents to see that she was weeping.

"You must tell them, Missa," Rabiah said. "They need to know so that they can begin to understand."

Timothy took a step forward, as if he intended to go to her. Rabiah stopped him at once with, "Sit down and stay down. *Now,*" and he did so at once. There was a second wingback chair not far from Yasmina and that was where he sat, on the edge, though, as if he would spring into action at the least provocation.

Nonetheless, he spoke gently, saying, "Missa, talk to us. Please."

She raised her head. Yasmina drew in a breath because on her daughter's face she saw at last the profound suffering she'd been hiding for months. Missa said, "I wasn't dressed when I woke up. I mean my skirt, my tights, my . . . I didn't know that at first but then he started shoving his . . . It was . . . I wanted to fight him but I was on my stomach and he put his hand over my mouth and he jerked back my head and then he was . . . he put his . . ."

"Oh God!" Yasmina covered her mouth.

"I could hear him grunting and grunting and it hurt so much it hurt so much . . ."

Timothy surged to his feet. "Who?" he demanded. "Who was it? Who?"

"Mum," Missa said, with tears falling that she didn't even seem to be aware of, "Mummy. It hurt so much and I wanted it to stop and I couldn't *do* anything . . . And Gran, don't make me, don't make me. *Please*."

Rabiah put her arms round the girl. Yasmina tasted the blood from where she'd bitten down on her fingers as Missa was speaking.

Timothy began pacing the floor. He said, "Who was it? You tell me."

"She doesn't know, for God's sake," Rabiah said. "She's never known."

He swung on her. "What about you? She says she was on the bloody *sofa*, Mum. Someone got into your house and did this to my daughter and *do* you understand? Inside your head is the name, so think!" He approached her. He grabbed her face and he squeezed as if it were a piece of fruit that he wanted to crush.

Missa cried, "Don't!"

Rabiah shook him off. "You're *not* understanding."

"Don't tell Justie." Missa made it a plea. "Please, you can't tell Justie. I talked and talked about being a virgin and how I wanted to wait because of what happened to Mum and how she got pregnant and how that made things so difficult for her because she wasn't ready and you weren't ready and . . ." She turned to her mother. "Mummy, I'm still a virgin, aren't I? Because of how he did it, I'm still a virgin, yes?"

Yasmina felt every particle of the horror attached to that moment. "This was why you wanted to come home," she said. "But I was the one who knew better than anyone . . . And all along, my dear God, this was why." She wanted to slap herself repeatedly. She understood the inclination of women to chop off their hair in mourning and pour ashes over themselves from head to foot. Could she have at the moment, she would have done so. "Oh, blessed God, Missa," she cried. "Tell me, please. What can I do?"

Rabiah was the one to answer. "You can listen to the rest of it. Both of you."

LUDLOW
SHROPSHIRE

Lynley's thought was that he should have seen it sooner. He couldn't blame Havers. She wasn't a churchgoer as far as he could recall, and although there had been a funeral service for her father, how would she be expected to know that there was meaning behind the colours worn by the clergy? On her own admission, Isabelle was not a member of any congregation either. But he? He couldn't say he believed in anything divine, but he'd attended church services until he was at university. Once he'd ended his long estrangement from his mother, he'd also attended at her side when he was in Cornwall. So he should not only have seen that the stole on the floor next to Druitt's body was red, he should also have realised what that meant.

He gave Havers time to put herself together while he returned to his own room and thought about their next move. They had an assortment of half-mad evidence that told them it was highly likely and practically assuredly murder, but while what they had might suffice to reassure Clive Druitt that his son had not committed suicide, it did not take them closer to an arrest, a charge, and what Druitt wanted and justice demanded: a prosecution. If he and Havers handed over what they had to the Crown Prosecution Service, the sheer incredulity of any barrister involved would end up shaming both the West Mercia police who'd allowed this to happen upon their patch and the Met who'd trotted up here in an attempt to pour oil upon the waters surrounding a rich man who had every right—as Lynley now knew—to be hauling in either a legal team or a national journalist with a bent for humiliation-producing investigative reporting. He could even hear the first question from the prosecutors that he would be called upon to answer should he present the CPS with what they had: "And a red stole on the floor proves *what*, exactly?" with the additional, "For all you know, Detective Inspector, the victim might well have been colour blind. Come back when you know that and when you also know why anyone might want to kill the man."

He and Havers could, Lynley knew, only look at each detail as it came up. They had little enough time and no manpower, so their next move had to be something that shed light. He was listing potential actions in his head as he went down to the breakfast room to meet Havers. She was waiting for him at reception, her expression telling him that a meal was the last thing on her mind.

She said, "Let's haul him in, sir."

"We're not quite there yet," was his reply, and he could see at once that this did not please.

"Sod it. What else do we need? A bloody dagger with his fingerprints on it?"

"That would be helpful," he said. "But first we need to speak to the vicar."

"And this would be for what bleeding reason?"

"He'll let us into the vestry."

"And we need to get into the vestry another time for . . . ?"

"For the assurance that what we think was done actually could be done. At the moment, we have nothing but supposition."

Arranging to have another look at the vestry was a matter of making a single phone call. The vicar said he would happily meet them at the church at a time of their choosing. They set off after breakfast, up the mild rise of Dinham Street and through Castle Square.

As he'd promised, Christopher Spencer was waiting for them inside the church, happy to help them. When Lynley asked the vicar if he might leave them alone in the vestry, he looked mildly surprised, but after a moment of contemplation he said of course, showed them back to it, and told them he would be waiting in the St. John's Chapel.

Before he left them, Lynley asked the man if his deacon had been colour blind. Spencer reassured them that Ian Druitt was not, as far as he knew. He'd certainly never donned the wrong vestments. And that would indicate he saw colours normally, wouldn't it? he asked.

Did the vicar know that Druitt had ostensibly used a red stole to hang himself? Lynley wanted to know.

Spencer did not. And he wouldn't have noticed a red stole missing, as the next time it was worn would be Pentecost, which hadn't yet arrived. After that, the vicar left them to it.

"We know Druitt was finishing up a service when Ruddock arrived to arrest him," Lynley said quietly when they were alone. "We also know that he removed his vestments and stowed them prior to setting off."

"Does a deacon do evensong in full fig?" Havers asked. "Does a vicar, for that matter?"

"I don't think we need to be concerned with that at the moment," Lynley replied. "We just need to keep in mind that the stole's size indicates it would go on last, as the final bit of *whatever* else he had on." He went to the large cupboards on one side of the room, opening them to reveal black cassocks and white surplices.

Havers, as he reckoned she would do, twigged at once. "If the stole goes on last, it comes off first. When you open the cupboards with the larger pieces, your back is to the set of drawers on this side, where the stoles are kept. But Ruddock would have seen him take off a purple stole, right? So *if* he's our bloke, why wouldn't he pinch the purple stole? Or any purple stole?" She opened the drawers to see how many stoles there were. "There was only one purple one. There's only one of each. So what happened? If Druitt took it off, why not just pinch it when his back was turned?"

"Perhaps Druitt didn't take it off over there with the rest of the stoles. Perhaps he removed it on this side of the room and placed it on the bottom of the cupboard while he hung up his surplice, removed his cassock, hung it where it went, and then turned to cross the room and put the stole where it belonged."

"Giving Ruddock time to ease the drawer open—"

"And perhaps it was even more than one drawer."

"—and pinch the first one that he came across. But why wouldn't he see the difference?"

"If he's not a churchgoer, he wouldn't know there *was* a difference. Besides that, he's not yet sure how he's meant to do away with Druitt. He only knows that he must."

"Then that means . . ." She seemed reluctant to say it, which was out of character in Havers and spoke of her reluctance, at the end of the day, to see how badly a copper can go wrong.

"Yes. Druitt wasn't brought into the station because of paedophilia. He wasn't awaiting transfer to Shrewsbury. Those nineteen days are what tell us that, Barbara. You saw that the moment you caught the date of the original phone call that set the ball in motion."

"Ruddock was obeying orders from the first. If he's our man, he's not the only one." After a moment of thought, she said, "Bloody hell, Inspector."

"Indeed," he replied.

He turned back to her so that they consider their next move. That was when her mobile phone rang.

ST. JULIAN'S WELL
LUDLOW
SHROPSHIRE

When Rabiah rang off, she returned the detective sergeant's card to where she'd shoved it after her first encounter with the Metropolitan Police. She went back to the sitting room, where Missa was huddled into a corner of the sofa, clutching a pillow to her chest like a child with a security blanket. She had made it clear in Ironbridge that she would go through the story another time only if neither of her parents was present. There was nothing that the police could do now, not at this extreme of time, she'd declared. Because of this, Rabiah had given the girl her full support when it came to returning to Ludlow without Yasmina. As for Timothy, he'd taken himself out of the picture at the conclusion of Missa's story.

It had been as dreadful listening to her tell the story a second time as it had been the first in the privacy of the Goodayle home. This time, however, had been made even more difficult by Timothy's reaction. Once he understood that what had happened to Missa had *not* happened at her grandmother's house, his demands of the girl became as furious as they were adamantine.

"Who was it?" he demanded past Missa's tears. His voice was loud and rocklike. "*Who*? Think! You *must* know!"

"Stop it!" from Yasmina, who'd risen to her feet and tried to move him away from their daughter.

Missa cried, "I don't know! It was dark and I couldn't—"

"Then who gave you the cider and why the *hell* did you keep drinking it?"

"Don't make this her fault," Rabiah ordered her son.

"We were celebrating." Missa tried to breathe past her terrible sobbing. "End of term. We . . . finished exams. We were . . . Don't tell Justie. Please don't tell Justie."

"You goddamn tell me—"

Rabiah intervened, for it was clear her granddaughter had had enough. She said, "Ding came to fetch her for an evening out. I told her to live a little for once. I went to bed because I knew she'd be out late. I'd already paid for the driver to fetch her to Quality Square and then to bring her home, so I thought everything was taken care of."

"I was too drunk," Missa wept.

"So she spent the night at Ding's, and that's where this happened."

"I couldn't go home to Gran, Dad. I couldn't *do* that to her."

"So she passed out on Ding's sofa, and someone inside that house sodomised her because she'd blacked out and if everything went as he hoped . . ."

"Oh, *Missa*," Yasmina cried.

"—she wouldn't regain consciousness during the act and the only way she would know exactly what happened was from the blood and the pain the next morning."

"Why didn't you *tell* us?" Yasmina cried.

Timothy said, "One of those boys in that house gave you that cider and you *will* tell me which one it is because he's going to pay for this. Who *was* it?"

"I *never* would have made you return to Ludlow if I'd known." This from Yasmina, who was extending her hands to Missa, but clenched as if waiting for handcuffs to be put on her. "Why did you never *tell* me?"

"It was my fault." Missa's voice grew louder. "Don't you see that? I was drunk because I liked the taste. No one made me drink it. No one drugged me. It's on *me* that I did it, and all I want is to forget it all, which is what I've wanted from the first. So I won't tell you anything else because it's my fault and I got what I deserved for being so stupid and drunk that I couldn't even go home."

"No!" Yasmina approached her as Timothy had done. Missa shrank from her advance. "You're punishing yourself."

"No!" Missa shouted. "No! No!"

"But Missa, my love, you must see now that—"

"Stop it!" she shrieked as she covered her ears. "Gran brought me here to tell you and I told you and I won't talk about it any longer!"

"Christ! *Christ*!" Timothy cried. He ran from the house.

And now, in Ludlow, Rabiah and Missa waited. Sergeant Havers had said to Rabiah, "We'll be there directly, quick as we can."

Twenty minutes after the phone call, they turned up. Rabiah had never thought she'd be grateful to have Scotland Yard on her doorstep another time, but she was now. She ushered them into the sitting room, where Missa remained. Sergeant Havers took a notebook and a mechanical pencil from her bag, depositing herself in a chair next to the fireplace. Inspector Lynley sat on the ottoman that served duty as a coffee table. He said with quite a lovely smile, "Ah, Missa. We meet at last. We've heard about you from Greta Yates and from your friend Ding. We understand you were an exceptional student here during autumn term."

Rabiah could see Missa's grip tighten on the pillow she still held. The inspector, perhaps, saw this as well, because he next said, "Are you well enough to speak to us? This can wait if you're not feeling up to it just now."

This, Rabiah saw, garnered him a look from the detective sergeant. It said, Are you mad? as clearly as if she'd spoken it.

Lynley then said, "I ask because sometimes speaking to the police is unnerving for an individual, especially for a young person. I know your grandmother has a solicitor. Would you be happier if he were present?"

This second bit from the inspector resulted in another look from the sergeant. This one appeared to be asking, Have you gone straight round the bend?

Missa said, "No! Gran, I don't have to—"

"No, no. You don't," Rabiah told her. "It's entirely your decision, my dear. He's my own solicitor, but you don't have to have him present. I'll stay with you, if you like. Or I can leave you alone with the police."

Staying was Missa's preference, so Rabiah joined her on the sofa as she'd done in Ironbridge. Missa told the story as she'd told it before. Sergeant Havers wrote at a pace suggesting she was taking down every word. Lynley merely listened gravely.

When Missa was finished, Lynley was silent for a moment. He seemed to be considering every aspect of what she'd said. Finally, he responded with, "I am so profoundly sorry." After another moment, he went on. "Am I correct that this was what you were talking to Ian Druitt about?"

Missa shook her head. There was fringe on the pillow she held and she began to twist it between her fingers. "He rang me because of my tutor." She went on to explain the chain of phone calls that ended up with Ian Druitt contacting her. "He asked did I want to meet with him, because the college was concerned how I was doing. I didn't want to talk to him but I did because . . ." She looked away. Her brow furrowed as if she were trying to sort out what had gone on in her psyche that she'd agreed to meet with Ian Druitt.

Rabiah offered the answer when she said, "Because that's what you've always done when an adult asks for your cooperation."

Missa gave a small moan. She nodded. "I talked to him about wanting to leave college. I told him about the coursework being too difficult, but he could see there was something more because, obviously, it hadn't been too difficult in autumn term. He probed and pressed. He was very kind."

"So you told him what you've told us just now?" Lynley asked.

"Not all of it. I just couldn't."

"Do you mean the sodomy?"

"I *couldn't* tell him that part. It was . . . too horrible. And anyway, it was too late to do anything. It was months and months too late and, really, all I want now is for Justie not to ever know."

Lynley nodded. "That's understandable. But can you tell me what you mean when you say 'too late'?"

"There wasn't any evidence."

Rabiah saw the sergeant raise her head quickly and look to Lynley, who said, "When something like this happens, there's always evidence. There wouldn't be any on your body by the time you spoke to the deacon, of course, as you would have healed and the DNA would have been long gone. But elsewhere . . . What did you do with your clothing?"

"That's just it," she replied. "I had it."

Sergeant Havers was the one to say, "You have it?" so quickly it was as if she couldn't contain herself.

"I put it in a bag," Missa said. "My underwear. My tights. I shoved them to the back of a drawer because . . . I didn't want ever to forget what happened to me because I'd been so *stupid* one night."

"You weren't stupid and you aren't stupid," Lynley said as his sergeant went on with, "Is all of it here? Is it in this house? Did you take it to Ironbridge?"

Lynley shot her a look that silenced her. To Missa he said, "You merely made a mistake, like millions of other young people your age. You were badly hurt from it—"

"Because I—"

"Not *because* of anything. That's where you're going rather wrong. You're seeing these two events as related. You were drunk ergo you were viciously assaulted. But while these events occurred one after the other, the first did not cause the second."

"I wouldn't've been—"

"That's what you can't know."

In the silence that followed, the sergeant said, "Sir . . . ," with an urgency that the inspector didn't seem to feel. Rabiah was conscious of gratitude sweeping over her at the compassion this man was taking the time to show her granddaughter.

Missa said, "I . . . I suppose."

Lynley said, "I've been a cop for a good many years so I feel confident about saying you must go beyond supposing." He glanced at Rabiah. She nodded and let her lips form the words *Thank you.* He went on. "Can you tell me about the clothing? You shoved the undergarments to the back of a drawer? Then what?"

"That's why I know it was too late. I gave them to Mr. Druitt. He said he would give everything to the police and they would test it and I wouldn't have to talk about it ever again to anyone."

"What happened to the results of the testing? Did he tell you?"

"He said he got told there wasn't any evidence. I mean there wasn't any evidence of anyone . . . you know."

Rabiah saw the sergeant start to speak but stop herself as Lynley lowered his head for a moment and appeared to consider what Missa had told him. Then he said, "What about the rest of the clothing you had on that night, Missa? What did he say about that?"

She shook her head. "There wasn't anything else. The clothes I was wearing? That night? They weren't mine."

Rabiah felt like someone seeing the dawn for the first time as she suddenly understood the rest of the story. "My God," she murmured, "of course they weren't yours."

LUDLOW
SHROPSHIRE

Ding could easily ride her bicycle to pay a call upon Francie Adamucci because Francie lived just beyond the old almshouses in Ludford, not far from the bridge. As it was fairly early, she found Francie still at home as she'd reckoned she'd be. She was about to set off on her own bike, but when Ding coasted onto the semicircle of gravel driveway at the house's entrance, Francie paused, looked wary—which was something of a surprise when one considered how casual she was about everything—and said, "Hey."

"Can we talk?" Ding asked. "You put me straight into it with the cops, Francie."

Francie looked behind herself at the windows of the house, as if she expected eavesdroppers or something. The only thing that was visible, though, was a deep windowsill that held a display of African-looking stuff: carved figures, a couple of tattered baskets, a truly hideous mask. Ding reckoned it was all there to prevent break-ins. With taste like that, who would want whatever else was inside?

"Yeah," Francie said. "I'm sorry, Ding. It more or less slipped out. It was all the rubbish with Ruddock. Gosh, that sounds like a song or something: the rubbish with Ruddock. Or the title of a book."

That was vintage Francie, Ding told herself. She could derail any conversation within ten seconds. Not that she intended to. It was simply how her crazy brain worked.

"So. Whatever. Can we talk?"

Francie shrugged. "It's geography anyway. Like I care? The world's going to be destroyed by some idiot shooting off nuclear missiles at some other idiot anyway. I don't know why I bother. Come on."

It hadn't been Ding's idea to go inside the house, but that was where Francie headed. Ding said, "Are your mum and dad . . . ?"

Francie laughed shortly. "You think they're here? It's the twenty-third of May. There's *got* to be some major ethnocultural-whatever event going on somewhere on the planet." She shoved her key in the lock and opened the door.

Ding left her bike propped up against one of the pillars in front of the house. She'd never been to Francie's, so she hadn't known it was a serious-looking structure probably listed by the government. She said as she followed in Francie's wake and found herself in a soaring entry, "What was this place?"

Francie looked round as if seeing the building for the first time. "Clueless. No central heating, no double glazing, plaster cracking, chimney's useless. All I want in life is to end up in a place built *anytime* after 1900. I'm out of here as soon as I can manage it."

"I didn't know that."

"What?"

"The house. I mean, where I live . . . my mum. You've seen it. Why'd you never say?"

"At least your mum's trying to do something with it. This place'll crumble round everyone's ears before my parents realise they might want to take a look round and see if it's even liveable. You want something?" She led them to a kitchen that at least had been modernised into what appeared to be postwar condition. "I can do us some toast. There's Marmite."

Ding had no appetite. There was a battered table in the centre of the room with stools round it, and she sat on one of these. For her part, Francie hopped onto the work top, found a banana hidden behind a pile of carrots and onions on the windowsill, offered it to Ding, and when Ding shook her head, peeled it for herself.

"The cops said you were seen with Ruddock like I was," Ding said. "Why'd you never tell me, Fran?"

Francie chewed the banana and scratched the side of her head. "It only happened once—I mean when he tried his game with me—so it didn't seem like a big thing. And anyway I dealt with him. It was totally different to how it was with you."

"How?"

"He couldn't threaten me." She waved casually round the kitchen but it seemed she meant the entire house when she said, "D'you really think my mum and dad were going to agitate themselves 'cause Frances is drunk? *That* would've required them to be involved in something beyond their 'ethnocultural-whatever experiences.' So he couldn't tell me that he was going to do something to force me to return home if I didn't play his game since I already live here. Swear it, Ding, I never had the first clue what that bloke thought he'd ever get from me."

"Is that why it only happened once? That he put you in his car?"

"Well . . . it was two times, but the second time I met up with him. See, I told him that first time that if I fancied blowing him—which at that moment I did not, officer—then I'd go ahead and do it. But *as* I didn't, he could just take me home if that's what he wanted to do."

"Did he?"

"'Course. I don't know what he thought was going to happen, but Mum and Dad were like, Don't wake us again, Constable, or whatever you are. And then when he left it was all Francie, for God's sake, give up the drink before you pickle yourself. And that was it. Sometimes, Ding, I got to tell you it truly helps to have parents who do maximum laissez-faire. They're bloody lucky, they are, that I gave up trying to get their attention directly they missed my tenth birthday."

There was no humour in Francie's laugh. Ding said, "That's awful, Francie. I never knew."

"Like I care about them?" Francie hopped down from the work top, tossing her banana skin into the sink and stretching her arms above her head. "Anyway, that first time he tried with me and it didn't work, I said he should give me his mobile's number and *if* I wanted to do it I'd give him a bell. I thought, as if? at first, but one night I was, like, totally blotto, and I decided to see what it was like to do a copper, so I rang him. That might've been when I got seen alone with him."

"Where'd you go? I mean where'd he take you?"

"Car park behind the college. What about you?"

"Police station."

"Shit. *Inside*?"

"Mostly the car park but it depended what he wanted."

"Fucking animal. You need to report him."

"I told the London cops. I more or less had to."

"They'll sort him, Ding." Francie had been prowling the kitchen as if she couldn't rest for even a second. But now she stopped to say, "I'm that sorry about it."

"You didn't know. I mean how bad it was."

"Oh right. I mean Brutus, though. I know I said sorry before but I s'pose I'm *sorrier* and all that."

"Oh." Ding wasn't sure she wanted to talk about Brutus, not after what she'd learned versus what she'd thought. But Francie looked so anxious about things that Ding decided to lay Brutus at rest as well. She said, "You don't need to be sorry. I never told you he was, like, that special to me."

"Yeah, but . . . well, I could tell you were totally special to *him* and I did it anyway."

"Believe me, Francie, I'm not special to him."

"Then you don't know him like you should. You're *absolutely* special to Brutus. He's got a lot to figure out, starting with why he's got this unquenchable woman thing going on. He might not ever figure that part of himself out since blokes like him gen'rally don't, right? *But* you're the special one. You're number one to him."

"Is that supposed to make me feel good: that I'm at the start of whatever bonking queue he's got going on?"

"Oh gosh, I didn't mean you should *stick* with him. What I meant is that how he acts? . . . That's got nothing to do with how he feels about you. Far as what I think you should do goes, I'd connect the toe of my shoe with his arse if I were you. He's a lovely bloke but really, why waste your time?"

"Yeah. Really." Ding found that she was able to smile at Francie, which she certainly hadn't thought she'd be able to do when she made the decision to come over the river to speak with her. But she now understood the other girl far better than she'd considered possible, and that told her something about looking more deeply at her friends than she'd done in the past by Googling them.

After their conversation, they were at peace with each other. They rode together over the Ludford Bridge and they parted at the bottom of Broad Street with the plan to meet for a Chinese meal in two days' time. Ding went in the direction of Temeside as Francie shifted gears to climb the hill.

At the house, though, Ding paused because the front door was open and she was certain she'd shut it upon leaving earlier. She hadn't locked it because they'd lost the keys months ago and there was nothing to steal anyway except their laptops. But even now she had hers in her rucksack and she knew the boys would have theirs as well if they'd left. Still, the door hanging open like that was rather much. It was one thing to be careless. It was another to send out invitations.

Once she was inside, she hesitated because when she shut the door behind her she could hear what sounded like pounding going on above stairs. Then there was a crash, a shout, grunting, and yelling. Then the sound of blows and someone's voice hurling, "You *bloody* touched her," at someone else.

Brutus, she thought. She ran up the stairs. It seemed he'd been caught at last by another girl's boyfriend.

Ding found him in his bedroom doorway. He was sprawled on the floor on his stomach, and his arm was at such a terrible angle to his body that she fell to her knees, crying his name. But when she touched him, he shrieked like an animal badly shot. She cried, "Is it Finn? Did you fight with Finn?"

But she became aware that the noise hadn't ceased and Brutus managed to say, "He's on Finn now," and she ran to Finn's room, crying, "Who? What's happening? Finn!"

The door was partially closed and it was suddenly quiet inside and she was terrified to see. As she was about to push it open, a man stormed out. He looked completely wild, and she thought a meth addict had broken into their house. She shrank back and covered her head to protect herself, but instead of attacking her as well, the man pounded down the stairs.

She saw Finn then. He was in far worse condition than Brutus. His head was bleeding from a terrible gash and his face looked torn up, as if someone had tried to rip off his cheek. She didn't know if he was still alive.

She flew down the stairs in the wake of his attacker, not because she knew what to do, but because she didn't.

LUDLOW
SHROPSHIRE

Lynley was concerned when he learned that Missa had told the story of the attack upon her to her parents only that morning. He became worried when he discovered that, at the conclusion of Missa's informing them of this attack, her father had left the house in an understandably wild state of mind and had not been heard of after that. But when he and Havers ended their drive to Temeside only to find both an ambulance and a patrol car in front of the house in which Dena Donaldson lived, he feared they were too late, the worst had happened, and another tragedy would be piled upon those that had already occurred.

As he pulled to the kerb, Lynley could see that the boy Brutus was being led from the house by a patrol officer. The boy's right arm was bound in a temporary sling against his chest, and Lynley might have thought that an arrest was occurring save for the fact that the officer paused to wait until a paramedic joined them, at which point he went to the driver's seat of the car, climbed inside, and started the police lights spinning. Brutus was then loaded into the car by the paramedic, who spoke to the boy, belted him in, and then trotted back to reenter the house. The car pulled away, the siren hooting twice to clear the roadway. The officer made a turn into Old Street, and as this wasn't the route to the Ludlow police station, Lynley reckoned he was taking the boy to the closest A & E.

The ambulance remained where it was. Havers said, "This is dead bad, sir."

Lynley said, "I fear the *dead* part, Sergeant."

They went inside the house. They were immediately stopped by another patrol officer at the door to the sitting room. He had a spiral notebook in his hand. He barked, "You lot stay right there. This is a crime scene."

Lynley and Havers both produced their warrant cards. The words *New Scotland Yard* produced no ready miracles but saved them from being thrown from the premises. The patrol officer said, "It's been phoned in if you think you're about to assist where you're not wanted."

"We've no interest in interfering in whatever's gone on," Lynley told him. "But we must speak to Dena Donaldson on another matter and it's essential we speak to her now. Is she here?"

"It's Finn. He got Finn!" Ding had been in the sitting room, Lynley saw, where the officer had been in the midst of taking a statement from her. She came towards them, wringing her hands.

"Did you see who it was?" Lynley asked her.

"Didn't I just bloody tell you lot—"

Ding cut into the officer's words by saying to him, "I only want to talk to *them*."

"You'll talk to who you're told to talk to," the patrol officer snapped.

"That sort of approach doesn't seem helpful," Lynley noted.

"To put it kindly," Havers muttered.

"D'you two want to be thrown—"

"Oh *God*! He's not dead, is he?" Ding clapped a hand over her mouth. She was gazing past them.

All of them turned. An ambulance's trolley was being carried down the stairs by two paramedics, its wheels folded, while from it a drip bag dangled above the form belted into position. A third paramedic shouldered a very large medical kit. The fact that there was a drip bag was reassuring as was the fact that there was no body bag but merely the blanketed boy himself. He wore a surgical collar and his head was wrapped with bandages, while half a dozen butterfly plasters held the skin together on facial wounds.

Lynley said quietly to Havers, "Follow the ambulance. I expect it's going to the same location as the patrol car. Talk to the boy if you can. Not Finn but the other. I doubt Finn'll be able to talk for a number of hours." When she nodded, took the keys, and left him, he turned to Ding and said, "He's alive, Ding. Brutus has gone with the other officer in the patrol car, by the way."

"But he didn't do anything! I saw. There was a man!"

"No, no," Lynley said quickly. "I didn't mean he's been arrested. I expect he's being taken to hospital. There wouldn't have been room in the ambulance. They'll need the space to work on Finn."

"Don't make me tell his mum what happened!" Ding said. "Please don't make me!"

"You don't need to worry about that. There are procedures to be followed and having you talk to anyone's parent isn't part of them."

"*If* you're finished," the patrol officer said meaningfully.

Lynley, however, had no intention of doing anything save remaining where he was. He said to the officer, "As before, it's essential I speak to Dena. I'm afraid it can't wait. It's on another matter but I think it likely that what happened here is connected." And to Ding, "Sergeant Havers and I have just come from speaking to Missa. She told us about the assault."

"There's someone who already bloody *knows* about this?" the patrol officer demanded. "Just what the hell is going on?"

"This concerns a sexual assault that occurred in this house last December," Lynley told him. And then to Ding, "It seems her grandmother got the story out of her and saw to it that she told her parents. I have to ask this, Ding. Did you see what happened here today?"

"I wasn't home." The girl first whimpered and then as she continued her voice started to waver. "Brutus . . . He was on the floor and I could hear from Finn's room . . . There was a lot of noise. I went to the door and . . ." Her eyes filled. "I'd gone to talk to Francie, see. I didn't think that anyone . . . It's just that we never bothered with locking up and anyway we lost the keys ages ago. Mostly, we just lock our rooms when we leave, but the house . . . That's why you lot got inside easy that one morning. Finn went mental about that and his dad said he would handle everything and I suppose we thought or at least I thought—" She stopped. It was as if she'd been struck. Then she suddenly began to pull at her cheeks as if she'd scratch out her eyes and she shrieked, "It's my fault! It's *my* fault! Only I didn't know I didn't understand I ran off because I could but she didn't only I didn't know and it isn't my fault that I didn't know only it *is*."

"What the *fuck* is she on about now?" the patrol officer demanded. "I want you out of here so I can get a straight story from her."

Lynley turned to him, surprised by the amount of anger he felt of a sudden. For the first time he took in how young the other man was, how inexperienced, how ineffably and inexcusably ill informed. He said, "Come with me, officer."

"I don't bloody take orders from—"

"I said come with me." His voice was louder than he intended. It was also steely. He was suddenly his father for the first time in his life, the last person he'd ever actually wanted to be. He took the patrol officer out of the house, speaking quietly now but with just as much iron intent. "We have a murder, a rape, and now both an assault, and an attempted murder," he said directly into the young patrolman's face. "All of these crimes involve the same individuals in one way or another. Now if you wish to stand in the way of an ongoing Metropolitan Police investigation because I'm on your patch, I suggest you think carefully before you take that decision. This isn't a turf war, is that clear to you? These are human lives and they're at risk and believe me I am only too happy to take down your details and make certain your career is finished by next week. Am I being clear? Do you have any questions? If so, ask them now because from this moment on, if you wish to remain in this house you'll do so with your mouth shut."

The officer opened his mouth but closed it at once as Lynley said, "Yes? What exactly do you wish to say?"

Apparently nothing, for the man went back into the house, where he retreated into the sitting room. He stood at something vaguely resembling attention at one side of the television, and from that moment on allowed Lynley to speak to Ding.

He had no chance to begin because once he was in the room with the girl, she at once repeated, "I *can't* tell his mum. Please don't make me tell his mum what happened."

"Both Finn's parents and Brutus's parents will be notified by the police or the personnel in casualty. You won't need to be involved." Lynley indicated the worn and stained sofa, and when the girl sat he joined her there as the only other choice was one of several huge beanbags, which he didn't fancy having to crawl out of when their conversation was at an end. He said to her, "Did you see the person who was beating Finn?"

She nodded tearfully. "I could see his back and he had a poker." She pointed to the wrought-iron stand upon which the fireplace implements were hanging. The poker was not among them, so it had probably gone with the bloke when he left the house. "He'd already hit Brutus and he was standing over Finn." Her eyes grew wide with realisation and she said, "But Finn's meant to know karate! He's always going on about how his hands are weapons of death and *why* didn't he use his karate?"

"Perhaps he's not quite as good as he's told you," Lynley said. "Or perhaps he simply didn't have time. He could have been asleep still and then suddenly someone was attacking him. Did you recognise the man? Or was it a boy, someone Finn might have met through his coursework?"

She looked away in that fashion people had when they were attempting to remember exactly what they had seen of a crime. She said, "A man, not a boy. Someone older'n us."

"Could it have been Missa Lomax's father?"

"I never met anyone from her family but her gran because Missa lives . . . she lived with Mrs. Lomax when she was here at college. But I never saw her dad."

"Would you recognise the intruder if you saw a photo of him?"

She didn't know, she said. All she knew was that he must've heard her when she ran to Brutus or maybe he believed he'd finished Finn off. In either case, the next thing she knew was that he was tearing down the stairs and Finn was . . . He was just there and his head was bloody and Ding managed 999 on her mobile once she ran out of the house. She was too afraid to remain inside, she said, because there might've been others and she knew she couldn't defend herself. "Please don't tell," she added in a low voice. "I was meant to do something like first aid or whatever but I was so scared and I thought it was maybe a meth addict who was wanting to rob us only there's nothing to steal."

"It's a good wager that this bloke wasn't an addict," Lynley told her. "If that's the case he wasn't looking for drugs or for something to flog in order purchase drugs. He was looking for exactly what he found: Brutus and Finn. I'm going to ask this officer—" Here Lynley indicated the patrolman who was still in the position he'd taken up, although, Lynley saw, he'd also written notes—"to fetch some photographs from Mrs. Lomax for you to look at. In the meantime, I'm going to ring your mum."

She looked struck by horror. "*Why*?"

He said, "This is a crime scene just now. There'll be officers coming to take evidence. Beyond that, I can't leave you here alone after what's happened." He took out his mobile and asked her for her mother's phone number. Ding tried to protest with, "But my mum'll make me—" and he cut her off with, "I'll explain everything to her. She won't be angry. No one's about to be angry with you, Ding."

"I don't want to go home. *Please* don't make me go home."

"It will be for a short time only, just until the crime scene people gather what they can. I promise your mum will understand that." He tapped her mother's number into his mobile and when he heard the ringing, he said to Ding, "I'll make certain she understands that this—here, today—has nothing to do with you." He waited until he heard a woman's voice before he covered the phone and added, "But that will be a lie, that last bit, won't it, Ding? So what I tell your mum when she arrives here to fetch you home is going to depend upon what you tell me now, at the end of this call." That wasn't fair: bargaining with the girl when she was so upset. But playing fair had gone by the wayside and playing fair would remain there as long as it took for him to get to the root of all that had occurred in Ludlow since the previous December.

He assured Ding's mother—who turned out to be not Mrs. Donaldson but Mrs. Welsby—that while her daughter was perfectly all right, something had occurred at her Ludlow residence that would require her to be fetched home for a day or two. Could Mrs. Welsby manage that as soon as possible? No, Ding couldn't speak with her at the moment as she wasn't present. But she would be waiting for her mother's arrival.

When he rang off to look at Ding, he said, "Now tell me about the end of autumn term: about the celebration and about what happened after the celebration."

ROYAL SHREWSBURY HOSPITAL
NR SHELTON
SHROPSHIRE

That they made it to Royal Shrewsbury Hospital in astounding time was owing to Clover's getting them there in a patrol car. She'd commandeered an officer who was happy to go at the road as if the devil were on his tail, sirens blaring and lights spinning. He'd barely braked at the entrance to casualty before they were out of the car and bounding towards the doors.

"My son," Trevor said to a receptionist behind the check-in counter. When she didn't look up at once, he slapped the counter's surface and said, "Where's my son?"

Then Clover was next to him and from the corner of his eye, he saw she had her police identification in her hand. She was wearing her uniform, so this seemed unnecessary. But it got them action enough when Clover said, "Deputy Chief Constable Freeman. Our son's been assaulted in Ludlow."

Reception jumped to. She picked up a phone and said into it, "George, is that copper still with? The one kid's parents are here." Then to Clover, "Name? I mean yours."

Clover looked as if she wanted to reprimand the receptionist since she'd already given her name and accompanied it with her police rank, but she merely said, "Clover Freeman. Trevor Freeman. Our son is Finnegan."

"Freeman," reception said into the phone. "Right. I'll tell them." And then to Clover, "An officer's coming out to have a word."

"Why can't we see him? What's happened to him?"

Trevor well understood her panic. Clover would know perfectly well that having an officer come out to "have a word" was how the worst possible news was passed along to the parents of a youthful victim.

It was probably only two minutes that they had to wait, but time slowed as it does in the midst of a nightmare. Then the last person he expected to see came from within the depths of the hospital. It was the woman detective sergeant from the Met, Havers. She carried a notebook as if with the intention of interviewing them, which Trevor knew that Clover would not countenance.

She joined them, saying, "He's alive," for which Trevor was so grateful he thought his knees would give out.

"What happened?" Clover asked. "How bad is he?"

"Not sure how bad his injuries are." Her tone sounded as if she was making an attempt to be quite careful with what she told them. "As to what happened, it looks like a break-in. My guv's with the girl who rang it in and there's another officer there as well."

"Gaz Ruddock?" Clover asked.

Havers knitted her brow as if the question were not only unexpected but also revealing. She said, "Not Ruddock. It's the patrol officer who got called from the centre. I've been talking to the other lad—This is the housemate. Know him, do you?—and from what he's said he got attacked by some bloke swinging a fire poker or a tyre iron, he's not sure which. He reckons someone got into the house by means of the front door not being locked."

"Christ. Why won't they lock that bloody door?" Trevor cried.

"Kids. Yeah. Well. It wasn't a break-in in the usual sense. The boy—" She glanced at her notebook—"Bruce Castle he's called. He came out of his room to use the loo and this bloke started swinging the poker thing at him. He lifted his arm to protect himself like you do, and that was that. His arm was smashed. He yelled for your son to ring 999 but before that could happen, the intruder had got into your boy's bedroom and was on him." She lifted her head, and for a moment Trevor thought she was finished. But instead she seemed to study them intently before she added, "Bruce says this bloke was shouting about someone getting his daughter drunk, stripping her, then raping . . ."

Trevor heard nothing after *raping*. He looked at Clover. For a moment his ears were filled with roaring as a number of what had appeared to be disparate pieces slid into place. *This* was what Clover had been intent upon hiding. This was what she must have learned at some point on the twenty-sixth of February. This would demand any number of phone calls between Gaz and her. This is what she had been dealing with ever since.

Trevor came round as Clover was saying, ". . . talked about a daughter? So the intruder was an older man? Was Bruce able to give you a description?"

"Fairly good one. I reckon he'll recognise the bloke when we bring him in."

"You know who it was." Clover spoke sharply.

Havers waited a moment before replying, as if assessing Clover's tone. "Since the bloke was shouting about his daughter being raped, I reckon once we know who the daughter is, we'll know the attacker."

Trevor got himself together enough to say, "Are you saying my son—*our* son—"

"Have you taken a statement from Finnegan yet?"

"Emergency staff are still working on him."

"And the girl who made the call?"

"Like I said, my guv's with her. She's the girl who lives there as well."

"Did she—"

"Thank you, Sergeant," Clover cut him off, and Trevor felt the anger like a band round his forehead that tightened and tightened, not only at this public slighting of him but also at his allowing this sort of thing to happen again and again, resulting in where they were at the moment. Clover added, "May I ask how you happened to be on the scene?"

Again that unnerving pause, in which the sergeant tapped her pencil against her notebook. Trevor became aware of the life of A & E going on round them: another trolley being rushed through the corridor, a white-coated Indian woman calling out from a doorway for a series of drugs and procedures.

Havers finally said, "My guv and I had gone to interview the girl. Dena. Called Ding? D'you know her?"

"About the rape?" Trevor asked.

"We've met her," Clover said, "but we don't know her well. She wasn't also attacked, was she?"

"She wasn't at home when it started. It was all going on when she got there."

"Thank you, Sergeant." And then with a turn to Trevor, she said, "Darling, let's have a word with the staff."

She took his arm, and they walked back towards the reception counter with Trevor saying tersely, "Darling, let's have a *word*? That's the bloody conversational conclusion that seems reasonable to you?"

She drew him to one side, quite near to the wall. She spoke in a voice that sounded low with fury. "I have no intention of getting into anything here, and neither should you have. We need to know what happened and—"

"We just got bloody *told* what happened: Someone got into Finnegan's house, and that someone believes his daughter was raped. Or did you miss that part?" When she looked away from him, he wanted to force her somehow to meet his gaze. Instead he said, "*This* is what you've been protecting him from, isn't it? For months now, you and Gaz. You think Finnegan set out to get a girl drunk and when he had her completely defenseless, he raped her. You actually believe our son—"

She whirled to him. "Stop it," she hissed. "Stop it, just stop. Do you have *any* idea how often it happens? There you are in your precious fitness centre with absolutely no clue what goes on in the rest of the world. Well, let me tell you: This is going on everywhere. Brainless girls drinking too much and brainless boys taking advantage of that. Sometimes it's only drink involved and sometimes it's more. Sometimes it's something slipped into the drink to speed things along. Do you *not* understand that?"

"What I understand is that you appear to see Finn as someone who could do this in the first place."

"I see it because it happens!" She spoke fiercely, and her expression told Trevor she'd be happy enough to beat her point into his head with her fists. "Perfectly nice boys talk to other perfectly nice boys and they cook up a plan or they see this sort of thing reported on the Internet and they think, Shall we give it a try? So they take a decision and they don't think there might actually be consequences because boys that age *never* think there might be consequences to anything they do. And when they do something like this, something that's completely beyond the pale like this, and it's reported, then their lives are shattered. I'm talking about *his* life, Trevor, Finnegan's life. *Do* you understand now? We—you and I, his parents—can't lift a finger to protect him if he's charged with this. We can find him a solicitor and we can make absolutely bloody sure—if he will even let us, which is seriously open to doubt as it has always been—that he will not say a word to *anyone* else when he's alone with them. But that's it. And if there's evidence involved in what he's been accused of—because, believe me, there is no girl alive who wants to be sodomised, so there *will* be evidence—then a solicitor means nothing because there is also no solicitor alive who can fight DNA no matter how good he is."

Trevor had heard it all without hearing because everything halted when she said the word *sodomised*. She apparently read his reaction on his face because she said, "Yes. *That's* what happened. Are you happy to know it?"

"How the hell . . ." Trevor licked his lips. They were dry as stones. "How the hell do you know all this. Christ, Clover, did Finn tell you?"

She looked beyond him, to the wall, before she replied. Then it was to say, "Ian Druitt turned evidence over to Gaz."

"*Druitt*?"

"Druitt. Now do you see what we're dealing with?"

LUDLOW

SHROPSHIRE

Once the patrol officer had left to fetch the photographs for Inspector Lynley from Mrs. Lomax, the detective took Ding upstairs to gather what she would need for a few days at home. She knew that her mother would be hurtling down from Much Wenlock in order to cart her back to Cardew Hall, and she understood that she was going to have to cooperate as fully as she could with the detective in order to escape having to live there permanently. So she would look at the photos fetched from Missa's gran and if Missa's dad was in any of them, Ding was going to have to point to him if indeed he was the person who'd broken Brutus's arm and mangled Finn's head. As for Cardew Hall itself, it wasn't as if a sudden understanding of her nightmare reaction to the place had altered anything. She still had come upon her father's naked body strung up to a bedpost. She still had buried everything inside her head and for years acted *as* she'd acted because of that. Having to stay there with her mum and stepdad while things were being sorted here in Ludlow was going to be bad enough. Having to live there till she got to university was something she knew she couldn't cope with.

Lynley instructed her to be careful and not touch anything as they went up the stairs. Everything, including every surface, he said, held potential evidence. Inside, he asked her to look round first to see if anything had been disturbed. When she told him that it looked the way it always looked, he handed her a pair of latex gloves and said that she could take three changes of clothes. She had a duffel and as quickly as she could, she stuffed into it what she thought she might need. He waited quietly, and she could feel him watching her every move. When she glanced his way, his expression told her that although he could be compassionate, he wasn't about to sign on as her friend.

They went outside when she had her belongings gathered. They paused in what went for the front garden, which was just the concrete square upon which she and Brutus stood their bicycles. She was glad enough to be out of the house, but less glad when she saw that a small crowd had gathered across the street.

A gent that Ding recognised as their next-door neighbour was among them, she saw, and he crossed over quickly as she and Lynley emerged. There was no crime scene tape yet—no one apparently had had the time or perhaps they didn't carry it about in their cars—so he started to come onto the property. His name rose to her brain unbidden: Mr. Keegan, he was called.

Lynley stopped him with, "This is a crime scene, sir. You'll need to stand back across the street."

Mr. Keegan said that he had information. He was fertilizing his roses just over there—he indicated the next tiny plot of garden—and he saw the bloke in question making a run for it, heading in the direction of Old Street. He was carrying a stick or something, he was. Mr. Keegan couldn't quite see as the bloke was at a distance by then and he himself wasn't wearing his distance specs, but whatever it was the man was carrying, he well could have thrown it over the wall and into the river. It might be in the water as they spoke, and it also might be on the bank. He added, "Watch the telly, I do, so you lot might want to do a search. Not the girl, 'course. You and th'other coppers."

That was extremely helpful, Lynley said politely. An officer would inspect the entire area as soon as SOCO arrived.

Mr. Keegan looked dead pleased at that, a citizen doing his duty, not to mention making a contribution to whatever the coppers intended to do to resolve what had occurred in the house.

Ding said, when Mr. Keegan crossed back to the other pavement, presumably to watch whatever proceedings he reckoned were going to happen next, "Do you know if Finn . . . ? Will he be okay?"

Lynley appeared to be waiting for Mr. Keegan to be among the other onlookers once again before he turned to Ding and said, "My sergeant will ring me once there's news. Tell me about the end of term in December. Do your best not to leave anything out."

"But you said that Missa . . . ?"

"We need to hear every version, Ding. Sergeant Havers will be talking to Bruce—to Brutus—at the hospital. She'll talk to Finn as well, if he's able."

"So you'll know if someone's lying."

"So we have every possible bit of information."

She gave him the details as she recalled them: the large gathering of college students at the Hart and Hind on a snowy night. Freezing cold, it was, but Jack Korhonen—"he's the publican"—always put out heaters for the smokers and for the overflow as well since he wouldn't want to lose the business. They'd arrived early enough to get a table inside—"least, Brutus got there early enough"—and Finn arrived round forty-five minutes later.

"How did you get there?"

Missa's gran had arranged for a car because of the weather and all that and so they wouldn't have to worry about getting back home at the end of the evening if they were . . . well . . . sort of lit up. Mrs. Lomax wanted Missa to have a nice time because she mostly studied and—being honest?—she's so dead prim and proper, and it was time for her to have a bit of fun. That's what Ding thought and it seemed to her that Mrs. Lomax thought the same.

"I don't think she'd ever been inside a pub," Ding said. "Missa, I mean. Her dad's something like a drunk, I think. She doesn't say much about it but I got that idea and one time she said her uncle's the same. She was way seriously concerned about how drinking might get to her as well, so she never did. Drink, I mean. Never."

"What was different about that night?"

"We wanted—this is me and Brutus—we wanted her to loosen up a bit. We did it for a lark. We didn't *mean* anything by it. And it wasn't like her gran didn't *want* her to live it up or whatever. She even said. Like 'live a little' or something. See, all Missa ever did was study, and of course her marks were super amazing because of it. And there was her boyfriend 's well, I s'pose."

"A college boyfriend?"

"Oh no, not from the college. This is her at-home boyfriend. They were meant to be taking a break from each other while she was here at college, but it didn't work that way since he rang her, like, every day and he texted her . . . I don't know . . . p'rhaps six times a day?"

"How did she feel about that? Did she tell you?"

"Not really. I know her gran wasn't, like, totally on board with the idea of the bloke. Missa told me that, something like 'at least I'm not at Gran's' one time when he rang her. It seems like everyone in her family wants her to . . . I don't know . . . meet someone else? And she wasn't going to do that, was she, if she didn't break away from him for a while, you know?" Ding was still holding her small duffel. She set it at her feet. Then she picked it up again because she found she needed to do something with her hands and this was as good as anything. She said, "Anyway, that was part of what we wanted to do, me and Brutus. We wanted her to see there was fun to be had if she just let herself have it. So we told each other we'd have a go with cider and see if she liked it. And she did and she was on her way to having a fun evening but then Brutus kept on."

"'Kept on'?"

"Sorry. He kept on giving her cider. She would drink one and there would be another in front of her. When Finn got there, he joined in—except he was drinking Guinness, not cider—and we all got pissed out of our minds. Which is how we were when Gaz Ruddock showed up." She twisted the canvas handles of the duffel as she recalled the evening and how it unfolded and knew how much she was responsible for and how little she *wanted* to be responsible for. "I think he was there to check on Finn or something like that because when Finn saw him, he got all . . . *super* annoyed. But then Gaz saw me and how I was and he grabbed onto me and said, Right, then, I'm taking you home to your mum 'cause it's time she learned what you're up to in Ludlow."

"Did he intend to take you home, or was this more of the usual, as you explained yesterday?"

"I *reckoned* it was worse this time 'cause he talked about my mum. For things to work for him, though, he had to take everyone home since it would look dead odd if we all were pissed and he chose only me to cart off. So he grabbed the lot of us. Only there wasn't room enough in the back seat so he put me in the front, which is how I made a run for it once we got to Temeside. The rest of them he shoved into the house—"

"Missa as well?"

"I expect she didn't want to go home to her Gran in that condition only I didn't know that, see, because I was running fast as I could away from him. I just didn't want to have to . . . you know . . . with him."

"Where did you go?"

"It was slippery and everything because of the snow and I knew he could catch me up fast if he came after me, so I ducked into where the rug shop is? Just along the street?" She pointed in the general direction. "There's wheelie bins there and I hid behind them. But it was freezing and it started snowing again so I was there maybe a quarter of an hour? Twenty minutes? Something like that. When I couldn't stand it any longer, I went to the pavement and peeked round and there was no patrol car in front of the house, so I went home."

"And Missa was there, on the sofa, in the sitting room."

"I didn't *know*," Ding said. "I didn't even look in there. I reckoned that she'd rung the bloke who took us up to Quality Square. She had his card and all that. So I thought she'd gone home. All I did when I got to the house was run upstairs."

"You found her the next morning, I presume?" Lynley said.

"Not even," Ding told him. "See, she wasn't there. She'd . . . she must've rung the bloke to fetch her at some point, like I said, because she wasn't there in the morning either."

Lynley looked away from her. He'd had his eyes fixed on her so steadily that Ding felt as if he'd been reading her brain so that, no matter what, he'd know the truth. As she was waiting for what would come next, a white van stopped in front of the house and out of it hopped three blokes who went to the back of it, opened its cargo hold, and began pulling white boiler suits over their clothes. She'd seen enough detective programmes on telly to know this was the crime scene team. The inspector told her to wait, went over to have a word, and then returned. Shortly thereafter, the first two of them went into the house carrying impressive toolkits while the third unspooled the yellow crime scene tape that they were always unspooling on telly.

Once all of the crime scene team were inside the house, Lynley spoke to her again. He said, "When did Missa tell you what had happened to her?"

"A few days later. I could see that something was wrong, and when she told me, see, I thought it was Brutus. He'd kept on with the cider, see. He knew it would get her completely wrecked. And he has . . . Brutus has this thing for girls. He can't leave 'em alone."

"Beyond that, is there anything else that told you it was Brutus?"

She had to look away. It was his eyes, she reckoned. He was a handsome man anyway, but his eyes made one want to . . . She didn't know, only that they were deeply brown and they wanted her to tell the truth. When she looked back at him, the eyes were still waiting. She said, "When I got up to my room, he was there."

"Brutus?"

"We slept together most nights, and there he was like always. He woke up when I came in and he wanted sex, like usual. But I didn't. He was annoyed for a bit but we fell asleep. Then I woke up later and . . . You see, he wasn't there. After Missa told me what she told me? I thought it was Brutus who did it to her only it turned out he was in the bathroom and he'd passed out and slept there in front of the loo. He said sometime during the night he woke up because Finn was peeing over him and not being especially careful where it all went. And he was laughing the way Finn laughs like sort of a *gotcha* laugh. Only, you see, I never knew any of that. I only knew that Brutus wasn't there when I woke up."

"You didn't look for him?"

"I didn't think to. Why would I? Only when Missa told me what had happened, I worked it out. Or at least I thought I worked it out. But I couldn't ever be sure, could I? And Missa didn't know."

"Missa explained to us that she told Mr. Druitt. He could see something was very wrong and he got the story from her. She seems to have wanted no one to know, as she considers it her fault. So how did you get the story from her?"

"Oh, I could tell . . . like Mr. Druitt, I expect. Plus, she felt dead bad about my top because she knew it was expensive and I don't have a lot of money for clothes."

"Your top?" He looked perplexed.

She explained how she had lent Missa clothing for the evening, how she'd even brought her a fancy bra as a Christmas gift. Missa had worn her own knickers and tights and the like, but the skirt and top were Ding's. "Missa didn't even *own* anything that said party, if you know what I mean, so I gave her something to wear. She knows I've been buying my own clothes since I was something like eleven years old. I like to keep them nice. When she gave them back, she apologised because the top got ripped and then she started crying."

"So she told you then."

"She was so out of . . . I don't know. She was *way* beyond how she should've been about a ripped top, which I reckoned I might be able to have repaired anyway. She told me because that's what I said, that I could maybe get it repaired and it was okay, but she wouldn't stop crying and I kept asking and the story came out. She asked me please *please* not to tell anyone because she was so . . . I guess humiliated, which is how I pretty much would've felt as well. I promised not to tell and I put the clothes in my cupboard but I couldn't stop wondering if Brutus . . . you know. Then she talked to the deacon and he wanted her to hand everything over for testing—what she was wearing—and I . . . I'm sorry but then I lied. Because . . . see, I couldn't face it might've been Brutus. I just couldn't. So I lied to her and I know it was wrong to do that but I did. I told her I chucked the top into the rubbish and I'd worn the skirt so much after what had happened that it finally needed to be dry cleaned."

"But that's not what actually happened?"

"I kept it. I kept both of them—the skirt *and* the top. And then one day I lost my temper bad and I threw them at Brutus."

"What did he do with them? Do you know? Did he take them from your room, for example?"

"Oh, I threw them at him in *his* room, not mine." She hated to tell the rest of it because of how dumb it all had been for so very long between Brutus and her. But she continued. "See, Brutus brought a girl home to spend the night, and he'd never ever done that before.

I'd been protecting him for ages because, like I said, I was scared it was him who'd hurt Missa. Then all of a sudden there he is, fucking . . . sorry . . . doing it with this random girl and he'd let her spend the night, like right in my face? I was over the edge at that. So I got the clothes and I banged on his door and I threw them at him and screamed about how I'd been protecting him when all along I could've just turned the top in to the cops. The skirt as well. He might've tossed them out after that, but I don't know."

Lynley nodded. He looked back at the house. He looked at some ancient pocket watch. Then he said to her, "Take me to his room, Ding."

Which was what she did.

ROYAL SHREWSBURY HOSPITAL
NR SHELTON
SHROPSHIRE

After Finn was moved from casualty to a hospital room, Trevor told his wife he would spend the night at their son's bedside. It was, at that point, after ten P.M. He said to Clover that one of them needed to rest and to be clear-headed should any crucial decisions about Finn's treatment need to be made in the morning. He would ring her at once should anything change in his condition. He would also ring her if Finn regained consciousness. That latter was unlikely, they'd been told, so far as the night went. As to Finn's recovery, there might be some memory loss, but that would be assessed once he was fully conscious, and it was likely to be only temporary.

Clover didn't want to leave at first, but Trevor managed to convince her of the good sense of doing so. She wanted a police officer posted at the door to Finn's room in the event his attacker showed up, and while Trevor didn't think that was necessary, he accepted it. Since the female detective from the Met had been the person to explain the incident to them, there was a chance she was still hanging about and Trevor definitely didn't want her gaining access to Finn.

Clover was in a state of anxiety when she finally departed. Trevor assured himself this was understandable. He couldn't consider anything else about Clover's concerns just then because he wanted nothing to play on his features other than his disquiet about her level of exhaustion and the need for her to have her wits about her should a crucial decision need to be made. The reality, however, was that he wanted to be completely alone with his son should Finn regained consciousness. He was attempting to come to terms with what Clover apparently believed: that Finn was capable of sodomising a girl.

Before they'd been allowed to see Finn, Trevor had insisted that Clover give him every detail of the supposed crime. So he knew that the housemates had been drinking heavily in a pub on the night in question, which had been in December after exams, that they'd been carted home by Gaz Ruddock, that one of them—Ding Donaldson—had done a runner, and that later that night someone had attacked another girl who was passed out on the sitting-room sofa. At the end of her recitation, Clover had said, "Do you understand my concerns now?"

He had said that he did. When he went on to tell her that this wasn't something Finn would have done, however, she raised her hands in defeat and spoke about the matter no further.

Trevor remained silent and watchful in the room with Finn. The hours crept by with no change. A member of staff came into the room now and then to check the boy's vital signs, and when a police officer arrived to take a position outside the door, she popped her head into the room to let Trevor know all was well, whatever that was supposed to mean. He was thus mostly left with his thoughts, and he directed them towards trying to dredge up anything at all that indicated to him there was a part of Finn that he did not know.

Finn regained consciousness just after four in the morning. Trevor was dozing in a chair next to the bed in the darkened room, but he was instantly awake when he heard the boy's voice murmur, "Mum?" Trevor rose, switched on a dim light, and reached for the plastic container of water that had been placed on the side table.

"I'm here, Finn," he said. "Mum's getting some rest at home. Thirsty?"

"Yeah." Finn went for the straw and drank the container dry.

"Thanks," he said. And after a moment, in an exhausted and somewhat blurred voice that reminded Trevor so much of his son as a child awakened from sleep, "Dad, who was that bloke?"

"The man who attacked you? We don't yet know."

"I heard . . . a ruckus is what . . . what it was." Finn's lips were so dry that they looked painful. Trevor made a mental note to purchase some balm for him. There had to be a shop on the premises. "Firs' I thought it was some random girl's father? Like . . . beating on Brutus because . . ." He paused. "Any more water?"

"I'll fetch it. Finish what you were going to say."

"Jus' that I reckoned . . . it was . . . like Brutus fucked the wrong girl for once? An' here was her dad to do business on him? On Brutus?"

"Would that be like Brutus?"

"Fucking . . . like . . . the wrong girl? Oh. Sorry. About *fucking*, Dad. I mean, he does it to any girl willing."

"What if the girl isn't willing?"

Finn frowned. One of his eyes was closed and his head was wrapped in white bandaging. Aside from the injuries to his skull, he had a fractured clavicle, about which nothing could be done since it would heal on its own, a fractured shoulder, and a broken wrist. He said with a wince as he moved his head, "Far's I know, there's not . . . like . . . a girl been unwilling. Don't know what it is about him, do I. He's got, like, a magic dick or something. Could I have water?"

Trevor hastened to get it from the basin. He let the water grow cool from the tap, and he wondered about it all: truth, lies, actions, reactions. And then he wondered about his wondering. He returned to the bed and helped his son drink.

He said to him, "Finn, something happened back in December, at your house."

Finn rested his head back on the pillow and shut his eyes. "Wha'?" He sounded drowsy.

"A girl was very badly assaulted. She was on the sofa in your sitting room, and she was drunk."

"Ding, y' mean?"

"Another girl. She'd gone out with Ding, and apparently she didn't want to go home drunk. Does this ring a bell?"

Finn seemed to be searching for the correct memory. He said, "S'pose it doesn't make sense it was Ding. Far's I know . . . she always made it up the stairs. If she was too . . . pissed and all that? Brutus would help her." He was quiet for a moment before he added, "They were like, you know, sleeping together? When Brutus wasn't doing some girl on the side? He can't resist women like they can't resist him."

"Do you remember this incident? When a girl slept on the sofa?"

Finn's eyes remained closed and Trevor wanted him to open them. While the room remained dim from the single light he'd switched on, it still seemed that if he could see Finn's eyes, he'd know the truth even though he told himself he did know the truth already. Finn would *never* . . . because he couldn't . . . because he wasn't the person his mother was declaring him to be.

Finn murmured, "Incident?"

"In December, Finn. It was all of you: getting drunk, being carted home, Ding running off, another girl being with you? She would have gone into the house with you. Ding wasn't there but this girl was."

"S'pose." Finn's voice was low. He was drifting off.

Trevor touched his undamaged shoulder and said, "Finn, in December, this was. Do you remember?"

The boy nodded. "December," he said. But that was all.

# 24 MAY

IRONBRIDGE
SHROPSHIRE

When Yasmina awakened, it was five A.M., two hours before her alarm would ring. She found herself in the same circumstances in which she'd gone to bed on the previous night: alone in the house. While she'd learned from Rabiah round half past eight that Missa would remain in Ludlow for the night, and she'd not actually expected Sati to return home if Missa didn't come to fetch her, Yasmina had thought Timothy would arrive back at some point, even if his return happened in the wee hours of the morning. But he had not done so.

Despite the hour, she rang Rabiah. It seemed possible that Timothy might have ended up there. But he had not turned up, and Rabiah's tone—when she learned from Yasmina that Timothy was missing—spoke of all the scenarios she was entertaining: drink driving, fatal accident, overdose of opiates, God knew what else.

"Missa . . . How is Missa?" Yasmina asked her. "Were the police difficult? Did they treat her badly?"

"They were quite gentle with her. It wasn't at all as traumatic as it was when she told you and Tim."

"Will you tell her I've rung? That I am so terribly sorry for . . . I don't know what, Mum. What I've put her through . . ."

"This is no one's fault but whoever it was who hurt her, Yasmina. But we all must prepare . . ."

In Rabiah's hesitation, then, Yasmina could tell that something else had occurred during the previous day. She could also hear her mother-in-law's reluctance to share the information with her. So she pressed her with, "Mum, you must tell me whatever else has happened. I can tell something more is going on. I'm that worried about Timothy. If it's to do with him, please tell me."

A patrol officer had come by asking for a photo of the family, Rabiah admitted. Specifically, a picture that had a clear shot of Tim was wanted. When Rabiah had asked why it was needed, the patrol officer said he didn't know, just that it was wanted.

"I had to give him one," Rabiah told her. "I did ask him where he was taking it. At that point he became quite cagey. Yasmina, my dear . . ." She was silent then, and in that silence it seemed that Rabiah knew very well why a photo of Timothy was needed.

"He's done something," Yasmina said.

After that phone call, she dressed for her workday because she could not think of what else to do. Her choices at the moment were severely limited. Should she go to Sati, Yasmina knew the girl would ask about Missa, but Yasmina had neither the strength nor the imagination to tell her youngest daughter anything at this point. Until she herself knew more, Sati was going to have to find the inner resources to get through the day alone.

It wasn't long after reaching this conclusion that Justin arrived to tell Yasmina what she already knew: Missa had never gone to work yesterday and, what was worse, she had not returned last night.

"She came upstairs to dress," he told Yasmina. "She said that Rabiah wanted her to speak to you and she didn't see any way other than doing it. And then she never came back."

"She went to Ludlow," Yasmina told him.

"Why? She'd been *crying*. When she came upstairs, her face was blotchy and . . . I could tell she was crying and she wouldn't tell me why, and what I want to know is what you lot did to her because she said she was meant to talk to you and let me tell you I know you don't want us marrying no matter what you say. I was that stupid ever to think . . . I want to know where she is."

"She's with Rabiah."

"You lot are trying to separate us. Missa told me you'd do anything to stop her, like maybe even making her go to India."

"That isn't true."

"And I rang her. Over and over starting when she didn't come to work. She's not answering, so what've you lot done with her mobile?"

Yasmina could sense the danger here: a strong young man filled with anger that she *knew* was righteous. She said to him, "I'm going to give you Rabiah's number. Ring it and she'll—"

"I'm not having that. You tell me what's happened!"

"Missa will have to tell you. I can't, not after everything else I've done. Things for which I am responsible and sorry. *Truly* sorry, Justin."

When he took in these last statements, Justin altered. He said quietly, "I love her that much. Is she coming back?"

"I think she is."

"You don't know for sure?"

"I don't know a single thing for sure. I don't blame you if you're unwilling to take me at my word, but it's all I have to give you."

It appeared to be enough for the moment—that pathetic "word" she was offering him—and he went on his way to Blists Hill to work. He told her he *would* ring Rabiah. Over and over if that's what it took.

Forty minutes later, she heard a car stop in front of the house. She hurried to the window in time to see Timothy get out of it. He paused to lean his head against its roof.

She went to the door. They opened it simultaneously: he from the outside on the top step, she from the inside in the silence of the entry. Because she was looking for it without wanting to look for it, she saw the blood. It speckled the left shoulder of his shirt, the right sleeve of it as well.

"A policeman was sent to Rabiah," she told him. "He asked her for a picture of you."

He looked utterly ragged. "I took care of things." He headed towards the stairs.

She planted herself in front of him and said, "What have you done?"

"I just told you."

"You must *tell* me. Did you hurt someone?"

The look he gave her was so contemptuous that she took a backwards step from it. "No more than Missa's been hurt," was his answer. He pushed past her and went up the stairs.

She shut the front door. Above her, she could hear him walk into the bathroom. She heard the water running into the basin, too briefly for him to do anything but fill the glass he kept next to the cold-water tap. She dashed up the stairs. She knew exactly what he was planning to do, but she swore to herself that he would *not* do it now. They were meant to talk to each other.

She was too late. He'd managed to get more pills and he was shaking two of them into his palm. She knocked them from his hand, crying, "Talk to me!"

He didn't react other than to shake two more into his hand. His fist clenched over them in such a way that she knew she wouldn't be able to wrest them from him.

"We've talked enough," he said to her. He slapped his palm against his mouth, downed the two pills, and left her.

She followed him to their bedroom, crying, "Why are you doing this? One daughter dead, another sodomised, a third afraid to come home, and *this* is what you do? I come to you. I beg you. I need you. All of us need you and this is your response?"

Timothy said nothing. He let the silence go on as if with the wish that she would be able to hear what she herself had said. Which she could not, of course, because what she'd said was no longer there. Which was, of course, the problem with speaking at all.

"You think that everything"—he gestured in the direction of the bathroom, by which she knew he meant his pills—"started with Janna. You see everything rolling along nicely in our family until her illness. We didn't cope with that well, did we, and then she died, and in your eyes we coped even worse."

"You did everything you could not to feel. You still do *anything* not to feel."

"No," he said. "I did not do everything and anything. But it seems that way, because in your eyes there is only one way to grieve and that's your way. What's gone wrong with us—you, me, the girls—is contained in your belief that you have some mystical power over everything that you consider an 'aspect' of your life. And the biggest 'aspect' of your life is every person in it and every circumstance that occurs."

"What a terrible thing to say to me when my entire life has been devoted—"

"Your life has been devoted to manipulating everyone in it. You haven't seen any of us as people. You've seen only how you could play us like chess pieces. But you can't look at that because if you saw it, you'd have to do what you want me to do and what you think I don't do: grieve and feel and . . . I don't know . . . howl at the moon at night in sheer rage because of what's happened and how it's all gone wrong."

"Blame me, then. Make me at fault. Because if I am, it's so much easier for you to walk away from us all and live with yourself afterwards."

He frowned. He rubbed his forehead. He tapped his fingers hard against it. "Yas," he said, "this isn't about fault. This is just what is." He went to the bed then. He lay upon it, turning his back to her. Within a minute, he was asleep.

And she was left with what she was left with: words forming accusations, accusations demanding guilt, guilt demanding reparation.

LUDLOW
SHROPSHIRE

When Lynley rang him that morning, Ruddock at once asked about the boys. "One of the Shrewsbury officers stopped at the station to use a computer yesterday," he explained. "He told me what happened. I tried to get on to the Freemans half the night, but they're not answering calls. Are the boys all right? Is Finn all right?"

"My sergeant was at the hospital with the family most of the afternoon," Lynley said. "This is Finn's family. We'd like to speak to you."

"Jesus. You're not thinking *I* attacked those two?"

"The attacker's been described, and he had reason. Or at least we presume that's what he believed."

"What kind of reason—"

"That's what we'd like to talk to you about. Shall we come to you? We're happy to do that."

No, no. Ruddock said he would meet them at the station as they'd done before. Could they give him thirty minutes . . . ?

They could give him fifteen, Lynley told him. If that wasn't possible, they were going to have to come to him. They would need his address.

He'd be there in fifteen minutes, Ruddock said. Lynley admitted to himself that over the phone Ruddock sounded normal: open about his attempts to ring the Freemans, speaking easily about the boys, ready to be helpful.

Once the crime scene team had allowed it on the previous day, Lynley and Dena Donaldson had done a search of Bruce Castle's room to find the clothing that she had thrown at him. Luckily, Bruce had merely kicked both the skirt and the top under the bed. Unluckily, they had lain there among various puffs of slut's wool ever since. Unluckier still, months had passed since Missa Lomax had worn the clothes, and during that time they'd not only been hung in Ding's clothes cupboard without protection, but they'd also been handled by Ding herself, along with Brutus—or at least his feet. But Lynley had a feeling they might come in useful, so when he and Ding had located them, he placed them in an evidence bag supplied by SOCO.

During this time, a photograph of the Lomax family had been fetched from Rabiah Lomax and shown to Ding. She was openly reluctant to identify Missa's father as the man who had beaten both Finn and Brutus. She said, "It's only that I saw him for maybe . . . I don't know . . . five seconds?" but when they explained that there would no doubt be fingerprints on the fire poker as well as on the front door, she was able to see that her word alone wasn't what was going to make or break an arrest of the man who'd assaulted her housemates. So then it was merely a nod, and "I feel that bad about it, see."

Then Ding's mother had showed up to fetch her to Much Wenlock, crying, "Ding! Oh, Ding! When I think what might have happened to you as well . . . ," and hugged her and kissed her and escorted her to the car she'd driven. She said, "Thank you," with a fervency that suggested she believed Lynley had done something to save the day when all the day saving had actually been accomplished by Ding herself. Had she not arrived at the house in Temeside when she had, one of the two boys probably would be dead.

He'd returned to the hotel at that point. He not only wanted to wait in order to hear from Havers and be told exactly what they were dealing with, but he also wanted to think. Barbara had certainly been right in her assessment of Gary Ruddock, but in the absence of compelling evidence, he had to consider how they were going to pin anything on him.

When Havers returned from Shrewsbury, she'd shared all the details she'd amassed from the hospital. They were few enough, as Finnegan Freeman remained unconscious. Brutus, on the other hand, had been able to describe the bloke he'd encountered as he'd left his room on the way to the loo. "Sounds like Timothy Lomax again," Lynley commented.

He told her about Ding's identifying Lomax as the man who'd entered their house. Thanks to an observant neighbour called Keegan, he said, they had the fire poker that had been used on both boys. Tossed over the wall that blocked access to the weir near to the Ludford Bridge, he told her. SOCO had collected it for fingerprinting.

Back at the hotel, they'd agreed to sleep on everything and meet in the morning. They would go to the police station then to learn why there had reportedly been no evidence on the undergarments of a girl who had been sexually assaulted.

Thus, they made their way there, within the time frame that Lynley had given Ruddock over the phone. The PCSO showed up within moments of their own arrival. He was well groomed, neatly dressed as usual, and he looked well rested.

Lynley removed the evidence bag from his own car. He saw Ruddock's gaze flick to it, but the PCSO voiced no questions. He nodded to them both, unlocked the station, and said, "Coffee?"

They both accepted. It would give them time to study the man. Had he not offered, they would have made the request anyway.

In the erstwhile lunchroom, they chose the two plastic chairs available. Lynley put the evidence bag on one of them; Havers hung her lumpy shoulder bag from the back of the other. Then she said, "I'll just fetch . . . ?" and took herself off to retrieve the desk chair from the office in which Ian Druitt had died. When she rolled it into the lunchroom, she did so wearing the latex gloves that Lynley had instructed her to don.

Ruddock had busied himself with the Nescafé, the mugs, the

appropriate accompaniments of sugar and, with apologies, a powdered substance that he called "whitener," at which point he turned with a smile. The smile disappeared when he saw the latex gloves on Havers.

Lynley said in a disciplinary fashion, "Sergeant, you're getting ahead of yourself."

"Fingerprints, DNA, the whole bit," Havers replied stoutly. "If he sat in this chair, there'll be evidence of it and evidence is what we need."

Ruddock said, "D'you mean Ian Druitt? He didn't sit in it. It was a plastic one was in the office, like I said before when you asked me about the SOCO pictures."

"Let's lay that aside for the moment," Lynley said to Havers.

"With those scuff marks smeared on the floor? With what we know now? You're joking, Inspector."

"C'n I ask what's going on?" Ruddock at last looked wary.

"Just sit for a moment," Lynley said to Barbara. "We'll get to things as they come."

She said huffily, "Oh too bloody right." She sat, not in the desk chair but on the plastic one. First, however, she took her shoulder bag from the plastic chair and removed her notebook and pencil. Lynley changed the location of the evidence bag from his chair to the table. Ruddock's eyes flicked to the bag, then away from it.

He said, "Something's happened. If you lot want my help, you're going to have to tell me what it is. All I know is that yesterday Finn Freeman and that other boy—"

"Brutus," Havers said. "He had his arm broken by some bloke shouting that his daughter'd been raped. He reckoned one of the two boys did it: Brutus or Finn."

"Why'd he reckon that, for God's sake?"

"Because it happened in the house."

"Jesus. *When*?"

"In December. After exams, this was. Binge drinking going on up in Quality Square that had to be dealt with cause the neighbours were complaining like they do. Everyone pissed to brainlessness. Since you carted the group to Temeside, I s'pose you remember?"

Ruddock said, "I've dumped that lot in Temeside easy a dozen times since autumn. If someone's saying I did the same that night, I probably did."

"This night was rather different," Lynley said, "because Ding ran off. Dena Donaldson, this is. That left the rest of them: Finn, Brutus, and a girl who didn't live there but who also didn't want to go home drunk. She's the girl who was raped. She told Ding about it but no one else, at least not at first. Please sit down, Mr. Ruddock."

"The coffee . . . ?"

"I think I'll forgo it. Barbara?"

"As well." She tapped her pencil against her notebook. She'd opened it to a pristine page.

Ruddock took no chances with pouring the coffee. Hands shaking? Could be, but it was difficult to tell. He said, "I'll do the same, then," and sat in the rolling desk chair. It moved a bit. He braced his feet on the floor.

"That would be why it had to be plastic," Havers noted to Lynley, indicating Ruddock's feet. "But we reckoned that earlier, eh?"

"We did," he replied.

Ruddock said nothing. One of his feet tapped on the floor, but when he seemed to realise that Havers had her gaze fixed upon his shoes, he stopped. He said, "I've my rounds to do this morning, so how can I help you just now?"

Points for bravado, Lynley thought. He said, "Aside from Ding, the raped girl told Ian Druitt about what happened that night. She saw Druitt a number of times—"

"Seven times, sir," Havers put in.

"—and it took a bit for him to get the story from her as she'd been seeing him for another reason entirely. After what happened, she'd wanted to end her enrollment in the college, not returning for the spring term. She'd been talked out of that by her parents, but her coursework began to suffer, which, through various means that we don't need to go into here, brought her to Mr. Druitt's attention."

Ruddock nodded. "That makes sense. He was a sympathetic ear from what I've heard."

"Hmm. Yes." Lynley took the evidence bag, removing it from the table and setting it on the floor.

Havers said, "We spoke to the girl as well, Gary. Yesterday, this was. It was a rough go for her, but as she'd finally told her parents what happened, it made things a bit easier for her to talk about it to us. Now, in the general course of things, you wouldn't expect—all those months later when she told Ian Druitt about the rape—that there would be any evidence of it. I mean, there'd be sod all on her body and everything else would be compromised from here to Jerusalem, if you know what I mean. Only . . . see, this girl'd never been drunk before that night and she was ashamed cause she thought she'd brought the rape on herself. So she wanted a reminder—although you ask me, it was more like a . . . what's one of those things that religious fanatics beat themselves up with, sir?"

"A scourge," Lynley said, his gaze fastened on Ruddock. "A cat-o'-nine-tails. That sort of thing."

"Right," Havers said. "But she didn't have a real scourge, did she? And anyway, people would've noticed if she started going round with blood seeping through her T-shirts and all that from using scourges on the back like people do. So she kept the underwear she was wearing that night, just like it was. She put it in a drawer and—although she didn't say this to us—I expect she brought it out now and then to give it a look just to remind herself what a tart, scrubber, minge bag, cow, or *whatever* she'd been that night. Some girls do that, you know. And this girl? Seems like she was brought up to do it."

"She gave her underthings to Ian Druitt," Lynley said. "When he reported back to her, it was to say that he'd been told there was no evidence on them."

"Which we reckon accounts for all those phone calls between you and the deacon," Havers said. "Sympathetic bloke like you said he was, he'd want to bring someone to justice if that person had raped this girl like she claimed. So he'd ring you to see where the forensic exam of her knickers and tights had got to. You'd tell him at first that there was no news, but he'd keep ringing, wouldn't he? Eventually you would have to say too bad, so sad and all the rest. And because you're an officer of law, Gary—because that *is* what you bloody are, right?—Ian Druitt would assume you were telling the truth, which meant that either the girl had cooked up the whole story for some reason or it had actually happened, leaving no evidence. And in either case, no matter what she said to anyone else after Druitt, it would have been her word against the word of whoever it was did this to her, especially if there wasn't any proof. Like you said, I mean."

"What she didn't tell Ian Druitt, however," Lynley added, "was this, Gary: While the undergarments were hers, the outer garments belonged to someone else. And that person—for all these months—kept them quite safe. She gave them to us yesterday." He touched his fingers to the evidence bag.

"We reckon the rapist's DNA is on them," Havers said. "What's your opinion on the matter, Gary? We'd like to have it from you. We've sorted Druitt's death, by the way. Sir?"

And Lynley gave him the caution, slowly and clearly. Ruddock offered no reaction to this aside from fingers tightening on the arms of the desk chair.

Lynley said to him, "Ian Druitt knew the identity of the girl who'd been raped. He knew about the evidence she'd kept. He passed that evidence on to you and then he relied upon you to do what you were meant to do."

"Which," Havers added, "would have been to log it in, put it into the system, send it off for an analysis that was going to show—"

"I had to protect him," Ruddock broke in. "I was *told* to protect him. I'd've lost my job if I *didn't* protect him."

"Are you talking about Finnegan Freeman?" Lynley asked.

"She asked me directly he came to Ludlow just to keep an eye out, so what could I do? Say no to the deputy chief constable? How could I do that? Would you do that? Would anyone? So when I found out . . . when Druitt told me what happened inside that house . . . I did what I could."

"Which was what, exactly?" Lynley said.

"I told her. Everything that supposedly had happened because for all we knew, it hadn't happened at all and the girl was lying, which is what I told Druitt at first. I know those boys, I told him. Whatever this girl is saying, it can't be true, I told him. This is about revenge or something or anger or whatever. You need to speak with her about *that.* So he did but then here he came with knickers and tights and I knew exactly what that meant."

"So he had to die?"

"I didn't think that! I never thought that! I reckoned getting rid of the evidence would be enough, so I handed it over and that was that. But not for her. She had to be sure that no one ever learned what Finn did to that girl when she was drunk. Only, Druitt *knew.* So—"

"So you killed him," Lynley finished.

"No! I swear to God that I never did *anything* to that bloke except fetch him from St. Laurence Church and bring him here to wait. Then I made my phone calls just like I said and in the meantime someone did him in."

"You've forgotten the part about the vestry," Havers said.

Ruddock licked his lips. The right foot tapped again. Again he stopped it. "What about the vestry?" he demanded.

"It's where Ian Druitt removed his vestments while you were in the room waiting for him," Lynley explained.

"I can't help if he took the opportunity—"

"You were the one who took the opportunity, Gary," Havers said. "You might've turned out to be less of an absolutely *pathetic* bloody tosser if you'd ever once gone to church in your life."

"That'll do, Sergeant," Lynley said mildly. And then to Ruddock, "You chose the wrong stole. The colours mean something. Ian Druitt didn't shove the stole he was wearing for the service into his pocket. He would have been wearing a purple one, for Lent. You chose red."

Silence at this. It would have been quite nice had Ruddock at any point started to look like a truly trapped and finished animal, but that did not happen. This suggested he had cards to be played and he intended to play them. What he didn't know and couldn't possibly know was that the ace was in Lynley's hand.

The back door to the station opened, and Lynley tilted his head in that general direction, indicating Havers should see to it. She rose to do so.

"She pressured me," Ruddock said when Havers was out of the room. "She wouldn't let up. Once I told her about Druitt and what he knew about that night from the girl herself . . . She was the one to ask about evidence, so I told Druitt there was nothing could be done unless there was evidence. He went back to the girl and there it was and he gave it to me and I had to tell her I had it at that point. If I hadn't done, it would be Finn arrested and Finn charged and Finn convicted and all because he made a wretched mistake one night in his life. The girl would heal up. It was bad for her, of course it was bad. But she'd heal and if she only kept her mouth shut, no one would . . . I *couldn't* let the boy go to prison. He'd've been branded because of what happened, and I knew it and so did Clover. The word would get out and he'd be used by the others. The lags would have him. They would line up, and how the bloody hell was he to survive *that* when he didn't have to if there was no evidence of a crime in the first place."

"I see." Lynley paused, frowning, eyebrows drawn together. "Making sure that I understand, the evidence couldn't go to forensics because it had never been worn after that night, so it held DNA. So you either have it still or you gave it to the deputy chief constable because you had to be sure she saw you as following orders."

"I gave it to her. Just like I said. But Druitt still knew it existed, and she couldn't let that rest. I had nothing against the man. He was only doing what he saw as his duty. But she didn't want to risk it."

"What?"

"That one of them—Druitt or the girl—might not believe the no-evidence story. That one of them might want to take their *own* story to the Shrewsbury police, ringing up and saying, 'Here's what happened, only we're being told there isn't evidence and how is that possible when a girl is sodomised?'"

"Ah." Lynley was silent for a moment. He produced an expression of deep thought: a man considering everything he'd heard and evaluating each bit of it. Finally, he said, "That's just the problem, Gary."

"What is?"

"That you know the girl was sodomised."

"Druitt—"

"No. Not Druitt and not anyone else. The girl never told a soul she'd been sodomised until yesterday. She was too ashamed."

"She had to have told."

"But she didn't. In her culture—or perhaps better said in the culture of her mother—a high value is placed on virginity. And while she was and is still technically a virgin, she couldn't bear the thought of telling anyone the exact nature of the attack upon her, in part because they might think she was no longer pure."

"It was Finn. I swear to you. It was Finn."

"That's certainly what you allowed the DCC to believe, isn't it? She needed to be in a panic about her son so that everything could be organised: moving the CCTV camera outside the station here; making a call to the control room that was just vague enough that nothing would be done immediately about it; making that call from here so it could look like someone was trying to frame you; and finally the call to Sergeant Gunderson once a big enough crime was committed that would occupy the patrol officers who otherwise would have fetched Druitt to Shrewsbury when the DCC asked that it be done."

"I'm telling you—"

"I'm sure you are. But once we got onto Druitt's mobile, things began to look worrisome for you, so you had little choice but to drag Finnegan into the story as someone Druitt was ostensibly worried about. But Druitt wasn't worried about anything regarding Finn, as he had both the truth and the evidence on his side. Until, of course, he hadn't."

"I was under orders. From her. DCC Freeman."

"Possibly. But I doubt any order she gave had to do with sodomising a girl. Sergeant?" He directed this last towards the corridor.

Havers came in. She was accompanied by two uniformed officers.

"These blokes'll take you to Shrewsbury, Gary," she told Ruddock. "There's a lovely custody suite waiting for you there."

ROYAL SHREWSBURY HOSPITAL
NR SHELTON
SHROPSHIRE

Clover arrived in Finnegan's room round half past nine. She wasn't dressed for work, and she said to Trevor, "Let me take this watch. You need some sleep."

Before Trevor could reply, Finn roused himself, saying, "Mum?"

She turned to the bed. "I'm here now, darling. Dad's going home to get some sleep, but one of us will stay with you till whoever did this is under arrest."

At Clover's appearance in Finn's room, Trevor had felt at once uneasy. He was reluctant to leave. He said, "I think I'll stay a bit longer."

"There's no need," Clover said. "And if anyone wants to speak with Finnegan, they'll have to deal with me."

Finn said in the same drowsy voice he'd had in the wee hours of the morning, "Cops, you mean."

Clover sat on the chair Trevor had risen from. She leaned towards the bed. "They're going to want a statement from you, Finnegan," she said. "Unless you've spoken to them already. Have you? About what happened yesterday? About anything else?"

Finn hadn't been looking at her but rather at the ceiling. Now, however, he turned his head, which showed his mother the extent of the injuries to his face, swollen and bruised and stitched up like a prizefighter. He said to her, "What?"

"They may want to speak to you about something that happened last winter," she said. "If they do . . . if they bring that up . . . But I'll be with you, so we won't worry about it just now. Unless they've already spoken to you. You haven't yet answered me about that." At this point, she turned to Trevor and said, "He hasn't spoken to the police, has he? Did that Scotland Yard woman manage to get to him at some point last night?"

Finn said, "Scotland Yard?"

Trevor said, "Your mum's worried you might speak to the Metropolitan Police again. Or for that matter, to someone else."

"But you said . . . won't they want a statement . . . ?"

"I don't mean about what happened yesterday, Finn," Trevor told him. "I mean the other. What you and I were trying to work out last night."

"Last night?" He squinted as if the daylight from the window bothered him.

"We talked about the girl . . . in Temeside . . . the assault," Trevor said. He could feel Clover shooting him a look but he didn't return it.

"What . . . was there a girl, Dad? Ding wasn't home when that bloke came at me. Least . . . I don't think . . ."

"That's a memory thing, Finn. It's fuzzy at the moment but the doctor's said it should clear up over time."

Clover said quietly, "So he can't recall anything just now . . . ?" and to Trevor she sounded far too relieved.

He said to their son, "The Met police are going to want to talk to you about a girl who passed out in your house last December. Your mum doesn't want that to happen as the girl was apparently sodomised."

Clover straightened from her position bending over the bed. She said to him, "Trevor, you'll not—"

But he stopped her with, "Your mum doesn't want you to speak to anyone about last December, Finn, because of where the questions might lead. Which means, I reckon, that she also doesn't want you to speak the police about who it was attempted to kill you yesterday."

Clover took a step from the bed. She said, "A word, Trevor."

But before she could lead him from the room to the corridor where, doubtless, she wanted the word to occur, Finn said, "But . . . who . . . Sodom . . . sodomised . . . Mum?"

Clover's tone became fierce and low as she said to Trevor, "That was foul of you."

Trevor said to their son, "You'll need to try to remember, Finn. Everything you can about that night in December."

"It's impossible. He *can't* remember," Clover hissed. "The doctor told us his memory will be faulty for a time."

"But he needs to try, doesn't he?"

"What he needs is to say nothing: to *anyone*. Are we clear, Trevor?"

"Dad . . . Mum . . . ?"

It came to Trevor not only how young Finn sounded, but also—when he glanced at him—how young he looked there in the bed, his head in bandages and his eyes so liquid that it seemed only a superhuman effort was keeping him from weeping in front of his parents.

"Your mum isn't going to allow you to speak to the police unless you're able to assure her, Finn, that neither rape nor sodomy is part of your repertoire when a girl is passed out from drink on your sofa."

Clover hissed in a breath between her teeth. She said, "How dare you."

To which he responded, "What did you intend to do? You can't keep him from the police forever. You can be present if he wants you present, but you can't answer their questions for him."

"They'll trick him. They know how to do that. Do you actually think I'm in the dark about how police detectives work?"

"If he tells them the truth—"

"My God, you are impossibly naïve. The truth means *nothing*. The truth *never* means a thing. When it comes to innocence or guilt, the truth is the very first casualty in an investigation. If he makes a single wrong step—"

"You think . . ." Finn's voice cracked as it had done in puberty. They both turned to him. "You think I did it. You think I . . ." He lifted his good arm and covered his eyes.

Clover's mobile rang. Trevor said, "Let it go." She looked at the screen and then at him. "I can't," she told him. "It's headquarters."

That said, she walked out of the room.

COVENTRY
WARWICKSHIRE

Yasmina wasn't oblivious to the irony of where her parents had chosen to live as pensioners since they had sent *her* to Coventry directly after she'd revealed to them, during her second year at uni, that she'd secretly married an English boy. They might have come round eventually to the idea of her marrying beyond their wishes, religion, and ethnicity, but that she'd become pregnant by that English boy *prior* to marrying him was another matter entirely. For a pregnancy declared she'd violated their cultural and religious beliefs regarding the vital importance of a woman's purity. More important than that, however, turned out to be their fury that—in getting herself with child at her young age—she'd jeopardised her future in medicine. The oldest of her parents' five daughters, she had been intended to show the way, acting as a beacon to the rest of them who might have had other ideas as to how they wished to spend their lives. All the girls were intended to be educated *first*, in possession of a career *second*, and married to suitable and equally educated husbands *third*. Everything else would follow from there: which meant a home, children, the trappings of success, and a list of accomplishments of which their parents could be proud.

They believed Yasmina would fail at all this once she violated the sexual strictures that had been part of the fabric of her life, so she was cut off from them all. She had seen them only twice in the intervening years: once when she attempted to present them with their first granddaughter and then again when she called upon them after attaining the goal of doctor of paediatric medicine. In neither case had she been allowed into their house. She'd come to Coventry now because there were ghosts she had to lay at rest.

Once Timothy had taken the drugs and gone to their bed, she'd climbed to the attic of the house. There, she'd unearthed an old chest and removed from it the garments. She'd ironed these carefully, and then she donned them. She wore them now in Coventry.

She'd chosen a sari of subdued hue from among those she'd kept for the important occasions that she'd hoped she would be invited to attend, such as the marriages of her sisters or the celebrations of births. Of course, she'd been invited to none of those, but still she had hoped that with time, all would be forgiven and her family would welcome her back.

Her sari was dark green, and she'd draped in the Nivi style. Her fingers had moved along the fabric by means of muscle memory, the pleats neatly tucked into the matching, firmly tied petticoat, the blouse adjusted above it, the gold-threaded *pallu* positioned over her left shoulder. She wore sandals on her feet and gold bangles on her right wrist. Her left arm was cuffed in a band of gold, and she chose heavy earrings fashioned with green tourmalines. When she'd gazed upon her reflection, she saw what she wanted her parents to see: an Indian woman who had not forgotten her culture.

Now she went to their door. The day was promising to be a warm one and there on the sheltered porch of her parents' home, she could feel the sun heating the back of her neck. She rang the bell. She had to ring twice before the door opened. Then her mother was standing before her, wearing a threadbare tracksuit and unlaced trainers.

In the years since Yasmina had seen her, her mother's hair had thinned and its colour had gone completely to grey. She squinted at Yasmina, and Yasmina thought the sunlight behind her was making it difficult for her mother to see her face. She took a step that would put her into the shade of the porch's gabled roof. She and her mother spoke at the same moment.

"Madhur?" said her mother.

"Mum," said Yasmina.

As if not hearing what Yasmina had said, her mother went on with, "Madhur, we have no cakes in the house. There *is* tea but there's no milk and the house itself—"

"Mum, it's Yasmina." Who was Madhur? she thought.

"—would not be a matter of pride to me as it is just now. Have you come to speak about Rajni again?"

"Mum, it's *Yasmina*. Your eldest. Yasmina. Will you let me into the house?"

"Oh, but I can't," her mother said. "You must forgive me. Palash said I must not allow . . . And Rajni . . . did you not know she has long since married, Madhur? She is no longer available although we do not see her. Palash did not approve the match as you had not made it, and he was very angry at the disrespect this showed." And then on the thin edge of a coin, the subject changed to, "Rajni, is it you who have come? But no. That cannot be. It would not be allowed. Rajni is heavy with a child now unless you have lost the child. Rajni, have you lost the child? Did you forget to take him when you were last here? But you were not here, were you? Is it Bina who has come?"

Yasmina began to understand. She said, "Is Palash here? Mummy, is Dad *here*?" because she could not imagine that her father might have left her mother alone as she was now.

"Rajni has done well," her mother said. "She is not what we intended for her but her marriage . . . Ambika says it has brought her wealth. Ambika, though, has done less well, and I had such hopes for her. But something has gone wrong in her head, Palash says."

"What has happened to her?" Yasmina asked. "Mum, is Dad at home? Please let me in."

"Oh so very sorry," her mother said and began to close the door. "Palash tells me I must not."

"Mummy!" Yasmina pushed lightly against the panels to stop the door from closing altogether.

"Madhur, Rajni, you must not! Ambika is not here. Palash says always—"

"Mummy, let me in!"

Her mother lacked the strength to keep her out, so Yasmina managed to get inside the place, but once inside she wished she had remained on the porch. Piles of newspapers, clumps of half-empty carrier bags, pictures dropped by cyclones on tabletops and floors, furniture stained, post unopened, magazines trampled underfoot, teacups and plates and glasses unwashed.

"Oh, you must not, you must not!" her mother cried. "Palash! Palash! Madhur wants Rajni, and Ambika will hurt herself if you do not come! Palash!"

There was a pounding of footsteps above them. Then an equal pounding as a large figure in a dressing gown hurtled down the stairs. Yasmina's father was saying, "Yes, yes, Vedas. Palash is here. But Madhur is dead. In India, Vedas. So long ago. You've only forgotten. Rajni and Ambika are gone, my dear. And who is this that you've opened the door to when I've told you . . ."

His words died off when he saw Yasmina clearly. And then it was only, "You."

Yasmina did not wait for any other reaction from him. She said, "What's happened? Mummy is . . . Dad, are you caring for her by yourself? How long—"

"Get out," he said. "*This* is what came of it all. Every one of them as if they were sheep and you the shepherd."

"Palash," her mother said. "Palash, when will Ambika come? And Sevti? Why do we not see Sevti? Did she not go to the market for us?"

He said to his wife, "Vedas, you must rest your mind. Go into the kitchen and wait for me there."

"But should we not offer Madhur tea?"

"Yes, of course. Fill the kettle, Vedas. Just water in the kettle. Do nothing more."

She looked as if she were concentrating on this idea of water in the kettle. She murmured "water" to herself as she wandered off, stumbling against a pile of newspapers in the sitting room, distracted enough by this that she knelt in front of them and began to sort through them, making an arrangement whose purpose was clear only to her.

Yasmina watched her with a sense of growing desperation. She said, "What can I do? Tell me what I can do. Where are they?"

Her father's nostrils flared as if he smelled an unpleasant odour emanating from her. He said, "Leave us. You are dead, and no spirit of any daughter of mine may enter this house."

Yasmina took in *any* and its larger implications. She said, "You drove *all* of us away?"

"You did this," he said. "If they are dead to us, it is as you wanted it. You have driven a stake into my heart. You have destroyed your mother's mind. And this is what's left: what you see before you. Now leave us to our grief and our shame." He turned her bodily, pushing her in the direction of the door.

She grew stiff with resistance. "It doesn't have to be this way. Why can't you see that?"

"Out!" And now he raised both his voice and a fist. He advanced on her as he had done in her past and as, undoubtedly, he had done to her sisters.

She backed away from him but still said, "Where are they? What has happened to my sisters? Where are they, Dad? Tell me."

"They are dead to us!" he roared. "Be gone with you and leave us in peace! Nothing has changed here and nothing will."

ROYAL SHREWSBURY HOSPITAL
NR SHELTON
SHROPSHIRE

Barbara Havers had been sorry to miss the Big Moment, but when Lynley had explained his plan to lead Ruddock into incriminating himself, she immediately recognised it as their best chance to sew up not only the death of Ian Druitt but also the rape of Missa Lomax. When she'd heard him call her name as she waited with the patrol officers in the corridor of the Ludlow nick, she knew he'd been successful.

The rest of their encounter with the PCSO was form rather than substance. He'd been handcuffed much as he'd handcuffed Ian Druitt, he'd been led to the patrol car, he'd been carted away at speed. She and Lynley would next see him inside an interview room at the Shrewsbury station, but before that occurred, they had to deal with Clover Freeman.

Lynley rang Chief Constable Wyatt from the nick's car park, with Barbara listening to his end of the call. After an interminable wait—and *why* did waiting for the CC seem to be de rigueur, for God's sake, Barbara wondered—Lynley revealed only that he and Detective Sergeant Havers were about to leave Ludlow for West Mercia Headquarters, where they would need to speak to the deputy chief constable on the matter of Ian Druitt's death. If Wyatt could see to it that she didn't leave the premises . . . ?

Lynley listened for a moment to whatever Wyatt was saying to him while Barbara waited like a horse at the starting gate. She was muttering, "Come on, come *on*," when Lynley rang off, saying to her, "She's not gone into work."

"Christ! She's done a runner."

"I don't think so. She's rung in and told them she was going to Royal Shrewsbury Hospital to her son. She said her husband spent the night with him and she needed to spell him there."

"So you think . . . what? She's sitting there waiting for us to fetch her?"

"I think she's still in the dark about what's going on here. If we can get to her quickly, chances are we'll still find her that way."

They set off at once. The distance wasn't great, but it had to be travelled on a road without a single dual carriageway, and twice they were significantly slowed by lorries. Without the benefit of lights or siren, they had to wait for opportunities to overtake the slower vehicles.

Barbara found her anxiety growing by the moment, made worse by Lynley's determined calm.

She believed that Clover Freeman would have long ago destroyed the evidence handed over by Ruddock, if Ruddock had handed it over at all, which was still open to doubt. They would then be reduced to he-said-she-said, because both of them damn well knew that even if Ruddock had rolled his body all over the clothes they'd found beneath Brutus's bed, there would be DNA from everyone else on that clothing as well. Since at her own admission Ding had performed sex acts for Ruddock in order to keep him from taking her home—drunk—to her mother, Ruddock's DNA could be explained away using Ding's own behaviour with the PCSO to do it.

Lynley took a different position about the evidence. He pointed out to her that if they had learned nothing else about Clover Freeman, they had learned that she appeared to maintain control over her son in whatever way she could. Ruddock had been employed as a virtual spy on her behalf, and the boy had been tasked with engaging in a mother-approved form of social activism by volunteering at Ian Druitt's after-school club. As he grew older and more difficult for his mother to manage, she was going to need something very special to keep him within her sphere of influence. Evidence of an assault upon an unconscious girl worked quite a trick at doing that.

"That would mean she reckons he did it," Barbara said to Lynley at the conclusion of his explanation.

"Ruddock certainly went to every effort to convince her of that."

"So why not get rid of the evidence once she's got her mitts on it?"

"Keeping it gives her power." Lynley eased the Healey Elliott into the right lane. He changed down gears and floored it, which allowed them to sail by a tractor and two cars. His own motor was ancient, but it had been built for speed. Barbara glanced at him as the trees along the verge became blurs of green. He looked quite satisfied with the car's performance.

"That's one bloody big risk, you ask me," Barbara said. She was not referring to overtaking the other vehicles.

"It is, but she would have seen the payoff. I daresay she's told herself that everything she's done has been for Finn's own good. That would make her actions easier for her to swallow."

"Makes one wonder, though," Barbara said as she thought everything over. "I mean, aside from whatever Ruddock told her, she must have a reason for thinking Finn was the one who assaulted Missa Lomax."

"He appears to be doing everything he can to alienate her," Lynley pointed out. "It's likely he's a decent sort at heart, but what he's done to his appearance alone suggests a form of rebellion that she wouldn't like. Doubtless there've been others over the years."

At Royal Shrewsbury Hospital, Lynley presented his warrant card at reception. A phone call brought a uniformed officer to speak with them. When Lynley assured the man that he wished to speak to Finnegan's mother and not to Finnegan himself, the officer said, "The dad's the only one here."

"We were told she's come to take over from Mr. Freeman," Lynley said. "Did she not?"

"She was here for a bit but then she left," the officer said. "I s'pose the dad didn't want to leave the boy."

"We'll need to speak to Mr. Freeman, then," Lynley told him. "It's a matter of some urgency."

The officer considered this one. He spent a moment sucking his teeth as if with the desire to clean them of bits of breakfast.

While he was doing his teeth sucking, Lynley added, "This will take less than five minutes."

"Right. It's only I'm not meant to let anyone into the room."

"We're happy with the corridor," Lynley told him, to which Barbara added impatiently, "Or the rooftop, the car park, the inside of a lift, or standing next to a wheelie bin."

The officer jerked his head to indicate they were meant to follow him. When they reached Finn Freeman's room, the door was closed. The officer told them to wait as he ducked inside. When he emerged, Trevor Freeman was with him.

Freeman looked like a man whose life had been steamrollered. He said, "You're not to talk to him. He's in and out of it, his memory's been affected, and unless—"

"We must talk to your wife, not your son," Lynley cut in. "He's recovering, I hope?"

"He will do, eventually. D'you have the bloody sod who did this?"

"We have a tentative identification made by someone who was in the house. The tool he apparently used has gone to forensics for fingerprinting as well. Mr. Freeman, we've been told that your wife was here briefly and then left. Have you any idea where she's gone?"

"She had a phone call," Freeman told them. "She said it was headquarters and stepped out of the room. I presume it was Wyatt asking her to come to Hindlip."

"Why?" Barbara asked.

"Because she left. I mean, she didn't come back into the room." Freeman looked from Barbara to Lynley, his expression becoming wary. "What's this about? I know what's been going on, by the way, and let me be clear. My son did not rape anyone, and he did not sodomise anyone. He didn't even know that a girl was passed out in the house that night. Someone got inside the place because—"

"We know," Lynley cut in. "An arrest has been made."

"Who?"

"I can't tell you more at the moment. There are interviews to conduct and the victim and her family to be informed. We do need to speak to your wife first, however."

"Shall I ring her mobile? Or her office?"

Lynley considered this. After a moment, he said no. Barbara knew that putting the wind up at this juncture was the very last step he would want to take. He would be seriously doubtful that Clover Freeman had actually been called to Hindlip, but he'd also be wanting to make sure of that without anyone's ringing her office or her mobile.

He thanked Freeman. He wished him well. He said he hoped Finn would make a swift and complete recovery. He said that he would be in touch.

Barbara followed him, then, as he retraced their route to the lift. She had a very bad feeling about what they'd learned. She was not surprised when, as they left the hospital, Lynley put in a call to the Shrewsbury nick and asked for the duty sergeant. For with its lights and siren, the patrol car carrying Ruddock would have made vastly better time from Ludlow to Shrewsbury than they had done, even with the Healey Elliott's speed and Lynley's dexterity at overtaking slower vehicles. Upon being booked, Gary Ruddock would have requested and been granted the phone call owed to him. There was little doubt he would have made that call to Clover Freeman who, from the hospital, was mere minutes from the station.

"She's going for the evidence," Barbara said, as Lynley waited to be put through to the duty sergeant. "She has to be, sir. She needs to get rid of it."

"That's one scenario," Lynley agreed.

"There's another?"

He didn't have a chance to reply as he began speaking, presumably to the duty sergeant. Had Gary Ruddock been brought to the station? Yes, he had. Had he been booked? Yes, he had. Had he asked for a phone call? Yes, he had. Lynley listened to what Barbara thought was an answer lengthier than was required. At the end of this, Lynley said, Has anyone asked to see him? Yes, someone had. Again he listened. Barbara wanted to rip the mobile from his ear or shout to put it on speaker, but she had to wait. Lynley thanked the man and ended the call.

He said to her, "She's been there."

"Did they actually let her see him?"

"It's not likely that a duty sergeant would refuse the deputy chief constable's request for a word with the bloke just brought in on charges."

"He did make his phone call to her, then."

"The sergeant didn't have it verbatim for me, but Ruddock evidently said to whomever he rang that he'd been arrested, and they needed to talk. The sergeant reckoned he was ringing his solicitor. But I think you and I can rely upon that constituting Gary Ruddock's message to the DCC that she was to come at once. Once she arrived and asked to see him, I think we can assume he told her everything, with a few careful lapses in the information."

"But he wouldn't have said he's the one who assaulted Missa Lomax. Would he?"

"I daresay he'd've wanted to keep her believing Finn did it. If he told her we're closing in on Finn, she'll get rid of the evidence. She might have kept it in order to keep the boy under her thumb, but with him now in the spotlight as a suspect in the assault of Missa Lomax? She'd want to be rid of it as soon as she could manage it."

"She can't risk dumping it anywhere near her home," Barbara said. "She'll know we'll search every dustbin, skip, and wheelie bin in Worcester if we have to."

"She certainly can't risk dumping it at work," Lynley pointed out, "for the very same reason. So where does that leave us?"

Barbara thought of the potential locations. They knew very little about the DCC. If she'd been carrying the evidence round in her car all these months, she could easily dump it anywhere. She could toss it onto a verge, she could fire up her barbecue and burn it, she could find a superstore and slip it into a wheelie bin there, she could take a flight to Timbuktu, for all they knew and there she could—

"The airfield, sir," Barbara said. "She's a member of that glider club along with Rabiah Lomax and Nancy Scannell. Remember the photo? If she uses a glider, she can easily get to a reservoir. Or to the middle of a moor. Or to just about anywhere. She can dump the evidence and as long as the place is remote enough or inaccessible enough, no one will find it."

"Where is this airfield?" Lynley asked.

"On the high moors above Church Stretton, middle of nowhere. Me and the guv talked to Nancy Scannell there."

"Can you find it again?"

"I can bloody well try. It's on the Long Mynd."

"Do you know the name of the airfield itself?"

Barbara searched for it in her memory. It had to do with the Midlands; she recalled that much. Then it came to her "West Midlands Gliding Club," she told him.

"Ring them, then. Tell them to stop her if she wants to take out the glider."

Barbara snapped her fingers, good cheer descending upon her as she recalled a delightful, vital fact. "The consortium's glider is damaged," she said. "That's what was going on at Rabiah Lomax's house when we arrived to speak to her. Remember? A meeting about the damaged glider. Clover Freeman may not know that that glider's going nowhere, no matter what she wants."

"They may well have extra gliders available for individuals who don't have the funds to purchase their own. Or for people wanting lessons. Or for people wanting to go up for a lark in the company of an experienced pilot. If that's the case—if there are spare gliders—we must stop her from using one, so make the call, Sergeant. Then get us to the gliding club as quickly as you can."

IRONBRIDGE
SHROPSHIRE

When Yasmina arrived home, she found that Timothy was not only awake but also climbing the slope towards their house on New Road, ascending from Wharfage. She pulled alongside him and lowered the passenger window, asking, "Would you like a ride the rest of the way?"

He looked towards her but shook his head. He gestured for her to go on, which was what she did. She was able to park in their garage for once, and when she got out and came round to the front door, she saw that he was two houses away, so she waited. If he was surprised to see how she was clad, he made no mention of the ethnic clothing. He merely went into the house, leaving the door open for her to follow.

She saw him pass through the entry and from there he made his way to the kitchen. She herself climbed the stairs. In the bedroom, she removed the sari and its accompanying garments. She folded them neatly for their return to the attic. Then she dressed as she would normally.

When she descended to the kitchen, she found him making a sandwich. He glanced round as she came into the room, saying, "D'you want something? Making two is as easy as making one. It's going to be cheese, pickle, onion, and tomato. I started to walk to the market but . . . I don't know. It seemed out of reach."

She said that she would be grateful for a sandwich. He made it in silence. She wanted to ask him what it was that had managed to get him out of bed, but she held her peace. Instead she put water in the kettle and set it to boil. She got out the tea—Earl Grey for him, Darjeeling for her—along with two person-size pots. She let hot water run into these to warm them as she made tea sachets for them both.

He finally said, "It was Mum. She rang one of the neighbours."

"What d'you mean?"

"Mum rang here. I don't know . . . three or four times? It didn't wake me. So when I didn't answer and you didn't answer, she rang the clinic. I expect at that point she panicked . . . as much as Mum ever panics. So she rang old Reg Douglas from the end of the street, and he came to see if . . . well. At any rate, he got me up. I was to phone her, he said."

"Has something happened to Missa?" Yasmina asked quickly.

"Reg couldn't say anything about anything since he didn't know. But seeing as Mum had been ringing the neighbours"—Timothy waved the knife he'd been using to spread the pickle—"he got me up." He glanced at her then. "I couldn't work out where you were. Once I rang the clinic, I mean. You didn't go to work."

"Timothy, what did Rabiah want? Why did she phone the neighbours?"

"Police liaison came by to tell her there's been an arrest."

Yasmina was almost afraid to ask, but she knew she had to so she said, "Of whom? For what?"

"For what happened to Missa."

"Did one of those boys—"

"It was someone else. Rabiah told me she asked who it was but the liaison officer wouldn't say. His remit was to tell her that an arrest had been made and the bloke was being taken to Shrewsbury. No worries that he might show up to do Missa any more harm."

The kettle clicked off. Yasmina went through the tea-making by rote as Timothy cut the sandwiches in halves and then in quarters. He carried them to the table on a single plate, fetching two smaller sandwich plates as if he and Yasmina were engaging in a ritualised afternoon tea. She went along with this: removing teacups and their saucers from a cupboard, fetching napkins, milk, and sugar. They sat at the table and said nothing for a moment until Yasmina told him where she had been.

"The sari," he noted.

"I thought it would help."

"It didn't, I assume." He poured her some tea, then did the same for himself. He took a quarter of a sandwich. She did the same.

She said, "I thought it might soften them towards me. But Mummy was only confused by it, and I don't think my father even noticed. All of them are gone now. It was the same for them."

"Your sisters?"

"All of them."

"Not pregnant, though. I can't think any of them would have made that mistake after what happened to you."

"That I don't know," she said. "Just that he's cut them off and there he and Mummy are, completely alone. Their house . . . It's like something one sees in a film, Timothy. They're . . . It seems like they've become hoarders."

He stared at his sandwich for what seemed like two minutes but was probably less than thirty seconds. He raised his head and looked at her just as long before he said, "I'm very sorry. That must have a blow to you, Yas. Where *are* your sisters? What became of them?"

"I don't know. I must begin a search." She picked up her own sandwich. But her throat was too dry because of what she knew she needed to say. She placed the sandwich onto her small plate and took a sip of her tea and then another. She said, "You were right about everything."

"I haven't been right about anything in years."

"That's not true. Regarding the girls, you were right from the first." She tried to find the words to explain what it had meant to see her parents, to learn how life had unfolded for them and for her sisters. She said, "Timothy . . . Seeing them . . . understanding for the first time . . . I don't know if I could possibly describe it to you."

"No need. I've still got enough imagination left to work it out."

"What I want to say . . ." At her hesitation, he looked at her and his expression altered and she wondered what it was that she was meant to read on his face: compassion, hope, worry, or merely resignation that all was lost. She forged ahead with, "I want you to know that this—who I would like to be instead of who I've been?—this will be a struggle for the rest of my life."

"I'm not sure what you mean."

"I intend to do whatever it is I need to do to become someone I can live with and someone you and the girls can live with. That's what I mean. I also mean that I am so profoundly sorry for where I've taken us as a family."

"It's not all down to you."

"Part of it is, and that's the part I can barely stand to think about, let alone to see."

She waited although she wasn't sure for what. Indeed, she wasn't sure she ought to be waiting at all. Wasn't the truth that she could only own the actions she herself had taken, the decisions she herself had made, and the blinkers she herself had worn? Timothy would have to do whatever he needed or wanted to do on his own.

He said, "Rabiah's bringing her home. That was part of why she rang. Missa's asked her to bring her here."

"To Ironbridge, you mean?"

"I mean here. Home. Here."

Yasmina took this in and turned it round in her mind, finally saying, "I don't exactly know how I feel about that. Frightened, I think. What does it mean that I'm frightened to see my own daughter?" When Timothy didn't reply, Yasmina said, "She'll want something from me, and I don't know if I have inside of me what she needs."

"I expect you'll need to ask her first if she wants anything at all," he said. "I expect both of us must ask her that."

THE LONG MYND
SHROPSHIRE

Havers kept ringing the gliding club once she had its phone number in hand. She kept saying that it was "a bloody recording" and then "doesn't anyone actually *work* in the sodding place? There's meant to be a receptionist. There was an office. The guv and I saw it. So where *is* this person?"

"Keep ringing," Lynley told her.

They were making decent time in their rush to the Long Mynd, but Clover Freeman had a very good start on them. Brief as her conversation with Gary Ruddock would have been, she would have known at its conclusion that she stood in every kind of danger. She'd orchestrated the deacon's death, she'd withheld evidence, she'd obstructed not only an IPCC investigation but also two additional investigations made by the Metropolitan Police. She was going to be occupying a cell at the monarch's pleasure for a very long time unless she could manage to rid herself of the evidence she was holding, which—she believed—marked her son as sexual predator. Aside from phone calls to and from Gary Ruddock made to her husband's mobile, they really had nothing on the woman save an argument that a nineteen-day wait to arrest the deacon existed in the first place because Ruddock and not a regular patrol officer had to be the one putting the handcuffs on Ian Druitt. But if she had in her possession the garments that Missa Lomax had handed over to Druitt, she would find it very difficult to explain them away in a court of law. And she had to have those garments with her. She was astute enough to understand that the walls were closing in. Doubtless, she'd kept the clothing nearby from the moment Ruddock had handed it over. The under things were not only a crucial element in the investigation. They also served a greater purpose in her malignant relationship with her son.

They swept south on the A49, passing neatly planted fields of summer wheat. They had better luck with the traffic this time, and with a distance that was shorter than their earlier drive from Ludlow, they were swerving into a right turn on one of Shropshire's lesser roads in quarter of an hour. The village of All Stretton passed as a blur, and they were fast coming upon the larger town—Church Stretton—when Havers cried, "Here, sir. *Here*."

Lynley nearly missed the turn, so thick were the trees and so narrow was the lane onto which Havers directed him. It quickly became a single car's width, and when the sergeant said, "Ouch. Sorry, sir,"

Lynley knew she was referring to the Healey Elliott. He wasn't reassured when she said, "It's going to get worse in a second or two."

Which it did. She said, "Here. Other side of that call box," when they reached a few farm buildings that went for the hamlet of Asterton. He saw that just beyond the red BT booth to their right, a track began to climb a hillside so steep that he wasn't certain his lowest gear could actually manage it.

He changed down gears. A plump ewe toddled onto the road, a lamb behind her. He hit the brakes with a curse. Havers said, "There'll be ducks as well. I'll see to it," and she got out of the car. She shooed the ewe and its offspring to the far edge of the road, giving Lynley what looked like six inches of leeway to pass the animals.

In the car again, Havers continued ringing the glider club. She finally managed to get through to someone. She identified herself. She said she was on her way. She asked about Clover Freeman.

She listened for a moment before she said into her mobile, "Can't you bloody well look for her? . . . What do you mean? You obviously *haven't* been sitting there in reception because I've been ringing and ringing and there's been no one—"

Lynley glanced at her. She was becoming quite red in the face as she listened to whatever she was being told. She finally said, "You listen to me, you sodding fool, this is—"

"Sergeant," Lynley murmured.

"—a murder investigation and that woman's in the middle of it, and what you're doing at this *precise* moment comes down to . . . All right. Do it *now*." She punched her mobile to disconnect and said to Lynley, "He's told someone to do a search for her."

"How large is the place?"

"Various wartime huts used as hangars, as well as outbuildings, barns, and a whole bloody caravan site." She cursed and then said quickly, "Turn here, sir. This is the last bit."

Lynley was glad of that as the last part of the route was down to mere tracks for vehicles' tyres. They were high on the open moor now, a vast and treeless expanse of land coloured at this time of year by the gorse, whose yellow blooms were interrupted by lacy bursts of bracken green in the spring and large swaths of heather that would turn the moor purple later in the summer. It was clear why the Long Mynd was a desired site for launching gliders. To the west Shropshire gave way to rolling hills, some comprising quartzite and some consisting of volcanic debris. The landscape rose once to form the mass of rock that was the Stiperstones, but other than that it merely undulated. One could sail in the sky straight into Wales if the air currents allowed it.

Havers cried out, "Here, sir, on the right!" at the same moment as Lynley saw the sign and then the gate of the airfield. He had barely braked the Healey Elliott before Havers was out of the car, shoving the gate open, and hopping back in to point the way to the main building, set back from a gravel-strewn area that served as car park.

Opposite this at a distance of some three hundred yards Havers pointed out the launching site for the gliders. Two were queued up, ready to take to the air. A third forward one was balanced with someone holding its wingtip while an individual with a clipboard walked round it, engaging in what appeared to be a preflight inspection.

Havers said, "Should I . . . ?" and waved towards the launching area.

Lynley said, "Go ahead. I'll check inside," and he set off towards the main building while Havers headed in the direction of the queue of gliders.

Once inside, he found the reception office. He learned to his chagrin that Clover Freeman had not been located at the airfield. No glider had been taken out in her name; no cursory search of the club's buildings had produced her; no response to announcements made on the internal and external public address systems had turned up either her or anyone who had seen her.

Lynley cursed quietly. It had seemed so probable. They knew she was a glider pilot. They knew she belonged to a consortium of other pilots. They knew this location was the only one in Shropshire from which the consortium members might—

Members, he realised. He asked if Nancy Scannell was at the airfield, if Nancy Scannell had checked out one of the gliders they had for hire.

The receptionist—a swarthy gentleman whose badge identified

him as Kingsley and who looked as if he'd spent his formative years walking the Shropshire hills in the blazing sun—had a look both on the sign-in sheet and then through the forms apparently filled out for taking a glider out for a flight. He shook his head. No Nancy Scannell. Sorry, he said. Fact was, the only glider hired out at the moment had been hired by someone called Lomax. He couldn't quite read the scrawl but it looked like . . . Rachel, possibly?

"Rabiah Lomax?" Lynley asked. And before the man could reply, he went on with, "Has she launched? Can you stop her?"

Kingsley said the best he could do was radio the winch operator. He said, "So you're not wanting the Clover Freeman?"

"That *is* Clover Freeman," Lynley replied. "Radio the operator. Tell him I'm on my way."

Lynley set off at a jog. In the distance he could see Havers hurrying towards the two remaining gliders. The earlier one had already been launched. It soared in the distance, circling now to head in the direction of Wales. The next was being checked over, its pilot already in the cockpit. Havers was steaming towards it.

But the glider was not important now. They had to stop the winch. He rang Havers's mobile then saw his error when Havers paused to dig for it. He cursed and cut off the call. She stopped her search but looked in the direction from which he was now running. That made things worse, as she hesitated. He waved her on. He shouted. If Clover Freeman was ready to launch, she still could not do it without the aid of the winch operator. Havers would know that. Surely she would know that. She was meant to stop the operator from whatever mechanism he employed to assist in a launch. She was not meant to stop Clover Freeman herself.

She misread his intent and kept on her path to the gliders. It was down to Kingsley in the reception office: his ability not only to radio the winch operator but to radio the *correct* winch operator, as there were two of them, one at each end of the grassy runway.

Havers ran to the glider still in the queue. She banged on the cockpit's Plexiglas cover. It lifted. She spoke. She turned to dash to the forward glider. At that moment, the closer winch flashed its lights at the distant winch. The glider began to move. Havers reached it. A horn of some kind began to shriek. She flung herself at the cockpit as if to open it. She managed to grab on to the edge of the Plexiglas in some way, but she was not in time to do anything else. The glider rolled forward, and then it was too late. Havers fell. The glider lifted off the ground as the distant winch drew it forward at speed. Aerodynamics did the rest. It launched within seconds. It climbed steeply. It would, Lynley knew, disengage from the winch as soon as—

It disengaged. But it did so at what looked like only five hundred feet. Not enough lift. Not enough altitude. It plunged to the ground.

Lynley heard the cries coming from all directions. Those in the car park watching the launch began running towards the crash. Havers had scrambled to her feet. She tore towards the glider as the winch operator leapt from his vehicle shouting, "She released! She released!" The pilot in the waiting glider climbed out and ran forward, hand over mouth. Others nearby dashed to the downed plane while a horn blared from the distant winch, perhaps alerting those inside the main building to the unfolding disaster outside.

Lynley made it to the glider at the same moment as Havers. Someone from the car park had reached it first. What remained of the cockpit cover had been removed, and the pilot had fallen half out of the straps that had restrained her. Voices came from every direction as more people arrived at a run.

"Who did the fucking rig check?" someone demanded as someone else declared, "I checked every fucking inch. There was *nothing*—"

"Is she all right?"

"Jesus, Franklin, what do you think?"

"It's got to be the cable release."

"I checked. I *checked*. That woman ran out of nowhere and all of a sudden—"

"Get her out of there."

"Don't touch her! She could be—"

"Oh too fucking bloody right, Steve."

"What woman? Where is she?"

"Don't you understand? She released it herself. There was nothing wrong—"

"Why the *hell* would she release at that altitude?"

"She might not've known what would—"

"Who is she?"

"Is this her first solo—"

"Didn't he stop the launch? I radioed! Oh God. He was told . . . the police are here somewhere. There they are. They wanted—"

"The *police*?"

Which brought about a stuttering into silence as every gaze sought out someone to name as the party responsible for what had occurred, and the police were going to be as good as any.

"She released the glider from the cable too soon, sir," Havers said. "I'm so bloody sorry. I thought I could stop her. But when she saw me . . ."

"She knew it was over," Lynley said. "She knew what came next, Barbara."

IRONBRIDGE
SHROPSHIRE

Rabiah thought at first that she would stop and fetch Sati. But when she reflected upon everything, she decided that bringing the little girl back sooner rather than later, while undoubtedly reassuring to her, would be an impediment to what needed to pass between Missa and her parents. So she went directly to Timothy's home, telling Missa that Justin would bring Sati down from the Goodayles' residence once she gave him the word to do so. He knew, she told Missa, that she was bringing Missa back to Ironbridge. He wanted Missa to know he was that worried, she continued. He wanted her to know he'd already been to speak to Yasmina. He wanted to learn what was happening because he was meant to tell Sati something. And had they not agreed that whatever else went on, they would never lie to themselves, to each other, or to Missa's little sister?

Missa took this all in but made no reply other than, "Thank you, Gran. For not telling him."

Rabiah said to her, "*Why* would I tell him? What must you think of your grandmother even to consider the idea?"

"It's only that if he knew about it all . . . I mean, I can see how you would think he might not want to marry me then."

"*I* would think that? How absurd."

"Mum, then."

"Equally absurd. If we know nothing else about life in general and our family in particular, we do know that Justin is devoted to you, has always been, will always be. And this includes your mother, Missa, despite what you might think of everything she's done regarding you, Justin, your marriage, university, and God knows what else. His love for you has never been in question. Perhaps in your own eyes? Never in ours."

Rabiah could tell that Missa took this in and thought about it during their drive from Ludlow. That had always been one of her strongest characteristics, as well as one of her weakest: She considered what other people thought, even when she should entirely dismiss what other people thought.

Knowing her daughter-in-law as she did, Rabiah expected Yasmina to come dashing from the house the moment she and Missa arrived. She reckoned Yasmina would have been watching from a window. Indeed, she thought she caught a glimpse of her as she pulled up in front of the house. But she did not come out, and when Rabiah rang the bell it was Timothy who answered the door.

He took Missa into his arms. For a moment. Missa stood statuelike, but then she returned the embrace. Arm round her shoulder, Timothy led her inside. He said, "Thanks, Mum," and Rabiah followed them.

Yasmina was in the sitting room, closer to the kitchen than she was to the entry. She held out a hand towards Missa but she dropped it quickly as if determined not to give the wrong impression.

Unsurprisingly, knowing the child as Rabiah did, Missa said, "I'm sorry for the trouble I've caused."

Which was enough to move Yasmina forward although she still seemed hesitant. She said, "Not one thing in all of this can be laid at your feet. I want you to see that."

Missa made no reply to this. She seemed confused by her mother's words. She looked first to her father, then to Rabiah.

There was silence then. Into it, Rabiah's mobile rang. She frowned at the number, which she did not recognise. She answered with a quiet, "What is it?" and heard the voice of the Scotland Yard detective, speaking about the assault upon Missa, the arrest of Ludlow's PCSO for the crime, and the death of Clover Freeman, who was one of the PCSO's superior officers. Although she had questions aplenty, she did not ask Inspector Lynley. She merely said, "Thank you. I've brought Missa to Ironbridge. Do you need her?" He said he didn't think so, at least not just yet, but he would be in touch.

Everyone's gaze was upon her as Rabiah returned her mobile to her bag. She said to Missa, "The police community support officer in Ludlow has been arrested by the Met detectives. He was the one, my dear." She did not look at Timothy as she spoke. Whatever he had done on the previous day, they would have to deal with it later. He did drop his arm from Missa's shoulder at that, though. He walked to the sofa and there he sat, his hands dangling limply between his legs.

Missa said to her grandmother, "The night it happened, when I was drunk . . . He was who took us home. But he left, Gran. We thought . . . I thought he'd gone to fetch Ding. She'd made him so angry. She wouldn't do what he said. I thought when she ran, he went after her."

"Perhaps he did, but I don't expect he found her. He came back at some point and entered the house."

"I shouldn't even have been there. I shouldn't have been drunk."

Yasmina said, "You've just laid this at your own feet, Missa. Do not do that."

"I knew better, Mum."

"What you knew was that your exams were completed, and you were meant to have a nice evening."

Missa lowered her head. It was as if she couldn't take in—let alone accept—what her mother was trying to tell her.

Yasmina closed the distance between them. "Missa, can you bear to look at your mum? If you can't, looking at me is not required. But I hope you'll listen." She didn't wait for a sign from her daughter before she continued. "I wish to hand you your life. With an open heart, I do so *want* to do that. I ask only one thing in return if you can manage it: that you forgive me one day. Not now. I don't even want that now because if you give forgiveness now, it will be given because you think you're meant to please me when in the deepest part of your heart you know that you aren't, which is what you've tried to tell me for so long. The sins I committed against you, Missa, were committed out of love, and I hope you will see that someday. But make no mistake, because I make none when I say this to you: the things I did and said and wanted and insisted upon? They were sins all the same."

"Mum, I never meant . . ."

"Faced with the mummy you've had for all of your life?" Yasmina said. "Believe me, Missa, you did what you needed to do."

Yasmina held out her hands to Missa. Rabiah silently urged the girl to take them, to make just one move to let her mother know that something of what they'd never had as mother and daughter might be constructed between them now. She did not do so. Instead she said, "C'n I ring Justie?"

Yasmina lowered her hands but her expression remained open, willing, and loving. She said, "Justin will be relieved if you ring him. Ask him to come for you if you would like that."

Still, Missa looked as if she needed more permission. She glanced at her father. He nodded. She glanced at Rabiah, who said, "He's that anxious for your call, Missa."

"Shall I ask him to fetch Sati home, then, Gran?"

Yasmina was the one to reply. "Only if Sati wishes to come."

Missa left them, then. Rabiah waited till she heard her footsteps on the stairs and, after a moment, her bedroom door close. She herself said nothing to her son and his wife. She merely waited for what needed to be said, and she prayed that there was enough courage left in the family for the words to be given voice.

Timothy rose from the sofa. He said to her, "I expect one of them gave you a card when they spoke to you?"

"The woman did," Rabiah said. "The detective sergeant."

He nodded and held out his hand. "I'll ring her, then."

"When they asked for the photo, there was nothing I could—"

"That's down to me, Mum," Timothy said. "It's time I got myself sorted, wouldn't you say? Whatever step's meant to be taken now, I'm the one meant to be taking it."

WORCESTER
HEREFORDSHIRE

Once the Met police left Royal Shrewsbury Hospital, Trevor had rung Clover's mobile again and again with the same result. He'd also begun ringing Gaz Ruddock, but there was no joy to be had doing that either.

He'd kept all of this from Finn. After the London detectives had put in their appearance at the door to his son's room, Trevor had determined to remain with Finn until he could work out not only what was happening but also that the boy was safe in every way, one of which was safe from being interviewed. As the hours had passed, though, it became progressively more difficult for him to remain calm. Something was happening, or surely Clover would have rung him to reply to his many calls to her. That she hadn't done so thrust Trevor into a morass of terrifying suppositions. When his mobile finally rang late in the evening, he grabbed it up and headed for the doorway to the corridor. Finn was dozing, and he wanted nothing to awaken the boy.

His caller turned out to be the same London detective who'd come to the hospital in search of Clover. He asked Trevor's whereabouts first and then requested a meeting with him in Worcester. To Trevor's reply that he was still in Shrewsbury with Finn, the man said that their encounter needed to be in Worcester, at his home. Was there still an officer in the corridor outside Finnegan's door? the man enquired. To Trevor's affirmative reply, the detective then pointed out that Finn would be safe.

"I've not been able to reach Clover," Trevor told him.

That was, Inspector Lynley told him, the reason he wished to speak to him in Worcester. He himself was, along with his sergeant, at police headquarters in Hindlip. They'd just finished up a meeting with the chief constable. DCC Freeman had not been at headquarters, by the way. As things had developed, she'd gone from Shrewsbury to the Long Mynd.

"What the devil?" Trevor said. "Are you saying she went *gliding*?"

Lynley, however, wasn't saying anything other than to express his intention of speaking further to Trevor in Worcester. When could Mr. Freeman manage to get there? he asked politely.

So there was little choice if Trevor wanted more information.

The two London officers were waiting for him when he arrived. They were in a car that looked nothing at all like something any police officer ought to be driving. He might have remarked upon the vintage motor had not he at once clocked the expression on the officers' faces.

He turned his head away, trying to ward off what was to come. He led them to the front door and inside the house. He switched on lights in the entry. He did the same in the sitting room. He went to the cabinet in which they kept spirits. He opened it, stared at its contents, and wondered what he would imbibe that might obliterate the reality he was about to face.

They waited, the Met detectives. When he turned from the cabinet, they were both watching him with a gravity he would not be able to dispel with a drink, with questions, with a report about Finn's progress, with anything. So he said because he knew what was coming, "How?"

"Her glider crashed almost at once when it was launched," Lynley said.

"Someone did something to it?"

"She released it too soon from the launching cable," Havers said. "She'd seen me, Mr. Freeman. She understood why we were there."

"I'm very sorry," this from Lynley.

"Was she . . . ?"

"She lived briefly after the crash, but not long enough to speak. Would you like to sit down?"

"Finn. I must . . ." He was suddenly angry. "*This* is why I had to come home? You couldn't be bothered to come to Shrewsbury to tell me so I wouldn't have to leave my son alone? It was so sodding important that . . . Why? What are you saying about my wife?"

They seemed to be willing to give him a moment, and he took it. He needed to do so because the walls shimmered, and the spot where their family photos were hanging suddenly went to black in his vision.

One of the two officers took his arm. When he regained his sight, he saw it was Lynley, who urged him to sit.

The London detective began speaking then. Trevor had no choice but to listen. He tried to tell himself that everything had been unknown to him. But wasn't the truth that early on he'd known without wanting to ask directly?

They spared him nothing. When Lynley paused, the woman Havers continued. So by the end of the recitation, he knew what Gaz Ruddock had done to the girl inside Finn's house in December, what he'd managed to persuade Clover into believing about the crime, how this related to the unfortunate Ian Druitt and to vital evidence and to an orchestrated arrest and an orchestrated suicide and all of it done because Clover Freeman could not believe that her son might have been not only innocent but also ignorant of the crime that had occurred on a night when he and his mates were drunk.

When they laid out for him what he thought was every possible horror, they ended with what he did not expect. "We've searched the glider and the vehicle she took to the airfield," Lynley said. "We've had a team going through all the buildings up there as well. CC Wyatt gave us access to her office, and we've done a search there. This—the house here—is our last hope of finding what we've been looking for."

He hadn't been married to Clover for more than twenty years to miss the detective's intention. He said, "Why the *hell* would she keep evidence here? That doesn't make sense if she believed Finn . . ." But then he saw that, to Clover, it would have made perfect sense if she believed Finn had assaulted the girl.

"With your permission, we'd like to have a look round," Lynley said.

It took them more than three hours. Trevor wouldn't have thought it possible for a search of the premises to require that much time, but they were as meticulous as they were thorough. They found what they were looking for, at long last, in the attic. Clover had kept the girl's tights and underwear in the evidence bag into which they'd been placed by Ruddock. She'd buried them in a cardboard box, among Finn's baby clothes. The irony of her choice was not lost on Trevor.

He said dully, "We'd always hoped . . . ," but there was no point in completing the thought. So instead he said to the officers, "How can you use this? Now, I mean?"

Lynley seemed to understand the implication because his reply was, "The chain of evidence is destroyed, of course. Your wife and Ruddock both saw to that. But the DNA on here will, we believe, put a full stop to the matter, especially when it comes to your son."

Havers added with a gesture towards the bag, "Once he knows we have this—with his DNA and not Finn's on it—Ruddock'll have something of a job explaining things. Especially as the girl in question isn't one he ever had anything to do with before that night. She'd never even been drunk, so she'd never been carted off by him, so she'd never been one of the girls who let him into her knickers to avoid being taken home to her parents. Under other circumstances he could have used that to excuse the DNA, you see."

"Are you saying Ruddock didn't know the girl he assaulted?"

"Yes," Lynley said. "That's what we think."

Havers put in, "He was dead cheesed off at Ding Donaldson, see. He went back to the house later, saw a girl on the sitting-room sofa, and since it was so dark he either thought it was Ding and he meant to punish her for running off or he didn't care one way or the other who he did it to, as long as he did it to someone."

Trevor took this in. He knew he ought to be experiencing something at this point—anything, really—but all of it was simply too much. He could barely feel his limbs when he moved, let alone feel his emotions.

He said, "I don't know how I'll tell Finn. Am I meant to say that right to her death his mum intended to have some kind of power over him? Right to her death, she saw him as a rapist?"

Lynley seemed to consider the possibilities before he replied with, "You might tell him she was human, as we all are. You might say that she believed something false that she was told by the PCSO and from that mistaken judgement on her part, everything else came."

"Why would she believe Gaz Ruddock and not her own son?" Trevor asked. He directed the question to himself, really, and he went on to give himself the answer as well. "She was afraid to ask him directly, wasn't she? She could tell at that point he wasn't about to be the person she wanted him to be, and since she didn't know who he was in the first place . . . It was easy enough for Gaz Ruddock to tell her. Christ. *Christ.*" Trevor's voice broke.

"Will you be all right here by yourself, Mr. Freeman?" The woman, Havers, was the one to ask this.

He got himself together so that he could answer and then act. He said, "I won't be alone. I'm going back to the hospital to be with Finn."

IRONBRIDGE
SHROPSHIRE

Yasmina was grateful that her mother-in-law remained. Once Timothy had made the phone call to the Scotland Yard detectives, once he'd been told that a patrol car would be sent to fetch him, once that car had come and he'd been taken, Rabiah's iron self-control had deserted her. Ages of grief had poured out of the woman. Every *why* she had never voiced demanded a reply that Yasmina could not give her.

Sati and Justin had not arrived till after Timothy had been taken, so there was a small blessing in that as Sati did not have to watch her father being arrested. As it was, she came into the house tentatively enough, as if fearing the worst from every quarter, and Yasmina's heart grew sore when she saw the child's expression and her reflexive step to hide behind Justin.

As for Justin, he'd entered in a state that said he was more than ready to know exactly what was occurring in the Lomax family. He'd said, "It's time you lot made a few things clear," in a tone that declared he'd had enough of them all.

Yasmina couldn't blame him, but she said nothing, and at that point Rabiah was not present. Missa was, though, and she said, "It's down to me, Justie. Can we go for a walk?"

That left Yasmina with Sati, the two of them watching each other across a chasm that only one of them was meant to breach. Yasmina said to her, "I have failed you, Sati. But from this day, no more."

Sati watched her, not quite comprehending. Yasmina could see her confusion in her lovely eyes and how they moved in her face, directing her gaze towards avenues of escape. She—Yasmina—had bought and paid for this reaction. She said to her, "Sati, listen to me. I want to hand your life to you."

Sati drew in on her lower lip.

"I hit you . . ." Yasmina stopped herself. "No, that isn't what I did. I punched you in anger. It happened in an instant and I have to tell you that I meant to do it. In that moment I wanted to hurt you. I thought if I did that you would see . . . I don't even know now what I thought you would see. That I'm right? That you're wrong? Who knows any longer. But what I did? It was viciously wrong and I have no excuse. And I tell you now that I will never attempt to come up with one. When you are years older and you remind me what I did for *whatever* reason that you remind me? Know in this moment, Sati, that as long as I have my actual wits about me, I will never deny what I did nor will I ever say that it was excusable."

Yasmina knew that what she was saying was probably too much for any twelve-year-old girl to take in, especially a twelve-year-old girl who'd been through as much as Sati had been through in the last two years of her young life. But these things needed to be said if they were ever to make the start they needed to make to repair their lives.

Having said all that could be said, Yasmina waited. Good-hearted as she was, Sati did not leave her long in suspense.

She said, "Mummy!" and ran to her. Yasmina crushed the child to her and murmured, "Thank you."

When Missa returned, Yasmina was upstairs with Sati and Rabiah. They were lined up on the bed that Timothy would not be sleeping in for a very long time. They were doing absolutely nothing. Everything felt beyond their capacity.

Missa stood in the doorway for a moment, observing them from the light shed dimly from a table lamp near to the bed. It came to Yasmina that her daughter looked uncertain, so she said to her in a murmur, "You find us at the end of our resources."

Missa said anxiously, "Mummy, is Gran . . ."

Rabiah stirred. She'd had her arm over her eyes but at Missa's voice, she'd lowered it. "Gran," Rabiah announced, "has managed to survive worse than this." And then after a moment, "Well, all right. Perhaps not worse, but I intend to muddle onward. What about you?" She moved over on the bed and patted the spot she'd vacated.

There seemed to be a long bout of breath holding before Missa moved across the room and joined the rest of them. Rabiah took her hand and pressed it to her cheek. Then she took Sati's hand and did the same. Sati, after a quick look to be certain it was acceptable, took Yasmina's.

They simply sat and breathed. They were as one organism, really. At this moment, together they had the strength to be one person. Later, perhaps, they could be more.

It must have been ten minutes, Yasmina reckoned, before Missa spoke again. She said, "He wants to wait. He says he can see what it's all been about. He says he'd like things to go his way eventually, but they can't go his way now. He says he's meant to build his business and I'm meant to . . . whatever."

"What did you tell him?" Yasmina asked.

"I said I would—"

"No," Yasmina stopped her at once. "I don't mean what did you tell him in reply to what he said to you. I mean what did you tell him about what happened in December in Ludlow."

"The truth," she said.

Rabiah said, "He wants to wait because of that, does he?"

"No. He says he wants to wait because it's the right thing for both of us just now."

"Is that what you think?" Rabiah asked her.

"I don't much know what I think any longer, Gran."

"Well, that makes two of us," Rabiah told her.

"Three," Yasmina added.

And Sati made it four.

# 26 MAY

VICTORIA
LONDON

It had taken the entire day following Clover Freeman's suicide and Gary Ruddock's confession to complete everything, even with a division of labour. Havers took on the job of sharing relevant fragments of information with the various parties who required them, if only for their peace of mind. So she paid a call upon the vicar of St. Laurence Church to reassure him of Ian Druitt's innocence in all matters, and she arranged to meet Flora Bevans not at her home but at the site of an installation of an impressive array of newly planted urns to give her the relief of knowing she had not been housing a paedophile beneath her roof. She found Brutus Castle and Ding Donaldson at home in Temeside; she took herself out to Much Wenlock to put Sergeant Gerry Gunderson into the picture of Ruddock's guilt. In the meantime, Lynley journeyed to Birmingham, where he returned all of his son's possessions to Clive Druitt with the acknowledgement of that man's true assessment of his son's character, and from there he went to West Mercia Police Headquarters to meet with the chief constable and to put into his possession all the material he and Havers had been given to use during their investigation.

CC Wyatt was understandably shell-shocked. The nature of the political and professional disaster he had on his hands was not going to fade from public memory any time soon. The public relations nightmare was only just beginning, and the judicial nightmare was on the horizon, ready to slouch in the direction of Hindlip as soon as the appropriate forces could be gathered.

They had only a brief encounter with the Lomax family, and this was when Lynley informed Rabiah by mobile phone that her son Timothy had given his statement to the Shrewsbury team handling the events that had occurred in Temeside. She was gracious about everything, blaming no one, least of all the police, who were "only doing what had to be done, Inspector." To his question about how the family were coping, she replied, "Just."

On the following morning, then, they left Ludlow. Clive Druitt would come for his son's car, Lynley informed the hotel. That being arranged, he and Havers set off for London.

They went directly to Victoria Street. They had not been in the building for five minutes when the unwanted but nonetheless expected call came through from Judi MacIntosh. They were wanted in the office of the assistant commissioner.

"You're to go straight in," Judi MacIntosh told them when they arrived in the assistant commissioner's office. She added, "No worries," as they passed by her desk. "Evidently the Home Office is pleased."

Lynley couldn't see how that could be the case, considering what they were looking at was everything from a police cover-up to murder. But it turned out that Clive Druitt had wanted his son proved to be just who his father claimed him to be: a decent man of God. That this had been proved, that an arrest of his killer had been made, that Ian's name had been cleared in every respect, that a prosecution would follow: These things were what his father had sought. As to what the news media made of everything, as to how the Met, the Home Office, and the West Mercia police intended to handle what the news media made of everything . . . that was out of his hands, he'd told his MP.

"The first head to roll will be Wyatt's," Hillier told them. "He made Freeman his DCC. He should have known, apparently, where that would lead. You did well, the two of you. You've Quentin Walker's thanks. I'm meant to pass them on."

That, evidently, was what they'd been summoned to hear, after which they were dismissed. Or at least, Lynley was dismissed. As he and Havers got to their feet to depart the AC's office, Hillier told Havers to remain where she was.

She looked alarmed and cast a glance of appeal in Lynley's

direction. But there was a limit to what he could do and being told to leave Hillier's office defined it.

He headed for the door, hearing only "We need to have a different sort of conversation, Sergeant," from Hillier as he opened it.

Lynley left them together. He didn't like the direction their conversation might take. Still, there was nothing for it but to return to Victoria Block and there to wait for developments.

He got only as far as the DCS's office when he arrived there, though. Dorothea Harriman called out, "You're wanted, Detective Inspector Lynley," before he had the chance to pass by. She added, "Judi-with-an-i just rang. She wanted Herself to have a heads-up that you'd been to see Himself." She lowered her voice to just above a whisper in order to say, "Did he really ask Detective Sergeant Havers to stay at the end of your meeting?"

"He was telling her he wanted to have a different sort of conversation when I left them," Lynley replied.

"*That* can't be good," Dorothea said. "Is that all you heard?"

"Lacking your talent . . . Alas," Lynley noted. "Shall I go in?" He indicated Isabelle Ardery's office.

"Oh do, do," Dorothea said. "Word to the wise, though? She's not exactly chuffed you spoke with Hillier before seeing her."

VICTORIA
LONDON

Isabelle had expected some form of chain of command would be followed. Lynley and Havers would report to her, she would report to Hillier, and Hillier would report to Clive Druitt's MP. What she had not expected was the short-circuiting that had occurred.

That this had happened was irritating. But that Barbara Havers had been asked to remain with Hillier once Lynley had been dismissed by the assistant commissioner was completely unnerving.

"Guv?" Lynley was courtesy itself, as usual.

"Why have you reported to Hillier without speaking to me first?"

She heard the level of annoyance in her demand and wished she'd schooled it. Too late now, she reckoned.

Lynley said in that maddeningly urbane way of his, "We'd had less than five minutes in the building before we were called to his office, guv."

"And, as I understand it, the detective sergeant is still there."

"Hillier asked her to remain."

"And his reaction to how everything's been handled?"

"No one's breaking out the champagne. A lawsuit filed by Clive Druitt's solicitors has been averted, but that's the extent of it. The amount of bollocksing up that's gone on since March has given journalists rather more political fodder than anyone's happy with."

"You're referring to me, I expect."

"I hadn't intended to. There's enough culpability to spread round. The chief constable—Patrick Wyatt—will have it worst, I daresay. Everything went on in his jurisdiction, so—"

Isabelle cut in with, "He's talking to her about my drinking, isn't he. We both know why he asked her to remain. He rang me one night when I wasn't in proper form to speak with him. I thought it was Bob or I wouldn't have answered."

Lynley said nothing in reply to this. He did move to the door of her office and closed it quietly, however, so Isabelle knew something was coming. She simply couldn't deal with more preaching from him, however. Nor could she deal with anyone—let alone Thomas Lynley—pointing out that if anyone was being hoisted on a petard, she was that person and the petard was hers.

She said, "I'm finished, then. That's it, as you warned me, Tommy. As Bob warned me time and again. As I've tried and failed, actually, to warn myself."

Lynley did that gentlemanly bit of examining his shoes to allow her to pull herself together, which she found rather maddening in that she *was* together, of a single piece, of a single mind, fully aware, and all the rest. He said, "May I sit?"

She said, "This doesn't need to be an extended conversation. I wanted to verify that Barbara Havers remained behind at Hillier's request. I've done that. We both know what it means. There's nothing more to be said."

"Isabelle, if you'll listen to me . . . ? You've failed from the first to—"

"I *know*. All right? There is *no* need for you to lord it over me, if you'll forgive the outrageous pun. I've driven myself to this destination, and that's that. I knew it the instant I opened the door to Dee Harriman's face and her bloody soup and sandwiches. She saw it all and I've no doubt she returned with the tale and passed it round."

"Dee Harriman," Lynley said, "is the embodiment of loyalty to this department, Isabelle, and she's—"

"She's governed by self-interest as the rest of us are."

"That's entirely untrue. She's completely loyal. And to be frank, she's—"

"Oh please. Stop trying to protect her."

"—not the only one. If you've not worked out by now that—"

"*Stop* bloody preaching at me!"

"Stop bloody interrupting me."

They were face-to-face and too close for her liking, so Isabelle strode to her desk. She sat. She gestured rudely for him to do likewise. She said, "May I say that you're as insufferable as you've been from the first. I *know* I've made a cock-up of my life, my career, my future, my relationship with my boys. Do you really think I need you to spell that out to me? I *don't* need that. *Do* you understand?"

"I do," he said, "but that doesn't prevent me from wanting you to see that—"

"When I said stop preaching, I meant stop preaching!"

"As I meant stop interrupting."

His voice had grown louder. He was a man who so rarely lost his temper that it was almost a pleasure to push him in that direction. But her hands had now begun to shake. She had other concerns that were meant to be dealt with.

He said, drawing in what Isabelle reckoned was a steadying breath, "What I've been attempting to say to you is that you've failed from the first to understand anything about Barbara Havers. Have that as you will because I've given up attempting to make it clear to you that

Barbara's a valuable member of the department. But I will have you know one thing, Isabelle—"

"I'll have you bloody *stop* calling me—"

"Isabelle," he said again and with far more emphasis than was strictly necessary. "The very last identity that Barbara Havers would take on is that of a common grass. That's neither who she is nor who she's ever been. As to you and your drinking? All of that is in your hands and no one else's. I suggest you leave Dee and Barbara out of whatever nonsense you've got running round inside your head." He rose and headed for the door.

She said, "I did *not* give you leave—" but he waved her off. He left her. The door gaped open in his wake.

Her hands were worse. She clenched them on the top of her desk. She clenched her jaw as well. She needed, she needed . . . After their conversation she bloody needed.

She swung her chair round and removed herself from the immediate vicinity of her desk, from the proximity to what she kept stowed in its bottom right drawer. She walked to the window. Blue sky rapidly clouding over, birds, the pavement, the street. She would *not*, she told herself, because she was the mistress of her life as she always had been, only now it would be entirely different, wouldn't it? She was finished with more than one element of her existence, wasn't she. She would, she told herself. And she bloody well could. All this time it had merely been a function of her brain. Her brain had been where the first falsehoods had come from, indicating to her that she needed something to help her relax, to help her sleep, to remove difficulties, to lighten the load. It was all about what she'd taught herself to believe that she needed when she didn't need it at all and never had done.

Only. It had gone beyond that now. She saw that in her shaking hands, which would not stop shaking till the vodka entered her system. She wasn't at all shaking because of a fiction she'd learned to believe, whether that fiction dealt with relaxing, sleeping, removing difficulties, or anything else. She was at this point shaking because the physical need had finally taken over. What had been desire was now necessity.

She couldn't bear it.

She would have to.

She approached her desk.

VICTORIA STREET
LONDON

Barbara didn't know what to make of it when Hillier began their conversation with a comment upon the improvement in her appearance. She would have liked to think that, in blatant disregard of the possibility of being accused of sexual harassment, he was taking note of her svelte body, courtesy of more tap dancing than she'd ever wanted to do in her life. Problem was that she wore nothing svelte-inducing at the moment if, indeed, one could induce svelte at all. Instead she wore baggy trousers, a blouse in need of professional help in the ironing department, and brogues. Since these were, however so humble, an improvement over her past garments, she thanked Hillier carefully. She waited for more. It was short in coming.

"I understand your overall comportment has undergone something of a transformation as well," Hillier went on.

Barbara tried to look earnest. She hoped for the best. She did wish Lynley were there, however. He was the only person she knew whose manners and breeding *might* run interference for her if it came down to Hillier's requesting an explanation for anything untoward she might have done.

"I'm additionally pleased that your second involvement in Ludlow produced a better result than your first," he said. "What do you think went wrong on that initial visit?"

Barbara's skin made an *aha!* jump. She said, after a moment to think about the various directions she could take and what each might cost her, "The situation up there was dead complicated, sir. Elements of the investigation that looked absolutely one way turned out to be absolutely the other." She hoped that his would suffice.

It didn't. "Can you be more specific? Since you were the only officer attending both Met investigations . . ."

"Oh. That. Well, the DCS and I didn't always see eye to eye, which happens, 'course. And it could be that I wasn't . . . Or that I didn't . . ."

His hawklike eyes didn't move from her face. He said, "Do spit it out, Sergeant Havers."

"It's only that I wanted to do everything right, sir. I mean, I wanted to be certain I coloured inside the lines, if you know what I mean. That probably kept me quieter 'n usual."

"What about the DCS?"

"Sir?"

"Colouring inside the lines? Outside the lines? What about DCS Ardery?"

Barbara didn't like the thinness of this ice at all. She said, "I'm not sure what you mean, sir. Far as I know and far as I've ever seen, the DCS does things straight by the book."

"Does she indeed?"

"Yes, sir. Absolutely. No doubt." Barbara swallowed. Perhaps three affirmations were two too many?

Hillier watched her steadily. It was like a game of stare-down. He said, "I know there's no love lost between you and Detective Chief Inspector Ardery, Sergeant Havers. And I don't want that to be an issue here."

"Oh, it's not, sir. I don't know what you might've heard and I'm not asking but aside from . . . well . . . an audio that the PCSO in Ludlow sent me after the DCS had already told me the transcript was good enough and then in my report—"

"That's not under discussion."

"Sir?"

Hillier leaned across the desk, a move that Barbara found distinctly unnerving. It was an indication that this was going to be a just-us-boys moment between them and what she knew beyond anything in her universe was that she and Hillier were not just-us anything. He said, "I'm going to ask you something directly, and I want you to answer me directly. Is that clear?"

Christ, was it ever. Barbara nodded.

"Good. It's my belief that the DCS was drinking to excess in Ludlow. It's my belief that she was altogether drunk on occasion.

Considering everything that's gone on since her return from Shropshire, I want you to confirm her Ludlow behaviour before I decide what's to be done."

Barbara hadn't expected to be presented with such a moment of praise God and sing hallelujah. The opportunity before her would do more than merely benefit herself. It would benefit the entire department. She'd be able to drink and dine on it for years. But . . .

She frowned. She nodded. She hoped her expression telegraphed very deep thinking. And then she said, "As far as I know, the DCS didn't drink at all, sir."

Hillier favoured her another hawklike examination before he said, "Are you certain of that?"

She knew his question had more than one meaning, but she also knew there was only one answer. "As I ever could be," she said.

VICTORIA STREET
LONDON

Back at her desk, Barbara had little enough time before her phone rang. She was loath to answer it, but had no choice. It turned out to be Dorothea Harriman placing the call. As Barbara heard Dee's voice, she realised she should have expected to hear from her. Tonight was, after all, their regular tap-dancing lesson and Dee would want to lay their plans.

So after their hellos, Barbara sought to head her elsewhere. "I'm begging off tonight, Dee. I need a rest."

"Tonight?" was Dee's unexpected reply. "Oh! You mean Southall. No matter. I'll catch you up tomorrow. In fact, I'll come to you. If we move your kitchen table outside, we'll have room enough. Umaymah's off the team, by the way. She's dropped the class entirely. Pregnant. There you have it. I've already adjusted the choreography."

"Dee—"

"Anyway, that's not why I'm ringing. You're wanted."

"I've just *been* in Tower Block."

"It's the DCS asking for you." And in a lower voice, "Word to the wise. You might want to come at once. She looks feather-ruffled and Detective Inspector Lynley just had one of those closed-door meetings with her that never go well."

So Barbara went as ordered. She'd not been alone with Isabelle Ardery since just after Ludlow and she would have preferred not to be alone with her now. But she saw no recourse.

Ardery was seated when Barbara walked into her office. Her only instructions were to close the door and to sit, neither of which sounded like particularly happy activities. But Barbara did as requested and found herself across an expanse of Ardery's desk. What she noted first was that it was beyond its normal orderly condition. It looked almost polished. What she noted second was Ardery's stillness. She sat with her hands clasped, unsmiling as Barbara joined her.

"DI Lynley tells me that you had a good result in Shropshire," she said. "Everything sewn up nicely, packaged, and delivered to Mr. Druitt."

Barbara sensed the DCS's hostility. She wasn't at all sure how to go at this, so she said, "Once we understood about the stole, guv . . . ? Its colour and all the rest . . . ? I mean, once you rang the inspector to tell him—"

"Don't patronise me, Sergeant. I fully understand how much of an impediment I was to the investigation. I've been told you've spoken to the assistant commissioner privately, by the way."

Barbara said quickly, "Right. I did, guv. He wanted me to stay behind in order to ask me—"

"Stop right there. At *once.*"

Barbara gulped at Ardery's tone. Her sweat glands began working overtime.

Ardery opened one of the side drawers in her desk. From it, she took out what Barbara recognised immediately: the folder containing her transfer paperwork.

Barbara said, "But guv, guv. *Please,* can I just say—"

"Did I not tell you to stop?" Ardery snapped. She opened the folder. She pushed the paperwork across the desk.

"But I . . . I did every single . . . I don't . . . Please."

"Take it," Ardery said.

"But—"

"*Take* it. I'm not asking you to sign the forms, Sergeant Havers. I'm telling you to take the forms. I'm giving them to you. Do you understand me? Do with them what you will."

"What? Do you mean . . . ?"

"I mean take them."

Barbara looked at paperwork. She looked at Ardery. "I don't . . . Guv, don't you want to know what Hillier wanted to—"

"I do not."

"But if I take the paperwork, d'you mean then I can . . . what?"

"Barbara. I meant what I said. I always mean what I say. Take the paperwork and do what you will with it."

Barbara reached for it. She kept her movements slow. It seemed to her that at any moment Ardery would fall over laughing at how she'd duped the ignoramus sitting opposite her. But that didn't happen. Barbara eased the documents onto her lap. She waited for more. There was nothing. She got to her feet.

She said, "Ta, guv." And when Ardery nodded, she headed for the door. But there she paused and said, "Can I ask . . . Did the inspector—"

"This has nothing to do with Inspector Lynley," Ardery said. "This—just now—is between the two of us alone."

VICTORIA STREET
LONDON

When the call from the assistant commissioner came, Isabelle was ready for it. She'd made the necessary arrangements, and she'd spoken to Bob. Her former husband had given her an informal reassurance and a formal blessing, both of which she was going to have to depend upon since there was nothing put into writing. Having finished up what needed to be finished up, then, what had remained was waiting for the phone to ring with Judi MacIntosh on the line, telling her that Hillier was ready to see her.

She gathered her belongings, chagrined by the paucity of them. They consisted of a photo of the twins, a photo of herself with the twins, a coffee cup, and ten airline bottles of vodka. Everything fit easily into her briefcase, which in other circumstances would have held reports on activities from the various investigators under her command. She took up her shoulder bag as well, and headed for the doorway. There she paused for a final look.

Odd, she thought. It was only a room in a building, wasn't it? She'd given it—and rooms exactly like it—too much significance over too many years.

She switched off the overhead lights, and she closed the door. She was lucky in that the hour was late and consequently there was no one nearby to see her. She could do without questions at the moment.

In Tower Block she went to Hillier's office, where the door stood open in anticipation of her arrival. Judi MacIntosh had left for the day, and Isabelle could see Hillier sitting at his desk, waiting for her. She was struck by the similarity: between his position behind the desk and what had been her position behind the desk when she had her brief meeting with Sergeant Havers. Like her, Hillier sat with hands folded. Unlike her, he played a pencil between his fingers.

When she entered, he told her to sit. She told him that she preferred to stand. He nodded. He did not rise to join her.

She said to him, "I wish I could tell you that meetings alone would be enough, sir. If I believed that, I would go to them daily. Twice daily if necessary. I've never been to one—although I've thought about it now and again—but what I know from where I am just now and what it's done to me physically, I'm going to need a supervised withdrawal. I mean a medically supervised withdrawal. I've found a programme. They say six weeks. They can take me at once."

"Where?" he asked her.

"Isle of Wight. It's a clinic and a recovery centre. First is detox and then . . . well, then there's recovery. They expect detox will take a week."

"And recovery?"

"A lifetime. What I mean is that no one actually recovers. One just learns the skills to cope."

"With . . . ?"

"The need first and what drives the need second. So after

detox—which deals with the physical part of it—there're five weeks of meetings and analyses and whatnot. After that, then, there are daily meetings. Morning, afternoon, night. It doesn't matter. They're everywhere in London and one can go to as many as one wishes."

Hillier nodded. He set the pencil to one side, but he kept his fingers on it and with one hand he rolled it against the top of his desk.

She said, "I'd like to swear to you that I can do this, sir. I'd like to tell you there will never be another occurrence. But the truth is, I don't know that."

"And is that meant to set my mind at rest?"

"It's only to tell you what I understand just at this moment." She did sit, then. She put her briefcase on the floor, but she kept her shoulder bag on her lap. "I've told myself before now that I can stop. I've done it, too. A month here, two months there, just to prove to myself that it doesn't own me. But the reality is that it's owned me for years."

He nodded again. She hadn't expected praise from the man, especially as she wasn't owed any. But she wanted *something* from him, and wasn't it a howling good joke that what she wanted from David Hillier was a form of humanity that she herself had been incapable of showing anyone for more years than she wanted to think about. It would be a humanity that demonstrated understanding or compassion or forgiveness or anything save the silence that now stretched between them.

She said, "I'm hoping for a leave of absence, sir. If I knew my job was waiting for me at the end of all this . . . It's that I'd have a light at the end of the tunnel. That wouldn't make it easier. Nothing about this is going to be easy. But it would give me . . . perhaps . . . a goal."

He rose. He walked to his bank of windows. June was coming fast upon them with its notoriously unpredictable weather, and the rain had begun to fall. Just now it speckled the windows. Another few minutes and it would streak them.

Without turning, Hillier said, "I wouldn't have given you the position of DCS had Lynley been willing to take it on. You know that, don't you?"

"I do, sir."

"I also wouldn't have given you the position had I not believed you can do the job. I still believe that, by the way. Not as you are now, but as you might be."

Isabelle said nothing. She was gratified to hear what he'd said, but he hadn't said it all, and so she waited.

He turned from the window and took his time about observing her, about returning to his desk, about sitting and folding his hands again.

"Granted," he finally said. "Conquer your demons first, and then you and I will talk about what comes next for you."

"Thank you, sir."

"When do you leave?"

"Now."

"Then God's speed."

She offered him the only kind of smile she could manage, which was faltering at best. She picked up her briefcase, bid him farewell, and walked to the doorway, where his words stopped her.

"Sergeant Havers said nothing, by the way. You ought to know that. I did ask her, but she wouldn't do it. Throw you to the wolves, I mean. She didn't even venture near it."

"Tommy said she wouldn't," she replied. And then because it was the truth and she owed the truth to everyone, "She's a good officer, sir. Bloody infuriating most of the time, admittedly, but very good all the same."

Hillier sighed. "Would that political life were not so difficult, eh?"

"Sir?"

"How I wish she were completely inept, but that will never be the case. Nor will it be the case for Lynley, and even on his best days he's only marginally less infuriating than Havers."

She smiled then, and she found it easy. As did she find her final words to Hillier: "I'd never disagree with that, sir, but it has to be said: They get the job done."

# 6 JULY

SOUTHALL
LONDON

"You aren't actually expecting Barbara to forgive you for this, are you?" Daidre asked him. "I know very well she told you and everyone else that this event was not to be attended by anyone who knows her."

"Barbara Havers will thank me in the long run. In the short term, she'll be furious, of course. But given time, all that will change."

"You're mad," Daidre noted.

"The wind, hawks, handsaws, and all the rest," was his reply. He cast a look at her in the passenger seat of the Healey Elliott. "I'm quite glad you're back in London, Daidre."

She hadn't been gone as long this time round, but during the last six weeks she'd been in and out of town, down to Cornwall and back again in a series of journeys that had eaten up virtually all of her free time. He'd protested when she would hear nothing of his accompanying her. This was her family, not his, she explained. So this was her problem as well.

Her birth mother had died, the miracle cure the woman hoped for denied her as it was denied so many others in her condition. The death had been a long one, made excruciating not only by her beliefs but also by the conditions in which she, her husband, and their two other adult children lived. Towards the end, she had still refused to be taken to hospital or, for that matter, to hospice. God would serve the purpose of handing her the cure she was intent upon.

Once the poor woman had passed, the issue had become Daidre's siblings and her father and the question of what to do with them, for them, and about them. Here, too, Daidre declined Lynley's assistance in any form it might take. To his protest of "What are we to each other then, you and I?" she replied, "What I must do bears no relationship to you and me, to us, to the whatever-it-is we share. As I don't intrude upon your family, Tommy, I ask you not to intrude upon mine."

But of course, he *wanted* her to intrude upon his family. Indeed, he'd been quite forthright in the matter of the two of them showing their faces at Howenstow so that she might be introduced to his brother, sister, mother, and niece. Daidre had dodged that bullet for quite long enough.

He'd assumed that at some point she would actually *want* to come to his family's home because she had lost her own small cottage in Polcare Cove once she made the decision that Goron and Gwynder Udy—the adult twins who were her siblings—would leave the caravan that their father refused to abandon, believing against years of evidence to the contrary that he *could* achieve riches through the expedient of tin streaming. They would take up permanent residence in their elder sister's isolated retreat, a small cottage that had been Daidre's off-duty refuge during her employment at Bristol's zoo. As he knew, the cottage was large enough, she'd told Lynley. A bedroom for each of the twins and they could share the bathroom.

To Lynley's, "But what about you, Daidre . . . ? I know what the cottage means to you," she had replied with, "I can sleep on the sofa when I want to go down."

"That won't do for a peaceful retreat."

"Perhaps not. We'll see. But I can't leave them in that wretched caravan. And this is the only solution I've been able to come up with. It's not likely they'd want to come to town."

"But do they actually want to move from the caravan?"

"They're frightened, of course. What else would they be just now? There they've been in that horrible place since they were eighteen years old after a placement even worse than living with our parents. They deserve better. The cottage offers them that. I'm happy to provide it."

"I hate to see you—"

"Tommy, our lives—yours and mine—have been too different for you ever to be able to understand."

"That's not altogether fair."

"Isn't it? Consider being taken from your parents. Consider ending up in Falmouth with a wonderful home and wonderful family and privileges you never expected to have. Consider discovering that what you were given is exactly what your siblings were *not* given in the homes where they were sent. And then consider how you would feel upon learning that."

"I understand."

"How can you? You haven't lived it so you can't know it. They—Goron and Gwynder—were robbed of every possibility in life, and I want that to be over for them. Call it guilt or whatever you'd like but I won't leave them in a situation that means the rest of their lives will be as horrible as the first part of their lives has been."

He hated how her words affected him, with their intimation of impossibility. This was a discussion between them that could go round and round for hours. He knew it was a moment when it was best to let the subject die. But although he was adept doing that much, he was without a single talent when it came to burying the corpse.

Eventually, he told himself that it could all be a good thing since, despite sleeping on the floor of her London flat for months on end while she renovated it, it wasn't likely that Daidre would be happy sleeping on the sofa in her own cottage when she went to Cornwall for a break from London. This meant, at the end of the day, that there was every chance she would at last consent to a Cornish retreat somewhat larger than the one she was used to: his family home near Lamorna Cove.

Havers would, of course, say, "I wouldn't wager any money on that, Inspector," but then that was Havers in a nutshell. No one would ever accuse the woman of oversanguinity.

As if reading his mind regarding Havers, Daidre said, "This could all work out very badly, you know."

He recognised her change of subject and lied to her blithely. "It could. I do know that." But he didn't see how that was truly possible.

He was certain that his plan would have a brilliant conclusion that Havers would thank him for in the end.

"I'm glad to hear that. But really, Tommy. Did *everyone* have to be in on this?"

"It seemed less awkward that way," he told her. "Beyond that, we do rather need Winston as a visual distraction, don't we?"

"But his parents as well?"

"That was something I could not have stopped had I tried. Winston keeps no secrets from his parents and, evidently, Barbara Havers in tap shoes promised to be as entertaining as was Barbara Havers taking a cooking lesson from Alice Nkata."

"And the others?"

"Others? Do you mean Denton?"

"Stop acting innocent. I mean Denton, Simon, Deborah, Philip Hale and his wife . . . Who else, Tommy?"

"I believe Dorothea's family are going, but you can't hold me responsible for that."

"You're quite impossible," was her conclusion. "I'd no idea you had such a naughty streak in you."

The dance recital was to be not far from where the lessons themselves were given. A community centre had provided its hall for the event. Havers, naturally, had been mute on the subject. Dorothea, on the other hand, was happy to direct him to the World Wide Web, where he gleaned every scrap of information she had regarding place, time, and number of tap routines they could expect to delight them.

And delighted they no doubt would be, he thought. No one was as ready as he to watch Barbara and Dorothea hoof their way into history.

SOUTHALL
LONDON

Barbara was beside herself. Not only had their bit been relegated to what was euphemistically being called Act II, it had also been placed as the penultimate performance of the event. This meant that her plan to escape the community centre within an hour of *arriving* at the community centre was completely scotched. What was worse, she'd spied Winston Nkata in the crowd when she'd peeked from backstage. It was difficult to miss him as he was six foot five and neither of his parents—both of whom were *also* apparently going to be witnesses to her humiliation—was much shorter.

That Winston had shown up was bad enough. No. That Winston had shown up was *maddening* enough. But then Barbara saw Simon St. James and his wife, Deborah—longtime friends of Lynley—and . . . was that Charlie Denton taking a seat near the aisle at the side of . . . that wasn't Deborah's *father*, was it, half hidden by three women wearing burkhas? At the sight of them, Barbara went from irritation with Lynley to jealousy of the three black-clad women. A large bedsheet of *any* colour on her own body wouldn't have gone down half bad. Anything rather than having to be seen in the costumes Dorothea had designed.

She had wanted Roaring Twenties at first. To hear her tell it, she'd had her heart *set* on the Roaring Twenties, and she declared herself devastated when she'd been told that Cole Porter's music was not part of that period of time. "Think thirties," Kaz had informed her. "Art Deco and all the rest."

So Dorothea had moved from flapper dresses to sailor suits. Barbara couldn't see this as much of an improvement, but at least she wouldn't have to show her legs.

They'd practised and practised since Barbara's return from Shropshire. Dorothea had declared that doing the steps properly was all about muscle memory, and the way to achieve muscles with memory was to force those muscles into repeating the same action until they automatically reacted to the music as they'd been taught to. "It's exactly like riding a bicycle," Dorothea said.

"Another activity I never intend to perform in front of an audience," had been Barbara's reply. But now, here she was. Having endured Act I, the interval, and now practically all of Act II, the time was nigh.

The next hapless group of dancers were about to take to the stage. Barbara and Dorothea were to follow. They stood ready: in their sailor suits, their sailor hats, with walking sticks in their hands. Barbara had tried to talk Dee out of the walking sticks as they didn't seem sailorly to her. What sailor went shipboard with a walking stick anyway? But they were an important part of the "overall effect, don't you see?" according to Dorothea. Barbara didn't see, but what was the point of fighting this any longer?

At least, she told herself, she wasn't a part of the group of eight assembling—fully if oddly costumed—on the stage in what looked vaguely like a deflating life raft but was supposed to be an enormous bowl. Someone, potentially more clueless than talented, had come up with the idea of fruit coming to life to the tune of "Hooray for Hollywood." Barbara would have felt sorry for the pineapple had she only possessed the emotional reserves required to feel sorry for someone other than herself.

When the audience cheered enthusiastically at the conclusion of the fruit bowl number—and this despite the fact that the melon and the banana crashed into each other and fell to the floor midway through—Dorothea was fast upon her. She clapped her hands, beamed, and cried, "This is it! It's what we've been working towards!" which made Barbara want to tell her that she herself had been working towards breaking an ankle with only limited success. She'd managed to come up with an ingrown toenail, but that was it. "We're going to be brilliant!" Dorothea exclaimed.

"Did you *tell* Winston where this was happening?" Barbara demanded.

Dorothea slapped her hand against her chest, saying, "*What*? Is Detective Sergeant Nkata here? Why would I tell him or anyone—"

"To ensure applause, I reckon."

"Detective Sergeant Havers, we had, have, and will have *no* need of bringing our own supporters to this event. We're going to be a sensation."

"I'm taking note that you didn't answer the question."

"What question?"

"The one asking if you told Winston where this stellar event was taking place."

Dorothea had bent to retie her tap shoes. She rose to say, "He probably learned from the detective inspector."

"*What?*"

Dorothea clapped her hand over her mouth. She went on with, "How could I *not* at least give Detective Inspector Lynley a hint when he asked? Especially when he said he meant to bring along a surprise for you. Don't you like surprises?"

"A surprise in the persons of Winston Nkata, his parents, and, I wager, everyone DI Lynley knows is not something I've been burning for. You're lucky I don't take off these shoes and throw them at you, Dee."

"But I *didn't* tell him. I mentioned the website, but that's all. I swear it. I told him that he'd have to do everything else on his own."

"Oh, he's managed that, all right," Barbara said.

"You're being very silly," Dorothea said. And then, "Ah. There's our cue! Time to Cincinnati."

Which was what they did, with Barbara asking herself how bad could it be to have her colleagues watch her make a fool of herself. They'd already seen her do so in other situations. What was one more?

A cheer went up as she and Dorothea Cincinnatied their way onto the stage to Cole Porter. That their costumes had nothing whatsoever to do with the lyrics appeared to make no difference to anyone. Someone started a chant of "Bar'bra, Bar'*bra*!" and while she wasn't about to embrace this as a sign of approbation, at least she was confident that what her associates knew about tap dancing could fill a teaspoon. If she made errors, they would be clueless. All she had to do was remain upright and act as if everything she did was part of the show.

It all went as it went: not entirely well, not entirely disastrous. She managed to remember the order of the opening bit, only once confusing a riffle with a scuffle. Smiling through it all was a challenge since doing that while also saying "riff, jump, shim sham, cramp roll" was more than she could consistently manage. So instead of beaming at the audience as Dorothea was managing to do, she accomplished a glance or three in that general direction as they went along.

But then the glue of her determination gave way. Her steps faltered. Her steps failed. She saw who was sitting next to Charlie Denton, and it was *not* the father of Deborah St. James.

She Cincinnatied directly off the stage.

SOUTHALL
LONDON

There were no dressing rooms. She'd had to wear the bloody sailor suit to the event. Only the pieces of fruit had not come already in costume, since they could don their various bits of gear directly over their street clothing. As for the rest of them, there would be no way that they could leave the premises incognito.

So she had to get away. She had to do it quickly. She didn't stop to wonder at the *why* of this. She was operating on rote fight or flight, and she was choosing flight.

Once backstage, she elbowed her way through a Fred-and-Ginger and a group of children wearing miniature top hats and tails. She heard Kaz behind her saying, "What *is* it?" but she didn't pause. He could think it was delayed stage fright coming at her at a gallop or a planned revenge against Dorothea for getting her involved in this insanity in the first place. He could think she'd twisted an ankle, been struck by food poisoning, or been hit with a visitation of the plague. It didn't matter. Nor did it matter that Dorothea was left on the stage to complete the number and to pretend it was all part of the show that her partner had executed a hasty removal of herself. Of course when it came to the end and Barbara Havers did not show up to receive her share of the applause, it would look strange. But she didn't care how it looked. She merely cared about absenting herself at once.

The worst was . . . She didn't know why she was doing so. The worst was . . . She didn't know what it meant that an Italian detective called Salvatore Lo Bianco was actually in the audience. He had to have been brought there by DI Lynley, and the absolutely bloody worst of this was . . . She did not understand why Lynley would seek to humiliate her in such a fashion.

She heard him call her name as she approached her Mini. He was no fool, Lynley. He might not have known a thing about tapping, but he knew a great deal about reading people. So he would have read her expression, followed by Dorothea's expression, and he would have put those pieces together with the kind of speed for which he was known.

She whirled on him. "Why *did* you?" she shouted. "Did you think I'd be chuffed? Amused? Thrilled to bits? I asked you not to come. I told you not to come. And not only did you decide to come anyway, you also decided to invite Salvatore, didn't you. And the rest of them as well: Simon, Deborah, Charlie . . . whoever else. *Winston.* Yes. Winston and his mum and his dad. What about my neighbours? Did you try them as well?"

He raised his hands in a defensive gesture, so she knew she'd got through to him at last. He said, "Barbara. Stop. Listen."

"I won't," she cried. "I bloody well won't. D'you think you know what's best for me? Like everyone else? Well, you *don't*, Inspector. You've just made me into a bloody joke in front of my colleagues, in front of friends, in front of . . ." She couldn't say the rest. She found herself so far beyond anger that she didn't even know the name for what she was feeling.

"I didn't invite Salvatore," Lynley said. And then, after a moment of glancing back at the building where the dancing continued, "No. That's not entirely true. I did invite him, but not to travel all the way here from Italy. He was coming here anyway. He's about to begin an English course."

"An *English* course? What's he want with a bloody English course?"

"I've no idea. You might want to ask him. I invited him to stay with me and once it was clear that he'd be here on this precise day—"

"You thought it was a perfect time to make me a laughingstock. That's why you brought him and everyone else."

"I can't even *begin* to understand how you managed to arrive at that conclusion. Why in God's name would I ever want to make you a laughingstock?"

"Because that's what I *am*," she cried, with a sudden knowledge of a truth she'd lived with and avoided for years. "Because that's what I'll always be."

"You can't possibly mean that."

"Just look at me. Think about what it's like to be who I am and where I've come from and how it feels to know that I have no chance *ever* . . . to ever . . . to . . ." She forced herself to stop because she knew she would begin to weep if she didn't, and there was simply no way on earth, in heaven, or in hell that she intended to begin weeping in the car park of a Southall community centre in front of Thomas Lynley while dressed in a sailor costume.

"You come with me at once," Lynley said. His voice had altered, not to the Voice, but to something that had an edge of roughness to it. When she didn't move, he said, "I said come with me. I'm giving you an order."

"And if I bloody well decide to refuse?" she said with a sneer.

"I wouldn't take that option if I were you."

That said, he turned. He did not look back to see if she was following him. She gave thought to disobeying his order, but there had been a flinty quality to his voice that suggested she might not want to do that. So she trudged in his wake.

By the time they got back inside, the curtain calls had begun. One by one, the dancing acts took the stage to applause and cheers from their families, friends, and supporters. Barbara had a feeling about what was coming, so she was not surprised when Lynley said to her, "When Dorothea comes out on the stage, you *will* join her, and you won't be doing it for yourself. You will be doing it for her because she's fond of you. As are we all, by the way, but I can see now is not the moment to argue that point with you."

"I can't go—"

"You damn well can and you damn well will," Lynley said. "Use the centre aisle to do it, and if you don't make the entire thing look intentional, you *will* be answering to me. Is that quite clear, Sergeant?"

She was stupefied. She wanted to say, How bloody dare you act in the right when you bloody well know you are in the wrong. She wanted to say, Don't you bloody throw your lordshipness at *me*. She wanted to say, You don't know me, you don't know anything, you don't know what's inside me and you've never known.

Only . . . that wasn't the reality, was it. That had never been the reality. Thomas Lynley knew more than anyone ever gave him credit for, and what he knew better than anything else was the nature of her struggle, and she *knew* he knew this for the simple reason that he never mentioned it, ever, even now. He spared her that. He had always done so.

Dorothea emerged from the wings, then. The crowd applauded. She smiled prettily but it had to be said, she looked tentative about it, which wasn't like Dorothea at all.

Lynley said, "Go," and Barbara understood that she could not hesitate.

She charged up the aisle. She leapt onto the stage with such momentum that she lost her balance. She fell and slid in Dorothea's direction, ending up at Dorothea's feet. And just as Lynley had instructed her to do, she made even that look like part of the show.

# ACKNOWLEDGMENTS

Whenever I begin the process of writing a Lynley novel, I locate the area of England that I would like to write about, I read about the area, and I spend time there scouting out locations and amassing information that I hope will help me in the development of the characters and the construction of the plot and the subplots.

For this novel, I must thank Chief Constable Anthony Bangham of the West Mercia police for allowing me to interview him, for explaining how the cutbacks in policing have affected the way the police now have to operate in that part of the country, and for graciously fielding and replying to follow-up emails when I ran into difficulties that only a member of the police force could solve.

Jon Hall, chairman of the Midland Gliding Club at the Long Mynd, was wonderful about showing me around the airfield complex, demonstrating how a glider is assembled, and explaining the details of how one flies a glider as well as the various ways in which a glider is actually launched into the air. I do regret not taking up his offer of a flight.

The mayor of Ludlow, Paul Draper, met with me in the town council chambers and explained what the cutbacks in policing were doing to the towns in general and to Ludlow in particular.

Swati Gamble of Hodder & Stoughton was, as she always is, incredibly helpful when it came to winnowing out information that I needed, and my editor, Nick Sayers, set me straight when I went off track in British English.

In the United States, fellow writer (and tap dancer) Patricia Smiley was extremely helpful when it came to tapping, my assistant Charlene Coe was resourceful and amazing when it came to doing research on far too many topics to list here, my editor, Brian Tart, was the personification of patience as he waited for this novel's completion, and my husband, Tom McCabe, could not have been more supportive or understanding of this lengthy process.

I've had additional loving support from my Sistahs as well: Karen Joy Fowler, Gail Tsukiyama, Nancy Horan, and Jane Hamilton. You four rock.

There will be mistakes herein, but they are mine alone.

*Elizabeth George*
Whidbey Island, Washington
27 August 2017

10 million world wibe

US
121,100 Death

534 places

3,000

7,149 CA
53,00 New Cases

21,243 - Cases CA
5,900

34,500 New CA

Fairy Grotto

Sleeping Rough